The Sinbad Novels
Part A

The Collected Novels of P. C. Wren
Volume 2A

Fiction Titles by P. C. Wren

Dew and Mildew. 1912
Father Gregory. 1913
The Snake and Sword. 1914.
Driftwood Spars. 1916
The Wages of Virtue. 1916
The Young Stagers. 1917
Stepsons of France. 1917
Cupid in Africa. 1920
Beau Geste. 1924
Beau Sabreur. 1926
Beau Ideal. 1928
Good Gestes. 1929
Soldiers of Misfortune. 1929
The Mammon of Righteousness. 1930 (U.S. title: Mammon)
Mysterious Waye. 1930
Sowing Glory. 1931
Valiant Dust. 1932
Flawed Blades. 1933
Action and Passion. 1933
Port o' Missing Men. 1934
Beggars' Horses. 1934 (U.S. title: The Dark Woman)
Sinbad the Soldier. 1935
Explosion. 1935
Spanish Maine. 1935 (U.S. title: The Desert Heritage)
Bubble Reputation. 1936 (U.S. title: The Cortenay Treasure)
Fort in the Jungle. 1936
The Man of a Ghost. 1937 (U.S. title: The Spur of Pride)
Worth Wile. 1937 (U.S. title: To the Hilt)
Cardboard Castle. 1938
Rough Shooting. 1938
Paper Prison. 1939 (U.S. Title: The Man the Devil Didn't Want)
The Disappearance of General Jason. 1940
Two Feet From Heaven. 1940
The Uniform of Glory. 1941
Odd—But Even So. 1941

The

Sinbad Novels
Part A

by

Percival Christopher Wren

ACTION AND PASSION
SINBAD THE SOLDIER

Edited

by

John L. Espley

Riner Publishing Company
Culpeper Virginia
2016

ISBN
9780692639382

The text of *Action and Passion* will be in the Public Domain as of 1 January 2029 since it was originally published in 1933

The text of *Sinbad the Soldier* will be in the Public Domain as of 1 January 2031 since it was originally published in 1935

Contents

PREFACE

The Sinbad Novels Part A and *The Sinbad Novels Part B* by Percival Christopher Wren are the second of a multi-volume series, *The Collected Novels of P. C. Wren*. The purpose of publishing this series is to make the novels written by P. C. Wren more available to the reading public. His novel, *Beau Geste*, is usually recognized by most of the book dealers I have met over the years, but his other works are not so easily remembered.

I have been collecting P. C. Wren for over fifty years, and have been working on a comprehensive bibliography for almost as long. The text of the twenty-eight novels were easily obtained from copies in my own collection. For that collection, I certainly need to thank the hundreds of used book dealers I have purchased items from, and I need to thank some by name: Steven Temple, David Mason, Walt Barrie and, especially, the late Denis McDonnell for the advice and help they have provided over the years.

Mr. John Venmore and Mr. Philip Fairweather, both descendants of the late Mr. Richard Alan Graham-Smith, Wren's stepson, and the executor of Wren's estate, have both been very helpful in providing information about Wren.

As it has been over seventy years since the death of P. C. Wren (November 21, 1941), Wren's works have passed into the public domain in the United Kingdom. In the United States fourteen of the twenty-eight novels are still under copyright. Thanks to information provided by Messrs. Venmore and Fairweather, the heirs to Wren's literary estate, Mr. Danny Adekoya Campbell and Mr. Christopher Oladipo Graham-Smith, were located and permission has been granted to reprint Wren's works.

I also need to acknowledge the help and guidance of my family members: my daughter and son-in-law, Dawn and Andrew; my son and daughter-in-law, Jared and Claudia; and my long-suffering wife, Cathy. Thank you.

In conclusion, I need to thank Percival Christopher Wren for the many years of great enjoyment that his stories have provided. I know that Wren is not a literary or critical success, but, for me, he is one of the great storytellers of the early twentieth century.

John L. Espley
Culpeper, Virginia
May 31, 2016

INTRODUCTION

Percival Christopher Wren is best known as a novelist, publishing twenty-eight novels from 1912 to 1941, the most famous being *Beau Geste* (1924). Wren also published seven short story collections; *Stepsons of France* (1917), *The Young Stagers* (1917), *Good Gestes* (1929), *Flawed Blades* (1933), *Port o' Missing Men* (1934), *Rough Shooting* (1938), and *Odd—But Even So* (1941), containing a total of 116 stories. There were also two omnibus collections, *Stories of the Foreign Legion* (1947) and *Dead Men's Boots* (1949), containing stories taken from *Stepsons of France*, *Good Gestes*, *Flawed Blades*, and *Port o' Missing Men*. All 116 short stories can be found in the five volume collection, *The Collected Short Stories of Percival Christopher Wren*.[1]

Wren was a man of mystery in that the more popular biographical statements about him seem to be more fiction than fact. A typical biography places his birth in Devon in 1885, educated at Oxford, and having a career of world traveler, hunter, journalist, tramp, British cavalry trooper, legionary in the French Foreign Legion, assistant director of education in Bombay, and a Justice of the Peace. Most of the above biography, however, has not been verified. Wren was born Percy Wren on November 1, 1875 in Deptford, a district of South London on the banks of the Thames. He did attend Oxford University, graduating in 1898 with a 3rd class honours in History leading to a Bachelor of Arts degree. He attained his "M.A." in 1901. In those days, a person acquired a "M.A." after a certain number of years (three in Wren's case) and upon payment of a fee.

After leaving Oxford, he married Alice Lucie Shovelier in December 1899 with whom he had a daughter, Estelle Lenore Wren, born in February 1901, and a son, Percival

---

[1] For further information on *The Collected Short Stories of Percival Christopher Wren* see http://rinerpublishing.wordpress.com

Rupert Christopher Wren, born in February 1904. Percy worked as a teacher at various commercial schools until 1903 when he and his family left England for India. From 1903 to approximately 1919 Wren was employed as an educator by the Indian Educational Service (I.E.S.). During that time he published a number of educational textbooks, some of which are still in use in Indian schools today. It was during this period that he started using the name Percival C. and Percival Christopher on the textbooks. From 1905 to 1915, he also served in the Volunteer Corps (Sind and Poona) in India (see the novel *Driftwood Spars*, which has a description of a Volunteer Corps), and was appointed a Captain in the Indian Army Reserve of Officers, the 101st Grenadiers of the Indian Infantry, in November 1914. He probably saw action in the East African campaign of World War I (see the novel *Cupid in Africa*, which takes place in East Africa), and resigned from the Indian Army Reserve of Officers in November 1915.[2]

Wren's first novel, *Dew and Mildew*, was published by Longmans, Green in 1912. His first novel of the French Foreign Legion, *The Wages of Virtue*, was written in 1913 and published by John Murray in 1916. One of the many questions about Wren is whether he did serve in the French Foreign Legion. Given the chronology of his documented biography it is hard to see where he had time to actually serve in the Legion. Wren himself always maintained that he had served, and his stepson, Richard Alan Graham-Smith, who died in 2006, "strongly maintained that Wren had indeed served in the French Foreign Legion and was always quick to refute those who said otherwise."[3]

The series, *The Collected Novels of P. C. Wren*, is intended to include all twenty-eight novels in seven thematic omnibus volumes. The final number of physical volumes might be as many as fourteen, depending on how large

---

[2] Most of the biographical information about Wren has been obtained through certificates, documents, and original research at the British Library, Bodleian Library, and the India Office papers. Detailed documentation and sources will be cited in the biographical essay to be included in the forthcoming publication, *An Annotated Bibliography of Percival Christopher Wren*.

[3] http://en.wikipedia.org/wiki/P._C._Wren

(number of pages) the later volumes are. The individual volumes will not be in Wren's original publication order, but will instead have a connecting theme such as characters or locale. The seven volumes are:

v. 1 - The Geste Novels
    Beau Geste
    Beau Sabreur
    Beau Ideal
    Spanish Maine
v. 2 - The Sinbad Novels
    Action and Passion
    Sinbad the Soldier
    Fort in the Jungle
    The Disappearance of General Jason
v. 3 - Foreign Legion Novels
    The Wages of Virtue
    Sowing Glory
    The Uniform of Glory
    Paper Prison
v. 4 - Other Novels
    Soldiers of Misfortune
    Valiant Dust
    Cupid in Africa
    Mysterious Waye
v. 5 - The Earlier India Novels
    Dew and Mildew
    Father Gregory
    Snake and Sword
    Driftwood Spars
v. 6 - The Later India Novels
    Beggars' Horses
    Explosion
    Man of a Ghost
    Worth Wile
v. 7 - The English Novels
    Bubble Reputation
    Cardboard Castle
    The Mammon of Righteousness

Two Feet From Heaven

*   *   *   *   *

Volume Two of *The Collected Novels of P. C. Wren*, *The Sinbad Novels,* is in two physical volumes and contain the four novels that have the character of Sinclair Noel Brodie Dysart, whose nickname Sinbad derives from the initials **S.N.B.D.** In the first three novels—*Action and Passion* (1933), *Sinbad the Soldier* (1935), and *Fort in the Jungle* (1936)—Sinbad is the narrator of his life story, much like an autobiography. The fourth novel, *The Disappearance of General Jason* was published in 1940, four years and five books after *Fort in the Jungle*. In *The Disappearance of General Jason* Sinbad is a minor, but crucial, character in the story.

*   *   *   *   *

The Sinbad Novels Part A

The two novels in *The Sinbad Novels Part A* are *Action and Passion*, first published in September 1933, and *Sinbad the Soldier*, first published in January 1935. Both of them are the first two (of three) volumes concerning the life of Sinbad (Sinclair Noel Brodie) Dysart. Like the mythical Sinbad, this Sinbad is also a sailor, at least in the first novel *Action and Passion*.

The "Prologue" is titled "Strands of the Rope" and introduces several of the characters that appear later during the three year voyage of the Valkyrie. The rest of the novel is the first person narration of "The Autobiography of Sinclair Noel Brodie Dysart". Sinbad is the son of a Royal Navy Captain, and he was intended to go into the Royal Navy, but instead, after his father's suicide, he has to go into the Merchant Marine. During his first voyage, on the windjammer Valkyrie, Sinbad goes from an apprentice to the captain, facing a series of adventures that include a mad captain, multiple murders, mutiny, bare-knuckle boxing, sea storms, and (almost) incest.

Action and Passion is a departure from most of Wren's other novels in that it is almost entirely a sea-based story, since the majority of the action takes place on the wind-jammer Valkyrie. A windjammer is a large iron or steel-hulled sailing ship built to carry cargo in the late nineteenth and early twentieth centuries. Possessing three to five large masts and square sails gave windjammers a very characteristic and majestic profile, and the name "windjammer" derived from the sound generated by these sails in strong winds.[4] The novel is full of nautical terms that can at times obscure the narrative text, indicating that either Wren must have done a lot of research on sailing vessels or was very familiar with them. Wren seems to have frequently sailed on ships, having spent fifteen years in India and embarked on several cruises in the 1930's.[5] But a more likely candidate for Wren's knowledge of sailing vessels is that in his youth he lived in Deptford near Greenwich, close to the River Thames. It is easy to imagine that the young Wren might have spent some time either on sailing vessels docked near Greenwich, or talking to sailors.[6]

Another aspect in the novel that might be auto-biographical in nature is Sinbad's disposition to visions, or "second sight". Wren also seemed to have visions as mentioned in at least two known articles penned by Wren— "I Saw a Vision" and "Meaning of Dreams".[7] Several short stories and novels with psychic overtones also lend weight to this inference. For examples see the novel, *Dew and Mildew* (1912), and the short stories "Not Seeing, But Believing" and "As in a Glass Clearly".[8]

Another possibly autobiographical theme might be that

---

[4] http://en.wikipedia.org/wiki/Windjammer

[5] Details and citations on this will be in the forthcoming publication, *An Annotated Bibliography of Percival Christopher Wren*.

[6] Wren was born in 1875 in Deptford, and he and his family were living in Deptford during the 1881, 1891, and 1901 Census.

[7] *The Collected Short Stories of Percival Christopher Wren*, Volume Five, pages 83-86 and 240-243.

[8] Both short stories appeared in *Odd—But Even So* (1941), and can also be found in *The Collected Short Stories of Percival Christopher Wren*, Volume Five, pages 87-99 and 229-239.

of boxing. Wren was supposedly a boxer while at Oxford, though no documentation has, as yet, been discovered to support that supposition. One of Wren's novels, *Soldiers of Misfortune* (1929), can be considered his boxing novel, and an excerpt comprising the final match was included in an anthology of boxing stories.[9] Sinbad's boxing prowess is an essential plot element in *Action and Passion*.

Action and Passion was first published by John Murray in September 1933, and contains the dedication "To Charles George Cowie, M.D. My dear Cowie, To whom could I more fittingly dedicate a tale of courage, than to you? Gratefully yours, P.C.W." *Action and Passion* was also published in 1933 by Stokes in the United States, Longmans, Green in Canada, and by John Murray (in their Imperial Library series). The novel was reprinted by Burt in 1935, and in 1972 by Stacey, and in 1976 by Severn House.

The second novel in *The Sinbad Novels Part A* is *Sinbad the Soldier*. In this novel, Sinbad, and his friend Dacre, decide to leave the sea. Since the farthest thing from being a sailor is to be a soldier, they join Her Majesty's Life Guards, a cavalry troop famous (nowadays) for being part of the "Changing of the Guard" at Buckingham Palace and other royal sites around London. Sinbad and Dacre are "gentleman-rankers", who only joined the Life Guards to receive the best possible training they could for a soldier. After a couple of years as Life Guards Sinbad and Dacre resign from the Guards and join a former Valkyrie seaman in a gunrunning adventure. That gunrunning adventure goes awry when Sinbad is captured by Arabs and sold into slavery. Sinbad eventually becomes a slave to a Sultan of a remote Saharan desert kingdom, who turns out to be a European who is looking for a trusted companion. The Sultan is the son of an Englishwoman who was taken captive during the Sepoy Rebellion of 1857, and brought to Mecca after the rebellion failed. The Sultan and Sinbad, along with some of the Sultan's entourage, go to Mecca for

---

[9] *Fifty Famous Fights in Fact and Fiction, selected, and with an introduction by the First Earl of Birkenhead.* London, Cassell, 1932. Pages 152-169.

the Hajj pilgrimage and to rescue the Sultan's mother.

The story of an Englishwoman taken to Mecca after being captured during the Sepoy Rebellion might be based on an actual event. One of the early European visitors (in disguise) to Mecca was a John F. Keane.[10] On his visit to Mecca, Keane encountered an Englishwoman who was allegedly taken prisoner during the Lucknow siege of the Sepoy Rebellion, and eventually taken to Mecca when the rebellion failed. After an investigation by the English and Indian governments, this Englishwoman, "Lady Venus" was found and she declined any assistance.[11]

Wren, a staunch Imperialist, also had some strong opinions about slavery. Sinbad, who in the novel goes from the lowest of slaves to the right-hand man of the Sultan, has some interesting comments on slavery. [12] In the description of his visits to Mecca's slave-market, Sinbad had these comments about slavery in general:

> Without saying one syllable in favour of the foul, shameful, and abominable institution of slavery, it is only common honesty to state that, in those civilized countries where slavery is tolerated, the ill-treatment of slaves is rare, as rare as the ill-treatment of children in Institutions and Orphanages in Europe.
>
> A slave is property, and is valued and treated as such. Moreover, an ill-treated slave has full right, and every opportunity, to complain to the nearest Authority; and if serious ill-treatment were proven, it is more than likely that the Kadi, the Magistrate or Judge, would order the slave to be

[10] Keane, John F. *Six Months in Meccah*: London, Tinsley Brothers, 1881. And reprinted as *Six Months in the Hejaz*: London, Ward and Downey, 1887, with additional chapters.
[11] Keane, John F. *Six Months in the Hejaz*: London, Ward and Downey, 1887. Pages 31-35, 42-45, 113-114, 132-137, 146-148, 154-157, and especially the Appendix, pages 300-307.
[12] Herein pages 629-633.

set free and the owner to be fined or otherwise punished. In every Asiatic Mussulman town like Mecca, Medina, Damascus, Sanaa, Jidda, Yenbo, Homs, Aleppo, or any other such, it would be almost as dangerous for an owner to flog a slave as it would be for a British householder to thrash a house-maid.[13]

Similar sentiments are expressed in the short story, "Mrs. Norleigh's Night Out", which is the story of a downtrodden housewife who one night desires to go see a movie. Her overbearing husband "allows" her to go to a lecture on slavery, where Mrs. Norleigh has a night out she will not forget. Besides being an entertaining story on some of the social evils of English life, this story is interesting for also providing insights into Wren's opinions about slavery, and the sometimes overlooked plight of the common poor in England. In a similar vein to what Wren wrote in *Sinbad the Soldier*, he wrote in "Mrs. Norleigh's Night Out":

An obviously careful, unbiased and open-minded-observer of social phenomena, this widely experienced explorer admitted that slavery as practised in the East, open, naked and unashamed, was not as black an evil as was sometimes supposed; that the slave in the Arab household was just about as happy as any of the paid servants, the members of the family, or the employer himself. And that if a sudden decree of manumission were promulgated and enforced, no one would regard it with greater consternation than the slaves themselves. He informed his deeply-interested hearers that in any country in which slavery is a part of the social system,

---

[13] Herein page 632.

there is, nowadays, no such thing as cruelty to slaves. Apart from the fact that they are of great value, they have their legal rights; and ill-treatment of a slave would be punished by Law in the same way as the ill-treatment of a horse, cow, dog, or other domestic animal would be punished in England.

They were regarded, he said, somewhat in the light of children—lesser children, of course—but still childlike dependants for whose welfare the owner was responsible. And with a wry smile, the lecturer informed his audience that it was only in England that there existed, so far as he knew, a Society for the Prevention of Cruelty to Children.

Slaves in all Mussulman countries could and would and did complain to the nearest *Kadi* if he or she had a grievance; and if the *Kadi* found the slave-owner guilty of real cruelty, he could and would punish him and free the slave. Not that anything that the lecturer said was for one moment to be taken as a plea in defence of a vile and abominable institution, the deprivation of any man of his freedom by any other man.[14]

Sinbad the Soldier was first published by John Murray in January 1935, and contains the dedication "To Kitty and the memory of Isaac MacAndrew." *Sinbad the Soldier* was also published in 1935 by Stokes in the United States and

---

[14] *The Collected Short Stories of Percival Christopher Wren*, Volume Five, pages 113-114. Wren wrote similar stories in "Bobball Again, and a Study in Contrasts" (see volume one of *The Collected Short Stories*), and in the novel *Two Feet From Heaven* (1940). "Mrs. Norleigh's Night Out" was first published in *Illustrated incorporating Passing Show & Weekly Illustrated* (March 4, 1939) and was reprinted in *The Australian Women's Weekly* (September 16, 1939). Its first book publication was as the fifth story in Part II, "Quaint", of *Odd—But Even So* (1941).

Longmans, Green in Canada. The novel was reprinted by Grosset and Dunlap in 1936. There have been no other English language editions since then, except for reprints of the Murray first edition in 1936 (3/6), 1938 (2/-), and 1958 (8s6d).

Both *Action and Passion* and *Sinbad the Soldier*, while not up to the caliber of *Beau Geste*, are both very interesting and exciting novels of adventure, and should be considered two of Wren's best stories.

*   *   *   *   *

The original spelling, punctuation, and grammar, except for obvious errors, have been preserved as found in the latest editions/printings of the stories during Wren's lifetime (1875-1941). The footnotes, in the novels, are also as found in the original source material.

ACTION AND PASSION

. . . that fatal and perfidious bark
Built i' the eclipse, and rigg'd with curses dark . . .
Lycidas.

1

TO CHARLES GEORGE COWIE, M.D.

My dear Cowie,
  To whom could I more fittingly dedicate a tale of courage,
than to you?

             Gratefully yours,
              P. C. W.

CONTENTS

PROLOGUE

STRANDS OF THE ROPE

I

Captain Sir Sinclair Brodie Dysart, R.N., sat at his desk in his big white-enamelled after-cabin, and stared, unseeing, through the wide aperture between the open steel doors that led to the "stern-walk", the balcony on which he might take his exercise in privacy, walking alone with his loneliness.

Through the door-way, the skylight, and the open ports, the sunlight streamed into the handsome chintz-furnished room, with its elegant, tiled, manteled, and fendered fire-place, curtains, pictures, book-cases, settee, and deep armchairs, making everything, save the Captain's face, to shine refulgent.

Of blue sea, blue sky, distant palm-clad islands and a city of bubble domes and slender minarets he saw nothing, nor did he appear to hear anything whatsoever when the door of the fore-cabin opened and his Secretary entered and asked whether he would 'sign papers' . . .

"Silence gives dissent, I think," said Assistant Paymaster Herriot to himself, as he laid the documents on the desk and retired.

Captain Sir Sinclair Brodie Dysart turned and looked at the young officer's retreating figure.

Yes, that was the Captain's Clerk going out through the fore-cabin, and that was the Captain's marine sentry in the lobby beyond . . . and this was the Captain's wife's letter. All real. All quite real.

And . . . he would read it again . . . and make sure that what he thought she had written was real.

Yes. There it was—real enough.

". . . and so I am asking you to give me my freedom. I cannot go on like this. One might as well be a widow. Far better in fact, for a widow is free. Yes, I know you'll at once say that I have had every freedom to do whatever I liked. I have—and to do everything I didn't like, too. Living alone in this house, neither married nor unmarried, so to speak, and bored to death. You know quite well that I cannot live in the Tropics, and I'm not going to try.

"As I just said, a widow is better off, for she is free—free to marry again. Free to marry somebody she loves, and whom she will see a little oftener than once a month, or once a year, or once in three years, as the case may be.

"Yes. *Somebody she loves.*

"I am truly sorry, Sinclair—but I came to the conclusion, when you were home on leave, that I no longer loved you. It was a terrible six months for me, really, and a dreadful strain, as I had to pretend the whole time. It nearly drove me mad.

"No, I haven't a word of reproach for you. Not a word. (Not even about 'Shanghai Charlotte', for I shall owe my freedom to her.) But we are incompatible—*now.*

"And you are so . . . so what shall I say—passionate —impetuous—overwhelming—possessive—ardent—enveloping—I don't know how to express it. But I do know that it is *awful*, tragic, impossible, when one of a pair is so insatiably loving, and the other is—quite the reverse.

"And what about when that other actually loves somebody else? It was your coming home after so long an absence—coming home and being so ferociously possessive—that showed me the truth, revealed to me what I either did not know or simply refused to know—that my friendship with another man, my feeling for him, is more than friendship.

"I have never really loved you, Sinclair—never really been in love with anyone—ever—until now.

"And now I am in love, and ask you to give me my freedom. You must give it me, Sinclair—or else I must take it . . . And you know I have good grounds for doing so."

Yes. There it was. Real enough. In her own handwriting. And when he had left her—only last year—he hadn't had the faintest ghost of an idea that anything was wrong.

Not seriously wrong . . .

"Never really been in love with anyone—ever—until now." . . .

That would be Fordingstane—of all poisonous people. . . . The noble Lord . . .

Well! Well! Love is blind. . . . He, himself, must have been blind indeed, to have failed to see why Fordingstane had always been about the place, like a sleek tomcat, the whole of last leave.

Fordingstane . . . The bankrupt fly-blown gambler.

What could Helen see in him?

A higher title presumably.

A Countess . . .

No. He mustn't be bitter and think harshly of Helen. There was a lot in what she said about being a sailor's wife.

But Fordingstane, who had left an ugly reputation even in

Shanghai and Macao . . . !

Of course he was just the type of man who'd come out East, be a guest for all the position was worth, collect scandal about his host, and then go home and use it to poison his wife's mind against him.

Yes, that's what he'd done; and Helen, by now, knew *all* about Shanghai Charlotte and a good deal more.

And so he must give Helen her freedom, must he, or else she would "take it". And that would mean ghastly scandal . . . Public . . . Terrible . . .

And how could he face the boy!

§2

. . . "You shall have your freedom, Helen," wrote Captain Sir Brodie Dysart, by the next mail, after a week's cogitation, wrestling, and black despairing misery, "if you are still of the same mind at the end of the year. You can wait till then, I hope. If I hear nothing further from you, I shall know that your purpose remains unaltered, and you shall have your freedom. I love you far too much to stand between you and happiness—but I'd give my right hand to feel convinced that it really will mean happiness.

"By every mail I shall most earnestly hope and pray for a letter from you—a letter telling me that this one was written in a dark mood of discontent when you were out of sorts, and that you don't really mean it.

"Helen—suppose I gave up the Navy and left the sea, and came home for good—would that help? I'd do anything for you— and I'll do that, if you like. I daresay I could get a job of some sort."

The letter concluded with the words,

"Be sure you know your own mind and that you won't regret what you do; and if you are still of the same mind, you shall, as I say, have your freedom in the New Year. But how I shall look for a letter—or a cable.

"If only you knew how I worship you, Helen. As to what Fordingstane has doubtless told you, I suppose it is utterly impossible for you to grasp that a man may have a deep abiding unchanging love for one woman, and, at the same time, when separated from her by thousands of miles of space and years of time, can have a brief passing passion for another woman—a passion utterly devoid of love, a mere physical matter of the senses?

9

"You are the only woman I have ever loved and I shall love you to the end of my life."

§3

By the next mail, Captain Sir Sinclair Brodie Dysart received the copy of the London Gazette that announced his promotion to the rank of Rear-Admiral; and orders to proceed to England to take up a new post.

II

The Dean of Wellingbury sat in his beautiful library enjoying his customary after-lunch hour of rest and thought. It was his habit to think with closed eyes, bent head, folded hands, and regular audible respiration; but at the least sound or movement—such as the opening of the door—he would be found alert, wide-eyed and receptive.

A light foot-step on the worn stone of the terrace.

That would be his Elizabeth—on her way down the garden to meet The Boy Next Door.

The Dean opened an eye and saw his small daughter pass the french-windows. There would be a whistle in a minute.

The Dean closed the bright blue eye that had followed Elizabeth.

The sound of a discreet whistle faintly disturbed the stillness of the lovely summer afternoon, and a smile disturbed that of the face of the Dean, "which did cream and mantle like a standing pool."

A very kindly smile as he thought of Elizabeth and young Brodie Dysart . . . poor boy.

If only his father had lived . . .

A queer case that. Whoever heard of the Captain of a battle-ship being "lost overboard" on a night of moderate weather? Suppose he were suffering from insomnia most nights and somnambulism on the others, was it likely that a man like Captain Dysart would walk in his sleep—from his bedroom-cabin, through his fore-cabin and after-cabin, out on to the stern balcony place, and fall overboard?

Yet that was what the Fleet-Surgeon made of it.

Said the Captain had told him he constantly found himself walking in his sleep . . . Tell that to the Marines. . . . But nevertheless, tell it to his son. It would be a crime to let him think that his Father had committed suicide rather than face the music—discordant and unpleasant music. Perhaps it was for the son's sake that he had committed suicide—if he did. No-one could prove anything either way.

And how could the widow of Sinclair Brodie Dysart marry a creature like Fordingstane? . . . Brodie Dysart a splendid Viking of a man. Fordingstane no sort of a man at all—except a nobleman.

11

. . . A very nasty fellow. And undoubtedly he hated the boy. Probably because he was such a chip of the old block, such an authentic Brodie Dysart.

Well, well; the Deanery had been like a home to the fatherless and almost motherless boy, and Elizabeth had been as good as a sister—and an adoring puppy, follower, pal, confidant and companion. . . . Both motherless.

Very good for each other indeed.

§2

Arrived at the Roman Wall, and the great tree that overhung it, Elizabeth pursed her lips and emitted the low "secret" whistle that should announce her presence to him who heard and understood its message and portent.

The whistle was answered and a head appeared—the head evidently of one who lay flat upon the broad stone-parapeted top of the Roman Wall.

This was not that empire-guarding wall of Hadrian, nor perhaps that of the persistent Balbus, but the boundary wall between the Dean's Garden in the Precincts of Wellingbury Cathedral, and that of Lord Fordingstane whose house lay just without the sacred ground. The wall's foundation was certainly of Roman tile, its lower course of Norman stone, its bulk of Tudor brick, and its projecting coping of Queen Anne flags—a broad, time-stained, sun-warmed retreat, where a boy could lie hidden and remote, safe and unsuspected while domestic storms blew o'er. . . .

"Hullo! Elizabeth! Shall I come over?"

"Yes. Come on, Sinbad. Daddy's asleep, so we won't make a row on the terrace. Anything the matter?"

The boy climbed along a branch of the big beech and dropped into the Deanery garden.

"Navy's off," he said, and then moistened his lips and swallowed. "Let's sit on this seat a minute and I'll tell you. . . . I am not to go into the Navy . . ."

"No! Oh, *Sinbad!* What a wicked, wicked . . . Oh! Sinbad! They can't mean that you . . ."

"They do," said the boy. "*His* doing, of course. . . . Mother told me last night that we can't afford it! I am to go into the Merchant Service . . ."

"Can't *afford* it! . . . What *did* you say?"

"Nothing. I never say anything. . . . But I turned Atheist.

12

Perhaps you'd better not have anything to do with me, any more. I believe I've Committed the Sin Against the Holy Ghost . . . and the Dean mightn't like you to be . . ."

The girl put her arm about the boy's waist.

"What have you done?" she asked. "Do tell me, Sinbad."

"Done? I've given up God."

"But you couldn't. You can't. Why?"

"Because God's given up me. So I've turned Atheist. And what's more, I'm an Idolater."

"Golly! How did you do it?"

"That idol Fordingstane brought home from China—I think it's a Buddha, or Confusions, or something Chinese—I said my prayers to it."

The girl regarded her admired and beloved comrade somewhat anxiously.

"Daddy could make it right, I expect," she said, her face clearing.

"No fear . . . I mean, I've fairly done it, this time."

"But Daddy's a Dean, and he'll be a Bishop and I expect he'll be an Archbishop."

"Oh yes," agreed the boy. "Of course, if anybody could do anything, your father could, but . . ."

The girl snuggled yet closer and tightened her arm about him.

"Tell me," she said.

"Well . . . when I went to bed I asked God to help . . . to change my mother's mind and make it all-right, and reminded Him that we've been in the Navy List since Alfred the Great was his own First Lord and Admiral of the Grand Fleet, too."

"Yes," agreed the girl. "Daddy said there prob'ly was a Brodie Dysart, Commodore of the Coracles, to Boadicea."

"I prayed like blazes. Nearly all night, or it seemed like it. This morning I waited about, till Mother came downstairs, and went and asked her to say she'd only been joking and that she was sending my name in to the Admiralty. . . . She told me I could put the Navy out of my mind, once and for all, as I was most certainly not going into it. That was final, she said, so I need not pester her any more . . ."

"Sinbad! . . . What *did* you say?"

"I said I didn't want to be troublesome and all that, but if she really meant what she said, I should have to run away to sea."

"Oh good! What did she say to that?"

"Said I needn't trouble. Because I'm to go into the Merchant Service, since I must go to sea and am fit for nothing else. Go to some beastly training-ship, and then be an Apprentice on a sailing-ship. Sort of cabin-boy, I suppose, instead of being a Midshipman in the Queen's Navy.

"It's Fordingstane, of course," continued the boy. "He hates me like poison.

"So do I him," he added.

"So do I," agreed the girl, "and I don't care if it is wicked. I hate him. I'd like to kill him."

"Mustn't say that. Your father wouldn't like to hear you say . . ."

"I'll tell him myself. Daddy hates him too. I'm sure he does. I believe Daddy would like to kill him himself."

The boy smiled drearily.

"Tell me about the Idolatry."

"Well, I went nearly dotty when I knew it was hopeless. I couldn't believe it, and yet I had to believe it, because when Mother says a thing she means it—and nothing will ever make her change it . . . especially if Fordingstane has put her up to it. So I knew God had gone back on me, and it isn't true that you'll get what you ask for, if you have faith. I had faith all right, for I never dreamt it was possible that I shouldn't get what I prayed for, so I turned Idolater. I rushed out of the room, straight to where the idol is—you know, above the settee at the top of the staircase—and said my prayers to it: and now of course God hates me worse than ever."

The girl pondered the terrible situation for a while, as the boy stared gloomily before him, visualizing a ruined life and a wrecked career.

"What did you do it for, Sinbad?" she asked. "You don't think heathen gods and graven imidges and golden calfs could do anything, do you?"

"No, of course not, but I felt just awful. I've got nobody else, you see. I've got nobody at all."

"You've got me," said the girl.

The boy looked at her and refrained from reply.

III

Mr. Hung Toon Chang sat deep in the most comfortable armchair in Charlotte's most comfortable room.

All the rooms, in point of fact, were comfortable, and Charlotte's House was, by common consent, the most comfortable in Shanghai.

"No, those are my terms," repeated Charlotte. "A hundred thousand gold yen, the jade Buddha, and the pearl necklace—the pink one."

"She's a good girl," smiled Mr. Hung Toon Chang, "and so her price is above rubies, eh? But one could get a lot of rubies for ten thousand pounds, my jade Buddha and the pink pearl necklace, Charlotte."

"Yes, she is a good girl and a lovely girl," replied the fond mother, "and as pure as the lily.

"And what's more," she added, "she's a virgin."

"Vergin' on sixteen, you mean," he whispered. "Quite so."

Mr. Hung Toon Chang smiled, and although his clothes were the product of Savile Row and his speech the English of Oxford University, his smile was definitely of China.

"And marriage," insisted Charlotte. "You can have any Chinese flummery you like as well, but there's to be a marriage ceremony."

"But certainly, certainly—if we come to terms," agreed her friend. "We will be married in church—Protestant, Roman Catholic, Baptist, Wesleyan, Presbyterian, Congregationalist—whichever has the honour and felicity to receive your support. Or indeed, all of them *seriatim* if you would prefer it. Respectability. Nothing like it. I am all for it, as you know. *Toujours comme il faut.* Respectability for ever!"

"Time you thought so," observed Charlotte, a trifle sourly. "Do you agree to my terms?"

"Well, my dear, I must think a while. Never do business in a hurry. Ten thousand pounds and my jade Buddha and *the* pink necklace, eh? Definitely above rubies. You could get a hatful of rubies for that lot, you know. . . . When I was studying at Oxford, a very small ruby indeed sufficed to . . ."

"Well, this is Shanghai," interrupted Charlotte, "and my girl is none of your . . ."

"No, no, exactly," interrupted Mr. Hung Toon Chang in turn. "She's everything that's lovely. Well-bred, well-educated, charming and delicious . . .

("Like her dear mother," he bowed.)

". . . and that is why I want her for the mother of my son who's going to be English from top to toe—like his father—as well as half English by birth.

"And he's going to marry an English girl in turn, and I shall live to see my grandson three-quarters English by birth and more English than the English by education and training."

"Then you'll have to pay my price," was the reply, "and if you don't, Macao Monty will. Why, even Lord Fordingstane . . ."

"Ah, the good Lord Fordingstane. He was at the House when I was at Balliol."

"What house? The Big House? The Work-house?"

"Well, I don't think he did much work—but he did me, the poor heathen Chinee! . . . But I got my own back, Charlotte, and he left China in a hurry—and did not take that trunk full of nice little stuff for Streaky the Steward to peddle."

"Sure. You butted in there, Hung. But for you, either I or the girl might have become Lady Fordingstane, some day."

"Velly likely, velly likely; p'laps not, p'laps not. Anyhow, that's all over, and hard cash is more than coronets, and jewels pay for Chinese blood. We must have a talk with the little one. We *may* find that she's in love with me already. . . . You know, my dear, if she were positively to fall in love with me—love at first sight, a consuming flame, *la grande passion*—she might want to run away with me. And then what of the gold and the jade and the pearls, eh? Not even rubies . . ."

If it be possible for a refined, beautiful, and gracious lady to grunt, it may be said that Charlotte's reply was a grunt.

"And what about the English Consul," she sneered. "What about a British gun-boat nosing up your muddy little river and blowing your fine *kongsi* to Hell, eh? You call it a castle. It'd be a sand-castle by the time they'd done with it."

"And what about the newspapers!" she added.

" '*Beautiful English girl of fifteen kidnapped by Chinese millionaire.*'

"What do you . . . ?"

"By the way," interrupted Mr. Hung Toon Chang who appeared to be paying less attention than strict good manners might demand, "you *are* English, aren't you? I have spent some time in America and once or twice I have fancied I've heard you use expressions that . . ."

"Of course I'm English," snapped Charlotte. "Didn't I marry an Englishman on purpose to get English nationality, and a damned rascal he was—and is."

"A rascal? How he must jar on you, my dear Charlotte. He isn't our little angel's father, is he?"

"No, he's not."

"Nor I?"

"Does she look like it?"

"No, my dear. I was only having my little joke. You know what a funny man I am."

"Yes," agreed Shanghai Charlotte, "I should certainly say you are. A definitely funny man. What about my offer?"

"Well, first of all, Charlotte my darling, tell me, who is her father?

"If you know, that is," added Mr. Hung Toon Chang, with his most Chinese smile.

"Well, since you put it like that, my friend, I do know—and can prove it. He was a British Naval Officer. Can you beat that?"

"No," replied Mr. Hung Toon Chang. "That's good enough. Now tell me his name and give me some proof, and I think we can close the deal."

"Brodie Dysart," replied Shanghai Charlotte. "He was Commander then; took me with him to Japan. I was alone with him for six months . . . six months leave . . . what they call 'language leave', I think."

"Yes, the British Navy is noted for its language, I believe," smiled Mr. Hung Toon Chang. "Now I wouldn't doubt a word you said, my dear Charlotte, but I expect you have some letters . . . eh?"

"Oh, any amount . . . dating from that time. And some a little later, giving instructions about his daughter's upbringing and education!"

Shanghai Charlotte laughed, and Mr. Hung Toon Chang smiled.

"Oh yes, plenty of letters then—and one regularly every quarter now."

"A little blackmail?" lisped the Chinese.

Shanghai Charlotte laughed again.

"A little—or a lot," she said. "Let's call it maintenance."

"And you'll show me those letters—now?"

"Before I've had time to get them forged, do you mean?" smiled Charlotte.

Mr. Hung Toon Chang waved a deprecating hand.

"Yes, I'll show them to you now. And what's more, I'll show you his signed photograph with a real red-hot loving message on it . . . the silly fool."

"Many other people know?" enquired the Chinese.

"Nobody but he and I—and his trusty friend, Lord Fordingstane!"

"Always careful of your reputation, Charlotte," smiled Mr. Hung Toon Chang.

"Always careful of a good investment, anyhow," replied the woman. "He's going to be worth half his income to me as long as he lives."

"I wonder how many other flies you have in your web, Charlotte?"

"I wonder. Now you know who she is, what about my offer?"

"Well, get those letters. And send the girl in, and leave us alone," replied Mr. Hung Toon Chang, and in his usually silky voice was that peremptory note that Charlotte knew and feared.

As she said, she could understand, and cope with, a steel blade, but the strangler's silk handkerchief gave her the whimsies. . . .

Charlotte departed in search of her daughter.

§2

The very lovely lass, known in Shanghai as Charlotte's Own, stood before Mr. Hung Toon Chang and regarded his fat face without enthusiasm.

"*Marry* you?" she said. "Marry you? I'd sooner stick a knife in my stomach—and ten times sooner stick one in yours."

Mr. Hung Toon Chang laughed merrily. A girl of spirit this.

"No, no," he chuckled. "You wouldn't stick a knife in kind old Hung. Why, he's going to take you to London and Paris and Rome and Berlin; show you New York, show you the whole world; give you the loveliest frocks and jewels—and all you'd have to give him would be . . . kisses."

"I'd give you ground bamboo-root in your birds'-nest soup and ground glass in your puppy-dog hash," replied the young lady. "Marry *you*!" she scoffed.

Mr. Hung Toon Chang chuckled delightedly.

"But look here, my darling, your mother wants us to get married, and we have to do what Mother tells us, don't we? You'd hate to have a real row with her, wouldn't you? Mother cuts up very rough when she does cut up rough. . . . And you don't want to spend your life in Shanghai Charlotte's House, do you? And become another Shanghai Charlotte? . . . Why, we'd be married in church, swell. Now come and sit on my knee and see what I've got for you in my pocket."

The girl, feet astraddle, arms akimbo, fists on hips, stared with narrowing eyes.

"You can certainly give me what you like," she said, "but if Mother dragged me into church to marry you, d'you know what I'd say when the parson asked me, 'Will you take this man to be your wedded husband'?"

"You'd say, 'Sure thing, boy, go to it,' " hazarded Mr. Hung Toon Chang.

"Wrong again," corrected Charlotte's Own. "I'd yell 'Wedded husband? Wedded nothing.' I'd yell 'No' three times and then some. I'd turn round to the people in the church and shout, 'Look at this fat little Chink. He ought to be what he is.' "

Mr. Hung Toon Chang smiled Chinesily.

"Ought to be what he is?" he asked.

"Yes," replied the girl. "You're Hung, aren't you?"

"Yes."

"So you ought to be!"

IV

In his ten by ten "humpy" of frame and canvas, Mr. Jake Walfisch sat at the receipt of custom. His customers were gentlemen who did ill by stealth, and would almost have blushed to find it fame.

The hour was small and early, and Mr. Jake Walfisch yawned with abandon. Unless someone came by four o'clock he would shut up shop until to-morrow. Unless Mister Dirty-Wight, Mister Yellow-Wight, Mister Half-Wight, who called himself Mr. Orlando Wight, soon brought some more money, he'd have to shut up shop until—well, until he did come. For, curiously enough, you cannot buy gold with gold—in Mr. Jake Walfisch's walk of life, that is to say.

In the cellar of the humpy—a hole in the ground covered by a sort of wooden raft upon which stood Mr. Jake Walfisch's bed—there was pure gold to the value of at least five hundred pounds; and yet, curious irony, Mr. Jake Walfisch could not go about his unlawful occasions of buying stolen gold, until Mr. Orlando Wight should arrive.

Very annoying of him to be overdue. Goddamned bad luck if Baldy Stammers turned up with a nice sack of telluride ore, and he couldn't buy it; or if Tommy Hanks of the Waverley Mine Battery House, faked a burst grating, hung up five head of stamps and cleaned out the mortar-box to the tune of a big ball of amalgam . . . twenty pounds of it, and fifty per cent pure gold; or old Chuck Witje came in with his usual stuff—oxydized surface ore that only wanted a short spell in the crucible with a little borax and nitre. . . .

Why should Jake Walfisch lose commission because Orlando Wight was on the booze somewheres?

Cripes! Suppose Mister Dirty-Wight had skinned out with the boodle! No, he wouldn't dare. He'd know Charlotte would get him, sooner or later—and probably a damn sight sooner.

Mr. Jake Walfisch yawned again, and was about to lay his head upon his folded arms to dream of lovely Shanghai Charlotte, when a slight sound brought him up, alert as a terrier. The sound had been made by the raising of the latch of the wooden door. As Jake sat erect, his head was now supported on one arm, the elbow of which rested on the table, the hand beneath Jake's chin.

The door opened and a burly man stepped into the light of the lamp fastened to the wall, close to the doorway. In his hand he held a heavy revolver.

"Put 'em up, quick," he snapped, and Jake pulled the trigger of the yet heavier revolver that he was holding beneath the table.

As the man staggered, Jake fired again. Then, rising, extinguished the light, thereby shutting up shop.

But his day's work was not complete, for ere his head might seek its pillow, he had the laborious task of carrying the dead body . . . that of a plain-clothes gold-field detective . . . a reasonable distance from Jake's humpy, situate near the track, half-way between Kalgoorlie and Boulder.

When, next morning, he mentioned the matter to Mr. Orlando Wight, the firm's Visiting Agent, that gentleman bade him skip as soon as possible or, indeed, a damn sight sooner.

No good, as Mr. Orlando Wight pointed out, ever came of having trouble with the Police, and shooting-up a plain-clothes "dick" undoubtedly amounted to that.

V

Mr. Giuseppe Pollegrotto sat taking his ease in his favourite Inn.

His "favourite Inn" was MacGurk's Place in the Bowery, New York.

MacGurk's Place was the unofficial Club of Mr. Giuseppe Pollegrotto and his more intimate friends, known to themselves and certain others, including the Police, as the Brass Knuckle Ring.

For reasons of their own—reasons which may or may not have had connection with Mr. MacGurk's bank-balance—the Police but rarely entered MacGurk's Place, and only then, after due warning conveyed to Mr. MacGurk.

To Mr. Giuseppe Pollegrotto entered Stringer Corinaldo, Mattio Crema—so wittily known to his friends as "Ice Crema"—and Bugsy Dormio, gentlemen all.

"Room empty, Sam?" enquired Giuseppe Pollegrotto of the man behind the bar, and receiving a peculiar nod, wink and "Sure thing!" from the barman, proceeded with his friends to a private room, a room so private that perhaps not more than a score of persons at any given time knew of its existence.

Having seated themselves on wooden kitchen chairs about a wooden table, the members of the Brass Knuckle Gang got promptly to serious business, without preliminary or loss of time.

"Stuff safe?" asked Giuseppe Pollegrotto, who had taken the chair at the head of the table.

"Sure," replied Mr. Bugsy Dormio, "safe all-right all-right. His Royal Highness Mister Desmond O'Moore Hartigan can light out for home and Momma to-night."

"Light out nothing," growled Giuseppe Pollegrotto.

His friends gazed upon his yellowish negroid countenance with renewed interest.

"The bucks is all-right, quantity and quality, and his Jane's to pick him up at the road-house at midnight, as arranged."

"Pick up nothing," growled Giuseppe Pollegrotto.

"What, don't we let him go then, Giu?" said Mattio Crema. "I allow Mrs. Hartigan can't raise another cent."

"No, Boy," smiled Giuseppe Pollegrotto, "but I guess His Royal Highness Mister D. O'Moore Hartigan can—once he's out."

"And why should he—once he's out?" asked Stringer.

"To ransom *Mrs.* Royal Highness D. O'M. H."

And with a quizzical look in his eye, Giuseppe Pollegrotto whistled a little tune across the end of a key that he drew from his pocket.

The other man, Stringer Corinaldo, smote his huge thigh a resounding smack, and broke into a loud guffaw of hoarse laughter.

"I get you," he laughed, "Jiminy Gees! You've thought up a good 'un."

Mattio Crema giggled a quiet and sinister laugh.

"Christ!" he observed, "you've sure said something, Giu."

Bugsy Dormio stared blankly.

Suddenly the light of understanding dawned upon his fat face.

"Hell!" he crowed suddenly. "Let her come fetch Hartigan—we pinch her—and then let Hartigan go and raise her ransom!"

Giuseppe Pollegrotto smiled triumphant.

"You've said it all," he growled.

"Now Ma Hartigan has ransomed Pop with every cent she can raise, let Pop return the compliment. Let him go ransom Ma with every dollar *he* can raise—and I guess Desmond O'Moore Hartigan could raise a million."

"He'd better, anyhow," he growled, "if he wants to see Ma again, hale and hearty, healthy and wholesome."

"An' by Gee, she's a lovely lump, too! Purtiest cutie I ever set eyes on. I'll say he'd better ransom her—quick," observed Stringer.

Mr. Giuseppe Pollegrotto, without moving his head, turned his eyes and favoured the glowing countenance of the speaker with a long look—a look that caused the glow and rapture to fade from his face.

"Sometimes a little of you's a lot," he said.

"All right, Chief, all right," grinned Stringer uneasily.

"Better be," observed Giuseppe quietly.

"Thought our first law was 'share and share alike'," observed Bugsy Dormio.

"*You* thought?" replied Giuseppe Pollegrotto with faint surprise. "Don't think no more, Bugsy. 'Tain't always a healthy pursuit.

"Anything outa you?" he added, turning to Mattio Crema.

"Nix," was the terse reply.

"O.K." . . . nodded Pollegrotto grimly. "Mrs. H. will be *my* business. Get me?"

The House then went into Committee of Ways and Means for the release of Mr. Desmond O'Moore Hartigan, a well-known New York business man whom they had kidnapped, and his replacement, in their custody and care, by his wife Moira O'Moore Hartigan when she came to receive him, bound, gagged and blindfolded, from their charge.

THE AUTOBIOGRAPHY

OF

SINCLAIR NOEL BRODIE DYSART

PART I

CHAPTER I

One of the things that I remember only too well after leaving my training-ship, the *Leicester,* is the period of waiting in my mother's house; waiting to find a letter on the post-box table in the vast comfortless stone-flagged hall in which so much of the family life was lived.

Another, is my mother's pleasant friendly morning smile; a little satirical, a little quizzical, a little surprised, as though to say,

"Is this charming guest still here? I thought he'd gone long ago. Tut, tut!", and my step-father's morning scowl that said all he had to say.

And one day, with a leap of the heart, I found a letter, the only letter addressed to me and bearing the Glasgow post-mark.

I had already signed Indentures in which I contracted faithfully to serve Messrs. Dobson, Robson and Wright, Scottish ship-owners and "to keep their secrets . . . not to embezzle their goods . . . not to frequent taverns and ale-houses, nor play at Unlawful Games", in consideration of which faithful service and abstinence from indiscretion, embezzlement, beer-drinking and illicit sportiveness, Messrs. Dobson, Robson and Wright, ship-owners, did bind themselves "to use all proper means to teach the said Apprentice . . . the whole Business of a Seaman . . . and to provide the said Apprentice with sufficient of Meat, Drink etc. . . . ."

Incidentally, I learned later that as the said Apprentice generally received no tuition whatsoever, and rarely so much as saw more than sufficient food to keep his soaring soul within his growing body, Owners almost invariably broke their contract—though I never heard of any of them being sued on that account.

In my own case, my ill-used step-father had been constrained to pay Messrs. Dobson, Robson and Wright a premium of Thirty pounds. But, on the other hand, Messrs. Dobson, Robson and Wright, moved to munificence by this and the thought of my own continual and unstinted labour, did, of their own good will and bounty, agree to pay me a wage of Nine Pounds per annum. Yes, Nine Pounds per annum—without deductions.

Nay, more, not only was this sum of nine pounds to be handed to me intact, but thereunto was to be added an allowance in lieu of laundry-bill payment.

The allowance for the year was twelve shillings and sixpence.

Why, a dishonest idle Apprentice could spend a shilling a calendar month on laundry alone, and keep sixpence for himself!

On the other hand, of course, a reckless waster from the wrong side of the Border could spend a shilling a lunar month and find himself faced with a budget deficit of sixpence at the end of the year.

But what were considerations of a salary of nine pounds a year, with an annual twelve and sixpence for washing, in face of the glorious fact that I was going to get away from home, and be a real sailor in a real windjammer? What mattered it that I had bound myself to serve a three-years' sentence of hard labour, hard-lying and of semi-starvation, saving my owners a seaman's wages, and having worse accommodation and food than any tramp in any casual ward, in face of the glorious fact that I should be free, independent and self-supporting; should be leaving the prison of my luxurious home! . . .

At lunch-time, my mother, with evident amusement, read aloud a letter which she too had received from Messrs. Dobson, Robson and Wright, and having done so, re-read, with peculiar intonation, in a kind of vocal italics, the sentence,

"The young man will join the ship, *Valkyrie*, now lying in Prince's Dock at Glasgow, as early as possible."

"As early as possible," echoed my step-father, Lord Fordingstane.

"Rather," said I.

§2

With an excellent and typical canniness, Messrs. Dobson, Robson and Wright refrained, in their letters to my mother and myself, from any mention of the fact that the *Valkyrie* had not even begun loading, and could not sail for at least a month. Why lose, for a month, the services of an industrious Apprentice?

That very night I took train for Scotland with some loose silver and five sovereigns of gold in my pocket and five cigars—of some kind of tobacco presumably—in a cigar-case that had belonged to my dead father, Captain Sir Sinclair Brodie Dysart, R.N.

I remember every incident, almost every thought, connected with that journey.

I was not unhappy: I was definitely excited: I was full of hope and of determination to get to the very top of the tree which I was about to climb.

I could never, now, become an Admiral of the Fleet and lead

it into battle against the Armadas of my country's foes, but I might and could and would become a Commodore of some great Line and . . . Oh, to be joining a battle-ship, as a Midshipman . . . Anyhow, what did it matter? I was going to sea!

Having the compartment to myself, I indulged in foolish glorious dreams in which I played a leading part in quelling mutinies, foiling plotters, felling burly ruffians, saving the Captain's life, rescuing the Captain's fair daughter, and weaving many a wild romance.

I even went so far, I remember, as to draw from its place of concealment at the back of my belt, my highly-prized "Green River" sheath-knife, and go through the motions of sharpening it on my boot.

Incidentally, it is an interesting fact that the most foolish of those dreams and the wildest of those romances fell completely short of the actual truths of the story of the *Valkyrie*.

From day-dream and from nightmare I awoke to find dawn breaking over Edinburgh station.

At Queen Street Station, Glasgow, a porter, dour and serious, eyed me disapprovingly, put my sea-chest and clothes-bag on a cab and received my modest honorarium in silence. The cabman, old, dour and serious, in silence received my instructions to drive to Prince's Dock, but with a down-drawing of the lips and a shake of the head seemed ominously to imply that many were called thither but few were chosen to return.

Arrived at the Docks, he eyed my full-fare-and-tip sadly, gloomily, and found voice to ask for "anither saxpence" for himself. I replied that I had paid enough and more than enough.

Once again, the poor man painfully found voice to repeat the request for "anither saxpence"—if not for himself, at ony rate for the puir horse.

Replying that the horse was not worth sixpence, I turned away.

I imagine that, while memory lasts, no sailor ever forgets his first ship, nor, ignoring her faults while recognizing her merits, fails to attribute to her every virtue that she does not possess.

While admitting this, I can, nevertheless, most truthfully say that the *Valkyrie*, if not a beauty, was a witch, a most unusually handy ship; and I doubt whether there was ever an iron vessel afloat that shipped less water in bad weather.

Being jubilee rigged, she crossed neither royal nor skysail yards, thus saving work for the Apprentices who, in addition to making up gaskets and stopping buntlines, are generally called upon to furl the upper sails. Also, in addition to the big double-purchase capstan amidships, both to port and starboard she carried a smaller one for'ard, which, with the windlass capstan on the fo'c'sle head, lightened the labour of All Hands.

In point of fact, her stump to'gallant masts and short jibboom did not make for beauty; nor did her square box-like hull display any graceful clipper lines. But as I stood and gazed at her, I cared for none of these things.

She was my ship.

My future home was a lofty sailing-vessel, carrying double the number of the training-ship *Leicester*'s spars, and, to me, a noble sight. My heart warmed to her; I may almost say leapt in my breast, as I caught sight of her golden-crowned figure-head, and saw Neptune's trident pointing me the way to perilous seas and faery lands forlorn.

It was one of those rare and priceless moments that come at times to the adventurous and the romantic, and are commonly his chief, if not his sole, guerdon and reward.

For a minute I dreamed . . .

Being practical, as dreamers mostly are, I came quickly back to earth and the Glasgow Dock.

Leaving my dunnage on the quay, I climbed a ladder and, jumping down on to the ship's deck, found myself in the midst of a surge of violently active bawling men who seemed bent on my destruction.

A hive of industry . . . and though far from "immemorial elms", I undoubtedly heard "the murmuring of innumerable b——s" by busy workers when hindered or obstructed by the idle drone, myself.

Taking a flying leap to avoid a cask that suddenly swung over the rail with the obvious intention of knocking me into the hold, I saved my life only to lose it, nearly, for a coil of rope that hissed down from aloft came within an ace of beheading me.

A crowded minute of inglorious death.

Stevedores were loading cargo, as though for dear life and high wages; riveters were savagely hammering ironwork as though they bore it a personal grudge, which probably they did; carpenters were caulking decks; riggers were reeving gear. Everyone was doing everything with the maximum of violence. And I, a useless atom in a world of uses, could, amidst all this babel, find no-one to take the slightest interest in my arrival or in me.

As quickly as I could, I sought a place of comparative safety under the after boat-skids, and there asked guidance of a red-faced dungaree-clad gentleman who shouted a stream of, to me unintelligible, instructions to men aloft, pausing to point and punctuate his high discourse by ejecting tobacco-juice over the rail and into the dock, a most remarkable distance.

I was constrained to admire the apparently effortless skill that covered such force and precision.

I may here state that I was not surprised when, later, I learnt that the riggers, of whom he was foreman, professed the belief that it was he, and he alone, who thus, and thus alone, extinguished the Great Fire of Chicago.

And yet I fear that I remember that gifted foreman rigger to this day, not so much by his skill; his eloquence; his astounding voice, amazing face, colossal chest; his single sound but blood-shot eye, and his bull neck from which hung a steel marline-spike, a wooden fid, and a skein of roping-twine, as by the fact, alas, that he was the only man aboard the *Valkyrie* who addressed me as 'Sir'.

This, in the confusion, he nevertheless did; he spoke at leisure and repented in haste.

I suppose that my "educated" voice, my well-cut clothes, and my three inches and a fathom of height deluded him into thinking that I was an Officer in mufti, or some other person of importance. On finding that he'd been respectful to a mere boy and a miserable first-voyager at that, he became most illogically resentful and angry with me, as though I had, with intent to deceive and malice aforethought, inveigled him into politeness.

He out-distanced himself, broke his own record, I am certain, expectorating at Glasgow as though that city was now on fire also.

He turned his eye upon me.

He called me a bluidy binnacle-boy.

He spoke of skelpin' my hinterlands.

I picked up the near-by blacksmith's-anvil, not with any intent to do violence. *Au contraire*. And indeed, the obvious ease with which I did it, certainly had a soothing effect upon this man's wrath.

Even through the red mist of passion, his cyclopean eye seemed to perceive a possibility that the issue of assault and battery might be in doubt.

He spared me, and growled the opinion that the sort of person I needed was the "lang feller, a chiel i' th' saloon." . . .

Coming from the sunlit deck into the comparative darkness

31

of the passage, or port alley-way, that led in under the poop to the Officers' quarters, I stumbled over one of those wooden square-holed gratings that happily are found nowhere save in ships.

From the darkness ahead, a voice called,

"Who are you, damn you?"

A few more hesitating steps brought me to the door of a room lit by a smoking oil-lamp, for most of the daylight that should have come through the open port-hole was intercepted by the cargo-shed roof.

Overhead, the wooden deck was strengthened by a thwart-ship angle-iron which bore the inscription,

"To acomodate I Ɛeaman."

As I looked at the giant who seemed almost to fill the room, the "acomodate" struck me as faintly, and a little grimly, humorous.

Coatless and bare-armed, the "I Ɛeaman" wrote at a little table, attached to the bulkhead and littered with pipes and photo-frames, the man's enormous fist obviously finding no facile joy in penmanship.

As I looked, the light flickered on a weather-beaten face with high cheek-bones and fine aquiline nose. But the mouth—which betrays so much when closed, and more when open—was hidden by a drooping moustache, some shades fairer than the man's fair hair.

Being six feet and three inches tall myself, I take an interest in big men, and here was a grand specimen indeed. I felt that he, with his vast wide shoulders, mighty forearms and great column of a neck, was a worthy re-incarnation of a Viking sire. When he looked up, I should see that his steady fearless eyes would be of the blue of a deep still fjord, and that over his austere face a slow smile would break and spread and glow, as doth the dawn upon the mountains of his home.

I felt that if he were to sail with us as one of my officers, it would be a joy, a pride and a privilege to serve under him, to deserve under him, and become his trusted right-hand man.

Which, in the light of after events, was all very funny, and shows how eager and enthusiastic a Romantic Ass I am—or, let me say—I then was.

Suddenly he looked up and my enthusiasm was quenched as a flame thrust into water. My soaring spirit fell, and doubtless my face fell also. For though the eyes were undoubtedly blue, they were anything but steady, and everything but fearless. They were shifty, mean, uneasy, sarcastically appraising, cold, cruel. Definitely they were bad eyes, the unclean windows of an ugly soul: and, above them, was a minimum of forehead.

Then, from that deep grand chest, a barrel worthy of a champion heavy-weight boxer or professional Strong Man, there issued forth a mean voice, a petty voice, high-pitched and petulant.

My disappointment, as the man raised his head and spoke, was so great that, as I say, it must have been patent. Visibly and obviously I must have wilted. For the sneer upon the face before me—a sneer that I soon found to be habitual—increased and deepened.

Alas, this giant, with head of clay, was Second Mate of the *Valkyrie*.

"New Apprentice come aboard, Sir," I said.

"Aye," was the reply, and the amount of unpleasant meaning conveyed by that monosyllable was astonishing.

Possibly a wiser lad would have been sufficiently diplomatic to mistake this officer for the Captain. In my case, however, it would have availed me nothing, for I learnt later that the Second Mate, watching my arrival and summing me up, had observed to the coloured Steward,

"Here's another of these damned 'gentleman's sons' that know everything before they're born," and took a violent dislike to me forthwith.

Once a fisherman, the Second Mate, whose name was Smeeker, had "come through the hawse-pipe": in other words, had served four years in the fo'c'sle in order to qualify as a candidate for a Second Mate's Certificate.

This was in every way creditable to him, of course, but surely a poor reason for his burning hatred, blind and implacable, of Apprentices.

And if there were one kind of Apprentice that he hated more than another, it was one from a training-ship, particularly if he were well-spoken and well-born, in addition to being well-educated.

All this, and very much more, was related to me by the delightful negro, who, on the *Valkyrie*, combined the duties of Cook and Steward, and was, like all coloured sea-cooks, known and addressed as "Doctor".

Poor dear old Doctor. He really was as primitive and child-like as his African ancestor who endured the unimaginable horrors of some eighteenth-century slaver's stifling hold on the long, long tropical passage from the Gold Coast to Trinidad.

Almost as ignorant as his slave forbears, Doctor could neither read, write nor cipher, and I believe that the really pathetic dog-like worship that eventually he accorded me, had its origin in my teaching him to scrawl the words "Alexander McGrath" which was his incongruous incredible name.

I liked him so much that, through many a precious watch-below, I hammered away at him, both metaphorically and liter-ally, until he had acquired this invaluable accomplishment, and so raised himself from the ranks of those who "sign with a cross".

Thereafter and thenceforth, instead of making a mere rude mark on the ship's articles after the manner of some other "black trash" and some "white trash", he could literally "sign on". It is true that the letters conveyed nothing whatsoever to him, and that he could not spell them out aloud, but that mattered nothing. He could put his signature to any document. And, indeed, it was not only to documents that Doctor put his signature, daily and hourly, whenever and wherever he dared, until the novelty and wonder wore off.

It was wonderful magic, strong ju-ju, and I was the remark-able person who had found time, patience, and kindness to teach him this wonderful magic, endue him with this strong ju-ju.

CHAPTER II

My first intimation of the then true status of the indentured Apprentice—or his total lack of it—came that same day with the opening of the "half-deck".

The half-deck is the room that should be reserved solely for Apprentices, and is far too often shared by them with such petty officers as the Bosun, Carpenter, and Sail-maker, any one of whom may be a coloured alien.

This deck-house may be anywhere fore or aft, except under the fo'c'sle-head, but is generally placed near the poop, and sometimes right under the poop-deck—for Apprentices are too useful, and too much in demand, to be allowed, in most ships, to berth at any distance from those in authority.

In the *Valkyrie*, the half-deck was separated from the poop by little more than the length of the after-hatch, and when its door was open, the Officer of the Watch could actually see two of the bunks.

As I stood waiting for the Second Mate, Mr. Smeeker, to bring the key, this small square iron deck-house seemed to me to offer very limited accommodation for two Apprentices, and I'd been told that four was the minimum number usually carried. The depth of my ignorance was quickly gauged.

Having crossed the very high step—which in bad weather proved to be none too high—I saw that the actual "half-deck" of the Apprentices was restricted to the after end of the deck-house, and that the for'ard half was partitioned off and inaccessible from the door-way by which I had entered.

Later exploration through the for'ard door-way showed that this section was divided into two rooms for the Carpenter and Sailmaker, who thus had very much more accommodation than we Apprentices who paid premiums.

Thank God I never again saw the *Valkyrie*'s half-deck as I saw it then.

Although I am big and powerful far above the average, I am, I suppose, sensitive, or what is called "psychic", and as, with an ugly sneering grin, the Second Mate opened the door, I beheld not only the beastliness and horror that were there, but beastliness and horror that were not.

I fancied that I beheld a materialization of the Spirit of

Cruelty. Horrible callous hostile faces seemed to watch me intently from the shadows; watch me furtively, cunningly, as though the spirits of incredibly evil ruffians, knowing that fear always makes the flesh of my scalp creep and my hair to feel as though about to rise, waited . . . waited . . . until they had me in their power, at their mercy, for the overwhelming of my soul.

It is a curious fact that I was then quite unaware that the room and the bunks had only just been vacated by a gang of "runners", some of the worst and foulest scum of the slums of Hull, dock-rats of the basest type.

By the light of three small and filthy ports, I could dimly distinguish six curtainless bunks, and assumed that six persons might be expected to live and sleep in a compartment smaller than a horse's loose-box.

The floor, absolutely black with encrusted yet greasy filth, gave insufficient space for an adequate table.

Across the room, only a few inches above my head, passed a bare angle-iron, red with rust at its lower edge, and, in the lower bunk nearest to the door, was an unattractive collection of enamelled plates and mugs, evidently used daily and washed annually.

From the overhead deck-seams hung drops of discoloured moisture where the recent rain had percolated. As I looked at the filthy grey-black pillows and the frowsy blankets, vilely dirty, and wet from contact with the sweating sides of this iron pig-sty, I thought of my room at home, my deep armchair, the firelight gleaming on foils, "pots", weapons and other trophies, and it now seemed to me the most desirable place in all the world.

Then I thought of the kind of welcome that I should receive from my mother and my step-father; her quiet, enigmatic smile, his unquiet, unenigmatic frown.

Again I looked round the foul room, and although I had then never seen the interior of a gaol, I felt quite sure that, in comparison with this loathsome hole, a prison cell would be a pleasant place, sweet, spacious and airy.

Doubtless consternation, disgust and hesitation showed in my face, for, as I glanced at the Second Mate, I saw his ugly sneer deepen and grow uglier; and although one cannot be certain—positively certain—I really think that it was his contemptuous sneer that sent me to sea!

I had turned to him to say the words,

"Don't trouble to have my gear put aboard, Sir. I wouldn't put a dog in there and I wouldn't go in there myself."

36

But the look on the man's face stopped me, kept the words from my tongue, and made it impossible for me to turn tail.

Cowardice or pride? Grit and backbone, or weak anger at contempt, and the fear of being thought afraid?

I don't know, and to this day I don't know whether I regret having looked round in time to see that bitter and sarcastic smile.

Life's little ironies . . . and the incredible smallness of the trifles that affect a man's whole career, and, with it, the career of many another. . . .

I said nothing.

"Not what the young gentleman is accustomed to, eh? After the fine family mansion, it is not so posh, eh?" he grinned. "Yes, the other gentlemen, from Hull, left this place in a hurry."

"And in a filthy mess, Sir," I agreed, ignoring the sarcasm and the reference to the fine family mansion.

"But if you'll have my gear put aboard, Sir," I added, "I'll change my clothes and clean this pig-sty out."

The Second Mate actually looked me in the eyes for the fraction of a second, and then, obviously disappointed, turned away without a word and left me in that Augean stable.

§2

An hour or two later I rose stiffly, stretched myself, and rubbed my wet sore aching knees.

With a bucket of water, a half-bald scrubbing-brush, and a scrap of desiccated mottled soap pried from the filth of a corner under the food-locker, I had made the floor of the deck-house several degrees lighter in colour, and my dungaree trousers a few shades darker.

In spite of Doctor's interesting and ambiguous remark,

"There's many a good flowah you's nebber scrubbed befoah, honey," I felt that I'd done pretty well, and had earned a rest and a smoke.

Pouch in hand, I looked up to see who blocked the light from the door-way.

It was an officer and a gentleman, or rather, by the brass buttons across his coat-cuff, a Senior Apprentice and a gentleman, and my spirits rose instantly and high.

I rejoiced the moment that I saw Dacre and knew from his face, voice, bearing, clothes and manner that he had been cast in the same mould, good or bad, as myself. For I heard his voice almost before I saw his face as, leaning forward, he peered into the half-deck and pleasantly, charmingly, conversationally enquired,

"And who the Hell might you be?"

I liked Dacre in that first minute, and have liked him increasingly ever since, even when Celia came between us. Indeed I could use a stronger word than "like" . . .

"The same to you," I replied politely.

"Well," he smiled, "very kind of you to take an interest. My name's Dacre Blount, and I've just served a term of three years' hard labour . . . in this ship. And like other silly criminals, I can't keep away from the scene of my crimes. Now, I don't know who you are and I'm damned if I care: but you're a fool or you wouldn't be here. And if you'll take a bigger fool's advice, you'll go away. You'll go away now. You won't serve a single day. Big and ugly as you are, I can see by your colour and your hands and your gear, that you're a First-voyager. Well, take my advice and be one-before-a-first. Be a no-voyager. Pack up and go repenting home, like the other prodigal calf, before this sea-faring gets you."

Grinning, I shook my head.

"The filth and dirt and foulness," I began.

"Now don't whimper like a wet monkey," interrupted Dacre. "Get up and let me sit there, and I'll talk to you for your good. And mine. I must always grunt like a passionate pig, for an hour, on the first day of rejoining ship.

"As you were saying," he continued, producing a cigarette case. "The filth and dirt and foulness . . ."

"Were what decided me to stop," I interrupted in my turn.

"What? Oh, Casabianca! 'The boy stood on the dirty deck. Then washed it as he'd wash his neck.' That's the sort you think you are, is it? Undeterred; hope deferred; filth preferred. Help! And I've got to sail with you for three years. When you saw how hell-awful it was, you hadn't the pluck to run away, eh? I know."

And Dacre's smile did there and then grapple me to his soul with hoops of steel.

"Now stop being funny and talkative and chatty, and listen to me," he said.

Then, pointing the moral and brightly adorning the tale, he did his eloquent utmost to persuade me to go straight back home and escape unpaid drudgery, frequent extreme danger, incredible discomfort, dirt, neglect, monotony, savage hardship and semi-starvation.

It was indeed a black picture that he painted, and when he had finished, his duty done and his conscience clear, he turned to me, clapped his hand upon my shoulder and said,

"There now, that's the plain unvarnished truth. Won't you clear out now, straight away, and go while the going's good?"

"No," I replied.

"Thank the Lord!" said Dacre, drew off his right glove, and extended his hand. . . .

"What's S.N.B.D. on that sea-chest mean? . . . Sinbad?" he asked.

"Yes," I replied, and once again became 'Sinbad', as I had been at home, at school, and in the *Leicester*.

Clad again, shod, and feeling like a dock-lumper, but now in far better heart, I was squatting on my sea-chest listening to Dacre, when the Second Mate came to the door of the half-deck.

To my great surprise, Dacre neither rose to his feet, straightened up where he sat, nor removed the pipe from his mouth.

The Second Mate stood and regarded Dacre's smart attire with a supercilious stare of contemptuous eyes that wandered from his feet to his head and back again.

"And good morning, Mister," Dacre greeted his superior officer. The suavity of his voice bordered on insolence.

"Good morning to you—perhaps—Blount," drawled the Second Mate sarcastically.

"And now that you have been so good as to come back to us, did you and the other young midshipman-gentleman think of turning-to to-day?" he sneered.

"We did not, Mister," replied Dacre promptly. "Both the young midshipmen-gentlemen have travelled all night and are entitled to a little rest."

"Aye, and is that so, now?" replied the Second Mate, his shifty eyes glinting. "Ah, well, then the young gentlemen must have their rest; but I'm thinkin' 'tis very likely the Superintendent himself will come and disturb their precious slumbers a little."

"Good. I'll be damned glad to see Captain Jackson, Mister," snapped Dacre. "I want to ask him who the Hell had the blazing impudence to put the Hull runners, those filthy verminous dock-side riff-raff, into our half-deck for the run round from Hull to Glasgow. We Apprentices left the place spotlessly clean and our bunks made. Now the place is poisonous, filthy, stinking—and my blankets have been used by God knows what diseased and lousy loafer of a down-and-out gutter-snipe."

Dacre rose suddenly to his feet. He took a step toward the Second Mate, and I was glad to notice that though he grew pale with anger, he did not raise his voice. If anything, it grew quieter as he added,

"Yes, Mister, I want to see the Superintendent, and I'll point out to him that it was obviously done by some swine who likes that kind of filthy slum scum—because he's one of the same sort —natural own-brother to them."

And Dacre's blazing eyes held those of the Second Mate, who now had, perforce, to look him in the face.

I felt most uncomfortable, deeply as I sympathized with Dacre's righteous indignation.

Was not this the rankest insubordination? Were not people "clapped in irons" who, upon the high seas, thus conducted themselves toward those set in authority over them?

And if we weren't yet on the high seas, we were on the ship, and the man to whom Dacre was speaking in this unpardonable manner was its Second Mate.

What awful retribution would overtake my new-found friend?

None. The Second Mate, his face contorted with anger, and looking as though he were about to spit, snarled,

"Bah! You young . . . Beginning your damned shenanikin' early, aren't you? . . . By God," he almost screamed, "the next thing you'll know, one day, will be that you're down in Hell where you belong."

"Beginning your promises early, aren't you, Mister?" replied Dacre with a more contemptuous and cutting scorn than the Second Mate's own. "Think of something fresh, or *do* something for a change.

"We're waiting," he added quietly.

Apparently taken flat aback, the Second Mate glared suspiciously at me, and ended the conversation by slamming the half-deck door.

"That man's a genuine dirty dog," smiled Dacre, "with my apologies to all dogs for saying so. That was just pure spite. Out of nothing but hatred, malice, and all uncharitableness toward Apprentices—just because they are Apprentices—he told those Hull runners to bring their muck and vermin, their fleas, bugs, and lice, their dirt and disease and filth, into our living-room and beds, instead of into the fo'c'sle. And that's rough enough on the decent clean sailor-men who are coming into it. I wouldn't mind *their* living and sleeping in here at all.

"And then he hadn't the pluck either to own it, or to deny it. Why couldn't he speak up like a man and a Second Mate and say,

" 'Yes, I put the dirty longshore loafers in here and you be damned'?

"Well, it's just one more of the millions of little things that have earnt him his name of the Long Snake.

"Sorry to have dragged you into it, Son," he added, "but you'd be up against him, anyhow. He loathes an Apprentice and he abhors a gentleman."

§3

"I'm extremely inexperienced, or rather absolutely ignorant," I said to Dacre, "so I'm only asking. Isn't it very dangerous, as well as rather bad form, to be insolent to an Officer—of whatever sort he may be? Apart from the Law Courts and legal punishments, what about the other things one hears of—hazing, belaying-pin soup, keel-hauling, flogging, bull-dozing (whatever that may be) and all the other horrible things that . . ."

Dacre laughed aloud.

"You've been reading books, Son," he interrupted, "stories about Yankee hell-ships and bucko Mates. Flogging and keel-hauling are things of the dim distant past, dead as Dodo.

"It may be just possible that the Mates of a few American and Blue-nose—they're Nova Scotian—ships still pack a gun after the old Western Ocean packet style, and are handy with knuckle-duster and belaying-pin. . . . They do call it 'hazing' I believe, and each hard-case thick-skulled ruffian thinks he's the dead spit and living image of Bully Hall who used to make such wonderful runs across the Atlantic in the *Splendid*, though Bully Hall only used brutality towards mutinous brutes.

"But all that's pretty well gone, even there. Any Officer who tried that game in a British ship would either get penal servitude or go overboard quicker than he wanted to, one dark night.

"As a matter of fact, with us the pendulum has swung too far on the other tack. To-day, under our rotten feeble Shipping Acts, an Officer's authority depends almost entirely on his personality and his ability to handle men—and to man-handle them, too, on the very rare occasions when it's right and meet to do so.

"If he couldn't do that when really necessary, the men wouldn't respect him, and then personality wouldn't carry him very far.

"For example, an Officer insultingly abused by a seaman can have the man logged five shillings, always provided that the Captain agrees to enter full particulars of the offence and fine, in the official log. . . . The entry must then be read to the offender and his reply duly noted!

"I heard one such reply duly noted. It was,

" 'Thank you, me lord. You can 'ave another five bobs' worth and stick me on yer bloomin' chart for a blinkin' light-'ouse.' "

I laughed.

"In point of fact," continued Dacre, "these threatened deductions from his far-off pay-day don't worry the sailor in the slightest degree. If he isn't going to desert at the next port and leave most of his pay mortgaged to the Old Man for clothes supplied from the slop-chest, he's going to spend the lot, whatever the amount, in a night or two.

"Moreover, lots of skippers will turn round and tell the Officer that 'when *he* was one, he never needed to have a man logged, for the Jack Skite had never been born that could take five pennorth of rise out of *him*, let alone five bobs' worth'.

"No, logging's no good. Captain jibs at it; Shipping Superintendent frowns on it; and the Fo'c'sle laughs at it, and at the officer as well. It's about as useful as giving a man a 'bad discharge'—which means that instead of putting 'Very Good' against *Character and Ability* on a man's Discharge Paper, the Captain writes 'Decline to report.'

"Naturally that wouldn't help the shell-back to get another ship, so the poor penalized down-trodden sailor-man loses it.

"Anyway, British Captains are very loth to give one, and Board of Trade officials, British Consuls and such-like hate to see one given.

"So there we are."

"Sad," I commented. "Seems I've got to spend my Apprentice years in working up a Personality and power to produce the impression that I can give a poke and a prod."

"Intelligent," encouraged Dacre. "That's just how you will maintain discipline in the Mercantile Marine when you walk the weather side of the poop. . . . And note, for your future safety and comfort, that only Officers are allowed to use that side, and the weather poop-ladder. Presumably you are already aware that the weather side is the side from which the wind is blowing, the side which the wind reaches first. In other words, my Son, the side exposed to the wind and the weather."

"And how about when there's a following wind from right aft?" I asked with a simple innocence that did not deceive my mentor.

"When the wind is dead aft, there is no weather side," replied Dacre with the professorial pomposity he was wont amusingly to assume when addressing his juniors. "So the Officer of the Watch makes one.

"And in the improbable event of his being below enjoying a cigar and a tot with the Old Man, you may observe the position of the helmsman. If he stands to starboard of the wheel, you will use the port ladder and regard it as being to leeward. Thank you. That will do for this morning. Open the door before you go out."

Dacre yawned long and loud.

"I, who've been to sea, man and boy for fifty years—you'll often hear that lying boast—will give you of my wisdom whenever you want it, and more often when you don't. . . . What I've been trying to tell you, if you had only kept quiet and listened, was that the Long Snake can't really do anything to me or to you, for anything we may say to him. He hasn't that Personality we were talking about and he can't give the impression that he can also land 'the prod and the poke'. He'd never hit anybody, sailor, Apprentice or boy, unless he were perfectly certain the other would never hit back. And he can't be certain, poor chap.

"Nevertheless, I hope and believe I'd talk to him exactly as I do, if he had all sorts of legal and illegal powers, and if I were certain he'd knock me down the moment I'd spoken. I only wish he would.

"And as for it being bad form to speak like that to an Officer—well, kicking's bad form, but I'd kick a Dago who ran at me with a knife, or a drunken fireman who came for me with a coal-shovel. Bad form! You wouldn't kick a dog, I'm quite sure, but you'd kick a mad dog to save yourself from hydrophobia.

"Of course it would be bad form—as well as damned bad policy—to be rude to an ordinary decent Officer, and of course I'd never do it. . . . But you wait till you know the Long Snake better."

"Sorry," said I.

"You'll be sorrier still before you've done with him," growled Dacre. "Anyhow, stand up to him and don't think of consequences.

"Provided you don't 'refuse duty' of course," he added.

CHAPTER III

"What are the other fellows like?" I asked.

"Well, here's one of them," answered Dacre with a heavy sigh.

For, even as I spoke, an amazing apparition appeared in the door-way of the deck-house; a caricature; something that might have come straight from the hand of a fantastically whimsical artist, and the pages of a really comic paper.

In the semi-darkness it seemed that the legs of a pair of vast calipers, such as a giant engineer might have used for measuring the outside diameters of his cylinders, had miraculously crossed the high half-deck step.

They were the legs of another colleague, Geordie Stowe, and surely this world's bandiest pair.

It struck me, even as I looked, that Hell itself could hold no terror that could ever make those widely sundered knees knock together.

"Yes," murmured Dacre, "the weight of the cap has bent them."

The theory seemed sound. Made of the thickest pilot cloth, heavily quilted inside and fitted with the visor-like peak favoured by bargees, the cap itself, naked and unadorned, must have weighed heavy as a load of sin. But with the added weight of gilt cord, braid and metal, all so dear to the wearer's childish heart, the resulting burden would surely have brought both headache and ecstasy to a nigger band-master.

Worn in conjunction with the Hungarian hussar uniform of a Vienna lion-tamer, it would not have been very noticeable, but in conjunction with the red tie, blue shirt, and yellow boots of the gnome-like Geordie, it was as conspicuous as a diamond tiara on a scarecrow.

I may here mention that, eventually, I became very fond of, and greatly indebted to, this queer quaint urchin, and I am glad to think that no sign of consternation or amusement appeared upon my face.

Equally expressionless was the face of Dacre, possibly because he was stunned. For although Dacre—declaring that the sole reason for a man's going into Sail is to wear out his old clothes—would use the oldest and raggedest of patched working-gear, his shore-rig must be faultlessly correct as well as perfectly cut.

Once, I regret to say, I borrowed and wore his best uniform, the better to impress an unimpressionable colonial maiden, and to my horror and dismay, tore it on barbed wire. When I confessed, Dacre neither reproached me nor would allow me to buy the suit, but he would never wear it again although I had it "invisibly" mended.

Immaculate nautical perfection was his shore-going standard. No less.

And here, straight from the shore, into the half-deck and the presence of its fastidious Senior, ever jealous of its honour, breezed the most un-nautical object that ever cumbered and defiled a ferry-boat. "Breezed" is the *mot juste*, for no diffidence nor shyness troubled this breezy newcomer. In manner he was airy, informal, and friendly to the point of familiarity. Producing a short clay pipe from his pocket, he stuck it in his mouth, threw the cap with obvious relief into a bunk, seated himself beside the pained Dacre, dangled his short legs and broke a somewhat stony silence with the announcement that he'd "coom".

"And when does the band begin, Conductor?" enquired Dacre coldly and unkindly.

"Reet noo," replied the sad-eyed imp, and, exchanging the clay-pipe for a mouth-organ, he gave us an extraordinarily clever imitation of the bag-pipes.

As I scanned his face, no longer overshadowed by the portentous obliterating cap, I realized that though far from repulsive it was curiously like that of a monkey; pathetic, miserable, and unhappy, though anything but sullen or disagreeable. It was the face of one who had had a hard and joyless life; of one who had really known sorrow and suffering . . .

"*The Cock of the North*" came to a moist and spluttering end.

Realizing that he was not truly *en rapport* with quite half of his audience, the musician turned a sadly enquiring face and mournful ever-disappointed monkey eyes toward the more disapproving part, and Dacre turned and looked at Geordie.

The two faces were in amazing contrast, and that of poor Geordie suffered badly from the juxtaposition. As the light from the door fell upon him, he did indeed look a most ill-favoured cadaverous gutter-snipe. In age, he might have been almost anywhere between fourteen and forty; the lead-coloured skin, that in all his sea-service never acquired the least trace of tan, suggested ill-health and disease; the rather loose-lipped ever-open mouth and always-drooping lower jaw seemed to indicate mental deficiency; the great hooked nose through which apparently Geordie was unable to breathe, more than hinted at adenoids, and the pale wavering eyes, full of a brooding sadness, haunted by an unappeasable sorrow and inspissate melancholy, gave an impression of timidity and vacillation.

Doubtless, thought I, in my wisdom, the airy breeziness and confident self-assertion are but the assumed defensiveness of a conscious inferiority complex, a submerged personality.

Wrong again.

Never was there a countenance that more belied its owner, an expression that less expressed his mind. In spite of a sad lack of education, Geordie was shrewdness itself.

Fore and aft, he became admired for dogged pluck. Never was he sick or sorry. In strange and piquant contrast with his melancholy expression, he displayed a gift of witty repartee, clever jest and humorous comment, that added considerably to the ship's gaiety.

And above and beyond these things, he possessed a great-hearted loyalty and devotion, a nobility of soul and a loftiness of spirit, amazingly housed in so queer a tenement.

Yes, in spite of uncouthness, lack of all that is known as culture, a stunted mis-shapen body, and a most unprepossessing physiognomy, our brave Geordie was, in the highest sense of the word, a man. I came to love him.

Dacre was a fellow of remarkably strong likes and dislikes, high pride and great prejudice. Geordie, offending his pride in his Service, evoked his prejudice and at first incurred his dislike.

Of the last fact, however, I believe that Geordie was simply unaware, or perhaps he was so accustomed to creating an unfavourable impression that its expression damped him no more than water does the back of a duck.

It was apparently a matter of complete indifference to Geordie whether Dacre addressed him as "Geordie", or as "Damned Dock-rat." . . .

"Yer savage breast doan' seem ower soothed, Matey," observed Geordie, violently demoisturizing the mouth-organ. "Shall Ah gie ye a step-dance?"

"Is there any reason why my savage foot shouldn't give you a step-dance—over the rail?" replied Dacre.

"Lots, Matey," was the insolent reply. "Ye'd mebbe find it a hard job, for one. And ye'd be dommed sorry ye tried, for another. And before Ah gie ye some more, what's wrong wi' me onyway?"

"Everything," replied Dacre. "And what's more, you're half-drunk. . . . The last child who came in here the worse for drink, I tied to the pin-rail and doused with buckets of water until he was sober. I'll have no drink or drinkers in this half-deck."

In point of fact, as long as Dacre ruled, the half-deck was strictly teetotal; and so keen was his sense of smell that he could detect the slightest odour of alcohol, consumed or otherwise.

"Also," continued Dacre, who was evidently beginning as he meant to go on, "I don't like your little ways. I say nothing of your person, for that you cannot help; but your manners and customs you can and will change—and there *I*'ll help. You barge in here, and without invitation or permission, plant your stern-post on my sea-chest, throw your Swiss Admiral's helmet into my bunk, make horrible grimaces, utter uncouth sounds, offend my nostrils with the stench of cheap whisky, and my ears with a sound like the death wail of a crimson cat. In fact, you've almost annoyed me."

I'm quite certain that none of the personal comment affected Geordie in the least. It was the criticism of his cap that hurt him.

Seething with indignation, he leapt to his feet, glanced at the cap, and then, with hard fierce eyes that no longer wavered, glared savagely at Dacre. Such ferocity in such a Lilliputian should have been ridiculous. In point of fact, it was not ridiculous at all. It was too genuine and dangerous. So much so, that Geordie seemed to me to achieve a curious and unaccountable dignity, and I was too impressed to notice the bow legs and queer stunted figure; for it was, at that moment, a figure of indomitable determination, courage, and audacity. I thought he was actually going to strike the huge and powerful Dacre, then and there. Instead, he burst into bitter and impassioned speech.

. . . Swiss Admiral's helmet be dommed. 'Twas a very fine cap —aye, and some there was as was jealous of it.

As for drunk, the man who said he was drunk didn't know a boiled baby from a burning bar-maid and was, moreover, a dommed leear.

Stench o' whisky be dommed! Some fowk'd do well t'weer a nose-bag. Even then they might die of the strong smell of some cold water that wasn't there.

Half-drunk! Why, he hadn't had enough to drown a weevil's orphan. He'd only had one nip from the bottle of a friendly blue-jacket on the train—and only that because the man was a Tyne-sider an' all.

Personally he hated booze and boozers quite as much as any

togged-up, psalm-smiting, brass-bound reefer's son of a gun of a bald sea-cook's nephew's relation. And what the Hell sort of a half-deck was it where a bloke canna gie friendly toons on t'mooth-organ and squat on t'other bloke's sea-chest?

Swiss Admiral's helmet! Eh well, he'd had more gradely welcomes i' the fo'c'sles of Sunderland schooners.

"T'Hell wi' all half-decks onyway," concluded Geordie, and banged out of the place.

"It was your insult to his hat that did it," I observed. "He'd have burst into tears in another minute. I think you're a little unkind, if I may say so."

"No—kind," answered Dacre, "for his good and our own protection. Don't forget we've got to live with him. Eat and drink and sleep with him for years. If life's to be bearable, either he's got to get more like us, or we've got to get more like him. . . . He'll want a lot of taming, I expect, but . . ."

The door opened and Geordie reappeared.

"I ask yer pardon," he said, "an' I mean it. Which bunk will I take . . . please?"

Which I thought very handsome of Geordie.

§2

As, without troubling about food, we had spent the day in yarning, in unpacking our gear, and in generally arranging and tidying, if not beautifying, our future home, Dacre now suggested that we should see what Glasgow had to offer in the way of refreshment and diversion.

We found that, *inter alia*, it possessed tea-shops innumerable and that these specialized in pretty waitresses, tempting cakes, excellent toast and really good tea.

Also, my boyish vanity was well pleased to observe the attentiveness with which the prettiest of them neglected other customers, for dalliance with the brass-bound men of the sea.

I noticed with some surprise, that Dacre received all blandishments, however innocent, and friendly overtures, however harmless, with definitely cold politeness.

I learned later that all girls, unless chaperoned, vouched for and formally introduced, were anathema to him. In fact, he was a natural, or unnatural, misogynist—as well as a teetotaler. Doubtless each of these (possible) virtues strengthened the other.

Anyhow, his aversion from alcohol and feminine society, from "Wine and Women" in fact, made him a most useful and wholesome companion for a dangerously unsophisticated youth, glowing with rude health and filled with normal curiosity and human yearnings for what is known as a good time.

Unable to eat another mouthful, we left the still kindly but somewhat disappointed waitress, who obviously and perversely preferred the unsusceptible impervious Dacre to me, and, by devious ways and interminable short-cuts, wandered into Argyle Street.

"The 'palatial buildings' seem to be mostly gin palatial," observed Dacre.

And it being Saturday evening, the garish public-houses were already reaping their harvest.

"When I think of what sights the moon'll see by midnight, I feel sick," growled my companion.

As he spoke, a pair of swing-doors suddenly swung violently open. A drunken ship-yard riveter emerged at high speed, and, for some unknown reason, took a sudden and passionate dislike to me.

"Yon's a white mon," he yelled idiotically, and literally flung himself at me.

I side-stepped. Dacre deftly tripped him up and we went on our way rejoicing while his equally drunken mates attempted to salvage him from the gutter.

Proceeding, we reached a neighbourhood in which two of the chief diversions appeared to be fighting and wife-beating, and more than once Dacre curbed my eagerness to interfere.

"I used to do it myself, my son," said he, "until I realized that the lady resented my intrusion even more than her husband did. You butt in, and she'll scratch your face while he kicks you from behind."

However, Dacre quite sympathized with my wish to go to the assistance of the door-keeper of a mock-auction room, a poor old man whose ancient bizarre uniform a gang of roughs was endeavouring to damage, destroy and, indeed, remove.

With them we had quite a hearty time, and I was delighted to find, as I quickly did, that Dacre was no boxer but a good fighter.

A cry of "Pol-ice" causing the flight of the "keelies," we also hurried away, and seeing the brightly lit front of a music-hall, took refuge within its hospitable walls.

Concerning this place it is perhaps enough to say that the price of the best seats was a shilling. I should not mention it at all, save for the fact that our going there kept us out sufficiently late to be witnesses of a queer incident—an incident that affected the future of us both.

Having alluded to this amazing music-hall, I may say that I have never forgotten the hours I spent in it.

The entertainment provided on the stage was bad beyond description. That afforded by the audience was good beyond belief. No less than four powerful and perspiring chuckers-out laboured unceasingly in the vineyard—or beer-garden—winnowing, or rather weeding, untiringly and without pause.

Through a specially constructed door that opened only outwards, and down a steep flight of stone steps, the chosen were flung . . . down to some bourne from which none of them returned.

To us, this was the real entertainment, being the higher manifestation of expert perfected skill.

Nor was it a case of "gentlemen only," when the somewhat arbitrary selection was made.

Many were called, many were chosen, and out they went, to a man, and alas, to a woman.

Suddenly a very big stout man, sitting immediately in front of us, leapt to his feet and turned about.

From an autumn-tinted forest or jungle of hair blazed a pair of bright eyes and an even brighter nose, while brightest of all, shone in the hand that he raised aloft, the blade of a butcher's knife.

"Ah wan' t' be hong—an' Ah'm gwane t' be hong," he yelled, brandishing the dangerous-looking weapon.

Whether his wish has yet been gratified, I do not know, for within a few seconds of the announcement of his desire and intention, he was gone from our midst, knife and all. The one-way-traffic door banged behind him and it was as though he had never been. . . .

§3

The queer weird incident that later affected our lives happened as follows.

Our return through the drab purlieus of dock-land and the Broomielaw took us past malodorous public-houses in which urgent pot-men were anxiously bawling,

"Time, gentlemen, time," and, doubtless moved by this clarion call to note the flight of time, there emerged from a distant beer-shop two of the gentlemen thus adjured.

One of them was in visible need of support. This, for a space, he received from his companion, a tall bulky man who frequently looked furtively around.

Failing to see us in the shadow of the high wall that we were passing, the taller man stopped, and carefully propped his slightly shorter companion against a lamp-post.

He then lifted the poor fellow's head so that his chin protruded, stepped back, and, measuring his distance, delivered upon it a tremendous blow which knocked the drunken man right across the street.

The brute then turned and walked rapidly away.

Dacre and I were off together, like sprinters from the mark when the flag falls, and I proved the better runner.

I had some running "pots" at home, and I was in splendid condition. In a very brief space I had outdistanced Dacre, and was rapidly overhauling the cowardly ruffian in front, who was now running for dear life.

I had not the slightest doubt of my ability to overtake him within a very short distance, nor did I in the least doubt my ability to hammer him handsomely when I had done so.

I was so close behind him that my right arm was out-stretched. . . . A second later, my fingers were actually inside the cur's shirt-collar, but even as they took hold, I was myself suddenly and powerfully seized as though in a Rugby tackle. . . . I was thoroughly winded . . . pulled up short beneath a street lamp . . . and my man was able to tear himself free and escape.

But the sudden tremendous heave and strain had dragged the collarless shirt and thin coat half off the blackguard's back, and in the light of the street lamp, a whitely glazed cone-shaped scar showed clearly glistening above the shoulder-blades.

It was only the briefest glimpse, but in that fraction of time and that swift flash of light, "the moving finger wrote, and having writ"—gave the craven runner less than three years to live.

But I knew only of the present, and turning to struggle with my assailant, found him to be a vast Highland policeman.

"Not so fasst, now," he chanted. "When I stepped from th' door-way, what wass you in such a tamn hurry apout for?"

"Pity you didn't 'step' a bit sooner," I panted, ". . . then you might have caught that swine I was chasing, instead of me. He's just committed a murder, or tried to."

And I pointed back down the long straight street where Dacre was bending over the body.

By the time we reached the spot, Dacre had loosened the

man's neckerchief, and was wiping his swollen bleeding face with it.

"Heart's going strong, Officer," he said to the policeman. "He'll be all-right when he comes round . . ."

Upon enquiry, the host of the beer-house that we indicated, confirmed our statement that the unconscious man had recently left there in company with a tall strong fellow to whom neither of us bore the slightest resemblance.

And when the ambulance departed for the Hospital, the policeman merely took our names and that of our ship. He did, however, inform us that, in the improbable event of an inquest becoming necessary, we should most certainly be wanted. . . .

That was the last we heard of this matter, and, since the battered blood-stained visage had been unrecognizable and the fugitive assailant's face unseen by us, I imagined that, if I should ever happen to meet either of these men, I should be unable to connect him with this unpleasant event—unless, indeed, I should ever happen to see that peculiar scar again.

CHAPTER IV

On returning to the *Valkyrie*'s half-deck, and lighting the lamp, we found a fourth member of our Mess, appropriately asleep.

"Who's that?" I whispered.

"That's Beauty," replied Dacre.

I wondered why, for the round fat face upon the pillow was anything but beautiful.

"He's asleep," I observed. "Hope we shan't wake him up."

"Of course he's asleep," replied Dacre. "Hence the name. And we shall not wake him up. I shan't, anyhow. I'm too tired. Beauty takes a lot of waking."

Dacre, as usual, proved to be right, and undressing and turning in, I quickly fell asleep to the undisturbed and undiminished strains of Beauty's snoring.

I do not think I had slept very long, however, before I was myself awakened by the sound of someone moving about in the half-deck.

Pulling aside the canvas bunk-curtains, I dimly saw the newcomer arranging his bedding.

"Hullo, Mate," quoth he, and replying,

"Hullo!" I left it at that, and quickly fell asleep again.

Daylight showed the fifth and, we hoped, last, arrival to be a youth whom Dacre addressed as Fagin.

When we were alone together he informed me that Fagin's name was William Sorder and should have been Disorder; that he was "no particular good", and not to be counted on in our imminent, inevitable, and endless war with the Second Mate.

"Why do you call him 'Fagin'?" I enquired.

"Well, ask yourself," replied Dacre. "Put a matted wig and long beard on him, and whom have you? Cruikshank's own model for Oliver Twist's old pal."

And it was so.

Once the fact was pointed out, one realized that Mr. William Sorder was Fagin himself, clipped, clean-shaven and rejuvenated. Especially when the long, thin-lipped, predatory mouth smiled beneath the long, thin, predatory nose, while the long, thin, Mephistophelian eyebrows, separated by a deep furrow, frowned above the dark, hard, predatory eyes, did the face of

Sorder invoke thoughts of Fagin.

So there we were—the five of us, the *Valkyrie*'s half-deck or mid-ship men:

Big, handsome Dacre Blount, the Senior Apprentice and Third Voyager.

Little bandy-legged monkey-faced Geordie Stowe, Tynesider, self-made man from the fo'c'sles of Sunderland coal-brigs.

Fat, somnolent, good-tempered Beauty, also known as Tubby Watton, Second Voyager, good sailor and good ship-mate.

Unpleasant, sinister William Sorder, alias Fagin, also Second Voyager, bad seaman and worse ship-mate.

And myself, Sinclair Noel Brodie Dysart—known as Sinbad—biggest and strongest of them all; also greenest, most inexperienced, eager, impressionable and enthusiastic: rendered self-distrustful, by my mother and step-father: and endowed, by them, with a fine inferiority-complex.

Not yet being accustomed to the garb of a casual labourer, my first "turn-to" was something of a nightmare, and although the foolish feeling of shame, due to boyish snobbery, soon passed, I could, at first, scarcely refrain from slinking into hiding.

I received help from the Second Mate of all people, for, at the moment when I was sympathizing with those sleepers who frequently dream that they are walking down Bond Street in most inadequate and ever-shrinking garments, he bawled to me to go at once to the Cook and ask for the "Key of the kelson".

"Keelson" or "kelson" being the technical term for the inner part of a ship's keel, its key is naturally mythical, and, by way of a little preliminary leg-pulling, a prolonged search for it is generally the novice's first job.

I believe that young army-recruits are similarly despatched in quest of the Key of the Half-Passage (an equine manœuvre) and sent to white-wash the Last Post.

Smeeker, the Second Mate, was unaware of my training-ship experience, which made me proof against such rusty traps. I accordingly left him under the delusion that the listening labourers were enjoying the joke against my innocence and ignorance, whereas, in reality, there was rather more than that behind their grins, for, with my back to my tormentor, I winked and smiled broadly with an air of artful knowingness, as I hurried away.

After enjoying a rest and a smoke in the half-deck, I returned and, in a loud voice, informed the Second Mate that unfortunately the Cook had gone ashore with the Key of the Kelson in his pocket.

"Would a corkscrew do instead, Sir?" I enquired innocently, but only to be answered with an angry scowl and a surly order to get down the main hatch, quick, and see that no cargo was broached. . . .

Never having been below-decks in a modern sailing-ship, I was greatly impressed by the tremendous spaciousness, which, to me, suggested that of a vast ball-room.

Unlike the average steamer, which is divided up into compartments, the windjammer's lower hold is completely open, fore and aft, right from the collision bulkhead—which must be situated not less than one-twentieth of the ship's length from the inner side of the stem-piece—to the transoms that strengthen the stern.

Much as I was interested in the vessel's construction, it was soon very obvious to me that, in this hatch, the cargo required careful watching. It consisted of beer and whisky, and was being stowed by eight men, exactly eight of whom were Irish.

With the exception of one "pipe" of one hundred and twenty-six gallons, in the port wing, the casks were hogsheads of sixty-three gallons, and I noticed that two of the labourers seemed very much more concerned with the stowage of the pipe than with all the rest of the cargo.

Quite frequently these men alternately considered it necessary to push heavily with his chest against it.

I thought it strange that they should each spend so long in this position, and then I thought it ominous that each should work with a neat straight straw in his mouth.

I sauntered over to the big cask, and the two scowled at me truculently, as though I were an impudent and unauthorized intruder.

What they had been doing was now obvious, and provided my first experience of what is known among cargo-workers as "sucking the monkey", slang for making a small hole in a cask and drawing out the liquid through a straw.

If the two thirsty thieves had not wastefully pierced the biggest cask of all, and had been less insolently threatening in their attitude, I might have taken no further action than making them securely plug the hole (which I could not actually prove had been made by them).

As it was, I quickly shaped a chip of wood with my sheath-knife, hammered it into the hole, dared them to touch it, and sent another man for the Second Mate.

While I sat on a cask and unhappily awaited events, the younger of the two free-drinkers, after talking at me to the other, and working himself up into a rage, turned and talked to me direct. He told me what he thought of me—and he thought quite a lot in that brief space, although he did not look like a thinker—and then described with exactness the things he would do to me when he had the good fortune to catch me ashore.

I hate ill-feeling, disharmony and quarrelsomeness, but, once properly in it, I love a fight: and having done a great deal of boxing, using gloves of various weights, I was interested to experience the somewhat different sensations, results, and technique of fighting without gloves.

So, jumping off the cask, I said, as my heart beat over-fast and my mouth went dry,

"Don't wait till you catch me ashore. Do it all now," and I "put them up".

This apparently surprised, not to say shocked, the man exceedingly, and I thought that the surprise was not untinged with consternation, for, as I have mentioned, I am both long and large.

However, after so many fervent promises, and before so many fervent admirers, Mike had obviously got to do something about it.

Mike rushed. I side-stepped and smote hard.

Mike sat. His friends laughed, and the Second Mate arrived.

On inspecting the cask, the Second Mate discovered an unsuspected fluency in a particular kind of English. It was good, strong and sustained, but, to my critical ear, faintly mechanical, a learned lesson, the speech of one using vain repetition as the heathen do.

It served, however, and spread consternation and alarm among the eight.

Having delivered himself, the Second Mate sent for the principal of the stevedoring firm, who was on board, showed him the damage that had been done; and requested him to deal promptly with the offenders, and adequately with such an enormity.

Forthwith this gentleman dismissed the culprits on the spot, and sent instantly after them a third man who blasphemously expressed his disapproval of such high-handed conduct and his fervent wish that quite early in the ensuing voyage I might suffer evisceration by "haythen sharks and dhirty dog-fish".

He departed condemning me and commiserating poor Mike.

"And him with a big family and a hungry wife, and now the beautiful face on him all shpoilt and him not uttering a wurrud . . ."

The gentlemanly head of the firm of stevedores then commended my alertness and attention to duty, and kindly promised that he would make it his personal care that no man employed by him should lay a finger on me in vengeance for what I had done.

I thanked him, and rendered cocky by success, assured him that, provided they did it one at a time, all his men were welcome to lay ten fingers each upon me—in the way of kindness and fair fight.

The employer laughed merrily, but it was obvious that this spirit of impudent independence in a "boy" was anything but pleasing to the Second Mate.

Virtue is sometimes more than its own reward, and, as a result of this incident, I was sent into the hold whenever broachable cargo was being handled.

Not only did I thus escape many far less pleasant jobs, but I was enabled to learn all about general cargo stowage, the proper slinging of goods, and the best methods of lifting heavy weights.

§2

While the main object of the Owners, in putting us aboard some weeks prior to sailing-day, was to take immediate and utmost advantage of our cheap labour, those gentlemen incidentally did us good service.

Not only did we "shake down" and get used to each other in comparative—shall I say—comfort, but the First Voyager had ample opportunity of becoming familiar with the ship and with the names and positions of the various ropes.

Also, without the added danger inseparable from the rolling of the ship, he was able to practise going aloft and accustoming himself to the sensations at first induced by dizzy heights.

In the half-deck, Dacre and I, coming from much the same kind of stock, having the same sort of back-ground, and a great deal else in common, naturally gravitated to each other and soon became firm, fast, inseparable friends.

Having made two long voyages in the *Valkyrie*, Dacre knew her from truck to keelson, and, in addition to being a really fine seaman, was as skilful at imparting his knowledge as he was willing and ready to do so.

To my great surprise I found that he knew no navigation. So, as I had a flair and an inherited aptitude for it, I was, during the voyage, able to teach him, fairly easily and quickly, much that he would have taken long to learn from his *Norie's Epitome*.

In return, he showed me knots, splices, and sennits that I had not seen aboard the *Leicester*, while what he taught me on the subject of running rigging and sails was invaluable.

I'm afraid that the Senior Apprentice's obvious liking for me, and our patent friendship, caused a certain amount of jealousy in the bosoms of Geordie, Beauty and Fagin; and it afforded me some secret amusement to watch the attempts of each of them to triumph in our sight over the other two, and to attach himself to us.

It was a little pathetic and quite unnecessary for we both preferred Geordie to the others, in spite of all; and liked Beauty very much better than we did Fagin.

To express it more exactly, we liked sad-eyed, self-made Geordie, so brave and so humble; tolerated fat, piggy-eyed, somnolent Beauty, so greedy yet phlegmatic and lethargic; and really disliked Fagin, shifty-eyed, nasty-minded and somehow evil.

In their competition, each of the three had his own idea of what might constitute a claim to some superiority. Geordie, in spite of his inauspicious advent, was strong on the fact of his sobriety and continence, and told us, truthfully I'm sure, of his saving a South Shields coasting schooner from total destruction, through being the only person on board who was not intoxicated in greater or less degree.

Beauty was wont to dwell on the power of his sex-appeal and the number and extent of his successes with the ladies who adorned his native place.

After the third or fourth repetition of his exclamation,

"Ah! How that woman loved me!", Dacre invented and introduced a toast which he was wont to drink—with a hard eye boring into the sinful soul of Beauty,

"Here's to the women who have loved us."

Fagin's strong suit was his cleverness, mental and physical. He told us many triumphant tales of which he was the out-witting hero, and showed us, in the shape of remarkable photo-frames and other alleged ornaments, proofs of his great manual dexterity.

I confess with shame that, frequently, when glancing from

Fagin's face to Fagin's nimble busy fingers, I thought of pick-pockets. Doubtless the unkind nickname with which Dacre saddled him had something to do with this.

The *Valkyrie*'s Plimsoll mark was nearing submersion when, one day, the Second Mate ordered Fagin and myself to bring the new Mate's[15] gear aboard.

On the wharf we found a florid-faced man guarding a sea-chest and a big clothes-bag, and never, in the whole of my life, have I seen another man so broad in the beam.

He was, in that respect, vast, enormous, colossal, gigantic, Gargantuan, Brobdingnagian. His rather shabby, obviously ready-made, blue-serge suit bulged, strained, stretched almost to bursting-point, and he soon demonstrated that his splendid generous curves were due to solid hard muscle.

Like himself, his speech was thick, and on our arrival he used it in sarcastic vein.

"Ho, you've come, have you?"

"Yes, Sir."

"Really *hic*come."

"Yes, Sir."

"To give me a liddle *hic*elp. I said 'help', didn't I? . . . *Hic*elp."

"Yes, Sir."

"Then you damn-well shan't do it. See? That'll learn you. I've waited here for minutes . . . for hours . . . for days . . . f'weeks . . . f'years . . . When I came, I wanted help . . . lot of help . . . *hic*elp. Now I've waited so long, I don' want any help."

And this fact he forthwith amazingly demonstrated by walking straight—if unsteadily—up the steep gangway with the great bag under his arm and the big box on his shoulder.

"Gee!" murmured Fagin. "I'm going to be civil to that bloke."

And I agreed that it might indeed be good policy.

Nor was this opinion weakened when, with booming voice and truculent mien, the new arrival informed the Second Mate that things in this ship needed waking up, and he, the new Mate, was the very crimson man to do it.

Comparing notes, that evening, on the Mate's conduct during his first day aboard, we agreed that while, in all probability, we were not going to love our new officer, in all certainty the Second Mate was going to hate him—a conclusion that, I regret to say, we reached with satisfaction.

---

[15] *The Mate is the Chief Officer.*

From my enemy, the one-eyed foreman rigger, I learnt that morning, that the Mate rejoiced in, or at any rate answered to, the somewhat ominous and entirely appropriate name of Blow.

"Aye, and it's mony a sair Blow he'll gie ye forbye, ere yer *first* voyage is o'er," prophesied he.

The prophesy was not fulfilled as the speaker intended, but during Mr. Blow's extremely brief sojourn with us, we suffered not a little from his pernicious and persistent facetiousness.

Each of the Apprentices in turn provided material for our Chief Officer's perennial and puerile humour, and thus in his eyes, at least, justified our existence.

I escaped lightly, if wearily, in being hourly bidden to keep well amidships lest my weight give the ship such a list that it share the fate of the *Royal George*.

Dacre, deputed to put a strop on to a threefold purchase-block, was advised to use a Spanish windlass because being "such a Spanish-looking bastard" he should be particularly familiar with that device.

Fagin, sent to put a new seizing to a foot-rope stirrup on the cro'jack yard, was advised completely to ensure his safety by hooking his big nose on to the jackstay.

Beauty, using more vigour than sense in clearing some tangled gear, was asked why he resembled a Portugee priest. And being unable to answer the conundrum, was informed that "he was never any good, but when he was any good, he was too perishing good to be any good . . . See?"

Geordie, being asked by the Mate whether he'd seen a runaway pig, and doubtless having more than once before been the victim of the stale joke that depends on the inability of a bandy-legged person to stop a runaway pig, gave us the first taste of his quickness and his courage.

"I didn't see you running, Sir," he said, and eyed the red-haired ruffian hardily.

This brought Mr. Blow up, all standing, and took him aback so completely that by the time he'd grasped the implication, swallowed and digested the insult, thought of an answer, and decided on his line of conduct, life in general and Geordie in particular had moved on.

When, a little later, the five of us were together within sight and sound of the Mate, he called us to him, and with heavy seriousness, bade us all instantly repair to the port lifeboat and remove the "oars" from it.

As we looked at each other, and a tired contemptuous smile

marred Dacre's handsome mouth, and Fagin sniggered with ingratiating approval, Mr. Blow burst into roars of delighted laughter. Obviously, he felt that he had attained the ultimate plane of true wittiness, but, as my unsmiling face confessed, it was a flight that I could not follow, a plane that was beyond me.

I mention and describe Mr. Blow because I learned from him. He broadened my horizon; he taught me things; he impressed upon my mind the truth of the great truism 'You never know, you know.' Had I been denied my brief experience of him, I might later have failed to do for the *Valkyrie* what I did do; I might all my life have been even less self-confident than I am; even less daring, less enterprising, less courageous.

I don't wish for one moment to suggest that I am daring and courageous in the slightest degree above the average, but I do say, and with complete certainty, that I should have had these qualities in even less degree but for Mr. Blow.

For he taught me that not every huge powerful bold-faced bully is as dangerous as he looks; that not every person in authority can, with impunity, abuse his power, should he wish to do so; that the well-grasped nettle does not always sting; and that most obstacles diminish and dwindle if you approach them with open eyes, firm lips and clenched fists.

It was an interesting little incident.

It was Mr. Blow's playful habit to address the Apprentices in terms of contumely which he spared sailors, riggers, stevedores and other labourers.

I believe that these expressions were as nothing in his sight— less than nothing. Possibly they were, indeed, terms of endearment. I, personally, didn't mind them in the least, and I don't think that my ship-mates even heard them. They were just the noises that come out of Mates, like the sounds that come out of volcanoes, thunder-clouds, syrens, railway-engines, elephants, mouth-organs and other such phenomena.

And none of us had the faintest objection to being told that we were a useless pack of highly-coloured hounds, utterly eviscerated, devoted to tripe, scarlet and not house-trained: utter soldiers of curious construction and strange deficiencies.

But I had the strongest objection to Mr. Blow's broadening the scope of his enquiry, mandate and commission to include my personal relatives; my father, my mother and, had I any, my sisters. . . .

We were unloading ship's stores from a van on to the quay, and the Mate, merely I believe in search of diversion and amusement, descended to the quay and superintended our labours. "Labours" is the *mot juste*, for it was very heavy work indeed, just unskilled hard manual labour, and I was feeling a little tired. Not exactly weary, but tired of the job and very tired of Mr. Blow. . . . And more than tired of his endless witticisms, each heavier than the last, and indeed heavier almost than the labour.

From time to time he addressed small torrents of abuse at me—interesting and amusing abuse, containing phrases far too intriguing and attractive to be original.

Suddenly, as I, with more violence than I intended or Mr. Blow approved, lowered an extremely heavy box from my shoulders to the ground, he assailed my ears with the comprehensive family insult to which I have referred.

I'd had enough.

I turned to my immeasurably superior officer, and told him that no doubt ancient sea-usage gave him the valuable right and high privilege of calling his subordinates anything he liked. But that, in my ignorance, I knew of no law that gave him any right to insult my parents. . . . That I did not like it. . . . Further, that I proposed to incur whatever might be the appropriate penalty for knocking Mr. Blow into the dock, unless he forthwith desisted. . . .

And, not entirely blinded by the red mists of passion, with sinking heart, I squared up to Mr. Blow.

I was aware simultaneously of at least three things. That the now speechless Mate's blue eyes beneath the bristling bushy red eyebrows, though deadly cold and murderous, blazed in a face from which some of the high colour was draining; that Doctor, the black Steward-Cook, raising hands and eyes aloft, exclaimed,

"De Lohd he'p us . . ."; and that Dacre, sliding down a fender-rope, jumped ashore to my support.

For a long moment the issue hung in doubt, and I had time to wonder what was going to happen to me—whether I should get both a tremendous thrashing and a term of imprisonment for striking a superior officer, or merely one of these.

I also realized that I didn't much care, and that if I were to be punished for striking Mr. Blow, I'd certainly do my best to deserve all I got and a little more.

I might be the lowliest of First-Voyage Apprentices and he might be the highest of Extra-Master's-Certificate Chief Officers, but, even so, I wasn't a slave and he wasn't my Owner . . .

And anyhow . . . as he rushed he'd meet the best straight-left I'd ever produced, while my right fist had a good look for the point of his chin.

As the Mate stepped back, Dacre thrust between us.

"No need to knock anybody into the dock, Sinbad," he said quietly, "though it might do some people a lot of good, if it washed the natural filth out of their mouths. . . . No, I think we'll all knock off work, take a walk up to the Shipping Office and see what the Owners think about it."

And planting himself squarely in front of the Mate, he added,

"Think it over, Mister—before we go to sea—for there are five of us and we hang together."

"Aye," spoke up Geordie. "That's reet, Mister."

And stepping up beside Dacre, he thrust out his little chest in the manner of a pouter-pigeon, and portentously tapped it.

As I have admitted, I am impetuous and not one of those good men who are "slow to wrath but terrible when roused".

I'm very quick to wrath, and probably ridiculous when roused.

Shoving Dacre aside with my right hand and Geordie with my left, I again "put them up" and glowering ferociously (ridiculously) at Mr. Blow, said,

"Well?" as provocatively as I could.

And then and there I learnt from Mr. Blow. The huge, powerful and truculent bully—immeasurably my superior, and terrifying both by reason of his known and his unknown strength and resources, physical, official and legal—simply climbed down.

I don't suggest that Mr. Blow was a coward, or that he was, in this instance, in any way cowed. Most certainly he was not afraid of me.

But there it was.

He did none of the things that he had so frequently and so freely promised to do to me "one of these times"—rope's-ending, kicking round the deck and into the dock, putting a head on, tanning the hide of, knocking seven-bells from, me, and so forth.

Whether he had sufficient moral sense to realize that he was in the wrong, sufficient legal sense to realize that we were in the right, or enough common sense to grasp the implication of the fact that we being five and he being one, we could make the *Valkyrie* something less than a happy ship for him, I do not know. But I do know that as a terror, a danger and a living menace, the Mate, in that moment, dwindled—deflated and reduced.

He dropped the fist that he had raised as I thrust my friends aside and squared up to him, turned his horrifying scowl into a half-contemptuous grin, and again stepped back.

"Gobblessmesoul," he said. "Whass the matter? . . . Called yer *that*, did I? Well, I'm one meself, ain't I? Perish me purple, what're things coming to? You fellers are too lady-like. You've come to the wrong place. What you want is a gals'-school."

Then changing his tone,

"Now, young *gentlemen*," he sneered, "get these stores aboard . . .

"And jump to it," he roared, "before I . . ."

On hearing from Doctor of this "disgraceful *fracas*", the Second Mate showed a certain impartiality of mind in expressing the fervent hope that Mr. Blow and I might kill each other at an early date.

His prayer was not answered.

Some twelve hours before the *Valkyrie* was due to sail, Mr. Blow did, under the influence of Scotch whisky, create so momentous a disturbance in Glasgow, and such an impression upon certain of the City's police, that six of them, not without difficulty, persuaded him to accompany them to another sphere of activity.

With not unmixed feelings we learned that our late Chief Officer was now a Government guest at Berlini, the curiously named Glasgow prison, which would be his address for some weeks after we had departed.

Before the end of the voyage I learned that Mr. Blow's historic binge was the expression of his joy at being bought out of his job on the *Valkyrie*. His place was wanted for Mr. Orlando Wight, and it was evident that Mr. Blow was more than satisfied with whatever arrangement was made to that end.

To Doctor, Mr. Smeeker observed that it was only when he thought of the Mate's admirably planned strategy and tactics for the future chastening of the Apprentices in general, and myself in particular, that he regretted the loss of Mr. Blow.

CHAPTER V

With amazing speed a month had slipped away, a month in which we had known long hours of the heaviest manual labour, very poor and extremely scanty food, thoroughly unattractive accommodation, perfect health, excellent high spirits, and a total freedom from every sort and kind of care.

Dacre had steadily risen in my admiration and esteem; Geordie had gradually lost and forgotten some of his fo'c'sle ways of thought, speech and action; Fagin had begun to realize that boastful swagger does not always impress, and that certain things that he had thought admirable, filled Dacre with contemptuous disgust; and Beauty, after a few vindictive cuffs from the Second Mate, had learned not to "take the fore hand"—in other words, not to stand in front of his seniors when hauling on a rope, but to go to the tail-end of the line.

Not for many a long week should we again adorn ourselves with smart badge-caps and brass-bound uniforms, evoking, as we believed, envious glances from men and encouraging smiles from women.

Beauty had said his last farewells to the girls he'd leave behind him; Geordie had spent his last penny in the purchase of a very wonderful musical instrument; and Fagin had, I was going to say, picked his last pocket. As I've no earthly reason for saying this, I merely state that Fagin had, for the last time, returned, smiling his Mephistophelian smile, from the conduct of some occult concerns of his own.

By what seemed to me a miracle, the roof-high piles of goods —that had seemed burdensome cargo for a fleet—had all vanished from the dock, safely stowed in the *Valkyrie*'s capacious hold, and the last raucous docker, seizing coat and bundle, had laid a course for his favourite beer-house.

The instant that the heavy thwartship hatch-beams thud into their sockets, a ship ceases to exist for the shore-gang, and to the Apprentices falls the task of fitting hatches and spreading stiff tarpaulins.

On the morrow, if sober, the Carpenter would oakum-caulk all loosely fitting hatches, and with innumerable wedges "batten down," so that neither tropic squall nor Atlantic roller could damage cargo.

With tugs ordered for three hours before next morning's daylight, it was our last night in Prince's Dock.

No more should we board a deserted ship after midnight, and, after tying the sleeping watchman's feet, shout to him to come aft and have a drink; or fire a revolver-shot to make the unprofitable and unfaithful servant jump nearly to the galley skylight.

That night, with three Mates aboard, there would be more than sufficient authority to prevent childish sky-larking. The new Mate, Mr. Orlando Wight, a middle-aged man, big, powerful, hard-bitten, with torpedo beard and but one sound eye, arrived quietly; and, staring vacantly, wandered about the ship, speaking to no-body and vouchsafing no reply when addressed. He struck me as being decently, self-respectingly drunk, and desirous of con-cealing the fact.

Later, we learnt that he had had the misfortune, when Second Mate, to receive upon his suddenly upturned face, a marline-spike dropped from aloft, and so to lose the sight of his left eye.

Before we saw the last of him, we wondered whether the marline-spike had been dropped with intent, and all-too-successful aim.

I like to look back upon my first impressions of Mr. Orlando Wight, and to compare them with my last: to compare what the man seemed, with what he really was.

Anyhow, he showed me nothing but kindness. I admired him, respected him, and became very fond of him.

Not only was he kind to me, but he gradually and increasingly gave me the impression that he was striving to teach me and train me—for some purpose of his own. It was almost as though he intended to adopt me, for, once or twice, when he either had, or had not, drunk too much, he would make dark references to the time when he and I were "on a better lay than this", the time when he and I would leave the sea and buy—oh, a lot of farms.

Knowing what I do now, I can see that Mr. Orlando Wight was a most unusual man; a kindly, pleasant, friendly—villain.

The Third Mate, an extremely foolish-looking youth who proved to be almost as foolish as he looked—his sole triumphant effort, we thought—came aboard, turned in immediately, and slept as he arrived, fully dressed, from cap to boots.

We Apprentices, aware that there was a very heavy day before us, wisely turned in early, but, thanks to the Second Mate, had but little benefit of our wisdom.

In the drear doleful early hours, the beast visited the half-deck, his speech, manner and appearance causing Dacre plainly to remark that he'd got more in him than he had on him. I wish to be just, so will add that, to give the Second Mate his due, this was the only occasion on which I saw him intoxicated.

He had lost his gold watch-chain, and nobody in the decorated ship was going to get any empurpled sleep before it was curiously well found.

And nobody did.

"Out, you blasted soldiers," he bawled. "Out, and find it."

I wondered whether disobedience to such an idiotic order, at such a time of night, could constitute the truly heinous and sternly punishable offence of "refusing duty."

Looking across at Dacre who had lit the lamp beside his bunk, I asked whether it were any part of our work to hunt, at three o'clock in the morning, for the Second Mate's private property, setting aside the question of whether he'd lost anything at all.

Dacre, looking more than usually like a volcano about to erupt, nodded his head and erupted from his bed with such violence, that the Second Mate staggered back.

"But we may also make it part of our work," he observed smoothly, "to hope that our superior officer catches his death of cold in that brief singlet."

Dacre also made it part of his work forthwith to haul the still-Sleeping Beauty from his bunk, and to throw him out on deck.

"Watch . . . chain . . . find it," he bawled in Beauty's ear.

And the idea of chains penetrating Beauty's dormant intelligence, sent him stumbling for'ard in the direction of cable and windlass.

In the morning we found him snoring on some coils of old rope in a "manger" over the hawse-pipes.

Fagin crept purposefully away, his face wearing an expression that induced in me the unpardonable thought that should he find the gold watch-chain, the Second Mate never would.

Geordie ambled forth on bandy legs, sarcastically peering up in the direction of the masts, as though expecting to see it dangling bright in golden glory, at the yard-arm.

Dacre and I thinking that "quickest done is soonest ended," and that the Second Mate had quite probably shed various belongings on his way down to the ship, searched with a lantern as far as the dock-gates.

On our return, we found that the Mate, the Third Mate and the Cook (and luckily for the Second Mate the Captain was not aboard) thinking much as Dacre and I did, had risen, cursed the Second Mate heartily, and, in the hope of later getting some sleep, joined the searchers.

It was the negro Cook, "Doctor", experienced and wise in drunkards' ways, who entered the Second Mate's room, searched the bunk, and found the watch and chain under the fool's pillow.

My head seemed scarcely to have touched my own pillow again, before the first day of my First Voyage had begun.

By the light of a hurricane lamp on the poop-skylight, the Captain was calling the muster and—a fact proclaiming the short-age of outward-bound ships—not only was every man present, but, with one exception, positively sober.

Moreover, they appeared to me fully to justify the Pilot's comment,

"A likely looking crowd, Captain, and quite half of 'em British."

Last on the crew list was the drunken man, a merry soul and a typical blue-eyed, mahogany-faced, ear-ringed sailor-man. In answer to his name, Church, he yelled,

"Aye, aye, Sir. Tha'sh me, Cap'n! Why, tha'sh me eggsackly. Tha'sh always me, ole Church."

I noticed that the Captain joined in the general laughter evoked by the drunkard's surprise at being himself—and I hoped much therefrom, considering it favourable augury.

I came to learn, however, that Captain Bryndal would have laughed at his own executioner—or had he been the hangman, at the man he was executing.

I came to learn that Captain Bryndal always laughed; that he laughed when there was cause for laughter, and when there was none; that he laughed to gain time in which to take thought for his answer; that he laughed to avoid answering; to deceive, to encourage, to disarm, to confuse, to propitiate, to annoy, to insult, to mock, to delude, to evade; in short to do anything rather than express amusement and the appreciation of humour—of the sense of which he was devoid.

With the crew practically sober, unmooring was the work of a few minutes, and, suddenly, with a sense of utmost surprise, almost of incredulity, I found that the ship was moving!

Yes, it was true; the weeks of waiting were over and at last I actually was aboard a moving ship. Good-byes and good wishes came across the widening gap of slimy water, but none were for me, and I was truly thankful to see the last of the receding quay.

At the swing-bridge, two butterflies, painted ladies from the sweet green Broomielaw—whether astir so early or awake so late, I know not—called shrill and ardent farewells to the Fo'c'sle.

Hearing the Call of the doubtless somewhat Wild, the drunken ear-ringed sailor-man, Church, dashed forth, and though by overpowering emotion, or alcohol, bereft of speech, vigorously waved aloft around his head a Garment.

Blowing warning blasts from their syrens, the urgent anxious tugs busily coaxed the *Valkyrie* out between the pier-heads, straightened her up to stem the rippling flood-tide, and so, to an accompaniment of ringing ship-yard hammers, my First Voyage began.

I was Outward Bound.

There is no voyage like the first, and nothing in its life becomes it like the beginning.

At starting, the cruel monotony, the heavy hardships and the base needless lack of all reasonable amenities, are as yet unsuspected. The uncertainty of the future is all-glorious; any romantic clear-calling Port of Missing Men may be among the First Voyager's destinations, and he may see Antofagasta or Antananarivo, Bombay or Brisbane, Callao or Calcutta, Durban or Diemen's Land, Volo or Valp'o, the Golden Horn or the Golden Gate . . . Quite possibly the Golden Gates themselves . . .

"For'ard with the fenders, you."

There was neither Romance nor uncertainty about the harsh and high-pitched voice of the Third Mate—only the loud arrogance of the weak Officer who seeks to cover his lack of self-confidence and his inexperience in handling men.

"Now send the gear down from the mizzen-top, you. And get a move on."

In an Officer, obviously very young and quite untried, such hectoring is folly, and likely to rouse resentment in the crew. Feelings of resentment in the crew are likely to lead to merited feelings of humiliation in the officer. . . .

A First Voyager is not expected to know the correct leads for buntlines, sheets and clewlines, but thanks to Dacre's competent and patient teaching, I was able to make quite a good showing, and inwardly I thanked the ill-meaning Third Mate for sending me aloft where I could enjoy the thrill of the morning panorama of the Clyde.

Hitherto such names as Clyde, Dumbarton, Renfrew, Greenock had been but names learned from maps, unwillingly, at school. Now they were realities materializing before my eyes.

These wooded slopes and mist-crowned hills belonged to that romantic Scotland which had always seemed to me a faery land forlorn, so remote from my school-room and my home.

Port Glasgow, birthplace of my staunch *Valkyrie*, was shrouded in a genuine Scotch mist, and although this cleared before Greenock was abeam, a fresh South-West wind brought us to anchor at the tail of The Bank, and gave the Mate a welcomed opportunity to smarten paint-work and clean away the soot and accumulated filth of weeks in dock.

In this we were greatly helped by a continual supply of clean fresh water straight from the sky.

While I'm not in a position to endorse Glasgow's professed belief that Greenock has, for armorial bearings, a duck *couchant* —under an umbrella—and has heavy rain for at least three hundred and sixty-six days in the year, I know that throughout the three days of our lying wind-bound, the rain did not cease for a minute.

At eight o'clock in the evening of that first day, the order was given to "pick for anchor-watch", and I assisted, with much interest, in working the sailor's ancient device for avoiding dispute about who shall have the first watch and get the most sleep.

Each of the twelve A.B.s[16] was to keep watch for an hour, and, to decide their rotation, a circle was drawn on the fore-hatch tarpaulin and divided into twelve sections.

I, being an entirely disinterested party, was now requested to turn my back while each man made his own private sign, hieroglyphic, brief crude drawing, or other mark, on a section of the circle.

When every section had thus been appropriated and labelled, I was invited to erase each of the chalk marks, rubbing them out in any haphazard order that pleased me.

My first erasure gave the maker of the deleted mark the first watch; my second erasure, the author of that mark the second watch; and so on . . .

It being to me an absolute novelty, my own watch from midnight till two a.m. was no hardship.

My watch-mate, a tall Glasgow youth named Hamblin, making his first voyage as A.B. advised me to sleep, offering to

---

[16] *Able Seamen.*

wake me in haste should I be needed.

The young seaman appeared surprised and flattered by my preference for walking the deck and yarning with him, and soon confided to me that he had terribly bad headaches—caused by a blow.

Noticing that I was not smoking, he kindly and warmly suggested that I should "hae a wheen draw at ma pipe".

Deeply regretting that I could not produce my own, and fearing that to refuse might be not only to commit a breach of nautical etiquette but to give offence in return for hospitality, I smoked the foul clay nose-warmer loaded with coarse black shag, until he allowed me to return it to him—not a moment too soon. . . .

Next day, in the process of making things ship-shape, I was ordered by the Third Mate to "go aloft and clear the mizzen of Irish pennants".

Luckily Dacre was near and whispered, as the Third Mate passed on,

"He means loose ends of rope-yarn and the like."

Having worked up to the lower to'gallant yard, I there found a fine example of the criminal negligence of rascally riggers—those scoundrelly knaves whose motto, according to sailors who know and fear their shameful slipshod work is,

"You can sink, *I'm* all-right."

At the break of the poop I saw the Mate and the Second Mate in conference, and from force of old *Leicester* habit, saluted the officers.

Ignoring the Second Mate's sarcastic sneering smile at what he doubtless considered a vile apeing of Navy manners and customs, I addressed myself to the Mate.

"The starboard lower to'gallant foot-rope is dangerous, Sir," I said. "The midship end is lashed to the stem of the truss with one end of rotten ratline."

The Second Mate's sneer deepened.

"And to what part of the truss would you lash the midship end of a starboard foot-rope, young fella?" he drawled.

And was obviously disappointed when, happening to know the correct answer, I said,

"To the port arm of the truss, Sir."

I imagined he'd been quite positive that I should fall into his trap and specify the starboard arm.

The Chief Officer, Mr. Orlando Wight, looked at me.

"Ho, and how long have you been at sea?" he asked.

"This is my first voyage, Sir, but I had some training aboard the Leicester," I replied.

His next remark gave me a thrill of pride.

"Well, they taught you to use your eyes, Son, and we'll make a sailor of you in two shakes of a duck's rudder. . . . Now let's see what you can do with a marline-spike. Ask the Third Mate for a fathom of ratline, and go you up and make a good job of seizin' that foot-rope—and don't forget that men's lives depend on your work."

Then, turning to the Second Mate, he added,

"Mister, you tell that Third Mate to look at every foot-rope in the ship, himself—fore, main, mizzen and jibboom—and do it quick."

Looking none too well pleased, the Second Mate departed and when, an hour later, he took the trouble to inspect the foot-rope seizing, disappointment again awaited him, for he could find no fault with my work.

After this little incident, the Mate, Mr. Wight, apparently took an interest in me. At sea, he not only gave me the forenoon and noon "sights", but taught me those little wrinkles and short cuts in Navigation which, though not to be found in books, and not allowed in the Board of Trade examinations, save so much time and trouble in ascertaining the ship's position. And although I sometimes foolishly and ungratefully begrudged a watch-below, given up to working out the problems that he set me, it was his tuition that later enabled me to grasp the opportunity of a lifetime.

I owe much to Mr. Orlando Wight—as well as to Mr. Blow.

In addition to favouring me with much wise counsel, he often pointed a moral by relating interesting personal experiences of his own. I concluded that, although drink may have caused some of his more recent troubles, it was undeniable that genuine misfortune had worked terrible havoc with this man's career, beginning with depriving him of an eye. His right arm (he said) was weak and painful, set at sea so unskilfully that, on arrival in port, it had to be broken again and re-set.

One ship he had lost by fire, and another by capsizing through having to sail with insufficient ballast.

Once part owner of a fine vessel, he had been ruined by litigation with unscrupulous charterers, and finally, so persistent and far-famed was his bad luck that the time came when Underwriters actually refused to insure any ship commanded by so notoriously unfortunate a Captain.

He contracted *beri-beri* and, after a spell in a Calcutta hospital, recovered sufficiently to sign Articles as Mate of a homeward-bound ship. The Captain of this proved to be a confirmed drunkard, the Second Mate a hopeless incompetent, and the resultant strain and loss of sleep throughout a long passage of severe and adverse gales so weakened the luckless Mr. Wight that all the symptoms of the disease recurred.

Now, he said, poverty had driven him to seek a berth on the *Valkyrie* and it was only Blow's arrest on the eve of sailing that had enabled him to obtain it.

Thus, at an age when he might have hoped to enjoy comfortable retirement and the reasonable fruits of his labours, he was obliged to follow the exacting profession of a sailor, and in a rank lower than that to which he had been accustomed. How I sympathized with him—until I learned that there was *not a single word of truth in his hard-luck story!*

But much as I sympathized with Mr. Wight, I was nevertheless thankful that he had taken the place of the ruffianly Blow, for, during the three months that he was our Mate, he proved to be not only my very good friend, but one of the kindest officers that ever walked the poop—albeit one of the most violent-tempered.

It was not long, however, before we—quite wrongly—concluded that his terrifying outbursts were due to his proclaimed suffering and ill-health, and that his ferocious bark was infinitely worse than his gentle bite.

Indeed, the graceless Apprentices quickly came to find joy in these sudden shattering explosions in which he cursed with such amazing fluency, using the quaintest of oaths and the rarest of strange expressions.

It was typical of his good nature that whoever might provoke him—and however uncontrollably—he sought relief in swearing furiously at the ship and not at the offender. Were it the failure of a blunt knife to cut a hard rope, or of a too-tightly stuffed pipe to draw, that aroused his wrath, he would dash the offending article to the deck, glare malevolently at it with his sound eye, draw a deep breath, and then curse the ship in one long swift torrent of tremendous objurgation.

Everyone within hearing would pause to listen and draw nearer to hear the better. At the sound of his uplifted voice, the number of jobs in his vicinity increased and multiplied amazingly.

And he invariably began with the curious exclamation, "*Great Purple Doings!*"

My first realization of the Mate's curious habit of blaming the ship for everything was when the Sleeping Beauty having failed to strike the bell on the for'ard poop-rail, Mr. Wight glanced at him, looked at the unnoticing heavens, gazed round the ship and suddenly raising his hands above his head, cried,

"Great Purple Doings! . . . Oh, the *Valkyrie*! She's the left-handed son of an illegitimate organ-grinder's mouldering monkey —a wandering wall-eyed panders' prison."

This was the beginning of the address, but it was all addressed to the ship and concluded with the words,

"Man and boy, I've been to sea for forty years and never in my life have I seen such a perishing portico of a left-handed Harriet's Half-way House of a floundering furniture-shop of a barnacle-bottomed barge of a sink-or-swim of a ship.". . .

Obviously he was not referring to the ever-Sleeping Beauty.

And actually—a thing I've never heard of before or since—Mr. Wight, while cursing the ship for Beauty's dereliction of duty, would strike the Seven Bells, or whatever it might be, himself.

When that young gentleman, suddenly awakened by a kick from Dacre, would gallop up too late to do his duty, Mr. Wight would generally take God and man to witness that he now really would mast-head the burning boy, Watton, every flaming night for a coruscating week.

But never did he do it. Indeed, only once did I know the Mate to swear directly at, and actually to punish, anybody. That was Fagin, and rightly he deserved it.

Sent aloft specially to make a preventer-brace fast to the main upper topsail yard-arm, in due course he sang out,

"All fast, Sir. . . . Haul away on deck. . . ."

And, lying well back to the work, two A.B.s, I and the Mate, hauled away. But the rope was by no means "fast," and, after one good heavy pull, we hauled it clean off the yard!

The Mate having, as it happened, taken the tail end, was knocked absolutely flat—with my heavy self and two even heavier A.B.s making a squirming and crushing pile right on top of his body.

The weight of three unusually big men falling suddenly, violently, and heavily upon his stomach, naturally rendered him speechless. But only for a brief space.

While he recovered breath, all who could, drew near and waited. Nor waited they in vain.

In a manner that would have made the most hard-case bucko blue-nose Bosun sick with envy, the Mate dealt faithfully with Fagin, forgetting not a feature of his face and form, nor a least detail of his nature, disposition, upbringing, education and character.

Not till breath failed him did he stop, and even then, with a dry cough, he used the last expiring whispering wisp of departing air to add,

"But after all, why expect anything better from a crumbling monument of fossilized guano!"

But while the admiring Apprentices frequently troubled Mr. Wight through youthful thoughtlessness and carelessness, the Second Mate, who above all others should have given every support to his senior colleague, showed, instead, the true beastliness of his miserable character by sneers and jeers behind his back, and by being as covertly insolent, obstructive and hostile as he dared, in his presence.

Probably this was because Mr. Wight promptly and flatly contradicted him when he observed in front of us that Apprentices were not worth carrying as bilge or ballast—and quite possibly because he had himself applied for the berth from which Mr. Blow had been induced to resign.

That the Mate was not quite as "easy" as he looked and not wholly unaware of the Second Mate's disloyalty and thinly veiled insolence, was brought home to the latter within a brief space of our sailing.

In the Bosun's locker under the fo'c'sle head, the Mate happened to find three or four fathoms of lower topsail "sheet"— a very substantial iron chain—and calling Beauty, who happened to be near and partially awake, festooned it around that fat youth's neck and arms. Having done so, the Mate spoke quietly awhile in Beauty's ear.

Faithful to orders, doubting nothing and thinking less, Beauty toiled painfully aft, to where the Second Mate stood in conversation with the Captain on the poop.

Unable to stand still and upright under the weight, Beauty, with a polite bowing movement, followed by a terrific clanging thud, crashed his burden at the Second Mate's feet.

"Please, Sir," quoth he, as bidden, "Mr. Wight says, " 'Is this the chain you lost last Tuesday night when you came aboard drunk and woke All Hands and the Cook?' "

According to Beauty he owes his life solely to the restraining presence of the Captain who, as usual, laughed.

As I look back, the more do I marvel at Mr. Orlando Wight—

wonderful actor, amazing deceiver, kindly mentor, accomplished scoundrel, dangerous criminal, fine sailor, and good friend to an inexperienced self-distrustful boy.

CHAPTER VI

With our fourth dawn off the tail of The Bank, light airs came from the South-East, and, weary of waiting for a good fair wind, the Old Man would wait no more.

So in the half-light of daybreak, the Third Mate swaggered for'ard, unwelcomed, unloved, and unadmired, vainly striving to put a bass note into his raucous cry of,

"Man the windlass."

Next to me, and heaving on the same capstan-bar, was the merry, ear-ringed sailor now entirely sober, and answering promptly to his name of Church.

With a fine deep tone he began the opening verse of a favourite capstan chanty, and I almost blessed aloud this rough shell-back who, in that moment, seemed to me the living voice of the blue ocean's deep enchantment. All the romance of the wild salt sea for which questing youth has ever yearned and sought and suffered—and so rarely found—is in that crude, rude, old sea-song, to me so new, so thrilling and so wonderful . . .

> *"Blow, boys, blow for Californy-oh!*
> *There's plenty of gold*
> *So I've been told*
> *On the banks of the Sacramento-oh! . . ."*

Whilst a magic name like Sacramento rose on the keen morning air there were, not very far away, young fools safe ashore, asleep in their beds; wretched youths who might seek the Sacramento and California's gold; strong and healthy youths who, laughing at the perils of the deep, might be enjoying the "hardships" of a life on the ocean wave and have the Seven Seas for their playground. Poor creatures, how I pitied them!

But soon we needed all our breath for breaking out the anchor. While adding his own weight to one of the long bars, the Mate exhorted us with such lovely salt-sea words as

"Heave a pawl!"

"Lift the man's bones!"

"Break her out, my bully boys!"

"Heave, Sons, heave!"

For to all Officers, even the most youthful, the men are

"sons".

Suddenly the strain ceased. The windlass clanked merrily round, and to a taut tow-rope, we forged ahead with "anchor aweigh." . . .

By tailing-on wherever men pulled, and by trying to be first aloft at the loosing of sail, I did my best to conceal my novice ignorance. What was my pride when coming off an upper yard, Blancke, a big bearded Dane, met me amidships and as he swung into the weather rigging, said in his soft hoarse voice,

"You vass not von First Voyager. . . . You yong liar. . . ."

Pride goeth before all sorts of falls and, in but a brief space, my breakfast fell from me.

Well, well; "we have fed our seas for a thousand years"!

Of the immediate hours that followed, I remember but little, save a fervent wish that I were dead, and a realization that the bright smile of Romance can swiftly sour.

I soon got better, and our food soon got worse. As my appetite increased in vigour, the food decreased in quantity and deteriorated in quality.

Milk disappeared entirely from the menu. We knew that the tea was tea only because Doctor said it was. Probably it was concocted by stewing the tea-leaves previously used in cabin tea-pots.

I can still see Geordie's long face wrinkled in piteous dismay and hear his plaintive

"Hooly Mither! Is theer na' burgoo (porridge) f'breakfas'?"

Although Dobson, Robson and Wright's ships were noted for good living, it was obvious that Bryndal intended rigidly to restrict us to our "pound and pint"—that minimum insisted on, by the Board of Trade, and generally conceded to be practical starvation for men engaged in heavy work.

Having a craving for sweet things after I had recovered from sea-sickness, I was astounded to find that my weekly fourteen ounces of sugar lasted for about three days, and during the rest of the week I had to content myself with milkless tea sweetened with tinned marmalade. And, strange to say, I almost enjoyed this horrible liquid.

The legal weekly allowance of sugar was actually sixteen ounces, but two ounces per man was retained by Doctor for sweetening our daily ration of lime-juice which, as a preventative of scurvy, must be issued as soon as fresh provisions are exhausted.

The for'ard end of his pantry alley-way was at the break of the poop where a port, about two feet square, gave access to the main deck. Here, each day at noon, Doctor's black face would be quaintly framed in the white bulkhead, and, with a large pannikin in my hand, I was generally his first customer. And if I did not receive extra large measure from the wooden bucket, Doctor was in a very bad humour.

With shame I recall how I told Doctor that he reminded me of a portrait of the Sultan of Zanzibar in a white frame. My emotion at the moment was not shame but sorrow, for Doctor immediately gave me short measure, in spite of my assurance that I had paid him a compliment, the ruler of Zanzibar being notoriously beautiful, intelligent, and accomplished, a man who could write his own name.

"I ain't no Sultan, so don't you go 'sultan me like that," grumbled Doctor, and Dacre instantly and warmly upheld him.

"Doubtless you're a walking scintillation of wit," he observed, as we left Doctor's port, pannikin in hand, "and it is a privilege to enjoy your society and sit at your feast of humour. But, in point of fact, I actually prefer the feast of gubbins—and if your brilliance so blinds Doctor that he makes a mistake and gives our manavalins to Chips and the seamen . . . well . . . I don't want to say or do anything unkind—but I'll say what I think of you and I'll knock you even sillier than you are."

And Dacre, of course, was right. No punishment was too bad for the fool who would imperil the half-deck's gubbins or manavalins (names of untraceable origin given to the meagre and normally undesirable surplus from the cabin meals).

Smitten with remorse, I sought Doctor out, apologized handsomely, placated him with a gift, and told him that the innocent half-deck was, to a man, angry and indignant at my rudeness to him.

Doctor may have been very black. He was also very white. And letting not the sun go down upon his wrath, visited no punishment upon the half-deck in general or me in particular.

For this, I was very thankful, and, if the whole matter seems infinitely petty, it is to be borne in mind that the problem of food is not a small one, from the moment that it becomes a problem.

In the tropics I made great efforts to save my allowance of sweetened lime-juice wherewith to help beguile the night-watch. But the strength of my self-denial was seldom equal to the strain, and usually I so far yielded to the temptation of sipping it, that, by sunset, the precious drink was all consumed.

Later in the voyage I discovered that Blancke, the big Dane, who apparently was impervious to anything so effeminate as scurvy, always sold his whack when he could find a purchaser. He found a regular one in me, plugs of Lucky Hit tobacco providing our standard of value and medium of exchange.

A somewhat unusual ration—and a very doubtful blessing— was a daily issue of soft bread.

In Sail, this is considered a very great luxury, but had we received the usual Liverpool Pantiles of hard tack (some kind of ship's biscuit) we should undoubtedly have had more to eat—and 'more to eat' was our cry. Infinitely would we have preferred a pound of ordinary dog-biscuits to half a pound of the best white bread.

As it was, being so foolish, in other words so ravenously hungry, as to eat the whole of our small rooti (loaf) at breakfast, we had no bread or, indeed, anything else, for the supper that was the third and last alleged meal of the day.

It was a cruel choice for growing hungry lads—that of almost no breakfast or absolutely no supper.

Kind Captain Bryndal certainly brought home to us the curious appositeness of the old sea expression,

"Oh, it's only a matter of form—like a sailor's breakfast."

Kind Captain Bryndal. . . .

Through his habit of laughter and of continually showing a perfect set of magnificent white teeth, this handsome bronzed upstanding English gentleman was at first known to the Half-deck as "Laughing Bryndal". But not for long. Soon, some of us were inclined to echo, and the rest did echo, the more perceptive Fo'c'sle's appellation,

"That perishing purple orphan of a grinning hyena."

For it took us not long to learn that Bryndal's most amiable, most warmly bright and flashing, smile was sure indication of his most devilish mood.

Kind Captain Bryndal. . . .

He had the most curious eyes that I've ever seen, and, often as I have looked into them, I cannot tell you their colour.

I think they were colourless, as though between the clear healthy white and the small black pupil was a belt of salt water.

Not deep blue sea-water; not shallow green sea-water; not the grey water that lowers beneath a leaden sky; but just water, and as I say, practically colourless.

His nose was big, strong and dominant; his mouth hard, thin, and perfectly straight; his expression when he was not laughing, ruthless, predatory, aquiline, though without any of the nobility of the expression of the eagle and the hawk. For the face, in spite of its strength, was mean and, in repose, gave the observer the impression that Captain Bryndal was, with inflexible determination, secret amusement, and complete shamelessness, planning some petty coup, some trickery, some minor villainy or other.

He was a hardy oafish brute, courageous and competent, base, cruel and evil. A man of ill-will.

My own first encounter with this ruffian, which roused misgivings eventually justified, was peculiarly damping and unpleasant to a slightly sensitive and over-eager enthusiast like myself.

Meeting him on the poop, I saluted him respectfully and said, "Good-morning, Sir."

Absolutely ignoring me, a yard from him, Captain Bryndal, his eyes flickering across my face, grinned up at the cro'jack yard, without a word or the suspicion of a movement, in acknowledgment of my salute and greeting.

And here I may as well tell you the sequel, though I don't much like doing so, and don't expect you to believe it. Still, if one is writing a book about oneself—well . . . one has to write about oneself.

So, suppressing modesty and a distaste for talking about myself, I state forthwith that I am a queer chap with a queer—what shall I say? Gift? . . . Disability? . . . Power? . . . Curse? . . . Blessing? . . . I don't know.

And what is more, I can't describe this curious attribute by any comprehensive term.

However, examples of its manifestation will be its best description, and here was one of them.

Even as I marvelled at such loutish gross discourtesy in a Captain, I began to experience somewhat similar sensations to those that troubled me on my first view of the filthy and empty half-deck.

For a second I not only seemed to see, I *did* see, Captain Bryndal fade, dissolve, change, from a man into a terrible skeleton that was not completely desiccated, but a ghastly thing of horrible corruption—which in turn swiftly faded, dissolved and changed into a ghost, a wraith, that grew transparent and disappeared, until there stood before me nothing but a uniform, empty as a suit in a shop-window.

This vision, waking nightmare, seizure, mental aberration, hallucination, call it what you will, must have lasted for a second or two, for an invisible hand knocked the ashes from the

Captain's finished pipe, against the taffrail; and then, strangest of all, as I blinked my eyes, this vision of an empty uniform changed into myself and there I stood, serenely smoking my pipe in that Holy of Holies by the mizzen rigging!

It seemed to me an eternity of time before I drew a deep breath, saw clearly what was actually before me, and was normal again. In point of fact, it had lasted as long as it takes a man to remove his pipe from his mouth, give it one tap and return it.

Well, that was that. Queer, uncanny and slightly disturbing, for, at the door of the half-deck on that first day, I had involuntarily looked into the past, and on this occasion I had equally involuntarily looked into the future.

§2

With all sails set, including our queer little spanker, and with sheets and halyards bowsed down to the last inch, we forged slowly southward, and the Mate confided to me that he was hoping to escape the "dusting" he'd almost invariably experienced here at this time of year.

In spite of her bluff bow, there was something about the clearance lines of the *Valkyrie* and her run aft, that enabled her to maintain steerage-way with canvas barely lifting. Given but a light quarterly breeze and every sail drawing, she slipped through the water in amazing style. Of course, it was foolish of the Mate to give voice to his optimism. The demons that ride the Westerlies naturally heard him, and equally naturally decided to "learn" him.

Coming on deck for the first dog-watch, I was amazed at the change wrought in so short a time. Black clouds raced in quick succession above the grey tumbling waste; there was a keen bite in the soughing wind, and, now and then, large drops of rain splashed heavily on deck.

Before Eight Bells was struck, the Mate, busy with some personal matter at the lee mooring-pipe by the break of the poop, saw me watching Geordie and Fagin who were making fast the mizzen lower to'gallants'l.

"You get into your oilskins, Son," he said. "Barometer's falling, wind's rising, and you're going to have your first taste of dirty weather. I was wrong about the weather, for the first time in my life."

And he laughed bitterly.

In my ignorance I imagined that dirty weather consisted

merely of strong winds and heavy rain, and that oil-skinned and sou'westered, like a picture-poster of a brave lifeboat-man, I should boldly defy the elements and be approvingly remarked by All Hands and the Cook.

I was soon remarked, all right: and, curiously enough, after smelling my beautiful new oilskins, of which I'd been rather proud, I felt neither bold nor defiant. I felt sick.

This ghastly feeling of nausea, returning again, made me somewhat slow, and I only had just sufficient time to pull on the oilskin trousers, button the now most peculiarly offensive jacket, and change into thick socks and a pair of bluchers.

Thanks to the gradually increasing Westerly swell, the *Valkyrie* began to behave in a particularly beastly manner, and as this seemed to inconvenience nobody but myself, I was forced to entertain dreadful doubts as to whether I was, after all, the born sailor that I had hitherto considered myself. . . .

Surely all the best people were only sea-sick once, just at first, and were then done with the horrible business?

. . . Listlessly joining the watch at the fore-starboard braces, I observed that, above the tops'ls, only the main lower to'gallants'l was set; and, from chance remarks, I gathered that the wind was no longer favourable, and that we were "bracing her sharp up on the port tack".

A few hours previously, I should have been eager to know what was gained by performing this mysterious manœuvre, and should have followed it with great keenness. Now, I was again so affected by the ship's motion that such matters as shifts of wind and the trimming of yards interested me not at all.

Really I think that if the Mate had come to me and said,

"Mr. Dysart, with your kind permission, I propose tying the steel mainyard into a figure-of-eight knot," I should have fixed him with a glassy eye and, without the least exhibition of surprise, have replied,

"Carry on, Augustus." . . .

At any other time I should have laughed at the slight discomfort of wet feet, but the water that now suddenly spurted through a scupper-hole and filled my boots to overflowing, seemed a last misfortune especially designed by an unkind heaven to complete my misery.

I began to think that Four Bells (six p.m.) and my watch-below would never come.

Yet, before being relieved, miserable as I was, I did actually laugh—and I laughed at Captain Bryndal, though I refrained from making the fact patent.

Perhaps because there was far less rope on that side, Hamblin, our tall Glasgow "keelie", had coiled the weather main braces on their pins, and had left me with a tangle at the starboard rail. Punishing him for taking the easier task, the *Valkyrie* chose the spot at which he stood as the one at which she would scoop up the first green sea of the voyage.

Right over head and shoulders Hamblin received a crashing shower-bath of "solid" water, and as he emptied his mouth of salt sea and strange oaths, he told the *Valkyrie* what he thought of her. After lurid Clydeside curses and horrid epithets, he fell upon anti-climax by calling the ship "a dirrty auld coo".

Suddenly, without warning, his abuse of the *Valkyrie* was quenched and drowned in such a torrent of terrible hair-raising blasphemies from the poop, that Hamblin's curses appeared but as the mild innocuous babblings of a child.

Had not Captain Bryndal stood there grinning pleasantly down upon him, Hamblin would never have supposed for one moment that he had incurred the Captain's wrath.

So kind did he look, so brightly did he smile, so friendly was his laugh, that as the youth stood there soaked to the skin, dripping and shivering, while the ice-cold water swirled round the after hatch-coamings and up my legs, we all listened, in utter amazement, to a scalding burning sulphurous harangue that—as Hamblin expressed it later—"wad hae raised a bluidy great blister on a frozen iron plate"; and it was not until Hamblin, his parents, his ancestors, his present family, his descendants, his person, appearance, intelligence, character and general failure to be either useful or ornamental, had been dealt with abundantly, that he, or any of us, had any idea of the nature of his offence.

But when he had finished his bitter savage indictment, biting, cruel and insufferably insulting, and had laughed merrily again, Captain Bryndal ceased his truly horrible swearing and, with a pleasant smile and flash of white teeth, asked in a friendly and pleasant voice,

"Where's your sense, you purple fool? How in the name of the Devil's dear daughter can we expect fine weather and fair winds if you *go and use language like that*, you hell-blistered orphan?"

I laughed.

§3

At Four Bells, I witnessed the first indication of the crew's growing dislike and contempt for the Third Mate who had the uncommon name of Prellott.

On the fore side of the after-house, I came, unseen by them, upon Prellott and the cross-grained Hamblin apparently about to do battle.

Each was telling the other what he thought of him, but both seemed afraid to strike the first blow, which I thought augured ill for the Officer.

After exchanging insults they parted, each assuring the other that the speaker could, if he cared to take the trouble, "put him to sleep" with the greatest ease.

A queer taunt of Hamblin's, if a just assessment, was his statement that Prellott was "nought but wind an' watter—like a barber's cat", and I passed on my way wondering why the hairdresser's pet should differ from others.

And very soon indeed after this, it was perfectly apparent to everybody that the Third Mate's fierce unnecessary truculence was the purest bluster, and that he was totally unable, and probably quite afraid, to carry out any of his violent threats.

Aboard ship, the reputation of being a "bluff" is completely fatal to an Officer's prestige, and that of Prellott rapidly dwindled to nothing.

Ultimately, while the poop-deck was being holy-stoned and "sand-and-canvased" one day, in the tropics, his complete lack of authority and control over the men was clearly and amusingly demonstrated.

On this occasion, he was working industriously aft, by the wheel-box, and, on all fours, presented a large taut southern end to the observant eyes of the port watch.

Hamblin, who hated the man bitterly, remarked that Prellott was a queer name for a sailor, "since a prelate was a priest", threw a piece of sand-stone the full length of the poop and scored a beautiful bull on the inviting target presented by the Third Mate.

Leaping to his feet as though stung, Prellott sprang round, glared at the row of grinning faces and knowing his man, bawled furiously,

"Was that you, Hamblin?"

Whereupon the young blackguard, straightening his face and raising his eyes to Heaven, replied in a solemn voice of awe,

"Ach! Goad forbid! Goad forbid that I should ever *stone a priest*, Mister, even with holy-stone . . ."

To return. . . . In the second dog-watch that day my only comfort came from changing into dry footwear. All the former symptoms of sea-sickness, with its accompanying fear and daunting lack of self-confidence were upon me again. And in spite of having eaten nothing all day, I refused everything but water.

In vain, the kindly and sympathetic Dacre impressed upon me that severe sea-sickness on a completely empty stomach might be a very serious matter—for the mere sight of black stewed tea and nasty scraps of cold meat (and there was nothing else whatever) was in itself nauseating.

On deck, the heavy crash of great seas rolling aboard was becoming ever more frequent, while the humming of the wind in the rigging steadily increased in volume.

To my inexperience it seemed a terrible storm, but I vowed that—unlike Beauty who had collapsed and now groaned in his bunk and probably in his sleep—I would carry on for just as long as my legs would.

I now know that had I given in at this point, I should have made a much quicker recovery.

Gigantic, in shining oilskins, at One Bell (fifteen minutes before Eight Bells) the Second Mate paid us a brief call. Having given Dacre, who was lamp-trimmer, instructions about lights, he suddenly produced from behind his back a great lump of rank, rotten pork-fat, hanging on a piece of string. Calling loudly to Beauty, he dangled this before the eyes of the wretched suffering lad, with precisely the results that the brute desired.

He then held it in front of my face, and asked if I wouldn't like to eat it. I closed my eyes, held on tight to everything, and faithfully promised myself that, when opportunity arose, I would endeavour to repay the Long Snake—and curiously enough, within half an hour I quite unintentionally kept my promise.

With one leg over the weather-board the callous and malicious ruffian bade me not only shut my eyes but open my mouth, and see what good luck would send me.

Finding me poor game, he changed his tone, loudly announced All Hands would "wear ship" at Eight Bells, and bade the lot of us be smart and ready.

Beauty was too far gone to care whether All Hands "wore" or sank the ship at Eight Bells. In but little better case myself, I burrowed in my clothes-bag for my sea-boots.

In the Nautical Outfitter's mahogany and plate-glass showroom, I'd felt that the possession of these boots would stamp me with the hall-mark of the genuine sailor-man. Rather would I have foregone glittering brass buttons and gold braid.

Tolerantly I had agreed with the shop assistant that the rubber boots, which I really wanted, are apt to make the feet damp and clammy, while secretly I marvelled at the depth of this landsman's knowledge and wisdom.

In point of fact, it would have been far better for me if I'd taken the rubber ones and risked the "dampness".

The atrocious boots with which this well-known house supplied me, proved most dangerous, lost those outfitters some custom, and became a by-word in the *Valkyrie*. According to Dacre, their one advantage was that they "let the water out just as fast as they let it in," and this kept my feet clean.

At the first contact with salt water, the uppers of these boots sagged and creased like a concertina; and the soles, becoming as slippery as soap, made it impossible for me to get any foot-hold on a wet sloping deck. Until I obtained rubber, and made additional soles, I had to glide and skate about the ship instead of walking, and when I screwed circular rubbers to the heels, their suction caused them to leave the deck with a loud plop, at each step.

At the moment, with Dacre away in the lamp-locker, there was no-one to advise me on the necessity and method of making sea- boots and oilskins combine to keep out water.

Thus, knowing nothing of the sailor-man's bad-weather "soul-and-body" lashings, I was soaked to the skin in my first two minutes on deck.

Later on, I learned to adopt those measures by which a seaman makes himself something like a diver, and which enable him, though knocked down, rolled and submerged in the lee-scuppers, to remain quite dry beneath his oilskins.

In really bad weather, he pulls his oilskin trousers well up the sea-boot legs, lashes them there with spun yarn, inserts oakum between oilskin and sea-boot above this lashing, and then puts a further lashing above the oakum.

Outside the short oilskin jacket, he wears his belt and sheath-knife, and from the back of the belt passes a lashing between the trouser-legs, and fastens it to the belt buckle. This properly done, no water can penetrate to the clothing beneath.

Knowing nothing of these things, and, in any case, feeling far too ill to care, I foolishly tucked my trousers into the vile boots, and even neglected the elementary precaution of tying the coat-sleeves at the wrist so that, when I raised my arms to haul on a sodden rope, water would not pour down the sleeves. I did not even put a woollen muffler inside my jacket collar to prevent water from going down my neck. As Blancke later remarked with some surprise, I went on deck "like I vos go to der church".

Most reluctantly I left the comparatively dry and warm half-deck, and, with the dazzle of its light still in my eyes, I tried to pierce the black darkness without.

White caps of foam hurtling swiftly past, were all that I could see; and they seemed to be terrifyingly near, big, and menacing. Gone was all my former confidence and, could he have known how I felt, Blancke would have been in no doubt about my being a First Voyager. Almost I wished that I were at home with my mother and my hateful step-father.

As I hesitated and wondered where I ought to go, both wind and sea seemed simultaneously to realize that here was a tyro, a greenhorn, a land-lubber, delivered to them for their sport.

The wind, seeing or feeling that my beautiful new sou'wester was not tied beneath my chin with proper strings, whipped it instantly from my head, and, in the light that escaped from the door-way of the half-deck, I saw my one and only storm-hat sail, majestic as a sea-bird, away into the night.

How was I to know that none save steam-yachtsmen ever had that puerile useless piece of elastic on their sou'westers?

As I stared, almost salt-eyed and broken-hearted, after my vanished sou'wester, the sea took its turn; a playful wave leapt the weather rail, almost knocked me down, drenched me, and turned my feeble curse to helpless spluttering.

It was a mere bathful of water and, a month later, I should have jumped on to the after-hatch and escaped wetting so much as my feet.

But that night I was indeed all at sea; and the icy water, first filling my boots and then whisking my feet from under me, rolled with me down to leeward and seemed to reach every inch of my shrinking skin.

Just as I gave myself up for drowned and lost, another merry wave floated me aft to the lee poop-ladder.

Grabbing the bottom step I dragged myself on to the poop, crawling, and looking, like a drowned rat, and feeling far too cold, wet, sick, and miserable even to be thankful for what I considered a hair-breadth escape from death.

Here, Fagin's ugly wolfish grin at my drenched and bare-headed condition saved me from any regret when he fell the first of my victims, on my memorable first night-watch at sea.

The water had, by now, soaked well into the porous soles of my disgraceful boots, and, the ship lurching suddenly, and they causing me to slip and slide, I fell heavily against him. Naturally he clutched wildly at me, and this brought us both down, but while my head was cushioned by his stomach, the back of his own head came violently in contact with the deck.

I was content with this arrangement.

And little did those who jeered know how soon their turn might come. For, without something to keep me upright, I was a source of danger to everyone near me. To me, the decks seemed like wet ice, and whenever I attempted to walk, I must seize the nearest support.

Frequently this was a man, and ere long I was not only hurt in body but also in mind—for I was cursed in several tongues. To imperil a sailor's foot-hold is to commit an unforgivable sin, and, apart from my clutching and grabbing at people, I was sliding about as uncontrolled and erratic, as dangerous and unwieldy, as a spare anchor adrift on the deck in a storm.

However, it's a good wind that blows nobody any ill, and my painful gymnastics had their climax, if not their end, in my inadvertently avenging Beauty and myself on the Second Mate. Literally on the Second Mate.

At the moment the ship was coming round, and had wind and sea on the starboard quarter. And though, to me, conditions seemed terrible, the weather was not sufficiently bad to necessitate ordering All Hands off the deck; or awaiting a "smooth" before bringing her to the wind.

Anyhow, with the Second Mate at the fore-hand, and facing for'ard, some of the men were tightening the weather fore-braces and I was making my painful zig-zag way to lend my countenance and weight to their efforts. The first part of my painful and erratic pilgrimage I took at a snail's pace; the latter part at a speed phenomenal—due to a mistake common to first voyagers.

Instead of leaping for the rigging when a sea deliberately hurled itself clear over the main braces at me, I attempted to run, or rather, to skate.

Taking me in the rear, a few tons of water suddenly gave me such an impetus that, with body bent slightly forward, I sped along as for the world's skating championship.

Had the ship remained on an even keel for but a few seconds, all would have been well. Graceful as a sea-bird I should have sailed past the watch, shot up the sheer of the for'ard deck, and come to rest under the fo'c'sle head somewhere near the starboard hawse-pipe.

But, in actual fact, things were quite otherwise.

No sooner was I well under way, and going very strong, than a sudden pitch of the ship sent me swooping down the deck like a sheering gull, and, at the same time, a heavy roll to starboard put me on a dead true course for the line of hauling men.

Except to yell,

"Look out, I'm coming," I could do nothing but come; and as though projected from a gun, I shot straight into the broad back of the unsuspecting Second Mate—and brought him down heavily.

Even in those days, I weighed about fourteen stone, and with the wet deck beneath him, no man alive could have withstood my onslaught.

Banging his face heavily against that of the man facing him as he clutched him, the three of us, in our lives united, charged, an irresistible battering-ram, upon the orderly line of hauling seamen, and reduced it to chaos. As though they were a row of lead soldiers, we swept their legs from beneath them, bowled them over, and mingled ourselves with them as part of a struggling spluttering mass of cursing, writhing men who fought and strove to sort themselves out, and to rise from three feet of swirling water.

Clever, cool-headed Geordie had jumped clear, and managing to keep his feet, had sprung on to the spare spar, and had had the presence of mind and good sense to catch a turn with the brace round a bollard—thus preventing the fore lower tops'l-yard from "taking charge" and perhaps doing considerable damage.

While his promptness undoubtedly saved some of us from serious injury—for had the brace been left free to run out through the blocks, arms and legs or necks would almost certainly have been jammed in its coils—Geordie did not receive praise for his quickness and presence of mind. For his sea-boots were heavy and he had reached the rail across the floundering bodies and sad faces of his shipmates.

The seaman, Church, being most hurt, was most aggrieved and, having given vent to the opinion that I was born and destined to kill All Hands and the Cook, turned to Geordie to say that, though it was possible he was not also a wanton and deliberate murderer, the fact remained that a British A.B.s head was not intended as a stepping-stone to higher things.

"Ye're dommed reet," said Geordie. "Lower things, or a

mile-stane on the road to Hell."

This exchange having given the Second Mate time to recover breath and to ascertain that his badly bruised nose, if broken, was not bleeding, he flung his hands aloft and addressed the sky. What he said I do not know, but Hate seemed literally to blaze in his pale eyes.

"Get you on to the poop and stop there," he snarled at me. "And if the Captain asks what ye're doing, say you've done it. Say you've half killed the Second Mate and maimed most of his watch—curse you. . . . And may the Devil fry you in your own fat, blast you."

Sore, ill, wet and very cold, I reached the poop and, leaning against the lee mizzen-shrouds, conceived a dislike for a life on the ocean wave.

I felt despondent.

But when I heard a loud coarse noise, followed by the voice of the Second Mate; heard him complain that I'd made him be sick and that he'd do it again, I felt less dejected.

CHAPTER VII

For three days the *Valkyrie* was compelled to beat about in the vicinity of Tory Island and the rightly named Bloody Foreland, until the wind, hauling to the nor'ard, enabled us to make a good offing.

On the second of those days, my foolish obstinate refusals to go below and admit myself beaten, brought the inevitable result of sickness, sleeplessness and starvation, and I collapsed in the mizzen rigging.

Fortunately for me, I'd only climbed a short distance, and just had enough strength to slither down to the rail. It was the Captain himself who, laughing merrily, grabbed my collar and hauled me inboard before I fell into the sea.

As I was half-dragged and half-carried to my bunk, he cursed me as he smiled, and then, turning to the Third Mate, overwhelmed him with a torrent of profanity; and, for sending me aloft when sick, cursed him violently, not on grounds of common humanity, but for risking the loss of my services to the ship.

No, there was nothing kindly or humane about Captain Bryndal, and he did not believe in "visiting the sick" in the half-deck a few feet away; and it was not until I was able to turn-to, some days later, that I saw his handsome face again.

A ship is the worst place in the world in which to be ill—except when the sufferer is a passenger in a big liner. Whatever sympathy may be felt for him, no help can be expected from the busy crew of an under-manned vessel, in which everyone has his own work to do. Nor, if there were anyone on board who had the time and inclination for nursing, would he be likely to have the skill. And, apart from the utter discomfort and hopeless lack of sick-room amenities, the conscientious sufferer is yet further troubled and worried by the knowledge that his absence from duty imposes extra duty on his hard-worked shipmates.

In this, my first and last illness afloat, a sensation of unrelieved hopelessness and misery gradually degenerated into something like terror, an awful fear that was caused and augmented by increasing physical weakness and exhaustion.

To my fevered imagination, every heavy sea that thundered aboard, stove in the hatches, and the imminent danger of death by drowning would find me undressed and unprepared to take to the boats.

As I lay sleepless in my bunk, weary of keeping my burning eyes closed as I wished to do, I counted again and again the deck planks above my head, watched the beads of sweat roll down angle-irons and the sides of the deck-house, and followed the voyages of matches adrift in the water that, leaking through the door, washed, inches deep, around our sea-chests.

But always the baleful light of the opposite port-hole triumphed, and, lured and fascinated, my eyes were compelled to stare at the grey heaving expanse that, stretching to the horizon, so daunted my soul and sickened my body.

My bunk was to starboard and when the port rail dipped, I seemed to be looking up the side of an immense cliff of grey water—a mountain of foam-flecked sea poised to topple over and obliterate our impotent puny vessel.

It was quite obvious to me that I was doomed, and at no distant minute, to a sudden end and a watery grave. Once again, almost I wished I was back in my mother's house.

Finally, I became so weak that I felt little and feared nothing, and Dacre, who had been doing his best for me, realized the Captain's utter indifference to my welfare and appealed to the Mate.

Mr. Wight came at once. Apparently from a great distance, I heard his voice say,

"My God, that boy's bad. Why couldn't you have come for me before?"

Going straight to Doctor, he told that poor overworked negro that I was very seriously ill, and not merely suffering from beginner's sea-sickness.

Immediately, Doctor took me in hand and showed the reason why sea-cooks are called by that honourable title.

Having purloined from the medicine-chest what he considered as the appropriate medicines, and administered them, he gave me, in gradually increasing doses, a mixture of beef-tea and brandy; and later procured from somewhere, undoubtedly by honest theft, a half-bottle of port-wine. I have not the very slightest doubt—and neither had anyone else on board—that Doctor actually saved my life, cured me of my illness, and restored me to health. What doctor can do more?

I picked up rapidly and, after promotion to rice-pudding, soon became well enough to hope for the best, to take an interest in life, and to derive some amusement from the respective attitudes of my room-mates.

Dacre was profoundly thankful, and in every unselfish way of which he could think, seconded Doctor's efforts on my behalf.

Geordie, I am certain, was as pleased as Dacre himself, and almost made me laugh by the way he would feel my pulse, lift my eye-lid and examine my eye, scan my features with anxious thought, and, taking my temperature with the tip of his finger, hazard the opinion that I was "aboot ninety i' the shade".

Beauty, when I first sat up and dangled feeble legs over the side of my bunk, literally "awoke" to the fact that I'd been ill.

Fagin, while not accusing me of deliberate malingering, made me feel what was doubtless true—that my illness, exaggerated or not, had been extremely inconsiderate; annoying to him, and discreditable to myself.

At last there came the memorable and wonderful day when I could get up, go on deck, and crawl along to the galley.

The *Valkyrie* was slipping sweetly along through a calm blue sea. I was returning to life and health and strength and had that best of all feelings that God's in His Heaven, and all's right with the world.

Doctor was as unfailingly glad to see me as I was to see him.

Poor old "Doc". I will refrain from quoting Gunga Din. He had never been very bright intellectually, but he was as brave as a lion, of perfect physical development, and had been of gigantic strength.

Curiously enough, it was to his strength and courage that he owed his position as Cook on the *Valkyrie*. Doctor had been Bosun of one of the Company's vessels; and, to maintain authority over white men, a "nigger" Bosun must be very fine. Aboard a ship partially dismasted in a *pampero*, all the wreckage, with the exception of a jammed main topmast, had been cut away and this spar was the only obstacle to the use of jury-rig.

Its removal, however, was not only difficult but highly dangerous, and the only man who would make the attempt was Doctor, the coloured Bosun. With no volunteer to aid him, he went aloft, at the risk of his life, and succeeded in dislodging the topmast, but his Herculean exertions so injured him internally that he could never again undertake arduous work, and, out of gratitude, and with delightful disregard for their crews, Messrs. Dobson, Robson and Wright made him Cook.

I am quite sure he was a splendid Bosun, and I'm even more sure he was not a splendid Cook. He was something better, though—a man of sterling honesty and of staunch loyalty.

Through writing his letters for him, I found that he had, for a long time, been in possession of a sum of money entrusted to him in a San Francisco boarding-house by a drunken sailor. Although the owner—probably shanghaied—had never returned to claim it, the idea of using this money had never entered Doctor's head, and, with my assistance, he made attempts at every port to find the man who, for all he knew, might have been dead for many years. I derived endless interest and much amusement from Doctor's observations on men and manners; life; death; and the Vast Forever.

Of one former officer he spoke very highly because, although on week-days he could and did out-swear, out-curse, out-blast and out-blaspheme All Hands and the Cook, and bring the blush of shame and the silence of shock to the faces of the ship's parrot, monkey, and cat, on the Sabbath he not only invariably and entirely refrained from swearing, but would permit no-one else to indulge in bad language of any sort.

Of another officer Doctor spoke most highly as a perfect gentleman and an honourable man because, when a Negro and a Dane were about to fight, he armed himself with belaying-pin and promised to brain messily any on-looker who, during the battle, uttered one word calculated to daunt or dishearten the Negro, inasmuch as the latter, though a goddam scoundrelly son of a gun of a gorilla, was the whiter of the two disputants.

It is an interesting and incontrovertible fact that Man, *homo* alleged *sapiens*, is far more prone to like, approve, and cherish those whom he has befriended than those who have befriended him. I suppose the sight of the person whom we have benefited inflates us subconsciously with the pleasant sensations appropriate to a Benefactor.

Having saved my life and nursed me back to health, Doctor evidently felt strongly drawn toward me, assumed a faintly proprietary air, did me most useful favours, and took me completely into his confidence.

In so doing, he showed how very thin was the veneer with which civilization had covered his natural mind and disfigured his simple soul. His own private God, with whom he was on the most familiar terms, was a strange Deity, tolerant, though in certain directions, prejudiced, jealous, and definitely vindictive.

Among other examples of His broad-minded tolerance was His clear view that any wicked man who was an enemy of Doctor deserved to die, and whether he died or not was a matter for Doctor's own private decision—a case of "killing, no murder".

Doctor's Deity, moreover, had not the slightest objection to his having a wife in every port, provided he treated them kindly and did not "pay them with the fore-sheet".

Nor did He mind having His name taken in vain. What He would not stand, and where He showed prejudice, jealousy, and vindictiveness, was superstition, such as any nonsense about drowning a cat, whistling for a wind, killing sea-gulls, or carrying parsons; idolatry, such as putting one's head inside a Mussulman mosque or Hindu or other "heathen" temple; and such sins as dishonesty, theft, lying, cheating, cruelty, and quarrelsomeness among the elect, His own followers; and the commission on Sunday of an enormous assortment of heinous sins that, on week-days, were permissible if not commendable acts.

I was not sure that Doctor wasn't the most interesting man on the ship—not only for himself but for his family history. His parents had been slaves in Barbados, and Doctor had documentary proof that the redemption of his mother had cost the Government eighty pounds. Of this, Doctor was very proud, for seventy-five pounds was the average price paid in those days for a human being.

His father, tired of waiting for the promised release in which he had no faith, fled to the jungle, and for his apprehension the unheard-of reward of ten *moidores* was offered.

Had it been known that the Government really was going to redeem him—and at the handsome price of ninety-five pounds—the reward would have been even greater.

Here was matter for pride. It is not given to every man to have proof that his parents are, or were, publicly assessed in open market at so high a figure—solely by reason of their ability and willingness to work hard.

Doctor's mother must have been a remarkable woman, for he had a clear recollection of his father being whipped soundly by her, for running away from so kind a master as herself—also of her compelling Doctor himself partially to disrobe to receive a sound whipping, before being sent to bed without any supper—at the age of twenty.

Doctor also remembered her telling him about her own father who had been one of a cargo of slaves shipped by Christian English gentlemen from Africa to Trinidad, in the brig *Prudence* of Liverpool.

Early in the voyage, cholera broke out in the hold, and, since Lloyds insured against loss of slaves by drowning—and by nothing else—the Captain had to see to it that they died in no other way.

An honest God-fearing man, he could not commit perjury. A faithful and zealous agent of his owners, he could not permit so heavy a loss to fall upon them as would be incurred through the deaths of the negroes from cholera.

So those who contracted the disease—drowned.

And the Captain could lay his hand upon his heart or his Bible and, with perfect truth, give his plighted word and take his solemn oath, that the slaves had died by drowning. Of two hundred negroes shipped, less than thirty lived to land at Port of Spain. Two of the survivors being bought by a visitor from Barbados received his surname in the usual manner, and became Mc-Graths. . . .

But this is the story of the *Valkyrie*, and, at this rate, it would fill a dozen volumes.

In fact, I must hasten along if I am to tell of the mystery and the tragedy of the *Valkyrie* in a book of reasonable proportions. Indeed, as one long voyage is very like another and its description an oft-told tale, I will say no more of this one, save that it was normal and fairly uneventful until the *Valkyrie* berthed safely at Sydney, where happened a series of events each of which played its part, great or small, in bringing about—that which happened.

But although there is very little to tell about the voyage itself, I must describe certain of the crew who remained with the *Valkyrie* until she reached home—or until they themselves left her for Davy Jones's locker and the Port of Missing Men.

Chief among these were Chips, Johes, Jake, and Müller, definitely of the one party; and Church, Carrol, Berghen and Blancke of the other.

Fluctuating between them, now attached to the one party and now to the other, were the Irishmen "Patsy Hooligan" and Foyle; "Baby" Axenstern, Olsen, Hamblin, and several "Dutchmen" under which heading, with large-minded tolerance, the British sailor includes Germans, Swedes, Norwegians, Danes, Icelanders and Finns, as well as the men of Holland.

Now, the first four of the above-mentioned were in their respective ways and spheres quite definitely Bad Men.

Bad Dutchmen are remarkably rare and, possibly because of this, when they are bad they are very bad—or seem so, by contrast.

"Chips", the Carpenter, a Scandinavian named Peddersen, was bad. His besetting sin was avarice; and ancillary sins to this master vice were disloyalty, treachery, theft and, finally, murder.

He was a big bold black-bearded man, lazy if competent at his job, gifted with unusual mental power for his walk in life, of very powerful physique, and a fair boxer. To him, a knife was a chest of tools and an armoury of weapons; he could throw it with the accuracy of a music-hall professional.

This man Peddersen played no small part in the tragedy of the *Valkyrie*.

The man who called himself Johes was almost certainly a fugitive from justice, and was generally believed to be a hireling labour agitator who had absconded with the Trade Union funds of some local branch of which he was the treasurer. Certainly, he had what is known as the gift of the gab, and was a most damn-able sea-lawyer, an inveterate trouble-maker, and a dangerous subversive element in the fo'c'sle. He was no sailor, and didn't look like one; a weedy, unwholesome creature, noticeable by reason of his jet-black hair, dead-white face, slate-grey shifty eyes, and big loose-lipped sagging mouth. He was a mean-hearted base rascal, one of those heroes who, having fomented real trouble, watch its course from afar and, in safety, see their dupes face the danger. In the event of success they will reap what reward there may be; in the event of failure, the loss, injury and punishment are to the dupes.

To the rest of his watch he was known as "Slim" Johes.

Jake, as he called himself—his other name being Walfisch—was patently a fraud from the beginning, for he pretended to be an American of English descent, and was obviously no more an American than he was a Hindu. In moments of great excitement or danger, he exclaimed and spoke in German. He also counted in that language. He was a bully, but, unlike most bullies, he was anything but a coward. He was also a "blower", a know-all fine-weather sailor, who might be difficult to find and more difficult to use in emergent dangerous weather; and (like his great friend Slim Johes) a bitter-tongued grumbler, a mischievous whisperer of lies, an unpleasant insolent dog when and where he dared to be. Jake Walfisch was definitely a rogue, and a thoroughly nasty piece of work. Incidentally, he was well known to Mr. Orlando Wight and something of a protégé of that officer.

To complete this quartette that was a misfortune to the *Valkyrie*, there was Müller, an anarchist, or what we should nowa-days call a Communist, a man with a grievance against the world, or rather against anybody and everybody in the world who was better off than Müller.

Being a Communist, he was naturally acquisitive, greedy,

miserly and avaricious. If there were one thing he loved better than gold, it was a grievance, and the poor ruffian's life was one long hymn of hate. He needs must hate the highest when he saw it, and as, aboard ship, the highest he could see were the officers, they were the inevitable and immediate objects of his concentrated passion.

It is an almost sufficient description of our Second Mate, Mr. Smeeker, to say that he was exempt from the hatred of Müller; that Chips Peddersen was his right-hand man, friend and protégé, and that the bad four were, of all the crew, his especial favourites.

In every way diametrically opposite to these unseamanlike and worthless scoundrels were Church, Carrol, Berghen and Blancke.

Church was the *beau idéal* of a British seaman, in skill and character as well as in appearance. He was a Mark Tapley of undaunted unfailing cheerfulness, a most seaman-like sailor-man, a lion of courage and as honest as Doctor himself. He was a man—and a sailor.

And like unto him was Carrol, a leathery, wrinkled, tough and defiant seaman who never spoke save to grumble. Indeed, in him, grumbling had become so ingrained a habit that he groused at everything—every happening, every person, every place. I'm quite certain that he will grouse in Heaven, a port which he some day assuredly will make, and wherein his rating will not be among the lowest.

Carrol grumbled at fine weather and at foul; at good luck and at bad; at his friends and at his enemies; at work and at idleness; at the accursed anxiety of having money and at the accursed anxiety of having none.

But as any officer with a grain of sense perceived, Carrol grumbled as automatically, habitually, and naturally, as he breathed, smoked, ate and drank, or slept. Simply, it was his nature "to", and it meant absolutely nothing.

But to the fool Slim Johes it appeared that Carrol growled, out of malice, hatred, and all uncharitableness; out of sheer bitter-ness of heart; out of base subversive loathing of all superiors, simply because they were superior to him. In point of fact there was no better seaman on the ship, none readier in emergency or steadier in prolonged tribulation. He could no more have com-mitted an unmanly, underhand, unseamanlike act than he could have refrained from his eternal grumbling.

Berghen and Blancke can be described together as easily as Tweedledum and Tweedledee. They were two of those fine, dependable, skilful seamen, amenable, peaceable and well-behaved, who are—I was almost going to say, alas—the backbone of the British Mercantile Marine. Certainly, they form a considerable part of it, are invaluable to it, and, strangely enough, seem to prefer it to that of their own respective countries. These four men, like the other four whom I have mentioned, formed another quartette of friends.

Of the others, men who might be influenced by Peddersen's gang for evil, or by Church and his friends in the interests of law and order, several left us at Sydney, San Francisco or Pisagua, and as they played no part in the tragedy of the *Valkyrie*, need not be mentioned.

Of the remainder who were of interest, were Hamblin and the two Irishmen, "Patsy Hooligan" and Foyle, who were real characters. Of Patsy, some said that he never wandered in his mind because there wasn't room, while others said that he'd never really go out of his mind as he'd never really been in it.

How far Patsy was a cunning actor and how far a simple idiot, I did not know. At times, one thought there was some method in his madness; at others, one was sure there was some madness in his method. A curious and wearisome habit of Patsy's was to state the obvious and then repeat it—sometimes *ad nauseam*.

Foyle was in a different category. There was no question of his acting or being cunning, for he acted the whole time; played to the gallery with everything he did and every word he said. And as for cunning, he was, in Dacre's words, twice as cunning as a barrow-load of monkeys and four times as mischievous.

Foyle did everything for effect, and when he raised the loudest laughter by his amusing actions and sayings, the humour was conscious and intentional, the situations arranged and the "impromptus" studied and memorized. He was the leanest, skinniest creature I have ever beheld.

Both Patsy and Foyle were good sailors and well-meaning men, though highly suggestible and apt to take their line of thought and shade of opinion from that of the last speaker and the nearest or strongest influence.

Hamblin, the long Glasgow lad, was a fine fellow—when he was himself. But he had a devastating recurrent head-ache, a temper, and an over-sensitive appreciation of anything savouring of injustice—and when in a temper, or suffering from a sense of injustice, Hamblin definitely was not himself. I hasten to add that there was nothing whatsoever in common between this idiosyncrasy of Hamblin's and Müller's hatred of his betters, and Slim Johes' base mean envy.

On the contrary, there was something noble about Hamblin's touchiness, as he was more often indignant on behalf of other people than he was on his own account.

Their own imagined "wrongs" made Peddersen's gang murderous. The genuine wrongs of other people made Hamblin indignant—and in his indignation he was apt to "raise Hell and break a tea-cup", as we used to say on the *Valkyrie*.

There was never much wrong with Hamblin and, rightly handled, there was nothing wrong with him at all.

CHAPTER VIII

Sydney Harbour . . .

In the first place, to my lasting sorrow and regret, we lost our Mate, Mr. Orlando Wight, who had become my staunch friend, patron and mentor. Grateful as I was to him, it was not until we lost him that I knew how much I owed to him, and what a difference to my happiness and welfare his presence aboard had made.

Just before we reached Sydney Harbour he fell ill, and to Doc's growing worry and anxiety, grew steadily worse.

"I sho dunno what's de matter wid him," he said. "He's like a man under a curse and a spell, like he got a debble in his stummick. Dreful pains, an' he sho am gettin' bery weak. Seems like he can't keep nuttin' on his stummick. I tell you, Sinbad boy, I got my 'spicions; *dark* 'spicions I got."

The night before we entered Sydney Harbour, Mr. Wight sent for me. I was absolutely shocked at the change in him, and, even to my inexperienced eye, he was a dying man—and he had sent for me too late. . . . If he had anything to say to me, that is.

And I believe he had.

I have often wondered what the result would have been, if he had sent for me sooner and told me everything.

Now he was semi-delirious, and, at times, did not know me.

". . . and mind you, when all's said and done, she's a good woman, one of the best. Never let you down—never. Only give her a square deal and she'll see that you get one . . .

"Hullo, Sinbad. There was something I wanted to say to you . . . Can't remember. Better to-morrow perhaps. And don't forget that any man who comes up to you may be a dick. You've got to know him before you do business or let him think you know anything about the business. . . . She's the best woman I ever met . . . Lovely . . . and what a brain! But don't you listen to Bryndal. He's nobody. He's not in it at all and if he says he is and can bring you in too, he's a liar. You watch him. . . . She doesn't trust him much—but it's too much, anyhow.

"She'd have done better with Smeeker—for he'd never have the guts to double-cross . . .

"And you look out for the engine, Sonny."

"What engine, Sir?" I asked, though I didn't really believe that poor Mr. Wight knew what he was saying.

"Hullo, Sinbad boy . . . something I wanted to say to you. Oh God, this pain . . . Can you remember a message for her?"

"For whom, Sir?"

"No need to name names and go shouting 'em about the place like that. But if I don't see her, tell her I said she'd do better with Smeeker . . . Yes . . . She's got to watch Bryndal. He's got a game, and he's a deep devil. Yes, a damned deep dog. He doesn't know how much I know and he's given himself away—to me, of all people. You tell her we'd better put him overboard, one night, between here and 'Frisco."

I felt dreadfully uncomfortable.

Of course these were only the unconscious meanderings of delirium, but I felt ashamed of myself to be sitting there and listening. People say anything when the conscious mind is dethroned and the unconscious takes complete control.

"Well, I'll be going, Sir," I said, "if there's nothing I can do for you."

"Bryndal," replied Mr. Wight, glaring at me, "if you try to double-cross her, I'll kill you. You've said too much, you hound, and you haven't done enough. And it's too late now. I've got your measure. You watch your step, Bryndal, if you want to live long and die happy. More likely you'll live unhappy and die long. I tell you, you're not fit to clean her shoes, you treacherous bastard. . . ."

I crept away, shocked and horrified and puzzled, and sought out Dacre.

"That's very queer," he said. "I know Wight has some sort of hold over the Old Man."

"How do you know that?" I asked.

"Well, I overheard something I was not meant to hear," Dacre replied. "I went to the poop to report, and the Old Man was grinning like a Cheshire cat in a cage, and I heard Wight say,

" 'Well, those are your orders, Captain Bryndal, and you'll do as you're told . . . like it or lump it . . . See?'

"Then they saw me and shut up."

"I don't know what to make of it," I said. "Wight's got some-thing serious on his mind—and he's very ill."

That night Mr. Wight died suddenly, and the day before we passed Sydney Heads he was buried at sea.

"An' why in such a hurry, Sinbad boy?" Doc asked me after the funeral. "I tell you for why. Because Mr. Orlando Wight was pizened. . . . I'se only a none-educated nigger, Sinbad boy, but I knows what I knows. Yessah. . . . And there's a queer spot ober his heart. . . ."

If the loss of the Mate, Mr. Wight, was bad, its sequel was worse, for, with utter dismay, not only on our own account but on that of the *Valkyrie* and all concerned, we learned that Smeeker, the Second Mate, was to be promoted and to be our new Mate.

The place of a really capable and competent Chief Officer was to be taken by one who was really bad, unworthy and incompetent—the Long Snake.

To the half-deck and myself especially it was a blow for, as I've said, if there was one thing that Smeeker hated more than another, it was Apprentices in general and me in particular.

As a fore-taste of what we might expect, Smeeker's first order as Mate was that all boat-work should be given to the Ordinary Seamen. This meant that while they, dressed in white, pulled the Captain ashore in the ship's dinghy, and then, at leisure consorted with the Apprentice crews of other ships' boats at the landing-stage, we five were put to cleaning out the filthy holds and then to tarring the rigging.

Fortune's next stroke was bad for Prellott, the Third Mate, now promoted Second, and good for us, inasmuch as his place was taken by a better man, a grand man; a fact for which we later had cause to be profoundly thankful. What would have happened in the event of the ship sailing under Captain Bryndal with the weak and evil Smeeker as Mate, and the weak and foolish Prellott as Second Mate, hardly bears contemplation.

Coming aboard late one night with a friend from another ship, Prellott had shown his authority by interrupting a private row in a hectoring bullying manner, putting up a bluff that deceived none of the brawlers and irritated them all.

So much so in the case of one of the A.B.s, a German named Kampe, that, drawing his sheath-knife, he pushed it to a depth of several inches, between Prellott's ribs.

With Prellott left behind wounded and apparently in a dying condition, Captain Bryndal refused to release Dacre whose Indentures had expired and who wished to sit for his Second Mate's "ticket". Instead, he ordered him to act as Third Mate—with an A.B.'s wages of three pounds a month, without any of the privileges of an Officer, and without having meals, according to custom, in the Cabin.

Moreover, thanks to Smeeker's unfriendliness, indifference

and lack of support, only the superior element in the crew accorded Dacre the "Mister" which is the time-honoured title and prerogative of all Officers. So long as he was only Second Mate, Smeeker's hostility was veiled, if only thinly, but directly he became Chief Officer, the veil was promptly rent, and the true nature of this mean-souled vindictive man became evident and revealed.

Some of the manifestations of his petty but dangerous spitefulness were incredibly childish, but as he now had nearly as much power over us as the Captain himself, life was rendered difficult. For example, in the hope that I should be late at the mustering of the Watches at night, he kept Fagin or Beauty—who should have come to call me from my watch-below—in his cabin, so that I should sleep on and miss roll-call.

When he discovered that the new Second Mate, Mr. Hammerson, made it his business to see that I was called, Smeeker simply resorted to plain malicious lying. He would declare that I'd not answered to my name, and so, in punishment, must lose half my watch-below.

Luckily for me, the new Second Mate had taken Smeeker's measure pretty accurately and liked him about as much as the Apprentices did; so as soon as Smeeker had put out his light, the Second Mate would whisper to me to "push off". As no bourne to which I should "push" was mentioned, I invariably selected my bunk, and so got my due, proper, and very necessary sleep.

I soon found other examples of Smeeker's mean unscrupulousness.

In every ship there's a great deal of overhauling of bunt-lines to be done.

Before a sail can be furled, it must be hauled up to the yard somewhat in the manner of a stage curtain, and for this purpose it is provided with ropes called bunt-lines. These are seized on to the foot of the sail, and passing up the fore side and through a block above the yard, are taken through various leads down to the pin-rail on deck. As every sailor is aware, the sail, being set, must not be allowed to take the weight of any of these long ropes, as the strain would soon chafe the canvas into holes.

Some of each bunt-line is therefore hauled up from the deck, "overhauled" down the fore side of the sail, so that it may hang in a bight, and the weight of the remainder is supported by a piece of twine fastened to the jack-stay of the yard, or to the rigging.

In such emergencies as a sudden squall or increase of wind, this twine can easily be broken by a pull on the bunt-line, without the necessity for anyone going aloft. But, as every Apprentice learns to his sorrow, the twine sometimes breaks, of itself, without any pull from deck. It does this for preference in the peaceful second dog-watch, or on the Sabbath Day itself—and an Apprentice must go up and replace it.

Personally, although I once saw Smeeker deliberately break a bunt-line-stop for my special benefit, I never succumbed to the strong but evil temptation of using anything more substantial than twine. In point of fact, I invariably kept twine in my pocket, for the sole purpose of stopping bunt-lines.

Therefore, I felt hurt, indignant, and very angry, when Smeeker burst into the half-deck with the entirely false accusation that by stopping the mizzen upper to'gallant bunt-lines with rope-yarns, I had very nearly caused the loss of the sail.

It appeared that, in the middle watch, the Second Mate was unable to haul up the to'gallants'l until a man had gone aloft and cut all the stops. According to Smeeker, the new Second Mate had accused me of the crime.

"I've never stopped bunt-lines with rope-yarns in my life, Sir," I replied when Smeeker had finished shouting, "and I've not been up the mizzen for the last three days."

"Don't you give me any of your damned lip, you young liar," was his astonishing reply.

And when I repeated, perfectly civilly, that I'd never stopped bunt-lines with rope-yarn, nor been up the mizzen for three days, he stepped outside the half-deck and again bawled at me to "stop my lying impudence and insolence".

I could only suppose that the man was drunk—until I realized that he was acting for the benefit of the Captain whom he knew to be close by, and an interested listener.

When the Mate had finished, I was called up on to the poop, soundly rated by Captain Bryndal for the crime that I had not committed, as well as for the insolence of which I'd not been guilty, and was docked of my watch-below in punishment.

As, with a pleasant smile and flashing teeth, Captain Bryndal excoriated me with invective, insult, and false accusation, he tried to "stare me out", and completely failed. I contrived to withstand the steady hypnotic glare of his horrible uncanny eyes, and to keep my own unflinchingly and steadily fixed upon them.

But enough of Smeeker for the moment.

To return to Sydney.

It was not long before we learnt some extremely interesting

facts concerning our new Second Mate, Mr. Hammerson. A Son of the Hammer he was indeed, and had actually been a professional boxer of very considerable repute in Australia and beyond.

Tiring of the sea, and knowing himself to be a boxer of much more than average ability, physique, and endurance, he had left his ship at Sydney, boxed for cash prizes, been taken up by a sporting syndicate, and had become Heavy-weight Champion of Australia.

Tiring of pugilism, and realizing that he wasn't growing any younger, he had now left the ring and returned to his first love, the sea.

As later he remarked to me, "if there's a worse and rougher life than wind-jammer lime-juicing, it's being knocked about in an eighteen-foot ring. And if there's a worse and rougher life than prize-fighting, it's being half-drowned, half-starved and half-paid in a three-thousand-ton lime-juicing wind-jammer."

"So there you are, Son," he said, "rough stuff, either way."

I don't know whether Mr. Hammerson found his sea experience of value in the prize-ring (though doubtless his muscles were the better for it) but undoubtedly he found his prize-ring experience of value at sea, and on at least one occasion it saved the *Valkyrie* and the life of every man on board.

As far as appearances went, Mr. Hammerson was a thick-set, burly, typical sailor, with a sailor's eyes and weather-beaten countenance, nautical roll, and tattoo-marks—a sailor, moreover, who had done so much boxing that his nose and his ears had suffered, the one being broken, broadened and bent, the others being damaged and thickened.

In fact he looked precisely what he was. His square, clean-shaven craggy face was redeemed by a pair of fine fearless eyes, blue, kindly, and penetrating; a good, firm, if somewhat grim, mouth; and a grand chin. Not a person of much education, culture, or the higher social graces and deportment, Mr. Hammerson was a man, and we liked and respected him. I personally got on with him splendidly from the first, even to the point, I fear, of making poor old Dacre quite unnecessarily jealous.

And among other tastes that Mr. Hammerson and I had in common was a very complete hatred of Captain Bryndal and the Mate, Smeeker.

CHAPTER IX

And now for the most important and far-reaching of the Sydney happenings, one that affected the lives and fortunes of all of us.

Eyes of a panther in the face of a tortoise.

No, a very beautiful woman.

She would be a beautiful woman but for her eyes, like those of a great cat.

No, they are wonderful eyes . . . glorious . . . almost golden . . . but how they could glare . . . tigerish.

She has been a very beautiful woman.

But no, she has no more lips than a tortoise has. Her mouth is a perfectly straight line . . . compressed . . . a steel trap.

The eyes of a fierce leopardess in the cold, hard face of a tortoise.

These were the thoughts that flashed through my dreaming mind as I came face to face with a lady who must have come aboard during the night.

Raising my cap and stepping aside, I then came face to face with a girl who could only have been her daughter.

No doubt about the beauty this time. Absolutely lovely, as such astonishing numbers of Australian girls are.

Eyes of a panther? No, of a nice panther cub, still in the fluffy pretty stage before it grows dangerous.

Not that the girl was in the faintest degree "fluffy" or pretty. She looked extremely cool and competent, and was quite definitely beautiful.

Mouth of a tortoise? No; a straight firm mouth, but not a hard one. Not like her mother's, suggestive of a steel trap. When she smiled, as she did when I raised my cap, there was nothing wrong with her mouth. It even acquiesced in a neighbouring dimple, unexpected and fascinating in so strong a face.

Beautiful: but nevertheless it was what the mother's had been twenty years ago, and twenty years hence it would be what the mother's now was.

I never in my life saw two women who looked more alike. . . .

"Mrs. and Miss Bryndal," whispered the Second Mate, with

raised eyebrows and a look expressing a belief that wonders would never cease.

That evening, in the half-deck, the two ladies were the sole subject of conversation.

Dacre was indignant.

"*Women*," he growled. "Sort of thing that grinning Hyena would do. . . . We've never been a happy ship, and before long we shall be a Hell-ship. You mark my words."

Geordie could find no words; but,

"Ba goom! But they're champion," was his endlessly reiterated panegyric, when he could.

Beauty, thoroughly awakened, found too many words, and bade us watch.

Fagin found a few, and bade Beauty watch. Watch out, lest Fagin should consider it worth his trouble to put Beauty where he belonged.

"She smiled at me, I tell you," protested Beauty.

"I know. I saw her," agreed Fagin. "But I should call it 'laughed'."

"Ah, that was when she nodded her head towards your face and then winked at me and laughed," countered Beauty.

"I'll nod my fist towards your face and see if *you'll* laugh," growled Fagin.

"That'll be enough for the present, thank you," interposed Dacre, and turning to me, added,

"Hell-ship stuff beginning already, you see."

§2

Whether the elder of these two women was not the Captain's wife, as Mr. Hammerson and Sydney gossip declared, I did not then know, though I knew later; but that the girl was not his daughter I felt perfectly certain, for she bore no faintest resemblance to him, and never behaved towards him as though he were her father. At the same time, one was bound to admit that she could scarcely have borne any likeness to whoever was her father, as she was so amazingly the living image of her mother.

However, the Mate and Second Mate were presented to the ladies and informed that they would make the voyage with us from Sydney to San Francisco. There they might leave the ship or, on the other hand, might accompany us to whatever place might be our destination thereafter. Possibly they might remain aboard until the *Valkyrie* reached home.

Whatever may have been "Mrs. Bryndal's" relation to the Captain, one thing was quite certain; she had some sort of hold over him, and that a very powerful one. It certainly wasn't love—as later events proved; and, as Dacre cynically remarked, if the Captain and Mrs. Bryndal were not married, it was a pity, for no married couple could have quarrelled more persistently, regularly, and intimately, than these two people did.

It was not a case of noisy wranglings and vulgar jars, but rather of a strong and steady undercurrent of hostility. With nothing that the Captain said did the woman seem to agree, and no view expressed by her ever seemed acceptable to the Captain, and we of the half-deck, as well as Mr. Hammerson (at least), all knew that there was one huge and lasting bone of contention between them, one matter to which she was always returning, with either urgent spur or contemptuous taunt. And one had learnt something about any human being, man or woman, who could use contempt and taunts toward Captain Bryndal.

That human being—man or woman—had courage.

As soon as conversation—gossip, speculation, scandal—concerning the two ladies themselves began to flag, it was revived with a new vigour by the subject of their luggage.

This was of the quantity and kind that might have been expected in the case of a couple of ladies embarking on so long a voyage as that which lay before the *Valkyrie*. It was all quite normal and ordinary, with the exception of one box or trunk, well-corded and sewn up in canvas or sacking.

The peculiarity about this package was its weight, which was utterly disproportionate to its size. Those who handled it averred that it was twice the weight of other packages of double its size, though these, being probably laden with clothes, were far from light.

Until the matter was put out of mind by more urgent things, speculation was rife as to what could possibly be the contents of a package so phenomenally heavy.

At the time I did not even smile when I heard Patsy Hooligan mutter to Foyle,

"Begorra, thin, phwhat's the heaviest thing in the wurrld? Oi'm tellin' ye it's goold . . ."

And Foyle's reply,

"Begob, thin, there's wan thing heavier than goold, an' thim's *corpses*."

§3

Happy is the country that has no history; also the ship.

But although the *Valkyrie*'s voyage from Sydney to San Francisco was uneventful, I cannot say that it was a happy one.

Nor could anybody have called the *Valkyrie* a happy ship. There were undercurrents, tension, a discomfortable feeling of something wrong, a sense of watchfulness, suspicion and strain.

Among the after-guard, this spread from the Captain, ever laughing, but surly and sarcastic when not savage; was disseminated by the Mate, Smeeker, hated and hating; and increased by the presence of Mrs. Bryndal and her daughter.

Among the fo'c'sle hands it spread from Slim Johes, the busy professional agitator and mischief-maker; was disseminated by the anarchist Müller, ably seconded by the lying trouble-making Jake; and increased by the countenance and support of the very man who should have been the first to check it (as his rank was somewhat that of a Petty Officer)—the Carpenter Peddersen.

By the time we reached San Francisco, Dacre and I were forced, incredible as it may seem, to believe that there was a certain sympathy and understanding between the worst elements in the fo'c'sle and the Mate, Smeeker, himself.

The connecting link between Cabin and Fo'c'sle was the half-deck, a part of which was occupied, as I have said, by Peddersen and the Sail-maker, instead of belonging to the Apprentices only.

Slowly, but quite definitely, there emerged a party, the unacknowledged and shadowy head of which was the Mate; the patron and protector, the Mate's friend and henchman, Peddersen the Carpenter; the active leaders and instigators, Slim Johes, Jake and Müller; the rank and file, the brainless lewd fellows of the baser sort, and all such as, with or without good cause, temporarily or permanently, held the opinion that they were under-fed, under-paid, over-worked, ill-treated, and proprietors of nothing but a grievance.

Until we reached San Francisco, this existence of a "party" was nothing more than a nuisance, a discomfort, a shame and a disgrace—to the Mate. He knew all about it and could have stopped it almost with a word, just as he had made it possible with a word at the wrong time, and of the wrong sort, to his crony Peddersen and any insolent half-mutinous rogue who, in the Mate's hearing, cursed the Captain and the ship.

Another contribution to our general lack of peace, happiness and comfort, was the fact that the wretched Fagin showed signs of joining the party, "making up to" the Mate, hobnobbing with the Carpenter Peddersen, and finding nothing objectionable in the words or acts of Slim Johes, Jake and Müller. Ever a trimmer, a turn-coat and one who knew precisely on which side his bread was buttered, his attitude to Smeeker changed on the day that, Mr. Wight having died, it became known that Smeeker was promoted from Second Mate to Mate.

From Glasgow to Sydney, Fagin could not curse Smeeker with sufficient virulence and venom. From Sydney to San Francisco and onwards, Fagin was Smeeker's man. The new Mate could do no wrong, and—bad downfall—from toadying the Mate and hobnobbing with the Carpenter, Fagin took to visiting the fo'c'sle.

This conduct on the part of Fagin naturally caused coolness between him and Dacre, acting Third Officer; and equally naturally, I supported Dacre. With shrill vehemence, Geordie supported us while Beauty wavered between the two sides. If Miss Bryndal appeared to be viewing Fagin with the eye of favour, Beauty was strongly on our side. If Dacre's star or mine appeared to be in the ascendant, Beauty promptly gave his valuable support to Fagin, agreed with him in his eulogies of the Mate, his disparagement of Mr. Hammerson, the Second Mate; his praises of Peddersen the Carpenter, and his contention that there was nothing wrong with Slim Johes, Jake and Müller, beyond a little honest and outspoken independence.

It was a curious state of affairs that prevailed on that apparently quiet run from Sydney to San Francisco. For, in addition to the atmosphere of disharmony and discomfort caused by the existence of this *imperium in imperio* ruled by Peddersen and encouraged by the Mate, there was trouble on the poop.

Relations between the Captain and the Mate were very curious; at times apparently very cordial, at times very strained; and whatever they were, it was common belief, if not common knowledge, that the two men hated each other.

Relations between the Second Mate, Mr. Hammerson, and his two superiors were as bad as they could be, the fault lying entirely with the latter, and the reason being that the Second Mate was a strong man, straight, simple, and a disciplinarian. Moreover, he was no dissimulator, and was patently disgusted at the Mate's unseamanlike weakness with slackers, grousers and insolents, and his unnecessary familiarity with the Carpenter.

Nor did Captain Bryndal support the Second Mate as he should have done when he was obviously in the right.

Despising and detesting the Mate as he did, he nevertheless, out of pure maliciousness, mischievousness and ill-will, either washed his hands of the whole affair and left it to the Mate; or else wrongly supported him against better men and his better judgment. And if the position of Mr. Hammerson, the Second Mate, was unenviable, that of Dacre was miserable, for he had not Hammerson's knowledge, his experience in handling men, his extremely tough appearance, nor his assured position as an Officer. The men knew that Dacre was still an Apprentice and the quartette of mischief-makers lost no opportunity of reminding him and them of the fact. Had he been properly supported by the Captain and Mate, as the Third Mate should be, all would have been well; but, having given him all a Third Officer's work, the Captain took care that he should have none of the Third Officer's prestige, prerogatives and privileges.

And here, at any rate, the Captain and the Mate were at one, for Smeeker hated Dacre almost as much as he hated me.

However, what a Second Mate can do for a Third, Mr. Hammerson did for Dacre, and Hammerson, albeit unsupported, if not hindered, by the Captain and the Mate, was a valuable ally.

And as is almost inevitable aboard ship, the presence of women caused further complications. In Sydney Harbour, Dacre, on being asked by Beauty why he presumed to object to the presence of the ladies, replied with his oracular air of wisdom,

"Women and Trouble are synonymous."

"What do you mean?" Fagin had growled.

"When you get near Women you get near Trouble," Dacre had explained.

And certainly, on the voyage from Sydney to San Francisco, Mrs. and Miss Bryndal had further complicated our complications, and further troubled our troubled minds. I don't say that this was deliberate. I merely observe that they were two exceedingly attractive women, one quite young and the other quite youngish, with nothing whatever to do, and quite a number of vigorous and personable men among whom to do it.

As the voyage proceeded, I came to the conclusion that Captain Bryndal hated them both; that the Mate, so far as he was capable of love, was falling in love with Mrs. Bryndal; that for this reason he and the Captain hated each other the more; that the Second Officer, Mr. Hammerson, had lost his head to both of them and laid it alternately at the feet of mother and daughter, whichever of them happened to be on the poop. When both were there, it was a case of "How happy could I be with either." . . .

For daring to make love to Mrs. Bryndal, Hammerson hated Smeeker the more—and later declared that if he ever "pawed" Miss Bryndal, he would render Smeeker's face unacceptable to her or any other woman.

Geordie literally worshipped Miss Bryndal—from afar, the love of the moth for the star.

Poor Geordie! Even for him the star twinkled invitingly, singed his wings and burnt him cruelly. Poor Geordie! He knew what suffering was, that voyage: and his efforts to "improve" himself in appearance, speech, manners, and general worth were pathetic beyond words. . . . Beyond words, and to the verge of tears.

Fortunately his anger at Beauty and Fagin was chilled by cold contempt of their presumption, unworthiness and impudence. Beauty babbled of her constantly, and told us of each step of his pilgrimage toward the inmost shrine of her heart and favour. Fagin, licking his lips, concentrated upon him the stare of his close-set eyes, said little, and smiled much—a most unpleasant smile.

And the ladies?

They loved it. They were a pair of shameless arrant flirts, and made the most of their happy situation, and of the man who was nearest at the moment.

Nor were the shafts of their exceedingly bright and truly beautiful eyes directed at Officers and Apprentices alone. There were some handsome men in the crew, notably Church and Hamblin, and there were at least a dozen of the crew, each of whom deserved the appellation "a fine figure of a man". But, of the crew, Jake Walfisch was obviously Mrs. Bryndal's prime favourite.

No, it was not a happy ship.

I will mention one incident of the voyage from Sydney to San Francisco which will serve to illustrate the state of affairs that existed, and foreshadow that to which we were drifting.

One day, both watches came aft to complain about the food. It was miserable weather, wet and windy, and the men were weary, quarrelsome and chilled to the bone after working for many hours at securing a yard broken adrift from the truss.

To Slim Johes it had seemed a good opportunity for inciting these big simple children to "demand their rights". Countenanced by Peddersen and ably assisted by Jake and Müller, Slim Johes had worked up a thoroughly mutinous spirit in the fo'c'sle.

Seeing the advancing mob, and scenting trouble, the Second Mate, Mr. Hammerson, smiled and slipped a belaying-pin under his coat.

He had served in Western Ocean packets, and it was thus that such emergencies were met, and dealt with, on such ships.

The Mate, Mr. Smeeker, who happened to be on the poop, and probably knew all about it beforehand, from the Carpenter, Peddersen, quietly disappeared.

Captain Bryndal stood and smiled at the crowd below as they clustered together at a short distance from the poop-ladder.

In the fo'c'sle, the men had cursed the Captain for "a grinning hyena; the perishing orphan of a cursed thief who robbed poor sailors' bellies and ought to be keel-hauled till he was half-dead, and then crucified upside-down on his own poop."

But down there, beneath his cold sardonic eye and beaming smile, the curses died away, the complaints and accusations hung fire, and the noisiest grumbler fell silent, each man waiting for someone else to begin the battle.

Most unwillingly pushed to the front and kept there, "Baby" Axenstern, the gigantic half-witted Norwegian, whose head was as noticeably small as his body was remarkably huge, looked alternately down at his tin of half-cooked oatmeal and up at the smiling debonair figure on the poop, while his expression of bewildered distress increased and deepened until he appeared to be on the verge of blubbering like a beaten schoolboy.

Maintaining his monotonous tobacco-chewing, Hamblin, the fiery young Glasgow keelie, red-haired, tall, and lithe as a leopard, had apparently forgotten his carefully rehearsed string of oaths, curses and complaints; and stood staring stupidly from under the shiny cracked peak of a battered old cap, childishly chosen and rakishly tilted especially for the occasion.

Patsy Hooligan, either mad or not mad, skirmished aimlessly round the group and, peering into the men's faces, asked them questions that they ignored. When not asking questions, he kept repeating,

"The divil himself has his roights, Oi say—begob he has . . . Oi say the divil himself has his roights."

All except Slim Johes and his clever henchmen Müller and Jake, were obviously thoroughly uncomfortable and wishing themselves safe back in the fo'c'sle.

It was the Captain who spoke first, and at the sound of his

voice Axenstern jumped visibly and dropped his pannikin.

Taking the initiative, Captain Bryndal addressed his crew,

"Thank you, men," said he, smiling. "This is the spirit I always like to see in the fo'c'sle of my ship. Kindly thoughtfulness and the share-and-share-alike feeling. I'm very glad that food in the fo'c'sle is so plentiful that you've got so much left over. Very glad, too, that you wish to share your surplus with the hungry after-guard. . . . But, as a matter of fact, all aft have already eaten. Nevertheless—I thank you. I thank you."

And with a bright and sunny smile, Captain Bryndal turned about and resumed his pacing fore and aft.

Secretly admiring this masterly effort while openly amazed at such queer doings, the Second Mate, Mr. Hammerson, as he afterwards told me, gripped his belaying-pin and prepared to use it. He had seen many similar emergencies, and according to his experience there should now be a lot of cursing and shouting, and then a rush.

Good officers would deal with that in the right way; knock down the ring-leaders, crack a few heads, and kick the rest of the roysterers back where they belonged. Thereafter, the Captain might see that things improved, or he might see that they were made worse, just to "learn" them to complain.

Or a soft Captain, especially if he had weak officers, might hear all that the men had to say, however insolently it might be said, temporize with them, make all sorts of promises, and then tell the Steward to "splice the main brace"—for Fo'c'sle Jack will do anything for a tot of rum.

But to quell trouble such as this, with bright smiles and pleasant words, was a thing quite outside Mr. Hammerson's experience. . . .

And in point of fact, but for Slim Johes, the trouble would have been quelled, and the revolt put down and ended, then and there.

Puzzled and disheartened, the men felt that it was impossible to hurl curses and abuse at this strange being; to wrangle and brawl with this novel and incredible Captain who gave them smiles, thanks, kind words and courtesy where they had looked for violent wrath, hostility and threats.

This was a new weapon, one of which they had no knowledge, and in the use of which they had no skill. They were defeated again and there was nothing to be gained by standing about there.

"Run away and play, little kid. He wouldn't trouble to spit on you," bawled Slim Johes to Red Hamblin.

Johes chose man and insult well, for Hamblin, with aching head, very uncertain of temper and easily led, was young enough to be extremely touchy and, moreover, extremely hungry.

"Ach, would he, b' Goad, the soapy old deevil," shouted the tall young Scot.

And seizing a mess-kid in both hands, he darted up the poop-ladder.

With a gleam in his eye, the Second Mate prepared for action with the belaying-pin, for obviously there was to be some fun after all, and it was about to begin. Between rushing the poop and rank mutiny, there is but a very short step. Clever Captain Bryndal might soon be very glad to have an experienced Western Ocean "packet rat", as he had once kindly called Hammerson, to stand beside him—or more likely, in front of him.

Had Red Hamblin waited at the top of the ladder, he might have met with a more sympathetic reception.

Walking aft, the Captain heard the rush behind him, and though he continued without turning his head, the expression on his face made the helmsman stiffen and grip the spokes. As the man said afterwards, it was the grinning face of a tiger with its teeth bared to tear at its meat.

At the relieving-tackle, the Captain turned about to continue his walk for'ard. Half-way to the ladder he stopped, to avoid contact with the mess-kid thrust at him by the long arms of the madly incensed Hamblin.

"Wull ye tak' a sup o' yere bluidy burgoo, ye grinning deevil, an' then tell . . ."

That was all Red Hamblin said. Captain Bryndal's uplifted hand shot forward as his terrible eyes glared into Hamblin's and held them.

There was no blow struck.

Before the Captain's blazing eye and pointing finger, Hamblin recoiled, stepped back, and with increasing speed, retired backward as the Captain advanced.

Reaching the ladder, Red Hamblin fell down it backward; his head struck the deck with a heavy thud, and he lay unconscious.

"Any other spokesman care to come up by the *lee*-ladder?" asked the Captain, as the men stared at the motionless body of Red Hamblin.

There was no reply, the men hastily returned to the fo'c'sle—their complaint still unvoiced—and Captain Bryndal's laugh was a sound to remember. . . .

§4

Our stay in San Francisco was fairly uneventful.

One day, I bought a set of boxing-gloves. Another day, Dacre and I were astonished to see Mrs. Bryndal lunching with a man, at the Kearney House. Two most pregnant facts.

The ladies went ashore several times with the Captain, and once or twice remained there without him for some days. A few men deserted, preferring to forfeit their wages rather than continue under Captain Bryndal and round the Horn in the *Valkyrie*, and in due course, we sailed again, bound this time for Pisagua, laden with coal.

PART II

CHAPTER I

Bound for the West Coast . . .

To the wind-jammer sailor these words bring visions of tier upon tier of lofty ships moored across open road-steads within sound of the booming surf; of flapping pelicans and barking sea-lions; of hot rainless days and cool refreshing nights; and most vividly of all, dreams of fandangoes, "vino", dark Spanish eyes beneath mantillas, and languorous music in shady piazzas.

These latter delights he evolves from a few isolated "liberty days" spent at different times in sundry dusty sun-baked *pueblos* at the foot of the bleak rampart of the Cordillera. Unconsciously romantic, he forgets the scarcity of fresh provisions and water, the sudden slipping of cables and sheeting home of sail to escape being driven rockwards by the dreaded "Norther"; the laborious man-handling of cargo from daylight till dark; and the monotonous months of unappeased land-hunger with the shore so near and yet so far.

Coming to anchor off Pisagua, the *Valkyrie* had carried her full complement, but not all the Captain's vigilance could prevent some desertions.

With most of their pay "mortgaged to the slop-chest" for clothing and tobacco bought at "sea-price", and with very high wages ruling ashore for sorely needed sailors, few of the men had any great incentive to remain in the *Valkyrie*.

The glorious peace of the lovely starry night following our arrival had been rent and ruined by revolver-shots, yells and curses. Rushing out on deck, we found the Captain blazing away and shouting threats of what he would do, not only to deserters, but to those who aided and abetted them.

However, four of the crew got away and their desertion made the task of discharging the cargo of coal a heavy one for the remainder. While the Ordinary Seamen lounged ashore in white ducks, the dolly-winch was manned entirely by Apprentices; and Dacre, as Third Officer, was expected to see that we hoisted the baskets of coal at a smart pace.

Our crafty Mate, knowing that sooner, or later, the A.B.s would cause trouble, and having no intention of being mixed up with it himself, put the Second Mate, Mr. Hammerson, in full charge of the unloading.

So, with Mr. Hammerson working on the stage rigged from the hatch to the bulwarks, and driving everyone hard, there was no chance for any slacking.

Soon after the floor, or, as the men called it, the "skin", had been reached in the main hatch, I fell and sprained my wrist, and, as this prevented me from heaving on the winch, I was sent down into the hold.

Throughout her full length, the ship was fitted inside with the usual wooden cargo-battens (sometimes called "stringers") for keeping perishable cargoes from contact with the dirt, rust and sweat of the hull.

As they stood some four inches away from the ship's side, coal had lodged in considerable quantities behind these battens, and I had the easy and monotonous task of removing it. Thus quietly employed, I had ample opportunity to watch the behaviour and gauge the characters of our men, new-comers and old hands, as they laboured under an ancient nautical system designed to prevent its victims from loafing.

At each corner of an imaginary oblong at the bottom of the cavernous main hatch, two men, half-naked and nearly invisible in a cloud of coal dust, sweated at shovelling the coal into a huge basket. No sooner was it filled, than an empty one dropped from above and replaced it. Hoisted above the hatch and seized by the Second Mate, the loaded basket was pushed across the deck, over the rail, and dropped into a lighter alongside.

Emptied and re-hoisted, the basket was then swung over the hatch and dropped into the hold; and, since rushing to and fro on a coal-stage, pushing heavy baskets all day long, does not sweeten the temper, any delay in hooking on a full basket evoked noises from our capable Mr. Hammerson, grimy, grim and powerful—and as hard-working as any of the labouring sweating men below.

Of the eight workers in this particular Inferno at the bottom of the ship, "Baby" Axenstern evidently considered himself the leader, aristocrat and *arbiter elegantiarum*. Whilst others must be content to wipe their steaming faces with a piece of an old shirt, a portion of flour-bag stolen from the Cook, or even with the back of a black hand, "Baby" Axenstern used the authentic article, the only genuine open-mesh sweat-rag in the ship.

In Axenstern, Nature had commenced to build a perfect spec- imen of a human being, and then, in cruel jest, had put, on the really perfect body of a man, the thin neck and tiny head of a small boy—a boy with a snub-nose, huge ever-grinning mouth and little piggy mischievous eyes.

It was a blessing for this magnificent giant that, while his enormous strength and occasional fits of terrible *berserk* rage saved him from the open expression of the ridicule he inspired in his shipmates, his lack of intelligence was sufficiently great to prevent him from realizing his defects, seeing his own folly, and from ever imagining himself to be the fool he was.

And although Slim Johes was the object of Axenstern's childish worship, Johes had taken good care, when nicknaming him "Baby", to imply quite falsely that he did so because the Norwegian was so huge, and that the nickname was a humorous tribute to his magnificent physique.

As like attracts like, Axenstern had paired with Patsy Hooligan, apparently as childish as himself—who, on one occasion, began work by wheeling his barrow upside down, with a view to increasing its carrying capacity by piling more coal on the bottom of it!

The mentality of each of these men was admirably illustrated in their respective methods of work. By dint of shovelling furiously and working with the strength and speed of two men, Axenstern managed to enjoy a few extra minutes of leisure before each empty basket arrived, and this time he spent in flourishing and airing his cherished relic of the stoke-hole, the open-mesh sweat-rag that was at once a proof and a reminder that he had seen better days. As none but a fireman ever possesses such an article, this showed that Axenstern had once been a genuine stoker.

Patsy Hooligan, on the other hand, by pottering about and stopping work, patently to admire and loudly to praise the Norwegian's Herculean efforts, contrived to do about one-third of his share of filling the baskets.

A typical weather-beaten bullet-headed old shell-back, round-shouldered and somewhat crab-like, Patsy was noted (and frequently cursed by his Officers) for adopting an air of owlish wisdom, giving unwanted and foolish advice, and monotonously reiterating the obvious.

To-day this last habit stood him in good stead, for Axenstern smirkingly agreed with Patsy's repeated,

"Begorra, ye're sthrong! But I say ye're sthrong! . . . Glory be, ye're sthrong! But I say ye're sthrong!"

Under the stimulus of this praise and approval, Axenstern redoubled his efforts, and Patsy slacked the more.

On the starboard side, and opposite to these simple ones,

the tall and athletic Hamblin, the red-headed Glasgow keelie, was, more or less, assisted by Slim Johes. In the dark blackness of the hold, this queer, stunted creature, ugly and gnome-like, appeared at home. It was his proper setting. He seemed to belong. His pale eyes, deep-set behind narrow slits, and veiled by overhanging lids; his huge protruding ears, his intractable hair and ugly tufted beard; might have been his heritage from troglodyte forbears. The very sight of his pallid matt-skinned face, equally unaffected by salt wind or tropic sun, suggested an underground worker—and this, in a truly double sense he had been. Determined to be the last of a long line of miners, Slim Johes had become a leader and an official, and had he had more courage and more honesty, he might well have become one of our Rulers, for to enter Parliament had been his high or low ambition.

But Trade Union funds and another man's wife had been too much for his honesty, while a place in the front row (when the results of his masked agitation and secret brewing of dissension led to cudgel-and-brickbat warfare and police baton-charges) had been too much for his courage.

Through old habit and natural inclination, his chief desire in life seemed to be the defiance, over-throw and destruction of all who held authority of any kind—particularly authority over Slim Johes. Hatred of his "betters" was his obsession, the motive for his actions, and the driving-force of his life. And as most men were patently his betters, he was a living Hatred, and the fact showed in his knitted scowling brows and twisted snarling lips.

Of his present companion, the suffering Hamblin, Slim Johes had high hopes. With cunning and patience, Axenstern and Patsy, and a new-comer, Villa, recently signed on at Pisagua, might be incited to join him with Peddersen, Jake and Müller, in disaffection, violence and mutiny, and Hamblin would be indeed a fish worth landing. There wasn't a man outside the ring-leader gang (Johes, Peddersen, Jake and Müller) to compare with Hamblin. In fact, he was worth any three of them, in courage, strength, fury, and stick-at-nothing determination.

Slim Johes knew the type and blessed it. Appreciatively, he watched the Scot's dour rancour and savage resentment of any wrong, and noted how, out of smouldering, pained, puzzled eyes, deep-set beneath a low receding forehead, the unhappy lad scowled defiance at a hard incomprehensible world, and a life that was too apt to "gang agley".

Poor Hamblin had scarcely been free from his splitting

headache ever since he'd been knocked on the head. Slim Johes saw to it that the headache was turned to good—or bad—account.

Suffering, sullen, and inarticulate, young Hamblin found in his older partner an eloquent mouth-piece for his discontent, and one whose fluent socialistic street-corner soap-box oratory expressed the things that Hamblin felt, but to which his compressed tight lips could not give words.

But in his admiration, Red Hamblin failed to notice the fact that Slim Johes' eloquence was rarely exhibited in the presence of an Officer.

As these two laboured, Slim Johes talked far more than he worked, whilst Hamblin worked far more than he talked, for he worked hard and scarcely spoke at all. . . .

In the next corner of their rectangle, worked Carrol and Church, and it was a pleasure to watch the silent neat efficiency with which these two genuine sailormen did their job. For these two, Slim Johes had little use and a professional contempt, as men without "guts". In other words, without a mutinous hatred of their superiors or any wish to join in making trouble for trouble's sake.

To him, they were spineless cowardly wage-slaves; down-trodden exploited fo'c'sle fodder; worthless expropriated hireings, who were but ornaments of the proletarian chain-gang lashed from cradle to grave by the big-bellied bloated plutocrats who "lived in luxury by grinding the faces of the poor".

On receiving this information, Carrol had replied that If Slim Johes had been a real man and a real sailor, he, Carrol, would have beaten him up. As it was, the poor fellow being but a gab-gifted mouth-flapping land-shark and no seaman at all, he would but hit him in the eye—which he did.

Church had only laughed at Slim Johes' oration, and remarked that it was as good as a play to hear him talk.

At the for'ard starboard corner of the hatch-way oblong, worked big Villa and little Larry O'Toole, new-comers who had joined in company together but were in amazing contrast.

I didn't like the look of Villa at all, and whatever he had been before, he hadn't been a sailor. I should think the *Valkyrie* was the first big ship in which he'd ever worked, if not the first on which he'd ever set foot.

And, incidentally, most profoundly thankful had he been to set foot on her. It was the opinion of the after-guard that if Villa were not a fugitive from Justice, none of them had ever seen one.

"Once aboard the lugger and the girl is—yours or anybody

else's", about summed up the situation, as Dacre said when it became known that not only did Villa desire no shore leave, but that no power on earth—save that of the police perhaps—would get him ashore.

In point of fact, for some days we quite expected to see a boat-load of the smart and dapper Chileno police pull out to the *Valkyrie* and visit her in search of Mr. Villa. . . . For some reason, his face puzzled me. . . .

He was a very big powerful man, swarthy, black-haired, black-eyed, black-moustached, with a greasy yellow skin, and ears pierced for the wearing of ear-rings. I imagine that he had removed the ear-rings to facilitate disguise when escaping from the police; from his gang; from his enemy, or whoever was pursuing him.

He looked, and was, a very dangerous man, dangerous in the way that a cobra or jaguar is dangerous. And like these creatures, he was amazingly quick, was well-armed, and master of his weapons of offence. His knife was to him what fang and claw are to the serpent and the leopard; and, in quiet baleful repulsiveness, he suggested the snake, while in sinuous litheness and in ferocity of face he reminded me of the jaguar. I fancy he began life as a gangster, continued it as an ornament of the underworld of certain South American cities, including Rio de Janeiro, Buenos Ayres and Callao, and had grown to his full prime and glory in Chicago and New York.

By the heavy weather he made of his pretence of labour, and by the look of his hands, I judged that he had been in the habit of using those large and useful members for anything but honest work.

Larry O'Toole, our third Irishman, in marked contrast to his companion, was light, slight, rather small, with an honest clear grey eye, and a general pleasantness of demeanour, voice and manners. He struck me, from the first, as being exactly what Patsy Hooligan pretended to be, a border-line case, a man simple to the point of half-wittedness, at times not very far from being a harmless lunatic.

And again in contrast to the man with whom he was working, he was a genuine sailor. He knew all there was to know about a sailing-ship from truck to keelson, and we had no better helmsman aboard.

The men laughed at him and he kept them amused. But it was noticeable that there was generally some shrewd and pithy truth behind his most foolish-seeming utterances, and he often reminded me of the medieval jester in whose folly there was wisdom, and by whom many a true word was spoken in jest.

With his long hair and untrimmed moustache and beard, he also at times reminded me of a Skye terrier, one of those nice dogs who can scarcely be called dumb animals, because their eyes are so eloquent. However fanciful, whimsical, or foolish the words of Larry O'Toole might be, his eyes were rarely vacant in expression. Indeed, as a rule, they were lit with keen bright intelligence and a look of knowledge, wisdom, and under-standing. But they were always sad, the saddest eyes I have ever seen in a human face.

At times I wondered if Larry O'Toole's brain had been turned by the shock or strain of some great tragic sorrow, some abiding grief which had been too much for him, some weight of woe that had broken down and crushed his mental resilience and resistance.

Quite frequently I wished I could get a barber to clean-shave his face and trim his hair. It would have interested me greatly to see what his face was really like; what sort of expression it habitually wore; what kind of a mouth he had.

During the illness that brought me to death's door, at the beginning of the voyage, I had known real horror, terror and fear—especially the fear of death—for the first time in my life. It had shaken me badly, and I had never quite recovered even my former poor measure of self-confidence.

As the result of this I had earned a reputation for a very gentle and quiet meekness, if not cowardice, which I think only Dacre, and possibly Doctor, believed to be undeserved.

Slim Johes had evidently come to the conclusion that, though big and strong, I was a spineless, soft and easy-going youth with whom, later on, he might do something, and for whom at the present moment he would do nothing.

Seated on the edge of a basket, the ex-miner informed his listeners that they were fools and slaves.

"Iss, I tell you, but we are fine fools to shovel coal all day for three poun'ss a month. On shore, look you, for this we would get fife poun'ss a week, I tell you, and that iss twenty to twenty-fife poun'ss a month instead of three poun'ss a month, look you. Inteed to gootness, it iss too pad now . . . and at elefen o'clock there was no smoke-oh whateffer. . . . And at four o'clock this afternoon there was no spell-oh for a smoke whateffer. That Second Mate Hammerson is a hammer-man, a slafe-drifer, py tamn. . . . Yess, it iss time that big stiff was put in hiss place, I tell you."

"Well, instead of talking so much, why don't you go and do it, you damned sea-lawyer?" I asked suddenly.

"Oh, iss inteed, and py tamn, I'll soon put you in yours too, look you!" shouted Slim Johes.

I jumped down from the ship's side and strode over to where Slim Johes sat.

"Yah, now vot you do?" laughed "Baby" Axenstern. "You vos alvays plenty say and noddings do, you Slim Johes."

Johes rose to his feet, full of bluster, but there was an uncomfortable look in his eyes.

"Knock off, below there," echoed down the hatch at this moment.

"Up you go, Slim. Now's your chance," laughed Church, the ear-ringed seaman. "I'll 'old your shirt while you go and use the Second Mate for a deck-scrubber. Come an' put 'im in his place, shipmate, come on."

On deck, the bold agitator found the redoubtable Mr. Hammerson standing at the corner of the after-hatch coaming; disgruntled, dirty, and dangerous. Under his smeared half-removed grime, Slim Johes looked paler than ever, but Axenstern and Hamblin were thrusting him forward, Church and Carrol maliciously egging him on, Villa and Larry O'Toole watching, while Patsy Hooligan monotonously chanted,

"Begorra, now's yeer foine chance to get him, I say. I say now's yeer foine chance, me bhoy. Now's yeer foine chance to get him, I say."

Emboldened by the presence and apparent support of his five shipmates, Slim Johes took his courage in both hands, and approached the unsuspecting Second Mate.

"Look you, why will you keep the men working all day without a smoke, Mister?" he demanded truculently.

And, thoroughly scared at having had the impudence and insolence to say "Mister" instead of "Sir", he tried to lash himself into a fury, and at least to appear dangerous.

"You haf no right whateffer, I tell you, and py tamn, look you, we will not haf it. I tell you we all sayss we will not work like thiss any more. We want our rights, and py tamn, we strike for them."

So amazed and almost amused was the Second Mate that he began to laugh; and then, seeing it was not a heavy joke, he turned his smile to a scowl, and protruded his jaw viciously.

"What?" he roared. "You? Are there no sailors aboard this

ship, that a worthless 'soldier' like you must open his head, you wind-bag? You useless chalk-faced mouth-flapping short-tailed swab. . . . Why, the *Calluna's* crowd over there discharges double our cargo, and never stops to ask for a smoke. You shark-headed sea-lawyer, I'll . . ."

"Begorra, the *Calluna's* only a barge," announced Patsy Hooligan, libelling a fine ship. "Begorra, it's a jolly-boat that the *Calluna* is. The *Calluna's* only a jolly-boat, I tell you."

And wandering aimlessly about the group, peering up into the men's faces, his monotonous repetition of this statement was his sole contribution to the proceedings.

"Yah, vot for ve haf no smoke?" squeaked the grinning Axenstern.

"We all wanna smoke," growled Villa, "and we gonna git it."

"Smoke . . . smoke . . . smoke . . . We . . . want . . . our . . . smoke-oh . . ." gleefully chanted Hamblin, and rattled a loose belaying-pin.

"Look you, we will not work without a spell and a smoke, I tell you whateffer," screamed Slim Johes.

"Oh, ye won't, won't ye?" snarled Hammerson and clenched his fists. "Smoke yer pipe, eh? If ye don't pipe down—and take up the slack of yer jaw-tackle, I'll leave ye just one wish in the world, and that'll be to get down to your graft. You watch out, Slim, or I'll trim you a bit slimmer. . . . As slim as a fathom of boat-lacing."

"The *Calluna's* only a blasted barge," Patsy Hooligan confided to the starboard shrouds. "I tell ye the *Calluna's* only a jolly-boat."

"We wanta the spell and the smoke-oh," growled Villa, his thumbs in his belt and his great shoulders squared back.

"Want!" growled the Second Mate. "Wanting's about all ye're fit for."

"Iss, I tell you. We want to strike," again shouted Slim Johes, encouraged by support, and emboldened by Hammerson's apparent patience.

"Strike!" sneered the latter quietly. "There'll be two in a second if you don't watch your step—one when I strike you and the other when you strike the deck."

Slim Johes stepped back.

"We'll have our rights," he shouted. "We won't work unless . . ."

"Aye," scowled Red Hamblin. "Ye canna get bluid fra a stane, Mister."

The fine-worn thread of the Second Mate's patience

snapped.

"No?" he yelled. "But I can get blood out of a lot of rotten loafing 'soldiers' playing at sailors."

And seizing Johes by the shoulders and thrusting his heel behind Johes' feet, he flung him heavily headlong into the group, and put up his clenched fists.

Hamblin started forward, belaying-pin in hand. Axenstern squared up in fighting shape; Villa put his hand behind his back as though for knife or gun; Carrol seized Villa's arm; Church shouted,

"Drop that belaying-pin, Hamblin," and Patsy Hooligan began to climb the rigging.

In the second that the issue hung in doubt, and just as I hopefully strode forward to support my superior officer, a smile like that of the Cheshire Cat shone upon the assembly, and the Captain stepping up, materialized beside Mr. Hammerson.

The men fell back.

"Chin-music—from Johes, eh?" he said pleasantly, with a gleam of bright white teeth. "Fond of music, like all sailors, eh? Vocal and instrumental. How do you like the note of this instrument?"

And bringing his right hand from behind his back, he jingled a pair of handcuffs beneath the ex-miner's nose, the bright steel no brighter than his kindly smile.

The agitator fell back as though struck, and muttered that the men were only asking for their rights.

"Here they are, rights and lefts," smiled the Captain. "Plenty for everybody."

With a pathetic air of casualness and indifference, as of men who had merely paused to look at something as they passed, the group melted quickly and quietly away.

"Inteed I do not forget, whateffer," whispered Slim Johes venomously, as he slunk off.

And,

"Begob, the Calluna's only a blasted barge, I tell you. I say it's only a jolly-boat the Calluna is," affirmed Patsy Hooligan, as he jumped down on to the deck.

From that day, Slim Johes' vicious hate increased, and his threats of vengeance became a by-word in the fo'c'sle; to some, a joke; to some, a matter of curious interest; to some, real prophecies actually foreshadowing coming events.

The earliest of these was to be horrific vengeance on the Second Mate; a vengeance in which Jake, Müller and Villa were promised a part; a vengeance in which Hamblin was told that he would wish to share if he were indeed a man, and should be allowed to share if he proved worthy.

*   *   *   *   *

"Noticed anything about the man Villa?" Dacre casually asked me that night.

I stared at him.

"Good Lord! You too?" I said in amazement. "You don't mean to tell me he's the man we saw lunching with Mrs. Bryndal at the Kearney House, that day in 'Frisco!"

"You've said it all, my son," replied Dacre.

As one man we whistled.

"Great Purple Doings! as poor old Wight used to say," murmured Dacre.

CHAPTER II

In spite of the men's incessant grumbling, and Slim Johes' continued efforts to stir up strife, Mr. Hammerson worked us so relentlessly that, in record time, it became necessary to "stiffen" the *Valkyrie* before discharging more coal.

The material used for this purpose was slag from smelting furnaces. Tests of strength and endurance come to most of those who use the sea, or rather who serve that enchanting cruel mistress; and among those that fell to my lot, the discharging of this terrible stuff from lighters into the ship was the most searching of all. It was by far the most strenuous labour that I have ever undertaken.

The eight men engaged in the comparatively easy task of filling our baskets with coal had been kept extremely busy; but now, in the lighter, only four men—two at each end—could find scant room to wield a shovel; and, in addition to having to bruise our elbows in the confined space, we had the strain of lifting the ballast over the rim of the basket.

So amazingly heavy was this slag, that considerable strength was needed to lift a shovel containing a couple of pieces the size of one's head; and, as an empty basket was always to hand, the ceaseless labour was really something of an ordeal.

In point of fact, I was pleased and proud to have been selected for this tough job as being one of the strongest members of the ship's company. Nevertheless, as, glorying in my unusual strength, I laboured at top speed in the heat of that fierce sun, while perspiration literally splashed on to the floor of the lighter, I was forced to regret, and to question, the foolish pride which alone kept me from demanding the periodical rests for which the others begged, and which some of them obviously needed.

Anyhow, it was magnificent exercise, and by the time those coal-shovelling and slag-shovelling days were over, I was in perfect condition; tough, hard, and strong as a man can be, and fit to fight for my life—or to run for it.

And thoughts of that heavy toil bring me one curious little memory.

With every bone and muscle aching to the point of agony, and my scanty clothing so soaked that I might just have stepped out of the water, I had stopped work while an empty lighter was shifted.

Happening to glance aloft, my eye encountered a lovely face, and for a few seconds Celia Bryndal's gaze held mine. As it did so, the expression on the face changed, and looked less lovely.

Undoubtedly I had surprised upon it a look—a natural genuine unconscious look—that she did not wish me to see, for it was a look of real interest, of admiration, of particular approval. It was gone within a second of my quick upward glance, and its place taken by one of boredom and distaste. Nevertheless, looked she never so superior and contemptuous, the other look had been there, and I had seen it, and she knew I had seen it.

§2

For a whole month, one of the hardest and roughest months through which I have lived, this work went on, and at the end of it, the last basket of coal-dust discharged, the holds were ready for a bagged cargo, and life aboard the *Valkyrie* became easier and—even more welcome change—far cleaner.

From Mr. Hammerson I received very handsome acknowledgment of the way in which I had worked, and adequate praise for the example that I had set the men, in literally two words.

"Good lad," said Mr. Hammerson, and this brief sufficient accolade made me glow with pride.

Sufficient also, though infinitely less valuable, reward he gave me in the easy task, restful and leisurely, of repairing bags broken in the hold. These were bags of nitrate, each filled to the weight of two and a half hundred-weight and slung aboard singly.

In the work of loading, our men were required for the hoisting only, and had nothing to do with the stowage.

This latter work is done entirely by one stevedore in each hatch, and I watched with admiration the practising of an art handed down from father to son. All the assistance required by one of these men is the placing of each bag on his shoulders. For this purpose, a stack of bags is built shoulder-high in the square of the hatch, and as each bag is lowered, it is seized and guided to the edge of the stack. The bag having been gently tipped on to his shoulder, the stevedore runs with it, drops it exactly into its place, and hastens back for the next bag.

So skilful are these Chilenos that the bags, once dropped by them, require no further arranging; and, with each slightly overlapping the next, they rise in perfect and level stowage, and form a flat-topped pyramid, which, gradually tapering away from the sides of the ship, serves to maintain her normal stability.

Very frequently have strong men of various nationalities attempted to earn the very high wages paid for this exacting work, but have invariably failed. Not being bred to it, they cannot endure the constant strain, even though apparently much bigger and stronger than the Chileno; nor, during the time that they are enabled to essay the task, can they ever acquire the necessary skill in quick stowage.

During these weeks of nitrate-stowing at Pisagua, there were innumerable rumours on the subject of our destination, and at so many various times were we bound for so many various places, that no port which ever received a cargo of saltpetre can have been omitted.

By the time the Plimsoll mark neared the water's surface, with no-one any nearer definite knowledge of our destination, the men, with increasing frequency, force, and openness, expressed their disgust at the Captain's reticence—a secrecy which they considered unnecessary, childishly foolish, and wantonly aggravating.

Although they said nothing in front of the men, the Officers quite obviously shared the general dissatisfaction; and even Doctor, usually the first to hear any news, was indignantly ignorant on the matter, right up to the completion of loading.

At last, the last.

Positively the last lighter to come alongside—and to distinguish it as such, the *lanchero* had decorated its topmost bags with a small Chilean flag—arrived, and was received with the cheering always given on the coming of *la ultima lancha*.

On this occasion, the crew of the dolly-winch needed no exhortation from the Second Mate, and the *ultima lancha* was emptied in record time, until but one bag was left.

That bag came on board with time-honoured ceremony.

Trying not to look as self-conscious as he felt, Geordie Stowe descended into the lighter and seated himself astride the sack. For the first time in his life, his shortness was going to raise him—above his fellows.

According to right and ancient custom, the rope-fall was unreeled from the winch, and, manned by all hands, was stretched along the deck.

To Church, who had the best voice, fell the honour of being First Chanteyman, and to the strains of *Whisky for My Johnny*, the absolute ultimate sack of all, rose slowly above the rail, its flushed rider waving the Red Ensign and our House Flag, the while he performed prodigious feats of balancing.

After our melodiously relating (among other very curious facts or fictions) that *Whisky killed my poor old cat*, that *Whisky made me go to sea*, and that *Whisky will not brew my tea*, Müller, unable to miss such an opportunity, made his version of *Blow the man down, Bullies*, the medium of expression of his extremely unfavourable opinion of the ship, her Captain and her Officers.

In view of the hope that a "tot" might presently be forth-coming, this was considered thoroughly tactless, and by means of more amiable improvisations, other singers sought to counter-act any possible ill-effects of Müller's lamentable lack of sense and diplomacy.

When the sack was up "two blocks", three cheers were given for the good ship *Valkyrie*, and, after the bag had been slowly and ceremoniously chantied down to the deck, there was, in joyous, loving, and trustful anticipation of the "splice the main brace" order, a great outburst of spontaneous and hearty cheering. This was followed by dead silence and a brief period of anxious waiting, a strained minute or so of discomfortable doubt and the dawn of fear. . . .

When it was realized that Captain Bryndal had gone ashore and had made no provision whatsoever for the rite of Wetting the Last Bag, the silence was broken. Indeed it was shattered, and I regretted that Bryndal, the mean dog, could not have heard the men's honestly expressed opinions of him, their threats and the curses they called down upon his head.

Discontent bordering on mutiny swiftly vanished, however, on the arrival of a boat bringing two new hands. Although the smallness of their clothes-bags and the absence of sea-chests indicated a long sojourn "on the beach", the new-comers were over-provided with a stock of that vile Chileno liquor known as *pisco*, and, in consequence, were made truly welcome.

In spite of the fact that one of them was a particularly villainous-looking negro and the other a dirty unshaven dock-rat, ragged and disreputable, the men immediately and loudly con-trasted them with Captain Bryndal—entirely in their favour: their manners, morals, appearance, characters and general worth with those of Captain Bryndal—also entirely and most markedly to his detriment.

The black man called himself Brown, which he was not; and the other dock-rat gave the name of Paulo.

135

Mr. Brown carried all his possessions, save for the ragged dungarees in which he stood—with a big bottle in each side pocket—in a red pocket-handkerchief.

The yellow-faced rogue, Paulo, seemed to possess nothing more than his rags, his matted hair and week's growth of beard, and his bottles of *pisco*. Later, he drew heavily on the slop-chest, and when I became better acquainted with the rascal, I did not grieve on hearing him whine that, there being no spare "donkey's breakfast" in the ship, he was obliged to sleep with nothing but some old canvas between him and his bunk-boards. . . .

Before nightfall further excitement was caused by a report from two Ordinary Seamen from another vessel that, while pulling the Old Man back to the ship, they'd heard him telling their own Captain that the *Valkyrie* was to proceed forthwith to Falmouth "for orders".

Optimistically assuming this to be authentic news, the fo'c'sle at once began preparations for the Homeward-Bounder's customary celebration of the last night in a West Coast port.

As soon as Eight Bells had been struck (eight p.m.) Church lifted up his magnificent voice and made the harbour resound with,

"*Good-bye, fare thee well,*" and as each of the four verses concluded, a lamp rose slowly from the fo'c'sle-head.

First there appeared a red light; then, nine to ten feet below it, and separated horizontally by a ten-foot pole, there hung two white lights, and, a further ten feet below this pair, a second red light completed the diamond-shaped pattern, the old traditional design for the occasion.

During the passage of these lights up to the block and down again, every chanty known to the crew was sung and adapted to hoisting and lowering.

Watching neighbouring ships looming tall and ghostly in the glorious starlight of the perfect evening, and listening to the deep-throated choruses echoing across the harbour, I felt deeply stirred as I enjoyed an experience that I shall never forget.

With the fore-light suspended high up the forestay, the big fo'c'sle-head bell was vigorously rung, and the chanty leader called for three cheers for the *Natuna*, the first ship in the landward tier. Her bell having been sharply rung in acknowledgment, a far-off voice called,

"Three cheers for the *Valkyrie*," and the volume of the response indicated that the *Natuna* was fully manned.

The next ship was then greeted by bell and voice from the

Valkyrie, and so, ship after ship, till all, each in turn, had been named and cheered, and had returned quick loud warm answer with bell and voice.

The last ship having responded, our cluster of lights was chantied down again, and the feeblest cheers of the evening were raised for Captain Bryndal. Possibly because he was entertaining other Captains in the Cabin, he was shamed into overcoming his meanness to the extent of sending a bottle of square-face to both watches, and many were the quaint expressions of genuine surprise that he had shown even this generosity.

"Bhoys," said Patsy Hooligan, "the Hyena has opened his hould. . . . He's opened his hould, I say."

And going from man to man, he repeated the statement as though it were interesting news known to himself alone.

We "boys" who did men's work without pay, and led the men in doing theirs, had to rest content with the subtler refreshment of the prevailing excitement. . . .

The morrow promising much and heavy work, I looked, for the last time, across the dark mirror of still water that glimmered with countless stars and golden shafts of brilliance from the ships' riding-lights, and at the lamps of Pisagua twinkling in the gloom of the mountains' vast dark mass. Then, wondering when and where our cables would once again roar out through the hawse-pipes, I went below to make the most of the last full night's sleep that I should be likely to get on this side of Cape Horn.

Coming events cast no shadows across my dreamless sleep and, in spite of my curious gift of second sight or prevision, I had no nightmare glimpse of the mystery and the tragedy, the drama and the horror, of the events which were to occur before our cables ran out again.

§3

With the first slow-creeping steps of Dawn across the mountain-tops came the task of running warps to other ships, and preventing our stern from swinging while we lifted the kedge anchors that, for fourteen weeks, had been sinking ever deeper into the ocean ooze.

Not until breakfast was long forgotten and the mid-day meal eagerly anticipated, were all after-moorings and stern cables aboard. The entire ship's company assuming that we were Home-ward Bound, there were no shirkers.

The sun was nearing the western rim of the ocean when we "boys" were sent aloft to loosen sail; and, the wind being very light, men from other ships readily helped us to set sail after sail.

Anon "Anchor's weighed, Sir," came from the fo'c'sle-head, and, at last, every warp had been let go, and hauled aboard.

With windlass pawls still clanking, cheers re-echoing and ensigns dipping, the *Valkyrie* gradually gathered way before the now freshening breeze.

Surely never did gallant ship make fairer start for fouler voyage.

From where I clung to make up gaskets and stop buntlines on the mizzen, I could watch the port's maze of mast and spar gradually coalesce into a blurred mass, and high aloft with none to hear, joyfully I sang,

"*Rolling home to dear old England,*" and whooped aloud as the *Valkyrie* curtseyed to the first Pacific swell.

Fortunately the merry and irresponsible youth that was myself—and at times, even now, it seems impossible that it could have been myself—had no premonition of the fact that less than two months of "rolling home" would bring him burdens that might indeed have overwhelmed and crushed an older wiser man—an experienced Officer.

By nightfall we were once more sailing in that great lonely and unbroken circle of the sea in which throughout the centuries, blue-water seamen have lived the greater part of their lives.

It was on this day that I took more especial notice of the Irishman calling himself Larry O'Toole, and found myself definitely disposed to like him for a friendly, pleasant and genial soul.

At the same time, I thought that he seemed rather frail for the hard life of a seaman, and that his soft Arklow speech, gentle brown eyes and quiet unassuming manner, seemed somehow to render him ill-fitted for holding his own in a ship's fo'c'sle.

In sharp contrast with Larry O'Toole, the man Villa loomed especially large and noisy that day, and indeed, when he could safely adopt the attitude, truculent, obscenely objectionable, and extremely troublesome.

Like the famous "Ranzo" of chanty fame, he was no sailor, and, while his bulk and strength saved him from ridicule and molestation in the fo'c'sle, it did not deter our Second Mate, Mr. Hammerson, from abruptly ordering him to cut short his first trick at the wheel, nor from assuring him that he was a rotten worse-than-useless soldier, who lacked the sense, the experience and the ability to steer a steam-ship on rails. This is at least a fair paraphrase of what Mr. Hammerson told Villa when he realized his worthlessness as a sailor.

This public humiliation Villa never forgot, and, in imitation of Slim Johes, Müller, and Jake, frequently dwelt on the complete-ness of the unique vengeance that he would one day wreak upon the Second Mate.

Nevertheless it was noticeable that he took good care not to be overheard by his appointed victim.

According to a tale that he told Fagin, who, I was sorry to discover, seemed rather to like the fellow, he had been shang-haied out of Portland, Oregon, a few months before joining the *Valkyrie*. This outrage had been perpetrated by his enemies because while practising his trade, profession, or business (unspecified), he had become so powerful in local politics that, at the next municipal election, he would inevitably have been made Mayor. This yarn would have been more credible if he had not, in unguarded moments, so bitterly inveighed against the Police, that it became fairly obvious that these were his real enemies. I thought that if he had indeed been shanghaied from Portland, Oregon, it was extremely probable that the Police had chosen an easy and profitable method of ridding their city of a crook, a gunman, and a pest. . . . Yet this was the man Dacre and I had seen lunching with Mrs. Bryndal in 'Frisco!

The two new-comers, Brown the negro and Paulo the more-or-less Portuguese dock-rat, were obviously good sailors and therefore bound to lighten the labour of the members of their respective watches. Whether they would eventually add to the peace and comfort, harmony and happiness, of the ship's company, I was quite early inclined to doubt. . . .

CHAPTER III

At the setting of the watches I was once more picked by the Mate.

Although it was quite obvious that this petty-minded vindictive man still hated the sight of me, he knew very well that I was quite as useful as any Able Seaman and far more willing than most of them; and, since Dacre was acting as Third Mate and was therefore bound to remain in the port watch, the arrangement suited me quite well. . . .

After standing to the westward for some time, we were fortunate enough to find regular South-East Trades which filled every sail from spanker to flying jib, and gave us a comfortable six to seven knots. Except for the daybreak "eye-opener" of putting the handy-billy on weather brace and sheet, we hardly touched running gear for days.

To me, the Apprentice without responsibility or a care in the world, that was a glorious time—literally, as well as metaphorically, a lull before the storm—tranquil days of that peerless Pacific weather, in which we could go happily bare-footed, bare-headed and clad only in shirt and trousers.

At the helm we could give the wheel a spoke each way, leave the good *Valkyrie* to steer herself and with an occasional glance at the compass-card, have leisure to wonder again at the frail and transparent beauty of the "Portuguese man-o'-war"[17] sailing merrily before the breeze.

Or, basking aloft in the languorous warmth, one could do his job of work in peaceful comfort, and pause to watch the vast circle of smooth sea, now and again broken into milky foam by the sudden uprising of shoals of flying-fish that sped like burnished arrows through the golden sunlight.

In such perfect weather as this, I and the giant "Baby" Axenstern, without first hauling the sail up to the yard, went aloft to reeve a new bunt-line, and, having passed it through its various leads in the rigging, we, from the upper yard, sought to drop the end through a bull's-eye half-way down the sail.

Unsuccessful in our first attempt to drop the end through the bull's-eye (a circular block of *lignum vitae* wood attached to the

---

[17] *A jelly-fish of brilliant colouring that hoists a membrane as a sail.*

sail by a few inches of rope) we lashed a marline-spike on to the bare end of the bunt-line, and tried to drop this through the bull's-eye. This, however, we also found to be impracticable, as the bull's-eye hung perpendicular, flat against the sail.

"Ah vas go down," said Axenstern.

"Not you," I replied. "I'll go."

For I knew that he, like many very strong but heavy men, could not climb upward, hand over hand, so much as his own length.

Even as I spoke, Axenstern, with a scornful snort, hitched the bunt-line round the jackstay and descended to the bull's-eye.

Quickly he had good cause to regret his rashness. To hang on with one hand and push the rope through with the other, was comparatively easy, but it absorbed some of his strength, and when he tried to return, he found that, even with hands and feet free, he was unable to climb up the rope for more than a couple of feet.

"*Mein Gott!*" he gasped, as he clung.

Looking anxiously down at him, I saw his bronzed face turn to the colour of an old sail.

"Ah gannot oop get," he groaned.

Thanking God for the stout gasket that lay along the yard, I said,

"Hang on, Axenstern. Twist your leg round the bunt-line and keep still."

Then dropping the gasket beside him, I slid down, hitched the end round his waist, climbed back up on to the yard, and bade him climb, if it were only a foot.

By catching a turn with the gasket and taking up the slack, I was able to support him when he had climbed a few inches, and so each time that he rested between his frequent struggles.

At length I got him on to the yard, and found that, on reaching it, the great "Baby" was infinitely more grateful for my not having called for help, and so proclaimed his failure, than for my having saved him from breaking his neck and every bone in his body.

"Von day Ah pay you. Ah get sqvare mit you," he panted as he rested on the yard.

He kept his promise—and little as I dreamed it, I saved more than "Baby" Axenstern that day.

Whether Axenstern straightway sang my praises in the fo'c'sle I do not know, and it may have been merely by chance that this incident coincided with a marked increase of cordiality between the port watch and myself. While I most heartily detested Slim Johes and knew that he hated me, we'd always been on speaking terms and now we spoke more pleasantly, and his easily-led crony, Hamblin, also became more friendly, and in his morose erratic way seemed at times to be very well disposed toward me.

In Axenstern I had hitherto detected a certain amount of childish jealousy of my strength, willingness and position, a slight enmity which, after the affair of the buntline, entirely disappeared.

Of the other men of the port watch, Larry O'Toole proved in every way a most desirable shipmate; with the clownish Patsy Hooligan and the foolish Foyle I'd always been jocularly, if somewhat contemptuously, familiar; and the unpleasant anarchist Müller I always consistently ignored as far as was possible.

In the starboard watch, the growling duets of Church and Carrol often provoked me to friendly banter, while for the solemn bearded Berghen and the hairy silent Blancke, I had considerable liking and respect.

By the blasphemy and bragging of the undesirable Jake Walfisch I was quite unimpressed.

Big Villa I grew to dislike more and more, until long before we reached the Horn, I think I preferred even Slim Johes and Jake.

These two were bad men and in many ways detestable men, but Villa was evil. It seemed to me that he radiated evil, as distinct from nastiness, envy, malice, dishonesty, blasphemy, laziness and shirking. These faults are bad enough, and a grievous disfigurement of character. But, to me, it seemed that Villa's whole character was a deformity, a disfigurement—sinister, bad for the sake of badness. For me he shed a new light upon the meaning of the line,

"Evil, be thou my good."

The worst of the other men thought and said and did wrong and evil things when tempted—or driven—by weariness, by fancied wrong, by envy, jealousy, or lust for that which they had not. But Villa thought and said and did evil things because he preferred evil for its own sake, and not only for imagined profit or pleasure obtainable therefrom.

Probably under no conditions whatsoever are the true characters and natures of men laid so bare to the watchful observer as they are under those that prevail on board a deep-sea long-voyage sailing-ship, where, day in, day out, week after week, and month after month, men live in such relentless inescapable proximity and intimacy—the paradox of the publicity of their privacy.

Brown the negro and Paulo the Brazilian or Portuguese I soon wrote off as low-type bad men who were fair-type good sailors.

§2

At about this time, too, I also discovered, from chance remarks and half-deck jests that, in addition to this increased friendliness, I had been gaining a surprising prestige.

The Fo'c'sle was beginning to talk of my boxing-skill—to them remarkable, unsuspected, and apparently amazing.

I had bought a second-hand set of gloves in San Francisco, and for the short time that they had been a novelty to the half-deck, we had all wanted to spar; but Beauty had proved too lazy to remain interested for long; Geordie had found that himself and his arms were too short for him to get much fun out of it; and Fagin, having bumped his long nose hard against my out-stretched left, had lost a little blood, a lot of enthusiasm and all desire to box with me again.

This left Dacre free to spar with me whenever opportunity offered, and throughout each dog-watch we practised continu-ally. Unlike myself, Dacre had never received any proper tuition and training, and, although he quickly became a good fighting boxer with a very useful punch, he was not in my class at all. Not only did he lack a cat-like lightness of movement which had always been considered remarkable in one so heavy as myself, but he had nothing like my natural gift, my acquired skill, and my power to hit equally hard with either hand, nor indeed my strength and endurance.

To avoid observation and comment from the Captain and the Mate, we used to clear a space amidships between the galley and the for'ard main hatch coamings. With a rope stretched from the corner of the house to the corresponding corner of the hatch, we formed a boxing-ring sufficiently large for freedom of movement but restricted enough to ensure that we practised side-stepping, dodging, and all other forms of foot-work. This suited me very well, for my own particular forte was the avoid-ance of blows by movement of the body—Entellus my exemplar. The more I could thus defend myself, the less I had to use my arms for guarding—and the freer they were for hitting.

At first our doings naturally attracted the crew's attention, but as we generally practised prescribed movements and seldom "mixed it" in spectacular fashion, the men soon lost interest.

Nevertheless, they had observed that I was the instructor, and overhearing some fo'c'sle gossip, I learned that it was there considered that "young Sinbad could use hisself all-right".

I also gathered that praise of my alleged boxing ability annoyed Chips (Peddersen, our Norse carpenter), who was the self-proclaimed Heavy-weight Champion of the ship, if not of the entire Mercantile Marine, and it was not long before he asked me, smiling his cunning ugly leer, if I would give him the pleasure of a friendly round. I was amused when he added that he would like the bout to take place at a time when we could spar unobserved. Obviously he did not wish to run any risk of being humbled before his shipmates, followers and admirers.

I agreed, and with only Dacre, Beauty and Geordie as spectators, we met in the ring.

In a very few seconds it was apparent to me that although probably a terrific and dangerous fighter, the fellow was not a first-class boxer. For one thing, he gave away all his great natural advantage of height and reach by adopting a crouching stance, and was very apt to leave his defence wide open to an upper-cut from any quick opponent.

Deliberately and intentionally, I "played light", refrained from taking advantage of numerous attractive opportunities, and gave Peddersen every reason to consider himself the better man.

At the same time, I took good care that none of his extremely powerful straight lefts, tremendous right swings, deadly hooks, jabs and upper-cuts should get home—for, far from "playing light" himself Peddersen did his best to knock me out. Some of his terrific "rights" would not only have done that, but would have knocked me out of the ring—if not out of the ship.

As it was, he scarcely hit me at all, did not knock me down once, and drew no blood.

On the other hand, I several times tapped him fairly lightly on the point of the jaw or on the mark, when I could, had I wished, have given him a blow that would have surprised him.

At the same time I had to admit that his fists were like sledge-hammers, his arms like pistons, his strength abnormal, his speed and skill considerable, and himself a very ugly customer to oppose.

Throughout each of our rounds I let him bustle me all about the ring, gave him the impression that I was fully extended and doing my damnedest, and that I was very relieved when he allowed me to rest.

When we had finished and Peddersen had gone, Dacre expressed his thankfulness that the business was over and that I was uninjured.

"I thought the swine was going to kill you," said Beauty and,

"Ba goom, lad, he might have!" agreed Geordie, "though ye're a reet guid boxer. Eh, 'twas champion."

So it was evident that I had played well my defensive rôle and deceived others as well as Peddersen.

The latter, I learned, boasted to his watch that he had "pasted me vell" and knocked some of the stuffing out of my cocksureness, big and strong as I was, and clever as I thought myself.

In one dog-watch, Dacre said he wanted to "mix it," and begged me really to box him, and for a two-minute round to go all out.

I humoured him, but refrained from knocking him out or giving him any really distressing body blows.

Dacre boxed well and fought splendidly, and at the end of a long and furious rally, we stopped at Geordie's cry of 'Time'—to find the Second Mate, Mr. Hammerson, watching us with the deepest interest.

"There's the makings of a fighting-man in you, Sinbad," said he, "and when I say a fighting-man I mean a fighting-man—a pro. . . . If you had a pro to teach you. . . ."

Knowing that Mr. Hammerson had himself left the sea to become a professional boxer, had earned his living in the ring for years and become a Champion, I very quickly assured him that there was nothing on earth that I desired more than that a "pro" should teach me.

"Well, perhaps I'll put you through the mill, some time," he grinned, "and see how you like it. See what you're made of."

To my surprise, the Second Mate proved as good as his word. Coming one day to our ring amidships, he bade me put on the gloves and took a pair himself.

"Now go for me," said he. "Knock me out, and I'll give you . . .

"I'll give you ten pounds and an inscribed gold watch," he grinned. "Three minutes."

For three minutes I went at him as though I were fighting for my life and his death; and, without boasting, I may say that Mr. Hammerson had to look out for himself.

While not forgetting that attack is the best defence, he boxed mostly on the defensive, replying with a quiet smile whenever I got home, which occasionally I did; and once with a punch that undoubtedly shook him.

I went all out indeed. I used every trick I knew. I boxed with my utmost speed, and hit with every ounce of my strength.

Mr. Hammerson paid me the compliment of quite obviously doing the same, save in the matter of hitting with all his strength, and using all his tricks, and of being the aggressor.

"Good lad," said he, when Geordie called 'Time'. "There *are* the makings of a fighting man somewhere about you."

"I'll come along again to-morrow," he added, as he turned to go. "Don't do any boxing till I come. I want you fresh."

Dacre, Geordie and Beauty eyed me, if not open-mouthed, at any rate with a new respect.

"Ba goom!" said Geordie.

"You're a blooming wonder," confessed Beauty.

Dacre pursed his lips.

"H'm," said he, and rubbed his chin thoughtfully.

True to his word, the Second Mate visited us amidships next day.

"Put 'em on," said he. "I'm going to knock you about and knock you out. If you're on your feet at the end of three minutes I'll give you . . ."

"Ten pounds and an inscribed gold watch?" I asked.

"No," grinned Mr. Hammerson. "A worse hiding to-morrow."

The moment we had shaken hands, I lashed out a straight left and a lightning right, struck the air where Mr. Hammerson's head had been, and received a rib-bender that made me gasp.

There was nothing of the defensive about the Second Mate's tactics to-day. Without giving me a moment in which to recover, he aimed right and left, almost simultaneously, at my face.

Ducking, and using both hands for hitting, I got in two beauties on the mark, a fraction of an instant before receiving an upper-cut and a left hook that sent me clean off my feet. Almost before I was on them again, Mr. Hammerson was at me, and it was only by the swiftest side-stepping, ducking, dodging, slipping, guarding with both arms and covering up, that I weathered the storm.

This I contrived to do, however, and rising suddenly from beneath and between his great arms, managed a few seconds in-fighting and, as he sprang back, drove a very heavy right through his guard, landing a blow on his cheek-bone that sent him staggering to the ropes.

Before he could recover, I sprang at him like a tiger, missed

146

him entirely as, with a laugh, he side-stepped clean away, and gave me a swinging left that, for at least some six or seven seconds, I thought had finished the fight.

"All-right?" cried Mr. Hammerson, as I got to my feet, drew the back of my glove across my eyes as though that might clear my sight, and then put my fists up.

I nodded.

"Now then," said my opponent, and came for me in a way calculated to show me that hitherto he'd been playing with me. It was a hurricane attack that taught me the difference between the professional and the amateur.

How much of the three minutes still remained I did not know, but every second of the time was a second too much for me. Mr. Hammerson seemed to hit me when and where he pleased, and as often as he pleased. I felt a fool, and before long I felt a weakling. Some of his blows I undoubtedly did evade, and some I stopped, and occasionally I got a real one home. Once as he rushed, and a cannon-ball straight left grazed my right ear, I countered with all my strength straight on his mouth, and was amazed to see blood follow my blow. But for that one I got a dozen such.

And yet somehow I weathered the storm, and at Geordie's raucous yell of 'Time', surely one of the sweetest sounds I ever heard, I was still on my feet—and no-one more surprised than I, unless perhaps it was Mr. Hammerson himself.

"Yes," said he, pulling off the gloves as I sat down in a state bordering on collapse, and breathed for dear life, "you've got the makings, my son."

He then shook hands with me, clapped me on the shoulder and gave me a smile that did me good.

"I'll have a talk with you by and by," he said as he turned away.

A day or two later he did; and an interesting talk it was, ending with nothing less than the suggestion that he should train me as hard as he could, teach me everything he knew, and if, by the end of the voyage, I could stand up to him for three rounds, I should turn professional boxer, with him as my manager and trainer.

"There's money in it, Son," he said, "and I believe you'd go far; and if you didn't, you could always go back to the sea, as I've done. . . . I know the game from A to Z in Australia, and could get you started. What's to stop your becoming champion of Australia for a start? You'd meet nobody bigger or stronger, and I'll say you won't meet a better boxer by the time I've done with you. You're a born fighter, and a natural fighter; you've got the heart and can take punishment.

"Then what about England? Lord knows they want a Champion. Then Europe, eh? Champion of Europe before you're twenty.

"Then we'd cross the North Atlantic and have a look at the World Champion. See what we thought of him, eh, Son?"

I laughed.

"What about you, Sir?" I grinned.

"What about me? Why didn't I do it? Too old. Began too late. Badly trained. And best reason of all—not good enough."

"And I?" I smiled.

"Yes, you could go a lot further than I. Quicker, taller, longer reach. And when you've done growing, a couple of stone heavier. And I could *make* you, Sinbad; teach you . . . tricks of the trade . . . ring-craft. And you've got breed . . . and sense. You keep off drink and . . . all the other things that ruin pugilists."

Mr. Hammerson fell silent and stared unseeingly through the port-hole.

"Anyhow," he said, "we'll make a start and see how things go. I'll teach you all I know, and train you till you can beat me. . . .

"And if as an amateur you can do that," he concluded, "you'll be a silly fool if you don't turn professional."

"Excuse me, Sir," I said, turning to leave the cabin. "Were you really going all out, the other day? Really doing your best to put me down?"

"I was," replied the Second Mate, "and that's why I'm talking to you now. . . . 'Nuff said."

Mr. Hammerson proved as good as his word, took me in hand, knocked me about—for my own good—most cruelly, and taught me systematically.

On moonlight nights when I should have been in my bunk; when he knew that the Old Man was asleep; and while the men of his watch dozed in odd corners about the deck, he drilled me in every sort and kind of blow and guard, feint and dodge and trick; showed me "specials" of his own; taught me methods and tricks of in-fighting; taught me blows which, though quite legitimate in prize-fighting, are seldom used by, or known to, the amateur.

After each lesson we would box, and box hard. Occasionally

he would bid me beware, and for a round we would really fight.

And gradually I learned from him that invaluable ring-craft, which is known, and known only, to the real professional pug.

With such remarks as,

"Now watch this. . . ."

"This would put your fancy amateur boxer to sleep for a bit. . . ."

"Stand by to guard with your left, and move quickly . . ." he would show me his devastating pivot-blow.

Or, observing that I might sometimes meet a bad 'un, he would, in a mix-up of in-fighting, cunningly pin my arms within his own and initiate me into the method of secretly administering the terrible stamina-sapping kidney-punch.

To my objection that this was a foul, he would reply,

"Quite so, and you've got to know how to deal with a man who fouls—in that way or any other. And when you know how a thing's done, you know how to guard against it. And if you are dealing with a swine that fouls, isn't it a good thing to be able to say,

" 'Oh well, if *that's* included—watch me . . .'?"

One lovely night, before loss of the Trades and a change in the weather put an end to our peaceful watches, Mr. Hammerson carefully taught me his own private upper-cut which, because (among other features) of a twisting motion of the fist at the moment of impact, was extremely effective, even at the shortest range in the closest of in-fighting.

After one of the last of the lessons and a very sharp two minutes in which I had held my own, my magnificent teacher admitted that I now only needed practice and ring-experience to make me equal to many a good professional heavy-weight.

"Don't get swollen-headed, Son," he concluded, "if I tell you that you're the quickest thing I've seen on two legs; that you've got a real punch in both hands—which so few boxers have; and that you fight as cunning as the Devil and with better foot-work. Now, with your physique, why shouldn't you get to the top—with me training you? . . . I tell you, if you don't turn pro, you don't follow the trade God meant you for . . .

"Not that you haven't a damn long way to go yet," he added.

§3

One day I was very surprised and not a little flattered by receiving a respectful request from the dour disgruntled Red

Hamblin that I would teach him how to box really properly.

Observing that he'd had many a "guid fecht and was no' sic a fule at scrappin' ", he admitted that he'd never had a chance to learn to box and really knew nothing about it.

Personally, and as it turned out, quite erroneously, I thought that perhaps this violent and fiery youth, unbalanced and discontented, would be better without a knowledge of boxing and a naturally increased desire to turn the knowledge to account.

However, not wishing to hurt or offend him, I did, in the fine night watches when Mr. Hammerson had done with me, and the Mate yarned with the man at the wheel (a bad habit in an Officer), box with the young Scot, by the bright light of the stars and the tropical moon.

In spite of his inexperience and awkwardness, Red Hamblin, with his long arms, quick movements, and fine general speed, gave me good practice; and, I must say, seemed very grateful to me for my tuition. I admit that I was very agreeably surprised by the fine hold that he kept on his temper, even when, as occasionally happened, he got a real hard blow.

I only "went for him" when he, feeling that he'd made good progress and wishing to test it, asked me to have a real round.

One night, owing to rather poor light, I accidentally landed with such force on his jaw that he was knocked right across the deck, before falling heavily.

I helped him up and apologized for hitting so hard.

"It was as well that we were using the gloves," said I, "for had my fist been there, you would certainly have been down and out for the full count."

"Och, aye," he answered, "an' well I ken it. I' Glasgae one nicht about three weeks before I happened to join the *Valkyrie*, some lang son o' a gun o' a sodden sea-cook did the like to me wi' his bare fist and pit me i' the hospital unconscious for forty-eight hours—an' gie me the headache that, whiles, I get to this day, and it drives me mad.

"I was tae drrunk to dae aught an' he juist took ma money and knocked me stane cauld, the dirrty cowardly hound. I can remember it a', him and me comin' oot o' the public, him proppin' me against a lamp-post and me smilin' foolish and daft-like whiles he took ma money; and then him raisin' his fist. I can see it a', but I canna mind his face, and that's a gey pity, for if I knew his face, I'd spend the rest o' me life lookin' for him. Goad love us, 'tis a pity, for I wadna ken the swine if I had him here the noo. . . . I'd gie him a headache that 'ud last the rest o' his life—and that wadna be five minutes. I'd juist say,

" 'D'ye mind a Saturday night in the Broomielaw when ye robbed and half-killed a drunken fule that had juist been treatin' ye?' . . ."

"What!" interrupted I, "the Broomielaw in Glasgow one Saturday night before we sailed? Stuck you up against a lamp-post and then knocked you clean across the road? Why, I saw it. I chased the man and nearly caught him."

"You did so?" cried Red Hamblin excitedly. "And ye saw his face? Ye'd know him again?"

"No, I didn't. He didn't run backwards . . ." I said.

On comparing notes we found that it was this same Red Hamblin whom Dacre and I had helped to put into the ambulance, on my return from my ineffectual chase of the taller man.

How Hamblin cursed when I told him that I'd actually grabbed the fugitive by the collar when the huge Highland policeman seized me.

Questioning him, I found that all he could remember of what happened prior to his waking in the hospital ward, was drinking with a dommed harrd-faced tinkler's bastard who talked a lot about his wonderful right-hand punch, plied Hamblin with neat whisky at Hamblin's expense, led him to a lamp-post, robbed him and struck him down. No, he couldn't remember his face at all, only that he was a big ugly deevil.

"An' it was ye that pit me i' th' ombulance . . ." mused Red Hamblin. "An' chased th' swine that hit me, b' Goad!

"Weel, weel! I'll no' forget you, ava!" said Hamblin.

"An' did ye no hae ony sicht o' th' face o' th' cur?" he begged.

I told him again that I never had a glimpse of the fellow's face —but suddenly I remembered, and described the big scar at the base of the runner's neck.

"Goad! If ever I set e'es on yon scarr, as sure's daith I'll gie that yin a double dose o' his ain medicine," swore Hamblin solemnly. "I'll gie him a scar on his dirrty heartt wi' ma knife."

Until some time later, the matter went right out of my mind.

CHAPTER IV

I found boxing a splendid pastime, and not only a magnificent diversion, but a most welcome relief from the monotony of ship-board life.

It was a thousand pities that my shipmates of the half-deck were not as keen and enthusiastic about it as I was. In point of fact they had lost interest altogether—in favour of a wholly different diversion. Love!

Dacre was now in love, while Fagin, Beauty and Geordie still thought they were.

Handsome and magnificent Dacre, the misogynist, had not fallen in love so much as flown into a sudden passion of love, as men fly into a sudden passion of rage. I verily believe that as quickly as a man may pass from complete good temper into fierce wrath, so quickly had Dacre passed from placid indiffer-ence to violent love.

Violent fires soon burn out themselves, and I fervently hoped that Dacre's fire of love would speedily burn out, mainly because Celia Bryndal was not the sort of girl to do Dacre any good, and partly because this new and sudden passion threatened to come between us, to cause a breach in our hitherto perfect and precious friendship.

Incredible as it seemed, this Apollo of a Dacre was actually jealous of me. It was too absurd to be believed, yet too real to be ignored; too ridiculous for acceptance, yet too patent for comfort.

How could so extraordinarily attractive, agreeable, accom-plished and truly handsome a man imagine that any girl, let alone such a girl as Celia Bryndal, would so much as glance at me while he was about; and how could so frank, clear-minded and honour-able a gentleman as Dacre flatly refuse to believe me when I told him that far from being a rival for Miss Bryndal's favour, I simply did not care a tuppenny damn whom she favoured; that her favours were to me a matter of the very completest indifference; and that, in point of fact and to be quite frank, so far as I had any feeling toward her whatsoever, I rather disliked her?

Dacre simply did not believe me. I suppose that in his abnormal condition of first love and blazing passion, he could not conceive it to be possible that anyone should be daily within sight and sound of his revealed goddess without falling in love with her.

When I said that on the whole I rather disliked her, I thought he was going to strike me. . . . To say such a thing was an intentional insult, and I ought to be ashamed of myself for my cowardice in denying that I loved her, and my caddish feebleness in pretending that I disliked her. . . . 'Why couldn't I admit like a man' . . . and so forth.

It appeared that the calf-love moonings and bellowings of the others were preferable to my 'lying pretence of indifference or dislike'.

Of course, we had all been shut up together far too long, and were getting on each other's nerves; and the presence of these women on board infinitely increased and exacerbated that irritation, exasperation and ill-feeling inevitably generated by prolonged contiguity.

But for Celia Bryndal we should have worked off the normal discontents in the normal manner, grumbled and growled spasmodically, quarrelled and made it up, and nobody a penny the worse.

I admit that I was exceedingly surprised and badly hurt at Dacre's attitude and behaviour. I'd thought him too experienced, too big, too fine, to have fallen so complete a prey to so miserable a passion as jealousy. And at the time the thought never entered my thick head that the inevitable cause of the mischief was, moreover, a deliberate and intentional maker of further mischief; that the girl was lying to him about me; was using me further to inflame Dacre's love; to punish me for my indifference; and to come between Dacre and myself.

I, of course, behaved foolishly, as the young are prone to do, and with false and foolish pride, took the line of hurt and angry silence, and the pretence that, since Dacre preferred the girl to me, preferred her word to mine, he was welcome.

My mental attitude was,

"All-right, have it your own way. If you are going to let this girl come between us—that's that. And if this is all your friendship is worth, it is no great loss."

Worse still, this foolish attitude of injured pride and aloofness degenerated into one of,

"All-right, since you insist on being jealous, I'll give you something to be jealous about", and forthwith began to show myself aware of Celia Bryndal.

But this proved a mistake.

Thinking over the incident, I concluded, later, that it was purely in a spirit of mischief that she invited me to visit her in her cabin.

"Oh no!" I said hastily, "I couldn't possibly do that."

She laughed at my evident alarm.

"All right . . . Don't . . . Stop outside—Little Joseph," she mocked.

I felt a complete fool.

Dacre himself was the first to exemplify the truth of his own remark that to bring a woman on to a ship was deliberately to turn it into a hell-ship, and now I heartily agreed with him.

A week ashore would have put us all perfectly right. . . .

§2

Nor was trouble confined to the half-deck. That would have mattered but little. There was serious trouble Aft—and trouble Aft is bound to mean trouble Forward. Unhappiness, suffering, and wrath in the Cabin quickly spread to the Fo'c'sle—being sooner or later, in some way or other, visited upon its occupants.

Things in the Cabin were evidently very wrong indeed. Repercussions of this position of affairs were quickly felt throughout the ship, and every one was, by now, in a state of irritation and discontent.

CHAPTER V

From this time, trouble came thick and fast upon the ill-fated *Valkyrie*—to the Cabin, the Half-deck and the Fo'c'sle.

Mrs. Bryndal now never appeared on deck at the same time as Captain Bryndal without a bitter quarrel developing between them. In fact, fierce and acrimonious quarrels were the order of the day; and the girl Celia seemed to be equally violently at issue with her mother and with her "father".

Mr. Hammerson, who, since the projection of our boxing partnership, had become increasingly friendly with me, confessed that he was thankful that he messed alone at the second table—because in these days the Bryndal family were more like a family of lions feeding, than three human beings.

"Or rather," Mr. Hammerson corrected himself, "like a lion, a tiger and a panther shut up together in one small cage."

Even the hitherto privileged Mate was now denied access to the chronometers, and his daily "sight" being sneeringly and jeeringly ridiculed by the Captain, Mr. Smeeker ceased to take any observations whatsoever, and gradually ceased to speak to the Captain unless absolutely obliged.

On the other hand, he lost no opportunity of addressing Mrs. Bryndal, spent every moment that he possibly could in her company, and indeed, if there were any truth in the allusive hints or scandalous statements of Fagin and Beauty, spent more time in her society than Captain Bryndal imagined.

On this subject Fagin was eloquent, for, incredible as it may seem, the creature declared that deeply and passionately as he loved Celia Bryndal, he wasn't sure that he didn't love Mrs. Bryndal "a damn sight more", and that his passion was returned!

The discontented crew suddenly asserting their legal right to have their allowance of food weighed in their presence at the time of issue, found that—if any difference there were—they received even less than before; and consequently they were yet the more discontented.

Their increasing and ever more vociferous anger and resentment and almost mutinous wrath, served to emphasize the strong contrast between the First and Second Mates.

Smeeker, having neither the personality nor strength of character to maintain his authority with men like Slim Johes,

Müller and Hamblin, actually condoled with them in secret, and when one of them was at the wheel, would stand and listen to his grumbling, agree with his statements, and sympathize with his views.

With Slim Johes and the foolish Patsy Hooligan, he gossiped maliciously about members of the half-deck and the quiet unassuming members of the crew, such as Berghen and Blancke, Church and Carrol, and the gentle and harmless Larry O'Toole.

As a matter of fact, I gleaned a lot of very useful information from this simple soul, Larry O'Toole, for whom I found myself entertaining a growing regard and liking. It was the easiest thing in the world to pick his poor brain, and lead him on to empty his somewhat feeble mind of its contents.

It was impossible for him to conceal anything, and while I was quite sure that Larry was the last man in the world to spy upon his shipmates and report their doings, he was wholly incapable of hiding anything that he knew—or so, in my wisdom, I thought at the time.

Certainly poor Larry O'Toole singled me out, made a friend of me, and took evident delight in my company and conversation. . . .

Pursuing precisely the opposite course from that followed by Smeeker, Mr. Hammerson kept his watch at arm's-length, laughed at the grousing and growling of Church and Carrol—the usual proper and normal grumblings of every right-minded shell-back—sharply checked any tendency to impudent criticism of black Brown and yellow Paulo, and showed his teeth pretty plainly to Jake Walfisch and Villa whenever those blackguards came athwart his hawse.

One fine night, finding Jake asleep when he ought to have been keeping a sharp look-out, he woke him in the proper manner and told him precisely what he thought of him—an art in which he was something of an adept.

Perhaps because he was only half awake, Jake was insolent and indeed blusteringly defiant. Hammerson, seizing him by throat and arm, ran him along and threw him off the fo'c'sle head. Villa, unwise enough to rush forward, protest, and interfere, received, and for some days bore, a vivid keepsake of the occasion in the form of a bright black eye.

Shortly afterwards, this alleged "hundred-per-cent. American" dropped a block from aloft. It missed Mr. Hammerson by a matter of inches. On reaching the deck, Villa admitted that he'd been careless.

"We're all careless sometimes, aren't we?" observed the Second Mate.

"Yeah," agreed Villa.

"Now I'm going to be careless," said Mr. Hammerson, and a minute later Villa fled, shouting oaths that were not American, and shut himself in the lamp-locker.

With Slim Johes and Müller, Villa and Jake, there were now two men in each Watch who exchanged confidences about what they would one day do to that unmentionable though much-mentioned Second Mate, Hammerson.

I am thankful to be able to say that, whatever our private differences—and they seemed to be rapidly crystallizing from mere differences to positive hatred—Dacre and I loyally supported each other in trying to keep the half-deck clear of the prevailing bickering, quarrelsomeness and tendency to split up into jealous cliques and warring factions. We insisted that the half-deck must be at one and act as one.

"We must hang together," said Dacre . . . "Hang together—or hang at the yard-arm," he growled.

Later, incredible as it seemed, I had occasion to remember his words, and thought of the trite truism that there's many a true word spoken in jest, as well as many a true jest not spoken in words.

Watching each other, with nothing of friendship in our eyes, we, for example, would join in pointing out to Fagin and Beauty, with crisp words and terse phrases, that the Half-deck was the Half-deck, the Fo'c'sle the Fo'c'sle, and never the twain should meet—save on duty. For these two fools were developing the habit of sneaking along to the fo'c'sle, hobnobbing with the men —and not the best of the men—listening to their grumbling half-mutinous threats, and repeating things that they had heard Aft, or that were reported to have been said Aft.

The asinine idiot Beauty had, I'm sure, no intention or idea of making mischief, and only visited the men because some of them flattered him; and because, whilst among them, he had the illusion that he, too, spoke and behaved like a man and a sailor.

Fagin's motives were much more open to suspicion, for he was the only one of us who talked with Chips (the subversive ill-conditioned Carpenter, Peddersen) and, moreover, he deliberately made trouble by inciting the least desirable of the men to break a strict though unwritten law, by returning his visits.

For Dacre, backed by myself, to stop Apprentices from going

into the fo'c'sle was quite easy. But with the Mate indifferent or worse and the Captain quite unapproachable, it was by no means so simple a task to keep Slim Johes, Müller, Jake and Villa out of the half-deck—and it looked as though Dacre, as acting Third Mate, was going to have serious trouble on his hands.

However, discovering that Dacre would fight to the last inch, and that the Second Mate—not to mention myself—would support him, the four seamen elected to accept Dacre's extremely blunt request to stay away—and to register a bitter grudge against Dacre and myself.

Not so Fagin. Observing that whatever Dacre might now consider himself, there was no question as to who and what I was (a conceited, bumptious, overgrown First Voyager), and that in view of what Dacre and I had impressed upon him as to the desirability of Apprentices avoiding the fo'c'sle, he would immediately forthwith and at once, rise up and—go to the fo'c'sle.

"I'll go with you," said I, glancing at Dacre.

Dacre nodded.

We went. As we were about to enter, I seized Fagin by the arm and swung him about.

"Listen," said I. "Go in there, if you like. When you've been in, one minute, I'll come in—and kick you out. I'll then kick you into the other fo'c'sle. From that one I'll then kick you forth, and then kick you all the way back to the half-deck. . . . Now then, Fagin, will you go in there, or will you put your fists up, or will you go back to the half-deck—and we'll say no more about it?"

"Who are you, you . . . ?" blustered Fagin.

I told him who I was.

"You think that because you can box with the Second Mate, you bullying . . ."

"Yes, yes, Fagin," I soothed him. "It's shameful. Hurry up. In there—or else put your fists up. Or come back to the half-deck."

Grumbling, cursing and threatening, Fagin came.

"That's all-right, Fagin," I said, quite kindly, as we arrived. " 'Nuff said. . . . But *don't* go into the fo'c'sle again."

I don't think Fagin disobeyed, but I cannot pretend that my very necessary action in the matter made for peace in the home, or inclined Fagin to lend more favourable ear to Dacre's homilies on the importance of union and strength in the half-deck.

§2

We now lost the Trades, and were constantly trimming the

yards to variable winds. Steady hard work is one of the best cures for brooding and discontent, but we got too much of it, too suddenly. There was now no sleeping or lazing while standing the night watches, and the voice of the grouser was heard o'er the water, ever more loudly.

After a few watches of pully-hauly, the wind came fresh from the Westward, and within a week, the sun's daily course was notably shorter and the nights too cold for sleeping on deck.

With other signs that bare-foot days and peaceful nights would soon be completely gone, there came the unbending of fine-weather sails, the substitution of heavier canvas, the reeving of new braces, the replacement of all gear considered unfit for the rigours of the dreaded Cape Horn.

But we were reeling off the knots and making our course for Home (as we thought), and, had we been a more normal ship's-company, the sullen spirit of ill-will that brooded fore and aft would surely have evaporated.

This, however, it did not do, either fore or aft, and a heavy swell now setting in from the South-West, the *Valkyrie* gave a first intimation of the wild and erratic behaviour that she was soon to display; and the crew, knowing that the Captain was to blame, at once decided that they had yet another weighty grievance against the "Grinning Hyena".

In Pisagua, Captain Bryndal had interfered with the loading. Either by his own instructions or by reason of the stevedore's not unnatural pique and resentment, a great deal of cargo that should have gone into the 'tween-decks had been stowed in the lower hold.

This had rendered the vessel so "stiff" that for the slightest cause, or none at all that was apparent, she would lurch violently either way, and so make going aloft a very uncomfortable, and indeed a dangerous, business. The old hands growled, groused and shook their heads ominously, observing that never before had they seen a Christian ship cut such capers. . . .

Perhaps the *Valkyrie* had ceased to be a Christian ship? Dacre likened her to one of those "tumbler" toys with which children used to play; little truncated cones of cardboard with a rounded leaden base, which, being knocked over, will immediately spring upright again and violently oscillate for a while.

Being myself on an upper yard when she gave her first exhibition, and momentarily expecting to be thrown off the foot-rope, I appreciated the aptness of this comparison.

During these horrible bouts of rolling, the sails seemed to

have no steadying influence whatsoever upon the ship, and the masts described arcs amazing in their length and the rapidity of their execution.

To the extent that it was feasible, we carried heavy bags of nitrate from the lower hold into the 'tween-decks, but having little room in which to work or rig hoisting-tackle, achieved very little appreciable improvement. Indeed, so little were we able to alter her trim and lessen the incessant heavy rolling, that, when the vessel was docked, it was seen that parrels and other gear had worn deep grooves in the plates of the steel masts. . . .

Our next trouble came with the capsizing of a pile of bags of nitrate in the 'tween-decks under the Captain's Cabin.

This made itself evident by putting such a strain on the deck-beams that it caused all the doors in the after-accommodation to stick fast. To rectify this, All Hands had to spend the Sunday forenoon watch in re-stowing the shifted cargo, and as the Port Watch should have been below, off-duty, Slim Johes' inflammatory whispering found ready listeners and fanned the smouldering fires of bitter resentment.

On emerging from the after-hatch, the sweating dirty crew observed the Captain smoking in cool and cleanly comfort on the poop; and, as they made their way for'ard, Johes and Müller, Jake and Villa exchanged audible remarks of the most insulting description concerning Stinking Beasts of Grinning Hyenas who robbed honest hard-working men of their hard-earned Sabbath rest.

That the Captain heard every word I'm quite sure, for, glancing in the direction of the ringleaders, his bright smile grew even a little brighter, as one or two more of his magnificent teeth were bared.

§3

And now occurred our second death, a suicide, and committed in the most extraordinary way. I've never heard of a similar case, nor met anybody who has.

The affair not only deepened the gloom already pervading the ship, but somewhat unreasonably increased—enormously increased—the crew's hatred of the Captain, and indeed of the whole after-guard.

The man was Foyle, the poor buffoon whom I have already mentioned—a very thin undersized, foolish creature, really rather solitary and friendless, now much given to brooding and bitterly resentful of slights and wrongs, fancied or genuine. To his shipmates, nothing in his life became him like the leaving of it. By his death he became a Symbol, as well as a martyr and something of a hero.

With or without good cause, Foyle had roused the savage wrath of the Mate, and it must be admitted that Smeeker was much more prone and ready to give vent to wrath and savagery when dealing with a meek and puny little offender, than when finding fault with powerful and truculent ruffians such as Müller, Jake, or Villa.

Undoubtedly, poor little Foyle was frequently given the rôle of lightning-conductor as well as that of whipping-boy, and suffered much that should have been directed to bigger men—and which they would have got had Mr. Hammerson been the Mate.

I had noticed that Foyle had been growing more and more dejected, broody and queer in his manner, but where practically every one in the ship was more or less discontented and abnormal, I thought little of it. Poor Foyle's cup of woe had been slowly filling and now it ran over.

Never too sane, he must have gone mad, for he did the maddest thing. Relieved at the wheel, he suddenly snatched a bucket from the rack at the break of the poop and sped with it down the port ladder.

With a loud hysterical sobbing cry of,

"Watch this, then, ye bluidy-minded divils," he thrust the bucket through the mooring-pipe against the ladder, as though pouring away its contents. He then stuck his head through the mooring-pipe and kept still, while those who happened to notice what he was doing thought he had gone insane—as indeed he had.

As the ship's speed caused the first upswirling sea completely to fill and heavily to tug upon the bucket, Foyle, with amazing determination and tenacity, kept a tight grip on the handle and, releasing all other holds, allowed his slight and slender body to be dragged into the sea.

It was Beauty who, doubtless three parts asleep as usual, witnessed this amazing tragedy, and, of course, such wits as he had, at once deserted him.

Instead of bawling in sailor-like manner,

"Hard down the helm! . . . Man overboard!" he wasted precious time in running for'ard screaming,

"He's gone through, he's gone through. He didn't jump overboard, he's gone through."

In an ordinary and accidental 'Man overboard' emergency, the delay would have been serious and might have been fatal, but as this was undoubtedly a case of most determined suicide, it is not likely that instant action would have effected a rescue.

To end his unhappy existence, the pitiably demented creature made the ocean serve a double purpose—its vast expanse for his loss from sight; and the extra weight of a mere bucketful for overcoming such buoyancy as he had, as well as his inevitable instinct of self-preservation. For doubtless he clung to the bucket as desperately in the sea as he did when hungrily it leapt to drag him down. . . .

The instant the Second Mate grasped what had happened, he acted like the seaman he was.

Simultaneously the helm was put down, a lifebuoy thrown overboard, and a man sent aloft, although there was scarcely sufficient light to make the last two measures of much avail.

Before the after yards had been run for'ard to bring the vessel to, All Hands were on deck, and the lifeboats being stowed above our half-deck, Dacre and I were the first to join Fagin and Geordie at the lee boat.

The Merchant Shipping Act lays it down that a ship's boats shall be "at all times fit and ready for use". So fit and ready for use was this boat that, working like fiends and using our knives to the cover and everything that could be cut, we lost a full twenty-five minutes in dropping the paint-stuck chocks, getting davit-falls out of the boat, and clearing the rope-swollen tackles.

Not until we were pulling in the boat did we know whom it was we sought, as, fully aware that our quest was now hopeless, we pulled to and fro over the dark foam-flecked water, fearing to go too far lest we ourselves should go adrift and lose sight of the blue lights burned at intervals aboard the ship.

Had it been an accident and Foyle a powerful swimmer and able to reach the buoy, our efforts would still have been in vain, for no glimpse of the lifebuoy was ever gained.

After a long time, reluctant, although we knew it to be useless, we gave up our search and pulled listlessly back. Nor did Hammerson protest or remark when Patsy Hooligan, after sobbing quietly for a few minutes, began to wail and keen like an old Irish woman.

Back aboard, the crew's natural sorrow and regret for Foyle quickly turned to a resentment which grew to anger and to rage; for unfortunately, the Mate, after punishing Foyle, had brought him up before the Captain to be logged, docked and fined and further punished; and the crew, probably unjustly, considered that what the Captain had said and done to Foyle had driven him to his death.

Imagine the opportunity presented to Slim Johes, professional agitator; to Müller, anarchist, rebel and mutineer; to Jake, ill-conditioned, ill-willed fisher in troubled waters; and to Villa, born criminal and crook!

The spectacular and unique details of Foyle's suicide had made the deepest impression on all members of the crew, and even the best of the men, Church and Carrol, Berghen and Blancke, lent ear to the wild and dangerous talk of the ringleaders of mutiny, while such men as Hamblin, Axenstern, Patsy Hooligan, Brown and Paulo, openly and loudly agreed with every word of Slim Johes' inflammatory oration.

A great hour for the gab-gifted fo'c'sle lawyer—and a most unlucky one for the ill-fated *Valkyrie*.

In his way, though quite innocently I'm sure, the half-witted Patsy Hooligan did almost as much harm as the malicious and mischief-making agitators. For days he went about among the men, peering up into their faces and saying,

"It was a could-blu'ded murdher, I say . . . I say it was a could-blu'ded murdher. If poor Tim Foyle took his loife for fear of the Hoyena, 'twas the Hoyena killed him. The Hoyena killed poor Tim Foyle I say, for didn't poor Tim Foyle kill himself for fear of the Hoyena?"

And the man to whom Patsy spoke would nod, growl assent, and spit.

A happy ship!

CHAPTER VI

And Captain Bryndal was puzzling us afresh.

He had done many inexplicable things since leaving Pisagua, one of the strangest of which was his refusal to give the Mate access to the chronometers.

Now, this undeniably courageous and competent skipper behaved as though nervous to timidity. This fine sailor who, laughing at the tow-boat men, had sailed the *Valkyrie* right through the Golden Gate and up to her anchorage in 'Frisco bay, behaved as though scared of a capful of wind.

Again and again, in fine weather, we furled cro'jack, mainsail and to'gallant sails as though fierce gales were threatening, wasting the good fair wind in a manner to sadden the heart of a homeward-bound sailor.

"Why the hell doesn't he put her under lower tops'ls?" growled Dacre, and the Mates themselves could barely conceal their disgust.

"Is he deliberately losing time?" I asked Mr. Hammerson, exasperated and disgusted.

"Ah, Sonny, now you've asked something," replied the Second Mate darkly, and with a world of meaning.

We calculated that Cape Horn lay about a thousand miles South-East of us, and every one was anxious to have the rounding over, and its buffeting done with.

It was most tantalizing, to say the least of it, to be continuously crawling along at two or three knots in a twelve knots' breeze.

What was the idea? What was his game?

Before long, the very elements seemed to take a hand in the said game, whatever it might be, for, the Westerlies failing, our unnecessary sail-drill came to an end, and without enough breeze to give her steerage-way, the *Valkyrie* rolled incessantly and heavily to the Easterly swell.

Sails and gear battered and thundered until we prayed for any wind, even a real Easterly gale, to stop the perpetual and erratic lurching that sent the water spurting through the scupper holes. . . .

Our prayers were answered—abundantly.

During the second dog-watch there was a sudden loud

164

whistle of wind, black clouds banked up in the West, and I was not at all surprised to hear the Mate remark that if the barometer fell any more it would be in the bilges.

By Eight Bells the wind was coming in strong puffs and bringing flurries of snow as a foretaste of what was in store; and by midnight, under foresail and lower top-sails, we were running before a proper Nor'westerly gale.

Expecting that the wind would back to the South'ard ere long, the Captain kept her before it; and, with the sea moderate, the *Valkyrie* made good weather—merely rolling her rails under.

Just before dawn the Captain was justified of his wisdom and rewarded for his patience for, after a short lull, the wind shifted, and, by daylight it was blowing so hard from Sou'-sou'west that, had we been outward-bound we should have been hove-to with a tarpaulin in the mizzen rigging.

Fortune was with us, and between fierce squalls of snow and hail, "Old Jamaica"—as Church called the sun—broke through and stayed out long enough for the Captain to bring his sextant to bear while he balanced himself on top of the skylight.

With a similar piece of luck at noon, he was able to verify his position, and with every confidence, put her stern to the gale and her head to the North-East.

The wind grew to real hurricane strength, and the Captain's skill and confidence and dare-devil courage seemed to grow with it, and to increase with every fierce gust.

As though he had decided that he had lost more time than he wished, he now started to recover some of it, and ignoring the dangerously heavy cross-sea that hurled huge masses of water aboard, till the *Valkyrie* resembled a floating swimming-bath, he drove her on through the towering crests and across the valleys of churned-up foam.

Those who had growled the loudest about wind-losing, time-wasting and sail-drill, were now the noisiest in favour of heaving-to while there was yet time. Bunched up under the fo'c'sle-head, both Watches stood-by for orders; and it was very interesting to see how the grumbling fine-weather "blow-hards" were now the first to tremble for their precious skins. . . .

"Gee! sailin's sailin', but this looks to me like some more wilful goddam murder," growled Jake. "Does that goddam Hyena want to send the lot of us to join Tim Foyle?"

And with shifty anxious eyes he canvassed the faces of those whom he knew to be genuine sailors.

"He'll crack on till he runs her under, I say, begob. I say, begob, he'll run her under," recited Patsy Hooligan monotonously, going from man to man pawing, and peering up at him.

"Py damn! We ought to go Aft in a body, look you. We'll go and tell him he's not going to murder us like he murdered Tim Foyle," said Slim Johes, expressing a sentiment loudly applauded by Müller, Villa and Jake.

"Oh, Hell. Leave him be," growled hard-case surly Carrol, fine sailor and true shell-back. "Leave the grinning old orphan alone, now he has started to carry sail—at last."

"Sure," laughed Church, "he's bin up to some game and now he wants to git home, and he wouldn't heave her to, not if the Infant Samuel and the Prophet Isaiah come aboard with Pomptious Pilot hisself and asked him, as a favour . . . Ar! There'll be more blue noses than warm backsides this night, I tell you."

"Well, 'tain't right," growled Villa.

"No, mate, nor are you. Not right in the head—nor yet in the guts," replied Church.

There was a laugh, and it was clear that the faint-heart blowhards realized only too sorrowfully that they were in the minority.

In the Captain's mind there was certainly no thought of heaving-to. To me it appeared that he was filled with a dark and cruel joy, though about what I could make no guess. His spirits rose as the *Valkyrie* made her swift easting, fleeing like a frightened bird across the narrow degrees of longitude that separated us from the Atlantic.

It was summer, and the nights were very short, but before complete darkness fell, even he was compelled reluctantly to realize that at least fore-sail and mizzen top-sail must be furled if the *Valkyrie* were to live. Throughout that wild black night—one that I shall always remember—we sped on dangerously, under main and fore lower topsails and main and fore top-mast staysails—which was canvas enough and to spare, in that fierce blizzard.

Cheerfully expressing the opinion that he could drown in his bunk as well as anywhere else, and much more comfortably, only dauntless Doctor went below that night. The rest of the ship's company spent the hours of darkness on the poop—comparatively safe from being washed overboard—where Beauty snored through the fiercest squalls, and Patsy Hooligan, making his way from man to man, monotonously chanted,

"She'll broach to, I say, begob. I say, begob, she'll broach to," until in the darkness, noise and confusion he said it to the Old Man himself.

Captain Bryndal, incalculable ever, laughed like a dog, his teeth gleaming in the dim light from the binnacle.

"Not if *you* keep away from the wheel, you sea-going crow," he snapped, and Patsy fell away into the darkness.

In point of fact, there was the gravest risk of the ship's broaching-to, and only the best helmsmen were allowed to take the wheel.

Sweating freely, they steered for their very lives—and ours—for had she run more than a couple of points off her course, the *Valkyrie*'s end would have been both sudden and soon. Or, had one of those mile-long white-crested mountains of water—that towered threateningly in our wake, licked greedily along our counter, and flung savagely their spume almost up to the gaff—but come over the taffrail, she would have been swamped like a child's toy ship of paper.

When, at long last, the pitch-black darkness paled, and men's faces—and women's—could be discerned, the Captain smiled, fresh, cheerful and merry, as though he had just stepped from his comfortable berth.

Women's faces . . . for there, close to me, clung Celia Bryndal, apparently strong, cool, and unconcerned as the best of us.

I stared in amazement.

"Morning, Little Joseph," she nodded curtly, and I returned her nod and said "Good-morning", reluctantly admitting that she looked marvellous, a wind-whipped, spray-dewed sea-nymph, a Venus . . .

No, nothing of the sort. There was Venus, being fussily coddled—I did not say cuddled—by the Mate.

Again somewhat reluctantly, I admitted that it could not have been long since Mrs. Bryndal could have posed to a great artist as the sea-born goddess herself, rising from the foam.

Anyhow, there she was, a slightly *passé* Venus, in mackintosh and sou'wester.

When had the women come up, and why? Cowardice or courage? And who had brought them up, or rather helped them up? Certainly not Captain Bryndal, I was sure. That stout seaman suddenly turned and, in the growing light, caught sight of his wife and his Mate.

He scowled ferociously.

"Mizzen lower tops'l, Mister," he suddenly bawled at Smeeker. . . .

Good Heavens! With the foresail set, we'd hoped and expected his shout would be,

"That'll do the Watch," but in his new-found driving mood, the Captain was evidently not yet satisfied with our rate of knots: and, plunging waist-deep in the icy water, we laboured to put a salvagee-strop and watch-tackle on the chain-sheets, and bowsed the clew well down.

"That ain't making her steer any better," cheekily shouted Church, as he toiled and strove at the wheel.

The Captain laughed aloud, and answered with apparent good humour.

"We'll soon cure that, m'lad. . . . Hoist the fore upper tops'l, Mr. Smeeker. . . . And then let the Watch get their breakfasts."

"Py tamn, py tamn, it's murder!" cried Slim Johes, and Carrol laughed.

"No, it's China tea in the *Cutty Sark*, that's wot it is," he growled. "He used to be on the China run . . ."

"He thinks he's a Clipper, racin' home, racin' home," shouted Hamblin, a little hysterically, I thought, but it may have been the result of working in the bitter cold water.

The yard hoisted, and handles unshipped from the halyard winch, we of the Port Watch went below to our breakfast of hard tack and salt horse. Shut up in his half-submerged galley, Doctor had, by some miracle, made hot coffee, glorious scalding coffee, sweetened with molasses.

I remember that particular drink of "hot-and-dirty" to this day.

In the half-deck, our bad and meagre breakfast eaten, Dacre and I were heavily contemplating the sad fact that it was our forenoon watch on deck, when, hearing loud hoarse shouting, we rushed out and saw, above a white fringe of surf, a dark cloud-like blur that could only be land.

Amid the excitement, discipline was temporarily relaxed.

"Begob, that'll be Cape Horn, I say. I say that'll be Cape Horn, begob," asserted Patsy Hooligan who was steering, or endeavouring to steer.

"No, m'lad, that's Staten Island. You're round the Horn," replied the Captain, grinning graciously. "Round it, safe and sound . . ."

And as though outraged by puny man's presumptuous confidence, the terrible *genius loci* of that treacherous Southern Ocean, that age-old grave-yard of good men and better ships, sprang, swift sudden and savage, from his ice-bound fastnesses —and, in comparison with the deafening scream of his rage, the feeble shrieks of the night's wind seemed a mere friendly hail, a zephyr's gentle whisper.

Never was Ship-master's vigilance relaxed at a more dangerous moment, nor in a more fatal position.

With the rest of the ship's company, I was intent on that
barren mass, the first land sighted since dropping the Andes,
weeks before—land that was a most welcome sign-post confirm-
ing and defining our position with absolute accuracy, and
marking the point of our safe departure from those southern
wastes, those perilous seas forlorn. . . .

And suddenly from where we stood by the overhang of the
poop, we heard the helmsman's cry.

"Houly Mary and God in Hiven!" screamed Patsy Hooligan,
and pointed in the opposite direction, seaward, where, like
charging cavalry, a black bank of lowering storm-clouds raced
towards us at an incredible speed.

With such vicious and terrific fury did that master wind cut off
the tops of the heaving grey-beard billows and fling their spray
high amid the snow, that, at first sight, I thought that the sea
itself had reared up to the very vault of Heaven.

"Faith, but here comes Cape Horn's own Hell-Hound, the
Black Divil Himsilf," murmured Larry O'Toole, who, as so often
happened, was standing near me.

And scarcely had his awed whisper passed his lips, than the
last narrowing strip of sky between us and that howling tempest
was blotted out.

With a sound like the tattoo of machine-gun bullets,
horizontal lines of hail spanged on our iron plates and forced the
very toughest of us to shield his face.

And then came wind beyond landsman's imagining.

Thanks to Patsy Hooligan's instinctive seamanship at the
helm, we were not caught full aback, or we must have gathered
stern way and sailed under—stern first. And well it was for us that
the *Valkyrie*'s masts were massive iron tubes stayed with stout
steel cables that had been hove bar-tight by the immense power
of screws and levers.

Had she been equipped with the old-fashioned dead-eyes
and lanyards, her top hamper would have been stripped from her
like a bunch of straw, and the ship must inevitably have left her
bones and ours, with so many more, beneath those storm-lashed
rocks upon our lee.

But although the stout handiwork of the builders' riggers
stood firm on the whole, web was never woven nor seam stitched
that could stand the ordeal of so sudden a blow from so fearful a
storm.

The last sail set was the first to go, and, as we heeled to the blast, the main upper tops'l burst into a hundred ribbons.

Then, like a land-seeking driven bird, the foresail left its bolt-ropes and flew over Staten Island. Within sixty seconds of the helmsman's cry, the fore and mizzen tops'ls had threshed themselves to rags, and the ship was under nothing more than main lower tops'l and fore topmast staysail.

In a gale of colossal strength and passionate violence, on a lee shore, beneath a cruel iron-bound steep-to and desolate coast, the stricken *Valkyrie* had but two tiny wings with which to attempt to fly from the hungry fangs protruding from that tormented surf.

On the foremast, the upper tops'l-yard had but the halyards for support, and at each heavy roll, the fractured parrel scored deeply into the mast; while with its truss broken and the greater part of its crane sticking through the fore hatch, the lower tops'l-yard swung wildly on the upper tops'l downhauls, and threatened to come down at any moment.

Yet, in the pyramidal cross-sea, colossal, treacherous, and terrible, raised by that sudden swoop and shift of wind, we could spare no thought for spars. Thundering aboard, mass upon mass, ton after ton of it, the water filled the decks up to the to'gallant rail. At times, with a great comber towering on either side, we wallowed deep down in the trough's momentary calm, as though instantly about to be engulfed or turned completely over. While the danger to every man of being maimed or swept clean overboard was great, the peril to the ship herself was awful, imminent, and apparently ineluctable.

Captain Bryndal was equal to the occasion.

"Head yards," he bawled in a voice of thunder. "Port fore brace. Jump to it, for God's sake."

And, taking our lives in our hands, Dacre and I plunged for the lee braces.

On the weather side, the pale and frantic Mate, clinging for dear life, and often submerged to the neck, also bawled,

"Port fore brace; port fore brace," and, as stunned and bewildered men hung back,

"Jump to it, blast your souls. Blount, Dysart, kick those swine along—and get the others out."

Even at such a moment and in his direst need, Smeeker must shirk the personal handling of refractory and frightened men.

For such they were.

Plunging, dodging and rushing to the fo'c'sle, Dacre and I found that, thanks to the example and infection of one land-lubberly white-livered coward, some of our normally stout-hearted men were the temporary victims of mob-panic.

Slim Johes was the plague-spot and the only-too-genuine cause of the rot, the craven fear, the miserable failure in the face of danger.

"My God, my God!" he screamed in abject terror. "It iss the end, it iss the end! We'll drown. Oh, kind Christ save uss."

This shocking exhibition of weakness and fright, in a British sailor, had completely demoralized Dutchmen, Dagoes and the nigger, as well as the mighty and loud-mouthed Jake.

The other Britons, cold, empty, exhausted by the labours of the night, were, to say the least of it, listless, fatalistic and indifferent—not terrified; not like Slim Johes, in a state of collapse through fright; but resigned, careless as to their fate rather than fearful of it; and sufficiently demoralized to accept death rather than put up a vain struggle against it.

I believe this to be a just estimate of the position of affairs in the fo'c'sle when Dacre and I dashed in, with a cry of

"All Hands on Deck."

"Come on, show a leg. Get a move on," shouted Dacre, and seizing the nearest man, slung him toward the deck.

"What's the good?" growled Carrol, and,

"What can we do?" agreed Church.

"There aren't enough of us to haul yards in such weather, are there?" shouted Hamblin, and by "us" he meant the Britons.

"No, dere vasn't enough of us, and anyhow vot's der good? It vos too late now," chimed in "Baby" Axenstern.

"Sure, 'tis niver too late to mend. Come on, ye cripples," cried Larry O'Toole, and made for the door.

"Good lad," I shouted, and smote him on the back.

But the fo'c'sle door-way was blocked. In it stood the man who shone in such emergencies. He also needed his Watch and, as ever, was not content to shout.

With a glare at Church, at Carrol, and at Hamblin, the Second Mate jerked his head and thumb toward the deck.

Church and Hamblin came to their senses and went.

"Must I sing out to you?" growled Mr. Hammerson, pointing at Berghen and then at Blancke.

Seeing their Officer utterly unafraid, shamed by the departure of Larry O'Toole, Church, Carrol and Hamblin, Karl Blancke and Hans Berghen needed no second bidding.

171

Sheep-like, "Baby" Axenstern followed.

And to the others, Mr. Hammerson lifted up his voice.

"Must I sing out twice?" he blared. "Move, you swine, before I move you. Out, every mother's son, and cant those blasted yards."

Slim Johes, insane with fear, flung himself on his knees before the Second Mate, raised his clasped hands above his distraught face and literally prayed to him.

His prayer was heard but not heeded, for, with no apparent effort, Hammerson swung his coward suppliant from the deck, flung him forth, and with a hefty kick, precipitated him among his departing shipmates.

Furious with himself, and still more so with Slim Johes, whose example had temporarily demoralized him, Church cursed Johes venomously, hauled him to his feet, struck him, and thrusting the brace into his hands snarled,

"Pull, ye whining land-shark, or I'll knock yer block off."

"Aye, stow yer bluidy gab an' pull, domn ye," bawled the equally ashamed Hamblin. "Pull, ye snivellin' stinkin' scalpin'," and even in my cold and sodden misery, I found myself wondering what a "scalpin" might be.

Only Müller, Jake and Villa remained, three very big, very strong, and truculent men; frightened, but made savagely defiant by their fear.

"What?" roared the Second Mate. "Must I sing out *three* times? . . . *Jump*."

Müller spat.

Jake raised a great clenched fist; and Villa's hand went behind him to the knife in his belt.

It was Hammerson who jumped.

Making an amazing leap into the fo'c'sle, he scattered the trio, and before they had recovered their wits and their balance, there was an almost imperceptible movement of his right fist, and having met the fatal twisting upper-cut, Villa sagged at the knees and collapsed groaning against the bulkhead, as his knife fell from his hand.

Had they not been badly needed on deck, Müller and Jake would doubtless have met with the same fate. But instead of striking again, the fist that had felled Villa, continuing through the air, grasped Jake by the neck. Simultaneously the powerful left hand grabbed Müller's throat, and the two heads came violently together.

Swinging him about, the Second Mate flung Jake out of the

place, and, whirling about on Müller, found that that earnest anarchist's one desire in life was to follow his admired shipmate.

The Second Mate in the fo'c'sle was more terrible than the storm on deck.

Without waiting to see whether Villa was sufficiently recovered to hear and understand him,

"If you're not out in two minutes, you back-stabbing scum, I'll come for you," he snarled, and was gone.

Amidships he bawled,

"Port main brace, Starboard Watch."

And by the time he was ready to slack the weather braces he had a full Watch.

Even the two with damaged faces knew that the Brutal Man-Handler, by his criminal exhibition of Western Ocean hell-ship driving methods had saved the *Valkyrie* and every soul on board.

. . .

It seemed too good to be true that we had braced her sharp-up in time and, without losing a man overboard, had dragged the yards on to the back-stays, and put temporary lashings on the damaged spars.

While battered and bruised, drenched, dazed and half-drowned, we hauled and floundered and fell, cursing beneath avalanches of green water, the snow came ever thicker and thicker, dropping an impenetrable curtain between us and the hideous rocks we dreaded.

It was now impossible to tell whether we were but a cable's length or a good mile from them, for in the deafening roar of the tempest, not even that surf would be audible.

When all was done that could be done, and the men were coiling down the gear, there was still stark terror in the eyes that strained to leeward, and glad I was that, in the Second Mate, we had a man who inspired more terror than the storm itself, and who, unlike the Mate, could drive the panic-stricken to the work that kept them occupied and sane; could, in an emergency, make the weak do impossibilities of strength; and the slacking shirker emulate the keenest and the best.

With the Captain, of necessity, rooted to the poop; the Mate, a bluffer with a yellow streak; and the Third Officer a boy, the crew that dreadful day could never, but for Mr. Hammerson, have been driven to save their ship and their own lives. . . .

On the poop—where, to keep her head to the wind, a queer goose-winged spanker had been set—Captain Bryndal, even with the compass and recent bearings to guide him, did not know

173

whether we were clawing off the land, or making lee-way towards it. But, beyond peering through his binoculars and giving an occasional warning to the man at the wheel, he showed no trace of the intense anxiety that must have racked him, and abated not the brightness of his eternal smile.

With all his faults, Laughing Bryndal was a man of cast-iron coolness and dauntless courage. At times he would look longingly aloft and slightly shrug his broad shoulders. With the tops'ls gone and no time to bend others, there wasn't a sail that he dared unfurl to speed us faster from the trap. Moreover, such was the fury of the storm that, had there been sea-room to spare, rather would he have hove-to than set more canvas.

"Houly saints in Heaven, phwhat're you looking so miserable about? Laugh, ye mouldy spalpeen, laugh!" I heard the voice of Larry O'Toole bawling in Slim Johes' ear. "She'll make it all-right. Bejabbers she will. . . . Never was such a ship for sailing to wind'ard. Just watch the ould duck tryin' to sail forninst the wind. It's a houly steamer she thinks she is. Phwhat's the matter, ye miserable divil?"

"I'm . . . hungry. That's all whateffer," growled the shamed Slim Johes.

"Faith now, think o' that. Hungry! Sure bhoys, that's the only trouble now. Whoy, me belly thinks me throat's cut."

And so did the excellent Larry O'Toole do his best to keep up the spirits of the shipmates to whom, for all his queerness, he was, at times like this, an example and an inspiration.

§2

And nobly did the staunch *Valkyrie* justify all Larry O'Toole's pride and faith in her, even though the dreadful wind was not her worst enemy.

Without let or mercy, the towering Cape Horn grey-beards swept in from the South and hurled themselves, vast ridges of vicious combers, cross-wise athwart her path to safety.

Hammer-blow upon hammer-blow they struck her broadside, and strove to drive her sideways and backward, and fought to rob her of every inch gained by the cunning of the Captain and the helmsman. Like a living thing, the poor ship lifted her streaming head after each relentless onslaught, and desperately battled to struggle back to windward and the open sea.

Ragged aloft and glistening with ice, labouring, pitching and trembling from shock after shock, crash after crash of savage wave, she drove heavily through the great walls of water that beset her; and after every staggering heart-breaking thrust to leeward, once again leapt ahead to snatch another foot of vantage amidst her million enemies.

Watching, helpless, that epic struggle, I knew why sailors swore that brave and noble ships had great and noble souls.

Suddenly, and almost as though shamed into sharing my admiration, the wind relented, left its base partnership with the cruel sea, edged back to its home in the West, and spared the suffering *Valkyrie*, depriving the great combers of their power, and leaving the sea to go down almost as rapidly as it had arisen.
. . .

With the knowledge that there was no longer any real danger of our being battered to pieces among the breakers, reaction came, and a great weariness.

All of us, save the Captain and the Second Mate, wilted visibly.

"Come on, jump to it, get a move on," cried Hammerson, "—you iron men who learned their trade in wooden ships. Come on, this isn't the place for wooden men in iron ships."

And though we reeled from weakness and for lack of sleep, he drove us without respite, and, urging the imperative need for sail on the fore, not only led, but himself did the work of two men.

At this hard haste and urgency, the Mate smiled sneeringly, interfered in no way, and gave no orders. Indeed, the only sound I heard from him was a hiccup; for, from some hidden store, he had drawn bottled courage, and had so drowned his fears that he reeled more than anyone.

Long before our escape from the rocks was an accomplished and established fact, Slim Johes, Jake, Müller, and Villa had succumbed to "Cape Horn fever", slunk to the fo'c'sle, and crawled into their respective bunks. The severity of their sea-sickness may be gauged from the fact that for three days they took no food nor raised their heads, and only with dry level decks and warm sunshine did the invalids return to work.

So, short-handed, the rest of us toiled almost blindly, to the orders of our tireless leader, and with white drawn faces, heavy sunken eyes and lurching steps, carried on, sustaining ourselves by munching biscuits, our only food.

Led by Hammerson, four of us of the half-deck (for Fagin had gone sick), five British sailors, Berghen and Blancke, Axenstern, Brown and Paulo slaved to turn reprieve into escape, respite into victory, as, with many turns of mooring-wire, we hung the lower tops'l yard from the cross-trees at the topmast-head, and, after heaving tight each turn with the capstan, painfully and laboriously lashed the yard with turns of chain about the mast.

Then having repaired the parrel of the upper topsail-yard, wearily we set to bending the fore lower topsail and the foresail. And when, after fifteen hours that we shall never forget, Dacre, Geordie, Beauty and I took off our sou'westers in the half-deck, we fell asleep with them in our hands.

But let me here put something on record.

Before we collapsed into huddled heaps on our sea-chests, we saw Dacre raise something aloft, smile at it, and thrust it under his pillow.

It was our reward from an appreciative Captain, our rich and munificent reward for fifteen hours of super-human labour (and fine example) in the saving of his ship. Freely he gave it, and with humble thanks we accepted it.

It was a rusty tin of canned rabbit.

*   *   *   *   *

Four hours later we wondered whether it had been rabbit.

§3

Four hours later still, Celia Bryndal came up on deck.

"It's been raining, or something, hasn't it, Little Joseph?" she said.

"Yes," said I.

"Would you like to come and see me, in my cabin, at seven bells, to-night? . . . *Tip-toe; and mum's the word.* . . . Would you, nice Little Joseph?" she asked.

"No," said I.

CHAPTER VII

After she had so magnificently and safely carried us clear of the perils and terrors of Staten Island, I loved the *Valkyrie* more than ever, and in the fine Atlantic weather that now compassed us about, I often spent part of my watch-below on the fo'c'sle-head or out on the boom.

With an arm round the flying-jib stay, I could imagine that I had no connection with the vessel, and, being so far out from the hull, I could view her as a beautiful spectacle, quite detached from myself.

On a moonlit night, the coarse canvas swelling aloft, tier upon tier, shone smooth and white as the petal of an Arum lily, and the upper to'gallant sail appeared to be a magic cloth gently brushing the star-sprinkled blue. At such times the *Valkyrie* seemed a magic phantom-ship gliding smoothly between earth and heaven, and belonging to one as much as to the other.

Incidentally my habit of remaining silent and still, on fo'c'sle-head or boom, was to have strange and far-reaching effects. . . .

But during the day there was no suggestion of Heaven-magic or Arum lilies or phantom-ship about her. No sooner were the dangers and hardships of Cape Horn passed and quickly forgotten, than suspicion, ill-feeling, bad temper and a thoroughly ugly spirit became rife once more. For'ard there was none of the former singing or yarning in the dog-watches. The men preferred to split up into small groups, arguing in low tones. If anyone approached, they would cautiously and resentfully look over their shoulders and abruptly cease talking. That they were by no means united on the subject they were discussing, was clear from the constant quarrels that were ever threatening or actually arising.

Life in the fo'c'sle must have been wretched, for trivial incidents became magnified. Words, and even looks, were misinterpreted, and if it were not the fact that no man trusted his neighbour, it was obvious that there was one party that did not trust the other.

Watching carefully, I was still convinced that most of the mischief-making, grumbling, back-biting and incitement originated with the two men who, in the best of crews, even in an all-British crew, would have proved "carriers", sources of infection, veritable plague-spots.

In Villa, Slim Johes had soon discovered that Fate or the Devil had sent him an ally after his own heart; a much cleverer, much wickeder man than even the ill-conditioned Jake, or the obsessed Müller. These latter, Slim Johes regarded, I believe, as savage dogs that could be "tarr'd on" to murder—but possibly might

"Snatch at the master that doth tarre them on."

Villa, on the contrary, would need no urging on—to any villainy, whether murder or greater crime. The only trouble with Villa might be a difficulty in holding him back, or, more serious thought, in preventing him from forgetting that he was an ally—and not a leader. Quite evidently, Villa had played this sort of game before, and knew all about it—had lived extremely danger-ously, done desperate things, been a member of a really tough gang, member of a gang that stuck at absolutely nothing—if, indeed, he had not been the leader of it.

But he was not going to be leader here. No. One leader was quite enough, and Slim Johes would be that one. . . .

Villa might be, and undoubtedly was, a professional criminal. Slim Johes was something much higher and nobler, a profes-sional mischief-maker, a trouble-brewer, a fomenter of rebellion and a mutineer—a professional agitator and leader of malcon-tents.

Very well. Let Villa stick to crime—under Slim Johes' direction, and let Slim Johes be leader undisputed.

Much of this I guessed at the time, and, later, not only found it to be true, but learned a great deal more.

At this stage, Villa amenable, the two played cleverly each into the hands of the other, and helped him to maintain a state of unrest, bickering, contention, quarrelsome ill-feeling, not only against the Officers, but between individuals and actually be-tween the Watches themselves.

Yet, when voices were raised and fists clenched, these two became the skilful mediators and wise counsellors who extolled the blessings of peace and good-will among shipmates—especially among shipmates who so soon might need to stand together.

"Stand together," growled Carrol one day. "Hang together, you mean," so deeply the envenomed barbs had penetrated and so widely the virus spread.

What, at the moment, the crafty agitators wanted, was to maintain just *enough* quarrelsome discontent, discomfort and strain, so that the crew would become increasingly difficult to handle and, in due time, ready to defy authority generally, and the Second Mate particularly.

Bitterly as all the men loathed Captain Bryndal, completely as they despised and detested the Mate, it was the Second Mate, Mr. Hammerson, against whom the wrath of the ring-leaders was really concentrated.

Loudly applauded by Jake and Müller, whom he had "assaulted", and Slim Johes whom he had "insulted", Villa openly proclaimed his intention of "getting" the Second Mate. He took an oath and made a promise, bidding the others watch him.

And when Villa said he would "get" a man, he merely and simply meant that he would murder him.

The better elements of the crew, men like Church and Carrol, laughed uneasily and bade him beware lest Hammerson got in first—"with another like the one that put him to sleep off Staten Island".

Hamblin bade Villa to bluidy well go and tell Hammerson what he was going to do, and asked why Villa hadn't done it on the day in question.

Then would Villa curse and scowl, sharpen his knife and bid the slack-jawed jabberers shut their heads—and watch.

In the half-deck, we too were about as happy a family as that in the fo'c'sle. Among Fagin, Beauty and Geordie the wrangling was incessant, the subject unvarying—Celia Bryndal. And I could not but admire the self-control and patience with which Dacre heard not only their miserable vulgar and noisy squabbling, but the sacred name of his adored idol, his goddess, bandied about, and none too gently, by these unworthy ones who, if not definitely disrespectful, were at least over-familiar in their reference.

Not only did I admire his forbearance and self-restraint, I wondered at it; and decided that Dacre regarded them in this respect, as beneath contempt, unworthy even of his rebuke on Celia's behalf; frogs whose croakings in their muddy swamp were unintelligible to the higher human ear.

For each spoke of her, and spoke of her incessantly, according to his kind. Fagin, lustfully, like the animal he was: Beauty, amorously and also appraisingly, as though an animal she were, an infinitely desirable animal, far superior to any hither-to encountered by that self-proclaimed Lothario: Geordie, sentimentally, mooningly, with the pitiful and ridiculous bellowings of calf-love, the first love of a starved but ardent soul.

All this must have been unbearably irritating, maddening, to Dacre—as deeply and loftily, truly and terribly in love as ever a man was. Nor am I sure that my absolute silence on the subject of Celia Bryndal did not annoy him even more. He probably felt that while the ravings of the vulgar ineligibles were nothing but meaningless noise, my silence was a meaning one, a purposeful silence, concealing the fact, although I denied it, that I was as deeply in love with her as was he himself: and in me he saw a rival to be reckoned with, a serious menace, whereas the other three were, in that respect, beneath notice and consideration.

"I say, you chaps, I believe there's something up between Mrs. B. and Jake Walfisch," Fagin flung at us one night in the half-deck.

"Yes," said Beauty, "I've seen 'em whispering together. S'pose she's not particular who it is, so long as it's someone."

"Rot," snapped Dacre. "I think, in future, we'll have a rule that no women are to be discussed in this Mess. It is not allowed in a wardroom, and we'll keep off the subject here."

"Well, if Mrs. B. looks my way . . ." began Fagin, but lapsed into sulky mutterings as Dacre half rose from his seat.

Later, when we were alone, Dacre spoke to me with his old friendliness.

"You know, Sinbad, what that beast Fagin said about Mrs. Bryndal and Jake was true. It puzzles me."

"Yes," I replied, "I've seen them whispering together, too. But I don't think it means what Fagin means."

"Neither do I," answered Dacre. "I have a suspicion that she's known him before somewhere."

"Of course we know she had met Villa," I mused aloud.

"That's no help towards solving the mystery," replied Dacre. "It only adds to the tangle."

Nor was Passion, in its varying degrees, our only trouble, for though Fagin had learned his lesson and no longer visited the fo'c'sle to hob-nob with the men, it was practically impossible for us to prevent him from fraternizing with the Carpenter, who berthed, as I have said, on the fore side of our deck-house.

For a time Peddersen had been laid aside with a sprained ankle, and I thought it grew to be a wonderfully long time. Fagin was most assiduous in visiting the sick, and spent more time in Peddersen's quarters than in our own.

Dacre and I gravely feared that no good would come of this, and although we knew quite well that Fagin told Peddersen everything that was said and done aft, and that, in turn, Chips retailed it for'ard, we were powerless to stop it.

Dacre's cold reference to that being Fagin's spiritual home and the company to which he was best suited, did not alter the fact that Fagin constituted himself the voice-pipe between the Poop and the Fo'c'sle.

And on the poop, conditions were obviously very similar to those prevailing in the half-deck and the fo'c'sle.

Captain Bryndal's autocratic aloofness grew more and more pronounced, and each day he seemed to hate everybody, including his wife and daughter, a little more, or a lot more, than he had done on the previous day.

Certainly Mrs. Bryndal reciprocated the sentiment, and most undoubtedly Celia Bryndal was, in that matter, if in none other, at one with her mother.

A happy family voyaging in our happy ship!

The Mates spoke to the Captain and to each other only when routine made it absolutely necessary; and while Mr. Smeeker hated and affected sneeringly to despise Mr. Hammerson, the latter returned these unsocial feelings without any affectation whatsoever. He did genuinely despise the Mate, and the fact is little to be wondered at, for, far from supporting Hammerson's authority, deliberately he strove to undermine it.

It was about now I realized an interesting fact concerning the expression of the Captain's eyes—for so small a thing as a facial expression was, in these days of strain and tension, not only interesting but portentous.

As I've said, Captain Bryndal's countenance was, as a rule, one bright and shining grin, a pervading and expansive smile in which his eyes took no part whatever.

I do not mean that he frowned while he laughed, for his fine brow was quite uncreased; but however merrily he laughed, however gaily he smiled, there was no laughter in his thoughtful calculating eyes. Generally they expressed nothing, and if they were the windows of his soul, blinds were drawn behind them, or the soul-place was empty.

But since leaving Pisagua, increasingly since the days of deliberate idling, and markedly since those terrible hours when Death had leered at us from the rocks of Staten Island, a new look, a new expression, had come on Captain Bryndal's face in the intervals between his bursts of laughter; a new look had come into his eyes.

Sometimes the grin would disappear altogether and this expression, this look, this air, usurped its place entirely. It was a look that said,

"Just wait and see what I have in store for you."

It was the facial expression of one who has up his sleeve a colossal jest that will do more than surprise all those who live to see it; the air of one about to bring off a tremendous *coup*, beneficial to himself and both amazing and detrimental to everybody else.

"Noticed anything queer about the Old Man?" I asked Dacre one evening when, throughout the day, this look, expression, air, manner, of the Captain, had been even more particularly noticeable.

"Who could miss it?" replied Dacre. "Looks like a cat that's not only drunk all the cream, but put a dead rat in the jug."

"Aye, ba goom! that's reet," agreed Geordie who was listening. "Or sooped a mon's whisky and put proosic acid in its plaace. Domned old deevil."

Beauty entering at the moment, Dacre repeated my question to him.

"Now you mention it, me lord," he said, "I don't mind telling you that that Hyena's Orphan gives me the perishing creeps nowadays. I tell you I don't like the cut of his jib at all. *Do* I think he goes about with a queer look on his ugly dial? I tell you he looks to me like a man who's planning to murder All Hands and the Cook—and thoroughly enjoying the job, damn him."

Shortly after this half-deck conversation, Celia Bryndal surprised and embarrassed me by raising the very same point.

Passing her open port, I heard her usual mocking,

"Little Joseph! . . . I want to speak to you. Come here, you'll be quite safe—as long as you stay outside."

And as I stopped and put my head through the port,

"What's in the wind?" she whispered. "What's the Old Man—the Old Devil—up to, now—or going to get up to?"

"Don't know," said I. "You should . . ."

"Yes, I know I should," she interrupted, "but I don't. He's got some game on. . . . He stands and stares at Mother, and then chuckles to himself—in a most sickening way. Gives one the creeps . . ."

Exactly the expression that the unimaginative Beauty had used. Yes, he did give one—the creeps.

"He does the same with me," continued Celia. "Sits and

stares at me all through meal-times, and when I feel his stare and look up, he drops his eyes—and chuckles. I see him do just the same with the merry Mate; and with my beloved Mr. Hammerson, too."

Celia could never refer to a personable man when talking to another, save as "beloved" or "darling" or something of the sort— a great believer in the power of jealousy as a weapon.

"Not but what Hammerson can take care of himself—and me too," she added provocatively.

"Why bother me, then?" I asked, with deliberate lack of grace.

"Because I love talking to you, you dangerous passionate Don Juan," she grinned.

I turned to go.

"No, stop a minute," she begged with a change of voice.

"I don't get the chance of a word in private with the Officers," she continued, "and I wouldn't speak to that mouldy Mate if I did . . . I want to ask you something. It's well known that you're a marvel as a navigator. I asked the Captain, and if a look could cut a throat, my head would have been off."

"What did you ask him?" I smiled.

"Why, whether we aren't making *far more easting than is necessary or reasonable.*"

I was instantly intrigued—not to say startled.

"I know more than you, my lad. I've been homeward bound round the Horn often enough to know what I'm talking about. . . . I made it my business to look at the chart in his room this afternoon, when he went on deck without locking the door."

"What made you do that?" I asked.

"The way he's been chuckling over it—as he always does when he thinks he's being specially clever. The Mate doesn't take sights or see the chart, but I believe he knows that we're too far East, from something I heard him say to Mother. I couldn't hear clearly, and I didn't hear it all, but I know he's worried. They both are. I can tell from the way that he looks at the Captain across the table at meal-times, that he's puzzled to death. . . . You can see him just going to say,

" 'Excuse me, Sir, but when are we going to stand to the Nor'ard?'"

"Well, if we don't alter course soon," I observed, "he's bound to raise the question, I should think."

"Then there'll be trouble," prophesied Celia.

"I can bear it," I admitted.

"Trouble?"

"Trouble for the Mate."

"Yes, but I mean trouble for all of us. Trouble for me—and Mother, and you and the whole lot of us, ship and all. . . . I tell you, Joey, there's something brewing, something bad."

I affected to laugh.

"All very well. You don't know him—and you aren't with him all day long as we are."

"Getting on your nerves, evidently," I remarked.

"Seems like it. I'm not afraid of the brute but I'm damned uncomfortable . . ."

"Fanciful, you mean," I jeered. "Don't you suppose so experienced a shipmaster and fine a sailor as Captain Bryndal knows what he's up to?"

"He's sailing East, I tell you, and there's more in it than you guess. I could tell you a lot that you don't know. . . . Give you the surprise of your innocent young life."

I received this in silence.

"I wish I knew what the artful devil's up to—what his game is."

"Isn't it extremely probable that by going further East than usual he's expecting to pick up stronger Trades?" said I.

"Bosh!" snapped Celia. "Stuff and nonsense. We ought to have been in the Trades days ago. Don't tell me he wants to go right across to Africa to find the South-East Trades."

"All-right," I said, "all-right. I don't want to tell you anything."

"Oh, Joey, don't be a pig," was the reply. "*Nice* little Joseph."

And two small hands, sunburnt and strong, came through the port to rest one on either side of my face.

"Give me a kiss, Joey."

"My name is not Joey, and I'd as soon smack you as kiss you."

"Nice Sinbad. Kiss me . . . Then you can come inside and smack me, too, if you like."

Whereupon Celia Bryndal, drawing my face towards hers, kissed me on the lips, a long . . . lingering kiss . . . warm . . . stirring.

Very nice.

Very very nice.

"I *beg* your pardon," said a voice as someone brushed past me—unnecessarily heavily, I thought.

It was Dacre.

"Break away," I mumbled, in boxing referee manner, as Celia, her arms about my neck, held me tightly, my lips to hers—and I struggled free.

"Dacre's turn now?" I asked, as I turned away.

Celia laughed.

"Isn't Little Joseph coming on!" quoth she, and shut the port.

Poor Dacre appeared to agree with her. . . . Coming on indeed.

He turned upon me savagely as I followed him into the half-deck.

"Am I to congratulate you, Dysart?" he asked, his voice cold . . . cold as ice . . . keen and cutting as a knife, and bitter as aloes; his eyes blazing, fierce and hot as fire.

"Why, certainly, if you like. On a fair fine kiss, the first I've had for years."

"The first you've had from Celia Bryndal?"

"Absolutely."

"You expect me to believe that?"

"Don't give a damn whether you believe it or not."

"I thought you swore to me that you didn't love her."

"I don't. Not a bit. Don't now—and never shall."

"You're a liar. You're in love with her."

"Not a bit of it, Dacre. I don't love her in the least."

"You're a damned liar, a lying, deceitful, sneaking, thieving. . . . I say you're a *liar*."

"Righto."

"Didn't I just see you kissing her?"

"You did."

It was on the point of my tongue to add,

"Or else you saw her kissing me," but it occurred to me, in time, that this would be a scurvy truth to tell, and likely to infuriate Dacre the more.

"Very well, then," he said. "Presumably you don't go and hang about there to make love to her and kiss her, because you *don't* love her. If you weren't in love with her, you wouldn't want to do it, and if she weren't . . ."

His face fell, as wrath for a moment gave way to pain.

"Is she in love with you too? Speak the truth for once," he asked.

And an idea occurred to me.

"My good ass," I interrupted, "you came along the alley-way and saw Celia and me—kissing. . . . Doesn't it occur to you that perhaps you were meant to see?"

"What d'you mean?"

"What I say. As you happened along there at that moment, it

seems to me just possible that you're in the habit of happening along there, at that time of day. . . . And that Celia is in the habit of sitting at her casement—or opening her beastly port—and that, expecting you, and catching me, she arranged a tableau for your benefit. She's quite equal to it."

"Look here," shouted Dacre who so rarely shouted. "Don't you say a word against Celia, damn you. You're a liar, a cheat, and a . . ."

"Oh, rats! Pipe-down, for Heaven's sake!" I growled, and flung out of the half-deck—sick and sore with my best friend.

§2

And within the next two or three days, I found that the peculiarities and vagaries of our navigation were being discussed elsewhere than Aft.

Going forward, and lying at full length among the jib-sheets by the starboard-anchor, I watched the fan of white foam under the fore-foot, enjoying the beauty of the ever-changing patterns that came and went under the *Valkyrie*'s gracefully curving stem.

Having for some time absent-mindedly, and yet coherently, cogitated the problem of our curious course, I decided that it was time to turn in.

"When next she dips the figure XXI right under, I'll go," idly I promised myself.

XXI suddenly being submerged, I straightened myself up, and was surprised to find that I was not alone. Karl Blancke and Hans Berghen were equally surprised, and I think filled with suspicion that I had been listening, intentionally spying on them.

They both scowled angrily at my greeting.

"Hullo, bully-boys, I thought I had the fo'c'sle-head to myself."

Seated on the anchor, they had smoked and talked without knowing that I lay close by, behind the coils of rope. With the sound of the sea and the crash of the "bone in her teeth", I'd been quite deaf to the noise both of their approach and of their voices.

"Haf you heard aboud vhat we sbeak?" asked Hans who prided himself on the fluency of his English and the purity of its pronunciation.

"I couldn't hear a word, and I wouldn't want to," I said curtly. "Didn't you hear me just say that I thought I had the fo'c'sle-head to myself? Why should I want to hear what you say?"

And I turned on my heel.

"Hi, but vait!" called Hans Berghen, softly, and to Blancke observed,

"Id is a good lad and freundly, und ve don't can't do no harm if ve it him tell."

And at a nod from the silent Blancke, invariably known as Dumb-Face, he forthwith began to tell me how, on the previous night, the weather being fine, the port over his bunk had not been screwed up.

Having pushed it open, not for the sake of fresh air but for the polite purpose of out-board expectoration, he had heard some interesting snatches of a curious conversation between Chips Peddersen and others, some of whom he could identify by their voices as Slim Johes, Villa, Jake and Müller. . . .

Now old Hans Berghen was not only a very fine sailor, but an exceedingly decent type of man, and I fully believed him when he declared that, but for hearing the word Dumb-Face and then his own name, he'd have taken no interest whatever in this or any other of the Carpenter's "committee-meetings"—which were now of quite common occurrence.

Because it was a weather port, nobody expected it to be open at night, and all spoke freely; but, being a weather port, the wind blew through it, and at times sufficiently loudly to prevent Berghen from hearing all that was said.

From the extremely uncomplimentary references to Dumb-Face and himself, Hans gathered that Blancke and he were expected to object to a certain course of action; to refuse to join in with the rest; to be spoil-sports, mar-plots and cowardly swabs. . . . Nevertheless, means would be found to make them only too glad to withdraw their objections, bear a hand, join in with the rest and take their share.

Somebody had observed that Blancke, Berghen and any other foolish son of a gun of a Burgher's Orphan would sooner feed his own silly face than feed the fishes.

Quite so, opined somebody else, for as soon as the rest of the crew (not only Berghen and Dumb-Face but Church and Carrol, and one or two more), knew for certain that the ship was not homeward bound, there'd be no difficulty in persuading them to agree to, if not take a hand in, whatever it was that Peddersen and the others proposed to do.

Another voice was heard to remark that the swine who hadn't the guts to take a hand in the job would stand by quiet enough for a hand in the pickings; to which someone else agreed that those who couldn't take a hand would get a foot—with a boot on it—for their share, when it came to dividing up. And it was, apparently, roughly settled that all who took active part should have equal shares.

Those who took no part, but merely acquiesced, would get nothing at all, or a bit less; while those who interfered could exchange the amenities of the *Valkyrie* for those of Davy Jones's locker. . . .

I wasn't amazed. I was far past amazement by the time old Hans Berghen had finished.

"But this is sheer nonsense, lunacy, penny-gaff tripe, bilge," I objected. "You misunderstood them; you got it all wrong . . . or else they were having a game with you."

"*Ja, ja*," smiled Hans Berghen. "Fonny game to play outside der closed port until quietly I open it."

"Could you tell me anything that any particular man said?" I asked. "I mean, do you remember the exact words said by any voice that you recognized?"

Hans Berghen said he did remember practically the exact words, and they were words worth remembering; and Hans Berghen now thoughtfully and carefully recalled them.

Slim Johes had expressed the opinion that while the Mate would certainly agree—under pressure—to fall in with the scheme and put his seamanship and navigation at their disposal, the Second Mate most certainly would not.

Whereupon Villa betrayed his presence, as well as his views, by announcing that neither Peddersen nor Slim Johes, nor anybody else for that matter, need trouble his head or his entrails about the Second Mate. . . . The Second Mate would be dealt with. Faithfully, fully and finally dealt with; and that dealing would be the business and the pleasure of the speaker. Let them leave Hammerson the Unspeakable to Villa the Invincible. . . . Trouble from the Second Mate! Huh! Let them watch and see what happened to Mister Second Mate; yo ho, and a bottle of rum!

Out of the silence that followed Villa's outburst, the voice of Jake was heard to observe that that blasted brass-bounder of a binnacle-boy, Blount, playing at Third Mate, might give trouble.

"Vell, you vas big enough to give him some trouble, vasn't you?" growled Peddersen.

Whereat Jake was heard to laugh and observe that he'd show the half-baked Third Mate how the good old larrikins used to pull the neck of that sort of chicken in Sydney. Whereupon Peddersen had agreed that the alleged Third Mate, then, might be left to the care of Jake while he himself would look after that goddamned First Voyager, Dysart, who fancied himself so much.

"Der Carpender said you vas von overgrown ape, Sinbad," smiled Berghen.

"Well, he ought to know all about apes," I said, trying to make my half-stunned mind do a little thinking.

Another voice, definitely recognized, and whose words he had clearly remembered, was that of Müller who had expressed his satisfaction, and fervent hope that the job of "fixing the hell-blistered Second Greaser and the two cursed lousy Apprentices would, at any rate, be properly done", whatever else was mucked, muddled and neglected.

Apparently Müller's observations had annoyed Peddersen who had invited him to pipe down, take in the slack of his jaw-tackle and wait and see what he should see, which had led Müller to remark that that might be a hell of a long time. . . .

I asked Berghen if, from this, he gained the impression that Müller was a candidate for the leadership in whatever it was that they were plotting; to which Berghen replied that he thought not. No, he felt pretty sure that Müller spoke thus to egg them on, by casting ridicule on the idea that they'd ever accomplish anything —except talk, bluster and bluff.

What had surprised Berghen, and more than surprised me, was the fact that Larry O'Toole's voice had been prominent in the discussion, incessantly asking questions and offering suggestions.

"Anything else?" I asked Berghen, when at length he fell silent.

"Ja, a big ache in mine liddle ear, by liszening drough de port in de cold night wind."

"But who the devil says we're not homeward bound, Hans?" I asked. "Who says we're not going direct to Falmouth, as we learned at Pisagua?"

"Sailor-mans was all vools—but not all pluddy vools," replied the old man, thoughtfully stroking his beard. "Ve gan zee der knots vhat ve log mit de course ve make und ve all blenty savee. If der Kapitan der course not alter, soon ve to der east gome of der Island vat it call Drisdan da Gunha, ain't it? For mineself, I not gare. 'More days, more dollars,' hein, ain't it? But vor dose udders—I dink drouble gome mit some of dem, if ve more East go."

"But, God bless my soul, man," I objected, "isn't there a Captain on board? Isn't his name Bryndal? . . . Trouble! If you'd asked me, I should think the trouble would come from him."

"*Ja*. He is der great man and der fine seaman. Und vhat gan one fine man und fine seaman do against a whole ship's company led by der Mate?"

"But—Lord give me patience, man—what do they think they're going to *do*? If they started anything with Captain Bryndal, they'd find even more trouble than they signed on for. Trouble? They don't know what it is. They would, though, if they came athwart Captain Bryndal—Mate or no Mate."

"*Ja*."

"Well, what is their game? Until we know that, what can we do? Didn't you get any idea as to what the scheme is?"

"*Nein . . . nein* and ve gan noddings do. Noddings but keep der eyes sharp and der tongue quiet."

"That's it," I agreed. "Now, if you hear anything more, you come straight and tell me, won't you?"

"*Ja*," nodded Hans Berghen.

And remarking that it was time I turned in, I left him solemnly stroking his beard and nodding his head at his *alter ego* Blancke, who had not once opened his lips.

As I went to my bunk, I was boyishly disposed to make light of the whole affair, to regard it as rather a lark, and to pooh-pooh it as another manifestation of that childish idiocy of which only silly sailor-men are capable—and that only after having been cooped up, overworked, overdriven, and underfed for long days at sea.

Nevertheless I meant to report it fully and faithfully to the Second Mate and to Dacre, and meanwhile intended to lose no sleep over it.

CHAPTER VIII

During the next few days, there was such unusual activity on deck, the Captain spent so much time on the poop, and Dacre was so ferociously haughty and uncivilly polite, that I had no opportunity of talking with the Second Mate, or inclination to talk with the Third: and the matter of Hans Berghen's report of "trouble" receded to the back of my mind.

Coming on deck for the forenoon watch, I was astonished to find that canvas was being sent down from the mizzen.

"Good Lord!" remarked Dacre to Geordie, "it's early days to be bending fine-weather sails. If it comes on to blow, there'll be some fun."

In spite of the fact that we were enjoying a remarkably long spell of very perfect weather, we were still hundreds of miles from the Tropics, and Dacre was only expressing the general opinion.

But, when all mizzen sails except the spanker were unbent, made up, put in the sail-locker, and not replaced, everybody was thoroughly mystified—and few made any secret of the fact. Those who ventured to sound the Mate on the subject, got nothing more than a sneering enigmatic smile, and the remark,

"Captain's orders, m'lad. Nothing to do with *me*. . . . Nor with you."

Sure signs that Smeeker was piqued, puzzled and annoyed because the Captain had not consulted him.

Quite obviously the Captain had not consulted him, and certainly he had not consulted the Second and Third Mates.

Utterly puzzled, the fo'c'sle experts expressed their wonder and curiosity in ironical surmise and suggestion.

"Blimey! The Old Man's going to give her single to'gallant and tops'ls to go 'ome with," grinned Church.

"Sure now, he's afther airin' the mast, I say! I say he's afther airin' the mast, begod!" was Patsy Hooligan's solution of the problem, freely offered to every man in turn.

"Garnaway! His heart's softened," opined Carrol. "He's so sorry for the poor perishin' Apprentices that he don't want them to have any more bunt-lines to overhaul."

But in spite of joke and jest, puzzlement grew and grew and grew, and in some quarters, settled into sullen apprehensive wonder.

Bewilderment prevailed on the poop, in the half-deck, and in the fo'c'sle; a cloud of bewilderment through which shone the bright smile of Captain Bryndal as, chuckling and grinning, he trod the quarter-deck 'without any amazement'.

"What the hell *has* he got up his sleeve?" whispered Dacre to me, breaking the ice of our estrangement.

In the end it was Geordie—cheekily insulting the whole crew, as he loved and dared to do—who earned great fame as a prophet.

Forbearing to mention that, taking his life in his hand and carrying eyes in the back of his head, he, peeping and prying, had seen certain plans and measurements on the Captain's table, he informed the crowd, who all stopped work and gathered to give ear, that they must be a poor brainless uneducated bat-eyed and blighted gang of dirty old shell-backs, if they couldn't guess what was about to occur.

"Happen Ah'm not half the age of the youngest of ye," he said, "but Ah'm twice the man of the ouldest of ye. Why didn't ye coom to me and get it reet? Ah'd have told ye streeght away how the Old Man had asked ma opeenion, and then decided to tak' ma advice and mak' this ship into a *barque*! . . . Aye, and a champion barque she'll be."

The men stared open-mouthed in silence.

"Why, I believe the young devil's hit the nail on the head," exclaimed Carrol at length.

"I'll 'it 'im on the 'ead," growled Church, more or less good-humouredly. "Comin' here insultin' 'is betters with 'is cock-and-bull story."

"Betters me foot!" bawled Geordie. "A gang of know-alls too big to learn from their superiors. Ah, weel, ye'll soon see who's reet . . ."

And see we did.

While the yards were being sent down from the mizzen, the best palm-and-needle men were set to work on a gaff topsail under the Captain's personal superintendence.

§2

If, knowing that the thoroughly discontented men were being deliberately incited against him, Captain Bryndal had wished to thwart his enemies and for a time to disarm them, he could not have adopted a better device.

With one or two exceptions, all for'ard were vastly pleased with the change to fore-and-aft rig on the mizzen.

As any sailor knows, spanker and gaff-topsail are much easier than cro'jack and other square sail, and it was immediately seen that the absence of yards and all their accompanying gear, would considerably lighten the labour of working the ship.

In this respect it was particularly beneficial to the half-deck, but that did not save Dacre from being yet deeper plunged in his savage dejection.

"It's a damned shame," he growled bitterly at table, to no-one in particular, "the old fool's absolutely spoilt our poor *Valkyrie*. He must be going mad. Who the devil ever heard of a barque without a spanker boom?"

A total absence of any comment from either of the Mates showed that they also held the same view. Their silence—and their faces—betrayed their deep disgust far more effectively than any strong language could have done.

I gathered that, for totally different reasons, Slim Johes and Villa were equally displeased. While they had no personal objection to less pulling-and-hauling, they strongly disapproved of anything that abated discontent and made the Captain less unpopular. A quiet Fo'c'sle was the last thing they wanted, and in the Captain's latest move they saw the undoing of some of their good work.

In the Port Watch, Slim Johes had an excellent and willing henchman in Müller, but with the others he now had need of all his cunning. Owing to his miserable exhibition of cringing cowardice off the Horn, the blatant fellow had lost much of his hold on Hamblin, while Larry O'Toole, always agreeable, always smiling, always saying but little, baffled and worried the busy agitator. And although he had no difficulty in persuading Axenstern and Patsy Hooligan that they were shamefully treated, he could distil no really dangerous venom into their discontent.

In the Starboard Watch, Villa, the leader—candidate for the leadership of the whole crew—was experiencing similar difficulty with Church and Carrol.

Carrol's endless grousing seemed to be a safety-valve through which all genuine ill-will and malice escaped, while, from loudly applauding and encouraging the grumbler, echoing and burlesquing his growls, Church derived much more amusement than Villa liked to see. In fact, Villa, I know, had an uncomfortable feeling that these two, Carrol and Church, secretly admired his hated enemy, the Second Mate, the bully whom he professed to have marked for death; the man who had quietly knocked him out, for laying his hand upon his knife.

Indeed, Villa was by no means certain that there wasn't a faint trace of respect in the attitude of these two seamen toward the Laughing Hyena himself.

Hans Berghen and Karl Blancke, Villa could only regard as hopeless pacifists, soulless spineless clods on whom any Officer of any rank could wipe his boots at will. Thus, in his own watch, with the exception of Brown the black and Paulo the yellow, who were coming along nicely, only Jake was definitely an ally, a congenial spirit, a man after his own black heart, and a useful tool. . . .

For a while the "syndicate"—whom I now knew to be headed by the wily Carpenter, Peddersen, and to consist of Slim Johes and Müller of the Port Watch, and Villa and Jake of the Starboard Watch—was temporarily embarrassed, hampered and forced to play a waiting game.

As soon as the excitement aroused by the work of altering the vessel's rig had somewhat subsided, I made an opportunity of telling the Second Mate all that I'd heard, as well as all that I had suspected.

He heard me in silence, occasionally nodding his sagacious head.

"I've always had my doubts of Peddersen," he said, "the two-faced reptile. Talks to you polite as though he lived on soap and oil—and *that's* how he talks behind your back, eh? . . . Yes, I've thought for some time that there was trouble coming. That wind-bag Slim Johes makes the noise, and that snake Villa backs him up—and although he'll keep in the back-ground, it'll be Chips who'll run the show when trouble comes."

"But after all, what sort of trouble can a square-head Carpenter make for a man like Bryndal?" I asked.

"What trouble? I'll tell you, Son. I'll tell you what trouble a man like Peddersen can make in a ship carrying a gang like Villa, Müller, Jake, Johes and a crowd of dangerous fools like Brown, Axenstern, Hamblin, Hooligan and Paulo. In the first place, he can do what I expect he's been discussing on the weather side of the fo'c'sle—urge the crew to lay aft in a body and demand that the ship be put on a Northerly course at once. . . . And what'll the Old Man do then? Laugh like a mad dog, grin like a hyena, and ask when he ever told anyone that the *Valkyrie* was ordered to Falmouth. Then he'll smile some more and observe that he proposes to take the ship exactly where he thinks fit—and suggest that they now get to hell out of this . . . back to their kennel before he kicks 'em there . . . and go while the going's good. Adding every sort of insult he can think of—and he'll be able to think of quite a lot."

"Well, what then, Sir?" I objected.

"What then? Why, Peddersen will hold another meeting—and at his instigation the men will approach the Mate, and ask him to supersede the Captain and take the ship home. . . ."

The Second Mate fell silent, gloomily ruminating.

"Whether the Mate would have the pluck to do it, is another question, but I know he's hand in glove with Peddersen—and I believe he's quite capable of leading him on and encouraging him, even in stirring up real mutiny, in the hope that he could snatch some advantage out of it. . . .

"Yes!" he continued, "take the ship home and be given the command as a reward for faithful loyal conduct and the display of great discretion, wisdom, and ability in most trying and dangerous circumstances! . . ."

Mr. Hammerson laughed bitterly.

"Yes, presentation gold watch and binoculars thrown in," he sneered.

§3

Yet for all the Second Mate's wisdom—and I believe that he accurately summed up the situation as it then was, it was not Peddersen who actually started the trouble.

The Carpenter later, played, for a time, a leading rôle in the terrible tragedy of the *Valkyrie*, but the man who really fired the train was Captain Bryndal himself—and the match that lighted it was his alteration of the ship's rig; and the light of it illuminated all his subsequent acts.

For a brief space, a most deceptive atmosphere of peace prevailed aboard—a peace that was but the calm before the storm that was to burst within the ship itself and prove far more dangerous than that which, at Staten Island, had broken upon the *Valkyrie* from without.

Not in my worst nightmare could I have visualized such a storm of human passion as was soon to overwhelm us. With a not uncommon irony its first murmur came with a very prosaic incident of routine.

The Mate, having set Patsy Hooligan and myself to paint the lifeboats, gave us instructions to leave the names untouched so that, later, the letters could be renovated with black paint.

While I was engaged upon this not unpleasant and purely mechanical work, my unemployed mind was free to range whither it would.

Among other high matters I idly cogitated whether slapping paint on boats and doing other unskilled labour would either reasonably or legally be *"considered, held, and deemed"*, good examples of *"using all proper means to teach the said Apprentice the full business of a Seaman"*, which, according to my Indentures, Messrs. Dobson, Robson and Wright had contracted to do for me.

My thoughts then reverted to the interesting piece of information, imparted to me by Dacre, that when a boat is painted, the laying-on of the brush-strokes up and down instead of fore-and-aft would take at least a knot from her speed through the water, or, in the case of a ship, between two and three knots.

It seemed to me impossible that friction between water and a boat's side could be as great as that.

What a lot he knew and what a splendid chap he was; and what a desperate pity that he and I should be so estranged. Since he had made a complete *volte face* from the misogyny so unnatural to his years and calling—for is it not well known to the landsman that every proper sailor has a wife in every port—why on earth, or on water, could he not have bestowed this passion of love on a worthier object? . . . And since he had done so, why couldn't she return it? . . .

And who was I to decide that Celia Bryndal was unworthy? Well, I hadn't said she was unworthy of me, had I? No, only that she was unworthy of Dacre.

Why? Jealousy on my part, probably. . . . Then I *was* worthy to be his friend—though Celia Bryndal wasn't. . . .

Nice modest conclusion. Still, love and friendship were two different things, and a man-friend and a wife two different people. Not that Celia Bryndal would ever become his wife—and thank God for that.

And why thank God for that? Jealousy on my part or unworthiness on hers? And so round again, full circle.

But of course Captain Bryndal's daughter wasn't 'good enough' for my splendid Dacre. And as a father-in-law, Captain Bryndal——

"Slipshod work! Scrimshanking hell-blistered young hound! Look at *that*," said he from behind me.

The Captain had walked along the bridge to the after house.

I glanced up at him and then stared hard at my excellent work.

"Look at it, you; look at it," he rasped.

I was looking at it, but honestly could see no fault of omission or commission. To my perhaps not unbiased eye the work was admirable, without spot or blemish.

"Look at that 'holiday' you've left there," grinned Captain Bryndal and pointed at the flawless area of paint.

"I'm afraid I don't see it, Sir," I truthfully replied, staring hard at my handiwork.

"Blind as a boss-eyed bat. . . . Here, give me your brush," replied the Captain.

And taking the brush from my hand, he dipped it in the paint-pot, touched a totally imaginary bare patch on the newly painted side of the boat and then, to my amazement, carefully obliterated the name *Valkyrie* from both bows and, immediately stepping across to the port boat, did the same to the name on that one!

Coming back and returning my brush, he gave me one of his brightest smiles as he concentrated his piercing hypnotic gaze upon my eyes.

"Listen," quoth he. "When that's dry, give it another coat. D'you hear me? D'you understand? Give it another coat," and turned away.

"Now why the devil did he do that, Patsy?" I asked as soon as the Captain was out of earshot.

But Patsy Hooligan's mentality, while sound and sane as far as it went, was entirely incapable of considering such abstractions as motives, particularly the motives of a superior.

He was concerned only with the results.

"Begob, the Mate'll raise hell, I say. I say the Mate'll raise hell, begob," he muttered, and frequently repeated his interesting prophecy, as he stopped to stare with stupid blue eyes at the Captain's handiwork, and to visualize the Mate's reactions to it.

When he did come aft, and stared with incredulous eyes whose evidence his mind at first rejected, the Mate's mouth fell open. When he could find words, he proceeded to justify Patsy's prophecy until, with quite obvious disappointment, he realized that I was not the culprit.

From the savage expression of his morose face as he walked aft, we gathered (and earnestly hoped) that he was on his way to "raise hell" with the actual offender.

Whether he would have found the courage to do so, I don't

know, for on the poop he was intercepted by one who laboured under an even greater sense of grievance than he did himself. This person being Dacre, we of the half-deck received that evening an unvarnished account of the Mate's behaviour—behaviour that, in the light of subsequent events, was to prove significant and illuminating.

What had happened was this. Dacre, the acknowledged artist of the ship, had been exercising his undoubted talents in the decoration of the lifebuoys.

In accordance with the usual sailing-ship practice, these were distributed at intervals round the poop, and hung in beckets seized with twine to the rails. As, in port, they always attracted the attention of passers-by, they bore, in addition to the ship's name at the top and her port of registry at the bottom, the Ensign and the Owners' House-Flag painted opposite to, and on a level with, each other.

In the skilful painting of these latter decorations, Dacre revelled and excelled; and it appeared that, having this morning completed one lifebuoy to his satisfaction, he was using it as a model for the rest. Not only had he accurately placed and stencilled the names without a blur, but his bright-hued flags were depicted most realistically waving and shivering in the breeze. Thus, when Captain Bryndal came and stood grinning behind him, Dacre had every right to expect that, if comment there were, it would be at least appreciative.

This being so, Dacre's feelings may be imagined when suddenly, with amazed indignant eyes, he saw the skilful work of his loving hands entirely wiped away with a piece of cotton waste.

"Very pretty, my lad, very pretty," smiled our merry Captain, "but I want nothing on the lifebuoys—nothing whatever. Just leave them blank."

And while poor Dacre stood, himself looking far more blank than any lifebuoy, the Captain *threw the stencils overboard*.

By the time that Dacre and the man at the wheel had finished gasping at the enormity of such an outrage—for even from a Captain it was an incredible and monstrous deed—the Old Man had departed and the Mate arrived on the scene. And the conduct of the Mate proved to be the most amazing feature of the whole astounding business.

He listened to Dacre and then, regarding the defaced lifebuoy with astonished anger, stepped clear of the wheel-box in order to look once more at the despoiled boats, and asked Dacre to repeat his statement that the Captain had thrown the stencils overboard.

Having heard Dacre's reply, and gazed once again at boats and lifebuoys in blank bewildered incredulity, he suddenly emitted a long low whistle that expressed, as plainly as speech, that understanding and realization grappled with wonder and amazement.

And then,

"By God!" he said, apparently forgetful of Dacre's presence. "I see! I see! Oho! Oho! That's the game, *that's* the game, is it? Oh, that's it, is it, Captain Blasted Bryndal! . . . I see . . ."

And walked away like a man in a dream.

All these things Dacre told us in the half-deck, as we hacked away at the salt horse with our sheath knives, and puzzled heavily over the Old Man's unbelievable conduct.

" '*Why* did the Old Man paint out the names and chuck the stencils overboard?' " replied Dacre to the fiftieth repetition of the question. "When we know what made the Mate whistle like that, and talk like that, and then walk off the poop as though he'd seen a centipede with a sea-boot on every foot, and no shadow of doubt about it, we shall get the answer to the riddle. Whatever that may be, the Mate grasped it the moment he properly realized that the Old Man had actually dumped the ship's stencils. It was quite plain that a great light had suddenly shone into the Mate's mind—and lighted up that dark hole wonderfully."

"Whatever it is, he's on to it then, eh?" observed Fagin.

"Yes," agreed Dacre, "he's got it, all-right."

"Happen he's got it wrong, though," mused Geordie.

"Eh, but we live in stirring times," he added, taking his cap and going out, followed by Fagin, leaving Dacre and me alone together, save for Beauty, who was sound asleep in his bunk.

As always, now, we were polite, if not pleasant, with each other. But suddenly, under stress of these new and thrilling wonders, it seemed that we laid all other matters aside, and looked each other in the face, as an extraordinary suspicion simultaneously occurred to us.

And then we looked away, for obviously each thought the idea far too fantastic to put into words. One part of the mind can entertain, or at least tolerate, a nebulous notion that another part refuses to take seriously, to analyse, arrange, codify and set forth. What we were both thinking was too fantastic, too silly to put into words.

But not a very great many hours were to elapse before we knew that it had been put into words, and that our fantastic suspicion, our silly idea, was held by a good many other members of the ship's company. We had forgotten that Axenstern at the wheel knew as much as Dacre and I; had heard the Captain's words, and had actually seen him throw the stencils overboard.

And, of course, even Axenstern would view such doings with amazement, and recount them in the fo'c'sle—with corroboration from Patsy Hooligan as to the painting out of the boats' names. The fo'c'sle would buzz like a hive. And, moreover, how long, we wondered, would the Mate refrain from telling the whole unbelievable story to his bosom friend and toady Peddersen, the appointed ring-leader of fo'c'sle mischief?

CHAPTER IX

And so the peace of the last few days—the last sane and reasonably normal days of the voyage—slowly but surely gave place to that uneasy tenseness, that tense uneasiness, that sense of watchful anxiety and strain, that pervades a vessel awaiting a terrific storm that is certain to burst upon it, and may break from any point of the compass.

The glorious weather without, made more painful, more deplorable, more terrible, the brooding sense of imminent catastrophe—the imminent catastrophe of the storm about to burst within.

The old spirit of suspicion, distrust and disaffection reappeared, darkened and intensified, and with it came again all the guarded watchfulness, the whispering in corners, the conspiratorial air of secrecy, of planning and of plotting.

Again warned by Hans Berghen, I watched and spied, and soon discovered that the Peddersen syndicate secretly conferred together at every opportunity. With Hans I agreed that "somedings vas in der vind".

In the light of what the Second Officer had said, I had little doubt as to what the "somedings" might be, and felt pretty sure that the Peddersen gang was endeavouring to force the rest to lay aft in a mutinous spirit, and agitate, among other things, for an alteration of course.

To my surprise, however, watch succeeded watch without this being done, and I grew more and more puzzled as to what was really happening. When I tried to discuss the matter with Dacre, he coldly observed that "he didn't know and didn't care, as he had better things to think about"; and with some difficulty I refrained from pointing out that the welfare of the "better thing" might be involved.

From the Second Mate I got nothing but a growl to the effect that we would wait and see, and those who lived longest would see most. To so brave a man as he, it was idle for me to point out that it was partly because I wanted him to live long that I was worried by what I saw and heard.

At first, the prevailing uneasiness and unrest might not have been apparent to a stranger nor to an unobservant member of the ship's company (such as Beauty, for example), and was

201

indicated chiefly by the complete absence of the usual rough jokes, and an entire lack of anything approaching joviality in the song of the chantey-man of the moment.

Even the Cockney humour of the irrepressible Church was in abeyance, as he went about chastened, subdued and obviously preoccupied with anxious thought. Only the clowning of Patsy Hooligan and the whimsical lunacy of Larry O'Toole remained unaffected by the black cloud of depression, for these two poor fellows must inevitably remain themselves. . . .

Then, almost suddenly, and with increasing speed, the subversive elements in the fo'c'sle obviously gathered confidence from a source unknown to me; and, while the others remained watchful and wary in varying degrees, Villa and Jake in the Starboard Watch, and Slim Johes and Müller in the Port Watch, developed a kind of jubilant knowingness and conceit that, at times, came near to absolute insolence.

Villa and Jake being in the Second Mate's Watch, and having that redoubtable man to contend with, were a little more careful than Slim Johes and Müller, but it was very apparent that something had greatly lessened their fear of him.

But this new and disturbing air of,

"You stand from under! You keep your eyes skinned. I've got something up my sleeve for you!" was most marked in the Carpenter.

As I have previously mentioned, Peddersen generally took his orders directly from the Captain, occasionally from the Mate, and never from the Second Mate. This made him far less disciplined than the other men, for obviously he had some understanding with the Captain; had little but contempt for the Mate; had no concern with the Second Mate; and an utter disregard for Dacre, the acting Third Mate.

And now he began to behave as though nobody at all had any authority, whatsoever, over him. As this kind of delusion is contagious, and particularly apt to infect weaklings, certain of the waverers conceived a new admiration for the Carpenter and constituted themselves his admiring disciples and followers.

This taint spread even to the half-deck, for Fagin, long a crony and confidant of Peddersen, began to ape his ways and manner. He overdid it, however, for, ignoring sane pungent admonition and advice from Dacre, he persisted in his folly until he aroused the always dormant anger of Mr. Hammerson who, receiving an impudent reply, swung round about on Fagin with blazing eyes, high colour and low voice.

"You fool!" he said. "Let sleeping dogs lie—and let lying dogs sleep," and, seizing him in his tremendous arms, thrust him on his back, grabbed his ankles, swung him up and held him head downward, over the rudder, for a period so prolonged that the on-lookers became nearly as scared as the victim.

"Now," said he, hauling him back and dumping him roughly on the deck, "get off the poop before I kick you from here to the fo'c'sle where you belong and ought to be."

Unfortunately, however, there was only one Mr. Hammerson aboard, and, still more unfortunately, he had but little to do with those among whom the rot was spreading most rapidly, those foolish easily swayed children of the Port Watch who needed an iron hand to provide antidote to the poison of Slim Johes and Müller.

The pity of it, that instead of such a hand as his, the Port Watch had no other control than that of the flabby paw of the weak and flaccid Mate who, even if he desired good discipline (which I doubted), had not the personality or power to enforce it.

In the Starboard Watch, moreover, in spite of the perpetual grumbling of Carrol and the pugnacity of the good-humoured Church, neither of these was at present prepared to support the malcontents in actual insubordination, while Karl Blancke and Hans Berghen, apparently unaware of the prevailing unrest, remained aloof, quiet, efficient and amenable as ever.

So in the Starboard Watch, Villa and Jake, in spite of the backing of Brown and Paulo, at this stage made little headway. But in the Port Watch, the evil developed fast, and it soon became evident that Slim Johes had gained tremendous influence over all his shipmates.

Patsy Hooligan, now thoroughly corrupted, became childishly impudent in his folly; Axenstern grinned, giggled, strutted and grew vastly pleased with life and with himself; Hamblin, when-ever he sighted the Second Mate, glowered and licked his lips; Larry O'Toole gave voice to amazing indiscretions at most inop-portune moments, while Müller, growing more and more over-bearing, threatened ever less darkly and more frequently.

To poor Dacre, in his capacity of Third Mate, unconsidered and unsupported by the powers that should have been behind him, this state of affairs grew increasingly unpleasant and humili-ating, but it worried our excellent Mate not at all—rather did he seem to find open pleasure and amusement in the insolence and slackness of his Watch, and the discomfiture of Dacre whom he had always hated.

§2

All these things were by no means hidden from a person as experienced and observant as Celia Bryndal; and the little crease in her brow, that denoted anxiety, worry and anger, was now seldom absent.

During my trick at the wheel one morning, she came and stood beside me, and taking advantage of this public privacy (for the Captain, her mother, and the Mate were below, and no-one was within ear-shot) she talked to me in a way that interested me greatly and moved me not a little. For once, her defences were down; she came forth from behind her screen of follies, affectations, airs, graces and pretences, became her natural very attractive self, and spoke simply, sincerely, and straight from the heart.

She confessed that she was frightened, and I realized that affairs must be going badly when Celia Bryndal was not only frightened, but admitted it. Her three main troubles were the facts and implications of a terrible row between the Captain and the Mate; of an even worse one between the Captain and her mother, and thirdly, the Captain's attitude toward herself.

And it was now that Celia Bryndal put into words an idea that had been knocking at the back door of my mind for some time.

"Sinbad," she said, "I tell you the Captain's mad. I mean just that. He's a madman, and I don't believe it would be an exaggeration to say he's a dangerous lunatic.

"Look here, now. After breakfast, the Mate, who has been behaving very queerly since all those names were painted out, asked Bryndal to spare him a moment, and, giving him a long look and a frightful grin, the Captain took him into his room and they talked.

"What they said at first, I don't know, though I did my best to hear, for I'm beginning to think that the more one knows of what's going on in this ship, the better.

"Suddenly they both lost their tempers and raised their voices and began to shout at each other, so that I could hear them in my room—with my ear against the door.

"Well, what do you think of this? The Mate bawled at the Captain as though he was shouting at a fo'c'sle hand.

" 'Bosh, you silly fool! D'ye think I'm blind? D'ye think we're all blind aboard this ship? D'ye kid yourself that we haven't all seen through this game of changing names and altering the rig?'

"And the Captain bawled back that he hadn't changed any

names.

" 'No,' shouted the Mate, 'but you're going to. Or else why did you have the others painted out? Now then, if you think you can put this thing through on your own, you're heading for the rocks.'

" 'Well?' asked the Captain.

" 'Yes, and you'd better make it "well",' cried the Mate, 'so I'm asking you straight—where do I come in?'

" 'Where do you come in?' mocked the Captain.

"And d'you know, Sinbad, I was so worked up that I found I had gently turned the handle and was actually opening the door a tiny crack.

"I must have done it half-unconsciously, when their voices fell a little.

" 'Yes, where do I come in?' repeated the Mate, 'for believe me, you can't get away with this without my help, and if you try, you'll come to grief.'

"The Captain laughed, and you can imagine the sort of laugh it was, Sinbad.

" 'Oh!' he said. 'Ah!' he said. 'Come to grief, eh? Through you upsetting my scheme, eh?'

" 'Yes,' said the Mate. 'I will so. I'll be as glad to leave the sea as you will, Captain Bryndal, and if you think you're going to retire on the strength of this scheme, you take it from me that you're not—unless I come with you.'

" 'Unless you come with me, eh, Mister?'

" 'Yes, you heard what I said. You let me in on the ground-floor, and we'll bring it off.'

" 'Bring it off, eh?' said the Captain, repeating the Mate's words again, as though he were thinking of something else—temporizing.

" 'Yes. You can't do it without me—and don't you forget it.'

"Then the Captain suddenly changed his tune—and his tone and his manner. . . . I'm certain he's mad, and that covetous fool, Smeeker, is too blind to see that he's dealing with a lunatic. . . . Blinded by money. The Captain's sudden change of front should have told him something—warned him—surely.

"For he suddenly turned as friendly as friendly, grabbed Smeeker's hand, patted him on the shoulder and told him not to be so silly. *'Of course he was going to take his good Mate into his confidence!* Of course he'd intended from the very first to bring him into it. How could Smeeker have thought otherwise? Why couldn't he have had more confidence in his friend and colleague and Captain than that?

" 'Perhaps he'd been foolish in postponing this talk so long and in leaving the Mate to make the first move. But he had thought it wisest to confide in nobody until the deal was put through and completed—ashore.

" 'Naturally he'd been a bit annoyed to find that his clever Mate had spotted his game and guessed his secret. . . . Clever Smeeker! . . . Clever Smeeker! . . . But he should have been more trustful. Yes, yes, he had been a little upset and angry at first, and especially when Smeeker had shown himself so suspicious—but damn it all, when Captain Bryndal had got the fifteen thousand pounds in his pocket, he could afford to be generous. And by God, he would be generous, too!

" 'Wouldn't the Mate sit down and have a cigar? . . .'

"And then they got down to it.

" 'Yes, yes, he'd been planning this *coup* for a very long time, and had provided himself with all the necessary documents, and there couldn't be a hitch.

" 'And how much was the Mate to get?

" 'Well, taking even such an absurdly low figure as fifteen thousand pounds—and it was more likely to be twenty thousand—that ought to allow ten thousand for the Captain who had engineered the deal and brought off the *coup*; four thousand for the Mate—think of it, my dear Smeeker! Forty bags of golden sovereigns, a hundred in each bag—and a cool thousand shining pounds to be equally divided among those members of the Crew who had proved *reasonable*.

" 'And then All Hands could separate, go their respective ways and enjoy their well-earned wealth . . .'

"By that time, Sinbad, I could hardly believe my ears," continued Celia. "I took a peep through the crack of the door that I'd had the nerve to open, and I could see the Mate's eyes shining with greed in his white excited face.

" 'Aye,' whispered the Mate, 'but what about some as I could mention that won't be reasonable, Captain?'

" 'Huh,' barked the Captain, 'accidents will happen on the best regulated ships, won't they? I'll have 'em receipted and *filed* for reference.'

"They looked at each other in silence, the Mate slowly nodding his head.

"And then in a voice that should have warned the fool and that certainly warned me, the Captain added,

" 'Be careful no accident happens to *you*, Mister. Don't *you* get receipted and filed for reference.'

"But, in his greed, the Mate missed the point altogether, I think. He just nodded complete reassurance to his kindly Captain and then asked for more details of the sale of the ship in Cape Town. . . . They put their heads together then, and whispered so softly that I could hear no more.

"What do you think of that, Sinbad?"

"Think?" I said. "That you're quite right. The Captain's genuinely mad and the Mate is a gullible greedy fool."

"But surely, Sinbad, you can't actually pinch a ship nowadays, can you?"

"No," I said. "Of course not, even if you do change her name and alter her rig. Not even if you do alter the ship's official number, cut inside the after part of the main hatch-coamings —and he'd have a tough job to alter those . . .

"By Jove!" I interrupted myself. "Of course! That's why he and the Carpenter have always been hand in glove. . . . No, you can't steal a ship nowadays, I should say. But mind you, Captain Bryndal's no cheap tin-pot criminal, and no fool. He's got brains, and he knows a lot. It's just possible that, trusting to their not seeing the insertions, he may have advertised in the Cape Town shipping-press on behalf of Messrs. Dobson, Robson and Wright; or he may actually have had instructions from them to try to sell her abroad—and has decided to forget to post the cheque to Glasgow. . . .

"D'you think he might have told your mother this, and she might have consulted the Mate—with some idea of putting a spoke in his wheel and preventing such lunacy . . . saving him from himself? . . ."

"No, I certainly don't," replied Celia promptly, and with an edge to her voice. "Not the latter part, at any rate," she added bitterly. "If she did know what he was up to and told Smeeker, it would be so that she and Smeeker could defeat him. It's a funny position. No, my mother is in on this, differently. I'll tell you about her, after. What I don't see, is why the Captain should be altering the ship and her name if he's going to sell her, honestly or otherwise, on behalf of the owners."

"True," I agreed. "Of course he wouldn't."

"Perhaps he's trusting to finding some sleepy Shipping Official who won't take the trouble, or have the means, to find out that our registered number was originally given to a ship called *Valkyrie*; or, better still for his purpose, some corrupt rascal with whom he'll share the loot—of which Smeeker will never see a farthing, of course.

"What's most likely of all," I decided, "is that Captain Bryndal will find himself in gaol with a ten years' penal servitude sentence for barratry and attempted piracy—or in a criminal-lunatic asylum for life."

"And I don't know which would be the better place for him," observed Celia, with a snap of the jaw.

We fell silent, either occupied with our own thoughts, or too overwhelmed and bewildered for anything that could be called thought at all.

"Well now, about this row with Mother," said Celia. "Really, it was terrible—and they've had some pretty bad ones."

"What! Has she been interesting herself in the changing of rig and painting out of names?" I asked in surprise, for I'd always regarded Mrs. Bryndal as a person of very different preoccupations.

"Yes," replied Celia. "But the row was about the other matter. To my amazement she spoke to him about the ship's course. Called him into her cabin as he went by, and asked him where he thought he was going.

" 'Up on deck,' he said.

" 'Oh! Yeah?' sneered my mother. 'And where's the ship going?'

"Captain Bryndal came into the room and shut the door, and I nipped round and crouched under her port-hole in the alley-way.

" 'What d'you mean—if you mean anything at all?' he asked, and his voice wasn't at all good to hear.

" 'How much further East are you going?'

" 'How do you know where we're "going"?' said he.

" 'Er—I . . .' Mother seemed confused. 'The Mate . . .'

" 'Oho! Aha! The Mate! Well, well, now, isn't that interesting!'

"And he laughed.

" 'Exactly! . . . The Mate! . . . Hatching a plot, are you, with my clever Mate? The clever Mr. Smeeker!'

" 'Don't be a fool,' snapped my mother. 'Plot indeed. I only asked the . . .'

" 'Why didn't you ask me?'

" 'Because I don't trust you. And because I know you've got some game on.'

" 'Oh, you do, do you?'

" 'Yes, I do. And I'll tell you what it is, Captain Bryndal . . . It's to get this ship to Cape Town.'

" 'Think of that, now! Cape Town, eh? And while you're telling me so much, suppose you tell me why I'm going to take this ship to Cape Town.'

" *'To try and sell the stuff there.* That's why.'

" 'Oh, that's it, is it? To try and sell your bit of stuff there, eh? Your nice little, big little, heavy little boxful there, eh? Think of that now,' laughed the Captain.

"Just the sort of laugh he gave the Mate. You can imagine it.

" 'Yes,' she said, 'but you can't do it, you cheap get-rich-quick Bryndal, and don't you think it. No, nor a dozen like you. Yes, you can grin. . . . Why, you poor fish, d'you think you can fool me? Pull that bunk on *me*? Say, did you ever hear of the Breakwater? . . .'

"What *is* the Breakwater, Sinbad? For they both began shouting at once, and mother kept on about it."

"A prison at Cape Town, I believe," replied I, "chiefly populated by I.D.B. men—illicit diamond buyers."

"It was awful," resumed Celia. "Disgusting. I'm sure he's mad, and Mother's a fool to wrangle with him, or take him seriously. But isn't it utterly amazing? A tremendous row with the Mate about selling the ship in Cape Town, and a tremendous row with my mother about something extremely valuable that belongs to her. Something that would make him rich. I suppose the Mate told her he thought the Captain must be making for Cape Town—and Mother at once jumped to the conclusion that it was to sell something of hers there, because he couldn't sell it in England."

"Yes, and I remember she asked him what he thought The Others would do to him, if he brought it off, even assuming that that were possible."

"Others on the ship?" I asked.

"Oh no. I don't suppose anybody on the ship except Captain Bryndal knows anything about what they were discussing, not even her precious friend the Mate—loathsome brute! Oh no, The Others must be—well, er—some of Mother's business associates in Sydney and 'Frisco and Shanghai."

"What is the valuable property that she thinks he wants to divert to South Africa?" I asked, intrigued and filled with a very natural curiosity.

"I'm sure I can't tell you," replied Celia shortly. "Well, the quarrel went on, and got worse and worse, but although I heard every word they said, there was a good deal that I didn't understand, and, in the end, they parted with mutual threats. I really thought he was going to strike her, and I was just screwing up my courage to go in, when he went out of the room; and the last thing he said—and in his very nastiest voice—was,

" 'And now you talk it all over with your loving friend the Mate, the clever Mr. Smeeker. You tell that brainy fellow all about it. . . . And since you've been good enough to give me some advice, I'll give you some. Same as I gave your friend the Mate. Be careful of your dear self. Mind you don't meet with an accident. You might be receipted and *filed* for reference.'

"I wonder what he means by that, Sinbad?"

"He's mad," I said.

"And now about *my* row with him.

"He came straight from Mother's room out into the alley-way, and ran into me. I'd had just time to get up, and was walking toward him.

" 'Come in here a minute, my dear,' he said, quite pleasantly, and led the way into my room.

" 'Did you hear all you wanted to know?' he asked, with his brightest smile, the moment he'd shut the door.

"I was aghast.

" 'What do you mean?' I said.

" 'What I say. Were you able to hear everything that was said . . . ?'

" 'What . . . when?'

" 'When you opened my door an inch and poked your ear in, and when you went round and squatted under your Mother's port.'

"Isn't he a devil? He never turned his head a fraction of an inch toward his door when I was listening. And I suppose he must have come and looked out of the port-hole to see if anyone was about when he was talking to Mother—and grinned at my silly head down below. . . .

"I had to think quickly.

" 'No,' I said, 'I couldn't hear anything.'

" 'Clever girl,' he grinned. '*You* don't want to meet with an accident, do you?'

" 'No,' I replied, trying to stare him out. 'No more than you do.'
. . .

"He laughed out loud at that, and stepping close up to me, put his left arm round me and his right arm under my chin. I kept perfectly still, for he's mad, Sinbad, absolutely mad."

"What did he say?" I asked, as Celia stopped.

"I'll tell you, Sinbad, though it's hardly believable.

" 'Clever lass, aren't you?' he grinned. 'Mother's own

daughter . . .'

"And I thought he was going to kiss me.

" 'But you're not *my* daughter, you know,' he went on. 'Aren't you glad?'

" 'More than that,' I said, for I was getting angry as well as frightened. 'I'm thankful to God.'

" 'Good girl,' he grinned. 'Good girl. So'm I. *Most* thankful.'

"And he drew me still closer to him.

" 'No, you're not my daughter . . . nor my sister . . . nor my aunt . . . nor my grandmother. You're nothing to me at all, are you?'

" 'No,' I said. 'Nothing.'

" '*But you're going to be*,' he laughed, 'you're going to be. And you don't go off this ship until you are. And do you know what you're going to be?'

" 'Yes,' I shouted. 'I'll be your death.'

"For he suddenly crushed his beastly face against mine and tried to kiss me on the lips. He just held me and laughed, and the more I struggled, the more he laughed. . . .

"It was awful. . . . The beastliest thing that ever happened to me."

"He's not your father, then," said I.

"Thank God, no. I don't know who my father was, but he wasn't Bryndal. He never met my mother till I was ten years old and more. No he's not my father, but he's my mother's husband.

"Though it was only a business arrangement," she added cryptically.

"Well, I fought and struggled like a wild cat, and it was only when I said,

" 'I'll scream the roof off,' that he let me go.

" 'Ah,' he said, 'you won't scream by-and-bye, my dear, when you know what's what. . . . You know which side your bread's buttered as well as most women, and that's saying a lot.'

" 'You wait till I get ashore,' I told him—and he knew what I meant.

" 'You wait until you do, my dear,' he said, and went out of the room.

"He opened the door again almost as soon as he'd shut it, put his head in and said,

" 'You're a good listener, aren't you? Well, you stick to listening, and don't talk, see? And be careful of your dear self—and mind you don't meet with an accident. I don't want to receipt and file *you*, of all people.'"

Celia stopped with a little catch of the breath that, in her, was rather pathetic. I stared ahead, unseeing, tightly gripping the spokes of the wheel, and either steering subconsciously or leaving the *Valkyrie* to steer herself.

Someone came and did something or other near by. Celia took a turn up and down the poop.

"Why have you told *me* all this?" I asked, when she again stood beside me.

"Can't you guess, Sinbad?"

"No."

"Oh, well then. . . . Well, I trust you. Let's leave it at that. And I somehow trust *in* you, too, if you know what I mean. You're the first man I've ever met whom I felt would . . . what shall I say? . . . You know . . do something for nothing."

"But what can I do?"

"You can help me. . . . Be my friend. . . . I've got nobody."

"You've got your mother."

"My mother! . . . A friend! . . . I tell you, Sinbad, I'm absolutely alone. I feel as though I were absolutely alone in all this ship-load of men. . . . And that brute-beast is . . . Oh, I can't talk about him . . . he's mad."

"What about the Second Mate?" I said. "Can I tell him all you've told me? Why didn't you go to him?"

"Oh, Sinbad, don't you understand? . . . Yes, tell him, by all means—if you're quite sure he's not as bad as the rest."

"I thought he was 'your beloved Mr. Hammerson'," I reminded her.

"Oh, don't joke, Sinbad. I daresay I did, but what do I know about him? He may be as big a rogue as the Mate and that rotten Carpenter. The Mate talked as though they were all in it. Hammerson may be . . ."

"Well, he's not," I interrupted. "He's an honest man, absolutely straight. . . . A splendid chap."

"Well, tell him, then. The more he knows, the better."

"And Dacre too?" I said.

"Yes, Dacre as well," agreed Celia.

"I don't know why you didn't tell him yourself in the first place."

"Then you're a fool," was the uncompromising reply.

"Well, anyhow, *he's* above suspicion, I suppose," I replied. "So there are three just men—and probably ten—in the wicked city, and two of them Officers."

"But what can they *do*, Sinbad, if Captain Bryndal . . ."

Captain Bryndal approached and Celia turned away—leaving me with a good deal to think about.

For'ard, Eight Bells was struck—the time by the cheap American clock in the galley was keenly noted by the Watch on deck—and it was now my watch below. With a truly nautical roll, Geordie came to relieve me, and, gruffly echoing my "Full-and-By", took charge of the wheel that was taller than himself.

As I made for the lee-ladder, I ran into Mrs. Bryndal who, smiling, said,

"Isn't your name Dysart?"

"Yes, ma'am; it is," I answered.

"Brodie Dysart?"

"Brodie Dysart," I replied, wondering a little.

"Was your father Captain Sir Sinclair Brodie Dysart, R.N., and was he ever in the China Seas?"

"Oh yes," I replied, "I know he was, at one time."

"Then I once met him—at Hong Kong," said Mrs. Bryndal. "Well, well, well! You're very like him, you know."

"So I've been told, ma'am," I replied.

"Do you intend to stick to the sea?" she asked, and when I said I did, she remarked,

"You'll never make a fortune that way. But who knows—I might be able to help your father's son along some day."

Then she passed on, while I went below.

That evening, Fagin being absent, enjoying the society of the Carpenter, Peddersen, I took it upon me to tell Dacre, Geordie and Beauty all that Celia had told me. A silence followed the ending of my narrative.

"Mad?" said Dacre at length. "Not he. Not in the ordinary sense of the word. He's bad, if you like, bad as they make 'em, but he's not mad."

"Eh, but I doan't know so mooch," reflected Geordie. "Happen he's gone mad—sudden like."

"Why should he?" asked Beauty.

"Well, some sea-captains do. Perhaps he's never been the same since that champion storm off Staten Island."

"*Pah!*" was Beauty's only comment.

"Happen he went and had a squint into yon heavy box. D'you remember it? And found it chock-full of great big diamonds. And the sight turned his brain. Aye, fair addled it."

"*Pah!*" observed Beauty again.

"Ony way, I reckon all criminals are mad—and t'Old Man's a criminal all-reet."

"Yes, I'd say he's got the makings of a first-class criminal," agreed Dacre, "but I wouldn't say he's mad. There's a devil of a lot of method in his apparent madness. . . . Mad or not, he knows what he's up to."

"Aye, we know he's oop to summat wi' the ship, for a start, an' it looks as though he's oop to summat wi' a heavy box o' . . . treasure," agreed Geordie.

"Ba goom, lads," he grinned, "we're a treasure ship! That's what we are, and t'Old Man's goin' to find treasure and lose ship, or else steal treasure and steal ship too. Nay, he's goin' to steal ship wi' treasure in it."

"Strike me pink!" murmured Beauty.

But it was of his own treasure that poor Dacre was obviously thinking, and his bitter jealousy and resentment, that Celia should have made me her confidant instead of him, was swallowed up in his anxiety for her, and his savage wrath, jealousy and indignation against the Captain.

"We must have a talk with the Second," he said, at length.

"What can he do?" asked Beauty. "Suppose he decided to take charge, on the strength of what we'd told him? Have we—who've no shadow of proof that the Old Man intends to pinch the lugger, got to hold the Skipper and the Mate, while the Second puts them in irons?"

"Eh, ba goom!" agreed Geordie, "and if the Old Man turns to us and says,

" 'Blount! Dysart! Stowe! Watton! The Second Mate's a mutinous dog! A mad dog! Seize him at once and put him in irons,' do we go oop to Mr. Hammerson and ask him whether he's comin' quietly? Does the acting Third go and grab him by t' throat? Nay, there's a whole lot of fowk I'd sooner put the bracelets on, than Mr. Hammerson."

And Geordie laughed ruefully.

"Nevertheless we'll have a talk with the Second Mate," said Dacre.

We did, at the earliest opportunity, and left Mr. Hammerson a very puzzled man, deeply sunk in anxious thought.

CHAPTER X

On turning-to, at noon next day, it was difficult to realize that anything but perfect good-will could flourish in such magnificent weather, such truly glorious physical conditions of existence.

With just sufficient breeze to fill her canvas, the *Valkyrie* drowsed gently along through the sapphire placid sea, while, from a cloudless sky of ineffable deepest blue, the sun just pleasantly warmed the sweet and balmy air.

Truly, every prospect pleased and only man was vile.

In that very watch, the rabid all-hating Müller showed something of man's vileness, and it was only the influence of the anxious cautious Mate—as ever, willing to wound but afraid to strike—that saved the situation for the time being.

From amidships came the tapping of chipping-hammers, where the Starboard Watch was scraping and cleaning the insides of the main hatch-coamings and preparing them for a coat of red-lead.

Being an efficient officer, the Second Mate never allowed his Watch to go below without being properly relieved, nor before each man had given his relief full particulars of the work yet to be done.

At noon there was generally a little delay while the Watch Below drew its lime-juice ration; and due allowance was always made for this.

To-day, however, insubordination was in the air, and, with the exception of Larry O'Toole who had relieved the wheel, not one of the Port Watch was less than ten minutes late.

Knowing of Dacre's difficulties with the Port Watch, and his lack of support from Smeeker, the Second Mate made no comment, as, with an angry scowl, he observed the arrival, one by one, of the laggards of the Port Watch.

His patience and forbearance however, gave way when Müller, more than fifteen minutes late, strolled leisurely from for'ard—smoking his pipe.

Not giving Dacre a chance to speak, the Second Mate strode toward Müller.

"Put out that pipe, before I knock it down your throat, ye Dutch hog," he ordered, in a low but threatening voice, "and if ye can't relieve your man to time, I'll come and fetch ye—with both hands—ye lazy skulker."

And then, to my utter astonishment, the German, without hesitation, did what was indeed a noteworthy sign of the times—a thing that only a week ago would have been simply unthinkable —snarled defiance at the Second Mate himself!

Fortunately, or wisely, Müller used his own language.

"Say it in English, you square-headed shirker," said the Second Mate, and thrust his face close to that of Müller.

Knowing and respecting the power behind the Second Mate's clenched fist, Müller stepped back a pace, but abated nothing of his truculence.

Obviously he expected support from the other members of the Port Watch, and observing the faces and the tense attitudes of Slim Johes, Axenstern, Hamblin and Patsy Hooligan, I felt certain that, had the Mate not seen, heard, and hastened up, to prevent trouble, that support would have been at once forthcoming.

"Get on with your job, Sonny, and let's have no more guff," said the Mate pleasantly, and gave Müller a slight push.

Still glaring and snarling, Müller backed away, turned and dropped down the hatch on to the cargo.

"I'll have my Watch relieved to time, or I'll raise Hell's delight," announced the Second Mate to whomsoever it might concern, including the Mate himself.

And Müller's growled reply,

"You vait. Mine chance was pluddy zoon come," was plainly heard by those about him in the hatch.

Ignoring the Mate, the Second Mate walked aft, unaware of what was undoubtedly a genuinely meant vicious threat.

As soon as both Mates had passed out of earshot, the pregnant silence was broken by the voice of Patsy Hooligan.

"I say there won't be any raising Hell's delight," he said. *"Not when we're the Ship-owners.* When we own the ship, I say, there'll be no raising Hell's delight, begob, there won't."

All eyes were at once turned to the Third Officer, poor Dacre, to see the effect of this startling remark. Dacre continued his work and gave no evidence of having heard what Patsy had said. I also ignored the interesting observation.

Patsy seemed to think he'd said a good thing and that it would bear repetition.

Raising his voice and apparently addressing me,

"There'll be no raising Hell in this ship, I say, when we're Ship-owners. I say there'll be no raising Hell at all, at all, when we're

216

Ship-owners," he said.

Hamblin nudged him heavily.

"Ach! Wait till ye're a Ship-owner before ye blether, ye auld fule," he growled sullenly.

"Inteed, and you may not have to wait long, Patsy, I tell you whateffer," sang out Slim Johes in his high-pitched chanting voice.

"And look you, them that do not wish to be Ship-owners can just be down-trodden wage-slave Fo'c'sle-Jacks. Iss, py tamn, sick and sorry Shell-backs they can be. Iss inteed."

He looked at Dacre, and he looked at me, and I felt that we were being sounded.

"Miserable fo'c'sle Shell-backs they shall be, then—whether they now live aft or half-deck or for'ard, I tell you."

Following Dacre's example, I remained deaf and uninterested.

"Ja, und den dere vas be no more 'You Dutch hog' und 'You skvare-head skulker' in dis ship," burst from Müller. "Dat schweinhund Second Mate haf himself finished, ja, he haf himself put to death."

"Ja, ja," giggled Axenstern in cheerfully excited agreement.

"Und ven ve vas Ship-owners der vas vill be no more Officers, ain't it?"

And he leered at Dacre.

Dacre yawned and straightened his back.

"Ah, when we're all Ship-owners we'll raise wicked hell and break a tea-cup," he said good-humouredly, smiling at Axenstern. "Meanwhile, suppose we get on with our job, eh?"

Presently Hamblin brought his scraper and worked beside me.

"Wull ye no be a Ship-owner too, ma hearty?" he whispered, closing up beside me. "It'll be better for ye, Ah'm tellin' ye. It'll be a graand sicht better nor joinin' the Shell-backs. . . . This ship'll no' be a guid place for them as willna stand in wi' the crowd. It'll be a sair bad place, Ah'm thinkin', and them not long in it."

"Hamblin, my son," I whispered back, "I don't believe you ever 'owned' so much as a box of matches that you'd no right to. Don't be a damned fool. Haven't you more sense than to follow that lot—like a gull following an offal-barge, hoping for scraps? Are you a decent British sailor-man, or a dirty, thieving, mutinous . . ."

"Decent British sailor-man!" exclaimed Hamblin. "Aye, to be ony mon's dog until Ah dee.

"It's a' richt for ye to be sae smart," he growled, "but Ah'll never wa'k the poop as Captain—and so Ah'm oot for ony siller that wants to come my way . . . Goad! How ma puir heid hurrts to-day."

"You'd steal, Hamblin?"

"Ah'd tak' . . ."

"Oh well! Every man to his taste and 'different ships—different long splices' as they say. . . . But I suppose we can differ and still be friends."

"It's goin' to be gey harrd—for Ship-owners and Shell-backs to be freen's. We've fixed a' that oop a'ready."

"Oh? So when you're a Ship-owner and I'm a Shell-back, you'll be my enemy, will you?"

Hamblin looked me in the eyes.

"Nay, laddie," he answered. "Ah canna be that. Ye taught me to box, and ye pit me in yon ambulance i' the Broomielaw. Ah'll never be yeer enemy. Not yer pairsonnal enemy, Ah'm tellin' ye; but it's goin' to be gey harrd for Ship-owners and Shell-backs to swop veesitin'-carrds."

"Oh, don't be a fool, Hamblin," I said. "I suppose when you're a Ship-owner you'll be ten times harder on any Shell-back than any Ship-owner has ever been on you?"

"Aye, ye're richt. Ah'll get some o' my ain back an' a bit mair. Goad, how ma heid hurrts."

At Four Bells, the Mate appeared and gave some indication of what future 'Shell-backs' might expect from him.

"Hey, you," he said, pointing at me and speaking as though to a dog, "get you up to the wheel. I only want men on deck here. Any lubberly binnacle-boy can steer a ship in this weather."

It was a long time since the Mate had used this sort of tone to me, and I turned and stared him in the face.

"Lie low," whispered Dacre sharply, "say nothing."

So, giving the Mate a gruff,

"Aye, aye, Sir," and a pleasant smile, I went aft in anything but smiling mood.

Considering the matter later, I remembered that none of the men laughed, and for some reason I took comfort in the thought.

Finding Celia on the poop, I decided that, in the circumstances, there were worse hardships than this extra trick at the wheel, which the Mate had imposed on me.

According to my invariable custom, I waited for her to be the first to speak, if speech there was to be.

Wondering at her long silence, I took my eyes down from my job and glanced toward her. She put her finger to her lips, and with a jerk of her head, indicated as I thought, that someone was behind me.

Glancing about, I saw no one. . . .

A minute later, sauntering past the wheel-box, she showed me a piece of paper.

"Peddersen is under the 'counter' just behind you," I read.

Before I'd been long at the wheel, the Carpenter climbed up over the rail and slouched forward. Directly he had gone, Celia strode to the break of the poop and, leaning on the taffrail, appeared to be looking idly along the main deck.

Suddenly, after a swift look round, she ran towards me.

"Sinbad," she said quickly and rather breathlessly, "a job for you. I've just seen the Carpenter take two cups of tea from the galley to his shop. One of those will be for the Mate, I know. The Captain's having his usual nap. I'll take the wheel while you slip down to that 'Bosun's chair' over the 'counter' and see what Peddersen's been doing down there, to the stern. Give me the wheel."

"Can you?" I said. "Don't get her aback, or the Mate'll come aft with a run."

"Don't you worry, Sinbad," grinned Celia. "I was steering when you were at school. Over you go. . . . And don't fall in the water, and get your nice clothes wet."

I glanced down at my filthy dungarees, and back at the beautiful smiling yet anxious face beside me.

Plucky girl. . . .

"Catch hold, then," I said, and was over the counter in a second.

"Well?" she asked, as I dashed back. "Well?"

"Not so well," I said.

"Is he?"

"Yes," I said, "he is. He's unscrewing the letters of the ship's name."

We stared at each other in speculative yet incredulous wonder.

"Any further developments?" I asked.

"No, except that my mother is undoubtedly in a state of furious rage and the Captain in one of . . . I don't know . . . jubilation, joyous anticipation.

"Have you spoken to the Second Officer, Sinbad?"

"Yes. He's sound as a bell, solid as oak, and true as steel."

"Well, that makes Hammerson, Dacre, you, Geordie, Beauty . . . How many more?"

"Four more," I said. "At least, I think so. Perhaps five."

"Who?"

"Well, Fagin, I hope. Berghen and Blancke for certain, and I'm pretty sure Carrol and Church, though they're grumblers. Probably Larry O'Toole, too."

"H'm," pondered Celia, "only five really certain then. . . . Only two in the fo'c'sle."

"Oh, more than that," I comforted her. "Four or five in the fo'c'sle. . . .

"Anyhow, the Fo'c'sle's divided against itself. Some of the silly fools are calling themselves 'Ship-owners'," I laughed.

"No? Already? Spreading quickly, isn't it? From the Captain to the Mate; from the Mate to the Carpenter; from the Carpenter to his gang—Müller, Villa, Jake, Slim Johes; and from them, I suppose, to Brown, Axenstern, Paulo and Patsy Hooligan for a certainty; and from them to Hamblin and Larry O'Toole, probably, if not to Church and that old grumbler, Carrol. What a hope!"

"Of course there's a hope," I snapped.

"And not much else," said Celia, who as usual gave me the impression of knowing a good deal more than she told me—about a good many matters.

"Oh, don't talk rubbish," I said. " 'Hope!' It's an 'A1 at Lloyd's' copper-bottomed certainty. What hope could those silly fools have—of doing anything? It's ridiculous. That sort of thing doesn't happen nowadays."

"No?" said Celia, "Nor is a ship's rig changed on the high seas, I suppose, nor names on boats and life-buoys painted out— nor the letters unscrewed from her stern, eh?"

This took some answering.

"Well, bless me, if there is some game on, I don't see who's going to be a penny the worse, except the fools who try the game. And anyhow, what about when rogues fall out, and all that? . . . What a team to do a job together—all hating each other like poison! . . . The Captain absolutely loathes the Mate and despises him as well. The Mate loathes the Captain, and what is far more dangerous—for the Captain—fears him. . . . There's hardly a man of the bad gang who wouldn't watch the Captain drown, with pleasure. And throw things at him while he did it. And half of them would as soon tip the Mate overboard as look at him.

"And another thing, among the men themselves—among those half-witted Ship-owners, I mean—it isn't all harmony, by any means. There's quite a little feud brewing between Villa and Slim Johes, for example, each of them thinking the other's getting ahead a bit too fast as a ringleader; and by no means all of them are very fond of Peddersen. . . . Lord, what a storm in a teacup!"

"Yes, Mr. Eloquent Sinbad, quite so," mused Celia, her lower lip between her finger and thumb. "A storm in a teacup. Did you, by any chance, ever see a teacup in a storm? Because that's what I think you're going to see, Sinbad, and I'm going to be the teacup."

Later, talking matters over with Dacre, in the light of what we'd seen and heard that afternoon, I found him to be of opinion that, in the event of real trouble, while the influence of the Half-deck would be negligible, the Fo'c'sle, with the possible exception of Carrol and Church, Berghen and Blancke, would be Ship-owners to a man. And what could those four do, save keep themselves as inactive and inconspicuous as possible, and follow—in stolid non-committal silence—the way the rest went?

§2

At Eight Bells, I waited in the half-deck until Dacre had finished whacking up the fresh water from the pump amidships, this being his daily job in the first dog-watch. As, returning, he entered the half-deck, I saw that he'd been laughing, and remarked, as he chuckled to himself, that it was good in these mouldy times that somebody could find something to laugh at.

"I feel more like crying really," he answered rather coldly, for the shadow of his love for Celia lay ever between us, and the brighter the moment the darker the shadow. In dark times of trouble the shadow was unseen.

"Much more like crying. Poor Larry O'Toole has gone clean off the handle; I suppose the strain in the fo'c'sle's been too much for his weak mind. He actually came to draw the fo'c'sle water in a bottomless bucket! I really had to laugh as he held it out, and I splashed a little through it.

" 'Something wrong with that bucket, Larry, I do believe,' I said.

"He looked at me with those sad shy eyes of his—like a hare's they are—and said,

" 'Something wrong, is it? Wrong? Why, can't ye see the

bucket's no good at all, at all? Not a bit o' good for anything else, now. But it'll still do foine for drawin' me watter. . . . So don't ye iver be throwin' it overboard.'

"He then put the bucket on his head, told me that he was the Tower of London, and begged of me, as a personal favour, to warn him if Guy Fawkes came aboard to blow him up. He was in deadly earnest, too.

" 'Shure it's a plot,' he said, seizing me by the wrist and whispering in my ear. 'It's a plot. That divil Villa. Peddersen's in it, too, and Müller and Jake and Johes, to blow up the Tower of London. They're goin' to take Guy Fawkes aboard and thin phwhat'll happen whin they blow up the Tower of London? Why, the ship'll catch fire, the ship'll burn. Houly Mither, how it'll burn!'

"It took me quite a while to calm him down and assure him that if Guy Fawkes tried to come aboard, he'd be clapped in irons.

" 'Ah, but who'd do it? Who'd do it? The Captain? No, begorra! . . . The Mate? No, bedad! . . . The Carpenter? No, bejabbers!'

" 'Well, the Second Mate would,' I soothed him.

" 'Shure now, av coorse he would. Him and Sinbad, two foine strappin' young fellas. And yerself . . .'

"It's a case, I'm afraid," sighed Dacre.

"I say, that's bad," said I, for I was fond of Larry O'Toole. "If the poor beggar's mind has gone for good, we've lost a friend in the fo'c'sle."

"I don't know about that," observed Dacre. "I'm not so sure. He's always been frightfully thick with that swine Villa. . . . Anyhow, in this absolutely mad ship, one lunatic more or less isn't going to make a lot of difference. . . . And I don't think one friend more or less in the fo'c'sle is going to matter much, the way things seem to be going.

"Well, well," he added, getting up. "I suppose I must go and report it to the Mate. And talking of Mates, let you and me have a quiet talk together with the Second, shall we? He ought to know what those fools were saying down in the hatch."

But at Four Bells, Dacre was saved by Larry himself from the unpleasant task of reporting to the Mate that there was a lunatic in his Watch.

Patsy Hooligan should have relieved the wheel, but that lazy old rascal had no objection to being forestalled by Larry O'Toole if he wanted the job, and, finding the wheel relieved by Larry, he promptly sneaked back to the fo'c'sle.

Within two minutes, Larry O'Toole, the master helmsman of

the Watch, instead of steering "Full-and-By" as was the order, had the vessel off her course and running merrily before the wind.

The presence of the Captain on the poop made this all the more annoying to the Mate, and it was in no gentle manner that Smeeker, striding up to Larry with clenched fist, demanded what in the name of The Hottest Hobs of Hell he thought he was doing with the condemned and crimson ship.

"Whoy, it's thim binds, Sorr, ye see, Sorr," replied Larry O'Toole, smiling his gentle and disarming smile. " 'Tis the wind av theer wings does make her run off."

Captain Bryndal took a hand.

"Birds? What birds are you talking about, m'lad?" he asked.

"Look! See! Some av thim birrds is binds av prey, Captain. They're following ye—ye bein' a birrd av prey yerself loike. Dear, dear, whoy did ye shoot th' albatross that time, Captain? When it doied, me brain doied too . . . Ah, there'll be others doying as well, before long, Oi'm thinkin'. Aye, and ye'll be among 'em, Captain."

Behind Bryndal, Smeeker quickly made the sign of the Cross. For him, there was inspiration and dread meaning in the prophecies of madmen.

"Why, this man's raving mad," said Captain Bryndal. "He's mad, mad, mad," he shouted, and roared with laughter.

"Send another hand to the wheel at once," he ordered, and a minute later, grinning sheepishly, Patsy Hooligan came to stand his regular trick at the wheel.

§3

Later, under the influence of "thim birrds", Larry O'Toole did such dangerous things aloft, and became so much worse than useless on deck, that he was lent to Doc, who was glad of his help in the pantry and the galley.

Curiously enough, he proved to be an admirable cabin servant, waiting at table deftly and quietly, and with none but the most harmless evidences of insanity.

CHAPTER XI

There was no man for'ard whom I liked better than poor Larry O'Toole, and thinking of him, it was with a heavy heart that I went to tell the Second Mate that, as I had struck One Bell, there remained only ten minutes of his watch below.

I found him, reading, on his settee, and told him that the Third Mate and I were anxious to have a few minutes of absolutely private conversation with him.

"Can't you say it now, Sonny?" he asked, and I had to point out that, apart from time being insufficient, my absence from the deck would be noticed, and moreover, I wanted Dacre to be present at the interview.

"H'm, let's see," replied Mr. Hammerson. "Most private time will be between Four and Eight Bells in the first watch to-night. Either Blancke or Berghen, I forget which, will be at the wheel. Big-mouthed Fagin will be on the look-out and Fat-fool Watton will, of course, be soaking his head,[18] and dead to the world. I can send young Stowe to call you, provided of course the Captain's not on the poop and there's no pully-hauly. If you don't mind losing a bit of your precious watch below, you can come and talk to me then, and nobody'll hear or be any the wiser."

Thanking the Second Mate, I assured him it would suit me excellently.

As I returned to the deck, Dacre was just leaving the saloon, wiping his mouth as he came out.

"That's the queerest black draught I ever tasted, Doc," I heard him say, and from the dimly-lit pantry came Doctor's reply,

"Nuttin' wrong wit' dat, Boy. Sure, dat's goo' tack. Dat's wunnerful goo' tack fo' yo' innards."

As we turned in, I attempted to chaff Dacre about his weekly aperient dose of black draught, and accused him of becoming a drug fiend.

As he entirely ignored my little joke and remarks, I imagined that he was still showing his cold displeasure. Scarcely had the thought passed through my mind than I heard him snore, a fact that rather surprised me, for Dacre was as slow to fall asleep as

---

[18] *Asleep.*

he was to wake. Could it be that he was shamming—to protect himself against further annoyance from his former friend?

*   *   *   *   *

"Sinbad! Sinbad! Wake up, wake up, I tell ye. The Second Mate told me to call the pair of ye, and there's summat wrong wi' Dacre. Ah canna wake him! Ah canna wake him at all! Ba goom! ye'd think he was dead drrunk, or dead wi'oot bein' drrunk . . ."

"Eh what? What's that? What's the time, Geordie?" I asked, yawning and half sitting up.

"Ah've just strook Fower Bells. Ah tell ye, Dacre's bad, an' all. Happen he was took ill in the night. He's reet bad, Ah tell ye."

"Course he's bad," I grumbled, pulling on my trousers. "Born bad, I expect. Anyhow, being called at Four Bells in his watch-below is enough to make anyone bad—even me—almost."

But one look at Dacre drove all facetiousness and sleepiness from my mind. His face looked drawn and clammy and was of the colour of old ivory. When I raised him and shook him, his head rolled on his shoulders like that of a corpse.

"Get the Second Mate down here, quick! Jump to it," I snapped, and, until his arrival, I tried smacking Dacre's chest, face and hands with a cold wet cloth.

"Good God, he's dead!" whispered Mr. Hammerson as he caught sight of him.

"No, he's breathing, Sir," I said, "but he'll neither move nor speak nor wake; and look at his colour!"

"Here, show a light," said Mr. Hammerson, and raised Dacre's eyelids.

"H'm," he grunted. "I've seen opium smokers' eyes like that in Chinatown dives.

"Let's get him out and move him around," he continued. "Looks as though he's taken something—or had something given him. Looks drugged to me."

Suddenly I remembered my playful accusation of a couple of hours ago, that Dacre was becoming a regular drug fiend . . . because he took an aperient regularly once a week. And instantly thereafter I remembered what I had heard Dacre say to Doc.

"Why, he had a dose of medicine at Eight Bells, Sir," I almost shouted, "and he smacked his lips and then said it was the queerest-tasting black draught he'd ever drunk."

"That's interesting," mused the Second Mate. "And queer," he added grimly, "very queer. Now listen—keep him walking;

keep him walking while you can shake a foot. I'll roust the Steward out, and see what dope he gave him."

In his rush to the poop-ladder, the Second Mate stopped for a moment at the after hatch, and kicked the Sleeping Beauty into wakefulness.

"Up, you fat tyke," he barked, "and go and help Dysart. Quick."

And never before had Beauty sprung so quickly to obey an order.

Between us, he and I dragged Dacre fore and aft along the main deck; and in our efforts to rouse him from the stupor that had deadened his brain and nervous system, we slapped, punched, shook and pinched him till the stars could have seen few more curious sights that night, as roughly we knocked him about, thrust him from one to the other, let him fall, dragged him to his feet again, rushed him along with a short staggering run; did anything and everything but give him a moment's rest in which he might again fall asleep—for if he did, it would be the sleep of death.

Then, with starting eyes, the pyjama-clad Doc came running with an emetic. Mr. Hammerson had smelt the unwashed medicine-glass, examined the empty bottle taken from the medicine-chest, and found it to be marked Chlorodyne.

Suddenly Captain Bryndal appeared upon the scene.

"How the devil did you come to make this terrible mistake, Steward?" he growled, and for once the Hyena was not grinning.

Doc turned upon the Captain like lightning.

"Why, what mistake I done make, Cap'n? Who tole I done make any mistake, Sah?"

Doc might be illiterate but he wasn't a fool—and Captain Bryndal had spoken too soon. He had put his foot in it.

"Well . . . er . . . well, it's obvious that some mistake's been made, isn't it, and in the morning it must be enquired into," was the somewhat lame rejoinder.

It was particularly awkward and unfortunate for our excellent Captain that there was absolutely no-one whom he could claim as his informant on the subject of there having been a 'mistake'. How did Captain Bryndal know what had happened to Dacre, and that there had been a 'mistake'?

"Yes, there must be an enquiry in the morning," he continued, eyeing the unconscious Dacre.

"There will be," growled the Second Mate, "and if that lad dies, we'll see that a Court of Justice does some enquiring."

"Sure thing, Sah," agreed Doc quickly, "an' I'm gwine ter be right dar in dat Court and give some interestin' evidence, Sah."

Captain Bryndal turned on his heel, and retreated to the poop.

While silently I thanked the Second Mate and Doc, I swore that if Dacre's life could be saved, he shouldn't die.

Our united efforts having wakened him sufficiently to make him chokingly gulp and swallow the emetic, he had already given us considerable hope; and I told myself that if my great strength were any good at all, it should be of some good now. While an ounce of it remained, Dacre should not fall into the fatal sleep.

Bare to the waist, I worked as hard as ever I had worked at any physical labour in my life, and so I believe did Mr. Hammerson. One on either side of Dacre, we maintained our staggering lurching devious course, to and fro along the deck, while Geordie and Beauty struck Dacre continuously with wet cloths and from time to time pricked him with their sheath-knives.

At Eight Bells, even the powerful Second Mate was getting somewhat exhausted and was obliged to give in, and let Axenstern link his massive arms with mine, about the still unconscious Dacre.

Doc came and offered to take my place, but I told him I was good for hours yet, and until my friend was saved—or dead—I wouldn't leave go of him.

At length Axenstern fell out puffing and blowing, and dripping with sweat. And with a contemptuous smile which I wonder I did not hammer from his face, Smeeker carried on.

His heart not being in the job, he very soon gave way to Doc who helped me to half carry, half drag Dacre, shake him from side to side and treat him with every form of violence of which we could think.

Suddenly Doc had an idea. Giving Dacre a terrific slap between the shoulder-blades, he suddenly bawled in his ear, in a voice of thunder,

"All Hands on deck," and—blessed ever-memorable moment, incongruously most beautiful of sounds—Dacre put forth some faint muscular effort of his own, the first since he had got into bed the night before, hiccupped violently, and murmured,

"Whassay?"

"Up, Dacre boy," bawled Doc again.

"You's got to stan' yo' Watch," he shouted, and again slapped Dacre mightily upon the back.

Dacre leaned forward in our arms and was violently sick.

"Whass marrer?" he murmured sleepily, and I doubt if any sound ever gave me greater joy.

"Come on, Doc," I bawled, and again we went at it.

Gradually the leaden limbs began to move of their own accord, and occasionally the heavy head was lifted from my shoulder.

After another hour of exercise as violent and exacting as that of a twenty-round boxing contest, Dacre began to walk, spoke one or two coherent sentences, recognized us by name, and laughed.

Soon followed further sickness and more lucid words; and Hamblin taking his place, Doc rushed to the galley to make strong coffee.

By Four Bells, Dacre was holding the cup with trembling hand, and suddenly, as though I myself had also been drugged, I sat down and fell asleep—and knew nothing of being carried to my bunk. . . .

At the farcical enquiry, Doc testified that he had taken the bottle that should have contained black draught—and that always had contained black draught—from the place that it had occupied without change of position for more than ten years. In it he always kept a supply drawn from the big main bottle, and from this smaller bottle he'd given hundreds and hundreds of doses.

Could he read?

No, he could not read.

Then how did he know what was written on the bottle?

He didn't know and he didn't care, for he never gave any but black draught medicine, and never gave it from any but that same bottle which was always in that same place.

Yes, Sah, it was the only bottle he had ever touched, and he knew it not only by its appearance but because it was always in the same place, its right place.

Now then, what he poured out last night for the Third Mate was poured out from that same bottle, and taken from that same place where it always was, and if the stuff poured out was wrong, someone must have meddled with the medicine-chest, mixed the bottles, and put the wrong one in the right place. And as (ship's) chlorodyne and black draught are of the same colour, he had no suspicion that they'd been interchanged.

Ah, all very interesting.

And had the Steward any further observations or suspicions that he'd like to put before the Captain?

Yes, Sah, sure thing he had, and that was this. It might not have been a case of mixing bottles at all, though that would be funny enough monkey-business, de good God knowed. It might have been a case of somebody putting something into God's good black draught and sp'ilin' it into a poison draught. Black opium or some sech goddam thing. . . . Chlorodyne ain't pizen.

The upshot of the affair was that Doc received a severe reprimand and was strictly forbidden ever again to dispense medicine until the Captain himself had seen the bottle from which it was poured—though for what he was reprimanded, and the mystery of how the wrong bottle or the wrong medicine came to be in the place occupied for ten years by the black draught, was not elucidated.

Neither was something, possibly more mysterious and even more interesting, elucidated either. And that was the mystery of how Captain Bryndal had known, before anyone had told him, that Doc had given Dacre medicine and had made a 'mistake' in the giving of it.

Later in the day, when I paid a visit to the galley for a quiet talk with Doc, he delivered his verdict.

"Sinbad boy, it sure was done deliberate. Eberybody knows Dacre hab dat black draught ebery Sat'day night . . . ship's joke. . . . Some yaller dawg done try to kill Dacre. Now den, who want to kill dat boy and why? Yo' fin' dat, and yo' fin' de man dat changed dat bottle. Dat boy Dacre kin t'ank de good Lawd Jesus dat Geordie done wake him two hours befo' de time. By Eight Bells he would have been a co'pse. Now you's got to watch yo'selves, yo' boys. Yo' boys watch yo' step. . . . Remember Mr. Wight!

"Yep, an' Mr. Hammerson, he got to watch his step, too."

I suddenly thought of what Celia had told me concerning the Captain, and the words flashed across my mind, "Receipted and filed . . . receipted and filed . . . Had Wight been 'filed'? . . ."

§2

What Dacre said to me about saving his life and about our recent estrangement, is between ourselves.

When he had finished, and I could reply with no more than a hand grip, he said,

"And now I'll tell you something, Sinbad. I should have told you before, but for the damned currish jealousy and stupid anger that kept me from telling you everything as I used to do. We've been wondering who's got a grudge against me and who's . . . well, what I didn't tell you is this:

"I went and bearded the lion in his den; asked for an interview with the Old Man and lost my temper, saw red, said a lot of things that I was a fool to say. I hadn't slept since you told me what he said—and did—to Celia.

"I began by pointing out that it was hopeless for me to try to be Third Mate if I got no support from him, and less than that from the Mate, and I ended up by talking about changing the ship's name—and a lot of other things I was a fool to mention."

"What on earth did the Old Man say?" I asked, wondering that Dacre had survived the interview, and aghast at his temerity.

"Nothing," replied Dacre.

"Nothing?"

"Exactly nothing. And when I'd done and, having no more to say, dried up and waited in silence—there was just silence. I stood there looking the biggest fool on this earth—land or sea—and just when I could bear that ghastly silence and the Old Man's friendly smile no longer, the smile broadened, the Old Man yawned and stretched himself.

" 'Shut the door as you go out,' he said . . . 'And go on being careful. Don't meet with an accident, whatever you do. Don't get receipted and filed, my lad.'"

I whistled long and low.

"Meet with an accident, eh? . . . You too!"

"What the devil does he mean by 'receipted and filed?' . . . the old fool", said Dacre.

§3

As I worked aloft in the next forenoon watch, I pondered the extraordinary event of last night, and for the hundredth time asked myself whether the poisoning could possibly have been intentional.

Up there in the glorious sunshine it seemed utterly absurd to imagine that there could have been anything more in the affair than a piece of carelessness on Doc's part.

But Doc knew that he had never changed the position of the black draught bottle; had never had occasion to do such a thing; never dreamt of doing it. He knew that he'd taken the same bottle from the same place as he had done any time these ten years past . . .

Of course it was just possible . . .

And then, as Doc had realized when thrashing it out the night before, there were several people who knew that he came for that black draught regularly every Saturday night before turning in, and it had been quite a little joke at one time.

Then, throwing off anxiety and dull care with an almost physical effort, I told myself that I was a silly fool, making mountains out of molehills, imagining things, getting morbid. . . . We'd all been shut up together far too long.

Of course there was no such thing as murder on the high seas in British ships nowadays. . . .

For once, a useful and instructive piece of 'sailorizing' had been allotted to an Apprentice, and I was engaged in putting new lanyards on the main upper tops'l sheets.[19]

These were 'standing' sheets of wire-rope and each ended in an eye-splice about three feet above the maintop. Into each wire eye was spliced a manilla lanyard which was used to lash the sheet to a heart-shaped eye-bolt in the maintop.

With a temporary "preventer" lanyard on the starboard sheet, I had spliced a new length of manilla into the wire eye-splice, and, after cutting off the loose ends of rope-yarn, instead of returning my knife to the sheath on my belt, I laid it beside me where I sat. Now as the battens of the maintop platform on which the knife rested were all laid fore and aft and about an inch apart, this was a very careless action. I fully admit it.

The penalty of my folly came when "Starboard main brace" was called on deck. In jumping to my feet I accidentally slewed the knife round fore and aft, and even as I made a fruitless grab at it, saw it disappear through the top.

Although I knew it would fall inside the main fife-rail and clear of everyone on deck, I nevertheless shouted,

"Stand clear from under."

This quite unnecessary precaution on my part lost me my greatly prized "Green River" knife for, most unluckily for me, my shout attracted the Mate's attention, and he, coming forward and seeing the knife, promptly threw it overboard.

The fact that this is common procedure with knives that drop from aloft, and the knowledge that I deserved to lose it for my carelessness, did nothing to lessen my anger, and I quite inexcusably let it get the better of my discretion.

On reaching the deck I went up to the Mate and sarcastically thanked him for what he'd done, and idiotically reminded him that dumping the property of other people was a game at which

---

[19] *These "sheets" are ropes.*

two could play.

I was amazed at the result of my words. Either I'd said something into which the Mate read more meaning than it contained, or else his nerves had gone utterly to pieces, for he went white to the lips, thrust his face close to mine and actually said, in a voice that trembled with passion,

"You needn't worry about your damned knife, boy. You're going to have your work cut out to keep your dirty carcase from going after it."

I was aghast.

However, recovering my temper and a little of my common sense, I laughed as though the Mate had made a good joke.

A minute later we were squaring in the yards a trifle, and as we hauled, Patsy Hooligan lifted up his voice and set the time with a chanty, extemporizing as was not unusual when he had finished the words that he knew:

> "Way hay ho!" he sang.
> "Way hay ho!
> Ship-owners all.
> That's us.
> Way Hay ho!
> All-together-one-after-the-other
> No-more-Shell-backs
> Way-hay-ha
> We'll-all-be-rich
> And-buy-a-farm
> No-more-pully-hauly
> Way-hay-ho!"

Here was Indiscretion incarnate. This was "coming out into the open" with a vengeance.

Most of the Watch greeted Patsy's incredible lapse with the broad grins that his chanty-man fooling so often evoked.

No-one made any remark. But, happening to look aft, I caught sight of the Captain standing at the top of the weather poop-ladder, and his lips were twisted into something far different from, and far worse than, his usual grin.

A grin of sorts seemed to be frozen on his ferocious face, for he had bared all his teeth—but it was as a feral beast bares them in the act of springing on his prey.

Never before, and never since, have I seen such purely savage hatred as distorted that scowling mask, and I had a feeling that in fact it was not a mask, and that for once I was seeing the real face of the man—catching a glimpse of the real soul behind it, naked and terrible.

Suddenly, catching my eye, he gave me a look that I remember to this day, and then resumed his pacing.

When he again reached the break of the poop, we had gone to the fore braces, and I remember looking at Patsy Hooligan and feeling thankful that it was he, and not I, who had evoked that really dreadful look on the Captain's face.

Within a few minutes I had something else to think about. Our jerking of the to'gallant yard had evidently loosened a gasket. As I remembered later, Müller had been up there just prior to our squaring of the yards and—had he had secret orders to do so—could deliberately have left it slackly made-up, so that it would soon fly adrift.

Later, I also remembered that the Mate looked up aloft once or twice exactly as though he were looking for that flying gasket and fully expected to find it.

"Up, Boy," he suddenly addressed me with fine politeness. "Go and make-up that gasket, and be quick about it."

Thinking to myself that the Mate and I would soon be "having words", I climbed to the to'gallant yard.

It was the outside, weather, gasket; and, as the ship was as steady as a house, I put my right leg over the yard-arm and, balancing myself with my left foot on the foot-rope, I coiled the gasket, and while doing so, glanced round the horizon to see if there were any vessels in sight.

There was nothing whatever to be seen but blue sea and blue sky, and I was just putting the final hitch over the coil, when the yard—beginning with a slight trembling—started to slip! Happily for me, the upper to'gallant-sail was not laced so tightly to the jack-stay that I was unable to get my fingers between the head of the sail and the iron bar.

Dropping the gasket, I took a good grip with both hands, brought my foot back to the foot-ropes, and thanked God I had not been the fraction of a second later in doing so.

The yard fell and, although its descent could not have occupied more than a few seconds, I seemed to wait through long minutes for the final jerk that would, I was certain, throw me right off the yard. As it gathered momentum and the halyards whined over the sheave in the mast-head, the winch on deck set up a most terrific rattling, and every man on deck, being startled by the sudden loud noise, looked up, held his breath, and waited for me to be dashed to pieces.

Below, by the galley, I saw the dark upturned face of Doc, and had time to think how the good-natured fellow would mourn my death and, sadly shaking his head, relate how he had warned me to "watch yo' step".

Suddenly, after what seemed an eternity of time, the yard was stopped—and though it stopped with a truly terrific jerk, I was, to my utter amazement, not thrown from it.

Actually, I still stood unharmed on the foot-rope, clinging for dear life!

Being an iron yard, the spar had not broken amidships, and by one of those interventions of Providence that we are apt to call chance, only the lee lift had carried away under the sudden strain. And well it was for me that I was not on the lee side, for, losing the support of the lee lift, the yard had "cock-billed", and the lee yard-arm landing on the lower to'gallant yard would have smashed my legs to pulp and thrown me off.

Feeling very thankful, very shaky, and not a little sick, I regained the deck as quickly as I could, and went straightway to inspect the winch that had so very nearly caused my death.

With a spike that hung from the fife-rail, I drew out the split-pin that connected the two halves of the brake-band, and at once saw that their linings were missing!

Only bare iron had been gripping the brake-drum.

Now, on all our halyard winches these linings were made of *lignum vitæ* wood, and it was the Carpenter's duty to renew them just as often as wear made this advisable. In this case, I would have been more than willing to believe that the wooden linings had worn completely away—but for the fact that even the holding-rivets were missing, and there was not a vestige of wood visible.

I felt myself trembling. . . . Suddenly I remembered that Müller, as I have said, had been up on the yard before me. Thus it was absolutely certain that no-one had tampered with the winch since my coming on deck at Eight Bells—or Müller would have been the victim instead of me. . . .

And then I caught sight of a wooden wedge beneath the winch and at once realized that if this had been jammed into the cogs while Müller was aloft, the barrel of the winch would not revolve and allow the yard to fall.

Yes—and when I went aloft, anyone, while appearing casually to pass the winch, could quite easily knock out the wedge and leave my weight on the yard to do the rest.

Furthermore, it was absolutely certain that the brake-linings—which had been deliberately removed, rivets and all—could not have been missing for any length of time, for, otherwise, the brake would very soon have entirely ceased to function. Thus, much against my will and against the sturdy objection of instinct, experience, and everyday common sense, I was forced to the appalling conclusion that there had been a definite premeditated attempt upon my life—and that the Mate knew of it. Knew of it, if indeed he had not instigated it.

'Meet with an accident' indeed!

§4

Repressing an almost uncontrollable impulse to rush aft, denounce the Mate as a would-be murderer, and show him something in that line for himself, I remembered that I had not a vestige of proof against him.

The crafty Peddersen would act the part of a man thoroughly ashamed of having failed in his duty, and would appear deeply and honestly to regret having neglected the winch; and he would swear that the brake had been in precisely its present condition for months past.

Also recalling Dacre's experience with the opium "chlorodyne", I realized that a mighty lot of good I should do by denouncing the Mate to the Captain.

No, we had to accept the fact that the ship was commanded by a mad Captain, a lunatic who was probably criminal and possibly homicidal: also the fact that the Mate was a weak and despicable rogue, ready to turn criminal at the urge of greed or hatred: that, owing to their attitude, the Third Mate had no influence or power over the men whatsoever: that the Carpenter whose influence in the fo'c'sle was not only paramount but so bad that it could scarcely be worse—was, for some reason, the special protégé and ally of the Captain: that, among the crew were at least four unmitigated scoundrels, creatures of the Carpenter, and without fear or respect for the Captain or the Mate: and that the bulk of the crew were foolish men, easily swayed and easily led by the Carpenter and his gang.

And the men already openly talking about "Ship-owners" and "Shell-backs"!

The Second Mate, the Third Mate and I . . . Geordie and Beauty: perhaps Fagin . . . Would Berghen and Blancke, Carrol and Church, stand in with us whole-heartedly, if it came to a show-down?

No wonder poor Dacre was worried and anxious about the girl with whom he was so passionately in love. . . . It seemed to me as I stood for a moment in thought, that our only hope lay in being as cunning as the others—or a little more so.

By now the Watch on deck and the Carpenter Peddersen had gathered round the winch, and I proceeded forthwith to exercise some of that cunning that we so badly needed and in which I knew myself to be rather deficient.

I played the simple sailor-man, and, pointing out the absence of brake-linings to Peddersen, I addressed him in true ship-board style and as though I were entirely unsuspicious.

"Look at that, Peddersen! a helluva fine Carpenter you are, eh?" I gibed. "If I couldn't do my job better than you do yours, I'd jump over the side and pollute the sea with the carcase of a rotten useless soldier. . . . It's no thanks to you that I wasn't smashed to pieces, you square-headed shirker."

So relieved was Peddersen to think that his share in the crime was undetected—for he had never expected me to survive to confront him—that not only did he meekly accept my rebuke, but became almost apologetic.

By the faces of the others who stood around, I could at once distinguish those who were deceived by him from those who were fully aware of the true facts.

Slim Johes and Müller exchanged a rapid and most meaning glance, and the mouth of each wore a slightly sarcastic half-grin. Patsy Hooligan rotated among the group declaring that,

"Begod, the young fella was born lucky, I say. I say the young fella's born lucky, begod," and earned my gratitude by being obviously glad that I had been 'lucky'.

And it was with further feelings of gratitude that I heard Hamblin say to Peddersen.

"Chips, Ah'm tellin' ye—if ye'd gi'en me a skeer like yon, Ah'd ha' taken the livin' hide off ye. Ah would so, if Ah hong for it."

Before Peddersen could reply, the Mate considered it time to appear on the scene, for—either because the remainder of his conscience troubled him or because he hadn't the nerve to stay and witness the effect of his handiwork—he had disappeared, on sending me aloft.

"What's all this? What's all this about?" he asked, on joining us.

"I'm just telling the Carpenter exactly what I think of him, Sir,"

I replied. "While I was aloft, the winch-brake failed, and it was only by a miracle that I didn't break my neck and every bone in my body. . . . I say he's been too slack about his work—sprained ankle or not."

"Good God, Chips!" exclaimed the Mate, registering surprise and indignation quite realistically. "What the hell are you thinking about to let the brake-linings get like that? Go at once and look at the other winches—before somebody gets hurt."

It was quite well done, but why did he blush? Why did that slow dark red flush spread over his face as I stared at him?

"Now, Sons, get busy," he bustled on, in a great hurry. "Quit this chinning and get a move on. Now then, let's get the yard hoisted."

"You seem to have had a bit of a narrow escape, boy," said the Mate, as soon as we were alone, and it seemed to me that he was unable, though more than willing, to leave the subject or me alone.

"A narrow escape, a narrow escape," he added, as though, with nothing to say, he yet must talk.

"Quite a narrow escape—quite a narrow escape," he repeated.

"Oh, not really, Sir," I said, as though quite unconcerned. "I knew I was safe enough—but that didn't excuse the Carpenter's carelessness and laziness."

As I hoped, Smeeker rose to the bait.

"How did you know you were 'safe enough'?" he asked.

"Because I'm not to die at sea," I replied.

"What! How do you know?"

"Oh, we Highlanders have the 'second sight'. I have, anyhow, and so had my father and grandfather. We had an old Highland nurse too, who used to make wonderful prophecies that all came true, always. She foretold my father's death—both the time and the manner—years before he died."

"I've heard of that sort of thing," said the Mate. "Old Scotch people. . . . Old witches and gipsies and the like."

"Oh yes, it's true enough," I assured him, "about the Highland 'second sight'. So I'm perfectly certain nothing will happen to me on this ship or any other."

The Mate stared at me, looking the mean, ignorant, credulous fool that he was.

"Yes, and another thing," I meandered on. "She told me that not only should I escape the sea and die a natural death on land, but that anybody that ever tried to kill me by any means, would himself be killed by those same means, if you understand me. And anybody who tried to hurt me would himself be hurt in that same way."

"Very interesting," growled the Mate.

"Yes, Sir, very. She was a wonderful old woman, and nothing that she prophesied has ever failed to come true, so far . . ."

I thought this a very good effort for a person not greatly skilled or practised in lying. And fearing that the Mate might now ask questions difficult to answer, I observed that I ought to strike Seven Bells at once, and call the Watch Below in time for dinner.

As I walked aft, leaving the Mate standing obviously deep in thought, I wondered whether my first essay in meeting cunning with cunning had had any effect. I didn't want to make the foolish mistake of under-rating my enemy, but I did feel that the Mate was just the sort of credulous and weak-minded oaf to swallow tripe of that sort.

At Eight Bells, I found Dacre ready for dinner, apparently quite recovered, and intending to resume work at four p.m.

As we ate I related the happenings of the morning.

"Well, Sinbad son," said Dacre, smiling at me very kindly, "thank God you've met with your accident and are none the worse for it. We've both 'met with accidents' now. . . . Who's behind it?"

"And who's next, Dacre?" I pondered. "And will it be a case of 'third time does it'? God grant it isn't the Second Mate."

"Yes," agreed Dacre. "One has a sort of feeling that God's on His bridge, all's well with the ship, more or less, while Mr. Hammerson's all-right."

"Yes," I pondered, "but they've got the same sort of feeling, too, of course, and that makes it all the more likely that an 'accident' is staged for him. They know . . ."

"Who are 'they', Sinbad?"

"Yes, who are 'they'?" I replied.

"I believe his worst enemies are in the fo'c'sle; those four he man-handled for shirking in the storm and leaving the ship to sink—Villa, Jake, Müller and Slim Johes. . . . On the other hand, the Captain and the Mate know perfectly well that they could never corrupt him to join in any hanky-panky games of ship-stealing—if such a thing is possible."

"No, nor stand in with them over any funny business of disposing of something tremendously valuable belonging to Mrs.

Bryndal—if there were any such thing."

Further we discussed the Second Mate, the situation and our line of conduct, so far as it was possible for us to have a line at all.

"Good God," cried Dacre, suddenly springing to his feet. "What is this ship? A floating lunatic asylum? A thieves' kitchen on the high seas? It's getting fantastic, a hell, a nightmare. It's absurd, it's impossible. And that poor girl . . ."

"We never had that talk with Mr. Hammerson," I interrupted Dacre. "Geordie had come to fetch us to him last night when we found you'd been poisoned."

"Yes, we must fix up another . . ." said Dacre, "and we'll try to get it into his head that he really must watch out. . . ."

But as I was preparing to turn in, for my afternoon watch below, we had welcome proof that the Second Mate had not forgotten my request, and that he was wide awake to all that was going on in the ship.

With the extremely quick, neat and quiet movements that I had always admired in so big, powerful, and bulky a man, he stepped into the half-deck.

"The Steward tells me that the main upper-to'gallant yard let ye down this forenoon watch, Dysart," he said quietly. "D'ye suppose there was any funny business at the back of it?"

"There's no room for doubt, Sir," I replied. "And none for proof either, I'm afraid. The brake linings had been taken clean away—but the Carpenter will tell you that they've always been missing. And he'd be very hurt if anyone disbelieved him."

"Y-e-e-e-s," mused Mr. Hammerson, "and that yeller-faced snake is going to be hurt—real serious hurt—before long. Y-e-e-e-s, I can guess when he pinched the brake-linings. It was during all the excitement of the Third Mate's poisoning. I remember wondering how Peddersen came to be out of his cart just then—and him such a whale for soaking his head[20] . . . Y-e-e-e-s, there's some real bad men in this outfit . . . who think they're going to work some funny wonders.

"Perhaps so," he went on. "But when they start trying to lynch decent hard-working lads who never did them an inch of harm, they're coming up against me. . . . And I can play 'bad man' meself, some, when I'm put to it. . . . You two boys can trust me to watch out for ye."

---

[20] *Sleeping.*

I found this very good talk. Mr. Hammerson evidently saw and heard more than we had supposed.

"The slimy son of a sodden soldier," he growled. "I'll deal with him—salut'ry and sudden."

I wondered exactly to whom he referred—the Captain, the Mate, the Carpenter, Villa or Müller, and as I was about to ask him, Dacre suddenly remarked in an unnecessarily loud voice,

"Well no, Sir, I don't mind lending it to you, of course, so long as you'll let me have it back. You will keep an eye on it, won't you, Sir—it's a damn good fid."

And from the bottom of his bunk he produced his favourite green-heart fid.

Handing it to Mr. Hammerson, he bent over and pointed to it.

"The Captain's on the poop," he whispered, "and staring straight in here."

"Look, I'll have ye called in the middle watch," answered the Second Mate in a low tone, "and we'll have the confab that we missed last night."

As he went out, he added loudly, with a laugh at Dacre,

"All-right, all-right, Mister. I'll not lose the run of yer bloomin' fid. You can trust me."

CHAPTER XII

In the very next watch—the first dog watch—proof was forthcoming that the Second Mate's statement was not an idle one, and that he really could and would 'watch out' for us.

On that day, I seemed fated to spend most of my time in climbing the main rigging, and as he lounged on the poop, even the Mate smiled to see Dacre pointing to a main lower to'gallant bunt-line that was chafing the sail. But not being made to hoist, the lower to'gallant yard would not come down and, as it was Dacre who had sent me to the job, I went very willingly and without any qualms.

Already my escape of the morning seemed ancient history.

As I expected, I found that I could overhaul and stop the bunt-line without going on to the yard. With one foot on the ratline and my arm crooked round a shroud, I was able to work with both hands, and still be so secure that nothing could cause me to fall.

Whether Müller who was painting round the foot of the mizzen mast had actually broken that bunt-line stop—by order; or whether, seeing me, as he supposed, on the yard itself, he thought he had a good opportunity to succeed where the Mate had failed, I never discovered.

In any case, what he did not know was that he was being watched by the Second Mate. The Second Mate's room was just inside the starboard poop alley-way, and in fine weather the alley-way door, giving access to the main deck, was kept open and hooked back.

In the *Valkyrie*, it was customary for the Second Mate to relieve the Mate for meals, and on this particular evening, expecting the tea-bell to be rung at any minute, Mr. Hammerson was smoking by his door and looking out on to the deck.

Invisible to Müller, he could see that worthy's every movement.

And, when he saw our Mr. Müller stoop to take a good look up at me and then lay down his paint-brush, Mr. Hammerson suddenly sat up and took notice.

When the German lifted the coiled-up spare part of the main lower to'gallant brace from its pin in the mizzen fife-rail, Mr. Hammerson became deeply interested. When Müller carefully and silently laid it down on the deck, he stiffened to attention.

And then, convinced that Müller intended to let go the brace, so that—as he hoped and expected—I should be thrown clean overboard by the spring of the suddenly released yard, the Second Mate moved as only he could.

It was typical of Mr. Hammerson that although he could have got in the all-important first blow, he refrained from taking advantage of a man's surprise.

Müller had actually taken one turn of the brace itself from its pin, when he was seized by the neck and the seat of his trousers and thrown clear of the fife-rail.

"Put up yer hands, ye foul murderin' swine," said Mr. Hammerson, and it was also typical of Müller and his kind that he put up only his left hand, to guard, while with his right he drew his sheath-knife.

I've no doubt that, had he known the number of times that the Second Mate had faced that sort of situation, Müller would have leapt back and thrown the knife—a trick in which he was very highly skilled—but he did not, and as his right hand came round from drawing the knife from its sheath at the back of his belt, the hand was stayed, as a terrific kick on the right wrist sent the knife flying.

"Now we start fair, ye square-head skunk," growled the Second Mate, and a moment later his right hand feinted and his left shot out, catching Müller fair and square between the eyes with a blow that sent him staggering back.

Leaping for the knife, the Second Mate threw it overboard. Müller, too late, also scrambled for the knife, and then rose to his feet.

Seeing the scuffle by the break of the poop, and not then knowing what it was about, I slid down a back-stay, and arrived in time to hear the Captain bawl in an angry tone,

"Why are you assaulting that man, Mr. Hammerson?"

"Because he's a murderer," shouted the Second Mate. "Whilst Dysart was on the main lower to'gallant, I caught the swine in the very act of letting go the weather brace.

"Yes," he added, "and I'm now going to do to him what I'll do to any other murdering, back-stabbing bastard—*whether Aft or For'ard*—that tries to murder a better man than himself! Yes, and you can watch me."

Mr. Hammerson was certainly angry.

"Hands up," he said, as he swung round again on Müller.

And with an apparently harmless easy-looking movement, he gave the German his pet twisting right-hand tap on the jaw, and the big fellow sagged, insensible.

"And that's the way I'll handle any other bloody murderer on board this ship," he said, staring up at the Mate who had joined the Captain at the top of the weather poop-ladder.

"Ah!" said the Captain, smiling tremendously. "So! But be careful, Mr. Hammerson, do be careful. Mind you don't meet with an accident."

"Same to you, Sir," replied the Second Mate as with fists on hips he stood and outstared the Captain.

Brave words from a brave man, but . . .

For some reason my heart sank as I watched those two eyeing him from the poop, and the recovering Müller glaring at him from the deck like a broken-backed snake.

§2

Dacre evidently thought much as I did when I told him about the affair.

"Müller'll get him, I'm afraid," he said. "I'm afraid he'll get him. Mr. Hammerson is so chock full of confidence in himself, and of contempt for scum like Müller and Villa. . . . I'm dead scared they'll lay for him, some dark night, and get him."

"Well," said I, "we'll both try to warn him when he sends for us in the middle watch to-night."

"Yes," agreed Dacre, "we shan't get much sleep to-night."

"Well, we ought to have a pretty quiet time between eight and midnight," I said.

But before midnight, Dacre found that it was not only the Second Mate who had need of special vigilance in the night watches.

Just after Seven Bells had been struck, Dacre had occasion to go for'ard.

Returning aft and passing the for'ard house, his keen ears heard a curious whistle and what he thought to be a whisper, coming out of the pitch darkness just above his head.

On top of the house, a four-inch wire tow-rope and a ten-inch hemp "spring" had been roughly coiled on battens laid thwart-ship. The combined weight of these ropes amounted to something enormous.

Subconsciously aware of this, and affected by the prevailing tension, Dacre's mind was not only sharply alert, but filled with suspicion. As, hearing the whisper, he had instinctively and instantaneously stopped, he was, as he realized in a flash, in a position of great danger, if he were in any danger at all. Had not that sibilant whisper—neither too quiet to be unheard nor too loud to sound natural and realistic—been uttered with the idea and intention of making him stop?

To have got clear of the house by running aft or for'ard would have taken too long, if someone on the roof were aiming at him with a knife, a grain, or some missile of heavy weight.

So, almost as he heard the whisper, he made a dive into the scuppers. There, sheltered by the pin-rail, he escaped being so much as touched by the mass of wire and hemp that crashed on to the spot that he had occupied in the very second that it fell.

Hearing the crash, I dashed out from the half-deck.

Although the lifting of the ends of the battens, by which act the mass was dislodged, must have required the strength of at least three men, there was not a soul to be seen when he got clear, and though he dashed straight thence into the darkened fo'c'sle, there was neither movement nor sound, other than the breathing of sleeping men.

Informed that the weather fo'c'sle door was blocked, the Mate came and surveyed the obstacle with apparent surprise and loudly wondered how in hell, with a ship so steady, it could possibly have fallen there.

"We'll discuss the how and why with the Captain to-morrow morning," observed Dacre, and set about the clearing of the deck.

In order to obviate bringing out the Watch Below to help with the heavy task, the look-out man was called from the fo'c'sle-head to bear a hand as well—and I was not in the least surprised to find that it was Müller.

From the top of the house to the fo'c'sle-head was but a short distance and could be covered very quickly indeed by a man in a hurry. . . .

We were making good headway with the job of returning the wire tow-rope to the top of the house, when the Mate, with a tremendous oath, suddenly asked what that daft Irish orphan at the wheel thought he was doing to get the ship all aback. What in hell was he up to?

Patsy Hooligan was at the wheel and as he appeared to be making no attempt whatsoever to get the ship back on her course, the Mate went aft to let the helmsman hear something to his disadvantage. Close on his departure came a hoarse cry,

"A hand to the wheel!"
followed by,

"Lay aft, the Watch!"
and wondering what on earth had happened, we promptly and willingly ceased work and made for the poop.

There we found the wheel untended, and the Mate bending over a figure that lay huddled in a heap by the wheel grating.

It was so utterly unlike Smeeker to have the confidence—or the courage—to strike a man, whatever the provocation or offence, that I stood and stared in amazement.

The Mate looked up.

"You, there! Dysart!" he said. "Away and call the Captain and the Steward, quick."

But as was soon evident, poor Patsy Hooligan was stone dead before ever the Mate got to him—and neither the Captain's authority nor Doc's rude skill could be of any avail.

Patsy Hooligan was dead. . . .

With a look of intense surprise on his poor stupid face, he had passed beyond all earthly assistance. Never again would he haul on sheet and brace, and chant of giving up the sea and buying a farm.

"This poor Shell-back will never be a Ship-owner," said I to myself, and as the thought passed through my mind I again saw Captain Bryndal's look of savage—nay devilish—hatred when Patsy had sung his foolish verse about Shell-backs and Ship-owners in the forenoon watch. . . .

I experienced a beastly goose-skin shiver; and wondered of what Patsy had died.

News of the tragedy quickly spread, and someone—Doc, I suspected—had called the Second Mate.

Aloud he uttered my thought.

"I wonder what he died of," he said.

"Heart failure," replied Captain Bryndal.

"May be," mused the Second Mate, kneeling beside the body. "May be, but he don't look like it to me. . . . No. . . . I've seen just that look on the face of a man who had—heart failure—through getting in the way of a .45 revolver bullet. . . . H'm, with all respect, Sir, I think you'd be wise to have a kind of post-mortem to-morrow, by daylight."

"Of course," said the Captain. "But why talk nonsense about revolver bullets? Can't you see the man's absolutely unwounded, uninjured? There's no blood about him, is there?"

Silence followed the Captain's words.

No, certainly there was nothing to indicate death by violence —no blood, no bruise, no mark, no sign whatever of anything in the nature of a struggle. Evidently he had just slumped down from the wheel, dead.

The silence was broken by an eerie sound—the high-pitched voice of mad Larry O'Toole.

" 'Twas wan av thim birrds av prey," he wailed. "I saw ut wid me own oys."

The Captain whirled round upon him like lightning.

" 'Tis the Truth o' God," cried Larry again. "I saw ut . . .

"Aye," he added, "thim birrds av prey is hell on *Ship-owners*."

And again I saw the Mate cross himself.

Seeing that it was only Larry O'Toole who had spoken, the Captain turned back to the body.

"Lay this poor fellow on the after hatch, men," he said, and as Patsy Hooligan was laid to sleep his last sleep upon the hatch whereon I had so often slept, someone, thinking only of the living and of his watch below, struck One Bell on the taffrail immediately above the corpse.

"My Lord!" murmured Dacre, as we undressed a few minutes later. "Here's the beginning of real business. We've had battle, murder and sudden death in this hell-struck packet for some days, but I never thought that poor harmless old 'Ship-owner' would be the first to go. . . . And—what's more, Sinbad son—the Mate didn't, either. I watched him like a cat watching a mouse, and it was a real shock to him. He's a bewildered and a badly rattled man. He's got no objection to our being done-in, but this is a blow to him, for he feels that either the 'Shell-backs' have got one in first, or else that there's a traitor among the 'Ship-owners.'"

"Why? Don't you think a weak heart did cause Hooligan's death, then?" I asked.

"Yes, I do. A heart that somebody suddenly weakened for him," answered Dacre. "Weak heart be damned. Patsy Hooligan was as strong as a gorilla.

"Yes, somebody weakened his heart for him, all-right," he went on, "and the Second Mate thinks so, too. . . . I bet you he'll absolutely insist on that post-mortem being held in full daylight to-morrow."

"But there were no signs of violence on Hooligan's body," I argued.

"No, there were no gaping gory wounds. His throat wasn't cut nor his skull cracked—and he wasn't riddled with bullet-holes. But quite apart from giving a man a dose of poison in a tot of rum, or sand-bagging him in thug style—there are ways of killing a man that leave practically no mark—so I've been told. Anyhow, I'm certain Mr. Hammerson's got more than a suspicion.

"And another thing; we're going to get him to join you and me in a word with the Old Man about this epidemic of falling yards and tow-ropes. Mr. Hammerson knows all about my opium business and what happened to you—both Peddersen's effort with the winch and Müller's with the main lower to'gallant brace. When he sends for us to-night, I'm going to tell him all about that ton of wire tow-rope just missing me. I bet you he'll join us and make the Old Man listen."

For a minute or two we sat silent, busy with our thoughts, and doubtless Dacre was, like myself, pondering the really amazing past and perfectly incalculable future.

"But look here, Dacre," I broke out, "it's absurd. It's fantastic. These things aren't done."

"Anything may be done in a ship with a mad Captain, a weak Mate, a couple of pretty women, and a gang of criminal desperadoes."

"That was deliberate attempt at murder to-night."

"What, tipping the stuff off the house on to me?"

"Yes," I said. "But why . . . *why*? What's the idea? What's the game? After all, it is a ship—and not a criminal-lunatic asylum full of homicidal maniacs."

"What's the game?" echoed Dacre. "I think it's perfectly clear. The 'Ship-owners' are simply going methodically and quietly to work to exterminate and obliterate the 'Shell-backs'; that is to say, those whom they *know* to be absolutely incorruptible—utterly incapable of criminal practice of any sort. They pay the Second Officer and me and you, and probably Geordie and Beauty—if not Fagin—the compliment of counting us out. Therefore they've got to *knock* us out."

"Yes, but who, once again, are 'they'? Where do the Captain and the Mate stand?"

"Dunno, Son. It's a Chinese puzzle. Wheels within wheels. It seems to me there's one gang, which includes the Captain and the Mate, that is as inimical to the 'Ship-owner' gang as both gangs are to us; and I believe the gangs overlap, too, if you know what I mean."

"Yes, you mean that there are some beauties that do or may belong to all three."

"Just so. Take brother Fagin, for example. He's been fairly licking the Mate's boots, lately; he's hand in glove with Peddersen; and he's—our friend, and a member of our mess."

"Well, suppose we said there's a Captain's party, with a dangerous game of their own, and a Peddersen's party, calling themselves 'Ship-owners'. What's their game?"

"Exactly. What is it? Probably two dogs after the same bone."

"But I thought Peddersen was the Captain's white-headed boy."

"So he is; and so he will be, as long as the Captain's going *his* way. But d'you suppose either of them wouldn't cut the other's throat for his own advantage. . . . Really, it sounds like an idiot talking in a nightmare, but I do believe that the 'Ship-owner' gang are trying to dispose of us—as hindrances: and the Captain's gang actually are disposing of the 'Ship-owners' as not only hindrances but rivals; and I believe Patsy Hooligan was killed, as a 'Ship-owner' by a 'Captain-ite'."

"Captain's gang a bit more efficient, eh?" I mused.

"Yes. No bungling. The 'Ship-owner' gang bungled me twice and you twice."

"Well, who are the 'Captain's gang' then?"

"God knows. As I say, they overlap, and the biggest puzzle of the lot is provided by the fact that Peddersen, the leader of the Ship-owners, is up to his neck in the Captain's game—or he wouldn't have been unscrewing the letters of the ship's name on the quiet. . . ."

Too sleepy to continue the discussion, I resolved that, when he sent for us within the next hour or so, I would give Mr. Hammerson an unvarnished account of how Patsy Hooligan had sung his verse about 'Shell-backs' and 'Ship-owners', and of the fiendish expression with which the Captain had glared at him for doing so.

With that decision in my mind, I fell asleep.

§3

But without any orders from Mr. Hammerson, we were, alas, destined to an earlier and sadder awakening.

For scarcely had I shut my eyes, it seemed, when I heard Geordie's expected voice bidding me to "wake oop". But, as on the previous occasion, Geordie was obviously excited and perturbed.

"Good Lord, man!" I growled, confused and half awake. "Surely Dacre's not ill again, is he?"

"No, Son, I'm not," answered Dacre for himself. "Geordie

248

says the Second Mate can't be found. He's disappeared."

"Aye, he has an' all," wailed Geordie, who had a dog-like hero-worshipping admiration and affection for Mr. Hammerson. "Theer's not a sign of him. Ah seen him creep for'ard, quiet-like, and as he seemed a long time coomin' back, Ah thocht Ah'd go for'ard meself—an' th' man on the look-oot sweers he's seen nowt of him."

"You haven't called the Mate or the Captain?" asked Dacre.

"Naw," replied Geordie. "Ah'm not wantin' to look a domn fule, if th' Second Mate's havin' a quiet smoke somewheer, or gone doon the forepeak."

"Quite right," said Dacre. "Where's Fagin?"

"At the wheel."

"And Beauty?"

"Asleep b' th' wheel-box."

"Then go and wake him, and he can come for'ard with us and help look for the Second Mate. That'll make four of us—and in this mad hell-packet, there's safety in numbers."

A minute later, headed by Dacre, we sallied forth.

For'ard, we found Müller on the look-out, and to me this seemed ominous. If there were one blackguardly murderous ruffian on the ship who, more than another, hated the Second Mate, it was Müller—though Villa and Jake must have run him pretty close.

Müller, of course declared that he hadn't seen the Second Mate, and added that he didn't want to. Dacre curtly informed Müller that he wasn't interested in Müller's wants.

In the fo'c'sle, the Port Watch were apparently all fast asleep in their bunks, and the Starboard Watch, depending on Müller to call them when necessary, dozed on their sea-chests.

On being disturbed, Jake growled that he hadn't got the blasted Second Greaser; he didn't carry him about with him.

"No," said Dacre, "it would take ten men like you to do that."

The negro, Brown, with an impudent laugh, invited us to search him.

The Brazil nut, Paulo, affected to search himself. . . .

Becoming more and more anxious, we even went to such foolish lengths as to look in the lamp-room, the paint-locker, the Bosun's locker, and such places where Mr. Hammerson would only be if he were dead.

At length, having satisfied ourselves that he was not at the fore end of the ship, we went aft, hoping against hope, to see whether, unperceived by Geordie, he had returned from for'ard and gone to his room.

As we feared, there was no trace of him aft.

Looking at his pipes on the rack, and his oilskins hanging on the bulkhead, I resolutely thrust from my mind the intolerable idea that the burly masterful presence, that had so long occupied this room, would know it no more.

"It's the Old Man's pidgin now, Sinbad," said Dacre. "You go and simply tell him that the Second Mate cannot be found, and say that, until relieved, I'm on the poop."

Waking at the first light tap on his door, Captain Bryndal showed not the slightest surprise at what was surely strange news; and one would have thought it was a perfectly normal thing for the Officer of the Watch completely to disappear when on duty.

A minute after I'd left him, the Captain appeared on deck.

"Well," he said, "if four of you have made a complete and thorough search—there's nothing more to be done to-night. Blount and Dysart, go below. I'll keep watch myself until the Mate comes on at Eight Bells."

There was nothing for it but to obey the Captain's order.

Returning to the deck-house we sat down, silent, in the darkness.

Personally, I felt stunned, appalled . . . frightened.

I knew—I absolutely knew—that Mr. Hammerson was gone. . . . Our friend, our tower of strength.

I could have cried.

I felt more like crying than I had done since, as a small child, I had suffered bitterly from some slight, some coldness, some small injustice on the part of my mother . . . one of those little mental cruelties that can almost break a child's heart.

I felt broken-hearted then, as I thought of that straight strong man, simple, forthright, and fundamentally kindly and good-hearted.

> " 'He was my friend,
> " 'Faithful and just to me . . .'"

I said aloud,

I could say no more. My voice broke, and I laid down my head upon my arms that were folded on the table. I was glad it was dark.

And I hope that there was but little that was selfish in my emotion, frightened as I felt at the loss of him who but a few hours ago had said,

"You two boys can trust me to watch out for ye," and, defying the Captain himself, had punished the man whom he had caught trying to murder me.

Then anger came to my aid.

"Dacre," I said, jumping up, "I'll find out who did it, and I'll kill him with my bare hands . . ."

"You've taken the words out of my mouth, Son," growled Dacre.

Silence.

"Those murdering swine!" The cry suddenly burst from my friend. "They've knocked him on the head from behind and dumped him overboard like they would a dead rat. Aye, and perhaps before he was dead. . . . Our Hammerson . . ." And I heard choking sounds from Dacre that made me thrust my hands against my ears and again be thankful for the darkness.

"And those two filthy skunks aft," he said later, "the Captain and the Mate. If they didn't actually fix it . . ."

"One can't think that, Dacre," I interrupted.

"If they didn't actually fix it, they're rubbing their hands with glee that some of those skulking curs in the fo'c'sle—those 'Ship-owners'—have murdered the finest man aboard. . . . One of the finest men that ever stepped. By God, if I only had a gun . . ."

"Let's talk sense, old man," I soothed him, for Dacre and I had now got to keep our heads—if we wanted to keep our lives. "Which is the likeliest—that it's the private feud of Müller whom he twice beat up, and Villa and Jake, both of whom he struck and who swore to get him; or that it's what you might call the public feud of the whole of Peddersen's damned gang of 'Ship-owners'; or, again, that it's plain common murder, arranged by the Captain and the Mate, of the man who was the chief obstacle to the carrying out of their plan at Cape Town?"

"God knows," groaned Dacre. "If it was the last, I'll take my oath that Peddersen was the instrument—or found the instrument the Captain wanted."

"There'd be no lack of them," I said. "A nod and a wink to Müller, Villa and Jake, not to mention Slim Johes. . . . What are we to do, Dacre?"

"What *can* we do?" he answered.

There was no softness about Dacre and myself. We were strong; we were normally and sufficiently game and plucky, and up to that night we had been pleased to rate ourselves as 'tough chaps' and 'hard citizens', if not hard cases.

But I am afraid there crept into bed that night two daunted tail-down boys, their miserable minds divided between fear for themselves and grief for the lost friend whom they now realized that they had really loved.

CHAPTER XIII

Nowhere is the presence of a dead man less welcome than on ship-board, and by the first showing of the sun's rim above the horizon Patsy Hooligan had already been prepared for a sailor's grave.

There was none now who dared insist on the post-mortem that the Second Mate had demanded; and with the main yard aback, we stood in orderly array, reverent and bare-headed round the gangway.

Dignified and correct as a Bishop, the Captain read the Burial Service, but in spite of the beauty of the well-intoned phrases of that wonderful Service, my thoughts were elsewhere, my blood was boiling, and scarcely could I keep motionless and silent as I thought of my murdered friend, my patron and protector who, with all his mighty strength alive in him, had suddenly been struck down, suddenly made as nothing; and forthwith flung like a dog into the sea, cast forth into the depths without benefit of prayer.

He was a Man . . . and could be spared far, far, less than this poor old buffoon to whom we were giving Christian burial, and whom we were about ceremoniously to commit to those waters that he had always so detested and so feared.

I looked at the Captain's face; I looked at the body on the grating: I listened to the Captain's sonorous voice and looked once more at the canvas-sewn form: I looked again into the Captain's eyes, and I knew. I simply knew that he was reading the Burial Service over the body of the man whom he had murdered. I had a—vision.

'Second sight'? I don't know. But I did know that this solemn hypocrite had killed the man who lay at his feet. . . . I saw him do it. . . . From behind. . . .

Had he killed Mr. Hammerson, too—not with his own hand, but with that of some foul hireling? If only I knew *that*!

Well, and what could I do, if I did know it?

With a start, I saw the hatch tilted, and mechanically I joined in the mumbling of the Lord's Prayer.

We had finished with Patsy Hooligan.

"Trim the yards and let the men have their coffee, Mr. Smeeker," said the Captain. "After that, I want both Watches, aft."

"Huh! That means a thorough searching enquiry, carefully arranged and fully intended to discover—exactly nothing," said Dacre to me as we left the poop.

At Three Bells, according to order, All Hands mustered at the break of the poop, and, so that none from the fo'c'sle should be absent, Doc relieved the wheel.

Leaning over the poop rail, with the Mate at his back, the Captain addressed the motley assemblage below him.

"As you know, men," he said, "we had the terrible misfortune last night to lose that splendid officer, our Second Mate. I've called you aft to see if any of you can give me useful information that might help to solve this shocking mystery.

"Now then, I understand that Stowe was the last to see Mr. Hammerson alive. Isn't that so, my lad?"

"No! Ah never said that, Sir," piped up Geordie's shrill voice, sturdily. "How do Ah know who was last t' see him alive? Ah said Ah was t' last to see him leave t' poop. Who seen him after he got for'ard, Ah dawn't knaw. . . . But Ah'd like to," he added bravely.

"Do you know why he went forward, my lad?"

"That Ah do an' all, Sir," was the prompt reply. "Ah strook Two Bells, an' after a bit, t' Second Mate sings oot to knaw why bell wasna strook for'ard.

" 'Hi, are ye asleep on the look-oot there?' he shouts. An' when he gets no answer, he creeps quietly for'ard t' see what Look-out was oop to. . . . An' Ah never set e'es on him after."

Geordie's voice seemed about to break, and I saw that he swallowed two or three times.

"Very good. Now then, who was on the look-out?" asked the Captain.

"Me. I vas," growled Müller.

"Didn't you hear Two Bells struck, nor the Second Mate's hail?" asked the Captain.

"*Nein*, I vas hear not a sound. And I tells you for why, Cap'n. Yust about dat time, I go down for trim the port light. *Ja*, or else it vas go out."

"That's not his job, and he's a damned liar," said Dacre audibly.

"Oh, you went down to trim the port light, did you? Yes? And when you went back up on to the fo'c'sle-head, you neither saw nor heard anything of Mr. Hammerson?"

"Dat vas so, Cap'n. Me, I vas not see, and I vas not hear, *anyt'ing*."

During this dialogue I had been studying the expressions of the hard faces of the men about me, wondering whether it were possible to detect any signs of a guilty conscience.

Slim's air, genuine or assumed, was that of one who found the whole proceedings trivial, boring, and unworthy of his attention. Carrol and Church both looked stern, indignant, and at the same time, worried; Blancke and Berghen appeared anxious, shocked and somewhat scared; Hamblin's face wore a heavy frown, and a pulse beat in his cheek. I put him down as puzzled, amazed and very bothered. The giant, "Baby" Axenstern, stared vacuously at each speaker in turn, wide-eyed and open-mouthed.

In distinct contrast to the rest, Villa and Jake struck me as jaunty, pleased with themselves, with a devil-may-care attitude that would have been defiant if any defiance were called for.

Peddersen's countenance was utterly impassive, and, save for occasional gleams in his pale face, expressionless.

Larry O'Toole seemed most concerned of all—particularly with the need of driving away the "birrds" that apparently beat their wings continuously in the vicinity of his head.

Müller, the man in whom I was most interested of all, was wearing a mask of swollen, bruised and discoloured flesh, but maintained a perpetual scowl between his blackened eyes. And, while I had no means of judging whether his scowl was due to the anger caused by fear and secret apprehension, or merely to memories of his recent thrashing by the missing man, I did notice that the Captain's next question and its answer gave evident relief to the anarchist, and caused him to brighten up considerably.

"Then I suppose I must log the Second Mate's disappearance as an unsolved mystery?" asked Captain Bryndal finally.

"Looks that way, Cap'n," volunteered Jake. "Anyone c'd see a week ago that he was going batty, and we in the fo'c'sle got no kind o' doubt among ourselves that he's committed sooicide. He never been the same since the big storm. Guess he got a sanaka-towzer on the bean, or somethink. Why only yesterday he beat up Müller here something cruel, just because the man shifted some gear to get on with his paintin'. . . . That's the way we figure it, Cap'n."

At the first suggestion that Mr. Hammerson was insane, old Carrol spat in anger and disgust, and it was only Church's strong grip on his arm that prevented the fine fellow from stepping forward and cursing Jake. As he angrily jerked away from Church, I heard the latter growl,

"Stow it, ye silly fool! D'ye want to make the next bloomin' mystery yerself? Go overboard next dark night, like the Second Officer?"

And, taking the point, Carrol acted on Church's excellent advice, and "stowed it".

Meanwhile Captain Bryndal smiled brightly and kindly upon Jake.

"I think you are probably quite right, my man," he said. "I myself noticed that poor Mr. Hammerson was behaving queerly and I happened to catch him in the act of striking Müller. Certainly his manner was very strange when I shouted to him to stop it. . . . Yes, yes . . . Of course, when we arrive in port there will be a proper Enquiry, at which some of you will be required to state your views."

"Perhaps—and perhaps not," said a voice.

But as the Captain swung quickly round to see who had spoken, there was nothing but enquiring innocence on Dacre's face.

Still carefully watching the expressions of the faces of the Captain's audience, I came to the conclusion that his ready adoption of the theory that the Second Mate had committed suicide was very agreeable to the Mate and to the "Peddersen Committee".

I felt quite certainly that the Captain's endorsement of Jake's suggestion relieved them of any qualms they might have had about the findings of a Court of Enquiry.

And then suddenly I saw, and saw with pleasure, their visible satisfaction turned to stark fear—fear so obvious in the case of the superstitious Smeeker, that his face paled and he seemed to sag at the knees as though about to fall upon them in an attitude of prayer. And this change upon the faces of Smeeker and those hardened sinners, Villa, Jake, Müller and Peddersen, was brought about by nothing more than the words of poor harmless Larry O'Toole.

"Bedad now, Sorr," he cried in a sudden silence. "Look! Look! Look at thim birrds! . . .'Tis the Second Mate comin' back, Sorr. An' Glory be to God! If he isn't bringin' ould Patsy Hooligan wid him!"

And he pointed to where a great albatross, closely followed by a solitary mollyhawk, sailed up, leisurely and majestically, from the south'ard and seemed to bear down upon the ship.

With the doubtful exception of Captain Bryndal, there probably was not a man present who did not, in the depths of his heart, firmly believe that the soul of a sailor, buried at sea, invariably takes the form of a sea-bird, and, in that shape, haunts the waters beneath which his body sank.

And, moreover, as every man there knew quite well that it was unusual to find two such species of seabird so far North, these ignorant and superstitious seamen must have regarded the arrival of these unwelcome, portentous and sinister visitors as convincing evidence of the truth of what Larry O'Toole had said.

For an appreciable time, in awe and dread, they watched that stately menacing approach; and, in utter silence, moved nor hand nor foot.

The Captain found his voice and broke the spell.

"Don't talk such blasted bosh," he growled at Larry, and turning to the men suddenly roared,

"That's all. Get out of it, you. Go and get on with your work."

But, as the men turned away, there were still many fearful glances at the following birds, and many black looks at the poor lunatic—the lunatic who, willy nilly, could but speak the dreadful truth.

"Turn your Watch to, and let the rest go below, Mister," growled the Captain to Smeeker as, dismayed, disgruntled, and depressed, the crowd dispersed.

CHAPTER XIV

Dacre and I talked about it and about, and got no for'arder.

There it was, plain, clear and simple. There were three factions on board, two of which overlapped, so to speak. That is to say, some members of each were members of both. And it appeared to be the definite policy, intention, and business of each of these two factions to destroy the members of the third.

To that third we belonged, with such members of the ship's company as were honest, decent, law-abiding people, who merely wished to go about their business in peace and quiet. Of this party, Mr. Hammerson had been murdered, and, but for good luck, or the protection of Providence, Dacre and I would have been murdered, for two definite attempts had been made upon the life of each of us.

"Now then," said Dacre, "why shouldn't you and I go to the Captain and tell him as much?"

"Because he knows it," said I.

"Well, why shouldn't we go to him and tell him that we know it—and what about it?"

"I'm game," said I. "It might clear the air. It might give him food for careful thought, and it cannot do any harm."

And forthwith we concocted a plan.

$\star$ $\star$ $\star$ $\star$ $\star$

Imbued with the spirit that inspired Drake and Nelson, Dacre and I mounted to the poop at Eight Bells and, endeavouring to look much mightier than we felt, crossed to the sacred weather-side and respectfully begged the favour of a few moments of conversation with our Captain.

This favour being graciously granted and a truly terrible grin bestowed upon us, Dacre, as the elder of the suppliants, acted as spokesman. And although I was not in a state of mind fully to appreciate his courage and ability, I admired the skill and delicacy with which he delivered what was, in effect, a speech—and a bold and clever one.

"Excuse me, Sir," he said, "but I think, and Dysart thinks, that unless you can change our luck for us, you will soon be reading the Burial Service on this ship for a third and a fourth time."

The Captain smiled cheerfully.

"We've both had two very narrow escapes as you know, Sir, and we can't hope to go on escaping like this by the skin of our teeth."

"No?" said the Captain, as his smile widened.

"No, Sir. And—so that our people shall know exactly how we have been persecuted and hounded . . . ."

"*What?*" cried the Captain, and his smile turned to a most wolfish snarl.

"Persecuted and hounded by Fate, Sir, of course. . . . We've both written, in triplicate, accounts of our adventures during the last few days—and also accounts of the murders . . . I mean the deaths . . . of the Second Mate and Patsy Hooligan—and we have each given a copy to three different persons."

"Ah! And whom did you favour, might one ask?" smiled the Captain suavely.

"Oh, curiously enough, before they accepted the letters, they pledged us to the strictest secrecy, Sir," invented Dacre instantly. "The foolish fellows seemed to think that something might happen to them if . . . ."

"If what?"

"If it were known, Sir."

"And," continued Dacre, "as, in those letters, we have asked our parents handsomely to reward the bearer, we feel quite certain that, if neither of us sees the end of this trip, at least one of the three bearers will see that the letters are delivered. Naturally we have told them that they will be rewarded."

"Ah!" smiled the Captain.

"Yes, Sir. . . . Of course you may wonder why we are not looking to you, our natural protector, to perform such a service for us. Well—to be quite candid, Sir, we both feel, and a good many others feel, that, in the next port, you are going to be so occupied with the *ship's business*, that we really cannot hope that you will have time to trouble about anything so insignificant as our affairs."

"Now that's very considerate of you," smiled the Captain, and really it was difficult to tell whether he were being sarcastic.

"You have acted very wisely, I think—*very* wisely. But I also think that our two recent catastrophes have got on your nerves a bit and made you a little jumpy."

"Our nerves certainly have suffered, Sir," agreed Dacre gravely.

"Ah, both nervous, eh? Well, I'll tell the Mate to take

particular care of you, and to be sure to give you no dangerous jobs."

And leaving the matter at that, Captain Bryndal turned about and walked away.

"Well, that's that," observed Dacre to me as we descended from the poop. "Done no harm and probably done no good."

"I don't know, old chap," I replied. "I shouldn't be surprised if it's done a lot of good. I think the idea of those letters of ours may occupy a considerable part of his leisure thought."

"May do," agreed Dacre. "Let's write some, shall we?"

§2

"Look at the Captain watching those two sea-birds," said Dacre, nudging me as we sat in the half-deck. "Do you know, I don't believe he likes them a bit more than the men do. . . . Curious bit of luck that they should have blown along just when they did, and decided to follow us. I believe every single man jack of this superstitious crowd is wondering whether his soul is going to be the next one to have webbed feet and a hooked beak."

"Yes," I agreed, "for the present, at any rate, the 'Ship-owners' are too thoroughly scared to do much harm. . . . Out of the mouths of babes and lunatics! Poor old Larry did us a good turn when he set their minds thinking along those lines."

"Look at him," cried Dacre. "Just look at him. What's the poor beggar up to now?"

To the obvious interest, if not to the great amusement, of the Captain and the Mate who leaned over the poop-rail and watched, Larry O'Toole now approached the half-deck door as though crossing a stream by means of stepping-stones.

"What are you doing, Larry?" asked Dacre.

"Oi'm afther moindin' the birrds' nests, ye see. Shure now, ye niver know whin they'll be buildin' next at all, at all, an' Oi'm not wan to put me fut on the poor cr'atures; and now that thim birrds o' prey is off the poop"—and it was perhaps only by coincidence that the Captain and the Mate just then disappeared—"ye'll not be moindin' if Oi stop to tark wid two dacent bhoys loike yerselves?"

Being assured that he was very welcome, he sat on the step of the half-deck and discoursed to us of birds and their ways; and before he went to his duties in the cook's galley, he added two pieces of information that gave us much food for thought.

"Now ye'll niver foind the birrds buildin' and nestin' in the manger for'ard," he informed us. "Niver. I'll tell ye whoy. It's beca'se there's a bag o' sand on the porrt soide, and thim birrds have no loikin' for sand, misused, at all.

"Ye see, bhoys," and here he leaned forward and whispered most confidentially, "the birrds are afther knowin' that there's some that put sand int' a thick seaboot-stocking—and not for a nest at all, at all. No, but for phwhat they call a sand-bag. Wan bat on the head wid the stockin', and the man they strike will foight no more, and no mark left. Tis bad stuff, is sand—used wrongly. . . . An' it's bein' used wrongly on this ship Oi'm tellin' yez, bhoys. An' look out ye don't get in the way of sand *misused*."

Encouraged by our obvious interest and understanding of what he was driving at, Larry added knowingly, with cunning winks,

"Aye, there's some loikes sand and there's some loikes better a long thin shpoike av a thing—loike a long needle—that likewise leaves no mark to show how ye doied; unless 'tis mebbe just a small red shpot loike a pimple. . . . Lookin' at ut, ye'd say, 'Ah, t' Hell wid ut. 'Tis nought but where a flea bit him.' But nevertheless b' me soul, if that goes into the heart av ye, ye're dead as Barney's bull or David's sow. . . . Glory be, and the houly saints preserve us, but there's some bad wans on this ship wid their murdherin' tricks that thim birrds can tell ye av."

After Larry's departure, Dacre and I looked at each other half amused and wholly thoughtful.

"Seems to me," observed Dacre at length, "that 'thim birrds' tell the little man a whole lot. He's as mad as a hatter, of course, but there's enough method in his madness to run a hatter's business."

"Yes," I agreed, "and I firmly believe he's just given us both information and a warning."

"That's what I think," said Dacre. "A broad hint that we had better look out for stockings that kick a damn sight harder than if they had a foot in them. . . . Though I don't quite get the 'needle' idea. I think a knife belonging to any man on this ship would leave a mark that was anything but 'a shmall red shpot loike a pimple'."

"No, I didn't quite follow that," I replied. "I suppose we are to understand that Mr. Hammerson was sand-bagged and flung overboard? When Müller purposely did not hear Two Bells struck last night, and knew damn-well that Mr. Hammerson would slip for'ard to catch him sleeping on the look-out, someone watched in the shadows on the fore part of the house, and sandbagged the poor chap. So if Müller didn't actually strike the sneaking cowardly blow, I'll bet he helped to dump the poor stunned Second—whose little finger was worth the whole gang of them—overboard, still alive; and that's as much murder as if he had hit him."

"Yes, and I'll tell you something else," agreed Dacre. "While we've got the strongest suspicion as to who did the actual sandbagging, I shan't be at all surprised if 'thim birrds' tell Larry O'Toole the actual name of the swine. That little chap knows things."

"Fore and aft," I agreed. "He knows what's going on in the fo'c'sle; and he and Doc, as stewards, must hear most of what's said in the Cabin."

"I suppose it is rather bolting the stable door after the horse has been stolen," observed Dacre, "but there would be no harm in our pinching that sandbag. Anyway, it'll be interesting to see if there is a sandbag in the port manger for'ard.

"I wish he'd been a bit more circumstantial about 'the long thin shpoike av a thing'," he went on. "It would be interesting and useful to know who carries it."

"Yes, it would," I agreed. "I wonder if that had anything to do with Patsy Hooligan's death!"

CHAPTER XV

The next blow fell that night.

I woke from sleep with the thought—"How curious these dreams are, in which you think that you wake up, and in which you dream that you are dreaming, and know that you are dreaming. . . ." For Celia Bryndal was at my open port-hole, calling my name in a low urgent voice.

It couldn't be she, of course, but it was somehow quite pleasant to dream that it was. No young man, who is both young and a man, objects to being the person to whom a lovely girl turns for help; or dislikes hearing his name called in a sweet and glorious voice of deep appeal; or to seeing a truly beautiful face looking in at his window and . . .

I sat up.

What was this?

"What's up?" I said

"Sinbad! Sinbad!"

"What is it?"

"Murder!"

"*What*? Whom?"

"My mother's dead. . . . She has been killed. . . . She was in perfect health when she went to bed. . . . *Do* come!"

"One second," said I, and sprang out of my bunk.

Dacre and Beauty slept like the dead.

Pulling on two garments I dashed out of the half-deck.

"Tell me," I said, and crept with Celia into the darkness of the alley-way that led past her cabin.

"I was asleep," she said, "and woke suddenly, quite certain that I had heard a cry. I listened and heard a sound from my mother's room. I don't know whether it was mixed up with a dream, but I felt that the cry I had heard had been something like a scream or a shriek or a cry for help. Perhaps I hadn't heard one at all—but thought I had. But there was no doubt about the sound I heard after I sat up. I don't know why, but I felt sure there was something wrong. So I got up and went into my mother's room. She was lying in bed on her back. I said,

" 'Did you call, Mother?' and she did not answer.

"I went over to the berth. Sinbad, the look on her face was awful—fright and horror and pain. Dreadful! . . . And she was dead!"

"Have you called the Captain?" I asked.

"The *Captain*!" answered Celia. "It was he who murdered her. Who else would? He's after her money and he's after me."

"Have you called the Mate?" I asked.

"Called the *Mate*! No. I'd as soon call the devil. Oh, Sinbad, what shall I do! what *shall* I do? . . . I'm absolutely in his power . . . In *their* power. . . . And Mr. Hammerson gone! What can we do?"

"Let me think," I said, wondering what would be the best immediate thing.

What could we do?

In the first place, what right had we to assume that Mrs. Bryndal had not died a natural death—heart failure, stroke, burst blood-vessel on the brain, clot . . .

In the second place, supposing she had been killed? What right had we immediately to assume that the Captain was the murderer?

In the third place, what would be gained by giving the Captain legitimate excuse for wrath and vengeance? . . .

An idea came to me.

"Why not go back to bed and leave it to the Captain himself to 'discover' that he has killed your mother—if she were killed and he was the murderer?"

"Oh, I couldn't."

"Yes you could. Nobody knows that you know."

"I couldn't. Look here, Sinbad. You know something of what my mother was to me, what she did to me, what our relations were—and that I have little cause to love her. I *don't* love her . . . I *didn't* love her, I mean," she said, "but, after all, she was my mother and we are two women alone on this dreadful ship. . . . Oh God, I mean we *were* two women. . . . Oh, I cannot tell you what I mean—but that devil shan't get away with it. I'm going to accuse him—at the top of my voice. I'll turn every decent man in the ship against him. I'll make them kill him! I'll kill him myself . . ."

"Hush! Don't talk rot. Pull yourself together, Celia. First of all, who's to say there has been any murder, and secondly, who's to say that the Captain committed it, if there has?"

Celia seized me by the shoulders and shook me in her urgency.

"Come and look at her yourself," she whispered. "Come and see for yourself. Look at her face and you'll see whether she was murdered. If you feel that she was, will you help me, will you stand by me?"

"I will help you and stand by you, in any case, Celia," I said.

And seizing my hand, Celia dragged me towards the room in which her mother lay.

It was terrible, dreadful. It leapt to the eye that the poor soul had died in the extreme of terror and agony. There was no sign whatever of a struggle in the cabin; no disorder; no disarrangement, even of the bed-clothes.

After all, there was practically nothing that I could do for poor Celia, save stay with her and talk to her.

It seemed to me an unspeakably dreadful thing that the last rites should be performed for her mother by such men as Peddersen the carpenter, the sail-maker and Doc, worthy soul as the last-named was. . . . And that Celia should have the choice of leaving her mother alone in their hands or of assisting them: also of making the choice whether she should give play to her natural desire to make a scene, and denounce the Captain as the murderer of his wife; or hypocritically to pretend that she knew nothing, suspected nothing. . . .

"Come into my room and talk to me," begged Celia. "It'll be all-right if we whisper; and, in any case, if that devil heard anything he wouldn't dare to . . . And if he did, I'd denounce him and scream the house down."

Even at such a moment, it struck me as funny to hear anybody on board a ship in mid-ocean talk of 'screaming the house down'.

I knew what she meant and felt that, awkward as my own position would be in the circumstances, I'd sooner be me than Captain Bryndal—if he came into the girl's cabin while she was in her then state of mind.

We crept into her room and sat on her bunk, and, with my arm about her shoulders, I did my utmost to comfort her, and to get her to believe that no harm should happen to her on that ship while there were five hefty Apprentices and half-a-dozen seamen of good-will and good character.

Suddenly an idea entered my mind, and without stopping to consider it in all its bearings, I said to Celia,

"Would you be afraid to go back into your mother's room?"

"Good Heavens, no," replied Celia. "Why should I?"

"Well, would you be afraid to look and make sure . . . whether there are any marks on her throat and neck, as though she had been strangled? . . . If there were any red marks or bruises it would show that she had not died a natural death, wouldn't it?"

"Oh, but I know she couldn't have died a natural death. She was as well as you or I when she went to bed. We were talking together and . . . Why, yes, Sinbad, she spoke about you. . . . She said she'd tell me something about you someday. . . . I wonder what she meant."

Celia paused and then repeated,

"She was perfectly well when she went to bed. It was some noise from her cabin woke me up."

"Do make sure if there's any mark, Celia," I begged. "Look here. Supposing I go."

"Yes, you go, Sinbad dear."

And turning quickly, Celia kissed me.

There was no sign of any mark or bruise about Mrs. Bryndal's throat, and though I did not actually touch her, I depressed the pillow on either side, to expose the neck just below the ears. Definitely she had not been strangled.

I still dream of that terrible face.

Once more we had a funeral at sea, conducted with an almost unctuous decorum by Captain Bryndal.

Watching him carefully, I saw no sign whatsoever of grief, pain, anguish, distress, strain, or any other symptom that showed he was burying his own wife.

He was as composed, mechanical and indifferent as are some clergymen when reading the Burial Service in the course of their professional duties for the ten-thousandth time.

When the last Amen had been said, and the body had plunged into the sea, I heard Jake, just behind me, make a curious remark to Villa.

"Guess that lets us out."

"Sure thing, Bo," was the reply. "Guess you an' I gotta set down and do some hard thinkin'."

Turning, I looked at them; and, scowling blackly, they looked at me.

Celia did not attend the funeral.

Talking with Doc afterwards I learned that it was he who had "discovered" the corpse of Mrs. Bryndal, and instantly reported it to the Captain.

"How did he take it, Doc?" I asked.

"Sinbad boy," replied Doc solemnly, as he laid his hand upon my shoulder and brought his face near to mine, "I swear befo' de Lawd Gawd A'mighty dat man was expectin' de news."

"What did he say?" I asked.

"He said,

" 'My God!' just like he might say, 'My ole hat!'

" 'What she die of?' he say. An' I say,

" 'How I know dat, Sah? I sho dunno what she die ob, but it was from somet'ing terr'ble . . . sudden.'

" 'Send Peddersen to me,' he says."

Doc lowered his voice and glanced round. "And now I tell you somet'ing else, Sinbad," he whispered.

"When Mr. Orlando Wight died, dere was a queer spot on his chest, ober his heart. When Patsy Hooligan died, dere was a queer spot on his back, ober his heart. And when I go, reverent and respeckful, to make dat poor lady ready . . . dere was a queer spot—ober her heart."

Going on deck next morning, we found that the Captain, having appointed Peddersen to act as Bosun, had had the falls of all four davit tackles unreeved and the blocks taken adrift for overhauling.

"It'd be rough luck on anyone who fell overboard to-day, Sir," remarked Dacre to the Mate.

"Well, it won't be me that has that luck . . . Mister," snapped Smeeker, grudgingly giving Dacre the form of address to which he was entitled as acting Third Mate, and thereby causing me to wonder whether the Captain had had any conversation with him on the subject of our interview with him.

Curiously enough, in the light of what happened within the hour, the Mate repeated his remark.

"No, it won't be me that goes overboard, anyhow," and, proceeding to give his instructions, informed Dacre that three new sheaves were to be fitted to each block.

With one of his usual sneers at the Captain, he observed that these being of what he termed 'liggey-vitey' wood, and having expensive patented rollers at the pin-hole, they were of course, in the Captain's pew. It had always been a sore point with Smeeker that the Captain had a marked weakness for hoarding such gear and gadgets as are usually left in the Mate's care. For that reason he would never ask the Captain for them personally, feeling, I suppose, that to do so himself would be something of an indignity.

Thus it was that I was sent to requisition the sheaves for him.

Knocking at the door, and being brusquely bidden to enter, I found Captain Bryndal engaged in clearing a drawer of his desk and impaling papers on a large bill-file.

This consisted of a long piece of steel like a very big knitting-needle, mounted in the centre of a thick disc of heavy wood.

Captain Bryndal seemed to be working rather mechanically and as though his thoughts were far away. Instead of replying to my request for the sheaves that the Mate wanted, he looked up, and, for quite a minute, studied me reflectively.

Growing uncomfortable, I repeated the Mate's message.

Still ignoring my request for sheaves, the Captain pursed his lips, grinned at me, again pursed his lips, and continued to regard me consideringly, and apparently without either his usual contempt or animosity.

"Dysart," he said suddenly, "could you navigate this ship?"

What was this? Some sort of a trap into which I was to fall in order to give him an excuse to curse me from Hell to breakfast? If I said,

"Yes, Sir," I should hear something to my disadvantage, on the subject of modesty and truthfulness. If I said,

"No, Sir," I should probably hear as much, or more, on the subject of laziness, stupidity and general worthlessness, for he knew how hard Mr. Wight had worked with me, at navigation.

I must avoid it. What should I say? Probably the best thing to do would be to hedge and temporize.

"Well, Sir, given the books and instruments I might be able to."

"H'm, I wonder," mused the Captain. "The loss of poor Mr. Hammerson makes us terribly short-handed. I don't know what we should do if anything happened to the Mate."

I repressed a start, and endeavoured to keep my face void of expression.

So something was going to happen to the Mate, was it?

Rubbish! I was getting morbid. Trust Smeeker to take good care of himself . . . On the other hand, if the Captain intended that something should happen to the excellent Mr. Smeeker. . . .

Oh, morbid, morbid, morbid! I told myself.

But who wouldn't grow morbid in the circumstances—in this coffin-ship, this Hell-ship, off her course in the middle of the South Atlantic; with the Second Mate murdered by the men; obvious attempts made on the lives of two Apprentices; a helmsman murdered at the wheel by some person unknown; the Captain's wife murdered in her bed—by the Captain (?)—and a suicide . . .

And now the Captain was considering how he could best carry on if "anything happened to the Mate".

"The Mate isn't ill, Sir, is he?" I asked with a hypocritical air of alarm.

"No, not ill, but queer. . . . Behaving queerly. Haven't you noticed it?" replied the Captain. "I was only just thinking to myself when you came in, what a hole we should be in, if anything did happen to him. I shouldn't have an officer at all. After all, the acting Third is only an Apprentice . . . Suppose I fell ill myself!"

For want of something better to say,

"You aren't feeling ill, are you, Sir?" I enquired as the Captain eyed me thoughtfully, in silence.

"Good God, no! Don't talk nonsense, Boy. The question is whether you'd be any good . . ."

The Captain did not complete his reply, but, turning back to his desk, sat absent-mindedly swinging the bill-file to and fro, its point between finger and thumb.

"Mr. Wight said the boy would be as good a navigator as himself, by the time we got to Australia," he mused aloud.

"Hey, what is it?" he snapped, suddenly turning to me, his own bright self again and grinning the old familiar smile. "Sheaves? Sheaves? You'll find them in the locker under that," and, suddenly removing the papers from the bill-file, he picked it up by its base and pointed with it to his settee.

The blood rushed to my face as, thankfully and swiftly, I turned my back and crossed the cabin.

It was with trembling hands that I opened the locker. Having with difficulty secured an armful of sheaves, I could scarcely hold them and rise to my feet.

For what the Captain held in his hand was not only a bill-file but a murderous weapon—a murderer's weapon. That long steel point had been driven through the hearts of two men and the heart of a woman. I could hear Larry O'Toole's voice, his very words,

"And there's some loikes better a long thin shpoike av a thing —loike a long needle that leaves no mark to say how ye doied, unless 'tis mebbe just a small red shpot loike a pimple."

With the cunning, or the wisdom, of the mad, Larry had guessed what had caused the death of his compatriot Patsy Hooligan—probably had seen the puncture on his breast, or on his back, above his heart.

"*Receipted and filed* . . . ." Of course—*that* was what he meant . . . The mad wicked devil!

Should I suddenly feel the sharp and dreadful pang below my left shoulder-blade . . . ? . . . Filed . . . !

Somehow I got to my feet without turning my head . . . and felt the blood draining from my face.

As I rose with the armful of sheaves from the locker, and at last looked round, the Captain was passing out of the room; and as he went through the Saloon—where the table was laid for dinner—and mounted the companion way, I followed immediately behind him.

Definitely I preferred that he should be in front of me.

The Mate, lolling against the poop-rail and waiting, no doubt, for the dinner-bell, straightened up at the sight of the Captain and feigned to busy himself about clearing the signal halyards.

"Oh, Mr. Smeeker," said the Captain in a casual tone, and as I reached the lee ladder, he started to walk toward the Mate.

Hampered by my burden of sheaves, I faced aft with the intention of going *backward* down the lee ladder; and, chancing to look across at the top of the Saloon skylight, I saw that which caused me simultaneously to drop my armful of sheaves, utter a loud and meaningless cry, and take a tremendous leap aft. But, unfortunately, as the dreadful thing was done and accomplished in the very second in which I saw it done, my actions were naturally too late to achieve anything useful.

Was I dreaming? Were my eyes deceiving me, and was I no longer able to trust the evidence of my senses? Had I seen Captain Bryndal stroll up to Mr. Smeeker and, with the utmost deliberation, carefully choose the exact spot that he favoured, and then thrust the file with such force and precision in the left side of the hapless Mate's breast that even as I jumped, the wooden base rested like a grotesque medal on the injured man's coat?

At the sound of my voice, Captain Bryndal, who must have supposed that I had descended the ladder (and facing forward), turned his head, and again I saw the savagely glaring eyes and ferociously bared teeth that once had expressed his unbounded hatred of Patsy Hooligan. And from his mouth came a sound that was nothing but a wolfish snarl.

"You devil," gasped the Mate, flung his long arms about the Captain, lurched sideways, and, escaping my frantic rush by a few inches, rolled bodily over the taffrail, carrying the Captain with him into the sea. . . .

Although I turned and cursed him for the silly gaping dolt that he was, I was really devoutly thankful that Baby Axenstern was at the wheel. Nobody could possibly have foreseen the Captain's attack on the Mate, but any other helmsman would instinctively have seized the Captain and hauled him back from the rail—and, with a divided crew and no officers in control, there would at once have arisen the problem of dealing with an insane murderer, a homicidal maniac—who was the Captain of the ship.

As it was, Baby Axenstern—although the associate of violent, criminal "Ship-owners"—was so unnerved by this sudden horror that he stood trembling and gaping until I myself, having thrown a lifebelt overboard, put the wheel hard down and bade him keep it so.

My loud cry had brought Dacre from the main deck, and, not knowing exactly what had happened, he nevertheless was in time to see two men go over the side; and shouting to the helmsmen to "hard down", he sent the "man overboard" cry echoing through the ship with all the strength of his powerful lungs.

And while we worked as—on hearing that urgent warning—only seamen can, I suddenly remembered poor Smeeker's complacent sneer that he, at any rate, would not be the one to go overboard that day, and I wondered whether Captain Bryndal, with the dreadful cunning of the secretly mad, had purposely crippled our boat davits, for, with no tackle to lift them, in this emergency our two well-equipped lifeboats might just as well have been bath-tubs.

As I saw it, the Captain had intended to murder the Mate and fling his body overboard, that he might disappear as poor Mr. Hammerson had done. He had supposed himself to be alone with the Mate on the poop. But for my cry, the distraction of his attention and the turning of his head, his arms would have gone about the Mate's instead of the Mate's going about his.

Had Smeeker in a flash of revelation known that he had got his death-wound and determined that his slayer should die with him—or had he merely been trying to throw overboard the man who had attempted to take his life?

Anyhow, the Mate must be dead, and, facing facts, I hoped that the Captain was dead. Without shame, I hoped that our efforts at his rescue would be fruitless.

What I did not visualize, in the rush and hurry of those frantic minutes, was the possibly worse situation that would arise if we failed to rescue him.

In any case, do our best to save him, we must.

Our only other boat was the dinghy, lashed bottom-up on the for'ard skids, and in wonderfully short order we had it free and man-handled to abreast of the main hatch. As it happened, there was little sea on, and, lashing the lee clew of the mainsail to the yard-arm, and taking the clew-garnet to the midship-capstan with a long strop, we hoisted the boat over the rail and lowered away, so that Hamblin, Church, Carrol and myself could drop into it.

Unexpectedly and unchallenged, Peddersen slid down into the stern-sheets and took the yoke-lines. Dacre, who remained aboard to handle the ship as was now his duty, had, at the first alarm, sent the sharp-eyed Geordie aloft. But although the latter soon located the lifebuoy that I had thrown overboard, not once did he sight either of the two men.

Later we came to the conclusion that either the Captain had sunk with the arms of the dying Mate still pinioning his own, or that both men had been seized by sharks. . . .

Until it was quite obvious that they were not afloat, we searched diligently and conscientiously; and had the two been our best friends we could not have done more. In my own mind, there was no doubt that the dying Smeeker had drowned the Captain, and my state of mind on realizing that both my enemies had gone was a curious one, for, stunned as I had been, my brain had not grasped the implications and connotations of this great and dreadful fact.

Probably actuated by purely selfish motives, Peddersen was most unwilling to admit that we were beaten, and it was only after he had been well cursed by the others that he finally steered the dinghy for the ship.

"Don't you fret your fat, Chips. We can soon find another Captain for the old 'ooker," growled Church.

This remark I noticed—for I was facing Peddersen—caused him to fall suddenly silent, to look curiously at me, and to become very thoughtful.

With the boat safely landed on deck, I saw that, naturally most anxious to know what had happened, Celia Bryndal had come out of the poop alley-way door and was standing with Doc on the main deck by the after hatch. Only then, and for the first time I think, did I fully realize her truly pathetic loneliness and the extreme awkwardness of her situation.

Going up to her I said that we had done our very utmost to save the Captain and the Mate, but we had failed.

"Well, thank God for that, anyhow, Sinbad," she replied.

Realizing that she had only said what I certainly, if subconsciously, felt, I was not surprised by her frank bluntness.

"But what in God's name is going to happen now?" she said. "This changes the position absolutely—and we shall soon see some pretty dirty work."

"What do you mean?" I asked. "We shan't see anything dirtier than the Captain would have shown us."

"I don't know so much about that," said Celia.

And again I felt that the girl knew more about certain phases of the ship's life than I or Dacre did.

"Well," said I, "I don't see how we can possibly be the worse

273

for the loss of that pair of . . ."

But suddenly I did see. Who was going to maintain discipline now? Who command the ship? Who control such men as Villa, Müller, Jake, and Johes, to say nothing of Peddersen?

Worse? Our position might now be infinitely worse. For after all, Captain Bryndal had been a Captain, a terror, a disciplinarian, a man feared and obeyed. But what were Villa, Jake, Müller?

And there wasn't an Officer on the ship!

There was not a person of the slightest authority, for we Apprentices ranked as boys—boys who did men's work without getting a man's pay. And Dacre, as well they knew, was only an Apprentice temporarily acting, by the late Captain's orders, as Third Mate.

And, in any case, discipline is only maintained on a ship of the British Mercantile Marine by the personality of the Captain and Mate; by the moral weight of their personality and position; and, upon occasion, the physical weight of a fist. As anyone who has been to sea knows perfectly well, the fear of logging, with a shilling fine, never yet kept any sailor from doing anything.

"Oh, it will be all-right," I said. "Don't you worry. I'm sure everything will be all-right."

But there was a further surprise for me in Doc's most unusual pessimism. He had had less to do and more time for thinking, during the last hour.

" 'Gwine ter be all-right' now, eh, Sinbad?" he observed solemnly. "Ah sho' is glad dat yo' t'inks eberyt'ing's gwine ter be all-right, fo' Ah opines, on da contrary, dat trouble's just gwine ter start right now. I'se scared dat dere's bad confusion and disgruntletion and mischievousness brewin' just now, right dere, boy."

And he pointed to where the men conferred, with obvious earnestness, amidships.

Celia Bryndal turned and went to her cabin.

"Sinbad boy, Ah sho' is anxious about dat lubbly gal. . . . Who gwine gubborn dat gang? Yo' watch out dat Carpenter—him Bad Man; and dat Villa—him Bad Man; and dat Jake—him Bad Man. Ah sho' am worried anxious about her and I'll keep a sharp knife to ma hand."

This untutored old negro (wanted for murder in New Orleans), a brave soul and a gentleman at heart, was at that moment, I'm sorry and ashamed to say, more concerned, nay, worried, anxious, and sorely troubled, than I, by the dangerous position in which Celia Bryndal now found herself.

Proud of his seldom-accorded rank of Steward, he regarded himself as responsible for her as a passenger; and before my slow brain had properly grasped the terrible possibilities of the situation, he was thinking of her rather than of himself and the ship, and was prepared to protect her as long as he had breath in his body.

Dacre joined us.

"My God, this is a pretty state of affairs, isn't it?" he said. "What are we to do?"

"What is all the jabbering about there?" I asked him.

"You'll soon see," he answered grimly. "Here comes the Parliament that is going to lay down the Law—and make some brand new ones."

And he took his stand between Doc and myself.

I was aware that Celia Bryndal had returned, and that she sat suddenly down on the after hatch, as though her legs refused to support her when the "Parliament" arrived.

This, it appeared, consisted of two clearly defined sections (possibly Lords and Commons), and that the foremost, doubtless the Lords, consisted entirely of the "Peddersen Committee" and comprised Peddersen, Villa, Jake, Müller, Slim Johes, Axenstern, Brown and Paulo. Hamblin, holding his head as usual, tailed behind them, but his puzzled frown, strongly in evidence, showed that he was far from being happy in his mind.

"H'm, Ship-owners to the fore," muttered Dacre, and I observed the lagging Shell-backs. Church, Berghen and Blancke and Larry O'Toole seemed to feel the disparity of their numbers and, like Hamblin, to be anything but happy.

I also noted with regret that even in this crisis and upheaval, habit had asserted itself and sent Carrol to relieve Baby Axenstern at the wheel.

CHAPTER XVII

In the beady eyes of Peddersen, who came first as spokes-man and elected leader, there was a gleam that, although I saw no reason why it should concern me personally, I very much disliked.

In the many months that he had served in the *Valkyrie*, his English had very greatly improved, and only a word here and there betrayed his Norwegian origin.

"Cook! Splice der main brace," he ordered in a peremptory tone, "and jump to it. We'll begin well and go on better."

"Sure thing, Cookie," cried Jake gloatingly. "Set the drinks up, good and plenty."

"An' who's yo' to gib de Stooard orders?" growled Doc, and never had I seen his black face so ugly and forbidding.

"Who'm I? I'm going to tell you right now who I am, *nigger*," replied Peddersen. "We've held Parliament and talked the persition over, and as there's no Captain or Officers, the fellers has elected me to take command of this packet as is proper right and law."

"Iss, iss, dat iss goot law, surely to gootness. It is the law of the land—and of the sea, whateffer," crowed Slim Johes.

"Sure thing," growled Peddersen. "And who else is there, anyhow? De Captain—he's dead. De Mate—he's dead. De Second Mate—he's dead. De T'ird Mate—dere ain't any. Dis boy, Blount here, ain't got any ticket. He's an Apprentice. He ain't even on de Articles as an Orficer . . ."

This statement, thanks to the late Captain's grasping meanness, was, alas, true.

"Dis boy, Dysart, what is he? He's a boy and a First Voyager. An' de other boys—is boys. Now den, I'm Carpenter, I am, and ranks as a Petty Officer—and as a Petty Officer I'm de highest ratin' aboard. . . . What's *more*, I have sailed as Second Mate in coasters, and I guess I can take dis hooker into port. . . . An' what's *most*, I'm Captain by election of de crew—all accordin' to law. . . . I command dis ship now!"

Complete silence.

"I am sure we all ought to be very grateful to you for assuming the responsibility, Carpenter," drawled Dacre, "but before you shoulder the heavy burden, I wonder if you would be so kind as to tell us exactly how you are going to take us into port? . . . It is a drawback, you know, from our point of view, that if you tried to sail overland, we should have to go too."

Silence again.

"Another thing, too. Have you quite decided on which port you are going to favour?"

There was a shuffling of feet and a clearing of throats. To Beauty Dacre whispered,

"Go and relieve the wheel at once, and send Carrol down here," and, to his great disgust, Beauty had to go.

Cool, clever, crafty Dacre! Quietly, calmly and without any truculence, and with no apparent intention of doing so, he had, to those simple men, emphasized the colossal contrast and un-bridgeable gulf between an ignorant bullying blackguardly rascal, and an honest man of training and education.

This mode of attack upon his position was too subtle to be recognized, as such, by Peddersen; but it made him suspicious and restive. Nor was he soothed by Carrol's arriving and reporting the course to Dacre, as,

"East by Nor', three-quarters North, *Sir*."

Peddersen eyed Dacre angrily.

"What d'ye think ye're gettin' at, boy?" he growled.

"Only at the exact measure of your doubtless great skill in navigation, Carpenter," replied Dacre blandly. "Like everyone else I shall naturally be delighted to call you Captain if—like everyone else—I am quite certain that your navigation is not of the follow-the-ship-in-front and go-where-the-ground's-wet order. Coastal navigation won't do in the South Atlantic, you know, and I don't suppose any of us wants a navigator who will navigate us all to Davy Jones."

"Here, here!" ejaculated Carrol loudly, and was not in the least abashed by the villainous scowl with which Peddersen favoured him in return.

"But naturally you can soon set our minds at rest, Carpenter," continued Dacre. "Carrol has just reported the course by the port compass. Now tell us—if the wind shifts to the other quarter, how are you going to decide what course to steer by the starboard compass? As no doubt you know, it differs from the port compass and from the standard compass. Naturally *you* can plot the course on a chart, as easily as you can . . . make a bucket"—and making a wooden bucket was a thing which Peddersen generally bungled very badly—". . . but can you take azimuths and ampli-tudes, and can you kindly tell us whether our magnetic variation is increasing or decreasing? And do you know when to add and when to subtract deviation, *et cetera*?"

Silence.

"I'm not trying to trip you up, of course, Carpenter," continued Dacre. "But we'd be a pack of fools to trust all our lives to a man who is not familiar with these little details, shouldn't we?"

Hamblin spoke.

"Tae me, them wee 'little details' seems domn big 'uns. Hoo aboot it, Chips?"

All eyes were turned upon the Carpenter, and the Ship-owners' confidence in his ability to take command was visibly shaken, and they began to regard him dubiously.

"An' if my ploody navigation ain't good enough, who de Hell's is?" snarled the angry Carpenter.

"Ah sho' can tell you dat," replied Doc eagerly. "You call it your 'bloody' navigation, you low swearin' jack-skite, an' Ah guess 'bloody' is right. Absolutely bloody. Now you don't use dat word no mo', in talkin' to yo' betters. An' Ah tell yo' all, yo' silly damn-fools, whose navigation is good enough. When Mr. Orlando Wight was Mate of dis ship, I hear him done tell in the Cabin dat dis lad, Sinbad, was as good nav'gator as Mr. Orlando Wight himself; and as good nav'gator as any Cap'n he ebber seen. . . . Now you listen to me, yo' silly sailor-men. You listen to me what's been Bosun of as good ship as ebber sailed the seas. You gib Sinbad a chart an' a sextant, and yo' don't need no better Cap'n. You don't need no low-livin' foul-mout' dirty Chips to be yo' Cap'n. You want educated man an' good nav'gator. Ah'm tellin' yo' for yo' good and for yo' lives' sake."

" 'Ooray for Cap'n Sinbad," shouted Church. "Can you dodge the bloomin' rocks and take us home?" he asked.

"I can navigate the ship," I said.

"Aye, and what about the port we're goin' to make?" growled Carrol. "On this trip there's been a lot of damn-fool talk by liars, rogues and half-wits about ship-ownin', ship-stealin' and ship-sellin', and givin' up the sea and buyin' a farm. Well, I know damn-well, and so do all you, that even if we were fools and rogues enough to try, there's nobody goin' to buy a ship from a lot of old fo'c'sle-jacks like us! . . . No, nor from the young fellers of the 'alf-deck—not that they'd do such a thing. So what I say is, let's make for Falmouth where we were bound in the first place, and let's have for Cap'n the best man to navigate us there. I've got an old woman and two kids in Liverpool that'll need me, pay-day."

"Ah, and there's a damn fine Judy in Limehouse a-waitin' for me to bring 'er 'ome somethink—not to mention me wife in Wappin', and me two little dawgs, Charlotte the 'Arlot, an' Hemma the Haw. It'd break their little 'earts, all four of 'em, if I never come back. So I'm for rollin' 'ome," chuckled Church.

"An' for the best man to roll me 'ome quickest," he added.

But this development was obviously anything but acceptable to the Peddersen Committee. With their leader in nominal command, they would be practically their own masters, and some of them, bearing in mind the mystery of the Second Mate, must have recalled uneasily that on arrival at any British port, there would be a Board of Trade Inquiry into the loss of the Captain and Officers of the *Valkyrie*.

Who would sail for a British port to find a rope when he might sail for a foreign one to find gold?

For, quite apart from the question of any possibility of selling the ship, there was the matter of the "pickings" from it.

There must be money on board, jewellery and valuables belonging to the women-folk, and all sorts of other valuable things—liquor, for example. And ignoring Carrol's question, the crafty cunning Jake struck a note that he knew would make most direct appeal to the Ship-owners.

"Holy Gee, are we gwine to be bossed around by a goddam kid that ain't been a dog-watch to sea?" he jeered fiercely. "It'll be another ten year before the goddam orphan kin grow as much hair on his chin as there is on a he-man's chest."

"Who said anything about bossing?" I asked quietly. "What I said was that I could navigate."

"Ven I vas in steamers, der Old Man did noddings do," observed Baby Axenstern. "It vas der Second Mate what make all der navigations."

"Good for you, Baby," shouted Jake, slapping Axenstern on the shoulder. "Chips can be Cap'n, and the boy can shoot the sun and lay the course. How does that suit you, young Dysart?"

In point of fact it might have suited me very well, for although I was one of the biggest, strongest and heaviest people in the ship, I was, as Peddersen had pointed out, still a First Voyager— and exactly what Jake had just called me—technically only a boy. I had had no responsibility, and no experience whatever in handling men, and the Captain's job was the last thing that I wanted.

For the moment I saw no great objection to Peddersen's being allowed to consider himself as Captain, and to command the vessel.

"Well, if the Third Mate now becomes First Officer, I'm quite agreeable to that," I answered, and wondered why under his breath, Dacre cursed me for an indescribable fool. I was quite unaware that through my stupidity all his cleverness and finesse were wasted.

"O.K. then. I guess we'll reckon that fixed," said Jake, rubbing his hands gleefully.

"Now *Captain* Peddersen," he continued, "how about splicin' the main brace and whackin' out some tobaccer, eh? And then we kin all have a friendly yarn about where we're gwine to head for."

As the cunning proposer expected, this suggestion met with general approval.

"That's so. Grog-oh, Doc," called Peddersen, "and show me where der tobaccer lives."

But neither Doc nor Dacre moved from before the alley-way door.

"Jest one minute, *Cap'n*,"—and there was a wealth of sarcasm in Doc's 'Cap'n'—"Ah sho would like to know jest whar we stands. Yo' ain't der Carpenter no mo'—you's Cap'n, eh? Dacre Blount ain't Dacre no mo'—he am now Mr. Blount, First Mate ob dis ship. And Sinbad ain't Sinbad no mo'—he am Mr. Dysart, Second Mate ob dis ship. Is dat so?"

"Sure. You said it all, quite right, Doc," agreed Peddersen cheerfully.

"Ho, then whar's you-all gwine ter live?" asked Doc, with his dubious scowl; and inwardly I smiled. I thought that his extreme vehemence was merely because his simple soul was revolted by the bare idea of a Carpenter's plebeian presence profaning the purlieus of the sacred Cabin.

Before Peddersen could answer, Larry O'Toole spoke, for the first time; and his words brought discomfort, a kind of breathlessness, almost stupefaction, to most of those present.

"Now begorra, bedad and bejabbers," he said in a voice of awe and wonder, "look out, bhoys, and be careful, what ye say an' what ye do. For look, look! '*Tis the Captain and the Mate is watchin' ye.* D'ye see them, Peddersen me bhoy?"

And with staring starting eyes he pointed to where, a common phenomenon, if an interesting coincidence, a pair of ordinary large sea-birds lazily winged their way toward the ship. The fear that made the Carpenter's swarthy skin turn a shade or two lighter also made him furious.

Affecting to ignore Larry, he turned ferociously upon Doc.

"Hell's bells, and where d'ye think I'm goin' to live, ye blasted nigger?" he bawled at Doc. "Der Officers can doss where dey likes, but me, I'm Captain now—*Captain*, d'ye hear me?—and I'm damn well goin' to berth in the Captain's room and I entertains me friends in the Saloon Cabin when I likes, eh, fellers?"

Then, encouraged by the loud shouts of approval from his followers, the *soi-disant* Captain betrayed the foulness of his mind, the filthy rottenness of his character, and made the mistake of his life.

"Sure," he growled, "I feeds in the Cabin, and I sleeps in the Cap'n's room."

And slowly he added, as he turned to where Celia Bryndal sat,

"I berths in de Cap'n's room, I say, and then I kin see that de young lady ain't never lonesome of a night-time."

Following the direction of his glance, I admired Celia Bryndal's self-control. She regarded the man steadily, contemptuously until her silent utter disgust spread almost as an aura about her.

CHAPTER XVIII

In the dead silence that followed his words, Peddersen looked around at the faces of his followers, to gauge the effect of his vile words.

And by the various receptions of his suggestion were the characters of his hearers manifested.

Carrol, apparently the first of the men to grasp its significance, growled,

"Ye're not British, thank God, Carpenter; but don't forget ye're on a British ship," and he was promptly followed by Church with,

"To Hell with that talk, Chips. Be ashamed of yerself, ye foul-mouthed bastard."

Blancke and Berghen looked at each other. Blancke spat and Berghen shrugged his shoulders, and, turning their backs on Peddersen, they watched Larry O'Toole gesticulating and signalling to 'thim birrds'.

"Holy Gee," guffawed Jake, "the Cap'n's cottoned to his job, all-right, all-right! He surely is on to it."

"Iss inteet, py damn," giggled Slim Johes, "some people will learn that other people are not the tirt beneath their feet whateffer. T'will do them good, look you."

"Say, Cap'n," laughed Villa, "don't you be a greedy hawg. Fair's fair and share's share."

"*Ja*," agreed Müller. "Share and share alike vas goot law."

I glanced at the mighty Axenstern, whose strength was always something to be reckoned with. He looked puzzled, and I was glad to see that a frown was gathering on his foolish face. Still more glad was I when Hamblin, stepping forward, spat at Peddersen's feet and exclaimed, or growled rather,

"Ach, ye dirrty scum!" . . .

Psychologists and other learned men tell us that there is nothing swifter than the passage of a dream through the mind of a sleeper, but I think that in the second that had elapsed since Peddersen's remark, my thoughts had been infinitely swifter. Awake, I now dreamed dreams, saw visions, thought thoughts and formed determinations quite as quickly as any sleeper could dream. I looked at Celia Bryndal's white face and suddenly realized her position, understood what she must be thinking and feeling, put myself in her place, and shed my callous insensibility and unsympathizing indifference and stupidity.

In those seconds I think I grew up. I believe I stepped from boyhood into manhood and willingly accepted a man's responsibility.

Baldly stated, it sounds like mere swollen-headed conceit, the pride that goeth before the well-deserved fall, the complacent self-satisfied egoism and cocksure self-assertion so repugnant to the decent mind—but the fact remains that in that moment I felt myself the natural and proper champion and protector of Celia Bryndal; I felt myself the person most competent to lead and rule these men; the man best fitted to command and navigate this ship. I'm sorry, but there it is, and I can only blame the circumstances, ghastly, incredible and possibly unique, that had arisen.

Well, this girl must be saved; this ship must be saved; and these fools must be saved—from themselves. And I was going to be the man to do it.

I could almost hear Hammerson's voice,

"It's by personality ye keep discipline; and a heavy fist—or rather the knowledge that there's a heavy fist ready, behind the personality."

And, although I was ashamed of myself for doing so, I felt that I had more of that particular kind of personality than Dacre had, and most certainly a heavier fist.

I would take charge of the situation; I would control it; I would break Peddersen and make myself master of these men; I would get them to ask Dacre to be Captain of the ship; and I would support and enforce his authority, and would navigate the ship to Falmouth.

Were not my fathers "Admirals all", and should not I be a wholly degenerate and unworthy descendant of such seamen, were I not the best man now left on this ship? . . .

All that in a second or two! . . .

I looked from the girl to the evil upstart, knew him for what he was, and smiled grimly in my heart. I was a better man than he, anyhow, and would prove it here and now.

For lack of a leader with a spark of fire in his mentality, British men in a British ship had let this ignorant "Dutchman"—who, incidentally, trembled at the sight of sea-birds and listened to the vapourings of a lunatic—take command of them, pervert their minds, seduce them from their allegiance and duty, and now, unrebuked by most of them, vilely insult a girl.

Well, as it happened, I had got a spark of fire, and his foul breath had fanned it into a blaze. In its flames, the lingering remnants of my boyhood had died, and my "inferiority complex" been consumed.

Dacre, white-faced, shocked to the depths of his being, seemed to be paralysed and struck dumb.

Doc, who had been standing as though he too were turned to stone, suddenly woke up and roared in such a voice that some of the Ship-owners jumped and put hands to their sheathed knives,

"Yo' filthy fo'c'sle trash, Ah'll . . ."

And then choked with sheer rage.

"Now, now, Doc, that's no way to address your Captain," I said, "your newly and duly elected Captain, chosen for his merits by these wise men."

A leaf from Dacre's book, this.

"Always respect the Captain, Doc," I added, and then in as quiet and silky a voice as would be heard by all,

"Captain Peddersen," I asked, "may I put a question, please?"

I think that the Norwegian suddenly realized that he no longer dealt with a boy, and the glare of his restless beady eyes focused on mine with a menacing stare.

"What do you want now, boy?" he snarled in the style of the late Captain Bryndal.

"Have you ever heard of the old Western Ocean custom that the *murdered* Mr. Hammerson used to talk about?" I asked. "He told us that, aboard those Western Ocean packets, it was unquestioned law that the man who could thrash the Mate could take the Mate's job, and further, that no Captain dared to carry an officer whom he couldn't knock stone cold."

"*Ja,* "agreed Peddersen, "and very goot, too."

"Quite so. . . . Now, don't you think that just to show who's who, you'd better knock Seven Bells out of each of your Officers, beginning with the lowest? I suggest that you begin with your new Second Mate, Captain, as there's no Third now. It would give all the men a real treat, and at the same time show that you don't intend to have any nonsense aboard your ship."

Again there was a moment's dead silence, and it must be admitted that the roar of approval that broke out, came as much from the Ship-owners themselves as from the Shell-backs. It was indeed a case of 'loud cheers'.

"Sure. Slap the young sunnavabitch and send him to bed,"

advised Jake.

"Iss, you give him a goot hiding, Cap'n, I tell 'oo. It will do him goot, and put the poy where he pelongs," contributed Slim Johes.

"*Ja*, kill the young *schweinhund*," growled Müller.

"Beat him up, Cap'n, till he has to blow his nose at the back of his neck," advised Villa.

With great satisfaction I noted that neither Axenstern nor Hamblin offered any suggestion; while Carrol growled,

"That's a fair offer, Chips," and Church loudly asserted that all Britishers present would combine to see fair play—provided Chips had the guts to accept the challenge.

Peddersen, in the pride of his promotion, the giddiness of his elevation, and the glory of his achievement, was above himself; and, I believe, was absolutely certain that he could defeat me, beat me silly, knock me out—and kick me to death.

He laughed angrily.

"Why, ye young fool, ye poor fish, ye half-witted pup, I could lick ye blind, wid one hand."

"Splendid," said I, "then you can spare a minute or two as I shouldn't be troubling you for long."

I turned to Church.

"And the Britishers will see fair play," I quoted him, for I had no illusions as to the likelihood of a stab in the back, or a blow on the head with a belaying-pin, from Jake, Villa or Müller, if things should go badly with Peddersen.

"Come on, Britishers," I cried, "see fair play while the Captain licks me with one hand."

The first gleam of humour in the situation came when little Geordie Stowe scuttled across the hatch and took his stand behind me. Quickly he was joined by Carrol, Church and Larry O'Toole, while Doc and Dacre had, of course, been beside me all the time.

It said much for the loyalty, courage, and sterling character of Blancke and Hans Berghen that, although not British, they immediately followed.

With these six reinforcing Doc and Dacre at my back, I had little to fear from treachery.

"Iss, look you, but ther's plenty to see fair play for Captain Peddersen, I tell you," sang Slim Johes.

"Aye, an' yer plenty will nae be needed, ye yelpin' hound," snarled Hamblin. "Is not yer Peddersen fightin' a Britisher?"

Rarely before had I seen the sailor-man's sublime superiority to "Dutchmen" exemplified with such beautiful simplicity.

"Vell, vell! I vas see vair play, vor bode sides," grinned Baby Axenstern, and I was filled with high hope that I had already done something to drive a wedge through the middle of our foolish Parliament, and to cause defection from the glorious company of Ship-owners.

Had he not committed the unpardonable sin of foully insulting the girl whom he supposed to be in his power, I could almost have pitied the Norwegian when he swaggeringly threw himself into his beautiful boxing stance.

He was so pathetically sure that he was not only going to humble me before All Hands and the Cook, but, once and for all, turn me into his little whipped dog, docile, obedient and fearful.

Whereas, it was my hope, intention and determination, first (by making him appear the second-rate boxer that I believed him to be), to turn the laugh against him and destroy all the prestige which, under false pretences, he had gained; secondly, to give him as severe and merciless a thrashing as one man ever gave another; and thirdly, to make him, literally on his knees, apologize most humbly to Celia Bryndal and to renounce absolutely all pretentions to being anything other than he was—the thoroughly disloyal, objectionable, and lazy carpenter of the *Valkyrie*. . . .

All very fine. A most admirable programme. And supposing a lucky blow from his ham-like fist and enormously powerful right arm laid me senseless before the fight had well started?

Was I suddenly grown conceited, swollen-headed—a loud-mouthed boastful braggart?

No, I hadn't. I had grown up, and I had lost my self-distrust, my vice of diffidence, my complex of inferiority. "The hour brings forth the man." In this case the hour had made me into a man, and I again assured myself that I had rightly, worthily, and not vain-gloriously taken it upon myself to try to save the girl, the ship and the decent men.

The ring was formed, the battle joined.

"Well, Captain," said I, "you promised to lick me with one hand, but I think, if I were you I would at any rate start with two."

And, like lightning, I feinted with my right.

As I expected, he instantly abandoned the statuesque pose of his stance and fell into his stoop that gave away all advantage and benefit of height, and incidentally gave me ample time to swing my left, open-handed, with a most resounding and ridiculous slap upon his right cheek.

Doc crowed.

"An' if a man smite you on de right cheek," he chanted,

"Turn unto him the other also," I laughed, and side-stepping Peddersen's bull rush, I slapped him on the left side of his face as he passed me.

The crowd roared with laughter.

"Say, quit foolin' and get down to it and kill him," came in anxious tones from Jake.

"It's no' *Chips* that's foolin', an' Goad help him when the foolin' stops," volunteered Hamblin; and I realized that, in expressing their views, both forgot that they were speaking of the rightly elected and duly appointed Captain.

Sparring easily and lightly, moving swiftly, and refraining from using my arms for defence, I endeavoured to make the Norwegian look the second-rater that he was.

Hitting him lightly, freely, and incessantly, I strove to drive him mad, and the audience uproarious with amusement.

I then began to talk to him, hitting him meanwhile almost when and where I liked, and always informing him beforehand of my intentions.

"Now a poke in the right eye for calling me a young fool, eh, Captain?

"Now a prod on the mark for calling me 'boy'.

"Now a tap on the nose for calling Doc a nigger.

"Now rather a hard one on the jaw for removing those brake-linings.

"And now a sit-down for your damned impudence in thinking yourself fit to command these fine fellows," and cross-countering heavily, I gave him one between the eyes that sent him to the boards.

So far so good. But would it be a case of farther and faring worse?

Peddersen was, by the Hammerson standards, a clumsy boxer, but he was, by any standards, a tremendous fighter—enormously strong, with a chest like a barrel, arms like oak branches, and fists like hams. That he used those great arms like flails was only because he was flurried and mightily anxious to destroy me in the first minute of the first round. He was not yet set, had not properly got down to it, had not got his second wind, nor me where he wanted me.

In theory, and according to all the books, the boxer must beat the fighter in the long-run, but how long was the run going to be, and how long would my youthful stamina stand against his mature and mighty strength?

Anyhow, the first part of my programme had been carried through successfully, for the frequent loud roars of laughter had been at Peddersen, and with me. But the first part was the least, and would avail me little if the second part did not succeed.

Very nice and very useful to make a fool of the scoundrel and cause defections from the ranks of his followers; but I had got to do more than make him look ridiculous, I had got to beat him, and so beat him that he was finished, done for, his claims to leadership abolished. . . .

With as ugly a look on his face as ever I wish to see, he rushed, and drove at my face a right that, had it been successful, would have finished the business then and there and settled the question of leadership.

Side-stepping, I hit him, for the first time with all my strength, catching him on the jaw just below the ear, and sending him heavily to the deck. Had it been the point of the jaw instead of the angle, he would have been out.

Jake started forward, and thrust his great carcase between me and the fallen carpenter.

Like a fool I drew back my fist to hit him, and, had I done so, should doubtless have had the pair of them upon me at once.

Fortunately I had not time to do so, for Hamblin, with a roar, literally flung himself on Jake's back, his arms about his throat, while a growl of anger arose from the decent men present.

Taking Hamblin's part, Axenstern also seized Jake.

"De fight vas vair," he shouted, and placed under the nose of Jake, a fist so huge and gnarled and ugly, that the rascal promptly reconsidered the matter and allowed himself to be dragged back to his place by the rail.

"Is the laddie no' playin' fair, ye treacherous swine?" snarled Hamblin. "Next time I'll put a knife in ye."

"I'd attend to you later," said I to Jake, as the Carpenter rose to his feet.

"Now Peddersen," said I as he squared up, looking a little shaken, "let's stop playing, shall we?", and feinting with my right, drove a straight left that sent him staggering.

With a bull roar, he rushed, and remembering Mr. Hammerson's aphorism,

"Aye, and after all, the best trick of the lot is a straight left every time", I put all my strength and weight into a straight left that took him squarely on the mouth, splitting both his lips and painfully extracting at least one tooth.

"You vait, you vait," he roared, spitting out the tooth.

"I am," said I, and for a second visualized what would happen to me if one of his blows came home and knocked me out.

"You fool," I told myself, "suppose you contemplate a picture of what is going to happen to this foul blackguard."

And taking the fight to him, I evaded his thunder-bolt of a left by a swift duck, cross-countered with my right, hooked with my left, and hit, and struck him a tremendous blow just below the breast-bone—a blow that drove the breath from his body and, for a second, doubled him up. In that second I administered the Hammerson pivoting upper-cut in a manner that would have earned that splendid fighter's entire approval.

Peddersen staggered backward, stared glassily into the far distance, rocked on his feet and fell to the deck inert.

A shout of applause, a ringing cheer, went up from my party—Dacre, Doc, Church, Carrol, Blancke, Berghen and Larry O'Toole. The last-named I observed to be looking anything but mad—unless he were mad with delight, the Irishman's delight in a fight of any sort.

I was glad to see that Hamblin and Axenstern were cheering wildly.

From the Ship-owners came a murmur of what seemed to me consternation mingled with astonishment.

"Well, that's that, anyhow," said Carrol as the 'tumult and the shouting died'. "That's the end of . . ."

"Not a bit of it," I interrupted, "that's only the beginning. Somebody chuck a bucket of water over him—if he isn't shamming."

But Peddersen's twitchings were genuine, and he was not only taking the count unconscious, but taking time for two or three counts.

By-and-bye, he moved his hands and feet as though wiping the deck with them, rolled over, and sat up.

"My Gawd, what a gollya'mighty swipe," said Church in the silence, as all men watched. "Knocked the poor orphan into the middle of next week. Bet you 'e don't know the date."

Peddersen sat up, holding his head and staring around.

"Get up, get up!" said I sharply. "You can't lie there all day."

Peddersen got to his feet.

"You vin," he said, and his hand went behind him in a half-instinctive reach for his knife.

"'Of course I win," said I, "but you haven't finished losing yet. Put your fists up."

"I've had enough," growled Peddersen, and his look

supported his statement.

"Oh no, you haven't," said I. "Put your fists up."

"I ain't ready," growled Peddersen.

"Well, be quick and get ready. Would you like to put your head in a bucket of water?"

Whether to gain time or whether my proposal were really acceptable in his sight, I don't know, but Peddersen took the suggestion, and a minute later knelt and put his head into the bucket of water brought by Slim Johes.

"Take a good 'un, Chips," advised Church, and with a shove on the back of the Carpenter's head, gave practical assistance as well as kindly advice.

" 'Ere, don't drown him, lad. Sinbad wants him," crowed Geordie.

Peddersen rose to his feet, spluttering and shaking his head like a dog, and wiped moisture from his face with his arms.

"Ready?" I asked.

"I told you I'd had enough, didn't I? You had the luck that time. You wait."

"Put them up," said I for the third time, and mercilessly, scientifically, and coldly, executed justice, hitting the man as hard as I could hit.

The fight had become an execution.

But Peddersen, though a vile and evil knave, was, after all, a man, and a strong one; and, suddenly, from his face-protecting crouch he sprang erect, aimed at my head a blow that would almost have knocked it from my shoulders, and, as I ducked and upper-cut, flung his great arms about me, clinging to me like a gorilla to a tree, and working for a hold about my waist with some idea, no doubt, of breaking my back, a feat of which his colossal strength was doubtless capable.

If my intention were to turn the fight into an execution, his was to turn it into an all-in rough-house.

But the instant that he flung his arms about me I stooped, reached outward with my elbows, and rained short-arm blows upon his mark; and they were blows, not taps, a speciality in which Mr. Hammerson—God bless him—had trained me.

Peddersen sagged, releasing his hold; and, stepping back, I upper-cut him—once again in true Hammerson style. And once again Peddersen responded as any man must, who received that blow on the precise spot at the exact moment.

He sank to the deck, his head hitting it with so heavy a thud that there was no possible question of intent to defraud. No man who went down like that could be shamming.

And again my adherents cheered; and this time the Carpenter's following stood silent.

I swung about upon Jake.

"Now do what you can for your friend and leader and *Captain*," said I. "Throw that water over him and bring him round —for some more."

"It wass murder, I say," shrilled Slim Johes.

"It will be, if you don't keep your head shut," I assured him. "Life seems pretty cheap on this ship."

And before my ferocious glare, Slim Johes wilted.

Beneath Jake's ministrations, Peddersen recovered, though I was again interested, and quite definitely pleased, to note that it would have been to a count of fifty rather than of ten, that he opened his eyes.

Jake, aided by Villa, got him to his feet and held him as he swayed.

"Ready?" I asked.

"I'm done," growled Peddersen. "Done fer to-day, any'ow. I vas . . ."

"Done for to-day, are you?" said I. "Well, you're going to be done for this week, and this month and this year . . . and for this voyage . . . before I let you go," I assured him.

"Seconds aht of the ring," bawled Church in referee style. "Toime!"

"Stand away from him, you," I shouted at Villa and Jake, and for some reason they obeyed me.

"Now then, Peddersen . . ."

"I can't," he growled. "I can't fight no more."

"Then you must take it without fighting," said I, "for you are going to get it. You are going to get it for insulting that girl; for whatever part you had in the murder of Mr. Hammerson; and for trying to take charge of this ship."

And stepping up to him, I knocked him down.

"For Miss Bryndal," said I.

Myself I pulled him to his feet, set him swaying drunkenly on his bending legs, and stepping back,

"For Mr. Hammerson," said I.

And with a smashing blow I knocked him down again.

Myself, I pulled him into a sitting position, shook him, ridiculed him, cursed him and with my arms beneath his, lifted him up.

He would not or could not stand, and I had to drop him and

let him lie—gazing at me as might a cobra whose back I had broken.

"Get you up, you dog," I ordered. "Get up, you *Captain*, and fight for your ship. . . . Here, Doc," I added, "do you think there's any medicine in the chest that would get this thing up again?"

"No, Sah. Ah sho don't, but Ah sho can put sumpin' in the galley fire dat would get him up mighty quick."

"Ar, that's right," laughed Church, "put a red-'ot poker on his tail."

"Go on, get up, *Cap'n*," growled Carrol.

"Oop lad, we wants to see ye foight some more. 'Tis champion."

Peddersen sat up and said something in his native tongue.

"Le' me go," he said in English.

"Not under your own steam," I said. "Get up, if you are a man, and take what's coming to you. You asked for it."

I turned to Villa.

"Hey, Villa, put that on its feet."

Now this Villa was a big truculent strong man, something of an unknown quantity, but I was strongly of opinion that his favourite form of fighting was not with fists.

His reply, though metaphorical, remarkable, and unprintable, was definitely in the negative.

"I'll talk to you later," I said.

"Pick that man up and hold him up," said I to Müller.

Müller eyed Peddersen, eyed me, eyed the crowd, spat and shook his head.

"It vas not a fight," he said.

"Of course it wasn't," I agreed with him. "It was a punishment. You are going to get some by-and-bye, if I see fit to give it to you. Pick him up."

Müller again shook his head and growled.

I turned to Slim Johes.

Before I could speak he screamed—literally screamed,

"It iss killing, I tell you. It iss murdering slaughter."

"And not the first on this ship, by several," said I. "*Who killed Mr. Hammerson?*"

And with my open hand I smacked Slim Johes' face so heavily that he fell to the deck.

Behind me there was a sound of a blow and a scuffle.

Villa, creeping up behind me, his hand on his knife, had been knocked down by Dacre, and, knife actually in hand, was rising, with murder in his eye.

"I told you I'd attend to you later, didn't I?" I said to Villa, stepping between him and Dacre. "Can't you wait a minute?"

A surge of my adherents swept Villa to the rail, and kept him there.

"Axenstern," said I, "you are a friend of mine, I know. Pick that dog up, and hold him up if he won't stand."

Baby Axenstern giggled, and joyously swooping upon Peddersen, lifted him as though he were a boy, planted him on his feet and held him erect.

Peddersen stood, and Axenstern stepped back.

"I give you best," said Peddersen through swollen lips, fixing me with his unclosed eye, in which burned malevolent hate not unmixed with fear.

"And I will give you better," I replied, and stepping forward hit him in the face with all my strength.

"That's for the *Valkyrie*," said I.

Scarcely had he measured his length when I was upon him.

"Come up," I said, "come up. Come on. I've hardly begun yet."

"Man, man," cried Hamblin. "Hae maircy on the dog. He's got a bellyfu'."

"I'll be judge of that, Hamblin," I replied, and with all my strength shook and hauled at Peddersen until I had that powerful and burly ruffian on his knees.

"Stay there," I growled.

"Don't hit me, don't hit me . . . Mister," he whined.

"I'm not going to—until you are on your feet," I told him. "White people don't hit a man when he's down—and white men don't stay down while they can get up.

"Now then, get up."

And to my horror, disgust and delight, our bold ship-seizing ring-leader of mutineers burst into tears.

Without restraint, disguise, or shame, Peddersen blubbered.

"There's your *Captain*," said I, turning to his followers, and if anything approaching a look of shame ever visited the faces of Villa, Jake, Müller, Johes, Brown, Paulo, Axenstern and Hamblin, it did so then, as they stood and stared at the defeated broken snivelling blubberer, whom they had elected for their champion and leader.

"Ye domned greetin' bairn," spat Hamblin.

Hands on hips, frowning and trying to look less ashamed of myself than I somehow felt, I stirred the wretched Peddersen with my foot.

"Get you there—on all fours—you dog," I growled, and pointed to where Celia Bryndal stood on the hatch, the better to see the progress of the fight.

"Kneel in front of that lady and beg her pardon."

Celia neither spoke nor moved. "Say after me," I ordered,

" 'I humbly apologize for insulting an Englishwoman whose shoes I am not fit to clean.'

"Good! Now——

" 'I beg God's forgiveness, and the forgiveness of all my decent shipmates, for the part I took in Mr. Hammerson's death.' "

"I didn't . . ." snarled Peddersen, and I raised my fist.

Instantly he gabbled the apology.

"And now——

" 'I humbly apologize to the ship *Valkyrie* for bringing my filthy carcase on board of her and for trying to seize her.'

"Good! Now you can crawl to your bunk. Crawl, I said, *crawl!*" I shouted, as Peddersen went to get to his feet.

"Crawl there on your hands and knees."

And in dead silence Peddersen crawled away—every decent soul ashamed . . . of him and for him.

"Now," said I, "let's hear no more of *Captain* Peddersen. Step forward, Villa, I always try to keep my promises."

Villa did not step forward, but my friends and allies stepped from beside him.

With a spring I landed in front of Villa and used my momentum to add force and weight to the terrific blow I drove through his guard at the point of his jaw.

The back of his head struck the pin-rail almost as hard as I struck the front of it, and he dropped to the deck unconscious.

Müller and Jake closed in upon me from either side simultaneously.

"Yo' move, an' Ah'll brain yo' both, yo' Dutch trash," I heard Doc's voice bawl as I turned on Jake.

And the sight of his brandished belaying-pin combined with a howl of rage from all but the remainder of the Ship-owner gang, caused the pair to step back.

"You would, would you? Come out here in the middle, you swine," I addressed the burly Jake. "Come on."

The treachery had sent me *berserk*, and, provided my knuckles lasted out, and I did not stop an unlucky one, I'd whip the gang.

"Come on, you Jake. You want a fight too, do you?"

I cannot honestly say that Jake paled or flinched; but the look in his eye was neither of confidence nor joy. However, he put up a good show, doubtless impelled thereto by the necessity for maintaining the position of importance, the rôle of hectoring bully, that he had adopted in the fo'c'sle.

With some show of confidence he accepted my invitation.

Quickly I discovered that not only was he a powerful, active and dangerous brute, but something of a boxer.

Now, not only did I suspect this man of a hand in the murder of Mr. Hammerson; but I believed him to be far more dangerous than the Carpenter, and I felt, moreover, that, unless he too were absolutely hum- bled, his evil influence was even yet liable to corrupt some of the more decent members of the crew.

As a fighter he proved tricky.

Standing lumpish and inert before me, he suddenly flashed into violent action with a vile oath, sprang, and lashed out with both hands; drove me back to the pin-rail, and, showing some knowledge of ring-craft, sought to retain the advantage that he now derived from the camber of the deck.

There, thanks to deck hamper and the unmoving forms of Müller, Brown, Johes and Paulo, I was prevented from side-stepping to right or left, and for a few seconds was forced to fight entirely on the defensive and in a very awkward position.

Ducking a right and dodging a left, I smote left and right just above Jake's belt, thrust myself against him, in-fighting like a wild cat, and pushing him backwards as I did so. Although taking heavy punishment, he not only kept his feet, but upper-cut me with such force that he laid bare the bone above my right eye.

No matter; I could now side-step, and deal with him faithfully.

Now facing aft, I got a glimpse of Celia, on tiptoe, her eyes alight, her hands clasped, and it was almost my undoing, for the terrific blow that Jake drove at my face came so near to doing business that it tore my ear as I bent my head sideways.

But both my hands were free and both got home with blows that did Jake no good at all.

At that moment I felt splendid. The warm deck seemed resilient beneath my bare feet, and my limbs seemed to have the force and precision of a set of highly tempered springs. I was in no doubt whatever, and knew that Jake Walfisch's hour had come.

I felt that he knew it too.

So did Church apparently.

"I wouldn't be in old Goldfisch's dirty hide now for a fahsand pahnds," he shouted, and I proceeded to do my best to justify his confidence in me.

But this time I was not facing an untrained fighter who had deluded himself into thinking that he could box. He was proving something of a dark horse, and a cool and wary fighter who did not often uncover for a mere feint. He also discovered a very useful knack of eluding my hooks by throwing back his head in a manner that indicated considerable practice and experience. I began to suspect that, in his earlier days, he had contemplated, and indeed begun, a career in the ring.

From this trick of throwing back his head without moving his body, he derived some satisfaction by causing my first really serious right hook to miss his jaw and describe an arc that finished well to the right of his head. But the grin on his straight gash of a mouth was short-lived. Naturally, he was unaware that this head-tossing was a device with which Mr. Hammerson had been well acquainted, and that under his tuition I was well prepared for the inevitable ensuing upper-cut.

Blocking the latter with my left, I kept my right arm in its bent position, and pivoting bodily on my right heel, brought my right fist hammerwise on to Jake's nose.

Had I been wearing boxing-gloves, this blow would have had little effect other than moral, but, delivered with the bare fist, it brought tears to Jake's eyes, a stream of blood from his nose and, what was more important to me, mad rage to his heart.

"That one 'ad a return ticket," drily remarked Church and, simultaneously with the roar of laughter, Jake rushed.

And now for the beautiful straight left—"the best trick of all".

It took Jake clean off his feet, and gave me a rest of which I was glad.

The men stood and stared in silence at the prostrate rogue.

"Let sleepin' dawgs lie," observed Church, quoting Mr. Hammerson, and there was another roar of laughter.

"Yes," I agreed, "and let lying dogs sleep."

Having had all the rest that I wanted for the moment, I stirred Jake with my foot.

"Come on, man, get up," I encouraged him, and reached for the bucket of water.

Jake arose.

"Ready?" I asked.

He nodded.

Stepping swiftly and lightly round him, I repeatedly feinted at his face with my left, and drove home a heavy body-blow as he guarded high.

Winded and distressed, he lowered his guard to protect his mark, and, with a smashing straight left and a right-handed hook, I sent him down again.

As soon as he was on his feet, I made a swift whirlwind rush, hit him how and where I liked, and, having knocked his head sideways, gave him the Hammerson upper-cut—with the inevitable result.

Jake lay at my feet for the count, and a long count too.

Villa, in the scuppers, had never stirred.

And suddenly I was tired, sick, sorry and ashamed—more ashamed than ever I had been in my life.

Nor could all my remonstrances persuade myself to feel otherwise.

I was a boxing bully; a showman; a swaggerer; prancing about in front of a girl and a knot of brainless tarry-breeks; a cheap, posturing mock-heroic. . . .

Still, I must go through with it.

"Now then, Müller," I said.

And Müller backed against the bulwarks.

"Well, if you won't come to me, I'll come to you," said I, and stepping up to him, banged his head to the left with a right open-handed clout, and banged his head back to the right with a left open-handed clout.

"Any fight in you?" I asked. "Any mutiny? Any ship-owning?"

"*Nein*," growled Müller.

"And what about you, Johes?"

"*Me?*" squcaled Slim.

And there was a roar of laughter at the passion of indignation and protest that the word contained.

"Well then," I grinned, "let me ever hear another word of trouble out of you, and I'll put you over my knee."

A sudden loud shout caused me to turn swiftly about to find that Jake, leaping to his feet and throwing all caution to the winds, was upon me. There was more in this man than I had supposed, and I think that in this moment I finally learned, and laid to heart, the lesson, 'Never despise your enemy.'

However, if Jake were going to indulge in mad rushes he was thereby going to double the force of my blows. I again stopped his rush with a straight left, instantly followed by a very heavy right, and as he checked and halted, another straight left taught him wisdom and drove him to in-fighting.

297

As my knuckles were by now feeling the effect of hitting two hard and bony faces, I was willing to accommodate him.

Laying my head beneath his chin as he clinched, I again rained short-armed jabs on his ribs and mark, which quickly made him glad to go back, gasping and wheezing, to long-range work. . . .

A pause. . . .

I must make an end of this. My hands, though very hard, were not hardened to bare-fist fighting, were swelling badly, and bleeding at the knuckles.

Unfortunately, the left was the worse and could not be trusted to repeat the blow that had put an end to Peddersen, for fear it should not be completely final and should leave me one-handed to finish a fight with a man who was both a fighter and a boxer, endowed with a certain knowledge of ring-craft.

The fist that delivered the finishing blow of this fight would need to be backed by much brute strength as well as knack.

Realizing this, and giving Jake no respite, I drove at him with heavy body-blows and painful bangs about the face until, a battered and beaten man, with his back to the bulwarks, he could oppose to me nothing but the top of his head and a pair of wildly waving arms.

Had this been a mere quarrel I would gladly have let the wheezing, panting wretch give in, but I was fighting for something infinitely more vital than the mere satisfaction of man-handling an enemy.

With a right upper-cut I lifted his disfigured bleeding face, and, aiming for the point of the jaw, smashed in a terrific left hook which, had it reached its objective, would have ended the affair then and there, and would have prevented Jake from knowing pain and sorrow for some time.

Instinctively, however, I had allowed for his trick of throwing back his head, whereas, from sheer exhaustion he had dropped it and brought his right temple into such a position that it received the full force of the blow, and jarred my arm to the elbow.

It was as though I had struck the mast itself.

From the hideous pain, followed by the numbness of my left hand, I had a horrible suspicion that I had damaged myself more than I had hurt my opponent, and it was with great relief that I saw that my last effort, though in itself a failure, had brought me within one move of checkmate.

Jake shook his head and raised it as he drew back his right

fist for the last time.

Now or never! I upper-cut with my right as though I should never want that useful member again.

In that fight I did not, and it was well for me that this was so.

Jake fell like a log, and it was quite clear that the fight was over. What would have happened had he risen to his feet and attacked me, then and there, I don't know, for both my hands were out of action, my last blow (and thank God it was my last!) having reduced my right hand to the condition of my left.

However, since Jake was finished, no one need know.

"Well," I asked, "while we are about it—any more trouble? . . . Brown? . . . Paulo? . . . You all-right, Baby?" And I turned to Axenstern.

"I vas all-right," he giggled.

"Hamblin?"

Hamblin laughed.

"Ah wadna strike—a 'boy,' " he said, grinning, and shrugging his shoulders.

And there was another loud laugh.

And I fancied that there was something if not exactly hysterical, somewhat unusual, in the laughter. Undoubtedly the whole crowd was excited.

In his rare moments of great tension and emotion, Doc always found relief in quoting the Scriptures, and on this occasion he issued a general invitation.

"Behol' how de mighty am fallen," and added what I am sure was a misquotation.

"Dey was not beautiful in dere lives and in dere knock-outs dey are not divided."

(And certainly either Villa's knock-out had done him serious, if temporary, damage; or else he was taking an unnecessarily prolonged rest. I hoped that he had not, in falling, fractured or otherwise damaged his skull.)

"Is that any reason why we shouldn't splice the main brace, Doc?" I asked.

Very loud cheers.

"Sure t'ing, *Sah*," replied Doc.

"Will you take charge, now, Dacre?" whispered I.

"For the moment," he murmured, and at the top of his voice bawled,

"That'd do the Watch, Mr. Dysart. . . . Steward, splice the main brace."

And, followed by prolonged spontaneous ringing cheers, I

entered those sacred precincts where, hitherto, my profaning presence had been briefly tolerated only when sent thither to carry out the instructions of a superior.

CHAPTER XIX

Free to relax, and no longer the centre of observation, I suddenly felt weak, rather frightened, and, so to speak, unprotected.

Slumping down on the settee, I gazed round the Saloon with smarting weary eyes. God! I was tired.

Surely, if I ever carried a pile of sheaves past this dinner-table, it was many years ago? It must have been in a previous existence. For, since I had done so, I had seen two men go to their deaths, had fought two others to a finish, and had knocked another senseless. In fact, in the presence of a girl whom I was beginning to like, to admire and to respect—though I certainly had no wish to "worship her with noble deeds"—I had behaved like a Malay running *amok*, and like a swaggering pot-house bully.

Well, well . . .

And still more incredibly, I had assumed authority and tacitly undertaken to maintain discipline among men who were, some of them, old enough to be my own father, and others tough and "bad" enough to be unamenable to discipline.

Why had I, young, inexperienced and foolish as I was, dared to do such things? Sooner or later I must be utterly humiliated before Celia Bryndal, Dacre, Geordie, Doc, Carrol and such as were my friends.

After the physical and mental strain I had undergone, the reaction was heavy. I put my hand wearily to my forehead and found it wet.

Sweat? No, it was blood.

I must have taken one or two absolutely without knowing it. One does, of course, in a good fight.

Dacre knocked and entered the Saloon.

Knocked!

"Will you come up topside a minute, Captain?" he said.

"What's the joke?" I growled.

And then got to my feet.

"I beg your pardon, Captain," I said.

"Now listen," answered Dacre. "Let's get this clear, here and now. You take me for a man of my word when I give that word seriously—'letting my communication be yea or nay'?"

"Yes," I said.

"Very well. I will not accept command of this ship. I will *not*—do you understand? Not in any circumstances whatsoever—while you are alive.

"And for two good reasons," he continued. "One, the men want you to be Captain; two, you are the better man, the better navigator and the better enforcer of discipline."

I stared at him in silence.

"You have the better 'presence'—and the heavier punch behind it," he grinned.

"'But look here, Dacre," I objected, "this is absolute nonsense. I . . ."

"Listen," he said. "Do you think Geordie, Beauty or Fagin would make a better Captain; or that the men would accept them?"

"No, but . . ."

"There is no 'but'. They couldn't and I couldn't; and if you won't, we can serve under—whom? Church? Carrol? That suit you?"

"No, but . . ."

"Well, look here. There's been another 'Parliament' and it has passed another Act—and I, Geordie, Beauty and Doc were M.P.s, too—and by this Act you are *nemine contra dicente* appointed Captain, *vice* Peddersen deceased—pretty nearly. Come up topside and do the thing properly. Come on, it's the one chance for Celia and the *Valkyrie*."

"Dacre, old chap, I can't and I won't."

"Sinbad, you can and you will. Don't you see, you ass, that you have no choice? That the men have elected you, and therefore have elected to obey you? What are we going to do—with one half of the crew refusing to obey an unelected usurping Captain, and the other half rank mutineers against *any* Captain? . . . For make no mistake, old son, Peddersen, Jake, Villa, Müller, Johes, and the rest aren't the sort who are grateful for a hiding. They aren't the sort that says,

" 'Shake hands, make friends, and all trouble forgotten', after being licked.

"Are you by any chance afraid of them?" he asked softly, as I stared at him in doubt.

"Yes," I replied, "I think I am."

"That's the way to talk," was Dacre's curious reply. "Well, now come and tell the crew so."

The men had gathered at the break of the poop and, looking down on their upturned faces, I saw that Peddersen, Villa, Jake, Müller, and Slim Johes were absent.

Carrol had evidently been chosen spokesman, which struck me as a sign of the times.

"Well," I said, "Mr. Blount says you want to speak to me."

"Yes, Sir," replied Carrol, and he removed his cap. "We wish to tell you that we have duly elected you Captain of this ship and request you to accept same and to appoint Officers. We undertake to do our duty and obey you as Captain until we reach Falmouth or another British port to which we hope you will navigate us."

"But look here," I said. "Mr. Blount is acting Third Mate and has made three voyages in this ship and he . . ."

"Excusing us, Sir," interrupted Carrol, "but it was Mr. Blount called the meeting and began by telling us he didn't wish, and don't intend, to be Captain—not anyhow. We've elected you, Sir."

"Very well," I replied patiently, "and supposing I now recognize your rights of election, and appoint Mr. Blount, Captain, myself Mate, and choose a Second and Third Officer—what then? I can navigate the ship just as well in the rating of Mate, can't I?" I asked. "Let's have Mr. Blount as Captain, with myself as Mate."

"No, Sir," replied Carrol. "We have nothing whatsoever against Mr. Blount, and we'll be glad to have him as Mate, but we have elected you as Captain, and Captain you are."

"And you wouldn't go for to refuse duty, Sir?" cried Church in an agonized voice that brought a laugh.

Then Dacre butted in.

"Hands up those who want Mr. Dysart for Captain," he said.

Every hand was raised—literally every hand, as each man raised two.

"But you aren't all here," I objected.

"Be Goad! We'll soon put that richt," growled Hamblin, and disappeared forward at a run, to return a minute later holding Slim Johes by the scruff of the neck.

"Müller willna come—though Ah hit him on the nose t'encoorage him," explained Hamblin, "so Ah e'en brought this yin."

Again Dacre intervened.

"Church," said he sharply, with the authentic ring of authority in his voice, "go and tell Müller and Villa that the Mate wants them, and unless he sees them within a minute, he'll come himself and kick them from the fo'c'sle to the break of the poop."

"Blancke, go and tell the Carpenter I want him," he continued.

Without undue delay, Müller, Jake, and Villa joined the group. Apparently the position had been explained to them.

Blancke returned alone.

"Der Carpenter says he vas not comin'," he said.

"Then go and fetch him," replied Dacre. "Axenstern, lend a hand."

Axenstern must have lent two, for the Carpenter, a sorry sight, arrived in excellent time.

"Now then," said I, "we're all present."

And, save for Beauty, still at the wheel, and Dacre standing beside me, every soul in the ship was on the main deck and facing me.

"Listen. Mr. Blount declining to accept the command of this ship, you've elected me Captain instead. Every man who agrees to that, raise his right hand; and let every man who does so, remember that I shall consider that, in doing it, he takes an oath of obedience and loyalty to the *Valkyrie* and her owners—and that he will obey my orders and those of the officers."

Every right hand was raised save those of Peddersen, Jake, Villa, Müller and Johes.

"Shove yer 'and up, ye backbitin' bastard," growled Church, and gave Johes what must have been a very painful jab in the side with his left fist.

I heard a sharp *hsst*, and saw Villa glance at Jake and Peddersen.

Slowly their right hands went up.

"Elected unanimously," said Dacre. "Three cheers for Captain Dysart."

And there were three good hearty ringing cheers.

"Your hand is raised, Peddersen?" I said.

"Yes," growled the surly ruffian.

"Good . . . And lucky.

"Now I will ask you the question again," I added, "and you'll answer properly. Your hand was raised, Peddersen?"

"Yes . . . Sir."

"Your hand was raised, Villa?"

"Yes . . . Sir."

"Your hand was raised, Jake?"

"Sure it was . . . Sir."

"Your hand was raised, Johes?"

"Iss it wass, Sir."

"And yours, Müller?"

"*Ja*, it wass, Sir."

"Very well. That's that, then. From now until we reach Falmouth I'll act as Captain of this ship, and Mr. Blount will be Mate. . . . I'll appoint somebody to be both Bosun and Second Mate, and he'll berth aft; and I hope to God there'll be no more rough stuff of any sort, but that we shall be a happy ship from here to Falmouth. . . . That'll do."

§2

Returning to the Saloon, I began the exercise of my little brief authority. In doing so, I might discover that I was really awake, really myself, and things were actually what they seemed.

"Are you there, Steward?" I called.

"Sure, Capt'in, an' yer dinner's afther gettin' cold and him warmin' ut at the galley fire, Capt'in."

Larry O'Toole had come out of the pantry and apparently was not pulling my leg.

No, in spite of my dirty dungarees, blood-stained grimy face, bare feet and broken swollen hands, the little Irishman recognized my authority, such as it was, and whatever it might prove.

So much the better. I would experiment with it and carry on until it came to a dead end—as surely soon it must.

"Get me some friar's balsam or something, for this cut and some hot water to bathe my hands."

Although Captains but rarely say 'please' when giving orders, it was with some difficulty that I refrained. This also went, and not only did Larry bring me those things, but he proceeded to bathe the cut, wipe my face and apply the balsam with a soft brush.

To my surprise I found that his hands were as gentle and dexterous as those of a woman.

The cut turned out to be much deeper than I had imagined, and at the first application of the balsam, I was obliged to draw a sharp breath through clenched teeth, in order not to cry out with the pain.

Suddenly I felt unutterably tired again. Then somewhat sick, and quite definitely faint. I was glad to close my eyes and, lying back in comfort, let Larry bathe my damaged hands. The settee was very comfortable and the cushions soft. One could sleep beautifully here.

Sleep. Oh, to sleep and . . .

Apparently I did so, otherwise how should a feminine voice

mingle with my dreams, and then bring me up from them to consciousness?

"Are you sure he hasn't got concussion of the brain or something, Doc? He's dreadfully white . . . Oh, what can we do?"

Celia Bryndal.

I kept my eyes shut.

"No, Missy. He ain't got no 'cussion ob de brain. Alt'ough him Cap'n Sah dis afternoon, he was a 'prentice dis mornin', an' 'prentices don't get 'cussion ob de brain, even when dey got a brain."

"Well, he's got brains enough, anyhow, Doc . . . And I wish he'd come to life. What should we do if . . ."

"Cap'n Sinbad all-right, I tell yo', Missy. He'm just dead beat. Dis day he have smote de strong men, hip an' t'igh, and he am only a boy. Ob a ruddy countenance like David. An' he knocked out de Goliars widout no sling."

"My God! He's saved this ship, Doc," whispered the girl, "and me. . . . There's nothing I wouldn't . . ."

"Sure, Missy," interrupted Doc, "he saved de ole *Valkyrie* dis day, and all de decent fo'ks on board. Dat Peddersen dog and dat fo'c'sle trash would have cut de t'roats of all dat wouldn't do what . . ."

"Don't . . . it doesn't bear thinking of . . . I wish he'd come round."

"Come round, Missy? He's sleepin' and Ah guess we got to wake him. He's done hab his dinner, but it was only a half-deck dinner, and he suttinly hab earn a Cap'n's dinner—de one Ah got in the pantry fo' him. Ah guess he won't mind another. Den he goss to carry on de work dat he hab undertaken, and may de good Lawd Gawd A'mighty strengthen his right hand. Ah guess a drop mo' of de balsam am goin' to be good fo' dat cut and wake him up fo' sho'."

A touch of the stinging liquid 'woke' me all-right. Looking up, I met the gaze of Celia's clear lovely eyes and I arose, entirely free from the black mood of reaction, and from my recent forebodings.

Doc disappeared into the pantry and Celia Bryndal, with a glance toward the pantry door, literally sprang at me; and, throwing her arms about my neck, pressed her lips hard against mine. I kissed her warmly. In common courtesy and fear of churlishness I could no less.

Having kissed me again, she took my face between her hands and gazed into my eyes, rested her hands upon my shoulders and said with a catch of her breath,

"Thank you—oh, thank you, thank you, Sinbad."

And again she flung her arms about my neck, and kissed me hotly upon the lips.

I felt supremely foolish, lumpish, loutish, and the inexperienced novice that I was.

"Break away," quoth I, in the language of the boxing ring, and was ashamed to seem the mannerless clod that I felt myself to be.

Giving me a look that I could not quite fathom and understand, Celia drew back.

"Listen, Sinbad," she said, "and do, *do* believe that this is good advice. . . . They've chosen you Captain. *Be* Captain. Rule them with a rod of iron. You mustn't only answer to the title of Captain, but you must live up to it; insist on it; and keep it—for everybody's sake. If I thought it meant anything to you, I'd say for *my* sake. But anyhow, they've put it in your hands and you must hold it, Sinbad—if you don't, we're lost."

"Oh, that's all-right, Celia," I replied. "They've elected me Captain and want me to be Captain. I shan't have any trouble."

"My dear boy, you don't know. You don't begin to know."

"What?" I asked.

"Villa," she replied. "Jake. Not to mention the others—Peddersen and his gang. You think Peddersen is the leader. So does he, the fool. But he's *nothing*, compared with the other two."

I smiled.

"Sinbad, for God's sake listen to me. I know things about Villa and Jake and I'll tell you all about them—some time, when we are not going to be interrupted. The rest are just common ruffians."

"Common ruffians!" I said. "Peddersen nobody! Why, it was Peddersen who insulted . . ."

"Yes, yes, I know what he said, but I tell you, Sinbad, I'd sooner be in this ship, with Peddersen in charge, for a month than with Villa or Jake for an hour. *Peddersen!* He's their fool—and tool."

I was learning things, and the girl was so earnest, so certain, so vehement, that I could not but accept them.

"Well," I smiled, "since I've got to play the part so thoroughly, I'd better dress for it, for a start."

"Well then, send for your things and change in the Captain's room. Now you have been elected and have accepted the job, don't be seen again—as you were . . . Captain."

I smiled at Celia Bryndal.

"No, I'm not poking fun," she said gravely. "Far from it . . . Farther than you know. I want you not only to dress and act as Captain, but feel yourself to be Captain right now, and make All Hands and the Cook used to the idea at the earliest possible moment."

"I wish to God it were Dacre," I observed. "He is in all ways— well, in almost all ways—better fitted for the job and the position."

"No, he's not, Captain . . . er . . . Dysart.

"Good chap and loyal soul as Dacre is, he is not as well fitted for the command of this ship as you are, and he knows it, and is the first to admit it. It was he who called the meeting that elected you Captain, and he made it perfectly clear from the first moment that he was not a candidate for the post: and if he had been they would not have elected him. So just you say no more and think no more about it. You are Captain by the choice of the majority—and you be Captain, and behave exactly as though the owners had appointed you after twenty years of service in all ranks from Apprentice to Chief Officer."

"Well, what I shall like least about the job will be giving orders to Dacre," I said, "to whom I still look up as the better seaman, even admitting that he is not the more competent navigator and stronger man."

"Rubbish—and you hear what he has got to say about it."

"An' hab yo' dinner at de same time," came from the pantry where Doc was getting impatient.

CHAPTER XX

My first meal in the *Valkyrie* Cabin was certainly the strangest of which I had ever partaken.

The place of honour was on the comfortable settee at the head of the table; and this seat being naturally allotted to Celia Bryndal, the meal was, probably for the first time in the ship's history, presided over by a lady, and at the unusual hour of three p.m. She, the Captain and the Mate—the two late unconsidered trifles of Apprentice boys—sat and ate in those high places and held council, while Geordie, positively jubilant at losing his watch-below in so noble a cause, proudly kept a look-out on the poop.

It must have been a difficult meal indeed for Dacre.

He was the proper person to have inherited the Captaincy, being Third Officer at the time when the Captain, the Mate, and the Second Mate were killed. He was far senior to me, older, abler, cleverer, wiser, more experienced and a better seaman; but because he believed that I was better fitted to keep strict discipline among the "bad" men, was better equipped for leadership of the others, and was likelier to maintain that prompt and willing spirit so desirable in any ship, and so necessary in this one, he had stood aside.

This would have been fine, heroic, and altruistic in any circumstances; but to act so, beneath the eyes of the girl he loved, seemed to me something far out of the ordinary.

What must have been the temptation to claim his rights and to show himself to Celia Bryndal as the dominant male, the domineering master, the strong and competent man that he was!

But no; Dacre, feeling that the woman he loved, the ship he loved, and the handling of the whole affair, would be better and safer in my hands, put them there and left them there.

When Celia—who seemed to me to have grown up, matured and developed in the stress of the recent dangers and tragedies —spoke with ridicule of my diffidence in accepting the post of Captain, Dacre most emphatically supported her contention that I was the proper person to command the ship, both by reason of my election by the men and my claims by qualification.

Not only did Dacre most stoutly maintain that, even had he

wished to assume the Captaincy—and he warmly disclaimed any such wish—my disposal of the Carpenter's claims rendered me the person best calculated to foster a wholesome fear and respect in the "Ship-owners" and to inspire complete confidence in the better elements of the crew.

I could not then express—any more than I can now do so—my admiration of Dacre's cleverness, lightness of touch and diplomatic ability as he upheld Celia, though every word of her praise of me must surely have given him pain; for Dacre was but human and he was most desperately in love.

"So that's that," he concluded. "Signed, sealed and delivered. We'll admit I may have a little more experience in seamanship than you, but we'll also admit that you are much better fitted to navigate the ship, and infinitely better fitted to maintain discipline—in a situation where the maintenance of discipline is the one thing needful . . ."

"And don't let's go back to it again," interrupted Celia Bryndal. "Dacre's right, and you know it. So quit fooling and carry on from this minute."

Dacre bowed to the speaker.

"So I suggest," he continued, "that you leave the handling of the ship to me, and appoint Carrol to be my Bosun and Second Mate—and I will conduct affairs so that you will appear to be controlling everything yourself."

"Carrol?" I asked.

"Undoubtedly Carrol," he said, "and I will tell you why. I shan't be giving away a secret, for he'll tell you himself if you appoint him Second Mate. He's got a Mate's ticket, and was once a brass-bound officer in a passenger liner."

"Good Lord!" I said. "Carrol! Come to think of it, when he made his little speech to-day, he quite dropped the Fo'c'sle Jack style of talk. I remember noticing it. What's his trouble? Drink?"

"That's it," replied Dacre. "He'll tell you all about it."

I then proposed that the late Captain Bryndal's room should be sealed, that I should occupy the Mate's room, Dacre the Second Mate's, and Carrol the spare berth that was on the port side, and right away from our accommodation. Although nothing was said to that effect, we all three knew that this arrangement was made in order that either Dacre or myself should always be at hand and available, in case Celia Bryndal needed help and protection.

Before we left the table, I endeavoured, from a very full heart, and in Celia's presence, to thank Dacre for the trust that he was reposing in me, for the magnificent generosity and altruism of his action in the matter, and for the honour he had done me, an honour that honoured him even more than it did myself. To the best of my poor ability, I tried to tell him what I thought of him, and to show Celia Bryndal what he really was—since she did not seem quite to know it.

Summoning Doc, we then—not without secret trepidation on my part—entered the late Captain Bryndal's room; and while Celia made a list of the things removed, I took away all official documents, such as the Ship's Register, Official Log, Bill of Health, and Last Port Clearance, and the Captain's sextant, navigation books, charts and parallel rulers.

I had the chronometer installed in the Cabin, and when able, later, to take the necessary observations, I was glad to find that the chronometer was consistently maintaining the small error at which it was rated.

Finding, as we expected, that the Port Clearance from Pisagua showed that the *Valkyrie* had cleared for Falmouth "for orders", we decided to head at once for the Nor'ard.

Before making any announcement or change of course, I wanted to speak to all the men individually. To go with the crowd and to raise your hand, showing that you agree with the overwhelming majority, may or may not indicate your true private feelings.

I proposed to have an interview with each of them separately, while issuing tobacco, and, with this in mind, I requested Dacre and Celia Bryndal to sign, as witnesses, the Crew Accounts and the book in which deductions from wages were entered. Then, leaving these in the Captain's desk, I got Doc to lock the door of the room and take charge of the key, and to seal the lock with wax on which I would impress the badge of a uniform button.

Noticing that Celia Bryndal looked as though she were beginning to feel the strain of recent events, I suggested that she ought to go and have a nap, and this she did, after promising to audit the accounts that I intended to begin in a new book.

Whereupon Dacre, after taking a look round the deck, joined me in the Mate's room—now mine—where, with a few minutes to spare before One Bell, we enjoyed our new-found sumptuous comfort, and indulged in a smoke while we further discussed the amazing situation. . . .

§2

"There's One Bell," said Dacre, springing to his feet, "and before I go I'll call you 'Sinbad' for the last time on this voyage, and I'll say that I shall always be proud of the fact that Sinclair Dysart is my friend and that I had the pleasure and privilege of watching him save the dear old *Valkyrie* from becoming Hell Afloat—and saving a girl from what doesn't bear thinking of—by whipping a foul gang single-handed. . . . What wouldn't I give to have done what you have done to-day! . . . Captain."

And putting on his cap, Dacre gave me a naval salute and turned to go.

"Wait a minute, Dacre, and get this. From here to home I can do precious little without the help of my pal and instructor. I may be able to navigate her a bit, but it will be you who will run the ship, and who will save me from making a fool of myself and putting us in a worse plight than ever."

"Till you relinquish the ship to someone else, I'm *your* man, Captain," replied Dacre. "I'll obey you and treat you in every way as my commanding officer, and do my damnedest to see that All Hands and the Cook do the same."

Strolling along to the pantry I found Doc cutting up meat. With his knife in mid-air he watched me jump up to seat myself on one of the lockers. There, dangling my legs and smoking my pipe, I thought to have a little fun with the old negro.

"Doc," I said, without a smile. "This is a fine state of affairs when the boys are allowed to come into your pantry, sit on top of your lockers and to smoke there without a by-your-leave. What's come to you? You never allowed such a thing to happen before."

"Now don't yo' talk that foolishness," he replied, rolling his eyes. "No boys ain't comin' here, Sah, an' I hopes de Cap'n ain't comin' in here—like a boy—no mo'. Dis pantry ain't no place for de Cap'n, Sah. Supposin' one ob de men was t' see you a-sittin' up dere—damn fine Cap'n you gwine to look. You's goss to be Cap'n all de time now, Sinbad—I means Cap'n, Sah."

"Then you think I can do it, eh, Doc?"

"Cap'n Sinbad, Sah, you'se *goss* to, Sah," Doc replied, scowling fiercely. "If you don't, dere's a plenty of us had better jump ober de side ob de ship and go to de sharks fo' kindness. Yes, Sah. Dere is some sure bad men in dis ship, an' you ain't heard de last ob dem neither, Sah. You beat dem wid fistes, an' you could beat dem wid fistes all de time, Sah. But what could you do 'gainst a knife in de back or sandbag on de neck or belayin'-pin on de head, one dark night? You'se goss to watch out for de bad mans. You goss to put dem right where dey belongs and keep dem dere, and if you don't keep law an' order dere's no pusson else can do it. Ah'm tellin' you, Sah."

"Well then, you'll have to help, Doc," I assured him. "To make good in this job I shall need all the help I can get."

"Dat's de way to talk, Sinbad boy," he approved. "Becase you ain't got no swelled head, and becase you got sense and goddam heavy fistes, you'se gwine t' win t'rough, an' Ah'm wid you all de way. Yessah, I sho am, Cap'n, Sah."

For some time, Doc chopped away at his meat in silence and then haltingly, and with much hesitation, said,

"Sinbad boy, becase you can navigate dis packet Ah'm sho glad dat you am Captain, and becase you can whang de stuffin' outa dirty fo'c'sle trash, Ah'm sho glad. But Ah'm mos' glad becase you am a gentleman, Sah, and knows how to behave rightly towards a lady."

Then anxiously he added,

"While you am Cap'n aboard dis ship, a lady don't need to fear anybody, eh, Sinbad boy? You wouldn't hesertate t' hang him on de yard-arm? . . . Ah sho do lub de planks she's trod on, though Ah nebber would presoom to maintain I was fit t' clean her shoes. No, Sah."

"Doc," said I, "that's really why I have taken on the job. Of course, I want to see the *Valkyrie* safe in port, but that does not trouble me much. That's not the worry that's going to be with me day and night. . . . Until I put Miss Bryndal safely ashore or aboard a homeward-bound steamer, I shan't know real peace of mind. If I could put her off the ship, Peddersen or anybody else could have the job for all I care, but till then, Doc, yard-arm's the word —as you say. I'm ready, willing, and able, to murder any swab that says a wrong word to her."

"De Lawd bless you, Sinbad boy," said the old negro. "You sho is the bestest and most whitest boy Ah ebber see, and wid de Lawd's help, you an' me will watch ober her and get her safe ashore."

"And now look here—about helping. I don't ask you to be a spy or a petty tale-bearer; but I do ask you to tell me everything you know, of what goes on aboard the ship. Everything you hear— everything you think, even. For it might be the means of saving . . . us all. I wouldn't say this if I did not have an idea that you may be right, and that we are sitting on a powder-magazine."

313

"Sinbad boy, Ah'll tell you ebery mortal t'ing, Cap'n Sah."

"Good. Now put some Lucky Hit on the Cabin table, and as I give each man his pound of tobacco, I'm going to have a few words with him. If you stay in the pantry you can hear everything I say and everything that each man says—and afterwards, I want you to tell me what you think of it all. Just every thought that comes into your mind about each man."

"Sho Ah will, Cap'n Dysart, Sah."

And clapping the good chap on the shoulder, I returned to my room.

There, under Dacre's supervision, Beauty and Fagin were bringing in my bedding and sea-chest, and seeing me still in working-gear, neither of them quite knew how to regard or address me. I still looked like Sinbad—the "light-the-binnacle!" boy who had to go aloft and overhaul bunt-lines while the paid men loafed on deck.

With his usual impudence, Fagin decided that he would try to keep me on that footing so far as he was concerned.

"Wot cheer, Sinbad! Wot cheer, me noble Capt'in!" he grinned. "Any chawnce of a Mate's job?"

"Are you addressing me, my lad?" I asked coldly, wondering as I did so, whether I was over-biased in thinking Fagin totally incapable of loyalty and trustworthiness.

Would it not be safer to make him painfully aware that I had the Captain's power as well as rank?

"No, my lad," I said, "there's no chance of a Mate's job—for you. Mr. Blount is First Mate, and the post of Second Mate will be given shortly to a competent experienced and reliable man. Meantime, bear well in mind that any man—or boy—who shows any lack of respect or obedience to the Captain and Officers of this ship, will see his name in the Log-book and himself in irons almost before he knows it."

"Well, I didn't mean no 'arm," growled Fagin sullenly.

"Were you addressing me?" I asked him again.

Fagin's eyes shifted and fell.

"Yes . . . Sir," he replied.

"Ah, that's better, and don't you ever forget the 'Sir' again unless you are honestly seeking real trouble."

"Beg yer pardon, Sir. No offence, Sir," cringed the now thoroughly scared Fagin, and lest Beauty's goggling stare should make me burst into laughter, I abruptly ordered both of them from the room.

Fagin's heavy boots made much clatter, but from the other

side of the bulkhead I distinctly heard a feminine voice—*à propos* of something or other, presumably—cry,
   "Well done!"

CHAPTER XXI

Uniform, with a clean collar and tie, was so essentially shore-rig and reminiscent of evenings in port that, wearing this unaccustomed garb at the Cabin table, I half expected to wake up and find that I had been dozing on my sea-chest in the half-deck. I had a sort of feeling that I must be playing a great joke on some-one, and it was not until I had interviewed Carrol that I began completely to realize, and consider the seriousness of, affairs in general.

After I had given him his four plugs of Lucky Hit and watched him sign the book, I said,

"Carrol, you have been a good many years at sea, and sailed in all sorts of ships with all kinds of skippers. Tell me what you think of this one."

"The ship's all-right, Sir," he growled.

While his attitude was perfectly respectful, his speech was no longer that of the grousing old shell-back whom I had known and beside whom I had worked for so long. If I had shut my eyes and forgotten his dungarees, I could easily have imagined that I was talking to a man of superior station in life, and, acting on an impulse that I had no cause to regret, I decided to take him into my confidence.

"Shut both those doors, and then—sit down on that settee," I directed.

Carrol's screwed-up eyes opened rather wider than usual.

"Now then. Just try to imagine that you are sitting on a spare spar and yarning with—we'll say your friend Church, and telling him what you think of the new Captain and the position generally.

"In other words, Carrol," I went on, "I shall be very much obliged if you will tell me, as man to man, exactly what is in your mind. If you think I've been led into biting off more than I can chew, and have behaved like a silly young fool, don't you hesitate to say so. I shan't mind. What I honestly want out of you, is your real opinion."

After some moments of silence, Carrol spoke meditatively and with periods of thought between sentences.

"No, I don't think you've behaved like a fool, and I'm not sure that you have bitten off more than you can chew. That remains to be seen. I was bothered and uncertain at first, but now that I see

316

the attitude you are adopting and your avoidance of swank and swagger, I wouldn't use the word 'fool' at all. I'd be more inclined to say, rather, that you are a gambler—and a damned plucky gambler—and . . . what shall I say? . . . quixotic."

"Before we go any further," I interrupted, "I'd like to ask you, Carrol, whether you'd have used the word 'quixotic' to anyone in the fo'c'sle, and pronounced it perfectly correctly, too. I don't want to be inquisitive, but not many A.B.s use that adjective, and I'd like to know if you haven't, at some time, been something more than an A.B."

Carrol grinned somewhat sheepishly.

"More shame to me if I have," he said. "Matter of fact, I used to read a bit, and I've always had a liking for old Don Quixote . . ."

He fell silent for a moment or two, and I also held my peace.

"Well, I don't mind telling you, Sir . . . that I've been Second Mate on some crack passenger ships. 'Twas a long time ago though, and I don't advertise the fact. All the same, I'd like to mention that, although I never use it, my ticket was never suspended."

"Then would you mind telling me, in strict confidence of course, why you stopped using it?"

"Well, in confidence, I don't mind telling you . . . Sir," he assented after a pause, and I felt, with considerable pleasure, that he was beginning to warm towards me.

"It's the old story—the old, old, story. Something that I wanted to forget—had to forget—and turned to the bottle for help, for sleep, for oblivion, for something to come between me and the dreadful pain. Soon, though never drunk, I was seldom sober.

"After a time, Captains wouldn't give me a reference and I was more or less forced to go before the mast . . . I went—and there I'm likely to stay."

"We will discuss that presently," I said. "Thanks very much for telling me. . . . Now, why do you think that in taking this job I'm a gambler?"

"You want my candid opinion?" he asked. "Very well then. You stood up to Peddersen, Jake and Villa, and you invited Müller, Slim Johes, Paulo and Brown to stand up to you. Well, when you whipped Peddersen, Jake and Villa so handsomely you only opened the ball, you only began the first stage of what, to my mind, is going to be a continuous, as well as a damned tough, struggle for power.

"It did my heart good to see you knock Seven Bells out of that flap-mouthed, dirty-souled Carpenter—but compared with some on this ship, he's merely a big noisy tough, nasty and crooked, mean and rotten all through, but still only a common tough. And the Mate, Mr. Smeeker, plumbed him up that he was such a helluva fine feller, and made him worse, swelled his fat head a lot bigger.

"And he was in some fancy business or other, with Captain Bryndal. He was the Captain's tool, and thought he was his partner—in some rum game or other—and that didn't lessen his conceit of himself. But you've taken him down a peg—taken him down from the top of the ladder to the bottom—and if you only had to worry about a few Peddersens it wouldn't much matter. You wouldn't have a walk-over, but you'd win."

"Well, who and what are these others—and what can they do?" I asked, eager to learn every last and least detail about my crew.

"What can they do?" cried Carrol. "What did they do to Mr. Hammerson? What did they try to do to you—and Blount . . . Mr. Blount? Who and what are they? From what I've overheard, they are murderers and professional crooks, who'd cut the throats of their own parents for the price of a drink."

"Well, let's get down to brass tacks, and decide exactly which the really dangerous men are. You needn't be afraid to tell me anything you know, for I shan't repeat a word of what you say, to anyone—and I expect that I know them as well as you do. I'll give you a lead. What about the noisy Slim Johes? Poisonous as a snake, eh? A man who'll egg others on to anything—push them on to any dirty work—and never be seen in the front row himself, or do anything off his own bat?"

"You've got him right, to a nicety," replied Carrol. "He'll scheme and plot, and let others take the risks. At heart he's really a coward, but he's got such a gift of the gab that he can lead the men on. You can bet your life it was his suggestion that Peddersen should bluff his way into the Captain's berth, and that he talked the others into backing and electing Peddersen."

"Right. Now take Jake. I place him as a German who has been a good deal at sea—evading the police—and having made Hamburg too hot for him, has become bully, thug, yegg, pimp, souteneur, gangster, and probably assassin, in New York and elsewhere in the U.S.A."

"Just about it," agreed Carrol. "I've heard him talking German to Müller, and as you know, he gives himself out for an American. He's among the three most dangerous men on the ship, for he would stick at absolutely nothing. I doubt if he is as naturally and genuinely bad as some, but he's a whole-hogger, a wholesaler. What I mean is he would never draw the line at anything because it was too wicked. I believe he'd see a theatreful of people burned alive if he could get the cash out of the box-office while it happened. I know he put in some time in Australia though, for Mr. Hammerson tackled him over some word or phrase he used that you wouldn't find outside that country."

"Now Villa," I said.

"Ah, that's the man," interrupted Carrol.

"The real leader, eh?" I continued. "I put him down as a half-breed, probably Italian with a dash of Negro, and there's no worse combination in the world. I should say he has scarcely been to sea before and, like Jake, is evading the police—probably of Chicago. I think he's a genuine professional gangster and crook of the very worst type; the sort that goes in for blackmail, kidnapping, robbery, white-slaving, and murder when it's safe. Bad all through; as bad as a man can be."

"Yes," agreed Carrol, "and as bad as a snake can be. From what I've heard, and overheard, I think you are just about right. But, like Jake, the man's got pluck, mind you—as you found when you tackled him—and that's what I meant when I spoke just now. Don't you think you've done with him, nor with Jake, because you've given them a hiding and knocked them out. He'd fight you to-morrow if you weren't Captain—but he'd have a piece of lead in each fist, and whoever won, he'd sandbag you the very first time you passed him in the dark; or throw a knife the very first time he got you against the light. As I've told you, you have only just begun with him and Jake. I'll lay nobody ever beat either of them and got away with it, yet.

"My advice to you . . . Sir . . . is to put Villa in irons on the first possible excuse, and keep him there till we drop hook in Falmouth Bay."

"And Müller?" I asked. "I don't think he's as bad as the other two."

"He's bad enough, anyway," observed Carrol, "though when I say bad, I don't mean criminal. He's not a professional crook, a criminal and a murderer—but he's a killer all-right: an anarchist, he'd kill anybody who'd got more than he had, and naturally he'd take it from him when he had killed him. He's the sort of man that Slim Johes could work up to anything, and he's got a fine pair of teachers and examples in Villa and Jake. No, I don't think friend Müller would hang back from anything that the others were in, particularly when Slim Johes showed him that he was acting in a good and noble cause and doing as every right-minded anarchist should do—destroying the rich in the interests of the poor; overthrowing any sort of ruler in the interests of the ruled—in other words, killing you and your Officers, and pinching the ship and everything in it."

"And what is an anarchist doing on board a ship, anyway?" I mused.

"Same as one or two more of our beauties—lying low and dodging the police," said Carrol.

"Well, we are agreed about Chips and four in the fo'c'sle. We'll call them the 'Ship-owners', as that's what they call themselves. Now what about the rest? Let's see how many 'Shellbacks' we've got left."

"There are some that don't know, themselves, what they are —that's the trouble," growled Carrol.

"Then we'll tell 'em which they are. For instance now, there's a chap named Carrol. His grousing is merely a pastime to keep up his spirits, and I know he wouldn't be found dead in the company of the 'Ship-owners' if they succeeded in whatever game it is they've got on. Naturally he's not going round denouncing them openly—so that he gets a knife in his back—but he certainly won't join them against the Officers, eh?"

"That's just about the size of it," laughed Carrol, "and my chum Church is the same. He doesn't pray for the Captain and Mate every time he goes to bed, but I know he'd like to see the 'Ship-owners' where they would need a few useful prayers."

"And Hans Berghen and Karl Blancke are nice quiet chaps who merely want to get on with their job and be left alone, eh?" I suggested.

"Two of the best squareheads I ever shipped with," admitted Carrol.

"Well, that makes four 'Shell-backs' in the Starboard Watch alone. We're not doing so badly," I pointed out.

"Yes, but what about the Port Watch?" asked Carrol. "Larry O'Toole is as mad as a hatter. Foyle and Patsy Hooligan are dead, and we know all about Slim Johes and Müller. And that leaves Hamblin and Axenstern. Now, would you call them a pair of nice quiet Shell-backs? Because I wouldn't."

"No, I don't know that I would call them that just yet," I replied, "but I think that, before long, I shall be able to do that very thing. Suppose you send Hamblin along now. Just say that it's for tobacco, and you and I will finish this talk a little later on."

It was a puzzled and rather hostile Hamblin who came down the companion-way to the Cabin door. Events had moved too fast for the slow wits of his almost-perpetually aching head, and he was inclined to look with suspicion on an Apprentice who had so suddenly blossomed into a tobacco-issuing Captain.

"Come in here, Hamblin," I called cheerily.

And crushing his cap into a ball, he advanced a few steps toward me.

"Come closer, shipmate, and let you and me have a crack together," I invited; and was rewarded with a grin that definitely improved the appearance of the Scot's dour face.

With an answering smile I began,

"Hamblin, my son, a day or two ago you tried to persuade me to join the 'Ship-owners'. Would you give me the same advice to-day?"

"I wadna," he declared emphatically. "I didna ken the truth concerrnin' yon dirrty swine, and I'm tellin' ye richt noo . . . Sir . . . that I had naethin' t' dae wi' the dumpin' o' the Second Officer. If I had been a guid eno' mon wi' ma fistes I would hae knocked the heid off o' him—but I'm no bluidy back-stabbin' kill-i'-the-dark murderer."

"And you want nothing to do with murderers?" I asked.

"Ye can tak' yere Bible oath on that, Sir," he exclaimed. "I'm takin' no chances wi' yon cauld-bluided sons o' dogs. Decency apart, I'm no wantin' to stand in the dock at the Old Bailey."

"No, you can stand in a better place than that, Hamblin. Stand in with me," I advised earnestly. "Sooner or later, some-body's going to hang for the murder of the Second Mate, and you don't want it said that you belonged to the gang—or even knew anything about it before it happened. . . . And, besides all that, I'd like to think that you are a decent man, a decent sailor, a decent Scot—and one of my friends . . . for I'm going to need all the friends I can get, and the more of them that are like you, the better."

Hamblin gazed down, wriggled his toes and twisted his cap round and round in his hands.

"Do you think, Hamblin, that I've taken over this skipper's job for the fun of the thing? Believe me, I don't want it, and if you can show me a man who can take the *Valkyrie* home without loss of time, without bloodshed, and with no more deaths aboard, I'll gladly call him Captain yet, and go back to the half-deck."

While his slow mind cogitated these matters, I made an entry in the book and picked out his tobacco. Then looking up suddenly and catching his eye, I said,

"Hamblin, ye Scot, would ye like to see squarehead Peddersen doing this job, Captain of this ship?"

"Goad! Him!" was the scornful response. "The best sicht I ever saw was to see ye leatherin' hell oot o' yon Lang Moll's Ghost. Aye, an' yon Villa and Jake, forbye. Mon, 'twere a grrand sicht."

"Well, since Mr. Blount won't take the job, who would *you* make Captain if you had it all your own way and could do as you pleased? Somebody has got to navigate the ship and keep those damned 'Ship-owners' from taking charge. Who do you really think it should be? Take your time now, weigh up everybody, and speak the truth like the son of your mother."

Hamblin undoubtedly took his time, as invited.

"Ye're the mon that's needed," he decided at length. "There's nane ither ava—that I ken."

And having thus far committed himself, he fought, to my great satisfaction and secret amusement, another tremendous battle with his natural dourness and caution.

"Aye, ye're a real bonny scrapper, Sinbad boy. I beg yer parrdon—Captain. An' I'm wi' ye. I'm wi' ye all the way noo, an' oop t' the hilt. Aye, ye're the yin to clip the ears o' yon bluidy murderin' lass-insultin' thieves o' 'Ship-owners'.

"Ship-owners!" he repeated with withering scorn, and sought about for a suitable spot on which to spit, ere he remembered that he was in the sacred Cabin if not the presence of a particularly sacred Captain.

"Aye, an' I'm never forgittin' what you did for me yon nicht in th' Broomielaw, and what ye taught me wi' the boxin'-gloves."

And looking me straightly in the face and thrusting out his tarry paw,

"Fra noo on," he said with solemn mien, "what ye say, that I'll dae."

"Good man, Hamblin," I said, rising and shaking his fist. "You help us, and we'll win through. You are going to be my right-hand man and a great help to us all, if ever there's trouble in the fo'c'sle. Now send Axenstern along. If I can rope him in too, I think we can take care of the ship."

"An' ye willna hauld it agin me that I was yin o' them?" he turned and asked, as he went out.

"You never were one of them, Hamblin," I replied. "Damn it, man, you are a Scot."

And I thanked God that the question of Hamblin might now

be considered as settled, once and for all.

As is so often the case, where the greatest trouble might be anticipated, there was none. Apparently, the man who could knock folk senseless for the longest possible time and do it in the shortest possible time, was Axenstern's *beau-idéal* of a Captain. Of him he demanded no other qualifications, and, for this reason, he was at no pains to conceal his preference for me.

"*Ja*, Sinbad, you vas goot skipper," he assured me, shaking hands uninvited, and smiting me on the shoulder. "You vas goot fightin'-man—und I vas vork goot for you now always."

I returned his blow upon the shoulder, and running my hand over his mighty biceps, praised it and him, and assured him that he would be not only the best worker in the ship, but my right-hand man.

When he left, grinning childishly, I knew for a certainty that I had won Axenstern also, and I wondered how much my saving of his life on the fore upper tops'l yard had to do with it.

With Karl Blancke and Hans Berghen, as I expected, I was entirely successful. And when I thanked them for their recent support, each assured me that he was not a fighter, only a sailor, but that he would be my most obedient servant in everything that appertained to duty and to the maintenance of discipline.

Peddersen, Villa and Jake were reported to be indisposed, and the angry resentful Müller received his tobacco in a sullen silence which I did not attempt to break.

Slim Johes' equally sullen silence I did not respect: and to him, as a different type of man, I was intentionally truculent and fierce.

"I've only one regret about you, Johes," I told him, "and that is that to-day I didn't give you as good a hiding as I gave your friends. But mark you this, my man. If you give me the ghost of a chance, the merest shadow of an opportunity, I'll give you a better hiding than I gave any of them. It won't be a fight, of course, it will be a punishment. The punishment you've been earning and deserving ever since you stepped aboard this ship. I've only got to hear a wrong word or hear of your saying a wrong word behind my back, and I'll beat the head off your carcase and the soul out of your body. D'you hear, you mischief-making cowardly scoundrel?"

"Iss, I hear 'oo," muttered Johes, and as I half-rose from the settee, hastily added, "Sir."

"Aye, and you forget to say it again, my man, and I'll see you aren't able to say it—or anything else—for a week or so," I promised him. "Now get out, and if you value your health, you watch your step and be careful of what you so much as whisper. . . ."

The negro, Brown, I found somewhat baffling, and at the end of my interview with him I felt, as I had done at the beginning, that he would always do his best to be found on the winning side; and would, on the whole, prefer that the winning side was out to win loot, by fair means or foul, preferably foul.

"Rough ship this, Brown," I said, having failed to get on any sort of pleasant terms with the man.

"Yessah."

"Unhealthy place for bad men," I continued as I handed him his tobacco.

"Yessah."

"Enjoy watching the fight to-day, Brown?"

"No, Sah."

"Not? I thought all you people liked to see a good fight."

"Ah don't like dat sort of fightin' much mahself, Sah."

"Oh? What kind do you like?"

"Ah fights wid a razor, Sah."

"Oh, you do, do you?"

"Yessah. And my fab'rite song is,

> 'Get away . . . get away . . .
> Get away from de window, gals, you hear.
> Come out some other night, for dere's goin' to be a
> fight
> An' dere'll be razors flyin' in de air.'

"Hab you heard it, Sah?"

"No, I have not," I replied, "and I don't want to. And I'll just mention, Brown, that if ever you use a razor on board this ship for any other purpose than shaving your face, I'll attend to you myself, like I attended to your friends Jake and Villa—not to mention the Carpenter. And when you come round, if ever, you'll find yourself in irons—and in the dark somewhere. So take my advice and drop your razor overboard and grow a beard, if you can. . . . Do you hear me?"

"Ah hear you, Sah," replied Brown.

And most intensely I disliked the look in his yellow eyes and the cringing insolence of his manner.

"Of course you don't have to use a razor to get a thrashing, you know, Brown. You can get what will keep you quiet for a few days, by a mere whisper—of the wrong sort. . . . I don't know whether you can use your fists for honest decent fighting, as well as for your filthy razor-slashing, but you'll get the chance if I hear one word against you. Understand?"

"Yessah, Ah unnerstan's eberything."

"That's good. Then clear out—and watch your step."

Paulo, the Brazilian, if that's what he was, I found equally elusive, unsatisfactory and undependable. I could make nothing of him, and decided that, like Brown, he would remain neither proclaimed "Ship-owner" nor authentic "Shell-back" until he saw which side was really going to win. I felt I did him no wrong in believing that his heart and hopes were undoubtedly with the former.

Should the "Ship-owners" get possession of the ship, friend Paulo would prove as villainous a desperado as any of them. While the "Shell-backs" had the upper hand, Paulo would sit on the fence, or rather the forward hatch, and do reasonably well such work as he was unable to avoid.

His weapon, I judged, would be neither fist, razor, pistol nor sandbag, but a long keen knife which he would use with the intimate rapid skill of a butcher, or throw with the neat accuracy of a music-hall artist.

Unable to win him, I warned him, assuring him that the forces of law and order were now firmly and finally established, and that I (though not, as he had seen, too gentle and merciful a creature) would be sorry for him—genuinely sad and sorry for him and his plight—should he deviate one hair's-breadth from the path of duty.

I was beginning rather to fancy myself as a layer-down of the law and an admonisher of the wicked.

I was but young and very very foolish.

My interview with Church was amusing.

Entering without knocking, and coming straight up to the table without any form of greeting,

"Now don't you get up an' biff me in the eye, Sinbad, ole cock," he began. "Let me say me little piece 'cos, after this, I'm goin' to call ye Cap'n and touch me 'at to ye, like a gentleman . . ."

"You or I, Church?" I enquired. " 'When Adam delved and Eve span' and so on . . ."

"Now don' interrupt me, ole Son, 'cos this is me last chance. What I wants to say to ye is that, afore ye takes your plice on yer quarter-deck, I'd like to tell ye that I never seen better scrappin' in all me life, and I spent it lookin' fer trouble. The Christian way ye knocked out them heathen squareheads and Dagoes did me 'eart good. Why, I never see a bloke at a Whitechapel Wonderland as 'it cleaner or worked better. A punch in both 'ands, duckin' for guardin', wunnerful foot-work, an' an upper-cut like a kick from the rudder-end of a mule."

"That all?" I asked.

"No, mate. What I wants to say is, I'll be prahd to serve under you, an' I'll do what you says till I drops; an' in conkerlusion, I wants ter say I'd like to shake 'ands with me ole pal Sinbad afore he turns Capting, and also with the coming World's 'Eavyweight Champion."

"I don't know if there *are* any in the Coming World," I said, as I rose and extended my hand.

"Thank yer very much indeed, Sir," replied Church—about what I know not.

And, wiping his very dirty hand on the even dirtier seat of his trousers, Church took his desired hand-shake and immediately became perfectly serious.

Stepping back, he gave me a tremendous and slightly emotional salute.

"Thank you, Church," said I in turn. "You and I understand each other, and we're friends, eh? Now then, let's talk business, for I want to ask your advice."

"An ole shell-back like me can't give much advice to the likes of you, Cap'n," he remarked.

"Oh yes you can, Church," I assured him. "You can give me advice that I shall value, for one thing, now. I'm wondering about the appointment of the new Second Mate; and I should very much like to hear what you think about it. What you think will be what the Fo'c'sle thinks—the decent men—that is. Who do you reckon is the man who'd best suit the honest men for'ard, and at the same time keep the rogues and shirkers up to the scratch? For rogues and shirkers there are, as you very well know. Now what about Sorder—would he be any good for the job?"

"Fagin?" he snorted, and then laughed. "For one thing, Fagin's too blamed ignorant, and for another, he'd get his snout flattened before he'd been long on the job."

"I don't want to give it to a 'Dutchman', though Blancke and Berghen are both very good sailor-men."

"No, Sir," answered Church, "not with this 'ere bunch of pier-head stiffs, work-shy swabs who know more about pickin' pockets and pickin' oakum than pully-hauly, goin' aloft, or standin' their trick at the wheel. No, the best bloke, as fer as I kin see, is ole Carrol—if you can get him to take it on, which I wouldn't. He wouldn't stand no back-chat and buck, an' 'e'd stand up to any man 'alf his age and twice his strength. And 'e's got the 'ang of it, too. I reckon he's been Bosun before. When his back's up, he talks to 'em in the fo'c'sle as though he was Bosun a'ready. Yes, 'e'd do, Sir, an' you'd find him good at roustin' the 'ang-backs about and around."

"You're right, Church," said I, as though the idea were new to me. "Carrol's the man, and if he's willing to carry on as Bosun—and Second Mate—you'll back him up, eh? For he'll have all his work cut out."

"He will an' all," echoed Church, "but I'll give 'im what 'elp I can. Don't you fret yer fur, Sinb . . . I mean, Cap'n Dysart."

"I'm sure you will, Church," I smiled, "and the next thing is to persuade him. Send him along now, but don't say why I want to see him again—and thanks for all you've said, Church."

And rising, I clapped him on the shoulder.

"You're going to be my right-hand man and a great help to us all, if ever there's any trouble in the fo'c'sle," I said.

Framed in the Cabin door-way, Carrol looked, with his leathery wrinkled visage, seamed and sinewy neck, brown gnarled low-hung fists, such a typical old Fo'c'sle Jack that I nearly decided not to make my offer—until I remembered that it would have to be he or no-one.

"Come in, Carrol," I said, "and let's finish our talk. Sit down. Well, you'll be pleased to hear that I've got Hamblin and Axenstern. Without a shadow of doubt they are definitely 'Shell-backs' now, and of course there was never any question about Church."

"That's good news, Sir," he replied.

"Now I think you'll agree with me," I continued, "that—without the influence of Villa, Jake and Müller—Peddersen and Slim Johes would be very much less dangerous. Well, suppose I put the three worst toughs into the Port Watch, and sent Peddersen and Johes into the Starboard Watch—and make Peddersen and Johes live aft . . . and keep aft. What about that? That would, to a great extent, break up the gang, and give the Second Mate a decent Watch. Moreover, we should know that, compared with the five sound men in the fo'c'sle—of course I'm not counting Larry O'Toole—we should then have only three bad ones. Is that a good idea?"

"Quite a sound plan, Sir, especially as, if you count me, you'll have seven sound men to the other three."

"But I can't count you," I laughed.

"Why not, Sir?"

"Because you won't be in the fo'c'sle. Did you think that I was going to scorn a gift of Providence and waste a man who's got a Second Mate's ticket?

"You're going to be Second Mate of this ship, Carrol. . . .

"Now wait a minute, and don't get excited. Just think now. Apart from the fact that I badly need you and that it is your duty to take the job, it would be a God-send to you. The Owners would be bound to see that you got a Second Mate's discharge, and, in addition to being able to throw extra money into your wife's lap, you could show her a discharge as Second Mate. Just think of that. And most important of all, you take this on and make good—and you are a strong enough man to keep off the drink—and stay a Second Mate. Think of it, man, think of it!"

And there kindled a light in Carrol's eye that augured well for me.

"Well, Sir," he replied, a grouser ever, "I don't see me going up for another ticket at my time of life, and I don't see me at table, with the young lady and you young gentlemen about. I generally eat soup with a fork."

"Say the word, Mr. Carrol, and, if you prefer it, I'll tell the Steward to serve your meals in the spare berth—which will be your room—and Larry O'Toole can wait on you."

This being exactly what I wanted, I promised it willingly and offered it warmly.

"By the Big-Hook Block, you'd coax an albatross out of the sky, Sir," he grinned, "but I'm a prize mug to let you wheedle me."

"You would be a fool, a coward and a cur, if you didn't," I replied, "and you are none of those things. So that's settled, Mr. Carrol," I declared. "And mind you, you are going to be an *Officer*, and I shan't interfere with you in the slightest degree. I suggest that when the men are about, I give you instructions to do anything that you have already privately suggested to me . . . just as a matter of form and to maintain my status as Captain.

"Of course, at night," I went on, "if I am not on deck, you will use your own judgment, and, from what I know of you, you are not the man to reduce sail before it's necessary."

"No, I don't think I shall do that, Sir," he laughed. "My good God Almighty! It'll be wonderful, wonderful! . . . Old times come back—for me to walk the poop again."

Carrol rose to his feet.

"Sir," he said, "I'm very humbly grateful to you for giving me another chance in life . . . a chance to get back from the fo'c'sle to the Cabin—and I'll die rather than that you should regret it."

"I shan't do that, Mr. Carrol," I assured him.

"By the way," I added, "I don't think we can do anything at all for Geordie Stowe or Watton, do you? Though excellent chaps, neither of them is equal to handling a Watch or dealing with such people as Peddersen, Villa, Jake, Müller and Johes—not to mention Brown, Paulo and one or two more."

"No, Sir," agreed Carrol, "neither of them is what you might call man enough to put it across a lazy or impudent seaman, let alone some of those big stiffs. . . . As for Fagin . . ."

"The question doesn't arise," I replied. "One thing more—don't say anything about this, for'ard, and I'll give the men a chance to elect their own Second Mate. They will certainly either leave it to me or choose you, and in either case that will strengthen your hand."

"It will, Sir, and thank you," Carrol acknowledged.

"Right. I'll go up now and tell the Mate all about it."

At the pantry door I paused for a moment and let Carrol get out of earshot.

"Well, Doctor Alexander McGrath, what do you think about it all?" I asked.

"Ah t'inks yo' mind am a whole lot older dan de rest ob yo' body, Cap'n," he chuckled. "You done handle those men jest like you was as old and wicked as me, Sah."

Coming from Doc, this was praise indeed.

CHAPTER XXII

On the poop I had a vivid recollection of the vision in which I had seemed to see Captain Bryndal change into myself, and with some awe I pondered this curious gift of mine; and, with greater awe, the inscrutable ways of Providence.

As I stood and smoked by the mizzen rigging, I feigned to be quite unconscious of the curious glances of the men on deck, and no one, I trust and believe, knew what an effort was needed to compel myself to appear serenely at my ease in my new and exalted position.

At length the sensation of being a hollow masquerading interloper became so strong that I forced myself to stroll aft to the compass. There, I sternly ordered the helmsman, who happened to be Fagin, to watch his steering.

Then from the for'ard poop rail, I called in a voice that I endeavoured to make loud, stern and strong,

"Mr. Blount, come up for a moment, please."

And in the ensuing chat with Dacre, I lost some of the unpleasant sensation that I was moving in a strange dream from which I soon should wake.

Dacre was naturally quite delighted to learn that Carrol was willing to act as Second Mate, and he also heartily approved of my proposal to alter the Watches.

He made the useful suggestion that it would be to Carrol's, and his own, advantage to re-pick them.

Our plan of campaign settled, he sent Beauty to call All Hands aft.

Looking down at the assembled crew I felt sorely tempted to address them from the poop, and thus enjoy the great advantage of speaking from an elevated position.

"The Carpenter and Jake are laid up, Sir," announced Dacre.

"Then turn them out, Mr. Blount," I answered, so that all could hear. "No man shall say that he wasn't consulted about the matters we're going to settle."

And after a little delay, Peddersen and Jake shuffled aft, with their heads heavily bandaged.

"Well, you've all had time to think things over," I began, "and I want to know if any of you have changed your minds.

"Are you still quite satisfied, Peddersen?" I asked suavely, and the idea of the swathed Peddersen being satisfied proving too much for Geordie, that small youth sniggered audibly, and was promptly cuffed by the Mate, late his comrade of the half-deck.

"Well, are you satisfied, Peddersen?" I repeated shortly.

"Yes," he croaked.

"What did you say?"

"Yes . . . Sir," was the reply.

"Very well then. I take it that nobody has changed his mind as to my being Captain on this ship," I observed. "All-right. Mr. Blount becomes Mate, then, and we now have to appoint a Second Mate. Anyone make a suggestion?"

There was a fairly general cry of,

"Leave it to you, Sir."

"Very good," said I quickly. "Then Carrol, from this moment, becomes Second Mate, and Mr. Carrol to everyone on board."

"Good ole Christmas Carol," bawled the impish Church. "H'm . . . what I said was, 'Three cheers for Mr. Carrol'."

They were given cordially.

"Thank you. And that'll do you, Church, my man," growled the new Officer, but there was a humorous twinkle in Carrol's eye as he frowned upon his old mess-mate.

Then, with what I hoped was a stern and menacing glare at the knot of "Ship-owners", I approached the most vital matter.

"I have only one more question to raise, men," I said. "This ship cleared from Pisagua 'for Falmouth for orders', with ample provisions for the passage there. We're only one man short in the fo'c'sle—and the Carpenter will now go Watch and Watch—and I know of no reason why the vessel shouldn't complete her voyage as ordered by the Owners' Agents. Any remarks?"

"No, Sir, there ain't. We're for 'ome sweet 'ome," joyously exclaimed Church.

There was a chorus of assent from the "Shell-backs" and sullen silence from the "Ship-owners".

"That's settled," said I. "We're bound for Falmouth. And now pick the Watches, Mr. Blount."

"Aye, aye, Sir," answered Dacre. "Pick the Watches it is, Sir. Port Watch—you, Jake Walfisch, step over here."

"You to starboard, Johes," called the new Second Mate.

Both men opened their mouths to protest, but even as they spoke, Dacre called Müller to port, and Carrol called Peddersen to starboard.

And so, alternately, each officer chose his man.

As we had arranged, Jake, Villa and Müller found themselves in the Port Watch. Slim Johes and Peddersen were in the Starboard Watch.

Finally Dacre took Beauty, and Carrol took Fagin and Geordie.

Pretending to take no interest whatsoever in the formation of the Watches, I returned to the poop, and there quietly gave Fagin a bright brief sketch of what would happen to him if he were found fraternizing, in any way whatsoever, with any but his shipmates of the half-deck.

When Dacre interrupted with the information that the Watches were now picked, I said a final word to the men without again descending from the poop.

"You've honoured me by making me Captain, men," I told them, and most of them undoubtedly thought that they had. "But I warn you that I'm going to be Captain in dead earnest from now on, and I'm going to exact absolute and prompt obedience. And what's more, I shall expect you to obey Mr. Blount and Mr. Carrol just as you did Mr. Smeeker and Mr. Hammerson."

Then to Dacre I barked,

"Mr. Blount, please see that Johes brings his gear into the berth next to the Carpenter, and that on no account does he go for'ard unless ordered to do so. The same applies to the Apprentices. Any man found entering their half-deck or coming aft without orders, will be in trouble. . . . That'll do the Watch, Mr. Blount. . . . Stand by to check the yards, Mr. Carrol."

With the intention of consulting the chart, I now went down to the Saloon, and, at the same moment, Celia Bryndal entered by the opposite door.

"I've just told the crowd that we are going to be a very happy family right from here to Falmouth," I smiled.

"You think so, do you?" was the reply. "I heard every word through my port-hole. You've begun well, Sinbad."

"What did you call me?" I said.

"I called you 'dear'. Didn't you hear me, Captain?"

"No, Miss Bryndal, I didn't," I replied.

"Then listen, little man," replied my passenger, and stepping forward and flinging her arms about my neck, she whispered.

"Dear, *darling* Sinbad," in my ear.

Evidently this was going to be my next difficulty. Wasn't a gang of potential murderers enough for a man to handle, without having to cope with a girl as well?

§2

Youth is nothing if not adaptable, and after we had enjoyed—or suffered—our new authority for a day or two, Dacre and I agreed that we might have been in such a position for years. It seemed like years.

The weather that we had enjoyed, since suffering and surviving the perils of the Horn, continued in a wonderful sequence of perfect days, broken only and rarely by occasional tropic squalls: and as my excellent Mates took all responsibility for the actual working of the ship, I found myself virtually a time-killing passenger.

The most meticulously careful navigation-work could occupy only a fraction of the day; and it was not very long before I began to realize how it is that some sailing-ship Captains are liable to become morbid; some to drink more than is good for them; and others to become eccentric, if not actually mad.

The Captain of a ship is a lonely man. Surrounded by men, he is alone.

As far as possible, and, as I was forced to admit, under the influence and restraint of a curious kind of fear, I kept as aloof as possible from Celia Bryndal.

Nevertheless, I could not evade her entirely, whether on the poop or at table. But so far as I could, I avoided occasions of tête-à-tête conversations with her in the Cabin—mainly by shutting myself in my room, where assiduously I read such books (once the property of Mr. Orlando Wight) as *Darner's Seaman's Friend*, and that invaluable work *Treatise on Practical Scamanship*, wherefrom I learned much about the duties and responsibilities of a Ship-master, and gleaned useful items of knowledge concerning my profession.

My rearrangement of the Watches seemed to have worked perfectly; and even the members of the "Ship-owner" gang appeared to have become models of good behaviour, if not of energy, efficiency, and speed.

To my amusement, I noticed that Beauty no longer slept on every possible occasion, and, during his watch-on-deck at night, was to be seen pacing to and fro under the break of the poop; and when Eight Bells was struck, he invariably waited to be relieved by Geordie.

Commenting to my Second Mate on this phenomenon, I was surprised and touched to learn that, not trusting the "Ship-owners" in the slightest degree, they had constituted themselves my personal bodyguard and watch-dogs! I gathered that the better the "Ship-owners" behaved, the more suspicious of them did Beauty and Geordie feel.

Bluntly offering his opinion that it was a good job that everyone was not as trusting as myself, Carrol expressed the highest approval of their conduct, and, on my pooh-poohing the idea of any danger of that sort, replied with ominous shakes of the head, that, even yet, I little knew the gang.

"You are competent enough to command this ship, Sir," he said, "but you simply are not competent to understand men like Villa, Jake and Müller—not to mention Peddersen and Johes. They're beyond you."

I laughed.

Jocularly suggesting to Geordie that he and Beauty had less of an eye to my safety than to the delicacies that I caused to be sent to the half-deck, I fairly roused the Yorkshire lad's indignation and disgust.

Angrily he replied,

"Yere groob's nowt to me, nor yet to Beauty. It's juist that, though ye be the Captain an' all, ye belong t' the Half-deck, an' we're domn prood o' ye, Sir. We're prood that once ye were oor friend, and that now ye're a champion Captain, an' we'll see to it that none serve ye like Mr. Hammerson was served—an' ye can keep yer groob."

For this disrespectful speech I liked dear Geordie none the less. I tousled his hair, clapped him on the shoulder, swung him round, kicked him in the seat of his pants, and bade him lay for'ard. Also I saw to it that the 'groob' of the half-deck was yet further improved.

The days passed. . . .

In spite of the sharp look-out and the frequent sending of Geordie to the mast-head with binoculars, we were well north of the Line before a homeward-bound steamer was sighted. She proved to be one of the biggest of the Castle liners, and I was both delighted and thankful to have such an ideal means of ridding myself of the dangerous presence of Celia Bryndal, and of sending her home with the maximum of speed and comfort.

When, gleefully, I told Dacre the news, he tried to hide the undoubted ruefulness of his smile. However, smile he did, and unselfishly was glad, while broken-hearted, that Celia would now be beyond risk or thought of danger, as well as removed from this blood-stained tragic milieu to the peaceful normality of a luxurious liner.

§3

But we reckoned without our "hostess".

To my utter astonishment and chagrin, and to Dacre's well-concealed thankfulness and joy, the young woman utterly and flatly refused to be transferred from the *Valkyrie* to the liner, and calmly declined to pack her belongings or make any preparation for leaving us.

In vain I pointed out the delights of passenger-ships; spoke of noble bath-rooms; of magnificently fitted cabins with tryptich mirrors; of deft stewardesses; of a hair-dresser's shop; of a laundry; of seven-course meals; of deck games, and of beautiful young men as dance-partners; and of every other thing which should appeal to a young woman, and every other inducement of which I could think.

When I had, at length, completed my list and my passionate appeal to her higher—or lower—nature, Celia eyed me for a moment in silence with a look that appeared to mingle pity with contempt, and her reply was discouraging and cryptic.

"Wonderful," said she, "the monkey and the nuts!"

And then, with flashing eyes—and I was almost about to say, bared teeth,

"Is my presence here so very distasteful then?" she snapped or snarled.

In vain I pointed out that I had nothing but her comfort, welfare and safety in my mind.

"It is awfully good of you," she replied. "Look out for your own, for it's going to take you all your time, Mr. Clever Captain."

Believing, in my youthful innocence, that something of the kind was indicated, I informed Celia, without prejudice to the main theme, and admittedly as a digression, that the angrier she became, the more beautiful she appeared.

"Well, I'm likely to get more and more beautiful if you don't shut up and clear out," she replied.

"Is my presence here so very distasteful, then?" I quoted feebly, ere being reduced to mortified silence.

"Yes," grinned Celia, "you go to the liner yourself. Go, by all means, if you want to be rid of me. And let me inform you of this fact . . . I'm on this ship's Articles as Stewardess, and if you attempt to remove me from here by force or against my will before the completion of the voyage, you will be doing an illegal deed which will give me ample grounds for taking action against you, apart from any question of seizure, wrongful imprisonment, assault, battery, demurrage, jetsam, flotsam, tare, tret, *habeas corpus*, arson, and sea-sickness in a small boat. . . . You'd certainly do time for doing that—or those."

"I'll risk it," I said when she had quite finished.

"Celia, listen. As you know, we've got trouble aboard this ship . . ."

"Yes, I *do* know—and a good deal more than *you* know."

"Well, your going would more than halve it. We might have trouble but we should not have worry and anxiety and—fear."

"Oh, Sinbad . . . Darling Sinbad. Do you really feel worry and anxiety and fear—on my account? *You*—fear!"

And smart as I considered myself at ducking and dodging, her arms were about my neck and her lips on mine before I could move.

Or was it before I tried to move? Was I getting to like that stirring, exciting, inflammatory feeling of her soft warm lips on mine, her clinging loving arms about my neck? . . . I who had never been loved and had never loved. . . . Love-starved . . .

But of course I had loved Cragellachie, my Cairn, dearly, and the child Elizabeth. Yes, little Betty, of course—quite as much as Cragellachie . . .

Celia withdrew her lips from mine and looked me in the eyes.

"You really do fear on my account, Sinbad?" she said.

"Wouldn't any man, in the circumstances, fear that . . . ?"

"Oh, damn 'any man'," she cried, and flung away from me, to my instant relief, and decision that I did not like her kisses.

"Now listen to me. I'm not leaving this ship. Not on any account—not for anybody, nor for any inducement. And I'll tell you another thing. For all your cocksure cleverness, the time will come when you'll be damned glad that I didn't go.

"Now then, you signal that liner, and I'll go for'ard and raise a mutiny on you. Don't you think I couldn't do it."

I laughed.

" 'The face that launched a thousand ships,' " I quoted with banal and nervous foolishness.

"Yes, they couldn't get away fast enough," replied Celia. "Now, are you going to signal that ship? Because, if so, I'm going to do one or two things that will surprise you."

"I'll talk it over with the First and Second Officers," I replied, and left her.

Again Dacre undoubtedly tried to hide his real feelings, and said that he thought I should signal the Castle ship and have Celia transferred.

"And if I do," I said, "I'll give you the job of seizing her, scragging her down into the boat, holding her in it, and getting a rope from the liner hitched round her so that they can haul her aboard, for she'll never go up any companion or rope-ladder. She simply will not go. But no doubt you could take her as a sort of parcel, if she were gagged and bound, hand and foot, and perhaps lashed to a plank or something. . . . It would be a nuisance if she jumped out of the lifeboat."

Dacre looked scared.

"I couldn't use force," he said.

"Would you like to try persuasion?" I asked.

"Well—er—yes, if you don't mind. Not that I think I can succeed where you failed."

"Oh, never mind that. You go and have a try, my lad. Go and knock on her cabin door and tell her you have come for her."

And I strode the weather side of the poop, in what I hoped was true Captain style, while Dacre went below.

I didn't stride for long. Dacre returned in a very few minutes, with an all-but-visible "flea in his ear".

I smiled.

"Nothing doing?"

"Er—less than nothing," replied Dacre.

"Let's see what Carrol has to say," I suggested.

Carrol took the view that if Celia had said she wouldn't go, there was no point in our saying anything at all. Also that she'd seen what had happened, could be under no delusions, knew as much as we did, and quite possibly a good deal more.

Anyhow, after another appeal to Celia, I gave it up, and told her she should have her way.

"What did you think I should have?" she asked.

And the liner passed unsignalled.

CHAPTER XXIII

Peaceful days passed; things went splendidly; our sense of security grew; and more and more did Dacre and I feel as though we had held our respective positions for years.

So smoothly went the working of the ship; so contented, ready, and willing, did all hands appear, including even the "Ship-owner" gentry, that I should exaggerate but little if I said that my only worries, troubles and anxieties were provided by Celia herself.

Not worry, trouble and anxiety on her account; not fear for her—as in our now peaceful and happy ship that fear seemed absurd—but worry and anxiety caused by herself.

For Celia would make love to me. She became more and more openly affectionate, demonstrative, possessive, in fact aggressive

And the more she did this, the less I liked her . . . the more afraid of her I became.

I cannot explain why; I cannot satisfactorily analyse my own feelings, but the sound of her approaching foot-steps made me uncomfortable. The sound of her voice, calling my name, made me wish to creep away; and to be left alone with her made me nervous, self-conscious, apprehensive, and as I say—afraid.

Celia frightened me.

It was borne in upon me that I was no match for her.

One night, she entered my cabin after a perfunctory knock, just as I got into bed.

"Hullo, what's happened?" I cried, grabbing for my clothes and expecting I know not what. "What's wrong?"

"You, darling Sinbad," replied Celia, and came over to my berth.

"What do you mean?" I asked quickly. "Anybody been annoying you?"

"Yes."

"Who? . . . Who?"

"You."

"I?"

"Yes. I want to talk to you."

"Well, if it's really urgent and important, I'll get up and dress,

338

if you will clear out."

"No need for that, Sinbad. I'll talk to you here."

And folding her arms on the side of my bunk, which was some four feet or so from the floor, she bent over me, brought her face slowly down, and pressed her lips on mine.

For a moment, the sensation was alluring, ecstatic, delightful, and I raised my arms from my sides to throw them about her body.

Even as I moved, revulsion came—and fear. I did not like Celia. She amused, interested and, in a way, charmed me. If she would but leave me alone, I should probably like her—and more than like her. Her passionate kisses inflamed me—and yet frightened me almost to the point of dislike, nausea, revolt.

Instead of embracing her, I took her by the shoulders and thrust her from me.

"Get out of here at once," I said. "If you have anything of importance to say, I will come out and hear it."

"Oh . . . Of importance, Sinbad!"

"Yes—of importance, Celia."

"Oh, it's hardly important, Sinbad. Only my . . . life, happiness . . . my love . . . everything in the world that matters—to me. That's all, Sinbad."

I yawned.

"Well, we'll talk about all that to-morrow," I said, through a second yawn. "Now get out."

Celia drew back and turned to go.

Suddenly she wheeled round upon me.

"Now I'm for it," thought I, and prepared to be blasted where I lay.

But Celia was no ordinary girl. She laughed—actually laughed, and to me it sounded genuine.

"Do me a favour, Sinbad?" she asked.

"Certainly, within reason. What is it?"

"Do come and throw me out. Come and give me the sound smacking I deserve, and throw me out."

"Get out yourself," I growled.

And Celia went.

Yes, a truly remarkable girl. And let no-one think that I lay there feeling a St. Anthony triumphant. I felt wretched, miserable and ashamed—ashamed for myself and for Celia. And I had not the consolation of feeling that I had fought a battle with my baser self and won it. No battle at all. Before I so much as thought of resisting temptation, there was none. There was no temptation. A hot ecstatic longing, a delirium of joy, changed to distaste, dislike, and indeed, as I have said, to revulsion.

It was not even a case of *"the thing he loved so much had turned to dust and ashes at his touch"*. It was as though a thirsty man, extending his hand to take a ripe and glorious fruit, found in the act of touching it, that it was inedible. . . .

I fell asleep wishing that my pup were curled up on my bed; wishing that I could climb the wall that separated me from Elizabeth; wishing that . . . wishing . . . How warm, peaceful and comfortable it was on the wide stone coping of the Roman wall. In a moment I should hear Betty's whistle. What a lot I should have to tell her when I had dropped down into her garden, and we, our arms about each other, wandered off to our own place in the shrubbery . . .

§2

Suddenly I sat up—found that I was not on top of the garden wall but in my bunk, and listening, as though my life depended on hearing again a sound that I must have heard in my sleep.

From the deck above me there came no sound but the kick of the rudder-head, and glancing at my watch on the bulkhead, I saw that it was past one a.m.

From this I knew that Dacre was on watch, and hearing no sound of work on deck, I wondered at his lack of movement.

Also I had often observed that he always paced the poop, and could never stand still for more than a few seconds. I had an instinctive or sixth-sense feeling that something was wrong. So dead a silence seemed oppressive, unnatural . . . I would listen a while. Surely before long I should hear some reassuring sound, some familiar noise, to show that all was well, everything normal, and the night-life of the ship going on as usual.

No, there was no sound, and I did not like the prolonged silence.

Jumping from my berth, I pulled on some clothing and shuffled my bare feet into slippers.

As I did so, I heard a sound, and it came as a distinct relief in that curious and inexplicable silence.

But I realized that the sound had been the soft shutting of a near-by door, and the turning of a key in the lock.

That was strange. Who should be shutting—and locking—a door down here, at one o'clock in the morning?

Puzzled and perturbed, I stiffened and held my breath. That

sound must have come from Celia's door.

Now, even supposing that she had left her cabin and returned at this time in the morning, why should she lock her door? Why should she wish to lock herself in, when she knew quite well that a call would bring assistance almost as soon as it was uttered?

Also I happened to know that she was not in the habit of locking her cabin door; for, in point of fact, she had told me so, a piece of information which I had received in stony silence, and affected to misunderstand.

Pulling on my coat, I was about to go and ask if all were well with her, on my way to the deck, when the light of the door-way was blocked and, as I turned, a voice said,

"Put 'em up, *quick*. An' if you don't want some lead ballast, don't try to pull any funny stuff."

The voice was Villa's, and in his outstretched hand was a gleam of metal.

I thought quickly.

This desperado would think no more of shooting me than of putting his foot on a cockroach.

This must mean that the "Ship-owners" were now—owning the ship. This accounted for the extraordinary silence on deck. They must have seized the ship, and seized it noiselessly. If this were so, they would certainly kill me; and it was my business to postpone that event as long as possible.

While there's life, there's hope.

"Well, please yourself," said Villa, and I heard an ominous and disconcerting click.

I 'put 'em up'.

"So!" sneered Villa. "Right! . . . Now come outa that and get up on deck."

As I stepped from my room he blocked the way to the Cabin, and forced me to go to the for'ard end of the alley-way.

With his pistol pressed hard against my spine, he made me open the door that gave access to the main deck. He was too cunning to let me go by way of the dark cabin, and the winding companion-way that led up to the poop. There I might have given him the slip, or taken my chance by suddenly wheeling round upon him.

On deck, moonlight made the night nearly as bright as day and I saw that, with their hands behind them, Dacre and Carrol were lashed to the pin-rail. Beside them was a third man. Yes, as I had anticipated, it was Doc. Evidently they too had been caught napping, or legitimately asleep.

With myself helpless, the assembled "Ship-owners" now had the whole of the after-guard at their mercy; and, although I bore myself with what calmness, confidence, and dignity I could assume, I was frightened—frightened to death; and my heart was like lead.

I thought at once of Celia, and bitterly I regretted the rudeness and brutality with which I had spurned her offered love and ordered her, like a dog, out of my cabin.

And how utterly I reproached myself for not forcing her to leave the *Valkyrie* for the Castle liner, though even then I did not see how we could have done it against her will, nor how the liner's Captain could have accepted a violently unwilling and protesting passenger. Still I ought to have tried it.

We men could take our chance, but the thought of her in that locked room there behind me made me sick with fear.

Glancing round, I saw a prostrate figure by the port poop ladder.

It was Geordie, out-stretched, face downward. Before he could give the alarm, the poor little watch-dog had been silenced for ever—sandbagged, doubtless, from behind, by some bare-footed creeping fiend.

While the muzzle of the pistol remained pressed hard against my shoulder-blades, my hands were lashed behind my back by Müller, who did his job thoroughly.

"Get your back agin that rail," snarled Villa, and holding the pistol a foot from my face, waited while Müller lashed me firmly to it. While this was being done, I wondered whether he hated me enough to shoot me in cold blood. I doubted it, believing that he was probably too big a coward openly to put his neck into a noose by turning pirate and murderer before so many witnesses.

I soon learned that some of my youthful innocence and ignorance still clung to me, and that I had been as far as Celia had said I was, from realizing the full depths of these brutes' base vileness.

With the pistol now pointing at my stomach, the scoundrel seated himself on the after hatch and leered at me joyfully. It was his turn . . . and he was enjoying it, and evidently he was going to make the most of it.

I am thankful that I still believe, indeed know, that the terror, which I felt, was for Celia Bryndal; and the rage, which I felt, was for the murder of faithful Geordie. How I wished that I had been kinder to him in life, now that he lay there beyond the reach of kindness and unkindness—still in death.

"Now, me noble lord, how do you like the look of yer Jedge an' Jury?"

The latter laughed and I glanced at their grinning faces; at Jake who had seated himself on one side of Villa; at Peddersen on his other side; at Slim Johes; at the nigger, Brown; and the yellow Paulo.

"This is a Fo'c'sle Trial, this is—like the Fo'c'sle Parliament you heard something from the other day. Pity you didn't listen, wasn't it? If you'd listened then, and kept your fat head shut, you wouldn't have been where you are now."

"No," said I, "I suppose the decent and honest men would have been dead and overboard by this," and I wondered what had become of them.

Had they murdered the Apprentices, and Church, Hamblin, Blancke and Berghen?

"Decent and honest men!" growled Villa. "Bone-headed guys that don't know enough to come in out of the rain: don't know enough to take what's on their plates an' put it in their mouths. Silly-faced suckers that'd sweat their guts out for a thing like you, when they might be owning the ship and living like gentlemen."

"Gentlemen!" I murmured, and laughed quietly.

It seemed to me that my one hope and chance was to get free. Tied up like this I could do absolutely nothing at all. It might be possible to rile this creature into putting up a fight with me and turning me loose for the purpose of doing so . . . and could I win the crowd round to my side again?

No, this was not the 'crowd'. It was the scum from the top and the sediment from the bottom.

Again, where were the men who had promised to support and stand by me.

"Yes, *gentlemen!*" bawled Villa.

"Why, you rotten yellow dog," I sneered, "you're not even a man, let alone a gentleman. You don't even know what a man is, much less what a gentleman is. Why, you haven't the pluck and nerve of a cockroach. You're only fit to face a man when the man's tied up, unarmed, and you've got a gun."

But the crook refused to be angered, or at any rate to be drawn.

"Listen to the fool. Just listen to him, will you? He seems to think this is some sort of a fight."

"No, he sure hasn't got the Big Idea a-tall-a-tall," grinned Jake.

"No," agreed Peddersen, "he doesn't yet know that this vas a Court of Justice. . . . Didn't the Judge tell you," he shouted at me, "you poor dumb fish, that you are on trial?"

"And don't you know enough yet, even you?" asked Villa, "to know that Jedges don't carry out the sentences they pass?"

"Judges!" I laughed. "Sentences! You're going to know something about Judges and sentences before you've done, and so are those murdering swine beside you, and the fools they've corrupted. You're going to learn—if you live long enough—that those who commit murder in a British ship, live to dance at the end of a British rope."

"Prisoner in the dock can shut his head," replied Villa, "while the Jedge announces the verdict on him and his accomplices— and then leaves the Court to carry out the doings. So listen, me noble fightin' Capt'in, and learn how much fightin' there's comin' to you from now on—s'far's this Court's concerned. Any more fightin' ye do will be with the 'murderin' swine' beside ye, an' the 'fools they've corrupted'.

"An' what's all this talk about murders?" he continued. "Nobody ain't murdered you yet, have they, nor yer five-cent Officers? Look at 'em—like chickens just goin' into the oven."

At this point, Jake roared with laughter and smote his thigh.

"Sure, that's a funny one," he guffawed.

Müller laughed too.

"*Ja*, juist like chickens going into the oven—and juist what they are. *Ja . . . ja.*"

Peddersen and Slim Johes did not seem to see the joke.

Neither did I—then.

Nevertheless when the Judge honoured his own wit with a hoarse laugh, Peddersen and Johes guffawed as loud as any.

"Laughter in Court," observed Dacre, who hitherto had been silent.

"Oh, you'd open your head, would you?" growled Villa, eyeing him. "Wonder if you'll laugh when you've heard the sentence."

Dacre yawned.

"Probably," he said. "You're a funny man, Villa, funnier than you know."

"An' he sure has got a funny sentence for ye," sneered Jake.

"Well, take in the slack of your jaw-tackle, and get on with it, ye mouth-flappin' swab," growled Carrol. "Get on with it; it's all you're fit for. There's not a dog of you, sittin' there howlin' on your haunches and scratching your fleas, dare loose the Captain and stand up to him. No, nor two of you at once."

"Order there. Keep order in Court," replied Villa. "You Slim, go and smack that yapper across the chops. He's takin' your job away. Thinks he's got the gift of the gab, now. Go on, hit him, you, before the Jedge boots ye out of the Court an' over the side. What're ye afraid of—his hands are tied, aren't they?"

To be fair and honest, I think it was this very fact that made such a task distasteful, even to Slim Johes. However, Villa half-rising to his feet with an ugly scowl, Johes hastened to do his bidding, and with an open hand and all his strength, struck Carrol across the face.

"Take thatt, Mr. Second Mate," he screamed, and working himself up into a rage, struck Carrol again with the other hand.

"Thatt will teach you to call yourself an Officer over me and give me your orders, you tirty Jack Skite of a Shell-back, yess. There's something to remember me by, whatteffer."

"I'll remember you, Johes, never fear," said Carrol quietly.

"Now then, order being restored in Court, the Jedge will pronounce sentence," said Villa, and looked at me. "You reckon you're goin' to get a stiff 'un, I lay, knowin' what you deserve from this Court and what they got against you for breakin' every law of the Navigation Act an' maltreatin', strikin', maimin', woundin' and hazin' the poor sailor-men kermitted to yer charge. You wouldn't be s'prised if we sentenced you to death by shootin', hangin' or drownin' . . ."

"Not a bit," said I.

"No, because you know you deserve it, jedgin' by yer talk about murders on British ships. You got a guilty conscience. You know you deserve it and you expects it."

"Is this fellow going to talk all night?" asked Dacre of me.

"Shouldn't be surprised," I answered. "It's about all he can do."

"Now, now," expostulated Villa in a mild and reasoning tone of voice. "Don't say that. Think of all the things I could do to you, right now. Jest think of 'em, and then think of the sentence of the Court, which is—'Not Guilty'."

"Innercent, absoberlutely innercent," added Jake, "too bloomin' innercent to live."

"Much longer," amended Müller.

"But that's not a sentence, my good ass," I pointed out.

"Oh, ain't it? Sounds like one to me. You're found 'Not Guilty', and the order of the Court is that we are gonna leave ye alone—in full charge and command of yer ship. See?"

"No, I don't," I replied.

"Why, if this was one of them Navy Court-martials, ye'd now be 'anded back yer sword, an' discharged wi'out a stain on yer character, and with a drink in yer belly, to resoom yer dooties as Captain of this ship. See?"

"Well, what's the game then?" I asked.

"Can't you hear, boy? We're gonna leave ye in full charge, I say."

And, even more than the grim ferocity lurking behind the last remark, the accompanying laugh from Jake and Müller gave me the first inkling of how grossly and gravely I had under-estimated the inhuman callousness and fiendish cruelty of this bestial brute.

There was a silence while we at the rail wondered, and some of that triumvirate's henchmen obviously wondered also.

"No, Captain, we ain't no 'murderin' swine' nor 'corruptin' fools'. We ain't no mutineers nor ship-stealers," chuckled Jake in a voice that was horrible to hear. "We're not gonna take away yer fine new job of Capt'in. All we brought you right here to tell you is—that we're goin' to remove ourselves and the best of yer crew out o' range of yer cruelty . . . where you can't kick 'em an' hit 'em over the head with marline-spikes no more. That's all."

Müller nodded his head.

"That's all. A free and equal community is going to have all t'ings in common, and go where dere aren't any oppressors dat grind der faces of the poor."

"An' kick the seats of the pants of the poor," grinned Jake. "That's so. We're goin' to carry out the sentence of this here Court to wit, an' we're gonna cut loose the nigger and set him to loadin' up the starboard boat with all the best Cabin stores and all the cash an' pickin's, an' then . . . ! Sure!—an' then, when he's been tied up again all ship-shape, we're gonna lower away the boat and rescue from this ship that poor young female that you three dirty swabs got hidden in there."

"Ja," agreed Müller, "we rescue her from the low company she ban forced to endure. We set her free—to go mit us."

"All t'ings in common," he added with an ugly chuckle.

I could see that Dacre was straining at his bonds, the veins standing out upon his suffused neck like cords. My own shocked horror, fear, and rage, gave me some inkling of what he was suffering.

"And you, Johes?" I asked. "You were born a white man, weren't you? You are neither a mongrel square-head nor a half-breed dago, are you? Are you in on this? Are you going to try your hand at mutiny, desertion, theft and—you know what the other charge will be, if Miss Bryndal is taken off this ship, don't you? Think of the Old Bailey, Johes. Ever heard of the Long Arm of the Law? It hasn't troubled to reach out for you yet, but it will, my lad, and it'll get you. It'll get you all-right."

"Yes, and the lot of you," added Dacre . . . "Villa, if it takes me all my life, you foul hound, I'll see you hanged—or get you myself. And those two mangy mad dogs on each side of you. I'll follow . . . "

"Follow!" laughed Villa. "Fergit it, little man. You ain't goin' to do no follerin'. You're not going to get a move on to no Long Arm of no Law. You ain't gonna do nothing at all—only jest learn what happens to silly young suckers that set themselves up against grown-up men."

Villa turned again to me.

"No, me noble Capt'in, we're not goin' to do a thing to ye—nor ain't you to us. . . . When the boat's all ready and everything's hunky-dory, and we feel like *This Way for the Skylark*—and—when we have poured all the kerosene outa the lamp-locker down the after hatch . . . we're gonna drop a lighted match on it and then push off! . . . Holy Gee! I seen a nitrate ship a-burnin' in Kiki Harbour, and believe me, me noble Capt'in, it was *some* blaze."

There was a tense silence.

"Yeah," added Jake, "an' tied to that rail Cap'n, youse gonna be 'in full charge of the ship' an' of all the crew as remains behind—and enjoy the bon-fire."

Let me add at once that such utter incredible fiendishness was beyond the scope of the more petty villainy of Slim Johes and Peddersen.

"But py God, that would be wholesale murder, I tell you," cried Johes, "it iss too much, I say. We haf no quarrel with those men locked in the forecassel, nor with the Apprentisses in the half-deck. Especially we haf no quarrel with Fagin."

"Slim's right, Villa," declared Peddersen. "Wot the hell d'you wanta leave 'em all tied up for? Smash de other boats, an' after ye've lit the fire, let one of the Apprentice boys loose, before we push off. Dat gives 'em a chance to put the fire out . . . if dey are lucky."

"Iss, I tell 'oo," agreed Slim Johes. "That iss a goot itea—an' leave the young woman behind, I say. Yess, whateffer. Leave the girl behind, and one boy loose, to set free the men."

"What—you bat-eyed, lop-eared, big-mouthed bone-head? What? . . . Leave them with a good chance to put the fire out—or, at worst, to get picked up from a raft—and give us all away, you pair of goddamned rats. . . . You, Chips, I thought you was something almost like a man. For the half of two damns I'd have you tied to the rail beside the other sheep. Can't ye see, ye herrin'-gutted hounds, that we gotta be the poor unfortunate *sole* survivors of the ship *Valkyrie* lost at sea? Lost by fire? D'ye think I wanna do fifteen years in the Big House? Why, curse yer god-damned souls, another word, an' ye can both stop aboard."

"Oh, yeah?" growled Peddersen. "An' aind't de gal gonna give us away?"

"No, she ain't gonna give us away, smart clever-neck," replied Jake, leering at me and Dacre before he turned to Peddersen. "You betcha life she ain't."

"An' how you gonna stop her? Soon as we get picked up, she . . ."

"Can it!" growled Villa, "the poor thing's gonna die from her sufferin's—long before we're picked up . . ."

"No—don't you fret your fat, Bo, she ain't gonna give nobody away," grinned Jake.

CHAPTER XXIV

Such convincing proof of the awful depravity of these sub-human creatures left us, for a moment, speechless—speechless with, I think, sheer incredulity.

Then, losing all self-control, Dacre suddenly burst into speech and cursed those brute-beasts most terribly for the foul and loathsome things they were. There was not a dire insult, nor a vile term of contemptuous loathing in use among seamen, that he did not hurl at them—and in response, instead of the wrath and action for which he doubtless hoped, his words only evoked that same horrible mirth, shameless and beneath all shame.

Curiously enough, it was my own seconding effort, feeble and inferior as it was to Dacre's, that pierced their thick hides and brought the climax.

"So that's your measure, is it, you Villa, Jake and Müller? One might have known what to expect from deported square-head scum, and a police-dodging dago crook—who are only brave enough to kill from behind in the dark, and are scared stiff by a damned sea-gull."

I was amazed at the effect of my words.

There was no laughter from them now. Cursing wildly, Jake sprang up and rushed at me.

"I'm glad we didn't kill ye," he snarled. "I don't want ye to die quick, an' I guess we'll show ye a bit of fancy shootin' before we leave ye in charge, Capt'in. I'd shoot the top off yer port lug, an' then we'll see if the Judge can make t'other match it. . . . Fancy shootin', ye high-hatted young bastard. I'd show ye some fancy carvin', too, an' when I done, ye'll be a nose short. See?

"Sure thing," he growled, bringing his face within an inch of mine and glaring into my eyes. "An' if we get another word outa ye, I'll fix ye how there won't be any more. See? I'd cut the tongue outa ye as soon as look at ye. Manhandle *me*, would you?"

And putting his hand behind him, Jake produced his long sharp seaman's knife.

"Hi! Not so fast, Bo," laughed Villa. "You ain't Jedge, jury, cop and executioner, all in one, are you? An' if you wanna be hangman—you wait a bit. All in good time. He's gonna see a lot before he tells himself good-bye. You go an' sit down."

Villa and Jake crossed glares, as fencers cross swords, and it was easily to be seen who was the stronger character, the leader in this business.

Slipping his knife back into his belt, Jake laughed.

"O.K., chief," he said. "I ain't in no hurry," and resumed his seat on the 'Bench'.

"Naow then, what's the next business before the Court, that lill matter of trial and sentence having been dooly concluded—the strong box or walkin' the plank?"

"The box," growled Müller.

"*Ja!* Let's see what's in the box," agreed Peddersen.

"Box nothing," objected Jake. "Let's settle 'oo's for us, or 'oo's for a swim."

"Iss," chuckled Slim Johes. "For him that is not for us is up against us."

Villa laughed.

"You've certainly said something. He's up agin us all-right, all-right. Go get Church, for a start; and let's see if he's as full of himself as he thought he was a little while ago. You Brown, Slim and Paulo, go fetch him right along."

"Will three be enough, d'you think?" sneered Dacre.

"Go and give that pimp's by-blow a smack in the mouth, Müller."

Nothing loth, Müller obeyed, punching Dacre violently in the face.

Dacre said nothing, and I wondered whether Müller would work himself up into a rage and batter my friend's face until it was unrecognizable, or let his well-developed discretion get the better of such valour as he had—for, after all, the play was not yet finished, the half was not yet told.

"Brave chap," I sneered. "Splendid fellow. Real anarchist, eh? Not afraid of any man—if his hands are tied, eh?"

"Give him one, too," called Villa, but for some reason Müller did not obey.

Was it possible that such mind as he had was still open to feelings of shame? More probably the discretion theory was correct, as the "Ship-owners" had yet some distance to go.

The three messengers returned, bringing Church, whose hands were tied behind his back.

Held by Brown and Paulo, he was brought before the Court.

"Wal, how're ye feelin' now?"

"Fine," said Church. "How's yerself?"

And he took a quick look round.

"Don't you worry about me," replied Villa in a quiet and

sinister voice, "but get hold of this, and be quick about it. D'you join us, and sign yer name to a little document I've written out, or do you walk that plank?"

"*Walk the plank?*" ejaculated Church. "I've heard about that game somewheres! . . . Pirates in penny 'orribles, was it? Lor' bless me soul, I didn't know it was still extinct."

"Not so much out of you. Are you going to join us?" snarled Jake.

"*Me?*" replied Church. "Join *you?*"

"Then get on to that plank."

"Don't I 'ave no time to say me prayers?"

"D'ye know any?" sneered Villa.

"No, but you gimme a week an' I'll make one up—an' mention you in it too, you Gawd-blistered sunnavabitch."

Villa raised his pistol.

"Beat it then," he growled, "and go where you belong."

With great dignity Church marched to the inboard end of the plank that these amazing people had actually run out. There he stood a moment, his face raised to the moon-lit star-spangled sky, his lips working.

"I'm comin', Mother," he called, and strode to the other end of the plank, head erect.

"But not to-night, ole gal," he added, as he reached the far end, and turning about, marched back again.

"Come aboard, Capt'in," he announced, "if you are the Capt'in—just at the moment."

"You playin' funny?" shouted Villa, rising to his feet and raising the pistol to Church's face.

"Me? No. I've changed me mind. When I gets there to the end of the plank, it all looks different-like. I come all over queer-like, an' I thinks to meself,

" 'Henery, you're too young to die—an' not nearly wicked enough. You 'aven't had time.' . . ."

"Now then, quick, one way or the other. You goin' to join us, or shall I blow your head off?"

"Now look 'ere, look 'ere; you don't want to go about blowin' people. Shootin' their 'eads off ain't no way to git the best out of 'em."

"D'you join us, or don't you?"

"Course I do, ole pal. I was only frightenin' yer," replied Church.

"Stand over there by the port rail then, and watch yer step—if you wants ter share. Chips, keep an eye on 'im, an' bash his brains out with a belayin'-pin if he moves the wrong way."

Villa then gave orders that Hamblin should be brought before the Court.

Hamblin was brought. Judging by certain alarums and excursions, shoutings and scufflings, not without some difficulty, his three gaolers haled him before the Bench.

The prisoner was given the same choice as had been offered to Church.

"An' ye want my answer at once?" asked Hamblin of Villa, seated, arms akimbo, on the hatch.

"Right now or sooner," replied Villa.

"Here y'are then," replied Hamblin, and with violence and accuracy, squirted a stream of tobacco juice at the Judge.

"Join ye, b' Goad!" he shouted. "I'll join me fist t' yer dirrty face . . ."

Rising to his feet Villa struck Hamblin a violent blow in the face.

Hamblin shook his head.

"Wad ye hae done that had me hands been free, me little hero?" he asked in a quiet voice.

"Well, well," sneered Villa, glancing at his knuckles, "we can't all be heroes, but you can—right now. Git over and walk that plank, an' if yer nerve fails you as that bastard's did, I'll shoot ye off the end of it."

"Goad, Ah'd walk along a red-hot plank into a white-hot Hell to be away from ye, ye gang o' stinkin' scum-o'-the-warrld. You Villa, you Jake, you Müller—and you Peddersen, the worrst o' the lot, for ye ought to know better—are lower than the beasts of the field. Ye're the sweepin's an' scrapin's o' the gutters o' the slums o' the vilest quarters of the dirtiest cities of the airth; ye pollute the clean air ye move in and the salt sea ye use to its shame; yer feet foul the ship ye . . ."

Peddersen, who had risen when named by Hamblin, now struck, and Hamblin, sagging at the knees, slipped from his captor's hold and slumped to the deck.

"Chuck him over there, and we'll talk to him some more, later on," ordered Villa.

And Hamblin was dumped beside Church on the port side of the deck, opposite to us.

"Fetch Blancke and Berghen," was Villa's next order. "They're the lot, aren't they?"

"Iss," replied Slim Johes, "except Baby Axenstern, look you, who's on guard."

"Fetch the lot, then."

And a minute or two later Blancke and Berghen were brought before the Court.

"Now then, my hearties," said Villa, "you goin' to join us or goin' overboard?"

"Overboard?" expostulated Blancke.

"Sure. Dumped—right now—unless you'd rather join us and make your fortunes."

"Ve vas not vant no fortunes. Ve vas vant to do our vork an' draw our pay an' not have no troubles."

"*Ja, ja,*" agreed Berghen. "Ve vas vant obey orders and . . ."

"Well, you obey my orders then," replied Villa.

"I thought the young man Sinbad that vas Apprentice vas now Captain—by election."

"Well, now 'e ain't—by election. Look at him."

And with a jeering laugh, Villa pointed at me.

"Dat vas four Captains we 'ave in five minutes," grumbled Berghen. "Captain Bryndal, Captain Chips, Captain Sinbad—an' now Captain Villa. . . . Perhaps I'll be Captain next."

And he laughed uneasily.

"Not you, Son," replied Villa. "We got to the right Cap'n at last; an' they as don't like it can leave the ship, *pronto.* Goin' to walk the plank, or goin' to sign on, under me?"

As one man, Blancke and Berghen stated that they had no intention of walking any plank—and if anyone blamed them therefor, it was not I.

"Get over there with Church and Hamblin then, and look at here. You'll be treated as you behave. Bear a hand, and you will be all-right. Bear two hands and go willing, an' you'll get a share.

"Don't untie both their two hands yet, anyhow," he added with ponderous jocularity.

Axenstern, I was sorry to note, had evidently joined the "Ship-owners" once again. After all, he was but a half-wit, if that, and, what mind he had, was not only swayed and influenced, but made up for him, by the last person who 'reasoned' with him.

So there they were, the whole crowd, now a confessed gang of murderers and piratical mutineers; save for Hamblin, too hot-headed, rash and violent to be of any use to us; Church, our friend, but with his own skin to save; Blancke and Berghen, constitutionally averse from trouble and strife, and the last men from whom to hope for anything in the nature of help, through cunning ruse or swift attack.

Where were Beauty and Fagin?

"Now then, boys," bawled the raucous voice of Jake, "now for the bokkus. An' we'll show you somethin' that'll make yer dead-lights pop outa yer heads. We'll show you what those gets a share of, that stands in with us.

"*If they're lucky*," he added quietly, in what sounded to me like an enigmatical, if not cynical, aside.

"Go it, Chips; you know where it's stowed," he continued. "You an' Baby Axenstern, Brown and Müller kin carry it, I guess."

"You makin' a speech, brother?" enquired Villa, somewhat unpleasantly, of Jake. "You buttin' in to give a few orders?"

"Only to help us along like, Cap'n," replied Jake.

"I'll tell ye when I want any help," was the reply.

And the faintest gleam of hope came to me from this apparent rift within the loot.

"Sure you will! . . . Perhaps you got a little help when I told you what was in that box; and how it got there; and what I had to do with the doings and all, huh?"

"Well, let's see what *is* in it," answered Villa.

"And what d'you think is in it, boys?" bawled Jake, springing to his feet, waving his arms and obviously endeavouring to work up an atmosphere of excitement, enthusiasm, and expectation.

"*Gold!* I tell you, gold! And all for the takin'."

"An' share an' share alike," growled Müller. "All t'ings in common."

"Course we'll share and share alike when the Captain's 'ad 'is whack as Captain; an' I've 'ad mine as what you might call owner."

"*Ja*, an' 'oo might call you 'owner', an' why?" sneered Peddersen.

"*You* might; an' everybody else might, an' bloody well will!" was the truculent reply. " 'Oo told Cap'n Villa what was in it? . . . 'Oo 'ad the 'andling of it in Sydney? . . . 'Oo got it aboard? . . . 'Oo's bin in charge of it all the time?"

"I didn't know . . ."

"No, there's an 'ell of a lot you don't know; what you don't know 'ud make a damn great book."

"Cut it out," snarled Villa, "and go and get it—since you know so much about it."

And led by Jake, with joyful whoops, Peddersen, Müller, Brown and Axenstern scuttled below.

What was this?

I glanced at Dacre. He was watching the port-hole of Celia's room. At Carrol. He was glaring across to where Larry O'Toole, presumably regarded as too hopelessly mad to be worth notice, had sauntered up, and with a stick held like a rifle across his shoulder, had constituted himself guard over the prisoners, marching up and down, and giving himself orders. . . . Right turn! . . . Left turn! . . .

Berghen was helping Hamblin to his feet.

As I looked, Church, edging sideways to Hamblin, whispered in his ear.

Merciful God! Would they, or Blancke or Berghen have the strength to break the lashings that bound their hands? And if so, could the four of them do anything?

I doubted it.

Hamblin would fight like a tiger; and so, probably, would Church; but there was nothing tigerish about the other two. And what could Church and Hamblin do against the whole ship's crew, led by such determined desperadoes as Villa, Jake and Peddersen?

With joyous yells, the gang returned, bearing with quick short steps the big box which I recognized as having formed part of Mrs. Bryndal's luggage at Sydney, and upon the abnormal heaviness of which, Dacre and I had commented.

"There, me hearties, what d'you say to that, me bucko-boys? Takes four men to lift it—and bung full o' *gold*. Who'd be a Shellback when he could join the Ship-owners, and get his hooks into *that*, eh? . . . You Church, you Hamblin, you Blancke and Berghen, would you rather have enough of that in the bottom of your sea-chest to keep ye in comfort ashore for the rest of your life; or would ye rather go on sweatin' in summer and shiverin' wet through in winter, strainin' yer guts out fer a gang o' fat-bellied longshore swine that live by killin' poor sailor-men, eh?"

"It *is* your night to howl, ain't it, brother?" softly enquired the sinister voice of Villa. "Here, Chips, get that box broken open, and let's have less talk, for we've a lot to do. Give the fellas a glimpse of what's comin' to 'em, an' then let's get busy."

Hammers and chisels having done their work, and the lid of the box having been prised off, a layer of straw was revealed. Into this, Jake, self-constituted master of the present ceremonies, delved two-handed.

"*Gold!*" he screamed. "*Gold* in nuggets and bars and . . ."

"Pipes," jeered Villa, as Jake drew forth and unwrapped what certainly appeared to be—a length of lead-piping.

"What the Hell's this?" he said, looking like a crestfallen ape, as he stood staring open-mouthed at the object he held in his hand.

"What the blazin' . . . ? Try again, brother. Ye might get a nut," sneered Villa.

"Iss," screamed Johes, and grabbed for himself.

From out the straw, his frantic snatch produced—a length of lead-piping.

"Py God! It wass a swindle, I tell 'oo."

And so stricken was the expression of his face, so broken-hearted his wail, and so childishly disappointed the tone of his voice, that there was a general laugh, albeit somewhat rueful and wry, I thought.

In a moment every "Ship-owner" had a length of lead-piping in his hand and was examining it, squinting through it, and gazing upon it as though expecting it by magic alchemy to turn to gold in his hand.

"Well, you Jake, what about it? What's the game? What's the Big Idea of this frame-up?"

"Why . . . why . . . we bin *swindled*!" shouted Jake, and was most obviously puzzled and amazed almost beyond speech.

I could have laughed.

The tone of indignation, grievance, and protest in the fellow's voice was really funny. *He'd been swindled!*

"Of course you've been swindled, you poor fools," I shouted. "You, Axenstern, Brown, Paulo! Of course you've been swindled. . . . You Johes, you Peddersen, you Müller—what do you think you'll get from foul swine like this cowardly cur Jake, or that crimp's pimp there—that crook Villa? What do you *think* they'll do but swindle you; and where do you think they'll land you? In gaol, and on the scaffold! . . . You've been swindled!

"Now then," I bawled, "save your necks while you can. Rush them, quick. Tie them up and return to your duty—while you've a chance to save your necks. . . . Go on, Baby. You don't want to swing for swine like these. . . . Go on, Johes. You don't want to hang, do you? Now Brown and Paulo, save your lives."

"At them, boys," shouted Dacre. "A hundred pounds to the man who lays out Villa or Jake. . . . And *we* don't swindle!"

Axenstern looked from me to Dacre, from Dacre to Carrol, and stood undecided.

Brown, razor in hand, glanced at Paulo who, though already hefting a length of the lead-piping, drew his knife.

Peddersen sprang to his feet. . . .

Villa raised his pistol, swung about in an endeavour to cover everybody in turn, while Jake, nearest to me, with one of the vilest oaths that I have ever heard, his face demoniacal in its look of rage, disappointment and frustration, raised his hideous leaden weapon high above his head to smash my skull.

As he bent his body back, putting the whole of his strength, weight, and spring into a blow which I felt would reduce my head to a mess, I thought that here then, was the end of Sinbad-the-would-be-Sailor—the ridiculous Boy Captain—and . . . oh! my God . . . of Celia Bryndal.

I closed my eyes.

Crash! . . .

Or, rather—a shattering *Bang* . . .

I felt no pain.

I opened my eyes.

Jake was in the act of falling to the deck.

I glanced at Villa. Had he shot him to establish his own captaincy once and for all?

No! Villa, like everyone else, was staring open-mouthed at Celia's port-hole, from which a complete view of the starboard side of the ship could be obtained.

"*The girl!*" he shouted, and rushed toward the starboard alley-way.

Bang! . . .

And Villa sprawled headlong.

"Now's your chance, Axenstern!" I bawled. "Now Brown! Now Paulo! Change sides—and save your necks!"

Bang!

As though to accentuate my words, the pistol was fired again, and, simultaneously with it, came a rush from the opposite side of the deck, led by—of all people, *Larry O'Toole.*

Upon Peddersen, Hamblin sprang like a tiger, and with a blow that did credit to my teaching, laid him out.

A tremendous cuff from Church sent Johes reeling.

Müller, a length of lead-piping in his hand, started to rush to Peddersen's aid, just as someone—and, could I have believed my eyes, I should have said it was Larry himself—hit him a tremendous blow across the back of the head, with a marline-spike.

"*Here*, Larry!" I bawled.

"An' shure it's here I am," he cried, and with two or three slashes of his knife set me free.

Scarcely had he done so than he was at Dacre's side, performing the same office for him, and, as the lashings fell from Dacre's arms, Larry sprang to Carrol's assistance.

Snatching up a piece of lead-piping, I dashed into the fray—to find that fray there was none; for, with two of their leaders shot and the third stretched senseless on the deck, there was no fight in Axenstern, Brown, Paulo and Johes—nor any left in Peddersen.

With the first crack of that pistol, and within ten seconds, the tables had been turned and the mutineers overthrown, defeated, and outnumbered.

On the deck lay Villa and Jake, groaning and bleeding; Müller senseless; Peddersen at the feet of Hamblin, either afraid or, as yet, unable to get to his feet; Johes lay declining Church's earnest invitation to get up and have some more.

On the other hand, here were myself, Dacre and Carrol, free and unhurt; and equally so Doc, Church, Hamblin, Berghen and Blancke.

Seeing that the brief fight—to call it such—was over, and no more fighting likely to occur, I rushed up the poop ladder and bawled my orders, endeavouring to behave as though I had just come up on deck to take charge of the ship and the situation.

"Mr. Blount," I roared, "send Axenstern to the wheel; have Villa, Jake, Müller and Peddersen put in irons at once, unless too badly wounded. Also any other man who gives one word of trouble."

And then I remembered—Beauty and Fagin.

"Mr. Carrol, find out what's become of the other two Apprentices and get them on deck."

And then I remembered again—poor Geordie.

"Doc, see if anything can be done for Geordie Stowe, quick."

But Geordie was dead.

And swallowing the lump in my throat I vowed that his murderer should hang.

At that moment I felt that I'd wring confessions from those foul reptiles if I had to torture them, myself, to do it.

Beauty and Fagin were found by Mr. Carrol, trussed and gagged, in the closed half-deck.

As I afterwards learned, Fagin had awakened to find a pistol pointed at his face, and had no option but to submit without a struggle.

He then had to watch his captors dispose of Beauty, and declared that they had tied Beauty's hands and feet and begun to gag him, before he awoke.

With the devilish wanton cruelty and brutality that distinguished them, these scoundrels had then assured the unfortunate lads that the cargo beneath the half-deck would shortly be set on fire, and that they would be roasted alive where they lay, unable to move.

In a surprisingly short space of time, the life of the ship was once again proceeding as usual; the Captain and the Mate on the poop, the Second Mate about the business of his Watch, the man at the wheel steering carefully; the look-out alert, and the Watch-on-deck ready, willing, and able.

When the bell, struck at the break of the poop, was echoed from the fo'c'sle-head, and the Look-out's hail went forth upon the night, it was difficult to believe—I could not believe—that, an hour before, that peaceful deck had been a stage for mutiny and piracy; for battle, murder and sudden death; the ship in the hands of men who proposed, intended, and had made their plans, to set fire to it while ship-mates, abandoned aboard her, burned alive, and a helpless girl was dragged away to a fate unthinkable.

Well, that nightmare being over (and I would see that no-one dreamed it again) I could now leave the deck to Dacre, and go and thank Celia Bryndal; thank her and congratulate her; and admit that it was she, and she alone, who had saved the situation.

For the two shots that had ended the mutineers' regime like the bursting of a bubble, could only have been fired by Celia.

•

CHAPTER XXV

I tapped at the door of Celia's cabin.

"Come in," she cried, and as I unlocked, and half-opened, the door, added,

"But don't hurry—unless you think I might perhaps want to be let out and know exactly what's going on."

"Come into the Cabin, Celia," I said, "and let us try to thank you."

"Can't you come in here?" replied Celia. "Why should I get up again? Oh, *come in*, Little Joseph."

It seemed both churlish and childish to refuse.

"I don't know what to say, Celia. I don't know how to . . ."

"No need to say anything."

"You've saved us all—and the ship."

"And myself," added Celia.

"Thank God," I observed.

"Do you, Sinbad?"

"Of course I do."

"I did save your life, didn't I, Sinbad?"

"Of course you did."

"You admit you owe me your life?"

"Absolutely, Celia."

"Pay it, then."

"What do you mean?"

Celia laughed uneasily.

"You know what I mean—but we'll talk about that later. Come and kiss me, Sinbad."

I obeyed, and Celia clung about my neck.

"No, put your arms round me and kiss me properly. . . . *Properly*, I tell you."

I kissed Celia in a manner that she at least would consider 'properly'.

I must have embraced and kissed her warmly indeed, for Celia seemed satisfied and lay quiet in my arms, hers about my neck, her lips against mine.

Once again I felt a surge of passion, a rush of warm blood to head and heart, a tingling of nerves from toes to fingers, a wild longing to . . .

"My darling . . . darling . . . darling . . ." murmured Celia. "My

360

own . . . my lover . . . my . . ."

And violently Celia gripped me to her and crushed her lips against mine so that we were rendered dumb.

And as before, the full tide of passion turned and ebbed, and by the time Celia, relaxing, released me and drew breath, revulsion had set in—and Celia was but a ship-mate of whom I was growing fond; to whom I owed the deepest debt of gratitude —and of whom I felt afraid.

"I must go," I said, "I've got all sorts of things to do. I just wanted to thank you and see that you were all-right."

"Yes, I suppose you must . . . Must you? . . . Must you go, Sinbad? . . . Stay . . . Stay, Sinbad."

"Don't forget I'm the Lord High Admiral," I laughed uncomfortably, and added,

"I don't think I shall sleep again till we dock . . . after that little shock."

"What happened exactly?" I asked as I opened the door.

"I was reading," said Celia, "and dozed with the book in my hand. My door was open on the hook. That man must have taken it off the hook and locked me in, without waking me, though I half-heard or half-dreamed that somebody moved something. I suppose that, with the door shut, the room got close and stuffy, and prevented my going off to sleep properly.

"I must have tossed and turned for a while, I think, and then I sat up to throw off some of the bed-clothes, and noticed that the door was shut. When I went to open it and found it locked on the outside, I knew that something was up, and it looked to me as though there was going to be some dirty work at the cross-roads.

"Well, I was going to start hammering on the door and raising Cain, when, thank God, it occurred to me that that might be just the wrong thing to do, and I decided to see whether I could squeeze through my port-hole on to the deck, and creep around and do a bit of good with that pistol. . . . No need: for as it happened, Villa, Jake and Co. had chosen the starboard side of the ship when they tied you to the rail.

"Well, it was pretty clear that a good deal was up to me, and the most important part of it was—the right moment. If anybody was going to hurt you, or if they were going to take you away out of sight—to hang you or something—I was going to shoot. Or if Villa, Jake, and that man Peddersen were where I could get all three of them—that would be a good moment. What happened, you know."

"You're a wonderful shot, Celia."

"I'm pretty good. I'll hit a playing-card, every time, at thirty paces; or make the card into anything you like, from an ace to a ten, at fifteen. One of the few useful things my mother did teach me. She was a marvel with a little gun."

"I wonder if you've killed them."

"Good Lord, no! Much too good a death for them. If they haven't bled to death, they'll be all-right—though I was sorely tempted to give it them both in the head."

"Anyhow, you . . ." I began.

"Well, don't forget it, then, Sinbad. . . . And now will you listen to me when I tell you that you're a child—a dear, innocent, ignorant, idiotic lambkin of a child—compared with Villa, and Jake, and that you don't begin to understand men like those. Badly wounded or slightly wounded, you keep them in irons until the end of the voyage. Keep them apart and keep them from Peddersen and Müller and Johes. You'll want them to work the ship."

"Of course I'll listen to you, Celia. You shall have a seat on the Board and be present at all our Councils."

"A seat on the Board!" smiled Celia enigmatically. "A better joke than you know."

"Well," I said, stepping out of the cabin, "I hope you'll get your sleep."

"Oh, rats, rabbits and little rum-bottles!" I heard as I shut the door.

"Well, Dacre, let's have your story," I said as I rejoined him on the poop. "Fine Mate, aren't you?"

"Fine!" growled Dacre.

"I should say so," I continued, "Here I take it into my head to come on deck at night-time—and find both my officers in an undignified position, cheek by jowl with the Cook, and hobnobbing with the crew. What about it?"

"You 'took it into your head' to come on deck?" replied Dacre. "Or did Villa take it into his head that you should? . . . Well, to begin at the beginning, in the middle Watch, just as I was thinking it was about time that Geordie struck Two Bells, Müller came up here and said,

" 'Please, Sir, young Geordie Stowe vas fall down an' 'ave a fit.'

" 'A fit? What do you mean? . . . a fit? Where is he?' I asked.

"And then I nearly had a fit myself, and realized that Müller was only holding me in conversation; for I felt the muzzle of a pistol on the back of my neck, and heard Villa's voice say,

" 'Put 'em up, *quick*. Let a shout an' I'll blow yer head off.'

"The last time that I had seen the hound, he was at the wheel. Now he'd left the ship to steer herself, and he was pressing his pistol in under the back of my skull.

"With Müller in front—and I now saw he'd got a knife in his hand—and Villa behind me with his gun actually touching me, I didn't think I'd argue. I'm no hero, Sinbad, old chap, but I did have just enough pluck to turn my head to make sure that it *was* a pistol, and not any old lump of cold iron. As I did so, I felt the point of Müller's knife, and saw that the pistol was only too real, for Villa stepped back—lest I made a grab, I suppose—and bade Müller rip me up if I moved.

"To me, he said,

" 'Get down that ladder—quick.'

"And realizing that, dead, I could not be of much help, I got down the ladder—quick.

"While Villa pointed the gun at my stomach, Jake and Müller lashed me to the rail. I was sorely tempted to shout at the top of my voice, and take the consequences. In fact, I honestly think I was about to do so, when I saw the body of poor little Geordie lying a few feet away, and I knew that what had happened to him would happen to me. . . .

"That I didn't shout, was due partly to cowardice, and partly to the knowledge that, even trussed up like a spare anchor, I should be more useful alive than dead. . . .

"It all happened so quickly. Then Villa, handing Müller a belaying-pin, told him to brain me if I opened my mouth to make a sound, and promised him he'd shoot him if he let me do it.

"While Müller literally stood over me, with his arm raised to strike, Villa and Jake went off to the half-deck and fo'c'sle and, after some time, they, Johes and Peddersen, brought up Carrol, then Doc, and finally yourself."

"Smart bit of work," I said. "And but for Celia, they'd have brought it off, and we should now be standing there—waiting to be roasted alive."

"*Isn't* she a wonder?" breathed Dacre softly. "She saved us all, and saved the *Valkyrie*. . . . The coolness, the courage . . ."

"What's the damage?" I asked. "To the crew, I mean? We're going to have a rough time getting the old hooker home if the weather turns bad on us—short-handed as we're going to be."

"No great damage, after all," replied Dacre. "The only people really *hors de combat* are Villa and Jake—and I should think they'd pretty soon recover. Doc says they ought to be at work in a week's time, and hopes you'll see that they are."

"Trust me," I replied. "As soon as they are anything like fit for it, they are going to do their watch-on-deck with the rest, and their watch-below in irons."

Dacre grinned.

"No reason why they should be passengers, is there?" he said.

And it occurred to me that these two gentlemen would work as they had never worked in their lives, once they were on their feet, with Dacre behind them.

§2

"Well, are you going to log me?" enquired Celia, as I entered the Cabin where she was seated on the settee busy with some matters of her own, with pencil and paper.

"Yes," I replied. "What for?"

"Well, under the Merchant Shipping Act, a member of the crew is Liable to a Fine of Five Shillings for every day that he or she is in possession of any fire-arm, knuckle-duster, loaded cane, slung-shot, sword-stick, bowie-knife, dagger or any other offensive weapon or offensive instrument, without the concurrence of the Master," she informed me.

"You seem to know the Merchant Shipping Act very well," I replied, "but the difficulty is this. Since your wages are, according to the Articles, One Shilling a Month, I can hardly hope to secure from them a sum equivalent to Five Shillings a day. Secondly, by not requiring the surrender of the weapon to which we all owe our lives, I'm placing myself hopelessly in the wrong. Thirdly, at the paying-off table, the Shipping Master would probably declare that I ought to have known that a girl like you would possess a means of self-defence."

"Well—another question," smiled Celia, "are you still anxious to be rid of me?"

"No," I said, "and I'm only too thankful that you didn't leave the *Valkyrie* when we wanted you to go. As for your saving us all yesterday, once again it is entirely hopeless and useless for me to attempt to thank you, so I shan't do it."

"H'm," said Celia, "we'll talk about that later on."

"But I'll say this much, Celia. We'll make you an *ex officio* Officer of this ship, and ask you to give us the benefit of your advice—whenever we need advice, and that'll be pretty often, I should think."

Celia sprang to her feet, and knowing what was coming I evaded it.

"I'm going to call the Officers now," I said, as I turned to leave the Cabin, "and I hope you'll join us in a consultation."

At our Council of War I was surprised to find that Celia's wrath and bitterness were reserved almost entirely for Villa and Jake. Toward Peddersen, she now seemed to entertain but ordinary resentment, while the rest of the mutineers, including Slim Johes, she apparently regarded as negligible trash.

Remembering Peddersen's suggestion on the day that I thrashed him, I would gladly have hung him at the main yard-arm together with Villa—whose idea, suggestion, and intention it was, that we should have been burned alive, and Celia should have been carried off in his boat, to be murdered and flung into the sea as soon as they thought fit.

She gave her opinion that Peddersen, Johes, Müller, Brown, Paulo and Axenstern might, after an intimidating warning, and under constant watchful surveillance, be allowed to go free; but, whatever was done with the rest, Jake and Villa ought, in her opinion, to remain permanently handcuffed in the darkest and most uncomfortable part of the ship.

With regard to them she was frankly vindictive, and when the others had left the Cabin she amazed me by saying that she wanted, before long, to have an interview with each of them separately, and in my presence.

"What on earth for?" I asked.

"You'll know when I've had a talk with you and told you my little tale," she replied.

Before this took place, however, we called aft the five 'Shell-backs' and asked how it was they had been so easily overcome and trussed up.

Hamblin at once admitted that, with Villa at the wheel, Müller on the look-out, and Jake 'standing by', Axenstern and he had stolen a nap in the watch-on-deck.

Stretched out on their sea-chests, each had been separately awakened, with a pistol to his ribs; and, after being quietly and securely lashed by Müller, could only look on, in fear of the pistol, while the three men of the watch-below were made to leave their bunks for similar treatment.

Finding himself bound hand and foot, and threatened with sudden and certain death, by Villa, it had taken but little persuasion to make Baby Axenstern resume his former rôle of "Ship-owner". In point of fact, I think that Villa exercised an almost hypnotic influence over the half-wit.

These men having been dismissed, with a warning to sleep with one eye open in their watch-below, and to live in a state of alert watchfulness in their watch-on-deck, we had the prisoners brought before us, one by one.

But the most searching cross-examination of these scoundrels failed to throw any light on the identity of the man who had murdered Geordie.

Completely baffled, I sternly asked each handcuffed man whether he could give me any good reason why he should not remain in irons until I could hand him over to the English police at Falmouth—which could be nothing but the preliminary to their being tried at the Old Bailey for mutiny and murder on the high seas, and to their expiating their crime on the scaffold.

"You murdered Mr. Hammerson among you, and you murdered George Stowe among you," said I, "and you will hang by the neck until you are dead, every man of you, as murderers, or as being accessory before and after the fact of each murder."

As I expected, Slim was full of admirable reasons why so gross an injustice should not be perpetrated upon him. What had he done? And if he had done anything, it had been in fear of his life and under the unavoidable and inescapable compulsion of Villa, who had driven him to it at the pistol's point.

And I could almost admire the man's colossal effrontery, when he went on to declare that inasmuch as he had been forced to join the others, he would take legal action *against me* for wrongful detention, assault, and other ill-usage, the moment he got ashore, and never had poor sailor-man better grounds for legal action than he.

"I may improve those grounds yet, Johes," I said. "You cowardly cur, nothing would give me greater pleasure than to have you trussed up, and order Doc and Church each to give you a dozen of the best. . . . However, as you will assuredly hang for complicity in at least one foul and cowardly murder, I may hold my hand. . . . If I *do*, you may take it as certain that I have found enough evidence to hang you. . . ."

At this point Johes' nerve failed him completely. He begged to be allowed to turn King's Evidence; to be forgiven by me; to be set free; and to be allowed to go about his work.

Peddersen, at first, took the same line as Johes—pleading coercion by the armed force of Villa and Jake; and that what he had done he had been compelled to do. He reminded us that he had objected, when Villa spoke of leaving us tied to the rail to be burned alive.

"Quite a philanthropist, Peddersen, eh? But I'm afraid the fact that you objected to wholesale murder won't save you from the consequences of the complicity in retail murder. Until we choose a King's Evidence from among you, we shan't know whose hand actually struck down Mr. Hammerson and George Stowe—and it won't greatly matter. Even your lawyer friend Johes knows enough to be able to tell you that where a gang commits a murder as one man, that gang hangs as one man."

Then and there Peddersen offered to turn King's Evidence and tell the truth, the whole truth, and nothing but the truth; and, like Johes, swore that if we would forgive him and reinstate him, his conduct would be exemplary to the end of the voyage.

We then had Brown before us, and I think succeeded in putting, if not the fear of God, the fear of the Law of England, into the rascal. He appeared thoroughly cowed, and pleaded that Captains came and went so quickly aboard the *Valkyrie*, that a poor uneducated down-trodden nigger didn't know where he was or who was who.

His friend Paulo, with whom he had doubtless been talking on the subject, took the same line. Each of them, volubly apologetic and explanatory, was discharged with a caution and a somewhat blood-curdling promise.

After some discussion, we decided to have Müller brought before us.

Looking pretty sick, and with excellent reason, in view of the blow he had received from the marline-spike, he seemed subdued, if not altogether cowed; and though he refused to plead, he swore that if he were not kept in irons, but allowed to go about his duty, he asked nothing better than to try to give every satisfaction.

Him, we dismissed with the information that his case was under our consideration—and at Falmouth, it would come under the consideration of the English police.

Having interviewed everybody with the exception of Jake and Villa, we decided that, with those two in irons, provided we took the most ordinary precautions, we should run no further risk and have no further trouble, so far as the "Ship-owner" gang was concerned.

Later in the day, I sent for Hamblin, and laid upon him a sacred charge, a noble trust—a charge and trust that he accepted with a lip-licking grin of satisfaction.

This was the literal charge of Jake. Save when Jake was handcuffed, and not only handcuffed but chained to a staple in the wall of the sail-locker, and the door locked and padlocked, Hamblin was to be Jake's gaoler, warder, and keeper.

Similarly I handed the care and charge of Villa to Church.

To the watching, by day and by night, of Müller, I assigned Blancke; and to that of Peddersen, Berghen.

I was pondering the problem of having Johes shadowed, when Larry O'Toole (who seemed to me to have recovered somewhat, and definitely to have brightened up during, and since, the fight), approached me with the curious request that *he* might be appointed Villa's especial gaoler.

So earnestly did he make his request, and so pleased with him was I, for his conduct in setting free Church, Hamblin, Blancke and Berghen at the psychological moment of our "trial", that I agreed to his request.

"But watch him, my lad, watch him."

"Watch him, is it, thin, Sorr!" replied Larry. "Shure an' I'll watch him twenty-five hours a day. Thim birrds have told me somethin' about that black-hearted spalpeen. Begob, I'll watch him till he dies—an' mebbe he'll die o' my watchin'.'"

This seemed good enough, and I changed my arrangement, committed Villa to the care of Larry O'Toole, and Johes to that of Church.

"Right you are, Sir," grinned Church. "Every time Slim opens his mouth I'll knock it shut—without waitin' to hear what he's goin' to say."

"And see that he does his whack of work," I smiled.

"Work, Sir? Gor'blessyer, Slim's goin' to learn what it is. An' he's goin' to wish the seat of his pants was cast-iron.

"Walk the plank!" he growled. "I'll make the little bastard *run* a few planks before I done wi' him."

Well, if the "Ship-owner" people contrived to foregather and lay their heads together once again—they'd be clever folk, I decided; and, so long as Villa and Jake were in irons, we could feel easy in our minds and sleep quietly in our beds.

That night the crew of the *Valkyrie* witnessed one more

funeral at sea.

Personally I was too mentally dazed, too surfeited with incredibilities, to wonder at myself, as I, of all people, conducted the Burial Service over Geordie, who had given his life for me—for had he been in his berth like the others, he would merely have been trussed up—as they were—and would have survived.

I gave orders that every man of the "Ship-owner" gang, ill or well, wounded or unwounded, should be present at the funeral—present and kneeling, from the beginning to the end of the service, with bared, bowed head, and wrists handcuffed behind his back.

In a row there knelt at Geordie's funeral, Villa, Jake, Peddersen, Müller and Johes; and behind each of these murderous curs stood the man whom I had appointed his guardian angel (or devil) for the rest of the voyage—with orders that should his charge attempt to rise or, feigning weakness, pretend to collapse, he should be dealt with promptly, and very roughly.

How I got through the Service I don't know, but I do know that when I had pronounced the last words of it, I could have said no more.

Another word—and, to save my life, I could not have avoided breaking down, bursting into tears, and disgracing myself utterly and for ever.

CHAPTER XXVI

Next day, I discovered that, little as I had supposed it, I was still capable of being surprised.

The surprise was twofold. First, Villa, apparently almost entirely recovered from his slight neck-wound—he had been 'creased'—sent, by the mouth of his watchful frequent visitor, Larry O'Toole, an impudent-sounding message that he wanted a word with Celia Bryndal—and so far as I could gather from the indignant Larry, had hinted that it was not only entirely in Celia's interests to grant his request, but very advisable for her to do so!

And indeed it seemed to me that Larry had been so impressed by Villa's words and manner, that he thought there was something in it, and it might be a good thing if the man's request were granted.

While I was yet pondering the implications of this amazing piece of insolence, Hamblin came to me, and, while apologizing for doing so, informed me that Jake insisted that he must speak to Miss Celia Bryndal.

"Why do you waste your time and mine by bringing me such a message?" I asked somewhat sternly.

"Because havin' seen and hearrd the mon, and havin' thocht it over, Ah've coom to the conclusion that it was ma duty to tell ye, Sir, and to leave ye to mak' yer ain deceesion. Ah couldna see that there was any harm in tellin' ye, and Ah could see that there might be a lot o' harrm in not tellin' ye, and rememberin' all ye said to me when ye put the dog in ma charrge—well, Ah've told ye. An' if ye ask ma opeenion, Sir, there's something in it. Yon murderin' de'il is in real earnest."

I went in search of Celia, invited her to come to the Cabin, and told her of this—to me—amazing message, sent by each of these brutes.

Evidently Celia, unlike myself, was in no-wise surprised.

"About time I told you a few things, Sinbad," she said. "Can you spare an hour now, or . . . ?"

"Two, if necessary," I replied.

"Let's go to your room," said Celia. "I don't want us to be disturbed or interrupted by anybody until I've said everything I've got to say."

I suppose I looked doubtful.

"No, it's all-right," she said a little bitterly. "I want to talk 'affairs'—business affairs, Sinbad—not love affairs. . . . I promise not to take advantage of you."

"Oh, shut up," I said; and led the way to my cabin.

Celia seated herself on my settee, and, taking my hand, pulled me down beside her.

"Now I'm going to tell you everything," she said. "so don't interrupt—and don't think the worse of me. I suppose you hardly could do that, Sinbad," she added.

"Bosh!" said I.

"Well," began Celia, "my mother was very widely, and quite unfavourably, known on the China coast as 'Shanghai Charlotte'. . . . I'm going to speak bluntly, Sinbad, because I believe in it. There's no point in mincing matters, and I want you to know the truth.

"She first rose to fame, in Shanghai, as an extremely beautiful, accomplished, refined, educated, well-mannered and extremely expensive—prostitute; her 'friends' being Naval and Military officers, Captains of ships, wealthy *taipans* and people of that sort.

"There was even an English peer—a Lord Fordingstane who was a *great* 'friend' of Mother's for quite a long time."

I was too astounded to speak, and Celia went on,

"Behaving with the utmost discretion, she prospered, bought a house of her own—and prospered some more. In time, she owned not only her house in the French Concession at Shanghai, but another in Gay Street, Hong Kong; and a third in Macao in Chinese-Portuguese territory, and any *fille de joie* who got into one of her houses considered herself, not only lucky, but a success, a girl whose future was assured—always provided she gave satisfaction—to Mother.

"In Macao she had other interests; and went into partnership with a Chinese millionaire who owned a number of fan-tan houses, brothels, opium dens, and a fleet of smuggler junks. In point of fact, this side of his business included piracy—from Bias Bay—as well as smuggling.

"What he smuggled into China, and up and down the coast, was cocaine, morphia, hashish, opium and other drugs.

"He was a wonderful man, this Hung Toon Chang—highly educated, widely travelled, extremely clever, and most gentle-manly. He did me the honour of proposing for my hand—or rather offered to buy me from Mother, at her own price.

"But although it was an actual offer of real genuine wedlock, I did not, somehow, feel I wanted to marry a Chink, an opium-smuggling owner of gambling-dens and brothels. So the little romance came to nothing; and, not long afterwards, he came to an extremely timely end—a girl, who must have admired him about as much as I did, sticking a knife in his fat neck.

"Apparently, Mother retained big interests in Macao as well as her 'houses' in Hong Kong and Shanghai. But, as a result of the inquest on Hung Toon Chang, who most unfortunately had been killed on British soil (in her Hong Kong house), she felt that a little leave of absence would be good for her health, until the trouble blew over.

"So she went for a sea-voyage—notoriously beneficial to the health, as we have found on this one—and fetched up in Sydney, Australia.

"The Captain of the ship on which she travelled was named Bryndal, and the First Officer was Orlando Wight.

"In Bryndal and Wight she found two men after her own heart . . . and conscience . . . men who put money first—and the rest nowhere, except perhaps love of a dangerous gamble and plenty of pluck.

"Like most other men they fell in love with her . . . to call it 'love' . . . and quarrelled violently.

"Mother had no use for romantic and uncapitalized 'love', from the time she earned her own living at fourteen years of age; but she had plenty of use for Bryndal and Orlando Wight. They were exactly what she happened to be wanting at the moment. She took them both into her employ; Wight on shore in Australia; and Bryndal at sea, on sailing-ships (but I'll tell you more about that, later)—and in St. Andrew's Cathedral in Sydney.

"On the day that he sailed, she married him; the chief reason being, I believe, because she wanted British nationality just then, for some scheme or other, connected with the English Concession at Shanghai. I think her original reason for going to Sydney was to find talent . . . for her 'places of entertainment' at Shanghai, Hong Kong and Macao—procuring, in short.

"Here, both Bryndal and Orlando Wight were useful.

"Also, having pleasant business relations with a Sydney gentleman of wealth and fame—underworld fame—she looked into the possibilities and probabilities of a new line of business . . . gold-smuggling . . . and saw how it might be enormously profitable.

"Apparently it was the old and simple plan of buying in the cheapest market, and selling in the dearest; and the cheapest market is that of the thief and 'fence'. You can buy stolen gold wonderfully cheaply from all sorts of crooked rogues and scoundrels, who vary, from men in a position of trust in big mines, to the wretched hi-jackers who raid and rob the honest miner of his bag of dust, and the illicit gold-buyer of his swag.

"Mother learned about all there was to know, from her rich and fashionable 'fence', who had hoped to employ her to smuggle his gold out of the country—with the kind help of Captain Bryndal.

"When she knew all there was to know about I.G.B.[21] she went into the business on her own account, and made a very handsome thing of it.

"In almost every mining 'town', on practically every gold-field, she had her agents who bought stolen gold with her money.

"Orlando Wight took the money round and collected the gold.

"Getting it out of the country presented no very great difficulty now that she had a ship's Captain for an accomplice. Sometimes Wight took a consignment (he had an Extra-Master's certificate, you know); and it was on his way back from a run, at some point of which he had smuggled the gold ashore, that he was returning to Sydney on the *Valkyrie*.

"That was one of Mother's few mistakes—bringing Orlando Wight back on a ship commanded by Bryndal. They had loathed each other ever since they had quarrelled about Mother—and, no doubt, Bryndal killed him. . . . It was because of his death, that Mother came on this trip, personally to superintend the smuggling of the gold. She couldn't trust Bryndal, though she trusted Orlando Wight absolutely; and there's no doubt he was perfectly faithful to her in all his dealings, and an honest, reliable, and trustworthy servant."

Celia paused for a moment, and some lines, committed to memory in childhood, occurred to me—

"His honour rooted in dishonour stood,
And faith unfaithful kept him falsely true."

To me it seemed almost more tragic that this beautiful and capable harpy-syren, with her insatiable greed for money, power

---

[21] *Illicit Gold Buying.*

and love, should have corrupted Orlando Wight, than that she should have ruined the willing girls whom she procured for her 'houses'.

He had been very good to me. I had grown very fond of him, and every word of Celia's hurt me.

"No, she soon found she couldn't trust her 'husband', Captain Bryndal. In him she had an ideal invaluable tool, had it not been a tool that turned in her hand.

"I believe that he was not only constitutionally incapable of running straight, but that he had some disease that affected his brain. He was admittedly 'queer' before he went home with the *Valkyrie* last time; and you have seen what he was like on this trip. I haven't the slightest doubt that, with all the amazing cunning of a madman, he was planning to steal the gold that he knew was brought on at Sydney; and I've very little doubt that his plan included intimidating Mother into becoming his obedient wife and partner—or of killing her if he failed.

"I feel pretty sure that another part of his plan was to steal the ship—and, as I'll tell you by-and-bye, this would not have been nearly as difficult as you would naturally suppose. Quite easy in point of fact, I believe."

"How?" I asked.

"I'll tell you—by-and-bye."

"There's a good deal to tell me 'by-and-bye'," I smiled.

"Yes, but suppose we have one thing at a time, shall we?" said Celia.

"Well, as I say, Bryndal's conduct is explained partly by what one can only call madness, and partly by his intention to double-cross Mother in every way.

"But, clever as Bryndal undoubtedly was—apart from the madness that developed so suddenly—he was not nearly so clever as Mother. I doubt if he was Mother's equal in anything, ruthlessness, wickedness, organizing gift, power of command, and the ability to win other people's admiration, obedience and loyalty. No, he was superior to Mother in one thing only—physical strength—and by that alone he defeated her.

"In her hands he was a fool as well as a tool. . . . You know that engine that was put aboard at Sydney and of which Mother apparently knew absolutely nothing, and which was part of the cargo discharged at San Francisco?"

"Yes," I said, "I remember it well, for it gave me a long, anxious, and busy day before we were rid of it."

"Well, most of that engine was pure gold. All the thickly vaselined 'brass' parts were gold, and I believe its furnace-box or boiler was filled with black-painted nuggets. I'm not certain of the details, but anyhow there was twenty thousand pounds' worth of gold on that engine, which was railed from San Francisco to the works of Mother's agent at, shall we say, Pittsburg."

I stared at Celia in dumb amazement.

"Now Mother had the heart of a stone, or no heart at all. In fact, her internal economy was altogether deficient, for of bowels of compassion she was also entirely devoid. But she had a well-developed crook loyalty, if you know what I mean, and a very lively sense of the wisdom of taking care of her own—helping and protecting any employee of hers who was in trouble. And in view of what they had to do in the course of their professional duties, they were pretty frequently in trouble, either with the police or with rival practitioners.

"Well, this man, Jake Walfisch, is a case in point.

"Mother had told him to put a rival Illicit Gold Buyer out of business, on the Golden Mile; and Jake, who apparently has a sense of humour all his own, did it in a very noisy way. As soon as the man went off to hide his gold or to get some more money for gold-buying, Jake broke into his humpy that night, raked away the ashes from under his ore-reducing forge, and replaced them with enough blasting-powder or some such explosive, to blow the man to pieces. He then covered up his home-made bomb with the ashes, and departed to get on with his job. The rival returned next day and got on with *his* job until there was a tremendous report—and the subsequent proceedings interested him no more.

"None so surprised or sympathetic as Jake, until a colleague looked in to get a drink and to tell him that he was going to be arrested when asleep and harmless, that night.

"Apparently an informer had told the gold-fields detectives that Jake had been seen to enter the dead man's humpy carrying a parcel, and to leave, half an hour later, without it.

"Jake slept elsewhere that night. A hue and cry was raised, rewards offered, and Jake's sphere of usefulness so circumscribed that Mother smuggled him out of the country and sent him to Orlando Wight in England.

"This was rendered easier by the fact that Jake had been a seaman before he was a gold-merchant.

"Now the reason why Mother employed Jake was that he was a genuine desperado, a man who would stick at nothing whatsoever, a murderer, an ex-convict and a real criminal."

"One would hardly have thought that a person like that would have been very trustworthy," I objected.

"No, one wouldn't have thought it, but one of Mother's many and peculiar gifts was her ability not only to pick men who would be loyal, obedient, and faithful—to her—but also to keep them loyal, obedient, and faithful. . . . Doubtless she was helped by the fact that she never employed people until she knew enough about them to give her a hold over them. And if their past were blameless—she soon put that right.

"A corrupt woman with a terrible power of corruption.

"Anyhow, while Mother lived, this Jake was her slave, with no thought but to obey her and please her in all things."

"Had your Mother complete trust in such a creature?" I asked.

"I don't know; but if she had, she didn't exercise it. He knew nothing whatsoever about the gold on the engine. All he knew was that Mother was an Illicit Gold Buyer, and that he himself had bought a lot of gold for her with money supplied by Orlando Wight. He knew nothing whatever of the gold on the engine. What he did know was that, with tremendous secrecy, skill and fidelity, he had helped to smuggle on board a box of what he thought was gold, and which was—lead-piping."

"It was lead-piping, I suppose?" I asked.

"Heaven knows what it was—Mother being Mother," was the reply. "It's quite possible that the brass on the engine was brass, and that this was gold covered in some lead or zinc amalgam. By the way, what became of it after the mutiny, Sinbad?"

"I—er—chucked it overboard for safety," I said, in some consternation.

"It can't be helped," said Celia philosophically. "You weren't to know you were joyfully chucking bars of gold to the fishes. . . . But perhaps they were only lead, after all. . . . I don't really know."

"I suppose it must have been gold," I said. "Why on earth should she bring on board a box of lead piping?"

"A box of red herrings, stupid," answered Celia. "For the benefit of everyone interested, including the Customs. Any thieves about, it was there to be stolen."

"Your mother didn't tell you everything, then?"

"No. She told me a good deal—and a good deal that was false. Certain things that she knew I would never tell; certain things that she hoped I would tell; and a lot that didn't matter either way. So you see there's a little that I know, more that I can guess, and a tremendous lot about which I'm as ignorant as you are.

"Anyhow, one of the things I do know is that Jake is as bad and dangerous a criminal as there is alive—except Villa."

"I still wonder how your mother could have entrusted him with large sums of money for gold-buying."

"Why shouldn't she? He was visited at irregular but frequent intervals, day or night, by Orlando Wight, who brought the money and took away the gold; and he knew that, if he bolted with either the money or the gold, he'd be giving up a permanent job for one small haul. Also that Wight would have shot him as soon as look at him, and that nobody ever double-crossed Mother and got away with it.

"He knew that if he bolted she would have put not only her own employees on his track, but the gold-field detectives and police as well. For Mother always stood in well with foreign police; and, to British and Colonial police, she was known only as a lady of unimpeachable character and blameless life.

"And, as I say, nobody, whether employed-girl in any of her houses, or employed-man in Australia, China or America, ever attempted to play any funny tricks with Mother—except Bryndal, and all he could do with her was to kill her.

"I think, for the first time in her life, Mother had begun to be afraid: and that night she was telling me a good deal of what I am now telling you. I feel certain Bryndal overheard something, and that was the end of her . . ."

We both sat silent.

"Well, that's Jake," said Celia with a sigh. "Now about Villa.

"Before speaking about him, I must tell you of Mother's third —and worst—line of business.

"She was an importer, and wholesale and retail distributor of the most profitable commodities on earth—far more profitable than stolen gold—narcotics. She had practically a monopoly of the sale of morphia and cocaine on the China coast, and an enormous business in opium and hashish.

"The Chinese I told you of, Hung Toon Chang, was her chief customer for cocaine, and had, through her, a monopoly in Macao. Not only did she handle these drugs in China, but had agencies in America; while Bryndal, Orlando Wight and one or two others did a side-line on their own, small but pretty profitable, in various ports, including the Port of London.

"I fancy her business in Marseilles was nearly as valuable as the one run from San Francisco.

"In this business again, Mother must have been extremely

377

successful in her choice of agents; and her organizing ability must have been phenomenal. Being one of the vilest businesses on earth, it is naturally one of the most dangerous, especially in a country where the police cannot be squared. Even in countries where they can, there's still a good deal of risk and a lot of graft, palm-greasing and blackmail.

"The agents through whom she worked must have been creatures considerably lower than her illicit gold-buying accomplices. If possible, they were even lower than her white-slave traders.

"One of these drug-agents was Villa, a man whose side-lines were blackmail, kidnapping, murder for hire, gang-robbery, white-slave trading, and the vice-racket generally. His main business was to get the stuff ashore at San Francisco, take it to Chicago, and thence distribute it to the retailers—all this again a very expensive business, as so many palms had to be greased before an ounce of the stuff could be sold.

"Nevertheless, the profits were simply enormous and all passed through the hands of this man Villa.

"Mother met him as usual this voyage, at San Francisco, and he told her he might have to make a quick getaway. The police were after him. Some new broom somewhere had sworn to sweep him up, and get him a 'lifer' in St. Quentin, if he couldn't send him to 'the chair'—wherein doubtless he was highly qualified to sit. He had to bolt suddenly and got down to Pisagua.

"It was up to Mother to save him, and, as in Jake's case, the ship was the obvious means of doing so. He could make some sort of a show as a sailor, as he had grown up along the San Francisco water-front, had been on the sea a good deal, and, among his other activities, had done some 'blackbirding' in a schooner round the South Sea Islands, retiring from that honourable profession to run a crimps' boarding-house at San Francisco. I should say that Villa is a much worse man than Jake, more heartless, more dangerous, more absolutely devilish.

"Probably he has done a thousand times more harm than Jake has, with his blackmailing, dope-running and white slaving. I haven't the slightest doubt that it was he who had the bright idea of burning you and the others alive and . . . ."

"An idea that quite appealed to Jake," I pointed out.

"Yes," agreed Celia, "quite so. Nevertheless, it's not the sort of thing that would have occurred to him, and I maintain that Villa is, even if not the worse, the more dangerous and desperate of the two."

We sat silent for a while.

"So you'll see that they don't get another chance to seize the ship," concluded Celia. "Don't take the handcuffs off them."

"No, they won't get another chance to seize the ship," I said, "and they won't be free from the handcuffs except when they are set to work. . . . But it seems to me that they're bound to get a chance to do something else."

"What's that?" asked Celia.

"Talk," said I.

"To the men?"

"I wasn't thinking of that, and I shouldn't worry about it. But what about their talking to the Police when I hand them over? Your mother was able to count on the loyalty of both of them, if only because their interests were identical with hers; but what about them now that your Mother is dead? The first thing they did was to organize a plot to seize the ship; and, as we know, Jake promptly gave away the secret of the gold—or thought he did—as a bribe and inducement to the rest."

"Well, Mother is dead. What they say cannot do her any harm. Bryndal's dead. Orlando Wight is dead. Whom can they hurt?"

"You," I replied. "They are bound to try to do themselves some good by accusing you of being accessory . . . and not only accessory, but a ring-leader—the only remaining ring-leader, in fact. I should think that when they've told their tale to the Police and the Solicitor for the Defence, or in Court, you'll be arrested. I should think the Public Prosecutor would be bound to have you put on trial."

"What for?"

"I don't know anything about the Law, but it seems to me you'd be charged with being an accomplice, a member of a drug-selling, white-slaving, smuggling corporation."

"Do you think so?"

"Well, I don't know. . . . I don't know how deeply you'd be considered to be involved. You're of age; you were travelling with your mother, and presumably on this business. . . . You see, I don't know what they could prove. . . . I don't know how deeply you were involved. I may be absolutely wrong, but at first sight, it does look to me like a very real danger."

"What's to be done?" mused Celia.

"Don't know—yet," I replied.

"Well, I know what I'd do," asserted Celia.

"Yes?"

"I'd handcuff Mr. Jake Walfisch to Mr. Sea-side Villa—and chuck the pair of them overboard."

"Would you?"

"I would."

"Would you like me to do it?"

"Oh, Sinbad! Would you?"

"No, I wouldn't."

"Do you want to interview Jake and Villa?"

"No," replied Celia. "I don't . . . not at present, anyhow. I'll wait until I've thought things out, a bit further."

CHAPTER XXVII

The blessedness of routine. . . .

In a few days' time everything was going on smoothly, the past seemed like an evil nightmare from which we had awakened, and the ship life was as normal as it could be, in our short-handed condition.

The conduct of Peddersen and Johes was unexceptionable. Müller, if sulkily silent, was well-behaved and hard-working.

Villa and Jake, recovered from their wounds, spent their watch-below in irons, and their watch-on-deck under strict surveillance; and were not allowed to meet.

At noon, one day, I was the unintentional and indirect instrument of the solution of part, at any rate, of Celia's problem.

The penultimate tragedy of that incredible, fateful voyage arose from so minor a cause, so trifling a matter, as—a shortage of soft tobacco.

Smoking a cigarette that I had clumsily made from chopped hard tobacco, I leaned over the for'ard taff-rail and discussed with Dacre some details of the painting of the ship.

Below us, the men waited to draw their lime-juice. Suddenly, nearly all the tobacco, lumpy, loose, and friable, trickled out of my cigarette-paper, and, by chance, the smouldering burning pieces and hot ashes fell on to the head and neck of Jake.

With no inkling of the tragic result, we saw Jake put his hand to the back of his neck and cause a piece of glowing Lucky Hit to drop down into his shirt, and become pressed against his bare skin.

Greatly to the joy of the onlookers, this made him swear, jump, clutch, and wriggle, and send the burning tobacco farther down until he had to find relief by pulling off his shirt.

Not troubling to put it on again at the moment, he tied the sleeves loosely under his chin, and allowed the body-part to hang down his back.

Then, quite unconsciously, Axenstern played his childish part in the affair; and, as Jake turned away with his pannikin of lime-juice, Axenstern lifted the shirt and brought down his big dirty hand with a resounding slap on to Jake's bare back.

The shirt was lifted for only a few seconds, but they were

pregnant seconds for Jake Walfisch; for, in that brief space of time, Hamblin, who was standing beside Axenstern, caught sight of a glistening cone-shaped scar, between Jake's shoulder-blades.

Later, I learned from Fagin that Jake had told him how, in another ship, he had been sleeping, face downwards, when, owing to a heavy roll, a lamp had fallen on him and caused the burn—that left this fatal mark on his swarthy skin.

Not very quick-witted, and suffering from one of his frequent splitting headaches, Hamblin wondered why the scar interested him. Then suddenly he recalled my description of the scar on the back of the man who fled from me in the Broomielaw!

Yelling,

"Ma Goad! 'Tis him wi' the scar!" he leapt after Jake, and, as the startled man turned to see the cause of the outcry, they came face to face.

Opening and shutting his outstretched hands, Hamblin, mad with rage and long weary months of incessant suffering, screamed,

"Ye're the hoor that hut me i' the Broomiela' when Ah was drrunk! . . ."

And Jake, seeing murder in the eyes that glowered at him, lost his presence of mind.

Had he remained on deck, there were plenty to see that he suffered no more than a beating; more than one determined that the gallows should not be cheated of its prey; but instead of doing so, he flung the lime-juice contents of his pannikin straight into Hamblin's face, and, taking advantage of his enemy's temporary blindness, fled, and jumped for the mizzen rigging.

This was particularly foolish because, owing to his lightness, great reach and long powerful legs, no-one aboard was able to go aloft faster than Hamblin—certainly not Jake, doubtless some-what weakened by the days he had spent handcuffed in his berth, and hampered by some stiffness of his right shoulder-muscles.

It was in vain that I shouted to Hamblin to stay on deck, and, before those who were near thought to seize him, he was shaking the shrouds with the fury of his pursuit and making an animal snarling sound that was horrible to hear.

In all probability Jake expected to reach the mizzen-top, and there, with his sheath-knife, to keep the Scot from coming higher. But, by that day, his luck had gone, his evil angel had turned from him, and, with his face to the sky, he was hanging like a fly from the futtock-shrouds when a great arm, seeming long and powerful as the tentacle of an octopus, curled about his middle.

By putting his full weight on the encircling arm, Hamblin was able to pluck the struggling Jake from his hold.

Then, like a pair of fighting cats, clawing and clutching at each other, they lost footing, rolled and gathered momentum down the lower rigging.

I looked away. . . .

At the sheerpoles, men risked their own lives in seizing them, and saving them from falling into the sea; but, while Hamblin escaped unhurt, save for horrible bruises, a dislocated shoulder and a sprained ankle, Jake's skull was fractured against the to'gallant rail, and he lived for only a few hours.

So, for his cowardly, treacherous, and brutal blow, and his robbing of a drunken man who had entertained him, he paid with his life.

Before he died, he recovered consciousness, and either repented or was filled with a remorseful fear of the Hereafter; for, having asked my pardon for the trouble he had caused, he told me what was doubtless the absolute truth concerning the murders of Mr. Hammerson and of Geordie Stowe.

In each case both Villa and Müller had struck a fatal blow; and Jake, as he freely confessed, had helped them in every way; and had actually thrown Mr. Hammerson overboard, not knowing whether he were alive or dead.

He also told me that it was Peddersen who, at Smeeker's instigation, had removed the linings of the main to'gallant winch; that he, Villa, Peddersen and Müller had tipped the coil of wire tow-rope from the deck-house on to Dacre; that Peddersen had told them that it was he who had put 'knock-out drops' in the black draught bottle—at Captain Bryndal's instigation.

When I asked Jake why the Captain should want to get rid of Dacre and myself, he replied that, according to Peddersen, the Captain wasn't going to have any use for us when we got to Cape Town; that we didn't know on which side our bread was buttered; and were the sort of psalm-smiting, Bible-punching young pimps who would 'blow the gaff'.

Apparently it had been the Captain's intention that none should survive the voyage to Cape Town who could not be relied upon to stand in with him, and not only take their share but do their share, as well.

Smeeker also was in with the Captain and Peddersen, and

between them they had separated the sheep from the goats, the "Ship-owners" from the "Shell-backs"; and had decided that there was nothing to be done with Mr. Hammerson, Dacre and myself but to 'dump' us.

Our fate was probably to be shared by Geordie Stowe and Beauty, unless they could be prevailed upon, and relied upon, to 'act sensible'.

Within this plot was another plot organized by Villa and Jake *after* the death of Mrs. Bryndal; their idea being that, instead of accepting from Captain Bryndal a small share of the proceeds of the sale of the ship, they should seize it for themselves, and, laying a course for the nearest coast, abandon it, taking with them the rich booty that they believed it to contain.

I gathered that the general idea of this plot of Villa's was to use their shipmates to get one or two of the boats to some deserted part of the African coast, or to some uninhabited island, and there to bury their treasure, dispose of their associates one by one, themselves escape, and return later to 'discover' the buried treasure that they themselves had hidden.

Whatever may have been the cause—repentance, remorse, fear, or a loquaciousness caused by brain-injury—Jake certainly attempted to make the fullest confession of everything that he could remember, and a clean breast of all his crimes.

And not only of his own, but of those of his associates in so far as they endangered us; and, by the time he had finished, I think there wasn't much that I didn't know about the general situation.

Of Villa he bade us beware—even yet; and strongly advised me to do everything in my power to prevent him turning King's Evidence.

"He ain't a man," whispered Jake, "he's a devil. And he ain't a good devil, too; for he's got a yellow streak. When it come to the last show-down, he'd squeal to save his life. Not for nothing else, he wouldn't, but to dodge the rope or the chair, he'd cert'nly squeal . . . and he'd double-cross anybody—unless it was Charlotte. Anyhow, don't let him get where he can blow the gaff about . . . the dope business. It'd go hard with the girl, and it might go hard with you—and everybody aft. There's some of the stuff on board now, and he'd swear you helped him plant it. . . .

"Sure thing, if once Villa started in to save his neck, he'd say something."

The last coherent words of this sturdy rogue were,

"Look out for the bottles . . . He told me . . ."

Having uttered this cryptic remark, he suddenly fell silent, began to breathe stertorously, and never regained consciousness.

That night I had another long talk with Celia, telling her all that Jake had told me.

§2

With Jake gone, and Hamblin temporarily *hors de combat*, each Watch was now reduced to four A.B.s and one Apprentice; and although I ordered that *kalasi* watch should be kept for most of the day, there was as much grumbling and growling as might have been expected.

With a superiority of manner that made me smile, and the air of one who had never known the inside of a fo'c'sle, Carrol, formerly the most inveterate grouser on the ship, observed,

"Good! When Shell-backs stop growling, it's time to stand from under and look out for squalls."

Hence a certain anxiety and disgust overtook him when the growling of our "Shell-backs" diminished suddenly and noticeably, and they became curiously quiet.

Whilst hauling, they raised no more song than was absolutely necessary to get unison of pull; and, at night, there was no evidence of the usual desire to get as far as possible from the Officer of the Watch. Rather did they huddle under the break of the poop, and go for'ard only when there was work to be done.

Secretly and anxiously watching events, we of the after-guard were puzzled.

The two men who might have been dangerous were not only most amenable, but seemed to share the general uneasiness. In fact, Slim Johes gave me the impression that he was badly scared; and, in the end, he was the one to supply the reason for the prevailing gloom.

It appeared that, not having suffered sufficiently, we were now being persecuted by a *ghost!*

"Good God!" said Dacre when he heard the interesting news, "and was there ever a ship afloat that was more likely to be haunted?"

The first indication of this new trouble came when Johes begged to be allowed to keep his look-out from the fore-yard. At the time of the request, the Second Mate was not in a good humour and his reply was,

"Now what the Hell's biting ye, ye yapping tyke? How d'you think you're going to report the side-lights and strike the bell from up there? Get ye on to the fo'c'sle-head and stop there, ye ruddy rabbit."

"But there are two *voices*, I tell 'oo, Sir," wailed the sweating Slim.

"Voices?" bawled Carrol. "Voices? You wait till you hear *my* voice properly. My God, you'll sweat properly then. You'll start sweating your buttons. Damme, I'd say ye'd got something on your conscience, if I thought ye'd got a conscience, ye slack-jawed swine."

And not another word would he hear from the obviously distressed and terrified Slim.

But Carrol, not being entirely free from the superstitions that he affected so deeply to scorn, made discreet enquiries of his old crony, Church, and discovered that he also had heard at least one "voice".

Others were supposed to have heard it too, but Church observed to Carrol that,

"They're like a bloomin' lot o' perishin' sheep, and because that blubberin' jabberin' Johes thought he'd heard something, they've all heard it. Me, I'm lookin' out for the blasted 'voice' that *I* heard, and only hope I can catch hold of it—or the bloke it comes out of. I'll knock some 'voice' out of him. I'll learn him to pull our legs—if I pull his head off."

Carrol soon had to admit, however, that he was beaten. Not only did the Watch, the next night, profess to have heard mysterious voices in the vicinity of the fo'c'sle-head, but they were able to repeat the exact words that they had heard.

Well, what were they, the funny words, the adjectived words, that had penetrated the lop ears, the bat ears, the mud-bunged ears, the wooden brains, the bone brains, the no-brains-at-all of the scarcely ornamental and hardly useful Watch-on-deck, enquired Carrol.

What they had heard, every man Jack of them, was a woman's voice, calling a name that sounded Eye-talian and telling the Eye-talian who she was, what she'd come aboard for; and what she was going to do with him—the Eye-talian.

Well, what was the Eye-talian's name?

Joo-seppy Something.

All were agreed upon the Joo-seppy, but the Something varied from Polly-oh to Some-sorter-Grotto. That's the name she called, and she said she was *Marier*.

"A ghost named Marier, eh?" jeered Carrol, "Marier Monk who did a bunk . . . or was it Marier Martin straight from the Red Barn?"

But the men were serious, and resented the Second Mate's flippant ribaldry and scepticism.

No, it wasn't no Marier Monk and it wasn't that sorter Marier at all. It was more like Moh-rier, or Moy-rier.

"Myra?" asked Carrol.

Ar, that was right . . . Moyrer.

And what was the poor young girl's other name if it wasn't Monk nor Martin? Could they remember that much?

Ar, they could so. *O'Moore* it was, plain enough . . . and *Hartigan* it was, plain enough.

"Hearty *gel*, you mean," jeered Carrol. . . .

But there it was. Jeer, sneer or cheer, the men had heard a voice, obviously and unmistakably female, call upon an Italian whose Christian name was Giuseppe and announce herself to be Moira O'Moore Hartigan!

And what was one to make of that?

Carrol, in point of fact, made very heavy weather of it, assuring me that I could take it from him that the men were speaking the truth.

It would have been different if the voice had been that of a man, as it would have been easy enough to account for the whereabouts of each member of both Watches; but the voice was to be heard when the movements of everyone for'ard could be accounted for; and thus the possibility of detecting the "bloke what's pullin' our legs" must be ruled out.

It seemed to me that Carrol was getting as scared as the rest.

While Dacre and I were in the act of discussing the matter, the men came aft in a body.

My hand went to the pistol in my pocket, but I took it out again as I noted that Church was leading them, and evidently had been appointed spokesman.

"What's the matter now?" I asked shortly.

"We wants leave to keep our look-outs on the fore-yard, Sir," said Church. "We wishes to say as 'ow, beggin' yer pardon, Sir, and Mr. Carrol's pardon, the fo'c'sle-'ead ain't 'ealthy nowadays."

I laughed.

"No, Sir," he expostulated, raising his voice slightly, "an' no man didn't ought to be sent up there alone, for two hours."

In point of fact, I was so relieved to find that I was not faced with incipient mutiny—for I'd got mutiny on the brain by that time —that I could have roared with laughter—a laughter none too sane and normal.

"The fo'c'sle-head not healthy!" I scoffed. "Surely the air on the fore-yard is much the same, isn't it? But what's wrong with the fo'c'sle-head?"

" 'Tain't the air, Capt'in," said Church darkly. "I knows what I knows. Still, I'd like one of these clever know-all blokes, like Slim Johes, to say 'is piece. Now then, Johes."

"Thiss ship is haunted, Sir, I tell 'oo! It's haunted for'ard," cried Slim. "We all know that it iss haunted. Every man in the fo'c'sle knows it."

"Aye?" I said. "Can't you get the ghost to lay aft? What's it like?"

"It iss the woman again, Sir."

"Good gracious! This won't do. I'm surprised at you, Church, a married man; and Berghen, and Blancke; and you Hamblin."

"Of course you think we're a pack of fules, Sirr, but we're no' feart of what we can see . . . Ah'd wring her bluidy neck . . . It's what a mon canna see that makes him scairt. When ye can hear voices a' roond, an' can see naethin', Cap'n, it's no' canny. Ah'm no' feart o' any mon—but Ah'm feart o' this—Thing; an' Ah'm tellin' ye, Cap'n."

"But surely, Hamblin," I protested, "I should have thought that a voice must be produced by a pair of lungs, and that those lungs must be inside a human body. . . . What does *this* voice say, anyway? No swearing, I hope, or bawdy songs, or telling you to set the flying jib, or promising to splice the main brace, eh?"

But in speaking disrespectfully of the "voice", I had made a fatal mistake, and not another word could I get from the men.

Shuffling uneasily, they relapsed into sullen silence and I was forced to dismiss them with a promise that I would look into the matter. . . .

"Now what do you think of that, Dacre?" I asked, as soon as the crew had gone.

"Well—it's plain enough that somebody's got that crowd badly rattled," replied Dacre, "and it isn't only a mass attack of mob-nerves, so to speak. I should say there's something behind it; and that the sooner we scotch that ghost, the better—before there's more trouble in the ship. . . . My God! haven't we enough—or had enough . . . ? If Jake weren't dead and Villa shut up, handcuffed, in the sail-locker, I should have said that the 'Ship-owners' were on the war-path again. But while you were talking I watched

Müller, Slim Johes, Brown, Paulo and Axenstern, and I think I know badly frightened men when I see them."

"H'm . . . I wonder whether Church's sense of humour has become so perverted that he has engineered the whole joke," I mused.

"I doubt it. Fancy Church producing a delicate female voice and calling on Giuseppe Somebody in the name of Moira O'Moore Hartigan! . . . No, it wouldn't be Church, with his Cockney accent and all. Let's have another talk with him alone, shall we?"

"No harm, anyway," I agreed. "Send for him, Dacre."

Although he was no fool Church was as susceptible to flattery as most sailor-men; and my opening remarks caused him to inflate his chest perceptibly.

"I want your help again, Church," I began. "It's all right for Johes and the rest of that band of fools to talk about the ship being haunted; but you and I know better. Now tell me. Whom do you suspect of adding to the pack of troubles we've already had?"

"Honest ter Gawd, I dunno, Sir," he declared fervently. "The first time I 'eard it—that man's voice, I mean—I'd gone on to the fo'c'sle-'ead to cadge a box o' matches off of Müller. . . . It was his look-out, an' 'e was up agin the knight-'eads, and just as I got to the top o' the ladder, I 'eard it. It seemed to come from under me feet and yet, in a manner o' speakin', it was in the air all rahnd me. I thought it was some damn foolin' o' Müller's, but before I could blarst 'is eyes, 'e screams,

" '*Mein Gott*, vhat vas that?'

" 'You knows ruddy well what it is, you funny tripe-'ound,' I tells him severity. But I was only bluffin', meself. I knew blame well that 'e didn't know. 'E was tremblin' like a haspen leaf, an' could 'ardly git his words out. . . . Then I slips down the other ladder and looks under the fo'c'sle-'ead, but there wasn't anything there, and everybody in the fo'c'sle-'ead was dead ter the world. I was fair flummoxed."

"Has anyone else heard it?" I asked.

" 'Ans Berghen and Blancke was 'avin' a mike under the fo'c'sle-'ead the other night, an' they swears that a voice come in by the 'awsepipes."

"And who was on the look-out?"

"Now you mentions it, Sir, Müller was, and all the other times he was, now I comes to think of it."

"Well, don't you think you've settled the problem?" I laughed. "Doesn't it seem as though Müller has got some game on, and that he's a bit of an actor, and thinks he's a bit of a ventriloquist too?"

"No, Sir, I don't. He's no more actor than enough to act the silly fool. Besides, he couldn't talk both like a woman an' like a man, could he? And in plain English?"

"Well, how could you know that?"

"Well, any'ow, 'twasn't his voice I 'eard," declared Church doggedly.

"Oh, but look here, Church," I answered testily, "you and Müller were on the fo'c'sle-head, and though there was nobody near you, a voice spoke. . . . Now talk sense, man. If it wasn't Müller's voice it was yours."

"*Mine?*" he snorted. "*Mine?*"

Then leaning towards me and tapping the palm of one horny hand with the index finger of the other, he spoke slowly and solemnly.

"Cap'n," he said, "I wish it was mine, Sir. I'd sleep easier in me bunk, and so'd some o' the rest of us. Now you've said that, I'll tell you whose voice I did 'ear, and neither Müller nor me could speak with it. I tell you, Sir, an' if it was me last words, I'm tellin' you the trufe, it was the livin' voice o' Mr. Hammerson.

" '*I'm coming back . . . I'm coming back . . . I'm coming back . . .*' it says, slow and awful like. Well, I ain't mad an' I ain't drunk, Sir, but I'll be bloomin' surprised—and a bit more'n glad—if he *don't* come back."

"But why should Mr. Hammerson want to come back, Church?" I asked, deeply impressed, against my will and against my better sense, by his solemn deep sincerity.

"Don't ask me, Sir, ask Müller. An' whatever answer he gives, I wouldn't be that Dutch dog for all the brass in the Bank of England."

I was, by now, quite convinced of Church's good faith, and that, not only had he no hand—or voice—in the matter, but most firmly believed the ship was haunted, the sound supernatural. It was also quite clear that to try to laugh him out of his beliefs would be a waste of time, and following quite the wrong line.

"Well," I said, "I haven't heard the voice, Church, so . . . I don't know. Anyhow, I'm quite sure that you never heard Mr. Hammerson. Personally I think someone's playing tricks, and I'm going to have a good try at finding the man that's fooling you all. I'll let you know how I propose to do it."

And bidding him tell Doc to give him a heartening tot, I sent him away.

At the evening muster I learned that Blancke was going on the look-out, and, presenting him with a whistle, I told him to blow it hard, the moment he heard any unusual sound. If he were undisturbed during his watch he was to pass the whistle on to his relief.

"And as every man in the ship knows you've got that whistle, Blancke," I concluded, "I don't fancy you'll hear any 'voices'. But if you do, I can assure you we're going to catch that talkative bird and put something stronger than salt on his tail."

Although this raised only a very little feeble laughter, the possession of the whistle seemed to give these superstitious children some measure of confidence.

As they turned to go, I pointed out that it didn't seem to have occurred to them that they could hear a voice on the fore-yard as well as anywhere else, and this reflection seemed to make them more reconciled to keeping a look-out from the fo'c'sle-head.

Up to Seven Bells in the first watch I heard nothing unusual, and, having finished my book, I was contemplating changing into pyjamas, when, from for'ard, there came a sound that I took to be the high note of a whistle.

As I reached the poop, it was repeated nearer, and, with an involuntary shiver and a feeling of "goose-flesh", I realized that it was the shrill scream of a man crazed with pain, or in an agony of terror.

It was somewhat akin to the awful shrieks that I had heard as a child when a horse was trapped in a burning stable.

"Moses! What's that?" cried the Second Mate behind me.

"Come and see," I said, over my shoulder, but at the top of the ladder I stopped so suddenly that, from behind, Carrol nearly knocked me down the steps.

A man was racing at tremendous speed along the main deck and, without pausing at the foot of the ladder, he charged up on to the poop.

He had mounted by the weather ladder, and the training of a life-time asserting itself, Carrol at that moment could think of nothing but this offence against one of the strictest rules of ship-board etiquette.

"What the Hell!" he began, but, being shouted down by the insane shrieks of the thoroughly demented man, he got no further.

"*I didn't do it! I didn't do it!*" screamed the fugitive, in the voice of Slim Johes. "*Tell him I didn't do it!*" And flinging himself down and clutching Carrol, cried with hysterical frenzy,

"Tell him it was Villa and Müller! They both hit him from behind, and threw him overboard. It wass three of them. It wass not me. Tell him! Tell him it wass not me."

"Tell who, you blasted fool?" shouted the affronted Carrol, jerking himself free from the clutching arms. "Tell who what, you squealing swab?"

Weeping like a woman and panting like a dog, Johes scrambled to get behind the Second Mate's broad back.

"He iss for'ard there now, I tell 'oo, I tell 'oo," he shrieked, and pointed with a shaking hand. "His face iss green and there iss sea-weed in his hair.

" '*I've come back for you all*,' he sayss. '*Why did you do it?*' he sayss, and I sayss,

" 'It wass not me. It wass Villa and Müller bashed your head, and it wass Jake threw you overpoard, I tell 'oo.'

" '*I've come back for you all. . . . I've come back for you all*,' he sayss.

"And I sayss,

" 'It wass Villa plotted it! You hit him that day in the fo'c'sle, in the storm off Staten Island. He said he'd get you. Jake and Müller said so too. . . . So all three took a hand. . . . It wass not me, I tell 'oo. For the love of Christ,' I sayss, 'it wass not me, it wass Villa.'

"It wass, it wass," screamed Johes. "It wass, it wass . . ."

"Here, steady yourself, Johes," I said sternly. "Pull yourself together, you miserable hound. Tell us what . . ."

But the madman heard not a word.

Shaking his palsied hand and trembling finger at the fore end of the ship, he screamed in a voice that rose to a thin piping falsetto,

"It wass Villa, I tell 'oo. . . . I didn't touch 'oo. How could it be me whateffer, when 'oo was alive when Jake threw 'oo over the rail. . . . I didn't touch 'oo, and 'oo wass not dead on this ship. . . . You shall not haunt me, I tell 'oo."

Suddenly, I grasped the tremendous significance of the truth of what was being extorted from this lunatic by his own terror.

"Here, all-right; I won't let you be haunted, Johes," I said suddenly. "Now come down to the Cabin and tell me all about it."

And grasping his arm I led him to the companion.

"Send those men for'ard, there," I added, indicating the gaping group that clustered on the lee side of the ship. "And just see if there is anyone on the fo'c'sle-head."

I didn't stop to think what such an order meant to a man like

Carrol, and it said much for his loyalty that he searched right out to the flying-jib stay, and of course found no-one.

In the Saloon, I found Dacre, who was about to go on watch, and I requested him to knock on the Steward's door and then bring paper and pen.

Doc having heard my voice, slipped on his trousers and followed close behind Dacre.

Celia also, it appeared, had not retired, for she followed Doc into the Saloon.

"Now there are plenty to protect you, Slim—including a girl," I said quietly. "So pull yourself together, and tell us who frightened you; and don't get so excited."

This seemed to revive the memory of what he had seen and heard, for it brought back a fresh attack of hysterical terror.

"Lock the doors, look you," he sobbed. "Lock them, I say. Keep him out! Keep him out! . . . It was the Second Mate himself, I tell 'oo. *It was Mr. Hammerson.*"

"Now how do you know it was Mr. Hammerson?" I asked gently.

"I saw the prass puttons on his coat," wailed Johes. "Oh, God the Father, he came up out of the sea py the starpoard light, and his puttons was green and shining."

Even at that dramatic moment, Celia could scarcely forbear to smile. The tarnished brass buttons, thick with green verdigris, of the late Second Mate's old uniform jacket had been a joke, not only with her, but had frequently been roundly commented upon, in old Hooligan's chantys.

"I saw him, I tell 'oo, in the green light of the starpoard lamp, and it was his voice that said,

" 'Why did you do it, Slim?'

"But I tell 'oo it wass not me, it was Villa."

"Now tell us exactly what Villa did, Slim," I suggested. "Make a clean breast of everything, and then I'm sure the ghost of Mr. Hammerson won't come to haunt you again."

"Villa made the plan, I tell 'oo; and Villa hit him from behind with a stocking full of sand," sobbed Slim, "and when he fell, Müller hit him on the back of the neck with a belaying-pin. He hit him with all his might, and spoke in German and then said,

" 'Take that, you *schweinhund*. "Dutch hog", am I? How you vas like a hog's kick, eh?'

"Then Jake came down from the fo'c'sle-head and sayss, " 'Holy Gee! That's give him his. Dump him, quick.'

"And Jake pulls him to the rail and heaves him over.

"Sir, Sir," Johes sobbed, "I didn't know there was to be any real killing, I tell 'oo. Inteed, I thought we wass going only to give him the pest hiding he effer got. I didn't know, and I wass so scared . . ."

At this point there was a disturbance in the companion-way, and Carrol's voice was heard to say,

"Ye damned Dutch liar! When did the Cap'n send for you?"

"Whom have you got there, Mr. Carrol?" I called, as Dacre opened the door.

"This man says you sent for him, Sir," replied Carrol, and holding Müller in a firm grip, he appeared in the door-way.

"Oh indeed, and who told you I had sent for you, Müller?" I asked sternly.

The man's eyes blazed at Johes and then sullenly sank to stare at my feet.

"I vas vant to know vhat dat lying dog, Slim, have say about me," he growled.

"Why should he say anything about you?" I began. "What makes you . . . ?"

"Müller! Müller! Müller!" cried Johes. "I didn't kill Mr. Hammerson, did I? Tell them it wass a mistake. Tell them his plood is not on my hands. He shall not haunt me."

"I know not vhat you vas speak about," snarled Müller, but with fear staring from his pale eyes.

"Don't know? Damn 'oo for a ploody liar," shrieked Slim. "Did 'oo not hit him with a belaying-pin after Villa hit him with the sandbag? Yess, and did not Villa say it wass no need, and did not Jake drag him to the rail and dump him overpoard?"

"You would speak lies about me, *schweinhund*?" said the German as his hand went to his knife. "You stabbed him in the back."

And only Carrol's powerful hold prevented him from springing on the trembling, cringing Johes.

"You, Müller," I growled, "let me hear another word out of you and I'll close your mouth for a week; and if ever you come aft again without leave, you'll go back in irons and stay in them for a month. . . . Mr. Carrol, take that man's knife and let him have it back in the morning—with the point missing. Now lay for'ard, you Müller. . . . And watch your step, for I'd as soon thrash you as look at you."

Müller's ugly mouth opened to reply, but, catching my eye, he decided to remain silent; and, glaring with furious rage, he gave Johes a look that boded him little good, and dashed up the companion-way.

"So Villa arranged the murder, did he?" I asked the trembling Slim.

"Iss, iss, Sir. And look you, he told Müller that his part wass to decoy the Second Mate for'ard by not striking the bell nor answering the hail."

This gave me an excellent opening for the next, and most delicate, part of the proceedings.

With a sympathetic and contemplative eye on Slim, I meditated aloud.

"Yes, this Villa's a cunning devil," I soliloquized, for Slim's benefit. "Now that he's got to face a charge of being ring-leader in a mutiny, and one of murder, he'll try to prove that Jake was the ring-leader and that he himself was the quite unwilling accomplice of Slim Johes and Müller. . . . And he'll swear—the truth—that he never laid a finger on Mr. Hammerson (for he only touched him with a sandbag, and didn't help to throw him overboard)."

"But inteed to gootness it was him that arranged it all, I tell 'oo," howled Slim. "When Müller got his hiding from Mr. Hammerson for trying to jerk you off the yard, Villa sayss,

" 'Ye can get square with that man-eater, one night for'ard, Müller.'

"And then they whispered together, and Jake joined in. I tell 'oo, Sir, I thought that when the Second Mate came for'ard in the dark to see what was wrong with the look-out, we wass all going to set on to him and beat him up, and then run away. I never heard anything about murder whateffer, I tell 'oo."

"H'm," I mused without looking at the creature. "I wonder whether a Judge and Jury would believe that. . . . No, of course they wouldn't."

"What shall I do! What shall I do? . . . Py Gott, it iss a hanging matter," moaned the demoralized Slim.

"Of course it is," said I, turning to him, and added,

"But there's one thing that might help you. You can write and sign a statement of how it all happened, and so get your story in before Villa's and Müller's. If you'd like to do that, the two Officers and myself will witness your statement."

"God bless you, Sir. I thank you, Sir. I think thatt iss the pest thing to do whateffer," replied Slim.

Celia, who was a very quick writer, took down Johes' statement which, because it was inspired by abject fear, both of life and of death, both of the ghost and the gallows, seemed to me to bear the hall-mark of truth. Personally, I decided that Slim had been present—'willing to wound but afraid to strike'—and, though accessory, had, by cowardice restrained, borne no actual hand in the murder.

When the statement was signed with Slim's wavering scrawl, and witnessed by Dacre, Carrol and myself, I felt inclined to call down blessings on the thing that had put such terror into the animal. We had obtained the evidence that was to prove vital in bringing Hammerson's murderers to justice.

Before Johes left the Cabin, a little of his fear had evaporated, and he was evidently wondering whether he'd done quite wisely.

When daylight and reflection came, he offered to give Doc his pay-day if Doc would steal the document and return it to him.

CHAPTER XXVIII

"What's your theory, Sinbad?" asked Celia as I rose to leave the lunch-table next day.

"Got none," I replied, "unless you can call it a theory that a pack of superstitious idiots imagine 'voices'; one a woman's and the other Mr. Hammerson's; and that the unbalanced excitable Johes has had Mr. Hammerson constantly on his conscience until he has begun 'seeing things'."

"It's a funny business," pondered Celia. "It has never occurred to you that, as I'm the only woman on board, the female voice that they've been hearing must either be pure imagination —or mine?"

"No," I replied, "it didn't occur to me; and it doesn't."

"Why?"

"Partly because the idea is too silly to entertain; and partly because I happened to know that you were in your room on at least three occasions when the phenomenon occurred—or was reported to have occurred."

"Quite so. . . . On the whole it's been a good thing, hasn't it?" she observed.

"How?" I asked.

"Well, it's given troublesome people something to trouble them, for a change, hasn't it? Given them something to think about."

"Yes," said I. "I think they've all pretty well got their tails down now. I gathered from Church, that Johes, the great agitator, is about the most agitated person on the ship, and keeps as far as he can from his old pals Müller, Villa, and Peddersen; that Villa is positively wilting under the strain; that Paulo spends the hours of darkness in prayer; that Brown goes about more grey than black; that Axenstern has certainly got something on his mind, or rather on the place where his mind ought to be; and that Müller hasn't a growl left in him, not even for Johes. He just looks at him and licks his lips."

"Well—there will be no plotting this side of Falmouth, I should say," concluded Celia, and went to her room.

"Sah," said Doc, who had been busying himself clearing the table during this conversation, "dat man Villa go for die. Him bery

397

bad, Sah. Larry tell me him eat no food, and suddenly get bery weak. No sleep, no eat, only groan and ask Larry not to leave him."

"Why, what d'you mean?" I asked. "I thought his wound had healed up completely."

"Oh, sure t'ing, Sah. Him body all-right; him mind go sick, like man when Voodoo curse put on him."

"Since when?" I asked.

"Since dat first voice come, Sah. Dat woman's voice. It frighten eberybody bery bad, but it nearly kill Villa, right dere."

"Pity it didn't quite kill him," I growled, thinking again of Mr. Hammerson, and realizing that, but for Villa, he would almost certainly have been alive now and commanding the ship. From what Jake had said on his death-bed, and Johes had said in his terror, Villa had been the head and front of the offending, the source and centre of all the trouble since we had left San Francisco, the ring-leader of the mutiny, and the proposer of the ghastly fate intended for Celia and for all those who would not join him.

Two days later Doc reported Villa as undoubtedly being in a dying condition.

Accompanied by Dacre I visited him in his berth in the sail-locker; and, although Villa was what he was, I was shocked at the change in him.

He was wasted almost to a skeleton, was not more than semi-conscious, had a feeble and irregular pulse, scarcely perceptible breathing; and he was a dreadful colour. The expression on his face was fixed—and it was one of *fear*. Stark, craven, panic fear—superstitious fear. He was dying of fear . . . fear of the supernatural. His ancestry was negro-slave and Italian peasant!

Bidding Larry O'Toole remove his handcuffs and to stand by to do anything that could be done for him, I went to consult with Doc as to whether there was anything in the medicine-chest which might be helpful. We could think of nothing except brandy, and it seemed to me that the only thing we could do was to try to keep Villa alive with teaspoonfuls of brandy and beef-tea, when he was able to swallow.

"Sure, Sah, we gib that sick dog anyt'ing we can, to keep him alive and save him."

"That's it, Doc," said I.

"Yes, Sah," replied Doc, "sabe him for de gallows.

"But I'se afraid," he added, "dat nothing sabe him. De ghost come for him and call him, and suddenly he know he got to go. He gib up because he know he can't fight de sperits; an' when a sick man gib up, he die."

Villa died that night.

§2

With the passing of Villa, our troubles passed.

As Doc said, the hoodoo was lifted; a cloud rolled away; ghosts ceased to haunt and supernatural voices to declaim.

In the most perfect weather the *Valkyrie* sailed on; and so little pully-hauly was necessary, so rare was sail-drill, that we scarcely noted our short-handedness.

Almost we became a happy ship, and should have done so completely, could we have exchanged the murderous Müller, the sulky anxious Peddersen, and the miserable broken-spirited Johes, for three decent ordinary seamen.

With Dacre, Carrol, Beauty, Fagin, Doc, Larry, Church, Hamblin, Blancke, Berghen, Axenstern, Paulo and Brown, all seemed to be well, and chanty, joke, and laughter returned spontaneous and free.

And if the rest were sullen and silent, there was no danger to be apprehended from them.

So little had I to do, that it was only with difficulty that I could decently avoid Celia without obviously appearing to do so: and Celia was a young woman who was difficult to evade when she did not intend to be evaded. However developed—or undeveloped—was her sense of shame, she certainly had no false shame.

§3

As though under the special care of Neptune himself, we sailed, with the smoothest of seas and the most favouring of breezes, into the English Channel.

So swiftly was the *Valkyrie* reeling off the knots that, although the long grass could be seen under her counter, in watch after watch, the men had had to be called aft to haul in the log; and there had been days in which we covered over three hundred miles in the twenty-four hours.

At last had come the unmistakable signs that gladden the heart of the homeward-bounder. A change in the colour of the sea, an occasional land-bird in the rigging, glimpses of floating vegetation that was not of the sea. These and other things had come to assure us that there really were boundaries to the waste of waters on which we had sailed for so many long and dreadful days.

I, the Captain, for the first time in my life saw the 'Blue Pigeon' "armed" and passed forward, and heard the cry of

"Watch there—Watch!"

But I knew what I expected to find on the arming, and was not disappointed.

On the day that the cables were shackled on, and the chain-lashings cast adrift from the anchors, Dacre was nervous, miserable, and depressed—though it did not occur to me that he was beginning to wonder whether my confidence in my navigation was well-founded.

Myself, I had no doubt that, barring fog, I should make a good land-fall; and I was more concerned about Celia Bryndal, and about what to do with the criminals, Müller, Slim, and Peddersen, than with the land-fall.

With the certainty of gaol and the prospect of the gallows before them, would they continue to behave properly? Yet to confine men, who would so soon be in prison, seemed cruel; and, after all, what harm could three well-watched and unarmed men do?

I felt that the mainspring-and-half-the-works of conspiracy had left the ship with the bodies of Jake and Villa.

Carrol most strongly advocated putting all three in irons as soon as land was sighted, and again I wondered why officers who have come through the hawse-pipe are always hardest on Fo'c'sle Jack.

Dacre agreed with me that they were unlikely to make trouble, and he also wisely pointed out that, having only Slim's testimony as to Müller's hand in the murder of Mr. Hammerson, we were not entitled to assume his complicity until he'd been found guilty by a properly constituted tribunal.

On the other hand, all three—the question of murder apart— were obviously and admittedly guilty of conspiracy to mutiny; of actual mutiny; of refusal of duty; and of assault upon Officers.

Anyhow, I decided to leave them at liberty a little longer— perhaps the last liberty they would ever enjoy—and, rather strangely, it was Slim who, just before midnight on the one hundred and tenth day after leaving Pisagua, from the fore-yard, sighted the Wolf light, and thereby earned the usual tot.

Hearing the good news from Doc, Celia came up on to the poop and congratulated me on my navigation. She included the eager Dacre in the conversation, and then asked me if I could spare a few minutes, as she had certain exceedingly important matters to discuss with me—not only important but private.

As she stressed the fact that they were not only important but private, I invited her to come forthwith to the Cabin.

"So this is our last night on board, is it, Sinbad?" she said, taking my hand, as I seated myself beside her on the settee.

"Yes," I said, "and my last night as Captain. . . . Where are you going when you leave the ship at Falmouth? Can I—er—be of any service?"

"Lots," she replied. "But I don't know that I am leaving the ship at Falmouth; and I don't know that this is our last night on board."

I stared at her in surprise.

"Not leaving . . . ?"

"No, I think not. It depends. Don't look so alarmed, Little Joseph. . . . No, and don't look sulky, either."

And putting her arms about my neck she kissed me passionately.

"Sinbad," she whispered, "*do* love me. *Do* love me—just a little . . . If you will, this need not be our last night on board by hundreds, or thousands. It need not be your last night as Captain. How would you like to be the youngest Captain that ever had command of a deep-sea ship . . . permanent command, I mean?"

"Well, to tell you the truth, Celia," I replied, "I'm not sure that I ever want to see a ship again. Now that we are in sight of England, I have a sort of feeling that I've lost my nerve; lost my love of the sea, lost my desire ever to command a ship again, at any age. I don't think I want ever to set eyes on the sea again."

"Then what would you like to do ashore? Travel, be a country gentleman and hunt, shoot and fish in due season; go into one of the professions—you're still very young—be a doctor, lawyer, architect, soldier; be a sportsman, a patron of boxing, racing . . . How'd you like to have a string of race-horses?"

"Are you under the impression that I'm a person of means?" I smiled. "Should I be an Apprentice on this ship if . . ."

"No, I'll provide the means—and nothing else on earth would give me a millionth part of the pleasure. Do you know, I'm a very, very rich woman? . . . Oh, Sinbad, I know there's not enough money in the world to *buy* you, in any sense of the word. I'm only telling you that we could get married—if you'd marry me—and, of course, if you wanted to work, I'd be only too pleased. And see how I could help you. If you get over your present feeling about the sea (and I'm sure you will) we could live on the sea. We could live on this ship. You could be its Captain and make money—for both of us. Clean money."

"Mightn't the owners . . . ?"

"Darling, *I* am the owner. I own the *Valkyrie* at this present moment. It's my ship."

Had this girl gone mad?

"I thought Messrs. Dobson, Robson and Wright had a little say in . . ."

"Yes, darling, they had, until Mother bought the ship—just before it sailed, I think. She bought it through her London agent, and Orlando Wight, and Captain Bryndal. . . . It was bought in Captain Bryndal's name, and he was trying to steal his own ship, so to speak. The Agent and Orlando Wight saw to it that Bryndal made a Will leaving it to Mother; and, in the event of her predeceasing him, to me. . . . I suppose he could have sold it, quite easily and legally, at Cape Town. . . . The one tool that ever turned in Mother's hand. . . ."

I stared dumbfounded, gaping like a fish.

"But why didn't she buy it in her own name?" I asked. "Why Bryndal's?"

"Well, naturally Mother never appeared in these matters herself. The last thing in the world she wanted known, was that she owned the ship.

"As I told you before," continued Celia, "he was simply Mother's employee; and only in law, her husband. There was a time, when he first came to Shanghai, when they were 'lovers'; but the more Mother knew of him, the less she liked him; and I don't think she ever ready trusted him, though she had the highest admiration for his courage, power, personality, strength, and skill; and for the way in which he could handle a ship and crew. She'd made a note of that when she first sailed with him from Hong Kong to Sydney."

Celia rose, paced the length of the Cabin, thinking hard; excited, triumphant.

Suddenly she flung herself down beside me.

"Captain," she whispered, "what powers has the Owner on his own ship? Does the Captain have to take orders from him? If so, I'm going to issue some. . . . Captain, what powers has the Owner on *this* ship?"

"None," I replied.

"Suppose I forbade you to put into Falmouth, what would you do?"

"Put into Falmouth," I replied.

"What would you do if I . . . ?"

"In any case, I've only your word for it, Celia. I've no proof that . . ."

"And you don't believe my word? You want proof?"

"In point of fact, I do believe your word; but I've got to have proof that you are the Owner before I can—well, do anything. The last orders the Captain of this ship got, were to proceed to Falmouth, and I'm going to obey them. . . . By the way, who sent them?"

"Mother's Agent—on her cabled instructions to him."

"Well, I'm going to obey them."

"And has the Owner ready no power whatsoever on his or her own ship?"

"Only on business matters, I should say; destination, cargo, trade, and so forth. The Captain is responsible for the safety of the ship and the discipline of the crew, and such matters. Whatever orders he gave, the crew would have to obey—and would obey."

"And the Owner's orders to the Captain?"

"What I told you."

"And they include destination?"

"Certainly . . . if it's a port that can be reached."

"A-h-h-h," breathed Celia. "And if I give you a destination . . . a port that can be reached, will you go to it—Captain?"

Celia's eyes gazed into mine.

"To-night?" she breathed. "To-night?"

I pushed her from my knees and rose to my feet.

"Celia," I said, humbly, miserably, with a weak, wretched and shamefaced smile, "I have no proof that you are Owner."

"Sinbad," she said, "let me give you every proof that you are *my* owner. . . ."

"Hullo, what's that?" I cried suddenly, pretending that I had heard a disturbing sound from above, and fled, seeming, as I did so, to leave behind me a ghostly cloak in her hands, and to hear a ghostly mocking whisper—Joseph!

§4

That night Celia came to my Cabin.

It was impossible for me to be unaware that she was wearing nothing but a thin kimono.

Folding her beautiful arms on the side of my berth, without touching me or kissing me,

"Sinbad," she said, "is it the money you hate, the tainted filthy money that came from white slavery, drug selling, and stolen-gold buying? If it's that, I'll give every penny of it to any charity you like. I will do *anything* you say, with it."

"No, it isn't that, Celia," I said, feeling so touched and ashamed, that I sat up and put my arms about her, and for the first time, kissed her, uninvited. . . .

"Who could hold you responsible for what your Mother did, and for your being brought up in the middle of—all that?"

"Is it because I—I—am not—not . . . fit . . . ? Not been a nice good little girl like . . ."

"No, no, no," I cried, "I just don't love you that way. But I do like you . . . and *please* believe that I really am fond of you and admire you."

I sighed unhappily. This was awful.

"I did save your life, didn't I, Sinbad?"

"That's got nothing to do with it. For that you have my everlasting gratitude and admiration. The respect I feel is for you, for you yourself. Not on account of what you have done for us."

"Sinbad, I want to tell you there are some cases on board. Cases, apparently, of wine; supposed to be Mother's favourite wine, without which she would not travel. The bottles are heavily sealed, and they are thickly crusted and coated with the dirt of ages, and each one is protected with a straw cover."

"Yes?" I said, wondering what she could be driving at, to start talking of wine just then.

"Well," continued Celia, "those bottles contain about ten thousand pounds' worth of cocaine or morphine. Will you take Owner's orders to have the cases thrown overboard?"

"Yes," I said.

"And Sinbad; Sinbad, my heart's darling . . . Oh, I do love you. Can't you love me just a little? Why can't you. . . ? I'll do anything you say . . ."

"Oh Celia . . . Celia, my dear! *Don't* cry . . . don't cry, dear . . .

don't . . . We will always be friends . . ." I begged. . . .

"*Friends!*" she cried. "I wonder you don't say you'll be a *brother* to me!"

And Celia flung out of my cabin.

CHAPTER XXIX

In navigating the *Valkyrie* I certainly had had true 'beginner's luck'; and, in a light morning mist, almost ran down the Falmouth pilot-cutter. To my unspeakable relief, I learned that there were no further orders for us, and that we were to proceed to Falmouth.

"No need to sing out *'What ship?'* Mr. Mate," laughed the Pilot as he mounted to the poop. "You'm nearly saved us the trouble of puttin' out my boat. Is Cap'n below?"

"I'm all the Captain we've got, Pilot," I informed him. "We lost him and both Mates, far South of the Line."

"You'm not got 'Yellow Jack' nor small-pox aboard?" he asked anxiously.

"No, we've no sickness aboard, Pilot. It's police we want, not a doctor. Mutiny and murder have been our troubles."

"Well, well, Go'-bless-me-soul, if that don't go for to beat all I've ever heerd. Mutiny and murder—my dear soul. . . . Give her arl she'll carry, Mr. Mate. This wind be goin' to drop soon, now, the lazy toad. . . . And ye brought the *Valkyrie* home. So young and arl. My dear soul! . . . Why, reporters'll be storming round 'ee like gulls round fish-market, I tell 'ee. Navigate ship and put men in irons, and you not out of your time. Well, well! 'Tis a gold watch from the Underwriters for you, young Sir, for sure."

Actually, I received a most noble sextant, a gold watch and a very handsome sum of money.

Off St. Anthony's we lost our 'soldier's wind' but my luck held, and we fell in with a Watkins tug, bound into the harbour.

Her skipper was a true Cockney, and I had but to shut my eyes to imagine that I was conversing with Church.

Our Pilot proved himself a good friend, and whispered instructions to me that enabled me to strike a very fair bargain for a tow to the anchorage.

A little later, with the Pilot's permission, I bawled 'Let go!'—my last order from the *Valkyrie*'s poop—and to Dacre's answering 'Let go, Sir,' the heavy bower anchor plunged deep into British soil, and an equivalent burden seemed to fall from my shoulders.

My responsibility was ended, and I had brought Celia to dear safe England—in those days so safe and dear to all her sons.

§2

That evening I sat on the poop skylight and, smoking my pipe, looked unseeingly across the fair Cornish harbour.

Consideration of the events of the preceding hours ashore, provided more than enough to occupy my thoughts. Never before had I known such a day.

My depositions made, and the three "Ship-owners" handed over to the authorities, I had been slapped on the back innumerable times; had refused enough drinks to drown me; had been told, again and again, that I was a fair wonder and, to secure a measure of peace, had threatened sundry reporters with personal violence.

My lengthy telegram to Messrs. "Dobson, Robson and Wright" had brought a reply,

"Well done. Coming by next train. Bringing relief Captain," signed with a name that I did not know, and which seemed to have no connection with Dobson, Robson and Wright.

On showing it to Celia, she informed me that it was the name of her mother's confidential Agent, a man who knew all about the English side of her business affairs, had charge of all her investments, and knew everything about her money—except its origins.

So that was that; and it looked as though all that she had told me was true—as indeed I had expected.

And here was I, safe in Falmouth Harbour, and gazing up at the Hotel to which Celia had invited me to go as her guest. . . .

§3

It was strangely pleasant to waken next morning to a motionless ship and a glorious feeling of relief. . . . Freedom . . . Escape . . . Yes, escape.

Doc entered with my coffee. How I should miss his honest, friendly, ugly face.

On the tray was a letter addressed to me.

A love-letter from Celia?

No, something much more curious and interesting.

"Dear Captain Dysart" (I read),

"For a seaman to desert at the end of a voyage and, in addition to forfeiting his pay-day, to send a note of explanation and apology to his Captain (whom he genuinely likes, respects, and admires) is probably unique. But then I am sure that, after reading this, you will agree that the circumstances are probably unique.

In the first place, although I flatter myself that I very successfully concealed the fact, I am not mad. Nor, incidentally, am I a professional seaman.

Fortunately I have always been an extremely keen yachtsman; and when Villa escaped from San Francisco to Pisagua and the *Valkyrie*, and shipped before the mast, I decided that he and I must be shipmates.

Of course, 'Larry O'Toole' is not my name. That I could not use, for Villa knew it before he and his gang kidnapped me for ransom, and then my wife for further ransom (and caused her death from misery, cruelty, and vile treatment).

They were clever little fellows. They got me all-right, and fixed, as ransom, about as big a sum of money as my wife could raise. When she brought it to them, they let me go, and seized her—setting me free to do what she had done . . . raise the biggest possible sum of money to ransom her. It took too long, and, after I had paid it, I found that she had died in their hands.

Well, I did what no doubt you'd have done—devoted my life to getting them.

And I got them—one by one—Villa the last. And no vulgar murders either; no quick deaths by pistol, knife or black jack. Believe me, they died slowly—as Villa did.

In a manner of speaking, I let my wife kill them; for I killed them with her voice, as I did Villa. I was the "ghost" on board the *Valkyrie*, and do not apologize for any trouble that I caused you, because I did far more good than harm.

I rid you of Villa, who was still dangerous; and put the fear of God and the grave and flaming Hell, into the rest of the 'Shipowners'. I also gave some pretty useful help, as early as when Bryndal went mad, Peddersen's head swelled, and Villa and Jake used him as their tool, while pretending to make him their leader.

It was a queer and involved situation, for two sets of scoundrels were arranging two different fates for the ship, and were mutually antagonistic, while some of their members were mutually sympathetic, so to speak.

Bryndal's, Smeeker's, and Peddersen's party wanted to sell the ship and contents. Villa, Jake and Co. were not in this—until the death of Mrs. Bryndal, when they wanted to take charge, scuttle the ship, and land some very valuable part of the cargo in some unknown spot. At the same time there were, as you know,

Hammerson, the Apprentices, and a few of the crew, who were for making the best of life, and getting back to Falmouth.

Unfortunately for them, their programme suited neither the Bryndal-Peddersen party nor the Müller-Villa-Jake gang, who were out to get Hammerson.

Well, I went 'mad' and made all the trouble I could—on the side of the angels—while keeping my own end, aim, and object, well in sight, watching my opportunity to make hay while my private sun shone.

It shone brightest when you granted my request that I, as assistant-steward, might have charge of Villa, and so delivered him into my hand.

Awaiting my opportunity, I used my (you will admit) very considerable ventriloquial power, and from various dark places announced that Moira O'Moore Hartigan had come aboard, and had come in search of Giuseppe Pollegrotto.

My wife was Moira O'Moore Hartigan; and Giuseppe Pollegrotto was Villa, the man who (according to the dying statement of each one of his associates, and other witnesses) had planned her kidnapping, after my ransom had been paid; had carried it out, and had treated her so shamefully that she had died before I could complete payment of the ransom. It was only when this was paid in full that I was informed of her death.

When I think of what she suffered, I am sorry there are no more of them for me to torture—to torture and to kill.

Well, you may imagine Villa's feelings when, suddenly, on a dark night in mid-ocean, the very voice of his victim called him *by his own name*, a name that no-one on board could possibly know; and uttered, in her own voice, *the name of his victim*—again a name that nobody on board could, by any chance, know.

A superstitious brute, negro-Italian, the shock nearly killed him; and, night after night, the voice whispered to him, there in the barred and bolted sail-locker; named his dead accomplices, and told him how each had been called to his death by the Voice . . . told him that his hour had come, and that he would surely, and soon, hear her accusing voice beyond the grave, before the Judgment Seat, where he would also hear his eternal doom.

Having had a *succès fou* as well as a *succès d'estime*, as the disembodied voice of a ghost, I was tempted of the Devil to pay off a strong and righteous personal grudge that I had against Slim Johes (a very mean and slimy scoundrel), at the same time increasing the terror on board to a point which would make the subject of the 'ghost' one of paramount interest.

409

By borrowing poor Hammerson's coat and cap, mingling some sea-weed with the heavy beard (that I have now, I assure you, discarded), I suddenly appeared to the wretched Johes, apparently climbing up from the sea over the rail, in the ghastly green glare of the starboard light. He screamed like a woman and fled like a hare, pursued by what he must have thought was the authentic voice of Hammerson himself.

Well, although by feigning madness I put extra work on to my shipmates, both at the wheel and on brace and halyard, I think that, on the whole, I was infinitely more useful as the weak-witted under-steward. Knowing German very well, I learned about the plots and plans of Jake Müller and Peddersen in particular, and the 'Ship-owners' in general.

It was an anxious time for me—more anxious than for anybody on board.

I knew all that was going on, and was well aware of the fact that, when there are half-a-dozen potential (and very potent) mutineers on a ship, there is not only a danger, but an extreme probability, that the merely weak, foolish and ignorant will be drawn into a mutiny.

This nearly happened in the case of Axenstern, Hamblin, Hooligan, Paulo and Brown; and the loyal and innocent knew they were almost certain to be heavy sufferers, punished by the mutineers if they succeeded, and punished by the authorities, as accomplices, if they failed.

I fully admit that I kept my own private business—my life's work—in the fore-front of my thoughts and plans; but I also did my best for the ship; and it was only after some hard thinking that I decided that, if I were to come and go, fore and aft, use my knowledge of German and raise no suspicion in anyone's mind, I could best do so as a complete but harmless lunatic.

I think my introduction of 'thim birrds' into my vapourings, was a master-stroke; and it was a master-stroke of luck that I was promoted, as I had hoped, to pantry-boy, cook's mate, and second steward.

Not only had I free access to both ends of the ship, but, on any night that I chose, I could sleep in the galley, and so be in a position to slip out on deck without being observed by those in the fo'c'sle.

I used this latter advantage to the full.

By the way, when I was demonstrating for the benefit of the fo'c'sle in general, as well as for Villa in particular, I used a very valuable gadget which really gave me the idea of extending the range of my operations beyond Villa himself (to whom I whispered with the voice of my wife, in the darkness of the sail-locker).

Some time before, I had noticed that, by the foot of a stanchion at the aft end of the fo'c'sle-head, a fraction of an inch of tubing protruded through the covering board. A little later I observed a similar thing at the for'ard end of the poop, and this being in a direct fore-and-aft line with that of the fo'c'sle-head, I concluded that, when she was built, the *Valkyrie* had been fitted with a speaking-tube between poop and fo'c'sle-head.

You can guess the rest, and how eerie must have sounded, to those in the vicinity of the fo'c'sle-head, these communications from the dead.

In the matter of poor Hammerson, I made a terrible blunder. I knew that Jake, Villa and Müller had decided to sandbag him and to involve Slim. And I knew that their devilry was fixed for the next night.

Alas, they changed their plan and fixed it for that night, unknown to me.

I had been going, not only to warn the Second Mate of what was intended for him, but to see with my own eyes that he did not go for'ard alone in the dark.

I did what I could to lock the stable door after the horse was stolen, by talking to you and Dacre Blount about the 'birrds' and the sandbag and the 'long thin shpoike av a thing'.

I'd seen Bryndal fondling that letter-file, but I had only a suspicion that he had stabbed Patsy Hooligan, and I was puzzled by his lack of motive. I made it my business to examine Hooligan's body before he was sewn up for burial, and discovered that he had a tiny puncture in the left side of his back, as though something very thin had been driven right into his chest—from behind.

I wonder if Bryndal had that amazing weapon made to order and for the express purpose of murdering his wife—and others—discreetly?

I was sorely tempted at the time to say more to you than I did, but I judged that I had given you hints enough, and that these, in conjunction with the other hints I gave you, would be sufficient to put you on the alert, and keep you on your guard.

In the light of after events, I think it was as well that I left you partly in ignorance. There are things—even on a perfectly normal voyage and a happy ship—knowledge of which is not good for the Captain's peace of mind, and about which it is far better that he should not know.

Fortunately, when you dealt so faithfully with Peddersen, the bigger scoundrels—Jake, Villa and Co.—gave themselves away. As you had gained some idea of how dangerous they might be, there was no need for me to warn you that Peddersen was really only a figure-head, and far less desperate and dangerous than the men who instigated his attempt to become Captain.

Anyhow, having terrified Villa to death and Slim Johes into confession, I have brought one unspeakable scoundrel to the sort of death he deserved, and, I hope, another to the gallows; for I certainly think that Müller should hang, and Peddersen and Slim Johes have, at the very least, a long long rest, where they won't be troubled by 'thim birrds' at any rate.

Well, Sir, this letter grows too long and I will conclude by saying that when we meet again—as we shall—you won't know me, for I shall have no whiskers, beard or moustache; no brogue, no wild and matted locks, and no signs of ever having been a Shell-back.

Will you very kindly send me an address to which I may write you again later, for I have certain proposals to make to you which you will find, to say the least of it, interesting; and suggestions of an adventure which I think you will find very much after your own heart.

Please write to me at the above address, and you will, my dear Captain, hear more of me anon.

Yours sincerely, and with sincere admiration,
DESMOND O'MOORE HARTIGAN."

As I shaved and dressed, I pondered this remarkable story, and tried to remember all I could of "Larry O'Toole" in the light of this revelation of him.

To him I would certainly write, for any adventure that took me from the *Valkyrie*, from the sea, and from Celia, would be more than welcome.

At breakfast, Dacre and I again talked "about it and about", and discussed the letter in all its bearings.

It kept us from dwelling upon the fact that the end of our adventure was also the end of our present companionship. It seemed impossible to visualize a life in which we were not together, and our home was not the *Valkyrie*.

Going on to the poop after breakfast, I beheld a beautifully dressed gentleman whose distinguished features and autocratic manner were not those of a local reporter; though his refusal to give his name rather indicated that he was in some way connected with the Press, probably one of the big London newspapers.

I was soon undeceived.

"I wish to see the Captain," he announced brusquely, before I could ask his business.

"I am the Captain," I replied shortly.

"My name's Dysart," I added.

My visitor held out his hand.

"Well—er—Captain Dysart," he said with a smile, "you are a most remarkable young man according to Miss Bryndal.

"I'm your Owner's Agent," he continued with a twinkle in his keen eyes. "I'm your Owner's Agent, and I have come to see what kind of a lad has seized her ship."

" 'Seized' is hardly the word, Sir," I grinned, "though I can hardly plead that it was actually presented to me."

"That's what I want to know," he replied. "Can you tell me exactly how you justify being in possession of the *Valkyrie* . . . ? I've already heard the most amazing, astounding and incredible story from the Owner, last night, at the Hotel."

"The Owner?" I asked. "Miss Celia Bryndal?"

"The Owner, Miss Celia Bryndal," he answered.

"Will you come down to the Cabin?"

"Your story sounds very much more like highly coloured fiction than plain unvarnished fact, young man," my visitor said, at last. "However, Miss Celia Bryndal's account exactly confirms what you've told me. . . . I'm not given to exaggeration, but I think I may express what I feel, by saying you—ah—rose well to an awkward emergency."

So I had risen well to an awkward emergency, had I?

Perhaps I *had* risen well, and perhaps the emergency *was* awkward.

And, while somewhat absent-mindedly studying this admirable phrase, with its excellent restraint and lack of anything approaching enthusiastic hyperbole, I found I had accepted his invitation to lunch with him and Celia at the Hotel where she was staying.

Dacre and I parted with few words and a grip of the hand that said all there was to say.

"So long, Sinbad. . . . See you again soon."

413

"So long, Dacre. . . . We'll meet in London. I'll write when I get home."

And with a wave of the hand, Dacre, unsmiling, turned upon his heel, and walked quickly away.

CHAPTER XXX

I cannot write of my parting, that night, from Celia; but I can honestly say that it was the most painful episode connected with the ill-omened *Valkyrie*.

She made me feel—or, at any rate, I felt—a cur, a coward, a fool and an ungrateful brute . . .

But there it was—always that inhibition . . . that quick recoil.

§2

When I reached home my mother was seated by the drawing-room fire.

"Really," she greeted me, "you get more and more enormous every time I see you—positively too gigantic. . . . By the way, when did I last see you? Are you a Captain, or something, yet?"

"Yes, Mother, I'm a Captain—or something," I replied.

"And when are you going a-roving again?"

My step-father, Lord Fordingstane, I found in my father's study, enjoying a cigar and, doubtless, pleasant thoughts and the calm peace that only a clear and quiet conscience can confer.

"Ah, good evening, What's-your-name. Are you staying to dinner?" he said.

"Yes, I'm staying to dinner," I replied.

"Oh? Catching the morning train?"

"No, I'm staying to a good many dinners," I said, "and going to have a good many long quiet jolly chats with you—about Shanghai Charlotte . . . and things."

Lord Fordingstane's red face went almost white, his lips almost blue, and the ash fell from his cigar.

I thought for a moment that I had killed him.

Another disappointment.

When I had made myself as presentable as circumstances permitted, I went to call upon the Dean, our next-door neighbour, and received the kindliest and warmest of welcomes ever extended to a returned prodigal.

When he had made me feel that here was someone genuinely glad to see me, that here was a house that I still might

415

look upon as home, he said,

"I believe Elizabeth is in the garden."

Elizabeth was.

And when we kissed, I suddenly realized why I had been unable to fall in love with Celia Bryndal.

Darling, darling Elizabeth . . .

Passion without love . . . That is a furious consuming fire . . . Of Hell . . .

Love without passion . . . That is Light without warmth . . . Of Heavenly angels . . . perchance.

But, ah, Love *with* passion . . . That is warmth and light as well . . . Of our good kindly Earth—and the best of all God's gifts to Man . . .

Brave *old* world . . . !

SINBAD THE SOLDIER

To

KITTY

AND

The Memory of

ISAAC

MacANDREW

PART I

CHAPTER I

"What is the most absolutely opposite thing to a sailor that you can think of, Sinbad?" asked Dacre, smiling, yet eyeing me with anxious thought.

"A soldier," replied I promptly. "How many times have you and I been told to 'jump overboard and poison the sea with the rotten carcase of a longshore loafing soldier'?"

"Yes," agreed Dacre, "I suppose it's the biggest insult you can offer a sailor, and the best way of telling him how far he is from being one. Right. Let's go and be soldiers."

"And what is it that's most completely different from the sea?" he added.

"The desert," I informed him promptly.

"Right. Then let's go and soldier in the desert," proposed Dacre.

"We've got to learn the soldiering first," I pointed out.

"Which is the best school, d'you suppose?" asked Dacre. . . . "Couldn't we go and have a dozen lessons? Or what about a correspondence course?"

"We'll do the thing properly, my son," I assured him. "We'll go to the best place and take the full course. I believe it's seven years."

"It isn't for me," replied Dacre.

"Well, we needn't stay the course, if we don't like it."

"Jump ship, do you mean?" asked Dacre in some surprise.

"No; as you pay no fee on joining, you pay one on leaving. Called 'buying yourself out', I believe."

"Where shall we go?" grinned Dacre.

"Life Guards," I replied.

"What?"

"Life Guards," I said. "Learn soldiering properly. I imagine that, by the time they've done with you, you know something about riding, shooting, swordsmanship and . . ."

"And a lot of other things," agreed Dacre. "Come on."

§2

There was little wonder that both Dacre and I, at that time, felt that we never wanted to see the sea again. For we had together suffered a sea experience of a kind rare even in the rough island story of British seafaring; we had survived one of the most tragic voyages ever made by a ship of any nation.

Between two ports, the mad Captain had killed his wife and two members of the crew; he and the Chief Officer had killed each other; the crew had murdered the Second Officer; they had mutinied and seized the ship, and had attempted to set her on fire and abandon her, together with such of her personnel as refused to join in mutiny, piracy, theft, arson and murder.

Two, who began the voyage as Apprentices, and one Able-Seaman, brought her home in the roles of Captain and First and Second Officers respectively. In addition to the horrors, anxiety, strain and danger of this incredible nightmare voyage, Dacre, a confirmed misogynist, had for the first and last time in his life, fallen desperately in love; fallen in love, with the violence and passion of your professing woman-hater; and, of course, fallen in love with our girl passenger—who would have nothing to do with him.

No. . . . We never wanted to see a ship again.

What really put the idea of the Life Guards into my head was the fact that my detestable step-father, Lord Fordingstane, had served in that Regiment as an Ensign, in his youth; and that the brother of my admired and beloved friend the Dean of Welling-bury had, as it happened, been in the same Regiment. Thus I had heard a good deal about it, and knew that it was not only a magnificent school of soldiering, but the finest Regiment in the world, and blessed with various privileges. Troopers of the Life Guards could, I knew, wear mufti when out of Barracks, and combine the joys of civilian existence with those of the martial life.

Impulsive, rash, and foolish ever—albeit joyous and care-free—Dacre and I "made it so", pooled our resources, rented a room which was to be our civilian head-quarters and private place apart, and finally left Wellingbury where he had been staying with me.

"Good-bye, my dear Sinclair," said my mother. "Going to be a soldier instead of a sailor? I thought one had to go through Sand-hurst or Woolwich or something. . . . Life Guards? Really! I wonder if Lord Borrodaile still commands the First. He was doing so last time I met him at Ascot. And you'll remember that nice Mr. Tunni-cliffe? . . . And Mr. Blount going with you? How very nice. You'll join the Guards Club, of course. You must ask me to lunch at the

Guards' tent at Lords and Ascot some time. . . ."

Dear Mother—endowed with every graceful attribute and virtue . . . save motherliness and love—I wonder what there was where your heart should have been. A jewel of some other kind, no doubt.

To my step-father, my destination was of no interest whatsoever. Sufficient unto the day was the joy thereof—that I was departing. I wonder which of us had the greater pleasure from that parting. I'd hated him for his cruelty in the days of my childhood, and I now despised him as well—for, judging me by himself, he obviously expected that I should make a blackmailing use of certain facts concerning his past, that had come to my knowledge. He now feared me as much as he disliked me; and, since my return from the sea, fear had tempered his contemptuous rudeness to a false and greasy ingratiation.

Dear Lord Fordingstane—real cause of my father's early death, and of my not going into the Navy, as all my forebears had done.

CHAPTER II

The Recruiting-Sergeant could, I think, scarcely believe his eyes or his ears when two well-dressed, well-spoken young men, both over six feet, accosted him as, jauntily, he strode the pavement of Trafalgar Square outside the National Gallery.

"You want to enlist?" he said. "Both of you?"

And he stared from me to Dacre and from Dacre to me.

"Why, of course," he added quickly. "Couldn't do better. Splendid life. Gentleman's life. And all found. And a horse to ride as well. Cavalry, of course. Come and have a drink and take the shilling. . . . Dragoons is what you want—my old Regiment. . . . Bays. Finest Regiment in the British Cavalry, and that means finest Regiment in the world. Bays. That's the corps for young gentlemen like you. Why, it's a gentlemen's Regiment. Colonel'll shake hands with you."

"Afraid he won't get the chance, poor chap," said Dacre. "Rough luck!"

The beaming smile faded from the Sergeant's face, and it looked less like that of a loving uncle and more like that of a— Sergeant.

"Having a bit of a game, are you? Being funny, like?"

"No," said I, "we want to enlist all-right, Sergeant, but we're for the Life Guards."

"I wouldn't," he said, "Reely I wouldn't. Get a much better time in the Queen's Bays. Foreign service and all. You don't want to go and join the . . ."

"No, of course we don't," agreed Dacre. "We want to join the Life Guards."

"Life Guards or—nothing," said I; and, seeing that we were in earnest and quite firm on the point, the man gave way.

Doubtless he would have gained more credit and emolument if he could have taken two such likely-looking recruits as Dacre and I to his own excellent Corps.

"Well, come and have a drink, anyhow," he said. "Follow me, if you don't care to be seen walking with me," and turned to lead the way.

"My dear chap, we'll walk one on each side of you, and each take an arm, if you like," smiled Dacre.

And one on either side of the Sergeant, we marched off to the

424

bar he honoured.

Here, over a pint of beer for the Sergeant, a whisky and soda for me, and (brave man!) a lemonade for Dacre, we learned what we could from the Sergeant.

"Now then," he said in a business-like tone, his beer finished, "how old are you?" and added,

"You're somewhere between eighteen and twenty-four. Got to be. Let's make it twenty-one. Where d'you come from?"

"Pisagua," replied Dacre gravely, "with orders for Falmouth."

"Never 'eard of the other 'ole," observed the Sergeant. "You're both from Falmouth then. That's Dosset way, isn't it?"

"Used to be Cornwall," said Dacre.

"Dessay it still is, then," agreed the Sergeant. "Right, then, you are two Cornish lads from Falmouth, aged twenty-one—and don't forget it. Now give me your names, addresses and occupation.

"Very good. . . . Now that's the shilling—for you. . . . And that's another—for you. . . . And here's a doccyment which you got to read. Some reads the doccyment, some doesn't. Some pushes the shilling back to the Recruiting Officer. Some calls for drinks, and some dirty dogs puts it in their pockets. Pick it up, each of you, anyway. Right. Now you've took the Queen's Shilling,"—and here he obviously began to quote—"and take notice as a noo recruit that if you don't present hisself at the Barracks herein named at the time I say he is liable to be prosecuted as a rogue and a vagabond and dealt with by law as such and God-have-mercy-on-your-souls and . . . thank you, gentlemen. . . . I can see you are gentlemen both, and will make fine soldiers."

For, moved by a mutual impulse, Dacre and I had slipped our respective shillings into waistcoat-pockets, to be kept as souvenirs of an interesting occasion, and returned to the Recruiting Sergeant a larger coin.

"Do well, you will," he added. "Get c'missions in no time, bein' educated, handsome and well-set-up.

"Now, another spot of beer and a word of good advice, eh? I'll tell you. I'll tell you just what to say . . . *Nothing* . . . That's what to say in the Army. To all sooperiors, don't say nothing."

"A still tongue runs in a wise head, eh?" observed Dacre.

"No, my lad, it don't run at all," replied the Sergeant. "It don't gallop, canter, trot, nor even walk, see? Don't say nothing. Never back-answer nobody, and you'll get on. Keep clean, keep sober—reasonable sober, that is—and think of your 'orse before you think of yourself. Keep in well with your Corporal and better with your Sergeant; and always address the Troop Sergeant-Major as 'Major' and The Regimental as 'Sir' . . . I suppose you can ride?"

"No," we both replied.

"Good!" commented the accommodating Sergeant. "Nothink to unlearn. They'll soon teach you. . . . You'll enjoy it."

And with brazen eye he looked us both in the face.

We should enjoy it!

"Now look," he suddenly barked severely. "Cut the cackle . . ." as though we had done the cackling. "If you are still fools enough to want to join the Life Guards instead of going to my Regiment, where I could have done something for you, you meet me outside the gate of the Chelsea Barracks at ten o'clock to-morrow morning. You know where they are, don't you? . . . Right. . . . Well, see you're there. Don't forget you're recruits now, and though you can still choose your Regiment, you haven't got no choice about joining the Army. You've joined it. You've took the shilling. Ten o'clock to-morrow morning then, outside Chelsea Barracks, or else your names and addresses will be in the Police News."

§2

Next morning, at ten o'clock, Dacre and I found the Sergeant awaiting us outside the gate of Chelsea Barracks.

"Ah," said he, on catching sight of us, "still for this lot, are you? Come on then."

And led the way to a big bare room furnished with a scrubbed table and a number of iron-legged benches arranged round the wall, benches tenanted by a motley assembly of other candidates for membership of Her Majesty's Army. Some of these looked like out-of-work labourers; one or two like clerks and shopmen; two or three nondescripts who might have come from the nearest Rowton House, men who probably had seen better days if worser nights; one man, wearing a frock-coat and striped trousers, high collar, smart cravat and silk hat, who was obviously unhappy, nervous and aloof. Studying his face, I put him down as what he proved to be, a shop-walker.

An orderly entered and spoke to another Sergeant who was in charge of the room.

"Undress all," barked the latter; and having done so, each recruit was carefully and thoroughly examined by a Royal Army Medical Corps doctor.

Apparently this gentleman thought well of my physique.

"H'm," said he. "What trade?"

"Sailor, Sir," said I.

"Soldier, sailor, tinker, tailor, eh?" he smiled, and calling one or two notes and directions to his clerk, told me that I would "do".

Dacre also "did", and apparently intrigued the doctor considerably by announcing that he also was, by trade, a sailor.

"You and your friend left the ship—together—in a hurry, eh?" he observed.

"Yes, Sir," agreed Dacre. "We saw a large rat."

"Or smelt one!" laughed the doctor, and wished us good luck.

Having passed the doctor, we were informed by our friend the Recruiting-Sergeant that we must now "take a canter past the Beak".

We took this canter on foot, discovered that the Beak was a Magistrate, and were duly attested.

"Now for the Life Guards Barracks, since you will have it," announced the Sergeant. "This way for the tin-bellies."

And to the Life Guards Barracks we marched.

Halting at the Quarter Guard and looking round, we beheld a great square parade ground, bounded on the left by the hospital, on the right by stables and sleeping quarters, and on the third side by a kind of mansion with snow-white steps, a big verandah, and windows adorned with brilliant flower-boxes—the whole place surrounded by a high spike-topped wall.

"Here we are," observed Dacre, as the Corporal of the Guard came out and received us from the Recruiting-Sergeant who, with a brief farewell, departed.

The Corporal, a magnificent creature in his immaculate and beautiful uniform, eyed us critically, balefully; and less in sorrow than in anger, as he called upon his Maker to witness that the departing Recruiting-Sergeant had unloaded upon Her Majesty's Life Guards a brace of things unmentionable—though he mentioned us at some length.

"Gentlemen-rankers, so called because invariably they are neither gentlemen nor rankers—not what you'd call such. No good as gentlemen, and no good as rankers," he growled.

"But we're not gentlemen," stated Dacre, forgetful of the Recruiting-Sergeant's first advice.

"Then what're ye dressed up like one for? And who asked you to speak, anyhow?" enquired the Corporal.

Unfortunately Dacre and I were well-dressed, albeit I was in plain grey flannels, and Dacre, as usual, in a perfectly-fitting suit of blue. Our collars were clean, our hats good, our boots unexceptionable and, being in London, we wore gloves and carried walking-sticks.

"Imitation gentlemen, are ye? Well, we'll make ye a damned good imitation of rankers. . . . It's make or break here, my lad. So watch it."

" 'Ere, Maxted," he bawled; and, as a Guardsman hurried from the guard-house in answer,

"March these acrost to The Regimental."

Later, we learned that, in the Life Guards, there are no Sergeants; the non-commissioned ranks being Corporal, Troop Corporal-Major and Regimental Corporal-Major, the last-named dread personage being generally referred to as "The Regimental".

"Toffs, eh?" observed Trooper Maxted, as soon as we were out of hearing of the Corporal of the Guard. "Well, well, we'll soon put that right for you."

"Thank you," said Dacre.

"What is a toff?" I asked Trooper Maxted.

"You are," was the reply. "What was you doing before you come in here?"

"Minding my own business," said I.

"Ho!" replied Trooper Maxted. "Well, now The Regimental's going to mind it for you. You stop there, both of you, till I come back."

We stood and we waited. We waited and we stood.

"Wouldn't do to sit down, I suppose?" asked Dacre.

"No," I decided. "Create a bad impression. Shan't we look a pair of knuts when we're dressed up like the gentleman on guard."

"I wonder how you scratch yourself," mused Dacre, "when you've got that helmet and cuirass on."

"You don't. You just wriggle."

"I expect there are fleas here."

"Yes. Only the best though."

"Ah, but big ones. They'd have a height and chest measurement of . . ."

"Look out, here's the Commander-in-Chief or somebody."

The Regimental Corporal-Major was indeed a fine specimen of a man, in scarlet and gold. Handsome, immaculate, beautifully set up, and, although no longer young, a perfect figure.

As he halted in front of us, we, with one accord and a flourish, raised our hats and bowed, while Trooper Maxted, who had been following close behind the Corporal-Major, took a step to his right, a step to his front, left-turned by numbers and observed, somewhat unnecessarily I thought,

"These is them, Sir."

The Regimental looked us over.

"H'm," said he.

And it was enough. Not the right type at all. Probably better educated than he was himself. He'd learn us.

Having made searching enquiry as to our respective records—names, addresses, trades, careers, education, crimes, and reasons for wishing to join Her Majesty's Life Guards, he gave us to understand that, provided we showed ourselves extremely industrious, prompt, smart, intelligent, obedient, respectful and perfectly amenable to discipline, we *might* become good soldiers. He hoped we would, for our own sakes.

He then bade us follow him; and follow him we did—to the presence of a very tall square-shouldered flat-fronted slim officer, wearing a pill-box cap perched over one eye, a long dark-blue heavily-braided frock-coat and very tightly-fitting trousers strapped over spurred Wellington boots.

To my amazement, this gentleman, *beau idéal* of a Guards Officer, opened his mouth and spoke—with a strong Cockney accent. We learned later that he was the Adjutant, and that it is usual in the Life Guards for a suitable and senior Regimental Corporal-Major to be promoted to this rank.

"Aow, yes, Blount and Dysart," he said, consulting a document. "Which of you is which? Where did you come from? What trade?"

"Sailors."

"Aow . . . sailors? Well, you don't look like it. Haven't done a bunk from the Navy, have you? Don't call yourselves gentlemen, do you? Got no use for 'em here. Never known one of 'em do any good at all."

"No, Sir," I replied, as he was looking at me; "we're not gentlemen and we've not been in the Navy. We are genuine sailors and accustomed to hard work."

"Huh! That's lucky for you. Sure you weren't 'orse-marines? . . . Can you ride?"

"No, Sir," we both replied.

"Well, we'll teach you that much, anyhow. 'B' Troop, I think, Corporal-Major. Dismiss. . . ."

Trooper Maxted, who had been standing like a statue, now suddenly came to life, executed a quiveringly violent salute, left-turned by numbers and, marching from the Presence, led us in the direction of the stables.

§3

Our new home was, in fact, over the stables. Nice and near to the horses, and to the smell of the horses.

I have heard that those who live within the sound of the roar of Niagara never hear that roar, and I discovered that, somewhat similarly, those who dwell in a constant odour, do, after a time, cease to notice that odour.

Perhaps this applies also to the odour of sanctity?

Clattering heavily up a narrow wooden stair, Maxted led us to the barrack-room of "B" Troop. This was big, long, and low; its ceiling and walls whitewashed; its floor, what might have been expected of one crowded and continually trodden by the heavy boots of men who had come straight from the stable. Frankly, it was filthy, but it was the only part of the room that was not specklessly and beautifully clean.

Down the middle of the room was a long well-scrubbed table surrounded by wooden benches, while, around the walls, and close together, was a large number of iron cots, each supporting a rolled straw-stuffed mattress and neatly-folded brown blankets.

At the head of each cot was a shelf on which was arranged a brass helmet, a cuirass, big heavy riding-boots and other articles of uniform. At the foot of each bed, and fastened to it, was a locked box.

With the exception of these articles of furniture, the room contained nothing whatsoever but a number of men, a stove, and a coal-box.

The men, in all stages of dress and undress, sat about the room on benches and beds; some cleaning kit and accoutrements; one or two reading; others doing just nothing, but staring idly in front of them. Weary Titans and warriors at rest.

"Recruits, Corporal," shouted Trooper Maxted, leading us to a huge man, the typical heavy-cavalry soldier of the day, with huge moustache, well-oiled "quiff", and hard weather-beaten face. Corporal Higgett, our immediate superior.

This man's forehead was somewhat low, eyes small, ears protruding, nose thick, and general appearance that of a rough tough fighting-man of rather low intelligence. In spite of his great height, he was very finely proportioned, with great broad shoulders; columnar neck; and strong, straight, muscular legs, of which the knees neither inclined together as do those of some giants, nor dwelt asunder as do those of some cavalry-men who have ridden from early youth.

At first sight I did not like Corporal Higgett, and at second sight I disliked him. He looked at Dacre and me from head to foot and then from foot to head, weighed us and found us wanting—obviously wanting in those qualities that Corporal Higgett liked to see in the recruits committed to his care and charge.

Again he examined us both, slowly, from head to foot; slowly, from foot to head.

"Benk clurks or hartists?" he enquired.

"Neither," replied I, but,

"Both," answered Dacre in the same instant.

"Well, whatever you was, we'll make men of you 'ere," promised Corporal Higgett.

"Thank you," answered Dacre, while I held my peace.

" 'Ere, you Blissful," he suddenly called, turning to a man who lolled at full length upon his bed. "Come 'ere, Trooper Bloomin' Blissful. Take these two acrost to the Canteen and let 'em feed their silly faces, and don't *you* get a bellyful, Mr. Bloomin' Blissful."

Trooper Blissful hastily pulled on his scarlet jacket, spat upon his hands, smoothed his hair, assumed his cap, and with a muttered,

"Follow me, 'Orace and Jasper," again led us down the narrow stairs out into the fresh air—and Heavens, how fresh!

Having crossed the parade ground we entered the Canteen.

"What'll you have?" I asked Trooper Blissful.

"Beer," was the reply. "And after that—you and D.V. willin'—I'll have some beer. And after that, perhaps, for a change, some more beer. Are you and Jasper sporting characters?"

"We're bookies," I assured Trooper Blissful. "Don't we look like it?"

"Well, 'ave a bet with me, and I'll lay the odds for a change. Your change. And I'll back my stomach against your pocket. Both of your pockets. And if I win, you pays for what I drinks; and if I lose, I drinks what you pays for. Got it?"

"No," replied Dacre. "You get a pint of beer. What do we get to eat?"

" 'Am," replied Trooper Blissful, "and bread. Or you can have bread and 'am, if you're perticler. . . . Ar, and butter too. You'll think you was at 'ome again. And you can put the butter on top of the 'am and the bread underneath it. This is Her Majesty's Life

Guards. We wallers."

"Will you have some?" I asked, as we sat down on a form at a clothless table.

"No, mate. 'Ard luck. I bin and filled up to the brim with cold potaters, bread, a mutton-bone and a floating-battery. Eat I can't. Drink I can, 'Eaven helpin'."

"What is a floating-battery?" I asked.

"Lumps of bread floating about in cawfy. Army cawfy, y' know, made in the same tank with tea-leaves, bones and cawfy-grounds. Breakfus-time you turns on the tap and 'olds a cawfy-mug, says '*Cawfy*'—and it's cawfy; dinner-time you turns on the same tap, same way round, 'olds out a pannikin, says 'Soup'—and it's soup; tea-time you 'olds out the same mug, says 'Tea'—and be'old it's tea. If you wants a 'earty breakfus, you breaks up your bread into the tea—and that's slingers. This is Her Majesty's Life Guards. We wallers."

"I suppose one can buy extras from the Canteen, and have them for meals?" I asked a little anxiously, for my appetite is very good, my frame large.

"Money'll buy anything," replied Trooper Blissful; "and any time you wants to share a tin o' sardines, a sossidge, a pot of jam, or a thumb-top of bloater-paste, with me—you say the word and hand out the money."

We having made quite a good lunch of excellent bread and butter, ham, and slices of cake, and Trooper Blissful having finished his pint of beer, the latter gentleman arose. Then telling us that if we were not killed in riding-school, or sent to prison through the good offices of Corporal Higgett, we should "do", he bade us farewell and turned to depart.

"Here, what do we do now?" I asked as he turned his broad back toward us and swaggered off.

"Do?" he replied, halting and turning about. "Don't do nothing. What's the good of doing anything but nothing, if you ain't told to do something? My orders was to take you to the Canteen and feed your silly faces, and myself not have a bellyful. All which I've done, 'aven't I?"

And Trooper Blissful departed.

"Wonder if that's his real name?" mused Dacre.

"I should think so. A man like that would hardly invent such a name."

"Well, there's one person here who's always blissful," yawned Dacre. "Wonder what we'd better do."

"Go back to the pit whence we were digged, I should think,"

said I.

And having paid for our meal, and returned our chipped crockery, brown-handled knives and forks and thick mugs, to the Canteen-orderly at the bar, we made our way back to Troop B barrack-room.

Here, Corporal Higgett having gone out, several of our future comrades gathered round, plied us with questions, and more than hinted that it was customary for all rookies (recruits) who wished to live long and die happy, or not die at all, to pay their footing.

Promptly we signified our willingness to pay our footing.

The day being Thursday, and in the Army something more of a holiday than is Sunday, with its compulsory Church Parade, it appeared that almost all the occupants of the room were free to accompany us to the Canteen, and earnestly to drink to our good health if not to their own.

I was greatly interested in studying these men and comparing them with a gathering of sailors. I got the impression that, on the whole, Foc'sle Jack was a jollier, happier, more care-free individual, more amusing and more humorous, than Thomas Atkins. It seemed to me that the hand of discipline lay heavier upon the latter, and that, even in his hours of ease, he was, while sober at any rate, somewhat stiff and constrained, of narrower interest and outlook, more repressed, inarticulate and—shall I say—standardized.

And although, so far as I knew him, Foc'sle Jack was an inveterate grouser and grumbler, the soldier seemed to me to have a more genuine and abiding sense of resentment.

Cheerful men of sunny nature there were among them, but the average level of contentment seemed low.

I decided, however, to reserve judgment and to abstain from the folly of premature generalization.

However, when closing time came, all was merriment, noisy harmony, and somewhat rowdy jollification; and, as we once again clattered up the wooden stair to our malodorous room, we had made a number of fair-weather friends and acquaintances who, through the rosy or amber mists of alcoholic illusion, viewed us as good fellows and worthy assets to Troop "B".

Beds having been assigned to us by Corporal Higgett, we hastily and partially undressed, got into them in our underclothes and, speaking for myself, bitterly thought of the morrow.

Lights out!

I must confess that in entertainment of our new-fledged

comrades, I had gathered that, of all hard schools, riding-school was one of the hardest; and that among the hardest, that of Her Majesty's Life Guards was second to none, if not easily first.

Trooper Blissful, who, on the strength of having introduced us to the Canteen, had constituted himself our more especial friend of the later debauch, had told us somewhat alarming tales of tall men who, impelled by vaulting ambition, had transferred from Hussar, Lancer and Dragoon Regiments, yea, from Royal Horse Artillery Troops, to the Life Guards—only to find that they could not ride! Though each the pride, the bright particular star-turn of Hussar, Lancer or Dragoon Regiment, of Royal Horse Artillery Troop, he had found that, on joining Her Majesty's Life Guards, the Riding-master had honestly supposed him to have been transferred from a foot regiment. On his stating that he knew how to ride, the Riding-master had been constrained to tell him that Bank Holiday donkey-rides on Hampstead Heath or Margate beach did not count.

Having made fullest allowance for the obvious fact that Trooper Blissful was a cheerful liar, and having discounted nine-tenths of what he told me, I still found the residue discomfort-able. I suffered, that night, a return of something of the self-distrust that used to assail me on board the *Valkyrie* in the early days of my apprenticeship to the sea.

Although I had been bred and born in a hunting county and had listened to the jargon of hunting people from childhood, I had never been on a horse in my life; and I had heard enough to gather that riding is not only an art and a science, but a gift.

Had I been born with that gift? A seat may be acquired, but had I been born with 'hands'? Good useful fists undoubtedly, but what would they prove—in connection with a horse's mouth?

And Dacre. How would he get on?

Suddenly he spoke, and his words were most à *propos*.

"Sinbad! You awake? I say, won't it seem extraordinary to have the tiller-ropes in front of you and the rudder ahead? I suppose Port and Starboard are the same for a horse as for a boat?"

Two minds with but a single thought again.

"They'll teach us, old chap," I assured him. "That's what they are here for, and we'll see they do their duty."

"Yes, and I expect they'll see that we do ours—and a bit more," replied Dacre.

Soon after, I fell asleep, to be awakened from time to time as a drunken man staggered into the room, fell over things, and received the blessings, and occasionally the boots, of angry disturbed comrades.

CHAPTER III

I was awakened by the raucous voice of Corporal Higgett bawling,

"Out of it, there, you. Show a leg."

Half awake and woolly-witted, I sat up and yawned.

"What's the time?" I asked vaguely.

"Time you was up and dressed," replied the Corporal. "Get a move on. You're for the doctor, and you can't see him till you've had a barf."

"You too," he added to the semi-somnolent Dacre.

"Doctor?" he yawned. "I'm not ill."

"You soon will be, if you don't hop out of that quick," was the reply.

"Where does one wash?" asked Dacre.

"Which one?" growled Corporal Higgett. "You? Didn't I tell you, you got to have a barf before you see the doctor? 'Urry up now. 'Ere, you Blissful, show these two how to roll the beddin' and fold the clo'es."

As we struggled into our mufti, Trooper Blissful swiftly and deftly rolled up and strapped our straw palliasses, and folded the blankets on top of them.

"There y'are, mate," said he. "Better undo it again and do it yourself. Then you'll know how. 'Urry up."

Alarums and excursions without. The clarion call of the trumpet, and everybody scattered from the room, leaving Dacre and me alone.

"Let's do these beds again," said he. "I don't think the Second Mate likes us very much, so we won't give him a chance to show it, eh?"

Very little practice enabled us to arrange our beds and bedding as tidily as those of the other men.

Before long, the Guardsmen trooped back again, and evidently the next item on the programme was breakfast. As the men seated themselves on the forms about the long tables, an orderly entered, bearing in both hands a big pail of some steaming liquid, and I wondered what Cabalistic key-word he had pronounced as he turned on the tap, to fill it from the tank which Trooper Blissful had described to us.

Following him, another orderly bore, like Pharaoh's butler, a tray piled high with cakes—of bread. Yet a third swiftly dealt out basins along the tables.

When our turn came, I decided that the pail-bearing orderly had pronounced the word "Coffee", for I detected that flavour among others.

Not having a spoon, I refrained from launching a floating-battery, and alternately gnawed my bread and sipped the hot and steaming beverage—whatever it might be. Privately I decided to augment my breakfast in future, and gazed in some envy upon those troopers who had added to the regulation breakfast of coffee and bread, such adjuncts as chunks of cheese, slices of ham, paper-clad lumps of butter, small tins of bloater-paste and minute pork-pies.

I observed that the comely, if somewhat gross-looking, young man who sat opposite to me, devoured, with obvious enjoyment, two uncooked sausages.

Such little conversation as there was, consisted almost entirely of "shop", with occasional comments upon the conduct of non-commissioned officers and the misconduct of troopers. I was definitely surprised and alarmed to hear of the doings of a certain Major, until I remembered that in the Life Guards a Corporal-Major is generally alluded to as "Major".

I gathered that the Major was idle; far too active; perfectly conscienceless; much too conscientious in enforcing the letter of the law; apt to delegate his duties to others (deputing a substitute to pay the men on pay-days and choosing a man who might well make personal profit from the business); far too fond of taking other people's duties upon his shoulders instead of leaving them to do their job in peace; far too haughty and autocratic; much too servile and subservient—even to the most junior officer; very prone to use his ranker's knowledge for the confusion of private soldiers; much given to pretending he had never been a real ranker of the ranker class at all; and, on the whole, a mucking old swine who was really a damned good sort.

A little bewildering.

"Naow then," suddenly bawled Corporal Higgett. "Tibles."

And the room orderlies, swiftly clearing the tables of their impedimenta, bore them forth into the open air and set to work to scrub them clean.

Corporal Higgett then turned upon Dacre and me where we stood uncomfortably conspicuous in our mufti, with nothing to do, and promptly remedied that particular trouble.

" 'Ere, you," he said. "Ever done a job of work?"

"Oh, one or two I couldn't dodge," replied Dacre; and I half smiled at memories of coal-shovelling, hold-sweeping, cargo-shifting, ballast-carrying, ballast-loading, deck-scrubbing, rope-hauling, sail-furling and other forms of sometimes filthy, and always heavy, manual labour which had been our daily portion on board the *Valkyrie*.

"Ho! 'Ave you? Well, 'ere's one you won't dodge, as'll do your lily-white 'ands some good, too. You'll black-lead that there stove for a start, and don't let me 'ave to find no fault with it.

"And you," he said turning to me, " 'ave you ever done a job of work in your life—honest work, I mean?"

"No," I replied, with a mental glimpse of a slag-laden barge in Pisagua Harbour and the incredibly arduous labour of shovelling the stuff, heavier than lead, into baskets—work that, in so confined a space and such great heat, caused strong and hardy seamen frequently to beg for mercy and a "spell".

Corporal Higgett turned from me.

"Atkins," he called to a man who, as he sat on his bed, was polishing a cuirass, "drop that, and fetch these blasted ornaments a pail and a scrubbing-brush to . . ."

But Dacre evidently intended to begin as he meant to go on—to be put upon by no insulting and offensive jack-in-office.

"Nothing of the sort," he observed coolly and quietly, hands in pockets, and rocking himself gently on his heels.

"Absolutely not," I agreed with him aloud, while mentally I disagreed entirely. I thought it would have been far wiser to have done exactly what Corporal Higgett ordered, whether he were within his rights or not.

Corporal Higgett's face flushed and his fist clenched.

Thrusting forward his lower jaw and narrowing his eyes he stepped close up to Dacre who returned cool stare for hot glare.

"Ho! Looking for trouble already, are you? You've come to the right place for that, my lad; my Gawd you 'ave. . . . Lucky you're only an ignorant fool of a recruit. . . . What d'you mean, '*Nothing of the sort*'?"

"What I say," replied Dacre. "I haven't passed the doctor. . . . I'm not a member of this Troop yet."

A silence had fallen on the room, and men paused in the brushing of uniforms and the polishing of accoutrements, to watch and listen.

Corporal Higgett was taken aback, nonplussed and enraged.

Obviously he was not accustomed to this sort of thing.

Failing to stare Dacre out, he turned to me.

"You refusing duty, too?" he growled menacingly.

"No," I replied. "Never do that. It's my duty to go before the doctor and I'm waiting to do it."

Words failed Corporal Higgett—for a brief space—and when he again found speech it was, I felt, inadequate. Men looked at each other, covertly exchanging grins, as Corporal Higgett bade us wait and see. Only wait and see.

In respectful acquiescent silence we waited, while Corporal Higgett, with considerable noise, bluster and commotion exercised his authority upon those who rightfully and lawfully came under it.

"Dacre, my son," I whispered, "you're a damned silly fool."

"Oh, I don't know," replied Dacre. "I don't like that merchant."

"Nor do I," I replied. "But there's no reason why we should make him dislike us."

"Oh, I don't know," said Dacre again.

"Listen, you came here to be a Life-Guardsman . . ."

"And when I am, I'll blacklead his ceiling, or whitewash his stove, or paper . . . his face . . . if he tells me to. But I'm not going to begin before I need, nor spoil my clothes. Perfectly good suit, nearly new."

"Yes, but supposing we're posted to 'B' Troop and to this room. . . . You've made an enemy of that . . ."

"Well, he's made an enemy of me, hasn't he?"

"Oh, don't be an ass," I said. "He can make our lives a hell upon earth."

"Pooh," jeered Dacre. "Me—that's 'been to sea, man and boy, for forty years', and been half-killed by bucko blue-nose Mates—bothering about a mouldy swab of a soldier, like that!"

"It's he who'll bother about you, my lad. He'll make . . ."

"What you lose sight of," interrupted Dacre, "is the fact that, when I'm a Trooper, I shall be a model Trooper. A perfect soldier—like I used to be the Perfect Sailor. The Happy Warrior, who is he, whom every Life-Guardsman would wish to be! Once we're in uniform, you watch your Uncle Dacre and study to improve. I'm going . . ."

"Follow me, you two," ordered Corporal Higgett suddenly. "The sooner I gets you where I wants you, the better."

"For whom?" asked Dacre.

To which Corporal Higgett replied only with a look of promise, an unpleasant smile, and what was definitely a licking of the lips.

"Naow then," he said suddenly, as we reached a door at the

bottom of the stairs. "Get you in there, strip, and wash yourselves. Properly. Head to foot. And don't let me see no dirt on you when you done . . .

"Or," he added hopefully, glancing from Dacre to me, "would you like to disobey orders—again?"

"We never disobey lawful orders," I replied.

"Of course not," agreed Dacre. "Very anxious to see the doctor. Also to feel what a bath tastes like."

And in cold water, with the aid of mottled soap, we bathed.

Nor, thereafter, was Corporal Higgett able to discover any deep or extensive traces of dirt upon our persons.

"Dress yourselves again," ordered the Corporal.

Following our leader, we crossed the parade ground to the Hospital, where we were bidden to wait outside while the Corporal went to find out whether the doctor was ready to see us.

A minute later he reappeared and took us to an anteroom.

"Undress agin," he ordered. "Doctor'll see you first, Blount."

When my turn came, I found the Regimental Doctor to be a rather small, elderly man with the face of a satyr. I know nothing whatsoever against him—but that his face was precisely that which one sees in paintings and statues of cloven-hoofed satyrs; the same slanting eyebrows, fleshy nose, curious mouth with full under-lip and goat-like eyes—and that his manner was brusque, unfriendly and unpleasant.

His examination was thorough and searching, much more so than that of the doctor who had seen us on enlistment. I concluded that though the latter might pass a recruit as fit for Army service, this doctor might not necessarily pass him as fit for service in Her Majesty's Life Guards. However, it could not have taken him long to discover that, in Dacre and myself, he had two pretty perfect physical specimens, as we were both over six feet in height, and, owing to our seafaring life and its constant labour, of more than usual chest measurement and general muscular development.

"And 'ow did you like the doctor? Pleasant gent, eh?" sneered Corporal Higgett, as once again we dressed ourselves.

Evidently the doctor had a reputation for unpleasantness.

"Or did you refuse his orders to 'op, bend, and waggle your toes?" continued the Corporal. "How did you find him, eh?"

"Looked under the sofa," replied Dacre.

"You did, did you? Ho! Well, I'll tell you something, my lad. And that's this. Some as'll be looking for you, before long, won't be looking for you under no sofa. It'll be on a plank bed, in a little stone room. That's where they'll look for you."

"Hope they'll find me, General," murmured Dacre, tying a boot-lace.

Corporal Higgett smartly tapped his leg with his cutting-whip, and I had no shadow of doubt that he would have given his next pay-day to have tapped the bending Dacre's back with it, and with all his strength.

"They'll find you, all-right. Don't you worry . . . And now go and find the Colonel and give him some of your sauce."

"Charmed," replied Dacre.

"Delighted," said I.

And, after waiting for an hour or so, outside the Orderly-room, we were brought before Colonel Lord Borrodaile, commanding Her Majesty's First Life Guards.

A noble figure of a man; with as fine, truly fine, a face as ever I saw; the eyes clear, piercing and bright, stern and hard, though at the corners were those little wrinkles that come from laughter; a beautifully-chiselled aquiline nose; good high forehead; the big cavalry moustache of the day; jutting chin; close-fitting ears, and grey-flecked curling short hair; the whole head nobly set on a powerful neck, rising from magnificent broad shoulders.

On his right sat the Adjutant whom we had already encountered, and beside him stood The Regimental, otherwise the Regimental Corporal-Major, corresponding in other regiments to Regimental Sergeant-Major.

The Colonel favoured us with a long stare.

"H'm," he observed to the Adjutant, "pair of well set-up lads."

And if I rightly overheard his next remark, added,

"Look like gentlemen," at which the Adjutant shook his head sadly.

"Er—Blount and Dysart," continued the Colonel. "H'm. Where did you enlist?"

"London, Sir," we replied.

"H'm. What were you before you enlisted, Blount?"

"Seaman, Sir," replied Dacre.

"And you, Dysart?"

"Seaman, Sir," I replied.

Again the Colonel stared hard at each of us in turn.

"That's a term that covers a multitude of—er—sins," he said, and his stern eyes twinkled.

"Navy?" he asked.

"No, Sir," we replied, as one man.

"And how long were you at sea, Blount?"

"About eight years, Sir."

"And you, Dysart?"

"About three years, Sir."

"Satisfactory discharges?"

"Er—yes, Sir."

"H'm. What was your father, Blount?"

"A gentleman, Sir."

"Follow any other trade, profession or calling?" asked the Colonel with the hint of a rasp in his voice; as though he had found something possibly impertinent or otherwise unsatisfactory in Dacre's reply.

"Yes, Sir."

"What was it?"

"Soldier, Sir."

"Commissioned rank?"

"Yes, Sir."

"Have you been in the Army before?"

"No, Sir."

"Sandhurst?"

"No, Sir."

"Fail for the Army?"

"No, Sir. My father died and we couldn't afford it."

"Ah. You, Dysart? What was your father?"

"Sailor, Sir."

"Navy?"

"Yes, Sir."

"Commissioned rank?"

"Yes, Sir."

The Colonel's stare increased in intensity, and his eyes narrowed as he studied my face.

"Your name *Brodie* Dysart?"

"Yes, Sir."

"Was your father Sir Sinclair Brodie Dysart?"

"Yes, Sir."

"That so? Met him at the Army and Navy Club. H'm! Why didn't you go into the Navy?"

"Couldn't afford it, Sir."

"H'm . . . Pity . . . And so you went to sea. Mercantile Marine Service."

"Yes, Sir."

"Why did you leave it?"

"I wanted a change, Sir."

"H'm. . . . Why have you come here?"

"It was the biggest change I could think of, Sir."

The Colonel laughed, and his face looked exceedingly agreeable, pleasant and attractive.

"And you, Blount?"

"The same reason, Sir."

"Did you serve at sea together?"

"Yes, Sir."

The Colonel leaned back in his chair and eyed us both thoughtfully.

"Well now, look here, you two," he said at length. "I suppose you are both what would be called gentlemen-rankers. Well, generally speaking, we don't like them here; don't want 'em. As a rule they're bad 'gentlemen' and worse rankers. . . . Exceptions, of course . . . good fellows who've failed for, or at, Sandhurst, and tried to get a commission from the ranks. Is that your object, Blount?"

"No, Sir." replied Dacre promptly.

"What's your idea then—what have you come here for?"

"To learn soldiering, Sir. Like I learned to be a sailor."

"And then?"

"I don't know, Sir. I haven't looked very far ahead . . . Colonies, Mounted Police, perhaps. That sort of thing. Adventure."

"H'm. And you, Dysart."

"The same sort of thing, Sir."

"H'm. Either of you been in trouble? When I say trouble, I mean—serious scrape? . . . Danger of the law?"

"No, Sir."

"Either of you ever been in prison?"

"No, Sir."

"Well, both of you get your hair cut," was the curious conclusion of Colonel Lord Borrodaile's catechism.

The Colonel turned to the Adjutant.

"Mr. Jackson, let me know how these two men get on; and especially whether they get down to work in a satisfactory manner in stables and riding-school. They can stay in Troop 'B' ".

Turning back to us again, the Colonel concluded,

"Very well; since you've come here, I shall expect you to use the advantages that you've enjoyed—good upbringing, education, and so forth—to make yourselves better soldiers than those who've not been so fortunate. You'll succeed here by nothing but close attention to duty, hard work, prompt obedience to superiors, and perfect discipline. I hope to see you gain pro-motion. That'll do. . . . Dismiss."

CHAPTER IV

I cannot honestly say that Corporal Higgett warmly welcomed our return to "B" Troop barrack-room, but I can state with perfect truth that he was glad to see us back. He was very glad, and said so.

It appeared that the thought of our being posted to any other Troop had quite worried him. He would have missed us. Now he would not miss us—not by a jugful.

Personally he superintended the cutting of our hair, and although he did not dare to order us a prison-crop, he bade the regimental barber see to it that we should as closely as possible resemble shorn lambs, though that was not the expression that he used.

It was during this operation that we learned the origin of the curious admonition, "Keep your hair on." It first came into use in barrack-rooms, and was the advice offered by non-commissioned officers to those who walked in peril of the law. In plain English it meant "Mind you don't go to prison," for when a man is given "cells", his hair is cropped as closely as it can be done with any instrument other than a razor.

However, Dacre and I, not yet being convicted military criminals, kept a good deal of our hair on; sufficient, at any rate, for the manufacture of the satisfying and modish quiff.

I gazed at Dacre and he at me.

"The mirror of fashion and the mould of form," quoth my friend. "Let us now visit our tailor."

Having been attended by our *perruquier*, our next step along the primrose path was, in point of fact, to our tailor.

Still personally conducted by Corporal Higgett, we returned to "B" room, and were there bidden each to cop 'old of a blanket. And duly armed with the blanket, we followed him to the Quarter-master's store. Here we received everything necessary for the equipment of the Compleat Warrior.

I thought that my uniform fitted me very well, but Dacre's sartorial standards were higher than mine.

"Is this supposed to—er—fit me . . . here and there?" he enquired of the Corporal.

"Serposed? You close your potater-trap and wait till the

Corporal-Major's seen you. 'E'll have you fitted. Fitted till you can't breathe, if you said a word. Then, when your uniform fits you like a sossidge-skin, the Captain'll have a look at you, and 'e'll say,

" ' 'Oo's this bleedin' Guy Fawkes? What is it—a scarecrow? 'Oo 'ung those clothes on 'im? Trousers like a 'ungry elephant's. Take the perishin' clothes-'orse, and tell the master-tailor that I won't 'ave nobody in a blouse and skirt in my squadron'."

"Then what?" asked Dacre.

"Ar! Then what? Then your uniform'll *fit* by the time the Corporal-Major and the master-tailor's got annoyed at you. Fit? Ho, yes, you'll 'ave a fit all right, my lad. Ar, every time you puts 'em on."

"Good," replied Dacre.

In the event, it was not wholly good, but not too bad. For, when, taken before the Troop Corporal-Major, he observed that, although perhaps his memory was not what it had been, he *thought* he'd seen worse.

And on Dacre's venturing quite respectfully to point out certain deficiencies, the Troop Corporal-Major looked him up and down, fixed him with a bold and bright blue eye, and observed,

"We'll 'ave that put right, my lad. I like to see a young recruit taking an interest in hisself and his appearance. Yerss. We'll 'ave that put right—by plenty of setting-up drill. We'll see your clothes fit you, and your 'at too. Make a man of you in time. Yerss, you'll fit that uniform before you pass out. . . ."

To me, "pass out" seemed to have a slightly sinister significance, but doubtless the Troop Corporal-Major alluded to our being dismissed from recruits' course and riding-school.

"Do you know," observed Dacre to me, as we returned to "B" room, "I think we're going to enjoy life here. We're going to be up against all sorts of things that will prevent life from being dull. I rather liked that citizen, didn't you?"

"The Troop Corporal-Major?" I replied. "No, I can't honestly say I did. He struck me as a first-class example of what the French call the false good man."

"Struck you as *faux bonhomme*, eh?" said Dacre. "Oh, I should say he's a humourist; a bit of a character."

" 'H'm,' as the Colonel says," I replied. "Perverted humour and bad character."

Studying Troop Corporal-Major Threddle's face, I had formed the opinion that he was a type not unknown, if rare, in the Army; a man who had made his way to the subordinate command of a Troop by judicious hardness and softness. A hard master to subordinates, a soft-spoken and obsequious servant to superiors.

His smile struck me as false, his expression as cruel, his voice detestable, his physiognomy unpromising, his personality unpleasing.

Time proved that my estimate was more just than Dacre's. If a fine soldier, strong disciplinarian and invaluable subordinate, Troop Corporal-Major Threddle was, nevertheless, a nasty piece of work.

§2

After a meal of slingers, that evening, a basin of milkless tea in which we soaked our bread (and we'd had many a worse meal when Apprentices aboard the *Valkyrie*), we had our first experience of "mucking-out".

Clad in over-alls and heavy boots, we were marched, with the other occupants of room "B", to the stables, both of us amused by Corporal Higgett's obvious belief that we were now about to encounter real work, and moreover, filthy nauseating work, for the first time in our pampered lives.

"I always thought that horses had their supper and went to bed at about the same time as other people," observed Dacre.

So far as I had thought of the matter at all, I too had supposed that horses "went to bed at night", but I now learned that cavalry horses, or, at any rate, the troop horses of the Life Guards, are bedded-down at tea-time.

"You see cab-horses about at all hours of the night, don't you?" said Dacre.

"I don't," I informed him. "I'm in bed and asleep at all hours of the night. Besides, these aren't cab-horses."

"Silence there, you," bawled the Corporal on stable-duty, to whom Higgett had regretfully delivered us. "Get into that stall and muck it out. No, you don't want no pitch-fork. Use your 'ands. What d'you think they're for!"

Although not the most charming task conceivable, mucking-out a stall was as nothing in our sight; comparatively light, if not pleasant, labour. And we did our work as quickly, and I think as efficiently, as did any of the other troopers.

What I liked less than the task was the horse. He didn't seem to approve of me. He laid his ears back, and showed the white of his eye. Although totally ignorant on the subject of horses, I was certain that these were not signs of grace or gratitude; and, by the way in which he frequently stamped and seemed to say "Tut! tut!", I felt that in some way I had failed to please.

As I stooped beside and beneath him, he seemed enormous; and, for the first time in my life, I pondered the fact that a horse is, or may be, dangerous at both ends.

As, bent double, I laboured for'ard, I wondered when and where he would bite me; and, as I worked aft, I wondered when, where, and how far, he would kick me.

I felt safest amidships, but realized that even there I was still in peril—of being trodden on. I wished I was safe back at sea, outward bound, rounding—or failing to round—Cape Horn, in a six-weeks' storm.

Having finished my work, I stood trying to placate the horse, to ingratiate myself, and to give him a higher opinion of me, by gingerly patting his neck and calling him Dobbin, Cedric, Horace, Bucephalos, and a Cock-eyed Son of a Bald Sea-cook, when, from the next stall I heard voices.

"Who's that fella?" in a high mellifluous euphuistic tone.

"Wot's your name, you?" in a tone that was neither mellifluous nor euphuistic.

"Blount," in Dacre's voice.

"Stand to attention, can't you, and say 'Sir' when you're spoke to by an Orficer, can't you? . . . His name's Blount, Sir."

"Oh—ah—a recruit?"

"Yessir."

"Does he—ah—know anything about horses?"

"D'you know anythink about 'orses?"

"No."

"Put your 'eels together, and cut your 'ands back, can't you? And say 'Sir' when you speak to an Orficer, can't you?"

"I was speaking to you."

Dacre sounded tired; and I longed to be beside him and dig him violently in the ribs, for a silly fool.

"*Wot*? Can't you see there's a Orficer present? Lucky fer you you're a recruit. . . . Nossir. 'E don't know nothink about 'orses."

"Well, tell him he's groomed that one very badly."

"You've groomed that 'orse *very* bad."

"I haven't groomed it at all."

"No; nor it don't 'arf look like it neither. 'Old your 'ead up and look strite to your front."

"You'll have to watch that man, Corporal."

"Yessir."

"Doesn't seem to know anything about—ah—horses. . . ."

"Nossir."

"Seems lazy."

"Yessir."

"This won't do, you know, Corporal. You're responsible, you know."

"Yessir."

"That horse won't do, you know, Corporal."

"Nossir."

"Who's this fella?"

I sprang to attention, stuck myself out for'ard, drew myself in amidships, protruded myself astern, put my feet together, cut my hands back, raised my head, and looked straight to my front.

I was confronted by a tall lean handsome young man, fair-haired, blue-eyed, curly-moustached, who, in his beautiful array, looked quite out of place in a stable.

On his starboard quarter stood the Corporal, a vast man of forbidding aspect.

"Wot's your name, you?" enquired the Corporal in a manner that was an insult, if one chose so to accept it.

"Dysart, Sir," I said, looking over the officer's head into the roseate future.

"Get them feet apart, can't you," rasped the Corporal. "Naow, not your 'eels. Your toes. Keep your 'eels together."

Apparently my heels let no man put asunder, but my fore-feet, that is to say the fore parts of my two feet, must not be joined together.

I grasped the idea at once. Feet at right angles, the one to the other, the heels forming the apex of a triangle the imaginary base of which would be a line drawn from the left big toe to the right big toe, or conversely.

"Oh—ah—another recruit?"

"Yessir."

"Does he know anything about horses?"

"D'you know anythink about 'orses, you?"

"No, Sir."

"Nossir, he don't know anythink about 'orses, too."

"Seems to have groomed that horse—ah—pretty well, nevertheless," said the officer.

As, so far, I had only patted Cedric's neck, I valued this opinion from my superior officer, and did my best to assume a look of conscious virtue, modest but deserving of the praise bestowed.

"The Orficer says you 'aven't groomed that 'orse so bad," announced the Corporal, as though some wide and salt estranging sea, or transparent but impenetrable wall, divided that gentleman from myself, depriving us of the pleasure of hearing each the voice of the other.

"Don't waggle your 'ands about, can't you!"

In point of fact I was not waggling my hands about. I was feeling with my thumb for the seam of my trousers, having some-where heard, or read, that it is important that the same should be in line with the seam of the trousers, while the weight of the head should rest firmly upon the chin-strap, or something.

"Fella seems more promising. . . ."

"Yessir."

"Made a better beginning."

'Yessir."

"But you'll have to watch him."

"Yessir."

"Can he ride?"

"Can you ride an 'orse?" enquired the Corporal.

As I had already denied all knowledge of horses, I thought it would be in order and quite interesting if I now announced myself to be an accomplished horseman.

"Yes, Sir," I said, as a beginning to that end.

"Yessir. 'E can ride," stated the Corporal.

The breakers, the combers, the reeling rolling deck, the lurching swaying spar. . . . Having ridden those for years, perhaps I could ride a mere horse.

At that moment Horace the Horse stamped violently.

" 'Ere, don't 'op about like that," ordered the Corporal, but whether addressing Dysart the Recruit or Horace the Horse, I knew not.

"Get on with your work. . . ."

And officer and Corporal went to the next stall.

In my relief I put my head round into Dacre's stall.

"Peep-bo!" said I, and wheeling about, smacked Horace violently upon the bottom.

Later I learned that that was not the proper name for the stern-sheets of a horse.

CHAPTER V

Dismissed from Stables, brushed and in our right clothes, we sought the Canteen, food, rest, recreation, and the cultivation of the acquaintance of our fellow troopers in their hours of ease.

Seated on a form at a table, eating much and drinking little, we looked and we listened, while the crowd of tall Guardsmen, in their short tight scarlet shell-jackets, close-buttoned, coming to a peak at the waist behind, and to a point in front; long dark-blue overalls with very broad red stripe, half-Wellingtons and swan-neck spurs, came and went, and the tide (of beer) ebbed and flowed.

"On the whole, a bit rough and tough, eh?" observed Dacre quietly as we listened to the jests, conversation, arguments and roars of laughter.

The soldier of those pre-War days was rougher, and more roughly treated, than the soldier of to-day. He was not nearly so well-educated, came from a much lower stratum of society and was not—in times of peace—held in high esteem by the community generally.

Did not a gentle and gentlemanly, indeed noble, poet begin a eulogy of a brave British soldier with the complimentary statement

> "Last night he swore and jested with his fellow
>   roughs,
> A drunken private of the Buffs."?

"Well, what do you fellows think of it all?" said a pleasant cultured voice, abruptly breaking and contradicting my train of thought concerning my 'fellow roughs.' "Feel like your first day at school again?"

"Exactly," agreed Dacre. "Won't you join us? What will you have?"

"Oh, thanks very much. I rather wallow in strong tea after Stables. Nothing like it when you're tired.

"My name's Challoner," he continued. . . . "Yes, very like one's first day at school. It will be, to-morrow—your first day at riding-school. . . . Do you ride?"

We assured our new friend that we did not, and he comforted

451

us with the statement that a good many fellows who rather fancied themselves in the pig-skin; men who had done quite a lot of hunting, steeplechasing and point-to-point racing; found they had a lot to unlearn before they began to learn—in a military Riding-school.

"Well, we have certainly nothing to unlearn," said Dacre.

"Ah, well then, you'll have a fair start—from scratch."

"And get a few, I suppose?" I asked.

"Well, more bruises than scratches, with an occasional broken bone. But you'll be all-right."

In the course of the next hour, Challoner gave us invaluable information and advice, and did his utmost to be helpful in a most kind and friendly manner. I liked him exceedingly, and thought it extremely good of him to go out of his way to waste his time over a couple of recruits when he might have been better and more agreeably employed.

"I say, I hope we are not keeping you?" said Dacre, in a pause in the conversation.

"No," laughed Challoner. "The Colonel is."

"The Colonel?"

"Yes. The Colonel. Seven days C.B."

We laughed.

"What for?"

"Disliking Corporal Higgett as much as you do, and being reported by him as improperly dressed, lazy and slovenly, insolent in manner, and drunk. I happen to be a teetotaller, but perhaps he was right. I get drunk with words, sometimes, when contemplating the face of Corporal Higgett."

"And were you improperly dressed?" we asked, imagining Challoner as appearing in brown shoes and a bowler hat with his cuirass and riding-breeches.

"Oh, yes, I was improperly dressed all right. He spoke to me as I was hooking the collar of my tunic, and I turned round with a hook unfastened."

"And were you lazy and slovenly?" I enquired.

"I must have been, for Corporal Higgett said so, and it was proven by tape-measure that my bedding-roll was not at exact right-angles to the sides of the palliasse. It was a good thirty-secondth of an inch out."

"And were you insolent in manner?"

"Yes. I treated my superior officer as though he were a smell. You know, stood respectfully before him, twitched a nostril and held my breath. Great fun. But don't forget that having fun with your superiors here is quite expensive. Like *roulette* and *petits chevaux*. You can't beat the bank. It's heads they win and tails you lose. The system wins every time. Quite right too, or where would discipline be? Placate and propitiate your Corporal and Corporal-Major and especially the Riding-master, that thy days may be long in the land—and short in the ranks, if you'd win promotion."

As Challoner rattled on and turned from advice to reminiscence, we learned that he had been at a famous Public School and at Sandhurst, his present position and condition being due to a congenital inability to spell correctly.

Being a descendant of a long line of soldiers and the son of a General on the Active List, he was taking this way to a Commission, and was fairly certain of getting it. Evidently one of the cases to which the Colonel had alluded.

We both came to like Challoner exceedingly; a gentleman in every sense of the word; a sportsman; a most cheerful sinner; a man of sterling character, admirable wit, a fine sense of humour; and, incidentally, a tough and dauntless fighter.

§2

Our second night in barracks was very like the first.

Returning to our barrack-room, we set to work with pipe-clay and polishing-cloth, greatly assisted by Challoner whose kindness was unfailing.

I think we—especially Dacre—must have puzzled him considerably by our avidity and capacity for work, and by the contrast between our obvious backgrounds and our equally obvious acquaintance with manual labour; between the facts that we were respectively the sons of an Officer of the 13th Dragoons and of an Admiral, and that we had the hands and physical development of—navvies.

When Corporal Higgett entered the room and observed that Challoner had joined us, he came over and eyed our work in contemptuous silence, remarking as he turned away, that "birds of a fevver flock togevver".

"Yes," laughed Challoner, "and he'll pluck some of them when he gets a chance."

The "Lights out" trumpet put an end to our first lesson in pipe-clay and spit-and-polish; and, in spite of the frequent and noisy entrances of late-pass men, I slept soundly.

Next morning we went to school indeed.

Before breakfast came Stables, a similar experience to that of the previous night, save that we got a thorough lesson in grooming.

After breakfast we paraded with other recruits and some defaulters, and were marched to the riding-school, a vast echoing gloomy building, the floor of which was thickly covered in tan, a sort of chopped bark and fibre that provided not only soft riding and hard falling but an unpleasant and unwholesome dust.

It was with a mixture of pleasant anticipation, anxiety, thrill, high hope and low spirits (indeed, sheer funk) that I eyed first the bare-backed horses and then the bear-faced Riding-master.

This man, Braddall by name (and Gimlet by nickname), was a terror. I suppose it must be a wearisome task, trying to the nerves and wearing to the patience, to spend one's days in teaching clumsy beginners to ride, especially when one believes that the credit and reputation of one's Regiment is in one's hands.

And certainly Riding-master Braddall believed that the great and glorious reputation of Her Majesty's Life Guards was due to him and almost to him alone. The Colonel, Officers and N.C.O.'s might do something in the way of ordinary discipline; the drill-sergeants might do some setting-up work at foot-drill and "arm-swinging"; but the name and fame of a Cavalry Regiment depended upon the horsemanship and horsemastership of its troopers, and these things depended entirely upon the skill and ability of the Riding-master.

And undoubtedly Riding-master Braddall had very great skill and ability as a horseman and a horse-master, and in imparting his science and art to others. Personally, I thought that his success would have been easier, quicker, and possibly even greater, had he adopted other methods. But I may be wrong.

Braddall's slogan was "I'll make you or break you," and his methods of teaching and training were those of the trainer of performing animals. In fact, he regarded riding-school recruits as animals. The horse was one animal—a good one; the recruit was another animal—a bad one; and it was the Riding-master's object to weld the two into one perfect combination . . . a centaur.

But whatever view might be taken of the methods by which the Riding-master obtained his results, one fact was indisputable. By the time he had finished with a recruit, and passed him out from riding-school—that man could ride.

Braddall's way along the hard high road of efficiency and perfection was strewn with a certain amount of wreckage, and, by way of hospital, complete rejection, or transfer to "the Foot," certain congenital non-riders departed and faded from our midst.

3

Suddenly, obeying half-comprehended orders and directions, I found myself standing to port of the big black horse, dressed in nothing but a snaffle-bit and a single rein. I allude to the horse.

From the Rough-riding Corporal who acted as assistant ring-master, or as subordinate fiend to the devil-in-charge, I learned that I was expected to plice both my two 'ands in the middle of the 'orse's back, spring hup'ards until the weight of the body rested on the two 'ands and straightened arms, and symuletan-ously to throw the right leg over the 'orse and assoom a seated position, at the same time taking the rein in both 'ands.

Upon these somewhat long and complicated directions followed an extremely simple and swift manœuvre. I found it the easiest thing in the world to jump on to the back of the horse as directed. What was not so easy was to remain there.

Seated aloft, I watched the other recruits. Some, like Dacre and myself, had just naturally hopped up, like birds on to a twig. Others, self-distrustful, not having jumped hard and high enough, fell back. Others again had, like vaulting ambition, o'erleapt themselves, or the horses, and fallen on the other side, rather heavily.

All being mounted and bidden to sit up—to *sit hup*—with their hands low and feet forward, their heads high and their backs hollowed, "the ride" was ordered to *walk—march*.

Instantly the well-trained troop horses set off at a brisk walk, and half the riders promptly fell off. Doubtless, to Dacre and me, our long experience of swaying yard-arms was now invaluable. Like a limpet I clung to my horse with my knees and thighs, while strictly obeying the Riding-master's instructions to refrain from using the rein as a means of support—what, at sea, we should have called a life-line.

Order having been restored to the ride, and recruits to their horses, the line set off once more at a walk, and solemnly we followed-our-leader round and round the riding-school.

In time, we could all sit steadily on a walking horse, only the more specially gifted occasionally sliding forward on to the horse's withers, canting over to one side or the other, clasping it

455

about the neck, and dismounting without orders. But even these had, by now, learned to cling until their feet were safely on the ground.

To the very last performer of this feat, Riding-master Braddall walked up. Touching the man on the chest with his cutting-whip, he said, in his far more cutting voice,

"Do that once again, you clumsy clod-hopping hound, and by the living God that half-made you, I'll make you. Make you wish you hadn't; see?"

"I couldn't 'elp it, Sir," croaked the sweating, white-faced, dust-stifled recruit.

"No, but I can help you," replied the Riding-master. "Get up on that horse and stay there; and don't sit like a monkey cuddling a bag of nails, or I'll . . ."

The over-anxious fellow fairly vaulted over the horse, falling heavily on his shoulder.

"Ah," observed the Riding-master as we miserably watched the performance. "I'm asked to make a trooper out of *that*, am I?"

The man got to his feet, a big powerful fellow whose white face had suddenly flushed red. His fists were clenched and his eyes blazing.

The Rough-riding Corporal stepped forward.

"A trooper out of that, eh?" continued the Riding-master. "But I'll do it. . . . I'll make you or break you. I'll break your spirit; I'll break your heart; I'll break your neck—or I'll teach you to ride. Get on that horse."

The man opened his lips to speak; then, to my relief, swallowed what he was going to say, turned about and vaulted on to his horse, and round we went again.

It was not until every man in the class could ride a bare-backed horse—at a walk—in perfect attitude and position and to the satisfaction of even Riding-master Braddall, that the ride was promoted to the trot.

Promoted!

After explanation, exhortation, admonition and threat, there came the long-drawn order,

"*Terr-rr-ot!*"

And instantly the horses broke from the walking pace into the trot—sudden, sharp and staccato—and the tan was strewn like a battlefield with the forms of the fallen.

Personally, clinging desperately with my legs, I survived, and, for a painful minute, until Braddall's welcome roar of "*Halt!*"

brought my horse to a sudden disconcerting standstill, was jerked, bumped, jarred, buffeted and banged to a state of breathlessness.

Dacre, I was glad to see, was also among the survivors, doubtless aided, like myself, by yard-arm experience—a training which teaches balance, self-confidence and the useful art of clinging on. . . .

Among the fallen was a man who, in Riding-master Braddall's opinion, should have "known better".

In unmeasured—or perhaps measured—language, he told him so; told him that it was in an evil hour for the Cavalry that he had been kicked out from the Infantry, into whose ranks he should certainly have gone . . . and serve them right!

This curious locution puzzled me until I learned that the unfortunate man had been an Officer in a Line Regiment until, unable to keep pace with his expenses, he had sent in his papers and, being fit for nothing but soldiering, had enlisted in the Life Guards.

For some reason, the Riding-master detested him, probably because he was, in everything but horsemanship, a far better man than himself—better born, better bred and better educated; also, as a soldier, of higher training and wider experience.

I think that out of sheer malice and hatred, Braddall kept him in the riding-school long after he had attained the degree of proficiency required for passing out.

Later we learned that, on Braddall's instructions, the Rough-riding Corporal always saw to it that Maltravers, as the ex-officer was named, was given the most notorious horse in the Regiment —an intractable, incurable rogue; an iron-mouthed, rough-paced brute that, at its best, was sulky, slow, and heavy in hand; and, at its worst, a kicking, buck-jumping man-eater.

Probably because Maltravers was a good horseman, he was at the head of the ride, and his discomfiture was the more public and apparent.

"Who told you to dismount, you wobbling sack of potatoes?" said the Riding-master as Maltravers got to his feet. "What d'you think you're doing?"

"The horse bucked . . . Sir," replied Maltravers.

"Yes! Blame the horse! . . . What your sort generally does. You'll be in this riding-school till it falls down. . . . It'll do that some day, through watching you. Mount, you flat-footed ham-fisted tailor, and get to the end of the ride. Go on; fall in last. I don't want recruits copying you. Sit up, you bloody frog."

Maltravers lightly vaulted back on to his horse, wheeled it out from the line, and, as he rode past the Riding-master, the latter gave the horse a sharp slash on the quarters with his cutting-whip.

Instantly the horse plunged, reared in a way that would have unseated any but the finest horseman, threw down its head, shot its heels high in the air, twisted, jumped, bucked—and then sent Maltravers flying over its head.

For a few seconds Maltravers lay apparently stunned.

"Gone to sleep, have you?" the Riding-master broke the silence.

Maltravers rose to his knees, got slowly to his feet, straightened himself, and turned to the Riding-master.

"You cowardly hound!" he said quietly. "You ruffianly brute! Call yourself a Riding-master? You don't know the beginning of your job."

Like the rest of us, I could not believe my ears. I half-expected the walls to collapse, the roof to fall in, the horse to die.

What would happen? It seemed to me at the moment that the Wrath of God must fall upon Maltravers, if not upon us all, and that even then it would be as nothing to the wrath of the Riding-master.

The Rough-riding Corporal's mouth literally fell open, while the Riding-master's closed very tightly. For once, words failed him.

Maltravers, on the other hand, was inspired. Evidently his cup was full. It ran over.

"A Riding-master? . . ." he said, "Men and horses? . . . I wouldn't trust a pig to you, you swaggering loud-mouthed bully . . . you swanking jack-in-office . . . you horse-spoiling man-breaking ignorant lout. You make me sick."

And actually, literally, Maltravers was then and there violently sick, either by reason of his fall which had been very heavy; his rage, which was terrible; or his sense of utterly hopeless and shameful injustice.

As he stood bent and swaying, Braddall strode towards him, his whip much in evidence.

"I'll deal with you afterwards," he said, and I was surprised that he could speak quietly. "Mount your horse."

"I'll not mount that horse," replied Maltravers, facing up to him. "It's a dangerous buck-jumper, and I'll not get on it again."

"So?" replied the Riding-master, evidently pleased. "You

won't, eh? . . . Well, a rest in cells will do you good."

"Yes," replied Maltravers, "and so will a talk with the Colonel."

"You'll have that all-right."

"So will you, when I've been brought before him," replied Maltravers.

The Riding-master turned to the Rough-riding Corporal, "Take this man to the Guard Room, Corporal," said he.

And, escorted by the Corporal, Maltravers marched off. Before he reached the big double door, his wrath overcame him again. Swinging about,

"Take a challenge, you cowardly dog!" he shouted. "Get on that bare-backed buck-jumper yourself, and let *me* have a cut at it with your whip. . . . Dare you? . . . Not for your life!"

And was hustled off by the Rough-riding Corporal.

Scenes like this were extremely rare in Riding-school, few men having the courage, or the folly, to defy Riding-master Braddall.

When, some days later, Maltravers returned to the Troop, having very definitely failed to keep his hair on, Dacre and I sought his acquaintance and came to like him very much indeed.

Only once again did we hear words of defiance and contumely addressed to the Riding-master, and that was when a man, riding at a jump with stripped saddle, neither stirrups nor reins, was thrown with a heavy crash and instantly bidden to arise and remount.

"I can't," he groaned, in obvious acute pain. "Me leg's broken."

"Broken a leg?" snapped Riding-master Braddall. "Well, you've got another, damn you, haven't you?"

And although this had been but a jest on the part of the Riding-master, a fair specimen of his wit, it had been the last straw, and the man, glaring up at Braddall, had deluged him with a torrent of invective and abuse, dealing with him fully and faithfully, without fear or favour.

This particular man was carried to hospital and we never saw him again, though we heard what may or may not have been true, that he was maimed for life, the fractured leg being permanently shortened.

Yes, it was indeed a hard and rough school, but Dacre and I, who had been to a harder and a rougher, came through it successfully, and indeed with credit.

We were passed out and dismissed riding-school in the minimum time possible.

Similarly with foot-drill and the rather absurd and futile physical training which consisted solely of a number of violent "arm-swinging" exercises. Nor had we to linger unduly in ordinary school, having given early proof of our ability to read, write and cipher with sufficient skill to pass the education examination without having to sit on forms and face a schoolmaster and his blackboard.

CHAPTER VI

On the whole, the life was not too bad. Certainly it was not nearly as hard and rough as life at sea; and the menial tasks of sweeping, scrubbing and black-leading with which Corporal Higgett had expected to daunt, depress, and defeat us, were as nothing in our sight.

I doubt if "B" Troop contained a better pair of sweepers, scrubbers, polishers and black-leaders than Dacre and I.

Some aspects of our existence as Lifeguardsmen we thoroughly enjoyed. Early morning rides, for example. Distinctly I remember our riding in file, at ease, across Wimbledon Common at seven o'clock one May morning when Dacre and I, in the lightness of our hearts and the joy of physical well-being, sang sea-chanties, to the obvious interest and amusement of our comrades.

There were, of course, flies in the ointment, flies that, upon occasion, were more like crocodiles, and from time to time assumed the proportions of elephants.

Corporal Higgett was one of these anointed pests, and another was a disgusting ruffian, one Chatten, whose pastime it was to annoy, offend, insult, and bully Maltravers.

This Chatten had been attached in some capacity to a circus, was powerful and muscular beyond the ordinary, remarkably agile and acrobatic for his great size and weight, was a fair boxer, and a most aggressive, dangerous and determined enemy, violent, brutal, and very competent.

According to some accounts, he had been a tumbler or acrobat in the circus; a weight-lifter; a trapeze-swinger; and one of those powerful creatures who form the base of a living pyramid of posturing entwined humanity, gymnasts who, climbing up, support one another, standing precariously but with apparent safety, upon each other's heads and shoulders.

According to others, he had been the star turn of a Let-'em-all-come boxing troupe that occupied a side-show booth.

Another account of him was that, under a foreign-sounding name, he had given exhibitions of wrestling and been either a Terrible Turk or a Russian Bear; a Grappling Greek or some such portent.

He wasn't by any means a sort of old-fashioned bully of the school, a cock of the walk, or a barrack-room terror; for, in the Life Guards, his shrift would have been short—but he was a truculent nuisance to any individual who offended him, or whom, for some reason, he disliked.

And poor Maltravers he definitely did dislike, if for no other reason than that he was a gentleman and a man of education and intelligence. Perhaps, at some time or other—probably when he was a recruit—Maltravers may have been tactless and have used to Chatten the tone of an officer, the tone that he had been in the habit of using to his men—*de haut en bas*.

Through becoming friends of the unfortunate ex-officer, we automatically became, if not enemies, at any rate objects of dislike to Chatten; and he did as much as one trooper can for another, to injure, trouble and annoy Dacre and myself.

Now, however stout-hearted and undaunted Maltravers and Dacre might be—and the same applied to Chatten's fourth *bête noire*, Challenor—they were physically no match for this brute.

With regard to myself, I was not so sure. I had had the tremendous privilege, advantage, and good fortune to be trained by a man who was Heavyweight Champion of Australia, and who, had he taken to professional pugilism earlier, could undoubtedly have been Champion of the British Empire, if not of the World. And he, while training me with the view to my becoming a professional pugilist, with himself as my manager, had told me that I was "the quickest thing on two legs that he'd ever seen"; that he had met no-one who could punch harder with both hands; who was a greater adept at ducking and dodging; or displayed better foot-work.

Being now six feet and four inches in height, a little over fourteen stone in weight, and in perfect condition, thanks to my sea-training, magnificent health, and lack of a single redeeming vice, I had an idea that I could give a good account of myself if driven to a settling-up with friend Chatten.

Being essentially a man of peace, I was desirous of living in amity, accord and concord with all men; and I hoped that nothing of the sort would be necessary. Nevertheless, I was doomed to disappointment.

Settlement became quite urgently necessary by reason of the fact that, one evening, I just naturally hit Chatten in the eye.

Dacre and I, Challoner and Maltravers, were busy about our daily task of pipe-clay and polish, and Maltravers in particular was preparing for the Queen's Guard. And when a man parades for that purpose, he is the spickest-and-spannest thing alive—speckless and refulgent, from boot-soles to helmet-plume, as a new silk hat in its band-box, or a costly toy taken fresh from its tissue paper.

Maltravers was giving the last touches to his cuirass, already burnished, immaculate, and shining like a mirror, when Chatten came up and asked him for half a crown.

Presumably, in theory at any rate, it was to be a loan, but the tone was more that of a demand than of a request.

" 'Ere you," quoth Chatten, "len' me 'arf a dollar."

"What about the last one?" asked Maltravers quietly, "and the one before that?"

"Gorn where this one's going," replied Chatten, his manner sneering, jeering and contemptuous. "Come on, don't be mingy. I'll pay you back when me rich Uncle Halbert dies."

Maltravers shook his head.

"Shan't lend you any more till you've paid back the rest. Or some of it, anyhow."

"Mean to say you 'aven't got 'alf-a-dollar?"

"I mean to say I won't lend you one, anyhow," replied Maltravers, eyeing the fellow steadily.

"You won't?"

"No."

And Chatten, disappointed, and in a sudden access of liverish bad-temper, probably caused by the previous night's beer debauch, did an unheard-of thing.

Deliberately he spat on the cuirass that Maltravers was polishing.

And immediately, mild, peaceful and harmless creature though I am, I hit Chatten in the eye.

Such was my intense disgust at the filthy action of this beast, and so much petty annoyance, deliberate insult and wanton unfriendliness had I endured from him, that it really was a most tremendous smack. Very satisfying indeed.

The room was in an uproar at once. Everybody dropped what he was doing and crowded round. Sides were instantly taken; Chatten was urged to take a speedy and horrific vengeance that would learn me once and for all; I was loudly applauded; Chatten was called a dirty dog; and on only one point did there seem to be a general consensus of opinion, and that was that we should at once "come outside".

My blow had sent Chatten staggering. The end of a bed catching him at the back of the knees, he had sprawled across it and fallen to the floor.

Springing up, he ripped off his tunic, rolled up his shirt-sleeves—displaying a remarkably muscular pair of arms—and came for me.

His right hand dashed backward and then upward in a feint, and his left shot forward with tremendous force.

I moved my head to the right, countered with a straight left with all my strength, and caught him squarely on the mouth.

I did not follow it up because I had no particular wish to fight him, especially with bare fists. I had begun the fight by hitting him in the eye and doing him no good, and I didn't want to get him and myself into trouble for fighting in the barrack-room. Corporal Higgett might enter at any minute.

But things had gone too far. I had "loosed an act", and must take the consequences. Chatten was going to take me seriously, and deal with the matter properly.

"Come outside," he said.

He was a little shaken, I think; mentally and morally, as well as physically.

"Come outside; and I'll give you what you want."

I had a hope that he too wanted something—to gain time and breath—but realized that it was much more likely that he wanted a bigger space. The room cramped his style.

I was for it, and could take but little satisfaction from the thought that I had brought it on myself.

Behind the troopers' quarters was a small enclosed area, a kind of court-yard bounded by the barrack buildings and high walls; a place to a certain extent sacred to the privacy of off-duty troopers, where they could loaf about, smoke and talk in peace, seated upon the bales of hay and heaps of straw that frequently were to be found there.

This, on the very rare occasions when troopers fought, was the scene of the encounter; and thither, as quietly and unobtrusively as possible, we all proceeded.

§2

It was rather a messy business. Also a little unfair to Chatten.

I think that, so long as we both adorned Troop "B", Chatten regarded me as a cheat, a fraud, a whited sepulchre, and a dirty dawg; for Chatten was not only a tough fighter, but had had considerable mixed experience of "pushin' the raw 'uns", in other words, of bare fist fighting.

Hence he, not unnaturally, expected quick and easy victory over a wretched and worthless toff who spoke the Queen's English, wore well-cut mufti and, upon occasion, draped his superior person in evening-dress. And from Chatten's point of view I was indeed a fraud, a humbug, a delusion and a snare; for, as I have said, I had had the inestimable advantage of intensive professional training as a boxer, by a Champion.

And after three years (on a wind-jammer) of pully-hauly cargo-lifting, holy-stoning, climbing, sail-furling, and general perpetual hard labour alow and aloft, I was, modesty apart, a magnificent physical specimen in magnificent condition. Also on that same death-ship, I too had had experience of bare-knuckle fighting—having fought three separate pitched battles with desperate ruffians. . . .

With a sneering smile, an air of trickiness, and some fairly obvious feints, Chatten let go a thunder-bolt of a left, intended to settle the matter—and me—in short order.

With a sufficient movement of my head to the left, I allowed his fist to graze my right ear, and cross-countered with a right that had behind it all my strength and weight and the spur of my annoyance. This took Chatten squarely on the nose, knocked him flat on his back, shook him badly and began the messiness. His claret was generously tapped.

The man was astonished and he was angry—angry to the point of savage folly, for, forgetting what skill and finesse he had, he rushed blindly to his undoing. Rushed like a bull, and I had but to side-step and drive hard at the point of his jaw. Three separate times this happened; and, after the third, he arose so groggily that I asked him if he hadn't had enough, or at any rate enough for one round.

But Chatten was game, shook his head in refusal, and squared up.

Disliking the business intensely, I made as quick and merciful an end as I could; and, with a crashing straight left to the point of his jaw, again sent him staggering. I followed up like lightning, and, with a right-hook, put him out.

When he came round I helped mop him up, shook hands with him, patted him on the back, assured him that he was a fine fellow, invited him to the Canteen, told him that I loved him and hated fighting, and that any time he wanted another hiding he could have it.

It is frequently stated that, after such passages, the

protagonists are thenceforward the best of friends; and that the defeated man immediately forgives the victor, for evermore admires him, and is his unshakeable friend. This is an admirable and satisfying theory.

In practice it is not always so, and this was a case in point; for, if Chatten had disliked and despised me before the fight, he detested me after it, and lost no opportunity of displaying the fact —the expression of his enmity being limited only by his fear of going too far, provoking another fight, and getting another thrashing.

CHAPTER VII

Another man of a very different type, whom Dacre and I liked as little as we did Chatten, was an exceedingly queer fish calling himself Standesh. He was undoubtedly a man of education, birth, and breeding; and had, quite evidently, at one time lived in somewhat spacious style. I should think he was a scion of—if not a noble house—a county family, and parents of wealth and position. Definitely a black sheep. His manners were admirable, his morals his own affair and no concern whatsoever of ours; and yet none of our little party, Maltravers, Challoner, Dacre and I, had any use for him at all. It was instinctive too, for we had nothing whatsoever against him. Or had nothing until he began to pester us, somewhat persistently, to "come up to the surface and breathe"; "come and imagine we are gentlemen once again"; "come and see a bit of life."

More to get it over and done with, than in any hope of enjoying ourselves, we at length accepted his invitation.

I don't know that I should have mentioned this man, Standesh, as he was neither a particular friend nor particular enemy of ours, save for the fact that I came across him again, years later, in a most unexpected place and remarkable circumstances.

§2

"*Phew!*" whistled Dacre as we came out from the over-heated rooms and stuffy house into the cool night-air. "That'll be about enough of that, I think, don't you?"

"Do me nicely," I agreed. "Enough can be better than a feast, and a little can go a long way too far."

"We've been 'seeing life', my son, and the gilded halls of vice," observed Dacre as we fell into step and marched back to Barracks, silk-lined capes over our left arms, and opera hats pushed back from our heated brows.

It had been a queer experience, the result of our accepting this invitation from Standesh, to "come along with him and have some fun."

Fun is an elastic term. One man's amusement may be another man's boredom, and neither Dacre nor I was of the type that sees much fun in losing money at crooked gambling or watching other people do so.

What had amused and interested us had been observation of the curious and varied collection of men and women who had thronged the house, and of its presiding genius. Particularly were we intrigued by the subject of her exact relationship to Standesh.

And if she belonged to him—or he to her—what was friend Standesh doing in Her Majesty's Life Guards?

Some little time previous to this, Dacre and I had noticed an ever-increasing tendency on the part of Standesh to cultivate us and attach himself more closely to the quartette consisting of Challoner, Maltravers and ourselves. We had noticed that if he could do so, Standesh joined Dacre and myself when we were together, rather than when we were in the company of the others.

To Maltravers and Challoner he made no overtures. On more than one occasion he had repeated his invitation to Dacre and me to come with him to a place he knew, and have a real evening; and on our suggesting that we all five went, had replied that five were about two too many.

When talking about him one day, and commenting upon his preference for ourselves, Dacre had observed, with his frank and cheerful cynicism, that he did not for a moment suppose that Standesh preferred us to Maltravers and Challoner. What he did prefer was our better-lined pockets.

"He thinks we've got money, old son," said Dacre. "Thinks we're Missing Heirs or Wicked Younger Sons with Great Expectations."

"Oh, I don't know," said I in my youthful ignorance and guilelessness. "He's never tried to borrow money or anything of that sort."

"No," said Dacre, "and you see that he doesn't. Standesh is a lad worth watching, for your own sake as well as his."

And on this particular evening, Challoner and Maltravers being elsewhere, either on duty or on leave, Dacre and I having nothing worse to do, had accepted Standesh's oft-repeated invitation "to come with him to a place he knew and have a real evening".

Having changed into mufti evening-dress and met Standesh similarly arrayed, we took a cab to a West End address that Standesh gave the cabman. If I remember rightly it was the name of a street near Lancaster Gate.

The cab stopped in front of a quite large house of excellent quiet appearance, an imposing portico, and flight of stone steps. At the double front-door of this house, Standesh rang a bell, and the door was opened by a man in sober livery, who looked a typical footman.

"Good evening, Sir," said this man to Standesh, and after taking our hats and opera cloaks, enquired,

"What names shall I announce, Sir?"

"Er—Mr. Smith and Mr. Brown," replied Standesh, and the footman, bowing, led the way across a black and white flagged hall to a somewhat nondescript but well-furnished room to the right of the front door.

"Mystery deepens, eh?" laughed Standesh.

"Definitely," drawled Dacre.

"The ancestral home," he added.

Before Standesh could reply, the door opened and a strikingly handsome woman came into the room. She wore an elaborate evening gown, and was, even to my inexperienced eye, both well and expensively turned out.

Handsome is the *mot juste*. She was not beautiful nor was she pretty; but her white face, with its heavy black eyebrows, big bold black eyes, large mouth and pronounced chin, was definitely handsome.

"Good evening, gentlemen," she said, and her voice was pleasant, well-modulated, and free from accent.

Well-dressed, well-spoken, handsome, attractive, but somehow not quite right. Not a gentlewoman.

"My friend, Mr. Brown," said Standesh, indicating me.

And as she turned, glanced quickly in my direction and extended her hand, I saw that she squinted. Perhaps squinted is too strong a term. Let me say that she had a cast in one eye.

"How do you do, Captain Brown," quoth the lady. "So glad to see you. Delighted at any time to welcome a friend of my—er—friend, Mr. Standesh."

I bowed and gently squeezed the shapely be-ringed hand.

"My friend, Mr. Smith," said Standesh, indicating Dacre.

"How do you do?" said Dacre, eyeing the lady straitly.

"How do you do, Captain Smith . . . ?"

"Major Smith," corrected Dacre gravely.

". . . Major Smith. So glad to see you. Delighted at any time to welcome the friend of my—er—friend, Mr. Standesh."

"I'm sure you are," murmured Dacre. "So hospitable.

And I thought that the lady's squint, or cast, increased.

"Well, come along and have a drink," she said. "Come along

upstairs. Perhaps you will stay to supper with us and have a little music; or perhaps take a hand at whist. . . ."

"Or Snap," Dacre bowed gravely.

"Oh, anything you like," laughed our hostess. "Come along, come along. So glad Jimmy brought you in."

And, Standesh opening the door, the lady led the way across the hall and up a flight of broad shallow thickly-carpeted stairs, to a spacious landing above.

"*Whist!*" murmured Dacre to me.

"Hold yours!" I whispered back.

"Whist! Beggar-my-neighbour! Snap! Happy Families! Quite, quite!" murmured Dacre.

Big double doors at the other side of the landing gave access to a very large room, probably an old-fashioned drawing-room ball-room.

Across one end of this, ran a bar laden with bottles of every shape and size, glasses, and plates piled high with various kinds of sandwiches. In the middle of this profusion was a noble ham surrounded by cold roast birds, a tongue, and various baked meats.

Adjacent to the buffet were one or two tables evidently set for such as might desire a sit-down meal.

The greater part of the room, however, was occupied by a long green table at which were seated a number of men and a few women, all suitably and indeed fashionably arrayed, the men in correct evening garb and the women in *decolleté* gowns of various hues and styles; a gathering of obviously well-to-do well-dressed ladies and gentlemen—of a sort.

On the long green table was a thick and heavy oblong of painted oil-cloth, with numbered squares and columns; and, at the top of the table was a gadget that was new to me; a sort of large flattish rosewood basin in which span a horizontal wheel, between the innumerable spokes of which were tiny compart-ments.

Over this wheel presided a huge genial-faced fat man; and, as he span it, a tiny ivory ball rushed madly round its edge along the overhanging rim of the wooden basin, from time to time falling into a compartment, and being instantly flung forth again by the centrifugal force of the spinning wheel.

As the wheel slowed down to stopping, the little ball at length found rest in one of the numbered compartments between the spokes.

"Now would that be a kind of Whist, Snap, Beggar-my-neighbour or Happy Families?" speculated Dacre, "or is it what they call Poker? But I don't see any cards."

"Oh, no, this isn't a card game. We play cards in the next room," smiled our hostess, and I noted that an open door at the far end led from this room to another.

"This is a game called Roulette. Our friends often drop in and amuse themselves at it. Sometimes some of them have a little flutter. . . . You can, if you like, Captain—er—Smith."

"Major," corrected Dacre, smiling pleasantly.

"Major Smith and . . . Colonel Brown. . . . You can either put it on red or black. You see the ball must go into a red or a black compartment."

"Nowhere else for the little chap, is there?" said Dacre.

"Or you can put it on odd or even," continued the lady, her smile tightening and her squint increasing. "You see the compartments are numbered, and a number is bound to be either odd or even, isn't it?"

"Practically certain," agreed Dacre. "Almost any number is."

"Or you can put it on 'above or below'—passe or manque—so that you are betting whether it will be below or above eighteen. Or if you like, of course, you can put your money on a number. On one of those numbered squares. Then, if the ball goes into the number that you have chosen—you make real money, for you get thirty-five times your stake returned to you. You put a sovereign on Number Twelve, for example, and if twelve turns up, you get back thirty-five pounds."

"Or put on a thousand and get back thirty-five thousand pounds," said Dacre.

"Quite so. Or you can put it on zero at the bottom there. And we play double zero too. You'll soon catch on.

"Why, we were playing an 'eagle' the other night," she continued, indicating a square on which the form of an eagle was painted, "and Mr. Standesh here, put a fiver on it and got back seventy times his stake."

"Three hundred and fifty pounds, eh," said Dacre, glancing at Standesh and smiling artlessly. "That accounts for . . ."

"Accounts for what?" asked Standesh a little sharply.

"The milk in the coconut," replied Dacre, looking him in the eyes.

"Well, I'm going to try my luck again," said Standesh.

And taking a sovereign from his pocket, put it on the red line that ran down one side.

Other players placed their money on various parts of the

table.

The banker spun the wheel and the ball came to rest in a red compartment. Standesh took up his own sovereign and another which the banker pushed toward him.

The table being cleared and the *croupier* having cried *"Faites vos jeux,"* or rather, *"Fate voh jew,"* Standesh placed the two sovereigns on the compartment marked pair. The wheel spun, the little ivory ball, driven upon its agitated journey, came to rest, this time, in a black compartment numbered twelve. An even number had won and the banker pushed two sovereigns to add to the two that Standesh had placed on *pair*. Some of the other players lost, some won.

Standesh now put his four sovereigns on the place marked *manque*. Again the wheel whirled round, the ball leapt and bounded, and finally settled down in the compartment numbered three. This being less than the number eighteen, Standesh had again won, and the croupier's rake pushed four sovereigns across the cloth to join Standesh's four.

"What about it?" said he to Dacre. "What shall I do with the eight?"

"Put them in your pocket," drawled Dacre.

"No, no! I'm out to make a killing. I feel this is my lucky night. You fellows have brought me luck. I'm going to put the lot on my lucky number—seven. Always been my lucky number. Depends on the month you're born in."

And Standesh placed his eight sovereigns in a neat pile on number seven.

"Fate voh jew," called the croupier; and, anon, spun the wheel and cried,

"Rien va plus," or perhaps *"Reang var ploos."*

It was indeed Standish's lucky night, for, to the accompaniment of cries of excitement, envy, incredulity and surprise, the hesitant reluctant ball dropped at length into the compartment bearing the figure seven.

I stared open-mouthed. Not so, Dacre.

"He's won two hundred and eighty pounds," he murmured, and added coolly, "I knew he would."

"What d'you mean?" asked a black-avised beady-eyed man turning his thin hungry face sharply round from the table.

"Exactly what I said," replied Dacre and declined further comment.

"Well, well! Look at that!" exclaimed our hostess, smiling with what I felt was intended to be a rueful smile. "You mustn't clear us out of 'ready', before the evening has begun, Jimmy. I shall have to give you a cheque."

"Oh, rather," agreed Standesh with a light laugh.

"Yes, I thought it would be a cheque," observed Dacre *sotto voce.*

Standesh's run of luck seemed greatly to encourage the guests and to stimulate their interest and ardour in the game. Watching them, I came to the conclusion that they fell into two categories; the innocent and foolish, generally rather young; and the rest, who were certainly neither innocent nor young. The men might have been a mixture of silly young subalterns and wicked old Colonels (though I imagine there were more subalterns than Colonels present); and the women, foolish, dissipated, young Society women, and well-dressed, well-mannered raddled harpies.

"Well, well," smiled Dacre as the next game was called. "What a world we live in, and what wonders we behold."

"What's Standesh doing in the Life Guards if he can make two hundred and eighty pounds whenever he wants to?" he continued.

"Well, I suppose he loses as often as he wins—probably a good deal oftener," said I.

"Not he, my son," replied Dacre. "He never loses a farthing. Neither does he gain one—at roulette. All he gains is what *chère Madame* allows him for his valuable services—as a decoy. . . . But what I *don't* understand is how the wheel's faked. It really would be interesting to find out. Shall we have a rough-house?"

"We shall not," I assured him. "We are honoured guests, and will behave as such. Let's go and behold the marvels in the next room. More Happy Families Beggaring their Neighbours at Snap."

Strolling into the adjoining room we discovered that chemin-de-fer, baccarat and poker were in progress.

"Going to have a flutter?" said a dulcet voice at my elbow.

Madame again.

"No, not this evening, thank you," I replied. "I didn't come—er —prepared."

"And I haven't my cheque book with me, for once," drawled Dacre.

"Oh, that doesn't matter. . . . Any friend of my friend, Mr. Standesh . . . As a matter of fact, I happen to have accounts at several banks, and can probably let you have a cheque on your own bank. . . . Or what's wrong with a sheet of note-paper and a stamp? What shall we say—a hundred each?"

"Oh no, thanks very much, we'll do the thing properly," replied Dacre. "You're too trusting altogether, you know, Madame. Why, we might be a pair of swindlers."

And Madame favoured him with a long look, the cast in her eye very pronounced.

"Any friends of my friend Standesh . . ." she smiled, and drifted away to greet some new-comers.

"Tell you what," whispered Dacre to me. "Let's ask Standesh to give another exhibition and we'll do what he does."

"Lose!" I grinned.

"Yes, I suppose he'd have to lose if we put a fiver everywhere that he put a sov. . . . Shall we have a drink on them and a light supper?"

"No, I think not," said I, "though it would serve them right if we did ourselves well and then proceeded to lose some worthless I.O.U.'s to them. . . . Might be a bit awkward though, by the time we heard the last of it."

"Yes. Let's clear out," agreed Dacre. "Shouldn't be surprised if this place were raided one night. . . ."

In point of fact it was raided. Madame was arrested and remanded without bail; and, on the following day, Standesh was arrested by the police, and eventually sent for trial at the Old Bailey.

It was very lucky for Dacre and me that the house had not been raided on the night that we were there. We gathered from the newspaper account of the Old Bailey trial, that the place was a good deal more, and a good deal worse, than a gambling-den.

It might have been a very unpleasant experience indeed.

CHAPTER VIII

But soon thereafter we really did fall from grace.

Yes, we failed to "keep our hair on", Corporal Higgett being the cause, and our march to Windsor the occasion.

This, in fine weather, was a pleasant ride, as soon as London was left behind.

We rode in half-sections and, in order to avoid monopolizing the road and interfering with traffic, proceeded in single file on either side of the road.

Riding "at ease" there was no particular harm in a song, a shouted jest, a little chaff with passers-by or a girl at a cottage gate.

Dacre, wanting to borrow a cigarette, left the line and rode up beside me. While I was struggling to get at my cigarette case, Corporal Higgett suddenly clattered up, bawled an insult at Dacre, asked him who the Hell he was and what the Hell he thought he was doing, and bade him get back to his place.

Dacre, hot, thirsty, and cross, requested Corporal Higgett to keep calm, to consider his health, and to keep his hair on— forgetting the evil and unpleasant implications of the last suggestion.

The red face of Corporal Higgett went several shades redder, and such was his wrath that he actually dropped his voice almost to a whisper.

"Right," said he. "Right. Now see how long you keep your hair on, you. . . ."

That evening, at Stables, Corporal Higgett came to the stall in which Dacre was working, polishing away at his horse with the groom's authentic hissing whistle, as though to the manner born. To see and hear him, one would have imagined that he had been bred and born on a farm, and worked all his life in stables, instead of having spent all the years of his youth and young manhood at sea.

"Is that the man?" enquired Corporal Higgett, indicating Dacre with his thumb, and turning to Trooper Chatten who accompanied him.

"Ar, that's him," agreed the man.

"You identify him. You're sure?"

"Ar, that's right," agreed the grinning Chatten.

"You 'eard 'im swear at me, call me names, tell me to go to 'ell; and refuse to obey my order?"

"Ar, that's right," agreed the trooper.

"You was the file ridin' immediate be'ind, and saw and 'eard everything what transpired?"

"Ar, that's right."

Turning away from Horace, I stood up and took notice.

Dacre, half-turned from Corporal Higgett, was stooping and scrubbing at his horse's fetlock and pastern.

" 'Ere, you," said Corporal Higgett.

Dacre took no notice.

"*You*, I said," bawled Higgett, and touched Dacre sharply with his foot.

It would be something of an exaggeration to say that Higgett kicked him.

It was more than sufficient for Dacre, however, who, springing erect and whirling about, clenched his left fist and gave Higgett a tremendous smack in the eye.

Leaping out of my stall, which happened to be almost opposite to Dacre's, I sprang between them. Higgett was no coward, but he was going to get something better out of this than the pleasure of hitting Dacre back.

"You saw that! You saw that!" he shouted, clutching me by the front of the jacket. "You saw Blount 'it me in the eye—for nothing."

"It wasn't Blount, it was I," I replied, and hit him in the other one.

"You silly fool!" shouted Dacre, and thrust between me and Higgett.

For a moment I was afraid Dacre was going to repeat the offence, and I had visions of my intervening again, smiting Higgett a second time; Dacre once more intruding and also hitting Higgett a second time; my again intervening and repeating the blow; Dacre then intruding, and so *ad nauseam*.

However, Dacre was promptly seized from behind by Chatten and another, while I was also seized and held with unnecessary firmness.

"*Now* we'll see who keeps their 'air on," spluttered Higgett, almost incoherent with malevolence and rage, as he attended to his nose.

And from the stables we were personally conducted to the Guard Room.

§2

Next day, Dacre and I were marched to the Orderly Room ante-room, and in our turn brought up before the Colonel for judgment.

The Adjutant read the charge.

"Trooper Blount behaving improperly on the march and in a manner contrary to good discipline; using disrespectful, insolent and insubordinate language to a non-commissioned officer; Troopers Blount and Dysart striking a superior."

Colonel Lord Borrodaile eyed us both coldly, severely, and with a look of grave disappointment. Nevertheless I had an idea that he gazed upon us more in sorrow than in anger. Possibly my wish was father to the thought.

Having stared long and speculatively at Dacre and then at me, he eyed Corporal Higgett; and it seemed to me that he summed the man up very much for what he was.

"Anything to say?" suddenly he snapped curtly. "You, Trooper Blount?"

"No, Sir."

"Oh; nothing? H'm. Nothing at all to say in your defence?"

"No, Sir."

"Did you leave your place on the march."

"Yes, Sir."

"What for?"

"To borrow a cigarette, Sir."

"Did you return to your place when ordered to do so by Corporal Higgett?"

"Yes, Sir."

"Did you curse him; swear at him; abuse him?"

"No, Sir."

"What did you say?"

"So far as I can remember, Sir, I said,

" 'Keep cool, and keep your hair on'."

"Oh! . . . Did you strike Corporal Higgett during Stables last night."

"Yes, Sir."

"Why?"

"Because he touched me with his foot, Sir."

"You mean he kicked you?"

"No, Sir."

"Oh, he didn't kick you? Only touched you?"

477

"Yes, Sir."

"And you struck him."

"Yes, Sir."

"H'm. . . . You, Trooper Dysart? . . . Nothing to say? . . . You admit that you also struck Corporal Higgett?"

"Yes, Sir."

"Why?"

"I really don't know, Sir."

"Don't let's have any insolence, my man."

"I beg your pardon, Sir. I didn't for one moment intend to be in the least insolent. I don't know why I struck Corporal Higgett. I just thought I would."

"H'm. . . . You just thought you would, eh? . . . Well, I'll do some thinking now. I think I'll give you one hundred and sixty-eight hours cells, and twenty-one days C.B. . . . Same for you, Trooper Blount. . . . Perhaps that'll enable you to think a little more wisely. . . . Give you time to think, anyhow."

"Prisoners and escort . . . Left turn! . . . Quick march," snapped the Corporal, and back we were marched to the Guard Room.

And thence to the cells.

Here Dacre and I were parted, and I was ordered into a little ugly dark room, with an iron door and a heavily-grated window.

Here a Grenadier Guards Sergeant took down various particulars concerning me. Having done so,

"Outside," he ordered, "and take that with you," indicating a heavy wooden barrack-room chair.

"Put it there, and sit down facing the wall," ordered the Sergeant.

This I did; and immediately the Sergeant fell to work with what must have been a huge pair of scissors.

These were the days before hair clippers; but the Sergeant made remarkably good practice with the tools which he had, and to which he was evidently accustomed.

By the time he had done with me, my hair was shorter than it had ever been in my life. In fact, nearly as short as a two days' beard.

By the time he had finished, I had indeed failed to keep my hair on.

"What are you in for?" enquired the Sergeant in the conversational manner of the barber he was impersonating.

"Smacking a Corporal in the eye," I answered.

"Bit of a luxury," replied the Sergeant. "You has your fun and

478

you pays for it, eh?"

"Cheap," I murmured, my nose almost touching my chest as he sought my last remaining hair at the back of my neck.

"Well, well; all a matter of taste, as the monkey said when he chewed his mother's ear. Stand up. Turn out your pockets."

This I proceeded to do, and the Sergeant received into his care and keeping, a handkerchief, cigarette-case, matchbox, knife, watch, and a purse containing some silver.

"That all you got? Everything?"

"Yes."

"Put your hands up."

"Don't trust me, eh?"

"Don't trust nobody."

And experienced hands were run carefully over my body.

"Right," said he, "you'll do. Come on, and I'll show you your 'utch."

And the Sergeant led me down the corridor into a cell, closed and locked the heavy door, and left me to my own devices and little else but a plank bed, a flap table and a Bible.

Well, man needs but little here below, really, and this was a place infinitely preferable to the Apprentices' half-deck (as I first saw it) of the *Valkyrie*, the ship in which I made a three years' voyage to Australia and thence round the Horn to San Francisco and back to England.

The cell was clean and reasonably airy. On the plank bed one could lie. At the table one could sit; and the Bible one could read. Read it right through in one hundred and sixty-eight hours. . . .

Towards evening, the door was suddenly unlocked. The Sergeant appeared and bade me come forth and fetch my tea, dinner and supper, all three, from the kitchens. I found out that tea, dinner and supper—also to be described as tea or dinner or supper—consisted of a pint of gruel and six ounces of bread. . . . I should have been glad of it on the *Valkyrie*, any night in three long years. However, I should now be more than willing to augment it, for my appetite was great.

"I say, Sergeant, can I buy . . . ?"

"Hold your tongue," interrupted the Sergeant. "You can't buy nothing, and you can't talk neither. You take that into the 'utch, and don't make an 'og of yourself."

Escorted by a Corporal, I returned to my cell.

Moistening the dry bread with the wet skilly, I made my evening meal.

Anon the Corporal returned, unlocked my door, bade me

bring back my plate and mug, and fetch my blankets for the night.

This I did, removed my tunic and overalls, and settled down upon the bare planks with one blanket beneath me and one above.

Such was my daily programme. Bread and skilly twice a day and nothing on earth to do from morning till night, nor from night till morning, save read the Bible and sleep. Except on Sunday when, for the good of my soul, I was marched, a criminal convict under escort, to the Garrison Church, there to be observed by all good soldiers and virtuous civilians, for the wicked man I was.

Positively I started, when the falsetto-voiced curate began,

"When the wicked man turneth away from his wickedness that he hath committed, and doeth that which is lawful and right, he shall save his soul alive."

Turn away from my wickedness. My wickedness was Corporal Higgett. I must turn away from him. So must Dacre, the other wicked man, also brought, under escort, to Church, for the good of his soul. He must not get the Corporal-thumping habit. He'd be thumping a Corporal-Major next. Suppose he'd been an Officer. That would have been two years' hard labour at the least. But of course he'd never do such a thing as that. He'd been an officer himself; Third Officer of the *Valkyrie*. And after all he'd only hit one Corporal once; and a Corporal is only one degree better than a common man except that in the Life Guards he ranks as Sergeant.

Besides, who was I to take thought for Dacre's conduct? Had not I thumped the Corporal also?

Well, we mustn't do it again. The game was not worth the— skilly. No, definitely, neither Dacre nor I must thump Corporal Higgett again.

But when the long and weary week had worn itself to an end and we were restored, purged and purified, to Troop "B," we found that Corporal Higgett had been reduced to the ranks.

I had been right in imagining that the Colonel had about taken his measure, and had decided that the sort of Corporal that gets punched in the eye twice in one evening is not the sort of Corporal that is wanted in Her Majesty's Life Guards.

Reduced to the ranks; and now we could, within reason, thump him as much as we liked. Thump him to our hearts' content.

And straightway we found we hadn't the slightest desire to

thump the creature.

§3

The first year of our service passed with remarkable speed and by no means unhappily; but, by the time we could honestly, if with due modesty, regard ourselves as the Compleat Troopers, really first-class horsemen and horse-masters, first-class shots and swordsmen, good scouts and good soldiers—Dacre and I began to feel that it was time we left school.

We had never had the slightest intention of becoming peace-time soldiers, with a view to making the army a career. What we wanted was adventure, the open-air, spacious life in foreign parts, something vaguely in the Colonies or America; ranching, prospecting, gold-digging, or service in some Police Force offering a hardy life, fair pay and good prospects, visualizing ourselves as cowboys, Australian stock-riders, South African ox-team drivers, or, more probably, members of some such force as the North West Mounted Police, the Cape Mounted Rifles, the British South African Police, the Rhodesian Police, the Indian Police or other semi-military organization.

However, we were not going to be in a hurry to make the enquiries and necessary application for permission to buy ourselves out of the British Army.

And it was during this period of discussion and tentative application, that I received a letter that settled the problem, and, for good or ill, changed my way of life and affected my whole career.

On board the *Valkyrie*, in which I had made my terrible three-year voyage, had been an Ordinary Seaman calling himself Larry O'Toole. He had joined the ship at Pisagua and left her at Falmouth.

Having done so, he wrote me a long and amazingly interesting letter, in which he informed me that his name was Desmond O'Moore Hartigan; that he was a wealthy man; incidentally a yachtsman who held an Extra Master's certificate; and that he had joined the *Valkyrie* at Pisagua because a man named Villa, of whom he was in pursuit, had done so; this Villa being one of a Chicago gang of gunmen crooks that had kidnapped first himself and then his wife—who had died at their hands.

In the letter he had prophesied that I should hear from him again, and he was now keeping his promise. . . . Very interesting and very à *propos*.

"Dacre, my son," quoth I, as I finished the letter and glanced across to where he was vainly endeavouring to improve the mirror-like surface of his cuirass, "how would you like to do a bit of gun-running?"

"Love it," replied Dacre. "What's the idea—pawn our carbines?"

"No. Remember Larry O'Toole—on the *Valkyrie*?"

"*Alias* Desmond O'Moore Hartigan, who got his own—and a bit more—back on that dreadful devil Villa? . . . Rather. . . . Why?"

"He's got what he calls a proposition that sure will interest us. His latest form of sport without danger, or with a lot of danger, is gun-running; and he proposes to let us in on it, 'on the ground floor'. Apparently a mixture of healthy pastime and profitable employment."

"Listens good to me, as Desmond O'Moore Hartigan would say," replied Dacre, "except that I'm not particularly keen on providing gin and gas-pipe guns for brown brothers who are better off on cold water and bows and arrows. . . . Nor on helping some fat millionaire ex-President of a South American Republic to start a revolution against the current incumbent, all in the name of freedom. . . . '*Liberty, Equality, and Fraternity*' generally means liberty for the peons to slaughter each other, equality for the under-dogs in poverty and misery; and fraternity among the top dogs—until they evolve another noble Liberator to start the game all over again. Saw something of it myself in South America. . . . Good speech, loud cheers."

"Agreed," I agreed. "Absolutely. But Desmond O'Moore Hartigan is on the opposite tack. He's running guns for the benefit of the poor and the oppressed, the widow and the orphan, against the Oppressor. Lending a hand to exalt the humble and meek and to put down the mighty from their seat. Do noble deeds—not dream them all day long—and get that tingling glow that comes from a just sense of righteousness and twenty per cent profit. . . . Read his letter."

Dacre read the letter which had been forwarded to me from home.

" 'Nuff said, Sinbad," he decided with his usual promptitude. "We're on this. . . . Change, adventure, good deed for the day, high wages and a handsome bonus. My God, what a chance!"

That very day I answered Desmond O'Moore Hartigan's letter, told him of our recent doings and present circumstance, and promised to meet him, as he had requested, on a certain date at a certain inn near a certain quiet little South Coast harbour, which shall be nameless.

For the salt was in our blood, and the sharpness of the horrors of the *Valkyrie*'s nightmare voyage had faded from our minds. Back to the ocean again, Cap'n, back to the ocean again! And hey for a gun-running venture—the purveying of rifles to the brave, noble, and deserving victims of a ruthless land-grabbing Oppressor; the assistance of worthy patriots in their wholly admirable stand for Hearth and Home, for their desert and mountain freedom. A positive god-send . . . !

PART II

"In the name of Allah, the Beneficent, the Merciful. Praise is due to Allah, the Lord of the Worlds, the Beneficent, the Merciful, Master of the Day of Requital. Thee do we serve and Thee do we beseech for help. Guide us in the right path, the Path of those upon whom Thou hast bestowed favours, not those upon whom wrath is brought down, nor those who go astray."

CHAPTER IX

I don't think I was ever so surprised in my life. I don't think that anything so dramatic, vital, fatal, ever happened with such amazing suddenness.

And yet even as I stared, probably open-mouthed, there seemed to be an inevitability about it. And again, amazed as I was to the point of incredulity, my chief surprise was at my lack of surprise. It was almost as though I had expected the utterly unexpected.

From the ravine, the band of Arabs positively erupted, shooting forth as does the long figure of the Jack-in-the-box toy. And as they galloped forth at full tilt, they opened fire from the saddle.

And these uncontrolled undisciplined people evidently had their own definite and understood strategy and tactics, for, of the horde that streamed forth, some galloped in a semi-circle to our right, others to our left, while the remainder came straight on.

To run was hopeless, to fight impossible. Even as I turned to measure the distance between myself and the water's edge, and to calculate the chance of a dash across that soft yielding sand, that unpleasant low-tide quicksand, half liquid, half solid, with the prospect of a couple of miles' swim if one ever reached the water, retreat was cut off, the leading Arabs of both encircling horns being nearer to each other than the water was to me. From the racing pace at which their horses flew, it was quite clear that they would meet and close the circle long before I was half-way to the water's edge.

Trapped.

In the meantime, the ill-aimed bullets were striking the sand here and there at no great distance from me.

I glanced at Halling. Like myself he had evidently realized the utter impossibility of escape, and simply stood and stared. Even as I looked, the leading Arab of the party that was charging straight down upon us, bore down upon him with levelled spear.

What followed happened more quickly than I can tell it. Halling ducked low just as I thought he was impaled, and must have thrown himself at the horseman and seized his leg, for, a second later the horse was galloping on riderless, and Halling and the Arab were struggling on the ground.

Both sprang to their feet simultaneously, the Arab snatched at his sword, and Halling, with a *smack* that was distinctly audible, struck him so violent a blow in the face that he reeled back headlong and fell.

As the active and plucky fellow stooped and snatched at the sword that the Arab dropped, another horseman rode him down and, to my horror, passed on, dragging Halling behind him at the end of his long lance.

I think I shouted and sprang forward as though it had been possible to do anything for the poor fellow, when I was myself knocked flying, by the horse of an Arab who had ridden me down, doubtless with the intention of doing to me as his fellow had done to Halling. Probably the latter had, in a way, saved my life, as, no doubt, my springing forward at that particular moment caused the Arab to miss me with his spear.

Well, if this were the end, I might as well die fighting. Far better in fact than to be taken alive and tortured to death.

Springing to my feet as the Arab reined his horse back on its haunches and wheeled about, I received a sickening blow on the head, a blow that again knocked me down and for a few minutes knocked me out, completely stunned.

As I lay endeavouring to pull myself together and get to my feet, I was aware of horses' hooves, men's feet, shouting, heavy blows about my body, and then that a rope was roughly pulled over my head and down about my body, pinning my elbows to my side.

As I struggled to rise to my feet, I was once again thrown violently to the ground and immediately dragged along it.

Suffering horribly, and yet incredulous, I found I was being dragged at a gallop across the sand, and, a minute or two later, across hard earth, stones, rocks, and scrub.

How long this lasted I do not know, but it was long enough for me to wonder whether my captors had selected this particularly unpleasant and lingering form of death for me.

Just as I had decided that this was the case and was wondering whether it would be possible for me to regain my feet, and with a mighty effort, sprint for a few seconds with sufficient rapidity to overtake the horse, grab the Arab, and cling to him or the horse's bridle, the man reined in. As I sat up I saw that we had reached the ravine whither we were being followed by the rest of the band.

One glimpse I got of the little bay, a lovely morning scene; the ship safely and peacefully at anchor a couple of miles away; the sands, so recently the scene of tumult, violence and murder, empty and quiet as they had been when first I set eyes on them.

And then I was again jerked violently forward, but now at a pace not too swift to prevent my rising to my feet and following my captor at a jog-trot, as he led the way along the wide and winding *wadi*.

I was little better off, however, for instead of violent bumps, blows and bruises from rocks and stones, I now received them from the spear-butts and sheathed swords of my captors, it being the humour of each one of them to have his whang at me. This they did in turn, and I know not which was the more unpleasant—the brutal violent prod between the shoulder-blades from the lance-butt of a trotting horseman, a heavy cut across the head, shoulders or arms from a long and heavy sheathed sword, or a blow from the flat of a drawn one.

I felt that I would have given all I possessed, including my immortal soul, to have been allowed to deal with these cowardly swine one by one, and I would have asked for no sword or lance for myself.

Yes, thought I to myself, I'd take the brutes three at a time, were they unarmed, and kill them with my fists.

One filthy savage, not content with having had his whack at me, fired his long gun as though to blow my brains out, just missing my head, intentionally I suppose, by an inch or so. Suddenly, the fellow to whose saddle-bow the end of the rope was tied, spurred his horse, and I had to run over that rough broken stony ground faster and farther than I have ever run in my life, or again be dragged until the flesh was rubbed, scraped and worn from my bones, or the brains dashed from my head against a rock.

That run behind a trotting, if not cantering, horse was one of the worst experiences of my life. It seemed to me that I must have run for miles, and that I could run no more when, beneath the shade of a clump of palms, the troop reined up, my captor's horse came to a halt, and I sank to the ground gasping and whooping for breath. As I lay, all but dying, several of these heroes beat me unmercifully.

Tiring of this—at long last—they held what I supposed was a council of war or a discussion as to my fate. That it was the latter I realized when one ruffian, drawing his sword, pointed with it at me, harangued the rest, and then stepping up to where I lay, raised it above his head as though about to strike.

So exhausted and defeated was I that I felt more than half

inclined to raise no objection, indeed to give him every facility, by offering my neck to the blow. Better to have one's head hacked off and done with it, than to be dragged at a horse's heels until one bled miserably to death. Better still to die fighting, making them kill me. . . .

Again I staggered to my feet, only to remember that my arms were bound firmly to my sides. As I did so, a man who seemed to be the leader, so far as this band acknowledged a leader, stepped between me and my self-appointed executioner, thrust him back and, with a torrent of words, bade him desist.

I imagined he was saying to him in Arabic,

"Who asked you to butt in? Who the Hell do you think you are? You didn't catch the accursed *Roumi*, did you? You're too full of yourself. When I want your help in killing him I'll tell you so. Who's leader here? A little of you's a lot," and so forth.

Anyhow, the man grumblingly sheathed his sword, and the leader, producing a fibre cord from his saddle, bound my crossed wrists tightly together behind my back, and bade my captor unfasten the rope from my arms and his saddle-bow and tie it to a palm tree.

This done, the band off-saddled, camped and rested.

From the look of the horses, I gathered that they'd ridden all night, and I imagined that some spy or scout had seen the ship, watched our boat pull ashore, and ridden off to warn the others of this chance of booty. If this were the case, it seemed to me that the band had shown remarkably little foresight, sense or enterprise in not, themselves, scouting, spying, watching, waiting and endeavouring to make a real haul.

I decided that probably, however, they were mere semi-savage nomads who neither knew nor guessed anything concerning our gun-running activities; didn't see any advantage in attempting to attack a probably well-armed boatload of men, but were quite content and highly delighted, to kill and capture one or two defenceless *Roumis*, the accursed hated dogs of Infidels.

My reflections were disturbed by one of the nastiest, most disgusting and most painful of events. A man arose from where he had been eating and resting, walked over to his hobbled horse, took something from where it hung at the saddle on the side further from me, and approached.

It was the fellow who had wished to cut my head off.

And suddenly with a sinking heart and sick feeling at the pit of the stomach, I saw that what he bore in his hand was the head of poor Halling. This he placed on a stone close in front of where I lay tied to the tree.

"There," said he in Arabic as I imagined, "what do you think of that? Have a good look at it. That's what your head will be like as soon as I get a chance at you."

I took a long look at the Arab's face and licked my lips. Conceivably I might get a chance at him sometime.

As I lay there in considerable pain and great fear, the leader and a couple of other men came and looked me over, discussing me in a manner that gave me the impression that they were agreeing that I was a good specimen; that I should be more valuable, if not useful, alive than dead; that it would be a foolish waste of a perfectly good *Roumi* to hack my head off just for fun, and that the fellow who'd wanted to do it was a careless lad, impetuous, improvident.

And when he, too, strolled across with one or two friends, they told him so.

But unlike so many of the improvident, the impetuous, the wastefully spendthrift, he was not warm-hearted, good-natured, good-tempered. He was a violent man, apt to take himself over-seriously and to foam at the mouth on the slightest provocation. Undisciplined and uncontrolled, he shook his fist in his leader's face, spat at his feet, foamed, gesticulated, and suddenly, followed by his friends, flung himself bodily upon me.

Again I thought my last moment had come, but this time it was robbery and not murder that occupied his thoughts. Tearing and rending at my clothes, these filthy ruffians contrived to strip me almost naked without removing the bonds that bound my hands behind me and to the tree-trunk. In a very few minutes they had possessed themselves of everything that I had, sharing my property, not without violent quarrelling, down to the last button.

Evidently the fanatic's acquiescence in my being kept alive for sale had been obtained by agreement that he and those who were of his way of thinking, should share such loot as was to be obtained.

And there I lay, black and blue, bruised from head to foot, practically naked, bleeding in a dozen places, exhausted and all but dead of thirst.

Will it be believed that, the Arabs now leaving me alone, I fell asleep and slept soundly?

CHAPTER X

I was awakened by a kick and a blow from a stick, and, as I eyed my assailant, I wondered just how much I would give to have my hands free for a minute or two. Apparently the band was about to move on. Presumably they either feared pursuit and attack by an armed landing-party from the ship, or from the followers of whomsoever the ship was there to meet.

Once again the end of the rope that was fastened to my wrists was tied to a saddle, and I realized that if the horse to which I was thus attached, cantered faster than I could run, I should be dragged along the ground with my head to the horse, and that my arms would be pulled backward almost from their sockets.

However, the pace was only a walk, with an occasional trot, and although I was almost worn out with hunger, thirst and fatigue, exposed almost naked to the sun, badly bruised and cut about, filthy with dirt, dust, and sweat, I was able to keep my feet.

For one thing I was profoundly thankful; the ruffians had not yet taken away my boots.

For about a couple of hours the march continued along a dry level river bed to which my captors kept, as I supposed, for concealment.

Debouching from this, we crossed a wide sandy rock-strewn plain, eventually reaching a range of hills. Crossing these by way of what I imagine was a secret pass, as its entrance was invisible from the plain, owing to vast boulders and clumps of cactus, we came out upon a plateau, in the middle of which was a considerable village of houses built of stone and baked mud. In the *sûk* or central market-square of this place, I was exposed to public view, insult, injury, contumely and assault by all such as found amusement in reviling, stoning, kicking, striking, and spitting upon, the accursed *Roumi*, the infidel dog, contemptible and abhorrent to Allah and their noble selves.

When night fell, and sheer boredom on the part of my tormentors brought a measure of peace, I lay in the dust, fastened by means of a short fibre-rope to a palm tree, my hands bound behind me, and thought of the day, how recent, how incredibly distant, when I sat on my horse, a Whitehall sentry, a model of spick-and-spanness, cleanness, smartness and brilliance, for all

492

the world to see and to admire.

However, in spite of pain, rage, humiliation and an agony of mental, moral, and physical suffering, I slept until awakened in the morning by a heavy kick and the gift of a handful of filthy dates and a gourd of filthier water.

That day I was again subject for much discussion, as well as an object for gross brutality; and, in the end, so far as I could understand, I was sold by my original captors to the headman of this village.

Anyhow, the former departed and, to my lasting regret, I saw them no more. I am not of a particularly vengeful and vindictive disposition, but there came, later, a time when I would have given a very great deal to have rounded up this band and dealt with its members faithfully and one by one.

Their first orgy of cruelty over, and anti-Christian anti-European sentiments satisfactorily expressed, the inhabitants of the village—while treating me as the dog that to them I was— behaved with less wanton brutality than the nomads had done. And my fate was no worse than that of some bird or other wild creature captured by village lads, tied up, with a string about its leg, and left to suffer hunger, thirst, fear and the miseries of captivity. Tethered and exposed to the sun, I was able to understand and sympathize with the sufferings of a lark, linnet or chaffinch trapped by the abominable fowler, thrust into a cage just big enough to contain its body, and exposed without food or water to the direct rays of the sun. Man's careless or callous brutality to beast and bird, man's inhumanity to man, are incredible.

The days passed. My wounds, after all only superficial, healed, and I recovered a measure of health, strength and spirits, albeit desperately hungry, always thirsty, and in a chronic state of rage, resentment and apprehension.

Before many days had passed, I concluded that I had been bought from the nomads as a speculation, for, on a caravan setting forth one evening, I was kicked to my feet and fastened by a cord to a camel-saddle.

The caravan, laden with dates, stinking bales of sheep-skins and goat-skins, bags of dried peas and parched acorns, lentils, onions and so forth, and led by the headman of the village, set forth in a south-easterly direction for the purpose, as I discovered, of disposing of these goods for grain, oil and salt; and of myself for cash.

Yes, I happen to be one of the few living Europeans who have been exposed for sale in a market-place, been examined, prodded, appraised, priced, chaffered over, haggled about, rejected, bargained for, and finally bought with money.

I don't know how long this journey lasted, for I shall doubtless be believed when I say that I lost count of time and distance, lived in a sort of waking nightmare, and became almost an automaton, conscious of little but pain, hunger, weariness and a sense of desperation.

It may have been for many days, several weeks, or a few months that the caravan journeyed on, until at last it reached its destination, a considerable town of the unrelieved unbroken colour of dried mud. The great embrasured loopholed wall that surrounded it, some thirty feet in height, twenty feet in thickness at the base and ten feet at the top, was built of dried mud. The square box-like houses were constructed of dôm-palm beams and dried mud. The streets were of the same material, but the mud was baked so hard by the heat of the sun that nothing but a heavily-wielded pickaxe would make any impression upon it.

Here again I was exposed to the jeers and insults of the populace and to fair and reasonable injury, though not to serious damage, for I was now merchandise. I was for sale, and to be bought by any citizen desiring to possess an extremely strong, active and healthy slave, as well as to enjoy the pleasure of being the untrammelled proprietor of a European, a *Roumi*, a dog and infidel whom he could humiliate, beat, and ill-treat at pleasure.

Day after day, I was exposed with other slaves—all of whom were negroes of varying sort, age, and size, and of both sexes— chained to a staple in the wall of the slave-market. Night after night I slept, bound, and tied to a camel, in the caravan *serai* occupied by my present proprietor.

Escape was out of the question, my hands being tied behind my back or, when I was permitted to eat, fastened in front of me, my crossed thumbs being tightly and cruelly bound with copper wire that had doubtless at some time stretched between the telegraph-poles of civilization.

Although I had been in the hands of these men for weeks, I had never once experienced a kindly action, word, or look. No sort of tolerance, much less friendship, had resulted from daily companionship. Their attitude to me was precisely that of any donkey-driver to his herd of starved, beaten, ill-treated and over-worked *burros*. No-one ever saw an Arab pat his donkey or give it anything but the bare sufficiency of food that should keep it alive and fit for work. And so these people treated me.

The only suggestion of the faintest touch of that kindness that makes the whole world kin, was a shy smile bestowed upon me by a stout upstanding negro lass, daily exposed for sale, a few feet away from my employer's stand or pitch in the market-place.

One day, a tall dignified important-looking man, clad in snowy white, save for a coloured turban and striped *burnous*, considered her, and, while the vendor expatiated with violence upon her merits, and showed off her points, the prospective purchaser looked into her mouth, pulled down her eyelids, examined her hands, and, so far satisfied, bade her owner remove her clothing.

Refraining from comment, he then examined me in like manner, and never will he know how near he came to receiving the kick of a life-time in the pit of his stomach. My hands being tied behind me, I could have delivered no other kind of blow, and it was, I believe, only my inherent and inbred dislike of kicking that saved the Arab—and myself.

Having examined the goods, he passed on, like a Saturday-night house-wife at a street market.

I caught the eye of the negress and, as I have said, she smiled at me—the first smile I had seen since I had left the ship, left Dacre, Desmond O'Moore Hartigan and my ship-mates and comrades of our gun-running venture. A rush of gratitude welled up in my heart. I would have liked to take her hand and thank her. I could have kissed her comely face. Positively, a smile, a friendly glance, a comprehending sympathetic look!

Soon afterward, the dignified Arab, tall and stately, returned and, without noticing me, passed by. The salesman in charge of me again assailed him with a torrent of words, obviously expatiating upon my youth, health and strength and the piquant fact of my being a *Roumi*. Passionately he gesticulated, flung his arms in my direction; and the tall Arab, who, I believe, had intended all along to buy me, made a bid, probably of one-half of what the slave auctioneer demanded, and promptly it was accepted.

I was bought!

Money changed hands. I was hauled down from the low stone selling-block on which I stood, the end of my halter was handed to the servant who had been following my new owner, and, like a purchased horse or cow, I was led away.

And like a horse or cow I was treated. Without active intentional brutality, without kindness or consideration. I was property, goods for which money had been paid, and so not to be damaged, injured or destroyed while fit for work or possessed of market value.

As I was led along the street of that city of dried mud, I wondered whether I was about to become a slave like the Christian slaves of the Barbary Corsairs, doomed to labour until I was too old to be worth my keep, or until perchance I should escape.

Thoughts and hopes of ransom crossed my mind, as well as visions of flight upon swift horse or enduring camel; and I made up my mind that, as quickly as possible, I must learn Arabic with a view to explaining to my owner that he could make a considerable sum of money by way of ransom. Failing that, a knowledge of Arabic would enable me to play the part of some sort of native of the country, and facilitate escape.

But as I was soon to discover, I was once again an investment rather than a purchase. My new owner had bought me with the intention of selling me at a profit, or using me as a gift for the purchase of honours or other value to be received. This accounted for the fact that I was now well-fed and reasonably well housed, clothed and treated.

In point of fact, I have little recollection of the weeks spent in the house owned or rented by my new master, one Ali bin Ahmed.

I have dim memories of a high-walled court-yard in which there was a great, almost windowless, thick-walled mud house, in the corner of a down-stairs room of which I slept on a string and frame bed; a room sometimes shared by a favourite camel, a noble white ass, big as a small horse, an occasional dog, stray goat, or fowls.

Instead of labouring in the barley-fields; in the olive-groves, beating the trees with a long stick; at the oil presses; or on building-construction or road-making under an overseer's lash, as I had imagined and expected, I had light and little work to do. This was such as the grinding of corn in a hand-quern, the cleaning of cooking-pots, and menial odd jobs considered fit for women-folk and *Roumis*, and I was given the *haik*, *djellabia*, and *kaffieh* of a servant. Also I was free, within the limits of the compound, but hobbled by means of a short chain attached to iron anklets.

And at the rarely-opened gate, there was always on duty one of four big powerful and apparently dumb negroes, each of whom wore a heavy sword and a knife or dagger, long, curved and ugly. In these circumstances, escape was out of the question, for even if I could remove my hobbles, evade the gate-keeper and get out of the town, where could I go and how could I go there?

To escape from this lost sand-buried city, one would require camels, food, water, weapons, a compass, as well as some sort of map. For where I was, I had not the vaguest idea. I never even knew the name of the place.

Nevertheless, constantly I thought of escape. In fact, I thought of nothing else, considering ways and means of secreting food, obtaining water (for water there was scarce and valuable) and something in which to carry it; stealing a camel and escaping somehow from the town, by night, in spite of closed city-gates and watchmen on the walls; and of arriving somehow, some day, somewhere on the coast of Africa, by proceeding steadily westward. In the desert my knowledge of navigation would help a little.

But while I was still wrestling with these problems, and refusing to acknowledge the fact that escape was impossible—for did not Slatin Pasha escape from Omdurman after ten years' captivity—my owner, Ali bin Ahmed, assembled and provisioned his caravan, and set off on a journey, taking me with him.

This time, I rode like a gentleman albeit a captive and a slave; rode one of the baggage-camels when I felt like it, and marched beside the beast when so disposed.

Of this journey again I have but little recollection, and do not remember whether it was long or short. I should think it was a matter of weeks rather than months; that I was not terribly unhappy; that I had a fair amount of food and enough water. I seem to remember ineffably lovely sunrises and sunsets and, occasionally, quite good meals of mutton-stew, cous-coussu, smead bread, and a sort of tea. More often, of course, meals consisted of dates or parched grain or dried peas stewed in oil, and leather-scented water.

Ali bin Ahmed did himself well, and I must admit, did me pretty well too. A man who looked after his cattle.

Journeys end in many things beside lovers' meetings. This one ended in a vast camp, comparable only with that of the biggest travelling circus ever assembled, and in my presentation or sale to the Potentate who, as I learned later, was none other than he who was known throughout the Sahara as the White Sultan—His Highness el Sidna el Sultan Mahommed el Kebir.

Evidently my master, Sheik Ali bin Ahmed, was a person of some importance, as he was given audience of the Sultan, and his caravan allotted to tents and camel-lines in a sufficiently honourable and important quarter of the camp.

That night I slept outside my owner's tent and, next day, was given clean clothing—cotton pantaloons, shirt and *haik*—and taken before the Sultan.

CHAPTER XI

In a truly colossal and magnificent marquee almost big enough to be the Big Top itself of an itinerant circus, I stood face to face with The White Sultan el Sidna el Sultan Mahommed el Kebir, Kaid of Bab-el-Djebel, Warden of the Moroccan Marches, Ruler of the Western Sahara, Lord of the Border Tribes, and absolute arbiter of my destiny.

On a huge silk-covered mattress piled high with great cushions, sat cross-legged, a great sword across his knees, the man who could have my head flicked off, have me tortured to death, order me to be impaled upon a sharpened post, burnt alive, crucified, or merely hanged out of hand, for the *Roumi* dog and infidel villain that I was.

Although dressed more simply than many of the officers and officials of his *entourage*, there was no possibility of mistake as to who was the master. Though his subordinates wore ornaments of silver or gold and the "striped clothing" of Arab rank and importance, the Sultan's dress was unadorned. His shirt was of cambric, braided with black silk at the seams. Over this he wore a white silk *haik*, and above the *haik*, two *burnouses* of white wool.

Hanging from his shoulders was a cloak of black silk. He wore no gold chains, no necklet or arm-bangle or wrist-bracelet. Only one or two silken tassels where the embroidery ended. And yet he was by far the most striking and impressive figure in the great tent, quite apart from the fact that he alone was seated, and was the centre of the group of officials, officers and men of his retinue and body-guard.

I wondered whether I should do myself any good by prostrating myself before him and bumping my forehead upon the ground, or rather the magnificent carpet, in token of my realization of the regrettable fact that I was a slave.

I did not like the idea of doing so, but, had I been certain that such conduct would have saved my life, I should not have had the slightest hesitation about getting down to it. Paris was worth a Mass, and my life was certainly worth a kow-tow. No, I didn't like the idea at all, but I'm not a haughty hero of the sort that "will not bow the knee to save himself from torture and from death". Moreover, as I looked at this mighty potentate, who fixed me with a gaze level and steady, yet cold as steel and utterly uninterested, I somehow gathered the impression that here was a man who would be little swayed by that sort of thing, a man who—if he thought of you at all—would think the better of you for displaying courage, and who would be entirely unmoved by grovelling ingratiation. If he was going to have your blood he'd have it, whether you kow-towed or whether you spat at him; and, if disposed to show mercy at all, would show it to a man of spirit rather than to a coward.

So, trembling within, sick with anxiety and apprehension, I stood erect, folded my arms upon my chest, looked him in the face and awaited what should befall.

And, while waiting, I took stock of this new arbiter of my destiny; and, knowing nothing concerning him then, as I understood but little Arabic, I was amazed to see that the man was, beyond doubt, a European.

Although, as I came to learn later, he was known as the White Sultan, he was little, if any, fairer than the average pure-bred Arab, or townsmen, such as the Fezai; but his features were unmistakably Aryan. Nor was this due to his being a Berber of far-off Gothic descent. Fair-haired, blue-eyed Berbers, a throw-back to Viking ancestors of a thousand years ago, are not uncommon, but such are quite unmistakably natives of Africa.

This man's face was as European as my own. He might have been Spanish, Italian or French. He might, indeed, have been a deeply sunburnt Englishman.

Though no trained and experienced physiognomist, I am fairly good at reading faces, and but rarely make a mistake. This, I decided, was a clever face, an intelligent, nay, an intellectual face, that of a thinker as well as a man of action. The forehead was good, high and broad; the eyes rather large for a European, and widely opened; the nose thin, aquiline, Norman and aristocratic; the mouth—scarcely concealed by the moustache, clipped Mahommedan fashion, and the small double-tufted chin-beard—was good. . . . It was somewhat full, slightly sensual-lipped, but not hard and cruel, the lower lip having the outward thrust often seen in men of action. The soldier and adventurer type.

No, not a bad face at all. That of a very experienced man apparently in the prime of life, or early middle age. Not that of a saint nor of a scoundrel; not that of a gentle soul nor of a brute; not ascetic, not particularly sensual; not kindly, not especially cruel; not the face of a weakling nor that of a violent ruffian.

Second thoughts may be best, but first impressions are generally right, especially in the case of an intuitive person; and I decided, then and there, that here was a very average human sinner who, like myself, would do ill and do well; a patch-work of good and bad; a man who would both use and abuse his high position and great power. Anyway, I was perfectly certain he was a European and was somehow comforted by that thought.

Admittedly there is no black darker than a black and white, no savage worse than a renegade from civilization. But, studying this man's face, I felt sure that here was a white man who, whatever his history, was also reasonably white inside.

I was anxious to hear his voice, for that, to my mind, tells as much as does the face. But would this apply in the case of one speaking a foreign tongue? . . . What language would he talk, and was he waiting for me to speak first? . . . Knowing no Arabic, and having no idea as to what his native language was, if indeed he were a European, I remained silent.

The silence grew uncomfortable, tense, somewhat ominous and sinister, and I began to feel more and more uneasy.

Suddenly he spoke in some unknown tongue, presumably Arabic.

"I'm sorry," I blurted out, using no honorific title, "I don't understand Arabic."

The Sultan did not "start" but I was perfectly certain that my speech surprised him. It did more than that—it interested him deeply. Though his expression did not change, though no muscle of his haughty face relaxed in smile or contracted in frown, there came a gleam into his eye, and I felt that somehow I had changed from an insect into a human being.

The gleam departed, the faint suggestion of warmth faded, and, after a long bleak appraising stare, the Sultan spoke again—this time, to my utter amazement, in French.

"*Qu'est-ce que vous dites?*" said he. "*Vous ne savez pas la langue Arabic? Alors, parlez-vous Français?*"

Yes, by the mercy and grace of God I did '*parle Français*' to the extent of a good knowledge of *Bué's French Grammar* and the bitterly resented but firmly enforced table-conversation of the French governess who had afflicted me throughout my nursery days.

"*Oui—er—Monseigneur . . . Monsieur l'Emir,*" (how the devil should I address the man?) "*Un peu . . . Mais très peu.*"

Another long considering look, cold, appraising but definitely interested in what was, if still an insect, a louse worthy of notice.

Another long and most uncomfortable silence.

"*Vous n'êtes pas un Français, hein?*" murmured the Sultan.

"*Mais non, Altesse.*"

"*Donc . . . ?*"

"*Je suis Anglais.*"

Watching the man's face as though my life depended on it, I could see no change, no gleam of surprise in his eye, and I somehow gathered the impression that this was not news to him, that he had understood me, or at any rate recognized the language, when I spoke to him in English, in answer to his Arabic.

"*Vous êtes Anglais? . . . Eh bien . . . Anglais!*"

Another silence.

"*Soldat?*"

"*Oui, Excellence . . . Aussi, autrefois . . .*"

"*Officier?*" interrupted the cold quiet voice.

"*Mais non. Simple soldat.*"

"*Ah! À pied ou à cheval?*"

"*A cheval.*"

"*Regiment?*"

"*Corps du Garde du Roi Anglais.*"

"*Ah! Et apres? Légion Étrangère Française, sans doûte. Transfuge.*"

And the voice was definitely unpleasant, sneering.

"*Mais non, pas du tout. J'étais soldat Anglais et jadis j'était marin.*"

"*Officier?*"

"*Cadet.*"

There was no point in mentioning, even if my French ran to it, that I had made a three-year voyage as Apprentice and finished it as acting Captain of the ship.

The Sultan again studied me long and thoughtfully while I endeavoured to return look for look, as man to man, without staring him out. I did my best to suggest neither fear nor defiance.

Again breaking a long silence, he questioned me as to how I came to fall into the hands of the people who sold me to Ali bin Ahmed, how I came to be in Africa at all; and generally on the subject of my personal history, experience, social origins and general background.

Having found out all he wanted to know, or as much as I, in my halting French, could tell him, he suddenly lost interest.

"I will decide what to do with you later," I understood him to say, "but your fate will be to some extent in your own hands. I don't like spies, and I don't think spies like the fate I apportion them.

"What's that? 'You are not a spy'? Huh! They all say that."

"Ali bin Ahmed can prove it. He bought me in the market-place and brought me here himself."

"How do I know that; and how do I know that Ali bin Ahmed is not himself a spy?"

This was a question to which I could give no answer. Presumably the Sultan knew more about Ali bin Ahmed than I did.

Having concluded the interview, by giving one of the stalwart body-guard who stood behind his divan, the order for my removal, he again addressed me with the enigmatic perturbing remark,

"Meanwhile consider the desirability of embracing the Mahommedan religion. Your doing so might weigh with me, and favourably affect your end—though it might not save your life."

By comparison with my recent state I was now well-treated and, short of deprivation of liberty and the infliction of mental cruelty to the extent of being kept in ignorance of the fate in store for me, suffered little hardship. I received neither blows nor insults, had a sufficiency of reasonably good food, a corner of a tent in which to sleep, the clothing of an ordinary Arab of humble station, and was given no particularly rough, hard or heavy work.

The tent in which I was confined was another very big one, some thirty feet by twenty, and twelve feet in height. It was a combined guard-room and general store for rations, chiefly barley, bread and ammunition. Of the guard of a dozen men, no more than six were ever absent from it at one time, night or day, and escape from it was impossible.

Next to it was the Sultan's kitchen-tent, where cookery was almost continually in progress, and whence fragrant smells perpetually tantalized me. As I said before, I am a fine trencherman.

Behind this kitchen-tent, a hundred picked baggage-camels were parked, these being the food and water transport, and, on the march, heavily laden with sacks of barley and the unattractive biscuits, appearing to be composed largely of straw, husks, and dust, which were the soldiers' chief food.

On the other side of this great tent was another huge one, the Quarter-master's, almost completely filled with every kind of military stores, clothing and provisions, particularly the precious butter and oil.

Round about these tents was a broad circular ride, an open space on which was nothing save the Sultan's own horse-lines where always stood ten or a dozen horses ready for immediate use, whether by himself, his officers or swift messengers.

His own tent stood in the exact centre, and from it a wide straight road ran out to the distant edge of the camp, an avenue commanded by a gun. Though fairly ignorant on the subject of artillery, I could see that this muzzle-loading weapon was probably more ornamental than useful, more minatory than dangerous.

Behind the Sultan's tent was that of his own personal bodyguard. Behind that again was a big one accommodating the muleteers responsible for the transport of his private baggage, and close to that tent were the mule-lines.

In a great circle about this centre of the camp the tents of the cavalry were pitched. Each tent accommodated from a dozen to a score of troopers, and each had its own horse-lines, wherein from ten to twenty horses were tethered, and hobbled about the fore-feet.

In another great circle about the cavalry tents, and divided from them by a similar broad ride, were the tents of the infantry battalions.

In an enclosure near the camel-lines was a flock of sheep and goats, one animal being given to each tent every Friday—the Mohammedan Sabbath.

In addition to this meat and the biscuits, the soldiers got an evening meal of boiled barley. Only officers and officials got *cous-coussu*.

I was greatly surprised that in so huge and close-packed a camp, containing upwards of a couple of thousand men and hundreds and hundreds of camels, horses, mules, asses, sheep and goats, there was not more filth, refuse, dirt and stench. In point of fact, the whole camp was not only clean and tidy but amazingly free from smells.

It was obvious that, whatever the march and drill discipline of the troops might be, camp discipline was remarkably good.

The Sultan's cavalry were very smartly turned out, in a red zouave jacket, very baggy red trousers, blue *haik* and *burnous*, red turban and strong heavy-heeled slippers or shoes, to which were attached long ugly spike spurs. They were armed with rifle and sword, ammunition being carried in a cartridge-box slung over the shoulder. The horses were as smartly turned out as the men, the big wooden saddles, with their enormously high pommel and crupper, being covered with Morocco leather. Doubtless such saddles are a great aid to feats of freak horsemanship, but personally I far prefer the plain European leather hunting-saddle.

To my British Cavalry eye, the stirrup-leathers were ridiculously short and the stirrups absurdly large. Under the heavy saddle were great brilliantly-coloured horse-blankets, but although these were folded to a considerable thickness, I noticed that the great majority of the horses were badly galled, many of their backs being a disgraceful sight.

I thought of "Stables" in a British cavalry regiment, as I observed that the only idea these warriors had of grooming, was to throw a bucket of water over the horse when he was taken to drink, once daily at sunset. The water and a measure of barley was all the horse got, save what he could pick up.

I was not surprised to learn, later, that the working life of these beautiful Arabs was only from five to six years. Whatever kind of soldiers they might be, and however fine was their horsemanship, as horse-masters these troopers made my blood boil.

For the infantry I had nothing but praise. They were really good, and I was astonished at the steadiness of their drill, the cleanliness of their turn-out, and the smartness of their bearing. What they were like in battle I didn't know, but in camp they were second to none. Their uniform consisted of a kind of woollen jersey or sweater, darkish trousers cut like those worn by the cavalry, a curious black coat with hood attached, and strong heeled slippers. They carried rifles and cartridge-belts and a long knife which I noticed could not be used as a bayonet. Presumably, their Commandant knew what was best for them when it came to hand-to-hand fighting.

They had a band, and that band played three times a day outside the Sultan's tent, from which I concluded that he had a strong ear for music, if not a good one. The band had four tunes, and it played those four tunes regularly, relentlessly, one after the other, always in the same order. Their instruments consisted of tambourines beaten with a stick, tom-toms, oboes, *raitas* and *derbukhas*.

My chief complaint, beyond that of all prisoners and captives, was lack of privacy and absence of companionship of anyone who spoke my own language. I suffered neither bonds nor imprisonment and was free within the limits of the vast camp; free save for the invisible chain which for ever bound me to unobtrusive but ever-present gaolers, out of whose sight I found it wholly impossible to roam. Their ineluctable presence did little, however, to spoil my absorbing interest in the, to me, amazing life of this ephemeral city of tents, huts and reed-mat enclosures, a city around and about which encamped an absolute army of troops—at least a regiment of cavalry, a camel-corps, and battalions of rifle-armed infantry.

A few mornings after my arrival I was awakened before sunrise by one of the guards in charge of me, and bidden, by signs, to arise, array myself, and come forth from the guard-tent in which I lived.

It was with some uneasiness that I noted the fact that the squad encompassed me about in military formation, a man walking on either side of me, two in front and two behind, the party being led by the corporal or *chaous* or whatever he was.

Through the camp we marched, to where, on a biggish knoll, mound, hillock, or it may have been a rock, stood, black against the rising sun—a gallows . . . an unmistakable obvious nice Christian gallows, erected for the hanging of men. From it to the ground hung a rope, and, some five feet above the ground, dangled a noose at the other end of that rope. By the gallows, in a large hollow square stood a battalion of Arab soldiers, while behind them thronged people, soldiers in mufti and others, assembled to enjoy the spectacle.

As our little party approached, down the main street of the camp, my mouth went dry and my heart thumped painfully. Was this the end of Sinclair Noel Brodie Dysart, and had he amazingly escaped the perils of the sea, including mutiny and attempted murder, to die thus here, somewhere in the desert of the Sahara?

I was frightened, indignant, angry, and curiously conscious of a sense of bitter disappointment in the Sultan Mahommed el Kebir.

I had thought better of him.

Suddenly the Corporal grunted an order. The men beside me seized my arms, and the party halted. Each one of my seven guards—Nubians, by the way—was even bigger, and probably stronger, than I; and, just as I had made up my mind that, nevertheless, I would put up a fight for it, a wretched creature, his arms bound to his sides, appeared over the other side of the knoll, led by a guard somewhat similar to my own, and was halted beneath the gallows.

Promptly a man placed the noose about his neck. Having settled it to his (own) liking, he hauled, and the jerking twisting body of the prisoner rose from the ground until the head was a few inches from the top of the gallows. There he hung, jerked and gyrated, while I, (I believe) suffered every pang that was his.

When at length the body hung motionless, our Corporal gave

an order, the guard turned about, turning me with them, and we marched back to the tent, where I sat me down, sick, sorry and shaken.

Why had I been taken at break of day, at vitality's low ebb, to behold this murder? A foretaste, a promise, a warning, a threat?

That same day, and if I remember rightly, that same morning, I was again brought before el Sidna el Sultan Mahommed el Kebir—the sight that I had witnessed still before my eyes.

Again that silent stare, cold, appraising and very daunting; and thereafter I was subjected to a prolonged examination, searching, probing, relentless.

I answered all questions promptly, simply and truthfully, believing that there is no guile, no diplomacy, no *finesse* so baffling as the simple truth.

At the end of the interview the Sultan regarded me for a time in silence.

"You saw a man hanged this morning," he said in his slightly difficult bookish French, richer, I thought, in errors than in idioms. "The dog lied to me, endeavoured to deceive me. No man does that, and lives."

"Take him away," he added.

I was taken away, but was brought back again that same evening. This time there was a difference.

A group of remarkable, almost naked, negroes, if possible bigger and more powerful-looking than the members of the body-guard, stood about a brazier of charcoal in which were stuck various suggestive-looking wooden-handled iron instruments. In the hands of one of these men was a coil of strong cord, either of plaited leather or of greased fibre. Another stalwart bore what was obviously an executioner's sword. A third fondled a knife, razor-edged and needle-pointed. These men eyed me speculatively, the body-guard with interest, the Sultan with cold anger.

"Ali bin Ahmed has confessed," he said at length, his voice quiet and cruel.

Again I decided to show a bold front, and pretend to an ease and courage that I was far from feeling.

"Has he, your Highness? What's he been up to?"

"Oh, you take that line, do you? Well . . . use your tongue freely while you've got it."

I had a sensation of goose-flesh, a little chill down the spine. Had I misjudged my man? '*While I'd still got it,*' eh? Evidently Ali bin Ahmed had not lost his tongue . . . or had he—afterwards? And what had he confessed? Under torture people would say anything. Some people. Most people, in fact. Had Ali bin Ahmed invented some tale—any tale, if only his torturers would stop? He couldn't possibly have really thought I was a spy, inasmuch as he had seen me exposed for sale, and had bought me—like a mutton-chop from a butcher's stall. But of course, for all he knew, I might have been a spy, captured about my nefarious business by the Nomads who sold me to the village headman from whom he bought me. Yes, for all he knew, I was a spy—and naturally he'd say I was, if saying so would save his skin.

"Well, are you going to follow the excellent example of Ali bin Ahmed? Are you going to confess freely; confess under torture; or remain silent—and be executed on suspicion?"

Which was I going to do? Suppose I fully, freely and loudly proclaimed that I was a spy. Would that save me from torture? Yes, but it would seal my death-warrant. Out of my own mouth I should be convicted.

Well, better be executed neat, than with trimmings. Better be hanged out of hand, than tortured and hanged.

"Well, do you confess that you are a spy?"

"I am not a spy."

"Let me see, what was your story, again?"

"I am an English sailor. I was engaged in bringing rifles to the Kaid of Tezedelt, a Sultan, I believe, like yourself; a very old man and a patriot, defending his country against invasion. While waiting for his caravan to arrive and take delivery of the rifles, I was captured on the beach, taken into the interior, and sold to the headman of a village, who again sold me to Ali bin Ahmed. And that is the simple truth."

"*Peut-être*. I have heard the 'simple truth' from *salauds* like you before. We almost invariably induce them to sing a different song. My people are rather good—inducers."

"That's the truth, if you want it," I replied. "If you got anything out of me under torture, it would not be the truth."

"We'll risk it! We'll risk it! . . . Anyhow, we will hear the other song. Are you aware of the interesting fact that birds sing better when blinded?"

To this I made no reply, perhaps because my tongue was too dry and I found some difficulty in swallowing.

"And, if you weren't aware of that interesting phenomenon, you may accept my word for it that spies generally abandon their honourable trade when they can no longer walk, speak, see or hear.

"No," mused the Sultan in his cold quiet voice, a voice I now found deadly cruel, "I doubt if even the great French nation could find much use for a spy who had no eyes with which to see, no ears with which to hear, no tongue with which to report—what he'd neither seen nor heard; no feet with which to walk, no hands with which to receive his pittance . . .

"*Stretch out your right hand.*"

I was surprised to find myself obeying. Probably subconsciously, I knew that it would only be the worse for me did I not.

"Mahmoud . . ." and the Sultan glanced at the man who held a tremendous scimitar.

Stepping forth, the negro seized my out-stretched hand, opened it and turned it palm uppermost.

Across my wrist he laid the razor-edge of the sword, measured his distance and raised the shining blade high above his head, and back behind his right shoulder.

I had scarcely time to tremble, shudder, grow faint. I think I concentrated, in the second that elapsed, on making certain that I could snatch away my hand as the blade fell. I had had a certain amount of practice in that art when the threatening weapon was a cane.

"Do you confess that you are a spy?"

"I will confess anything you like, but the fact remains that I am not one."

"Ah, indeed! But that won't do . . . Hassan, Ibrahim . . ."

The man who held the cord, and the knife-expert, flung themselves upon me, each seizing an arm while another, grasping me about the knees, brought me to the ground.

To struggle was useless, foolish, and could do nothing for me but make matters worse. While three of these giants sat themselves on my chest and stomach, a fourth sat upon my knees while the executioner, kneeling beside him, fumbled and prodded at my bare legs just above the instep. Having satisfied himself as to the exact spot, he marked it with his thumb-nail, arose and drew the edge of his sword across the place.

Was he such an expert that he could sever both feet at the ankle joint with a single stroke?

"Will you confess that you are a spy?" came the soft impersonal voice again.

"Certainly. Anything you like," I assured him, "if it will save trouble—to me."

"No, that won't do, either. I want full confession with details. And details that agree with those given by Ali bin Ahmed."

A brief order in Arabic, and the man in charge of the brazier drew from it one of the wooden-handled instruments, a thing somewhat resembling a huge two-pronged fork, the prongs being some two inches apart and red hot.

Coming behind me as I lay upon the ground, this man knelt, placed his left fore-arm and all his weight upon my head, and the glowing points of the instrument within a few inches of my eyes.

"Now then," said the Sultan. "Speak the truth and the whole truth, or you will never spy again. You'll spy nothing, in fact. And if that doesn't make you find your tongue, I'll find it for you, and when I find it you will lose it. . . . Are you a spy?"

"Yes . . . I'm anything you like."

A word in Arabic and the glowing points came closer to my eyes.

"Are you a spy?"

"Yes . . . Yes . . . Yes . . ."

I could scarcely utter the words. For though my tongue did not cleave to the roof of my mouth as tongues are said to do, it was dry. My throat was dry and swollen and I could scarcely speak for terror.

"Ah! That's a little better. Now we'll have the whole story out of you before your tongue is cut out—unless you decide to have your tongue cut out first. Otherwise—you make up your mind to tell me everything, or to share the fate of the man you saw hanged yesterday.

"Take him away."

§2

It will be believed that I slept but little that night.

I was terrified, horrified, frightened to death, and yet with a curiously persistent feeling, a kind of sub-conscious idea, that there was a catch somewhere; a faint shadow of a possibility that things were not as bad as undoubtedly they seemed; a ghost of a little chance that there might be at any rate an element of grim jest somewhere in this tragic horror. Or else, why had my hand not been hacked off? My feet? Why had I not been blinded, to make me speak?

The answer was, perhaps, that I was being reserved whole and hale and hearty, full of life and strength and the unimpaired power to suffer—for some terrible and final torture, if the Sultan decided that I really was a spy and one endowed with a sufficient courage to carry him in silence to his dreadful end. But somehow I did not think so, for I was inclined to bank on my intuition and my ability correctly to read faces and assess character.

This man was not a brute.

Who could he be, this amazing ruler who, I felt certain, was a European; and who spoke French? He might of course be an Arab or an Egyptian, or, again, a Syrian.

Yes, did not the great Abd-el-Kader, the patriot who for so long defied, fought, and at times defeated, the French, go eventually to Egypt, and his son to Syria? Might not this Sultan be the son of Abd-el-Kader, whom the Arabs of North West Africa almost worshipped, regarding him as the Saxons did Hereward the Wake and the Scots did William Wallace and Robert Bruce?

And then another idea occurred to me. I had recently read in the papers of the amazing Voulet-Chanoine affair, of how two French officers of approved service and excellent record had, when entrusted with a desert column, renounced their country, thrown off their allegiance, turned their arms against France herself, and endeavoured to set up an Empire of the Sahara.

According to some accounts, both were killed by a pursuing column sent to put an end to their amazing activities and to their mushroom "empire". According to others, one of them, Captain Chanoine, had escaped with part of his force, and had become, if not exactly Emperor of the Sahara, a person of importance and power in the great hinterland that lay between Algeria and Central Africa. One story said that he was the mysterious Great White Sheik concerning whom many travellers' tales were told. Could this be he, this desert potentate to whom his followers referred as el Sidna el Sultan Mahommed el Kebir?

That would be a solution of the problem and I was strongly inclined to accept it—until I remembered that his French was not fluent, that, even to my ignorance it was, at times, palpably faulty, and that when speaking French he evidently was not talking his own language.

And that brought me back to the probability that he was an Arab after all. Quite possibly an Abd-el-Kader from Egypt or Syria where, of course, he would learn French.

And what did he intend to do with me? I felt quite sure that he would not merely murder me, much less torture me to death, as the average Bedou or Targui would have done, merely because I was a dog of an Infidel.

On the other hand, if for some reason he was suspicious of Ali bin Ahmed who had brought me to him, and decided that I was a spy, I should share the fate of the man whose body yet hung from the gallows.

A man in such a position as his would live in an atmosphere of suspicion and distrust.

If he were a European he would fear all Arab potentates who were not of the people whom he ruled, and a great many of those who were.

If he were an Arab, he would fear the French, the mighty Power slowly but surely spreading ruthlessly, remorselessly and relentlessly over Northern Africa, East, West and South. Like a cloud no bigger than a man's hand they had arisen from the sea at Algiers, and year by year the cloud had swiftly expanded. From its foothold in the city of Algiers, French dominion had grown ever greater and wider, until almost it threatened to engulf the Arab world, from Egypt to Morocco, from the Mediterranean to the Niger. . . .

And even when the Sultan considered the fact that my French was no better than his own, he would realize that I might be playing a part, that my halting French was part of my disguise. Any Frenchman, who was worth his salt in the Secret Service, could speak with an English or German accent, pretend to fumble for his words, and use idioms unknown in France.

On the other hand, of course, the Sultan himself might be playing a part. He might be Chanoine himself pretending he knew but little French.

Anyhow, I was infinitely better off than I had been in the hands of my first captors, far better off than I had been in the hands of Ali bin Ahmed; and, though a prisoner in danger of torture or death, and in certainty of a prolonged captivity, my position was not desperate. While there's life there's hope; and indeed I had many good reasons for hope. Chief of them was my feeling that, though this man had as much unlimited and untrammelled power over me as the urchin has over the mouse that he has trapped; and cold, hard, remorseless as he might be, he was no mere savage ruffian and brute rejoicing in cruelty for the sake of cruelty.

Besides, I argued, once he realizes that I am not a spy, surely he could make me extremely useful? And, sanguine ever, I at once had visions of myself becoming another Kaid MacLean, the great Scot who rose from Drill-Sergeant to Commander-in-Chief and Prime Minister to the Sultan of Morocco.

These wild fancies, too foolish to be hopes, unsubstantial fabric of a dream, ended abruptly next day. The Sultan sent for me; my warders conducted me to the great marquee, and handed me over to two of the giants of the body-guard.

Once again the uncomfortable disturbing silence, the cold baleful searching stare, the sudden questions:

"You still maintain that you are English?"

"That you have never served in the French Foreign Legion?"

"Nor served France in any other capacity? . . ."

"Have you ever lived in France? . . ."

"Have you ever been in Africa before? . . ."

"Do you still wish to call yourself a Christian? . . ."

"Very well. Now then, are you prepared to renounce such Christianity as you profess, and embrace the Mahommedan religion?

"Oh, you require time to think it over, do you? You shall have to-night, and give me your answer to-morrow.

"What, not to save your life? It's a matter of life and death remember . . ."

"Take him away."

§3

And not for a week did I again see the Sultan, and never again did I hear the word 'spy' upon his lips; my spiritual condition and beliefs remaining his pre-occupation, as, to my amazement, I discovered when next he sent for me.

There is no need to detail his harangue or our conversation, but, in short, he offered me my life in return for my publicly embracing Mahommedanism.

If I wished to live, I must become a Mussulman.

Whatever doubt there might be in his mind as to the truth of my story, there was no room for any as to my being an Infidel, inasmuch as I admitted and proclaimed the fact.

Naturally, I listened to all the Sultan had to say, in humble and respectful silence, and used what tact—and French—I possessed, in answering his questions as to what sort of Christian I was, and why I should prefer to remain one for the very brief span of life that would be left me in the event of my doing so.

And suddenly, like a bolt from the blue, came one of the surprises of my life.

Having, in slightly laborious French, praised Allah, Mahommed and the Mussulman religion; without pause or change of voice he said, in colloquial English and with a very good English accent and intonation,

"Which years were you at Sandhurst? Must have been about

my time. Or no—you'd be after me."

To say I was struck speechless is no exaggeration.

I had been right. The French-speaking el Sidna el Sultan Mahommed el Kebir was a European. And what was more, he was some sort of a Briton—pure-bred or otherwise. . . .

"You are English!" I gasped.

"Sounds like it, my lad, doesn't it?" was the reply.

"Then you are a Christian yourself . . . Sir."

"Not a bit of it. You jump to conclusions, ingenuous youth. First, because I speak English almost as well as you do—and thank God, you speak it admirably,—you assume that I am English. And then you take it for granted that, if I am English, I must be a Christian. . . . Well—I am a Mussulman. I worship Allah the Merciful, the Compassionate, and am a follower of Mahommed his Prophet, on Whom be Peace.

"Yes, get that right into the middle of your head; grasp it firmly; and keep it clearly in view. I am a Mahommedan . . . and you've got to be one too, if you wish to live. Meanwhile you haven't answered my question about Sandhurst."

"I never was at Sandhurst," I replied.

"Sure you weren't kicked out?"

"Quite sure."

"Failed to get in?"

"No. In point of fact, I was intended—by my father—for the Navy. He died just before I should have gone to Osborne, and I went into the Merchant Service. I did a three-year voyage as an Apprentice on a sailing-ship, and that sickened me of the sea—for the time being, at any rate. Being fit for nothing else, I wanted some sort of an active out-door life, and thought about Colonial Police Forces. Being nothing but a sailor and unqualified for the other sort of thing, I thought I'd learn soldiering, and I enlisted in the Life Guards to learn to ride and shoot . . . Drill and discipline and all that . . . After a couple of years or so, this gun-running adventure offered itself and I bought myself out.

"I was to be both sailor and soldier, helping to handle the gun-running ship at one end of the journey, and the guns at the other. Teach our customers how to use them, they not being accustomed to magazine rifles and machine-guns. My friend and I rather had the idea of trying our luck as Army Instructors to these people and . . ."

"Well, you fool," interrupted the Sultan. "Don't you see the chance you've got now? By Allah—you were absolutely guided here."

"Rough guides," I grinned.

"Guided here, I said, and here's your chance—and a thousand times better one. Now what about Army Instructor here, and rising to something worth while—provided you turn Mussulman?"

"No," I said. "Absolutely not. Anything in that line, I can do without changing my religion."

"Oh, take him away," growled the Sultan and added something in Arabic—and the faint suggestion of a ghost of a smile that had played about his eyes and lips changed and vanished, leaving his face as hard, cold, passionless and ruthless as before.

CHAPTER XII

A week later. . . .

The Sultan Mahommed el Kebir, motionless as a rock, upon his mound of mattresses and cushions, eyed me, long and thoughtfully. I returned his stare and imitated his silent immobility.

"Well?" he said, at length, in good English. "What is it to be? Death or—Allah? Are you going to be the Last Christian Martyr; or save your soul—and your hide?"

"I shan't change my religion," I replied.

"Wish to die for it?"

"Not a bit."

"Then why do so? Why not change? Probably you never gave a thought to your religion until I gave a thought to it for you. Did you, now . . . ? Why not change then?"

"I don't really know . . . I hate change—and I hate interference with my private affairs. Besides, I haven't the courage. That's the real reason, I think."

"Haven't the courage? What d'you mean? I should have thought it was the other way about—that you wouldn't have the courage to die a hideous death for it. A hideous ugly death—in private. No *réclame*, applause, approval, the sympathetic tears of admiring crowds, and all that. You won't get a head-line in the British, American or Continental papers, *Heroic Death of Intrepid Explorer. Martyr to his Faith. Briton suffers torture for his Religion.* Not a dozen people will ever know of your sad end—in this tent—and they'll be Arabs . . . and delighted. No-one but me will know why you died. . . . What d'you mean—'haven't the courage'?"

"What I say. Life wouldn't be worth living, and I haven't the pluck to face it. I should be annoyed—and ashamed of myself—for the rest of my days. Give me indigestion probably; and I might 'go all morbid', brooding on it."

"Yes . . . I see," mused the Sultan. "Well—you're honest. Or are you? . . . Anyhow, I prefer it to your striking an attitude, whether moral or religious. It won't save you though. It's death or Allah, all-right. . . . Screw up your courage and—come over. Deny Christ and abjure Christianity, in return for life, joy, adventure, a career . . . happiness. . . . What about it?"

"No. It would be known, sooner or later, in England. I should be a bit of a pariah. There are one or two people whom I shouldn't care to face, if it got about. I shouldn't have the courage to go Home—as the man who ratted to save his life. Converts are one thing—perverts are another."

"Well, personally I'm an honest spontaneous convinced Mussulman, for Mahommedanism is the best and greatest religion in the world. It's a man's religion; a fighting religion. No turning of the other cheek. No loving thy beastly neighbour as thyself. No *'blessed are the meek'*, *'the poor in spirit'*, *'the peacemakers'* . . ."

"Nor *'the pure in heart'* and *'the merciful'*," I observed.

The White Sultan fell silent.

"From my youth," he said suddenly, "from the days when I was old enough to think about such matters at all, I rejected the 'Pale Galilean' wishy-wash. . . . How could I admire and accept a kind of Mild Curate of a Christ when my earthly gods were heroes, brave men, real men—men like Saladin—and Vikings, Danes, Norman Knights, Crusaders, Red Indians, soldiers, sailors, adventurers. Where was Gentle Jesus beside the Heroes of India, Persia, Arabia; the Heroes of Greece and Rome; Alfred the Great, Hereward the Wake, the Scottish Chiefs, Richard the Lion Heart, Drake, Raleigh. . . . Had I not been brought up a Mahommedan, my Gods would have been The Red Gods of War; and Thor and Odin and the Great White Spirit of the Happy Hunting Grounds . . . Imagine giving a boy of any one of the world's fighting races this Gentle Jesus Meek and Mild—when every such boy loathes, detests and despises 'turning the other cheek' meekness and mildness, the accepting of blows and being spat upon . . . Cowardice . . . Why, I sympathize with the Wandering Jew and swear I'd have done the same as he did. So'd nine men out of ten. . . . No. Mahommedanism is a man's religion—and the finest religion."

"It may be," I agreed. "But incidentally I have yet to hear of a braver man than Jesus Christ. Christianity is a brave man's religion—but not a bully's. . . . No. I prefer my own religion—chiefly, I expect, because it is my own. Just as I prefer my own country. There may be better ones—but I prefer my own country. Same with my faith."

"Enough to die for it, eh? Well, well! *Chacun a son gout.*"

"Why d'you want to kill me? What does it matter to you what I believe, or don't believe?"

"Nothing, really. I don't give a tuppenny damn what you

believe—but I can't afford to favour *mlecchas*, unclean infidel dogs—now, and here. It would look as though my own Faith were not too fiercely and fanatically fervent. . . . Sad that you should lose your young life—but your loss will be my gain. I shall gain in prestige and popularity, increased odour of sanctity and virtue. Show forth good works and acquire merit in the sight of Allah and my people, by killing a foul Infidel, an Unbeliever abhorrent to the One True God. So you've got to adopt and profess Allah and Mahommet, His Prophet, or go to your own Hell. You've got to do it publicly too; and be received in the Mosque before the assembled *aalimin*, *marabouts*, *imams*, *shereefs*, *dervishes*, and all the congregation of the Faithful."

"Why?"

"To my greater honour and glory; to give me a sound hold on you; to make you useful to me—and to save your life. . . . You see, if you embrace the One True Faith, and become a genuine professing Mussulman, I can make you my personal servant without losing prestige; I can keep you about me, and—what I particularly have in mind—can take you with me to Mecca. I must perform the Pilgrimage and become a *hadji* some day, finally to set the seal upon my Faith; solidify my position once and for all; set the crown upon my work. . . . D'you know what I want and need more than anything—more than a caravan laden with gold? I want and need someone whom I can absolutely trust. Someone upon whom I can rely completely. Someone in whose loyalty and honesty I can have perfect faith. . . . Well—that man must be a white man and he's got to be a Mussulman—so that I can trust him and my people can accept him. Yes—so that not only can I place implicit reliance on him, but my civil and military *entourage* accept him as a co-religionist, my soldiers follow him as they would one of their tribal leaders. . . . They never really trust an Infidel you know. '*How can any undertaking succeed in the hands of an Un-believer—an enemy of God*'? . . . Look here—turn Mussulman and you might rise to be my Wazir or my Commander-in-Chief, or both. You have the ability. You can make the public protestation of Faith, go through the ceremonies of initiation, make the Pilgrimage with me—and still remain Christian if you feel that way. Say the same old prayers, and explain to your Christ that you only did this to save your life. . . . Well?"

"No. I'm not brave enough," I said.

"You really mean it? You would rather die?"

"I think so. . . . Hope so. . . ."

"Well—I'm sorry. You could have been very useful to me. And

have done yourself some good too. . . . So be it. . . . Would you rather have it *à la carte* and be hanged, carefully, after some very assorted tortures, or have our more usual *table d'hôte* bill of fare? The ordinary *plat du jour* is to have the hands and feet hacked off and then a little bon-fire is lighted over you. It's a toss-up whether you bleed, or burn, to death. Neither seems to be enjoyed—by the victim—and both seem to last about the same length of time . . . Think it over—till sun-rise to-morrow."

I did think it over; and the more I thought, the less I feared, the less I believed the Sultan's blood-curdling threats. Once again I assured myself, the man was no cruel Oriental potentate, blood-thirsty and brutish. He was a white man, almost certainly some kind of an Englishman. Nor, unless my intuition and study of physiognomy were grievously at fault, was the man a weakling of the type that is driven to cruelty through fear.

And if he were, what had he to fear from me? Judging by the patent and obvious evidence, he was an arbitrary ruler, of unbounded unlimited power, to whom his troops, *entourage* and followers rendered absolute obedience.

Of course he wouldn't enforce a choice that he described as "death or Allah." What was far more likely was a choice between welfare and Allah.

What an amazing history he must have. How on earth had he arrived at such a position? One had heard of such things before, of course, and had known that there were authentic cases of Europeans becoming "Arab" Sheiks, Kaids, Emirs, Sultans and Rulers; men of the type of Sir Richard Burton, Sir Harry MacLean, General Gordon, Slatin Pasha, Captain Chanoine, and several French soldiers who, whether one called them renegades or adventurers, were undeniably brave and able men.

Likely enough that such a renegade would condemn a compatriot to death, if he considered his death necessary or even advantageous. But surely there was no necessity and but little advantage, in this case.

No. I was not convinced, and not badly frightened. In point of fact, I was rather hopeful. What a magnificent thing for me, what a splendid adventure, if only he would drop this conversion business, take me whole-heartedly into his confidence and give me a chance to show what I could do in his service. I could certainly do something with his cavalry, for a start, since as I had already noted, although their horsemanship might be beyond compare and above criticism, their drill was certainly beyond compare and beneath contempt.

Anyhow, whether it affected my fortunes or not, I would stick to my religion, if only out of stubbornness and because it was my religion.

CHAPTER XIII

But on the subject of my being a Christian, as on that of my being a spy, I heard not another word from the Sultan.

For a time, thereafter, his conduct as regarded myself caused me no little puzzlement. Until enlightenment came, it seemed to me that he was indulging in a somewhat childish game of cat-and-mouse.

After ignoring my existence for a time, a period during which I was a fairly-well-treated prisoner, with little of which to complain save constant surveillance and confinement to the camp, the Sultan sent for me one evening. As usual, he regarded me long and thoughtfully before speaking. Suddenly he shot a question at me in English.

"Any good at figures? Know anything about accountancy, book-keeping, banking, actuary's work, the higher or lower mathematics—that sort of thing? Never had any ambition to be Chancellor of the Exchequer, I suppose?"

"No, I'm afraid not, Sir," I replied.

"Well, I suppose you can count?"

"Oh, yes."

"Well, you're going to spend the night counting. If you can't do anything more, you can do that—put down totals and add them up, I suppose?"

"I suppose so. . . . Yes. . . ."

"Well, I hope so . . . for your sake. And I hope you know what work means. For you are going to work all night . . . or will do so if you are wise. I'm going to let you loose in the Treasury like a mouse in a cheese, and you are going to count the contents of quite a number of fair-sized sacks—sacks of gold. Gold coins.

"In point of fact, you won't have to do any mathematical feats beyond counting and adding up. You needn't worry about values of Maria Theresa dollars, *majediehs*, *moussounés*, louis, napoleons, francs, rates of exchange and that sort of thing. As it happens, the gold coins are all of one denomination and I want to know the exact total. Be accurate, because it may be literally a matter of life and death for the Courteous Secretary and the Affable Treasurer of this Golden-Goose-Club. I have wanted a sudden surprise-visit and unexpected-inspection for a long time, but haven't been able to summon up the energy to do it myself.

There will be nobody in the Treasury tent with you, but there will be sentries and a brace of my body-guard outside, so you won't be interfered with by the Chancellor of the Exchequer, who might try to get at you—with a knife or an offer of a share in the loot.

"The guards won't let anyone in. Should anybody burrow in from the back, you'll find they will 'answer to *Hi!* or any loud cry' and your visitor won't get out alive.

"Don't forget that you've got to do the job at a sitting, and you won't come out of the tent until you've done; and as I said, if you are careless . . . or anything . . . the Courteous Secretary and Affable Treasurer will be the losers—by a head.

"Out you go," concluded the Sultan with a curt nod.

This was good. Definitely good. I had a chance to make myself useful, and to show that I could do so.

At some time toward the middle of the night, an Arab of superior rank, accompanied by two enormous Nubians of the body-guard, came to my tent, ordered me out, and led me through the sleeping camp to a tent-walled enclosure around which was camped a company of soldiers. After a slovenly but efficient challenge by a guard, we entered the enclosure to find ourselves in another one, the four sides of which were constantly patrolled by four pairs of sentries.

Another challenge and pass-word, and we entered a second enclosure in which stood a square tent, at the four sides of which stood four more sentries, watched by some sort of an officer.

To him my Arab conductor spoke, and I was shown into the tent and given a bunch of clumsy keys, a reed pen, a brass ink-bottle, some pieces of brownish paper—and was left alone.

The tent, like its surrounding enclosures, was well-lit and I saw that the Treasury consisted of twelve large strong trunks, arranged in a square about the central tent-pole. They appeared to be of native manufacture, and proved to be of very stout hard wood sheeted inside and out with iron. It did not take me long to find the correct key for the first of these that I tackled, and, on opening it, I found it to contain ten small leather sacks, each tied about the neck with a thong, the ends of which were heavily sealed.

I set to work and, thanks to three years of ship-life and watch-keeping, felt no sense of fatigue for the first four hours of my easy monotonous labour. I knew fairly accurately when four hours had passed, but contrived to fight off an inclination to rest, and temptation to sleep.

In time, exactly how long I don't know, I had finished, and had worked with such care that I felt perfectly certain of the accuracy of my total.

But when I had done I was tempted of the Devil. Here was I, absolutely alone, with a very large sum of gold, the exact total of which was admittedly unknown to its owner. Gold will buy camels, food, water; it will hire guides; corrupt guards . . . and is as much the sinews of escape as it is the sinews of war. This man who had bought me like an ox, or accepted me as a gift, who had threatened me with death and torture, and had kept me like a dog chained to a kennel, could hardly complain if I took what steps I could to escape. Even if he knew, that is to say. I could steal . . . no, take . . . a hundred of these gold coins and he be none the wiser.

And if I assessed the total at a hundred less than it actually was, what of the Secretary, the officer in charge of the Treasury, the men responsible to him? Suppose the Sultan knew, as very probably he did, that the total should be about a hundred more than I made it? They'd pay for my theft with the loss of their right hands, according to Arab custom, if not with their lives as well.

No, I couldn't do it.

And, apart from any question of another man suffering for my dishonesty, I somehow felt that I couldn't do it. My argument as to my having a perfect right to use any means in my power for escaping, was all very well, but the fact remained, a fellow-countryman, alone like myself among Arabs, had trusted me. Trusted me with his money, and with a job.

No, of course I couldn't do it.

Having completed my task, I shouted. The Corporal of the Guard entered, and I was conducted back to my tent.

Almost immediately the Sultan sent for me.

"Well?" said he. "Has the Secretary of the Slate Club got away with much? What is the total?"

I told him, and he favoured me with a long appraising stare, but for a time made no comment.

"Absolutely certain?" he said presently.

"Absolutely, Sir," I replied. "You can rely on it that that is the exact total. Neither more nor less."

"H'm. It is, is it?" said the Sultan. "You may go."

§2

Walking about the camp next day, observing what was still to me a show of thrilling interest, I met the Sultan riding in from the desert, followed by a retinue of officials and a troop of cavalry.

Coming to attention, I stood at the salute while he rode by. Halting, he beckoned to me and spoke—in his good idiomatic, but accented, English.

"Will you give me your parole not to attempt to escape?" he said.

"No, Sir," I promptly replied. "I shall escape at the first opportunity."

"You mean you will try to," was the cold reply.

"I do, Sir," I assured him.

"Once again, you are a fool. I was almost tempted for a moment to trust you, though I trust no one at all—and to take your word. You'd have had a very much better time of it, I can assure you . . . I regret having paid you the compliment."

I also was inclined to regret my too impetuous refusal, for I had a foolish feeling that I had rebuffed an overture, refused a friendly gesture.

"Anyway, you'd probably have tried to escape, parole or not."

This annoyed me, and without stopping to reflect how infinitely more important it was that the Sultan should not be annoyed, I promptly contradicted him.

"I should have done nothing of the sort, Sir," I assured him. "If I gave you my parole, I should keep it."

"H'm . . . Perhaps. Well, look here. Will you give me your parole for a period, say a month, new moon to new moon, that you will make no attempt to escape—take no advantage of an opportunity to escape?"

I felt, in a way, that this was generous, kindly almost, and that it was up to me to respond.

"Certainly, Sir. Or three months, or six months, if you like."

"Done," replied the Sultan. "We'll make it so. You won't regret it—and I hope I shan't. I'll take off your guard and give you a tent of your own, near to mine. Also the kit of an Arab of position, and a servant of your own . . . No, he won't be a spy. He will be deaf and dumb, and you will get much the same grub as I do."

"Thank you very much. I . . ."

"One condition. You will learn Arabic. Work at it like the Devil. I'll give you a good man who speaks some French. That will be a great help. Work at it night and day. Work at it until you can pass for an Arab. Then you will be some good to me—if you don't run away."

"I shan't run away, Sir."

"I meant, try to run away. Because if you do that, I shall hang you, and then you'll be no use at all . . ."

I had every reason to be thankful that I had accepted the Sultan's offer and given my parole. Life became definitely better and I had nothing whatsoever of which to complain—save captivity. I was a prisoner in the hands of a man who had complete and untrammelled control of my life and destiny, but save for that, my material circumstances were as good as they had ever been. I had everything but the only thing I wanted—freedom. I had a horse, a tent, a servant, good food and clothing, and much to employ and exercise my mind.

Whenever I could forget that I was as much a captive as a fly in a spider's web or an animal in the Zoo, I was not unhappy. And I worked at Arabic as though my life depended on it—which, indeed, before long, it might very well do.

As a matter of fact, I found it an easy language to learn, and I learned it by the best of all methods, as a living tongue without so much as a mention of the word Grammar. My *munshi*, a portly and comfortable *ekhwan*, was a born teacher and blessed with common sense. He would touch a thing and name it, making me repeat the name after him. When I knew the name of practically every concrete object that I could see, he proceeded to the performance of actions and the provision of the words that named them. Words grew to phrases and phrases to sentences, and I was amazed at the rapidity with which I gained the power to express myself in Arabic.

That we had a common medium in French was, of course, a tremendous help, as I could ask questions and mention difficulties in that tongue, and my teacher could give simple explanations.

I think the Sultan must have offered him some prize or reward if he could produce me as an Arabic scholar within a certain time, for he told me (in French) that His Highness el Sidna el Sultan Mahommed el Kebir was going to give me a test at the end of six months, by himself conversing with me in Arabic; and by making me repeat to him, in my own language, the tales told at an evening's entertainment by the Sultan's own story-teller.

I may here mention that when that day drew near, the wily old gentleman assured me that he had fixed that part of the test, all right. He had squared the story-teller to tell certain tales, and would now proceed to tell them to me, first in careful simple

French and then in careful simple Arabic. Nor could he fathom my folly and stupidity in requesting him to desist and let the test be a fair one.

However, eventually light dawned upon his simple brain, for suddenly he observed,

"Doubtless you are right. The Sultan would be up to that, and order the stories himself, one at a time."

Almost daily I saw the Sultan. I had been on parole for some weeks, and was growing to feel more and more like an Arab and as though I had been bred and born in the desert, when one evening he sent for me.

"I have another job for you," said the Sultan. "You are to go with a small caravan to Ain Boufra, an oasis about a hundred kilometres north west of here. You won't be in charge of it, of course, but you will be in charge of the money I am sending, and of a girl. I am buying some camels and horses. You will be met at Ain Boufra by the man from whom I am getting the cattle, and will hand over the money and the girl to him. She is going to marry his son. I'm sending you because I most particularly want the girl— and her virtue—to arrive safely. '*Clothed and in her right mind. Fragile. This side up. With care*', and all that. You understand? Also the money. I don't think there is any possibility of your being attacked on the way, so there will be no escort, and only you will carry a rifle. No, there is no danger on that score, but I wouldn't put it past the lad at Ain Boufra to try some tricks. He has some marvellous horses and camels, and he is a bit of a wild bird—as much raider as dealer. I don't want to be swindled by him, and have the choice of either 'losing face' or hunting him down and punishing him. I should have to chase him half-way across the Sahara. Nor do I want to show mistrust by sending a strong party to meet him. . . . Well, there you are. See if you can make a job of it."

I was delighted, and most certainly I'd make a job of it.

I was growing to admire the Sultan more and more. It would give me definite pleasure to win his approval, to show him what I could do, and that I was deserving of his trust and confidence.

Incidentally, it would be a most welcome change—as good as going ashore after nine months at sea.

At Ain Boufra I got a surprise . . . The leader of the caravan, one Kassim bin Ibrahim, the Sultan's Chief Courier, chief caravan-leader, Master of the Horse, and general camp Provost-

Marshal, showed himself a complete rascal and a worthy friend of the scoundrel who had come to meet him with a herd of fine camels and a drove of Arab horses. Incidentally the lady who was in my charge proved not only no better than she ought to be, but no better than these two worthies.

The journey to Ain Boufra was uneventful. The girl rode in a *bassoura*, a balloon-like hooped camel-tent, and the money was in a leathern sack strapped to the girth and saddle of my riding-camel.

Arrived at the Ain Boufra oasis, we found that the camel-dealer was before us. After the bustle of making camp, he, Kassim bin Ibrahim the caravan-leader, and I, sat down to a gorge of mutton-stew and *cous-coussu*. While sipping coffee thereafter, the camel-dealer, to my utter amazement, made a most outrageous proposition.

He calmly proposed that I should hand over one half of the purchase-money to him and the other half to Kassim bin Ibrahim, the caravan-leader. Whereat, the latter gentleman nodded his head vigourously in profound approval. Evidently the two knaves were in agreement, and had already laid their plans and hatched their plot.

While I stared in astonishment, scarcely believing my ears or trusting my knowledge of Arabic, the camel-dealer added that he and Kassim bin Ibrahim would also divide the caravan between them. My profit in the matter would be my freedom; for, as they would have to depart promptly from without the sphere of influence of the Sultan's law, they would travel fast and far. I should accompany them, and when they halted in safety they would set me on my way with a guide, camels, food and water!

Was I tempted? I don't really think so. Not really. Not for long, anyhow. Months ago, before I had given my parole, before the conditions of my captivity had improved, this was the sort of chance about which I had dreamed. Perfect, beyond my wildest hopes. Camels, food, water, a guide, Arab clothing, everything calculated to give one fair hope of success. And now I also knew Arabic, and something of the ways of the desert.

Thinking it over, but not toying too much with the idea of seizing the opportunity, I decided that it could be done. That these men could undoubtedly make off, that very night, with the camels, the horses, and the money, and that I could go with them. Naturally, I should not trust them further than I could see them, but I had got the rifle and bandolier of cartridges and they, though armed, had no guns. I had the whip-hand; and, provided I was wary and watchful, I could manage them. Moreover, I could promise them a good reward when I reached safety.

Was I tempted?

Anyway, having heard what the rogue had to say, I sipped my coffee in silence, and then invited Kassim bin Ibrahim to favour me with his opinion of this interesting scheme.

Kassim was all for it. He explained that he had long been discontented with the Sultan's treatment of him, that he had been going to leave his service anyhow, and here was an opportunity for doing it with grace and profit.

He took it for granted that although an Infidel, I was not a fool so afflicted of Allah as to let such a chance slip.

I was not invited to share in the loot—definitely I was not—and therefore should have nothing on my conscience. All I had got to do, was to go while the going was good.

Again I sipped my coffee in silence, not pondering the pros and cons of the proposition, but the best way of dealing with the situation. My rifle was with my saddlebags and rug in the *tente d'abri* pitched for me beneath the palms beside the water; and the dealer's men, not to mention Kassim's, were many.

Another time—if I were to live to see another time—I'd wear my rifle as I would my *kaffieh*, and when I took it from my back I'd lay it across my knees. What a fool I'd been, and how miserably I had failed in my first position of trust. Would the Sultan ever know that I hadn't gone off with his damned caravan-leader and the camel-dealer?

And what of the camel-men of our caravan? Presumably they'd follow Kassim, after being given the choice between a bribe and a slit throat.

Turning to Kassim, stroking my beard and eyeing him thoughtfully, I observed that I had supposed that trusted Arabs were true to their salt, whereat the man threw out open extended palms and shrugged his shoulders. He had eaten of the Sultan's salt, but he had earned it. He had also eaten of blows and curses.

"And doubtless earned them too," I observed.

Another gesture of contemptuous indifference.

To the camel-dealer I observed that the Sultan's arm was long, his horses swift.

"Yes," agreed the dealer. "I sold them to him. I have others swifter."

I reminded him that the Sultan's power was great, his soldiers many, his wrath terrible; and that the proposition was, in short and in Arabic, a mug's game: that it couldn't be done, and that if it could be done, it was not worth the doing. Who but fools would incur the anger, enmity and ultimate inevitable vengeance, of such a man as el Sidna el Sultan Mahommed el Kebir?

Having heard, in courteous silence, all that I had to say, Kassim observed that perhaps I was wise and knew best; perhaps I was a coward and a fool and knew nothing at all; that perhaps the thing could not be done—but nevertheless they were going to do it, and that I could either come with them willingly and helpfully, or stay where I was. But in the latter event I should, of course, stay under the sand.

Things looked bad. If this precious pair really intended to decamp with the money and the caravan, they could do it. I could not stop them. That being the case, should I not be well advised to make the best of a situation that was none of my creating—and for which the Sultan himself was responsible—and escape?

I should benefit neither myself nor the Sultan by attempting to put up a fight against such odds.

I had an idea. I would try a bluff.

"So you really think you could cheat and rob el Sidna el Sultan Mahommed el Kebir, as easily as all that, do you? He's a poor fool, is he not? He's the sort of man that any of his servants can swindle, that any horse-dealer can easily deceive and get the better of, isn't he?"

And again I laughed.

"Yes, he's a fool and you are two very clever men, aren't you?"

And I laughed a third time.

The two clever men eyed me unpleasantly.

"Now, I will tell you something. Something that shows what a silly unsuspecting innocent the Sultan is, and how really cunning and clever you two noble Arabs are. Listen, my wise friends. The Sultan sent after us a troop of the body-guard, to pay us a little surprise visit. If they don't ride in here to-night, it will be because they are picketing the place in a circle, and especially to the north-west.

And again I laughed merrily.

"You will look the clever fellows you are when the troops surround you and catch you with the Sultan's caravan and money, and without me, won't you?"

My hearers eyed me askance, their grave impassive faces immobile and expressionless, though I fancied that the ghost of a smile hovered about the corners of Kassim's eyes, perhaps in acknowledgment of the Sultan's astuteness, as he imagined, or of my own, as probably he preferred to think.

Anyhow, my bluff seemed to have succeeded. No more was said on the subject of trickery and treachery, and the incident seemed to be closed and dismissed by Kassim's profound,

"Kismet! That which is written will come to pass. *Inshallah.*" And the dealer's "We are in the hands of Allah."

Anyway, I thought it a sound plan to see that the rifle was in *my* hands as quickly as possible, and to let it 'come to pass' that I was not caught napping.

I passed a sleepless, anxious, and unhappy night.

Some time in the middle of it, I had one more surprise, and another shock to my ingenuous innocence.

Unheralded by any sound, a white-clad figure materialized before my *tente d'abri*, like a wraith in the light of the late moon.

An assassin? Well, I was ready; and slowly and gently I raised my rifle.

As the figure came closer, I saw it was that of a woman.

It was, indeed, the girl whom, as instructed, I had handed over to the camel-dealer.

Whether this Jezebel was put up to it by that scoundrel, or merely moved by original sin, I did not know, but, with a coy giggle and a whisper, she announced not only that she'd come, but that she proposed to remain.

Summoning my best Arabic and such terms of reproach, contumely, and abuse as seemed to fit the occasion and the sex of the offender, I endeavoured to let her know what I thought of her and her conduct.

This seemed to amuse her. She accepted my pungent rebuke and invective and returned them with interest—very great interest, methought—and I was privileged to hear an Arab lass really let herself go.

And at length she did go, and, in the going, turned, removed her slipper and flung it at my head. This, I believe, is the lowest and worst insult that a lady can offer a recalcitrant, contemptible and unenterprizing male.

CHAPTER XIV

The Sultan received me graciously and bade me tell my story with care, circumstance and detail. I did so, sparing neither Kassim, the camel-dealer, nor the girl.

For the first time, I saw the Sultan really smile, heard him make a sound which might have passed for a laugh.

Thereafter he eyed me thoughtfully.

"Good," he said, at length. "I almost begin to think you'll do. I am tempted to give you a trial, anyhow."

"As what, Sir?"

"As a man whom I can trust as I can trust myself—and a damn sight better, for I can't always do that. If you proved absolutely honest, reliable and trustworthy, I think I should have at least one of the many things I want in this imperfect world. . . . In point of fact I have got nearly everything, really—everything but happiness, that is. . . .

"I wonder if I can trust you."

"Yes," I answered, "you can. I don't say I have any particular ability and should be successful in doing everything that . . ."

"Successful be damned," interrupted the Sultan. "It's not men of ability I lack. It isn't brilliant cleverness and marvellous capability I want. It is honesty. Just common truthfulness . . . honesty . . . reliability."

"Well, I shan't cheat you or let you down—intentionally," I replied. "If it's only honesty you want, I can promise you that much."

"That much! H'm. It's the biggest thing in the world. My world, anyway, because it's the rarest. But I am inclined to try you. You have passed the preliminary examination pretty well. I can give you full marks in that."

"Examination?"

"Yes. You didn't pinch any of my gold in the Treasury."

I eyed the Sultan and concealed my thoughts and feelings.

"I knew to a farthing how much was there, of course, and how much of a temptation it would be to you to pocket enough to get you away from here. That was the first paper."

So that was it, was it?

"And you've done well in the second paper I set you. Quite well. That must have been a real temptation. I don't mind telling you now that Kassim bin Ibrahim had my clear instructions to do all that he did, and that the 'camel-dealer' is Hussein the Brave, my chief scout, spy, and intelligence officer."

I refrained from comment.

"Their story confirms yours in every detail."

"And the Arab girl?" I was moved to enquire.

"A boy, of course. Hussein's son. A splendid young rogue, and a damn fine actor."

"He's certainly that," I agreed, "and I'll break . . ."

"You'll break nothing. He did as I told him. And so will you, if you're wise. Now you'll go and sulk in your tent, like Ajax, was it?—and feel very hurt and sore. Well, you'll get over that, and you'll feel sorer before you've done, for I shall have some more tests for you. But, by Allah, if you come through all-right and I decide that I can trust you, I will trust you as . . . as . . . few men trust their wives. I will make you my personal and absolutely confidential secretary and friend; consult you on everything, have not a single secret from you; make you my confidant, and my—brother. By Allah, you'd save me from madness. . . . This loneliness . . . I'll do it, and if you've any military gift beyond the drill-sergeant's, the instructor's, I'll make you an officer. Make you my Commander-in-Chief, some day. . . . And if you've any administrative ability and power to handle men, I'll give you your chance. You could rise to be my Vizier.

"Anyhow, I'll push you as high as I can on the military, or civil, side—or both. And I'll take a risk from now. I *will* trust you. . . . And by the Ninety and Nine Sacred Names of Allah, I solemnly swear that if you cheat me, Dysart, I'll shoot you myself—or hand you over to the torturers."

"I shall not cheat you, Sir," I said.

"I hope you won't, for your sake . . . and mine."

"But I may fail you through inability, stupidity. . . ."

The Sultan waved this aside.

"All I ask is honesty, truth, reliability, loyalty—that's all. I merely ask the biggest thing in the world, I ask for a thing I have never yet found."

"And suppose someone comes to you with a false tale about me?"

"It will be the last tale he'll tell," was the grim reply. "I have made up my mind I'm going to trust you—and no-one but yourself shall shake my trust in you. Nothing but my own eyes and ears, and your own confession."

"A woman might say that I . . ."

"*A woman!*" growled the Sultan, and refrained from spitting.

"Well, now," he said. "Business. Will you freely and voluntarily take service with me on a 'gentlemen's agreement'? . . . For a term of years, say, giving me your parole not to—I won't say escape—but not to leave me without fair warning and due notice?"

"I will," I said, impulsively, impetuously. "I'd love to."

"For how long will you give me your parole?"

"Oh, don't let us say any more about paroles, Sir. I'll take service under you, for as long as you like. Indefinitely," replied I, romantic and foolish ever.

"Good," said the Sultan. "And how long notice of the termination of our 'gentlemen's agreement' will you undertake to give me?"

"Oh, as long as you like. . . . A year?"

"A year. So be it. Splendid. Allah be praised!"

"Now look here," he continued. "Henceforth, when we are quite alone together, we are Chandos and Dysart—friends and equals. Partners, perhaps, some day. . . . In public, I am His Highness the White Sultan el Sidna el Sultan Mahommed el Kebir, the Lion of the Desert and Lord of the Western Sahara. And you are my confidential scribe, follower, secretary, courtier and all that. I am your Lord and Master—and you will address me as such.

"And I will promote you just as quickly and as high as you are fit to go, and as it is possible to do without offending the susceptibilities of these people too much. They are jealous devils, and you'll have to walk pretty warily at first. And later on, when you have power, you will have to use it ruthlessly. Kid gloves aren't worn in the Desert."

No. No kid gloves in the Desert.

And suddenly I had a disturbing thought.

"But what about the necessity of my turning Mahommedan before I can be of any use to you?" I asked. "For I'm afraid I can-not do that."

"That was another examination paper, my lad. If you'd failed in that one, you wouldn't be here now. I've no use for a man who changes his religion to save his skin."

"But you are a Mussulman . . . I beg your pardon, I . . ."

"Yes, I am a Mussulman all-right, convinced and professing, and no ulterior motive about it. It's a grand religion and suits me perfectly. But I've no more use for 'cash' Mussulmans than I have for 'rice' Christians. It was when you refused to rat that I first had hopes of you."

"Then it won't matter my being. . . ?"

"Not a bit. All you've got to do is to avoid giving offence to the Faithful; and that, of course you'd avoid in any case. A few fanatics may look askance at you, but the average man will think the better of you—and of your religion—for sticking to it. You would not have won much respect by perverting under pressure.

"But I've got to go to Mecca, both for my own sake and the final strengthening of my position—and you've got to come with me. And that means you'll have to play Mussulman, anyhow—pretend to be a Mussulman while we are in Arabia. You'll do that, of course?"

"Yes, I don't mind pretending to be a Mahommedan in the same way that I shall be pretending to be an Arab. That is quite a different thing from denying one's Faith, of course."

"Quite so. . . . It will be a great lark. And probably we shall both be scuppered. Still, we shall see a bit of life, my son. This is all very rich and rare and new and strange to you at present; but believe me, an 'Arabian-Nights' Sultan's life is just as boring as a city clerk's. It'll be a real adventure."

"For a change," I grinned.

"Yes," agreed the Sultan. "For a change."

How we talked! . . . I believe a load of care and anxiety fell from us both. The Sultan—or Chandos, as he again bade me call him in private—changed completely. Not only did he thaw and become human, he became positively merry, jolly; and the happier he grew, the more delightful I found him. I liked him immensely and admired him enormously.

What a man, to have attained at his age, such a position as this! . . . Such power. . . . To have imposed himself upon these brave fierce men, these jealous difficult wild people, who worshipped strength and courage, skill and cunning, and all the military virtues.

Earnestly I hoped that, some time, he would honour me by telling me his story.

One day, I sent him a note from my own little camp, where in the course of my duty as Instructor of Cavalry, I was training a picked squadron to act as Mounted Infantry rear-guard covering a retreat, and signed my message with my initials S.N.B.D. Thereafter he called me Sinbad; and once again I answered to the name that had followed me from the cradle to school, to my training-ship and to the *Valkyrie* of unhappy memory.

CHAPTER XV

"Now, I'm not going to ask you to play the dirty hireling spy, Sinbad, because you are not the chap to do it," said the Sultan, as we sat at coffee, he on his divan of cushions, I at his feet on a rug, "and if you were, I could never trust you as I'm going to do. *But* I do want your considered opinion on one or two people."

"Of course," he continued, "it will be a very long time before your knowledge of the Arab—and Arabic—is going to make your opinion about them very useful, but I do want to know what you think of the Europeans—especially from the point of view of character."

"Europeans?" I exclaimed in some surprise.

"Oh, yes. Abu bin Zaka is a pure European. Not a drop of native blood in him."

"Good Lord!" said I in amazement. "I should have said he was the perfect Arab."

"Yes, the reason being that he was captured as a child, and was brought up by Bedoui. Can't speak more than a word or two of his own language."

"What is he, then?" I asked.

"Italian, son of Sicilian fisher-folk, although he ranks as Colonel. Have a talk with him, some time. You'll have to talk Arabic, of course. He's a very useful man indeed, and his European blood comes out, so to speak, in lots of ways; initiative, thoroughness, steadiness, ability and general . . . guts. But I don't absolutely trust him, and I've got an idea that another sign of his European origin is ambition. I fancy he can quite see himself sitting on these cushions, and me dangling on the gallows, though I wouldn't say so for worlds, not even to you. . . . And of course, he's no good to me as a—well—a companion. Peasant stock, no English, remembers nothing of Europe except glimpses of his village and a fishing-boat. . . . Well, see what you think of him, will you?"

"I'll give you my opinion of him for what it's worth, most certainly, and with the greatest pleasure. I want to help you to the utmost of my power in every possible way; but . . ."

"Yes, I know the 'buts'. . . . *But* if one of these people tried to nobble you, threw out gentle hints, or you came to hear of a plot, I suppose you'd tell me everything? I mean, you wouldn't be goat

536

enough to let anybody tell you something in confidence—and then feel you'd got to respect that confidence?"

"No," I said. "I won't accept anything in confidence."

"And if you decided that somebody was hinting, you'd lead him on, and then round on him?"

I pondered this for a moment.

"Well, short of being treacherous myself, I would," I decided. "Yes, of course I'd do anything in the nature of what you might call Intelligence duty—what you might call Secret Service stuff and police-work."

"That's it. Good. One's got to have that sort of thing in Europe, but it is ten times more necessary among Orientals; and if a man likes to be a treacherous dirty dog, he mustn't complain if he's treated like a dog."

"Would you have any objection," he continued, "to joining a plot—as a plotter, and working with the conspirators up to the last moment—keeping me informed the whole time?"

This I pondered also.

"No," I decided. "I think one would be entirely justified, provided it was treachery on their part. . . . It is difficult. . . . An informer—of the type that is always to be found in an Irish plot, for example, strikes me as being a loathsome swine. But, of course, that is different. The informer does his dirty work for money, and was actually in the plot in good faith before he decided there'd be more profit in being a Judas."

"Totally different," agreed the Sultan. "All the difference that there is between the detective and the rogue who turns King's Evidence to save his hide."

"Well, we know where we are then. Good. And We do hereby and forthwith appoint you sole and secret head of our non-existent Secret Service.

"Then there's Haroun bin Arrach. He's a German."

"Haroun bin Arrach a German?" I exclaimed.

"Yes, although you'd never guess it, from his brown eyes, bronzed skin, and black beard."

"Bred in the desert, too?"

"Not he. He was a Sergeant-Major in the Potsdam Foot Guards. Got into some sort of trouble, hopped over to Belfort, joined the French Foreign Legion, did four years, was twice decorated and promoted to Sergeant. He's a really first-class Sergeant-Major, though he commands my second Infantry Regiment with the rank of Colonel. A real stout lad, the fine and finished product of the German Army system, and invaluable to me—in his place. But there again, he is no use to me as a companion. I know no German and he knows no English, and, outside his job, which he does most admirably, we have nothing in common."

"But you trust him?" I asked.

"Well, no, in point of fact I don't; neither on his record nor on my estimate of his character. A German Sergeant-Major doesn't bolt to France by reason of his good character and conduct, although quite a few German privates do it. But a Sergeant-Major doesn't. And there's something queer about a man who, in the fifth year of his Legion service, with decorations and the rank of Sergeant, again does a bolt. . . . I give him full marks as a soldier—with his *Croix de Guerre* and *Médaille Militaire*—but, well, I want you to cultivate him and tell me exactly what you think of him. Yes, and more than that, I want you to watch him. I know that, put in plain words, it sounds like spying, but . . ."

"No; that's all right," I interrupted. "I see no reason why I shouldn't watch him and find out all I can about him. It might be entirely to his good."

"Quite so. Splendid. It will make all the difference in the world, to feel, and to know, that you will be not only passively honest and loyal, but actively helpful, in assessing the honesty and loyalty of others."

"The one thing I wanted," mused the Sultan. "The one thing needful. Someone who'd stand back to back with me against the ring of them."

"You fear treachery then? More or less expect it?"

"Constantly expect it," was the reply. "Live in fear of it. With noble exceptions they are flighty volatile beggars, the Arabs. And they don't view treachery as we do. The word itself is not much harsher in their ears than the word 'wily' is in ours. They're fickle changeable creatures. With them, nothing succeeds like suc- cess. You've *got* to succeed. You've got to understand them, you've got to humour them, and the velvet glove is as absolutely essential as the iron hand. No Arab ruler can ever be too certain of his own tribe, let alone of others. There is generally a brother, cousin, nephew or son, who thinks the Old Man has had a long enough innings. And when tribes amalgamate, the Chief who rules the lot is in a still more precarious position. There is terrific jealousy on the part of the other leaders, apart from treachery among his own people. And, of course, the whole thing is intensified when you get a foreigner trying, not only to govern a tribe, but to amalgamate a number of them, and build up a nation.

"In some ways, of course, and to some extent, he is helped by being above, beyond, and outside, the tribal jealousies, and in a position to apply the good old Roman *divide et impera*. Something like the British in India—but he is also open to the sort of thing that the British got in the Mutiny. . . . Well, my son, get on with the Arabic until you can tell a Lancashire Arab from a Yorkshire one, and speak it so fluently that any Arab would call you a liar if you denied being one. Then you will be worth your weight in gold to me as Chief of Police and Head of the Intelligence Department. . . .

"Meanwhile, cultivate the Europeans."

"Are there any others?" I enquired, "beside Abu kin Zaka the Italian and Haroun bin Arrach, the German?"

"Yes, I'm quite sure there is a third. But I can't place him, at all. He's a dark horse and an unknown quantity. Ben Abu . . ."

"Ben Abu?" Again I was astonished. "What, the Treasurer, the Chancellor of the Exchequer chap? Good Lord, what sort of European is he?"

"I don't know. I don't know anything about him, except that I'm perfectly certain he's a European."

"What makes you think so? I mean, how do you know?"

"Lots of things. I happen to know that his body is a great deal whiter than his face and hands. I've been informed more than once that he has been overheard counting, *not* in Arabic; and every man counts in his own language, when he is off his guard. And I was informed by one of my spies—of all of whom I am going to put you in charge when the time comes—that he gave a letter to the leader of a caravan that was going to Algeria, to be posted when the man reached there . . . and the envelope was not addressed in Arabic. In what language it was written, the spy, of course, did not know.

"Another spy has reported that Ben Abu sometimes talks in his sleep, and doesn't talk Arabic."

It struck me that the Sultan's spy-system seemed fairly elaborate and comprehensive if such details were reported to him. But then, I reflected, this probably would only apply to a man who was for some reason under suspicion and special surveillance.

"Oh, in a dozen little things, he gives himself away," continued the Sultan. "And, on the other hand, he never gives himself away. I have not the faintest idea who he is, whence he comes, or anything about him, except that he is a damned good

Comptroller and Treasury Clerk—and whatever his nationality, he writes Arabic as none of my Arabs can. Now, my son, see what you can make of Ben Abu. . . .

"Well, so much for my Secret Service and Intelligence. But, of course, your real job will be military—everything in the cavalry line from Sergeant-Instructor to Inspector-General. My luck really was in, when Ali bin Ahmed brought you along—for a European-trained Cavalry-Instructor I have never yet been able to lay hands on. The invaluable Sergeant-Major Hans Grünther, alias Colonel Haroun bin Arrach is an infantryman, and, so far as I know, had never sat on a horse till Hussein the Brave, my chief scout and intelligence officer, and his band of cut-throats, picked him up in the desert and brought him in. . . . By the way, Hussein will be your Chief-of-Staff when you are the fully-fledged and acknowledged head of the Secret Service and Chief of the Intelligence Department. . . .

"I have done my best to improve the cavalry on European lines, but I am not a cavalryman myself, and I have really had too much on my hands to find time for being Drill-Sergeant. That's where you will be absolutely invaluable, for, although the finest horsemen in the world, they are rotten at drill, and while the best of scouts, they are the most slovenly soldiers.

"And if drill and discipline are good for infantry, they are good for cavalry. So I'm going to look to you to do some Life Guard stuff with them.

"Still, go slow. Ca' canny. Walk before you run; and above all, look before you leap—for they are kittle cattle, and you've got to turn yourself into an Arab before you try to turn them into disciplined troops. You must get to know the officers of all ranks, for a start, and get about among the men. I'll think of a few 'reforms', improvements, boons, and benefits—though I can't raise their pay at present—and give you the credit. That'll help you a lot—make you popular—the Arab soldier's brains being in his belly. . . ."

Whence did the Sultan get his English? And what was its accent? It was not that of a man from any part of the British Isles, although it was good, idiomatic and colloquial.

Occasionally he used a word or a phrase that I'd swear he could have learnt only from a Scot.

§2

Abu bin Zaka interested me greatly, as did his story. Here was a man, a European born and bred who, without possessing one drop of Arab blood, was an Arab and a Mussulman.

Partly as another of my innumerable daily exercises in Arabic, I got him to tell me his story, after informing him that the Sultan had mentioned to me that he was an Italian by birth and parentage.

Abu bin Zaka seemed delighted to learn that he had been the subject of the Sultan's conversation; most willingly and readily complied with my request; and poured forth his tale with cheerful volubility.

I found it very interesting. As far as I could calculate from his somewhat vague use of Mahommedan time-reckoning (dating from the Hegeira), some time in the early 'sixties, his father, whose name he did not know, two uncles, and two older brothers, sailed from a small place of which he had a clear picture, but of which he knew not the name, on the South coast of Sicily.

They were about their business of coral-fishing and going to an island off the coast of Algeria, of which, again, he had forgotten, or had never known, the name. He must, at this time, have been some five or six years old. Why, at so tender an age, he should have been on board a coral-fishing boat, he did not know. Possibly in the capacity of a pet, or the voyage may have been in the nature of a treat.

"That, Sidi, I cannot tell," said Abu bin Zaka, "but among the many things I have forgotten, I remember the joy of my father, uncles and brothers over the richness of this bank of coral. Also, that our joy was somewhat damped on entering a tiny cove and discovering that another boat was there before us, a boat full of Arabs.

"As we drew near, however, my father recognized the leader of these people, a man who'd frequently visited the village from which we came, and whom my father had encountered in Algiers harbour. I think they must have done one or two jobs together, of the kind about which you don't shout in the ears of the Police.

"Either my father must have known Arabic or the captain of this boat must have talked some Italian. Both, probably, as they were always to and fro, between Sicily and Africa.

"An interesting fact is that I must have understood what they said, for I know that the Arab captain assured my father that no other boats but these two had been into this cove, and that no-one else knew of this bank of fine coral.

"On my father praising God on this account, the Arab captain went on to say that, not only was the bank unknown to other Arab coral-gatherers, but it was known to no-one but himself—until my father intruded. This was the Arab captain's own private coral bank and what did my father propose to do about it? My father told him there were no private coral banks, any more than there were private oceans, and that the island (of which I have forgotten the name) was uninhabited and belonged to nobody. Nor did the coral. The Arabs began to shout and gesticulate, but I don't think they out-did my relations in that respect.

"It looked as though words were going to lead to blows. But as we were a crew of five tough and hardy sailors, and the Arabs were not more than six or seven, the latter did not seem to wish the argument to proceed as far as that.

"In the end, it was agreed that we would join forces, all work together, divide the coral equally, and, in acknowledgment of the Arabs' prior claim, we should feed them while the work lasted.

"I remember being slightly dismayed at the idea of this arrangement, and eyeing hungrily our small store of biscuit, coffee, figs and dried grapes. Our small keg of brandy did not interest me, but it interested those unworthy sons of Allah profoundly.

"Well, we having come to terms, and given each of the Arabs a small measure of brandy, they all set to work; while I played about in the boat, pretended to fish and to row, and stole as many raisins as I dared.

"The work must have gone on for six days, for I remember one of my uncles saying to the Arab captain that two thousand lire worth—two thousand five hundred francs' worth—of coral in a week, wasn't bad.

"That evening, when we were all back in our boat, my father told my uncle that he had been a fool to tell the Arab what the coral was worth to us. Whether he was right or not, I don't know, but, during the night, the Arabs and their boat silently disap-peared, and, what first amused and then troubled my father, was the fact that they'd left all the coral.

"This, according to him, looked bad. Why should they go, leaving their share of the week's hard work? And he and my uncles had a long and loud argument as to whether it would be better to load up the lot and set sail. My uncles argued that, as the Arabs had left it, it was ours, and we might as well make off with it at once.

"My father would have none of this. Evidently he considered honesty to be the best policy—whether you liked it or not. And, moreover, he wasn't going to sail until he'd got all he could carry. Who could say when such a chance would arise again? Next time we came back, the place might be crawling with Arab boats.

"And now we were all shouting and gesticulating among ourselves, just as we had been doing against the Arabs. I don't know how it would have ended, for the matter was settled for us. Round the promontory that sheltered the little cove from the open sea, came a barque, and another, and another and another, and from them, as they closed in on us, came a fusilade of gun-shots. Quite a shower of bullets must have struck our boat, for I remember to this day the sound of their blows upon the wood as well as upon the bodies of my kinsmen, the flying splinters, the holes suddenly appearing in the sides of the boat, the groans and cries of my wounded brothers and uncles.

"We were unarmed save for our knives, and the treacherous Arab captain had brought a score or so of his friends and tribesmen, each of whom carried a gun as well as a yataghan and knife.

"As the Arab boats came alongside ours, men stood up in them and hacked at my people with their swords, inflicting ugly wounds.

"I saw my uncle's head cut from his body, for, as, either shot or stabbed, he fell with his head across the side of the boat, a man chopped and chopped at it with his heavy sword until it fell off into the sea—a nice sight for a young child.

"My father and brothers fought desperately with such weapons as they could lay hands on, with boat-hooks, tools, and their knives, but were soon overpowered.

"When the Arabs towed the boat ashore and threw the poor fellows out on to the beach, only my father and my eldest brother could stand. Finding that the others could not, or would not, get to their feet, the Arabs fell upon them and hacked them to pieces.

"They then looted our boat, shared the food, brandy, and money, and what else was worth taking, and set sail.

"All this time I had suffered nothing as to my body. A man pointed his gun at my head, but the leader interfered, doubtless remarking that I should fetch a good price in the right market.

"I suppose I was too dazed and shocked really to understand what was happening and to suffer much pain of mind at the thought of the murder of my uncles and brothers. Doubtless I could not have realized the truth. It must have seemed like a nightmare. Moreover, I was soon too utterly weary to think of anything but rest, for I was made to walk for miles and miles to a village whence the band had come. But, strange to relate, once inside the robber stronghold, my troubles were over, for I received nothing but kindness, care and affection from the women of the village. They exclaimed with delight over my beauty!"

Here Abu bin Zaka broke off to grin engagingly, his leathern face creasing with smiles, his grim mouth relaxing and expanding.

"How long I lived at this place, of which I don't know the name, I have forgotten; but when some big man, perhaps the Kaid of that district, paid the place a visit, doubtless to collect revenue, I was presented to him—doubtless, again, as a substantial part of that revenue.

"I must have been very happy among the womenfolk of this village, for I remember howling with grief at parting with them— but recovering my spirits promptly when I found I was to ride on a camel instead of being dragged, sore-footed, wearily along, at the tail-end of the Kaid's retinue, in the way I had first come to the village.

"Again I was treated quite kindly, and enjoyed the journey, being well-fed and sleeping at night on a rug in the Kaid's tent.

"And when we reached his *ksar*, he gave me as a present to his favourite wife and, once again, I was lucky and happy. To Allah the Merciful, the Compassionate, be the praise and thanks, for I, who had had a rough and hard life, now had a soft and easy one. I who had hitherto walked upon sand now sat upon silk.

"I shall never forget the love and kindness that I had from the wives and women-folk of the Kaid. The Prophet grant that they were allowed to slip into Paradise in the shadow of their husband and master.

"Not only were they good and kind to me, but the Kaid's wife had me taught. . . . Oh, yes, I am an educated man. I can read and write, and I know much of the Koran by heart. . . . I remember that I was puzzled a little, at first, to learn that there were no such Gods as Isa Christ and Miriam the Blessed Virgin.

"Yes, they soon made a good Mussulman of me, praise be to Allah and to Mahommet his Prophet, on Whom be Peace.

"So I grew up an Arab and a Mussulman, and forgot my country and home and parents. When I say I forgot them, I mean that I never thought about them. I could not have quite forgotten them, as I remember them to this day, and can see the faces of my father, uncles and brothers, of my mother and sisters. I can still see the little village climbing up from the tiny harbour where the fishing boats rode at anchor.

"And then my master, the Kaid, died; and his son, who had always been jealous of me, would have killed me, but that the Kaid's wife, my second mother, saved my life, helping me to escape in disguise, with camels, weapons and money. I travelled into Morocco and reached Fez where I traded for a time, until misfortune overtook me. I was falsely accused, thrown into prison by an unjust judge, a taker of bribes; and only saved my life by becoming a soldier, in the *hamsain* of the Sultan.

"From this service I escaped with one of the *chaous* of the squadron of *makhaznis* who guarded a convoy that brought certain things from the Kaid to the predecessor of our Lord, el Sidna el Sultan Mahommed el Kebir.

"After hiding in a near-by oasis for weeks, I was captured by one of his patrols and was brought before him. Finding I was a trained soldier, he spared my life and allowed me to take service with him, and in his service, and that of our present Lord, el Sidna el Sultan Mahommed el Kebir, I have been ever since. . . ."

Yes, thought I, and quite possibly maintained communication with the Sultan of Morocco ever since, too. Quite a good way for that wily potentate to plant a spy on Chandos, if he thought fit to do so.

Heavens, here was I already inhaling deep draughts of the atmosphere of suspicion that Chandos breathed! When I told him the story that Abu bin Zaka had told me, he congratulated me on my knowledge and understanding of Arabic, and asked what impression I had received of the man himself.

"Oh, I reserve judgment altogether," I replied. "He's interesting, amusing and likeable; but I imagine an Arab-trained Sicilian who grew up in a Kaid's *harim*, might well be a spiritual descendant of Machiavelli."

"Yes," agreed Chandos. "He might! And, in point of fact, he is. He's a very cunning bird indeed; but although I don't trust him, I have nothing against him, so far. Anything else occur to you?"

"Well, I did toy with the foolish and fantastic notion that he might be what is, I believe, called a stool-pigeon, a spy—really the employee of the Sultan of Morocco."

"Oho!" smiled Chandos. "Getting the jargon and the technical terms of your new job already, are you? . . . Bright idea too. I have a notion that that is precisely what he is. Not that it matters much, so long as he's also the other thing that he is—a jolly good infantry Colonel."

"His tale may not be absolutely true then?" I asked.

"Well, I believe it is the truth, but not the whole truth; and certainly not 'nothing but the truth'. I think it goes a little off the rails when it deals with Morocco and his experiences there. Watch him—when the next convoy comes from Fez. . . ."

CHAPTER XVI

Well, my son, what's puzzling you?" asked Chandos one evening, a few weeks later, as we sat silent, after talking of England, and more especially of London, and most especially of certain hotels, clubs, theatres and various haunts of the West End thereof—places of which Chandos evidently had some little knowledge.

At least, it was Chandos who did the talking.

And how he did talk—although he had at first given me the impression of a taciturn uncommunicative reserved man to whom speech was difficult, and who said the less and thought the more!

I had not then realized that this taciturnity was imposed by circumstance, and was unnatural and foreign to his nature. He was like a starving man led to a banqueting table; like a river long frozen throughout a hard winter, and now in spring-time spate.

Very useful as I undoubtedly was to him in many ways, I must have been a god-send to him in this; his chief deprivation having been the absence of someone to whom to talk in his own language (for English was his own language—however accented); someone approximating to his own age, tastes and upbringing, whom he could meet on common ground of mutual interests and outlook; someone with whom he could talk sport, games, books, drama, music, travel, politics, and life in general, and English life in particular. And religion, of course—a subject on which I, personally, had nothing to say, save that on no account or consideration would I change my own.

And the more Chandos talked on the subject, the more he praised Mahommedanism and attacked Christianity, the more I felt he 'did protest too much', arguing with himself rather than with me. Without accusing him, in my mind, of recusancy for profit or for safety, I still felt that he was not altogether happy in his belief, not wholly satisfied with it or with himself.

"What's puzzling me?" I replied. "Well, I've undertaken always to tell you the truth, so here it is. I was wondering where you get your money. No concern of mine, but—that's what I was wondering—since you ask the question."

Chandos gave me one of his long considering and appraising

looks.

"As you say, it is no concern of yours," he said sharply.

"Quite so," I replied, "and I had not the slightest intention of making it so."

"Sure?"

"Perfectly certain."

"Well then, I'll tell you. Of course I'll tell you. I'm going to tell you everything—gradually; be as open with you as you are going to be with me. Partly taxation, of course, and partly, very largely in fact, subsidy from the Sultan of Morocco and from three or four European powers. But chiefly from the Sultan of Morocco—who calls himself my suzerain. He really maintains my army for me, or for himself. I am, in a manner of speaking, his first line of defence or—what shall we say—his outlying picket.

"The stronger I am, short of being any kind of a danger to himself, the better, from his point of view. To liken small things to great, I stand to him in somewhat the position in which the Amir of Afghanistan stands to the Government of India—which pays him a subsidy in return for loyalty."

"I see. A sort of buffer state."

"Yes. A moveable buffer. In fact, my son, a highly mobile old buffer. Especially if I live long enough."

"Rather like a fender, in fact."

"Fender?"

"Yes, the fat thing made of rope that you hang over the side of the boat when it's coming up against the landing-stage or another boat."

"The seaman speaks," smiled Chandos. "Excellent. Exactly that, my son. Just as the sailor runs along, dangling the fender, and drops it in just where it will do most good, so the Sultan hopes and expects to use me in time of trouble—put me in between him and whatever is going to bump him. Yes, buffer state, but the state moveable like a feast—or a ship. In point of fact, I am waiting here for his next convoy. It will interest you. I want you to keep your eyes and ears open, too. Incidentally, shadow Abu bin Zaka, your Sicilian friend; keep an eye on Haroun bin Arrach, the German; and don't neglect Ben Abu—the mystery."

"Does the convoy just bring sacks of gold?"

Again Chandos, incurably suspicious by circumstance if not by nature, eyed me thoughtfully.

"Oh, by no means! Far from it. Being an Arab—and of course Moors are Arabs really, though they affect to despise them—he sends a lot of the promised subsidy in kind. Still, we rub along! We rub along! And, after all, I should have to buy a great deal of what he sends me, so it's as broad as it's long."

In point of fact, I discovered, on the arrival of the huge convoy from Morocco, that the long long line of camels, tied head to tail, brought a very mixed as well as valuable and useful cargo.

First of all was the subsidy itself, in gold coin; next, most important, was load after load of arms and ammunition. The arms varied from quite good rifles of European pattern (including, to my amazement, English Martini-Henry rifles, French Gras rifles, and others of German, Italian, and even Russian make) to terrible percussion and even flint-lock guns, presumably for the use or ornament of "friendlies" and highly Irregulars; the ammunition similarly varying from consignments of cartridges suitable for the rifles, to spherical bullets, gunpowder, percussion-caps and gun-flints for screwing into the hammers of the Belgian guns.

The next most important items brought by the convoy were hundreds of uniform suits of tunics, trousers and cloaks for the *hamsain*, and thousands of skull-caps, sandals, and slippers.

There were also bales of cotton, piece goods for the making of *haik*, *djellabia* and *kaffieh*, as well as large numbers of plain *burnouses*. There was also a considerable store of unattractive army-biscuit, and of salt. Also vast consignments of dried peas and lentils, barley, wheat, stinking dried fish, onions, olives and oil.

Small but valuable extras were sacks of coffee, tea, mint, cones of sugar, jars of honey, and dried fruits.

A special department of the convoy brought personal gifts for el Sidna el Sultan Mahommed el Kebir—rich silken garments and articles of beautiful Morocco leather work; quaint flasks of alleged perfume; sporting rifles and a handsome sword or two— with letters of loving greetings from his alleged over-lord His Serene Highness and Holiness Muley Idris Bou Moussa bin Haroun Ibrahim, Sultan of Morocco, Lion of the Atlas, Over-lord of Moghreb, Defender of the Faithful, Descendant of the Prophet, and Allah's representative upon earth.

§2

I may here add that, on the occasion of the arrival of this convoy, I watched Abu bin Zaka closely and carefully, albeit unobtrusively, and the conclusion at which I arrived agreed with that of Chandos's spies—that he held more (and more private) communication with the super-cargo, the Caravan Leader, and the Commander of the Escort than was at all necessary.

"Yes," said Chandos when I told him what I had observed and what I thought. "We will make it our business, one of these times, to find out what he says or writes; but so long as he reports the truth, it doesn't matter to me whether he is in the pay of the Sultan of Morocco, or not. . . . And I don't want to lose him until I can replace him.

"But I'll *lose* him all-right," he added, grimly, "if I catch him out."

§3

Colonel Haroun bin Arrach, elsewhere and in other days, Sergeant-Major Hans Grünther, was a difficult nut to crack. Seeking his society, the more I saw of him, the more he puzzled me. In the first place, he simply would not utter, and I found it difficult to decide whether his silence was due to his having nothing to say, or to his determination to say nothing.

Certainly he was of the stolid, solid, German type, rigid, stiff and machine-like; but no really stupid man could have attained to a position of power, importance, and trust under the Sultan Mahommed el Kebir and to the command of a regiment in his *hamsain*.

No, he could not be brainless; and there are few cleverer men than those who, being very clever, contrive to pass themselves off as fools.

On closer inspection I realized that Grünther, big, thick-set and heavy; although dark-haired, dark-eyed and sunburnt to brownness, could never really be mistaken for an Arab. He was too good a Sergeant-Major for that; too well-drilled a Prussian, with his flat-backed ram-rod carriage and air of suffering from suppressed goose-step. His ham-like hands alone would have given him away, in spite of their being, like his face, burnt to a uniform brown.

At first I found him extremely suspicious, and always I found him inclined to be jealous. He did not like Englishmen. He did not like other Europeans entering the service of the Sultan Mahommed el Kebir; and he did not like my sudden rise to friendship and intimacy with the Sultan.

While endeavouring to suspend judgment, my first impression was, on the whole, favourable. He struck me as being, purely from the military point of view, very good indeed—a Soldier of Fortune true to type; of the sort that is whole-heartedly and unshakeably loyal to its employer; that can never be bribed to bite the hand that feeds it; and giving of its best, unstintingly devotes all its powers and faculties of mind and body to doing its job and honestly earning its pay.

A man of little education and limited intelligence, he was, though admittedly a very fine soldier, nothing but a soldier; and with regard to subjects that had no military bearing he was not only ignorant but totally uninterested.

Very quickly I understood Chandos's complaint that he was no earthly use to him as a companion, and that conversation with him on any but professional matters was impossible.

I endeavoured to find my way to his heart and confidence by praising his regiment, a thing I was able to do, for I doubt if a better trained, drilled, and disciplined regiment of Arabs ever existed. They were a fine body of men. His hand was heavy upon them; they feared him; had no love for him; and, indeed, I am not sure that they did not hate him. Nor, in such circumstances, is this a bad state of affairs. Iron is a tough enduring metal; and the rod of iron serves best, wears best, and wears longest, when such people as desert Arabs are commanded by a foreigner, and he an Infidel, a *Roumi*.

I imagine that, had he endeavoured to rule by kindness, forbearance and mercy, he would not have ruled for long. He'd have had his throat cut. The Arab respects and admires strength, and obeys the strong ruler in proportion to his strength—and success.

By any military standards, Grünther's rule was not very brutal, unjust or cruel, but his punishments were heavy, sharp and certain—above all, certain.

Anyway, he had a fine regiment, and, from the military point of view, had done, and was doing, fine work. Probably it was the only subject on which he was open to flattery, the Achilles heel of the self-sufficient strength of his rugged, harsh and ruthless personality. And by the use of this golden key I was able to open at least the outer gate of his confidence, and penetrate the high thick wall of his suspicion and reserve.

Indeed, he told me something of his story—and, in a way, I was inclined to be sorry that he did so, for he stripped himself almost bare of all but military virtue.

I was reminded of certain former comrades who looked so

attractive and distinguished in uniform and so unattractive and insignificant in mufti. Fine feathers make fine birds.

As he told me his story, I could at times almost have stopped him and begged him, metaphorically speaking, to get back into uniform, for, as a civilian, he was detestable and despicable. It was a pity, of course, that from this point of view we had to talk in Arabic eked out by French, when not in French interlarded with Arabic.

Unconsciously but inevitably he thrust himself from whatever pedestal I was disposed to set him on, showing himself as a "creeping" private in the German army; a truculent and ruffianly non-commissioned officer; and a complaisant, favour-currying toadying subordinate to his officers. And while, as a soldier, he was the perfect non-commissioned officer, invaluable to, admired and trusted by, his officers; feared and obeyed by his subordinates; he was, as a man, definitely dishonest, and capable of the pettiest meanness and rascality.

Moreover, a thing that put me off—and militated against the good impression that he made upon me as Colonel Haroun bin Arrach—was the way in which he inveighed against his own country, speaking bitterly and contemptuously of Germany and all things German.

"*Ja*, I was bred and born in Potsdam," he growled and grunted in slow Arabic interlarded with German, "Drums and bugles for lullaby; and weaned on army soup and rations. Foot-guards, from recruit to Sergeant-Major in record time. Youngest Sergeant-Major in the German army. I should have been made an Officer in any *decent* army. . . . Well, they treated me wrong and they lost me."

And he proceeded to tell me, with righteous indignation which was obviously genuine, his mean story of favour-selling, profitable injustice, graft and peculation that ended in a Court Martial and reduction to the ranks. Also, obviously without shame or regret, the tale of how he thereupon induced his faithful sweetheart, a well-paid hotel-cook, to entrust her life-savings to him in the belief that he was going to desert, escape into Switzerland, and start life anew in the restaurant business; she of course to join him in the capacity of cook, manageress and wife. With the help of her money, he deserted, fled to France, had a good time, and then joined the French Foreign Legion.

In Sidi-bel-Abbès he banked the remainder of the money at the *Crédit Lyonnais*, against a rainy day, by which he obviously meant the possible occasion for another desertion.

In Algeria his outstanding ability as a soldier brought him to the front again, and once again he found himself a Sergeant-Major, having proved not only his quality as a drill-sergeant and instructor, but his virtue as a fighting-man—to which two decorations bore further witness.

And here, once more, his besetting sin—his fundamental dishonesty—caused his downfall. This terminated and ruined the success achieved by the exercise of his undeniable military virtues.

Also, without the slightest evidence of shame, regret, or remorse, he described the filling of his pockets by the emptying of his comrades' stomachs. As *fourrier-sergent*, he sold military stores, and, as catering Commissariat-Sergeant-Major, under a weak officer, he automatically put to his own account one-half of the mess-appropriation fund, expending in the meat and vegetable market the other half only. An even baser and meaner crime than this was a side-line which he was enabled to run when he combined the office of Commissariat-Sergeant-Major with that of *vaguemestre* or Military Postmaster. While he was acting in the latter capacity, none of his comrades received postal orders, cheques, drafts, or the pitiful sums in paper money which sons of poverty-stricken peasant families sometimes received from home.

Yes, Sergeant-Major Grünther, Colonel Haroun bin Arrach, puzzled me, while, in guttural staccato speech, he revealed himself as a base, heartless, thieving criminal, a competent distinguished heroic soldier. . . .

Again to escape court-martial and its inevitable *sequelæ*—disgrace, degradation and heavy punishment in the shape of a long term of imprisonment and service in a Penal Battalion, he deserted.

Once more, the proceeds of his crimes aided his courage, resolution, and fortitude, in successful escape; not only serving to purchase disguise, assistance, and means of transport, but the good-will and favour of the ruler of a considerable tribe of Arabs into whose hands he fell—or to whom, according to his own account, he made his way.

These people employed him to teach them European drill and methods, more particularly fire-drill and control, and the proper tactical use of the rifle.

With them, according to his own account, he was a great success until they suffered a sharp reverse in a skirmish with a French desert column which, on his advice and under his leadership, they attacked.

Shortly thereafter, having concealed his considerable knowl-edge of Arabic, he discovered the intention of the warriors under his command of shooting him in the back, at the first opportunity, thus ridding themselves of a man of whom they were jealous; an Infidel abhorrent to Allah; and a mis-leader of their infatuated ruler.

While making his plans to deal with the situation, bad luck befell him in the shape of the death of the Kaid, the strong leader whom his followers had reverenced, feared, and obeyed. Promptly they now seized Grünther and, under a flag of truce, took him to Zaguig, the nearest French garrison town, and handed him over to the military authorities there, thus combining business with pleasure, currying favour with the French and receiving the cash reward of their treachery.

Inasmuch as he was not only a convicted criminal and a posted deserter, but had now actually fought against the French, in the ranks of their enemies, the Court Martial could give but one verdict.

Once again, Grünther escaped, this time from the condemned cell itself. Concealing himself behind the door, he felled with a stool the warder who entered it. Having then killed the man, he dressed himself in his uniform, walked out, and coolly strolled across the dark yard through the gates, into the town and to the native quarter.

That night he treacherously killed an inoffensive Arab and arrayed himself in the dead man's clothing. He then committed a burglary, a highway robbery, and a swindle of the confidence-trick order; and, with the proceeds, equipped himself for a desert journey. Going from *ksar* to *ksar*, oasis to oasis, *sûk* to *sûk*, he travelled on toward Morocco, until he fell into the hands of Hussein the Brave and the Sultan el Mohammed el Kebir.

In his service, by sheer military merit and ability, he had risen to be commander of a battalion and Aga of the Infantry Brigade, he being, as Chandos remarked to me, too valuable as a whole-time Colonel to be used as more than a part-time General.

§4

Chandos and I, when alone, always spoke English, of course, partly because it gave him profound pleasure to hear and to speak his own tongue once again, and partly because there was no possibility of eavesdropping, there not being a single person,

European or Arab, in all that great assembly, who understood a word of English.

One evening, however, he said,

"Let's talk Arabic. I want to see how you are getting on."

And for the rest of the night we used only that tongue.

"Good," said Chandos, after a time. "You really are fluent. Let's see what you can make of the colloquial vernacular of the towns. I'll send for old Ibn Faka, my male Scheherazade—professional story-teller, you know. Professional liar too, doubtless.

"Now—you imagine I don't know a word of Arabic. And you interpret to me what he says; sentence by sentence. . . ."

Ibn Faka proved to be an elderly negro with a merry eye and laughing roguish face, a most cheerful old scoundrel and a wonderful actor. These public and professional story-tellers of Northern Africa are to the townsmen what the theatre, music-hall and cinema are to those of happier—or less happy—lands.

Seated in a corner of the market-place, they tell their tales, while a crowd, varying from infants to grey-beards, sits and stares, open-mouthed, silent, rapt and admiring. From time to time a copper collection is taken up by the entertainer, generally just before the climax of a thrilling story. . . .

Although Ibn Faka talked rapidly and colloquially, with dialect words and allusions that were beyond me, I fully understood his stories, and apparently pleased Chandos with my translation.

I was interested to note that not all of the tales were wholly unfamiliar, and that some were reminiscent of Hans Andersen; others of Æsop. I should like to know whether the former made their way to Africa from Europe or whether from Africa to Europe and the ken of Hans Andersen and the brothers Grimm.

Doubtless the Greek fables came to Mauretania with the Romans. Some tales, again, were definitely reminiscent of the Baghdad of Haroun al Raschid. Two or three of the stories made me laugh, and have remained in my memory. I rather liked the following:

Know then, Sultan, that once there dwelt in your own city of Bab-el-Djebel a rich merchant who, as such men do, took to wife a young and beautiful girl. But, alas, after he had expended vast sums upon the wedding feast, the girl fell sick and was like to die.

The merchant was distraught, for she had cost him much, and was most fair to look upon.

Nothing that his other womenfolk could do was of any avail;

nor could the prayers and ministrations of the holy marabout bring her back to health. One night, when it seemed that soon she must breathe her last, the distracted merchant rushed forth from his house to go in person and beg the great, famous—and expensive—Doctor, Hakim Ishak bin Moussa to come quickly; yea, to name his own fee, and rise from his bed and come at once.

But on his way he met a holy Dervish who, accepting alms from him, asked whither he went in such haste.

The merchant told the Dervish of his trouble, and begged that he would use his, doubtless miraculous, powers to save the dying girl.

"No," replied the Dervish to the merchant's prayer. "I can do nothing for any woman; but, in return for your faith and charity, I will confer a boon upon you. I will give you power to see the Invisible. Go in peace."

Hurrying on, the merchant turned a corner and saw, before him, a great crowd that surged about the door of the house of the most famous doctor of Bab-el-Djebel.

"Who are ye? Who are ye?" he cried as he made his way through this great assembly.

"We are the souls of the dead, slain by the hakim, the famous doctor who dwells in this house."

"Then he has slain his thousands?"

"Yea, his tens of thousands," was the reply.

"Then he's not the doctor for me," cried the merchant, and blessing the gift of the Dervish, he rushed on to the house of another *hakim* of lesser fame.

Outside the house of this learned man—the Hakim Yacoub el Barka—was another angry crowd of men, women, and children, who shook their fists and hurled curses at the house.

"Who are ye? Who are ye?" cried the distressed merchant.

"We are the souls of the dead, slain by this charlatan *hakim*."

"But he must have killed his hundreds," cried the merchant.

"Yea, his thousands," was the reply.

"Then he is not the man for me," said the merchant; and again ran on, to the house of a third doctor, one Hakim Saleh-ud-din of whose wondrous skill he had heard.

About this house thronged yet another crowd of people, of both sexes and all ages.

"Who are ye? Who are ye?" asked the merchant, as he joined the crowd.

"We are the souls of the dead, slain by this rogue who calls himself a *hakim*," was the reply.

"But he must have slaughtered his patients by scores," gasped the merchant.

"Yea, by hundreds," was the reply.

"Then this is not the man for me," cried the merchant; and once more ran on, this time to the house of another recommended doctor, Hakim Abd-el-Rahman.

Almost as the poor merchant had come to expect, there again was gathered a mournful crowd.

"Who are ye? Who are ye?" again he asked.

"We are the souls of the dead, slain by this poison-peddling butcher," was the reply.

"But he must have killed you by dozens."

"Yea, by scores and scores," was the answer.

"Then he shall not kill my wife also," vowed the merchant, and ran on. . . .

Where should he go. What could he do?

Suddenly his eye fell upon a sign painted in black letters upon a white wall. Scanning it by the light of the moon, he read the words,

"The far-famed and learned Hakim Abdullah el Kerim, late Court Physician to the King of Arabia, dwells here."

And at his gate there stood, not a crowd to be numbered by hundreds of thousands, by tens of thousands, by thousands, by hundreds or even by scores. At his gate there stood but two people!

"Who are ye? Who are ye?" cried the merchant.

"We are the souls of the dead slain by this *hakim*," was the reply.

"And there are but two of you?"

"There are but two of us," was the reply.

"Then *this* is the doctor for me!" cried the merchant joyfully, and raised loud clamour at the gate.

Being brought to the Hakim Abdulla Kerim, the merchant besought him to come at once to his house, and save the life of his young, beautiful, and valuable bride.

"But what fee do you offer me, to rise from my couch and go forth at this hour of the night?" asked the doctor.

"Don't haggle, but hasten. Come."

And after a moment's struggle with himself, the merchant added,

"And name your own fee."

Hastily springing from his divan, the doctor flung on his

burnous and cloak, took certain phials from a cupboard, and bade the merchant lead the way.

Almost running they came to the merchant's house.

Having examined the bride, the doctor wrote a certain verse of the Koran on parchment, and steeped it in a mixture of the contents of the phials that he had brought.

"There," said he. "Give her one-third of that potion now, one-third at dawn, and one-third at mid-day to-morrow; and she will recover. In seven days she will be in perfect health."

In gratitude the merchant prostrated himself before the hakim and clasped his feet. Rising, he led him to an outer room, paid him his heavy fee, and himself conducted him to the gate of the court-yard.

"I marvel, oh *Hakim*," said he as they parted, "that thy fame is not even greater in this city than it is; for I happen to know that your treatment has been incredibly successful—indeed marvel-lous!"

"I thank you. I thank you," replied the physician. "But how did you know that—since I have but newly come to this city of Bab-el-Djebel. I arrived only last week."

"*What?*" cried the merchant. "*What?* Then how many patients have you attended here?"

"*Two*," replied the doctor, and hurried off, clutching his fee.

This was a fair sample of the story-teller's longer tales. Many of them were terse anecdotes, brief and witty; most of them relating the clever sayings and cunning verdicts of more or less just judges. For example:

Know then, oh Sultan, that a certain man was seized by the police of your city of Bab-el-Djebel, and haled before the judgment-seat of the wise and upright Kadhi Wulud Zeki Bey.

"What is the charge?" asked the Judge.

"We caught this man lying outside the house of Samsoun the Money-lender. He had made a hole in the wall, and when we came upon him, he had thrust his right hand and arm through the hole, doubtless in an attempt to reach the treasure which Samsoun keeps beneath his bed.

"What is the defence?" asked the learned Judge, eyeing the criminal.

"It is my right hand, oh learned Judge," replied the man. "I cannot control it. As the police themselves admit, I was outside the house. It was only my right hand that was inside. That unruly member is a curse to me. I am a poor man. What can I do?"

"You swear that you yourself are innocent?" asked the Judge.

"I do. I swear it on the holy *Koran*. I swear it by the Beard of the Prophet. I am innocent. It is my hand that is guilty."

Stroking his beard the Judge eyed the prisoner awhile.

"Poor fellow!" said he at length. "The Court pities you. It will help you. Recognizing *your* innocence, we sentence only the hand—to twice seven years' imprisonment. You can go with it or not, as you like."

Another pawky police-story that amused me, was:

Know, oh Sultan, that a certain man sat daily in the *sûk* of your city of Bab-el-Djebel, selling *kaibobs* of hot mutton which he cooked over a brazier of charcoal. A poor widow-woman who tasted meat but rarely, and on many days tasted nothing, was wont to sit near and inhale the fragrant odours of cooking meat. Hungrily, and with great yearning, she inhaled the incense of roast mutton.

One day, the surly dog of a *kaibob*-seller, turning to her, cried,

"Woman! Why should you get this pleasure for nothing? Do I spend money on charcoal and meat, and time on cooking it, that you may benefit? Nay, do not rise and go away, but pay me what thou owest. Pay me—for all these days and days of pleasure and profit."

And rising to his feet, the fellow seized the poor widow.

"Pay me! Pay me, at once," shouted the man, "or . . ."

The woman screamed.

"Here! What's this? What's this?" said the voice of one of Your Highness's police.

Bawling angrily, the man explained.

Weeping miserably, the woman explained.

And, as becomes one of the servants of el Sidna el Sultan el Kebir, the policeman gave wise decision.

"Have you any money, mother?" asked the policeman.

"Two copper *flouss*," replied the woman.

"Good. Then rattle them together in your hands and let this miser hear them in payment. You have smelt his meat—let him *hear* your money. . . ."

§5

The invariably quiet, self-effacing, pleasant Treasury Clerk,

Ben Abu, defeated me altogether. I came to the conclusion that he was an extremely clever man indeed. He was pleasant, agreeable and quite conversational, but I think I never met anyone who could tell one so little in so many words. Not that he was garrulous—far from it—but that he gave not the slightest impression of reticence. There was only one thing he gave less and that was information.

On somewhat inadequate grounds, I came to the conclusion that if he were not a Frenchman, he understood French.

I thought it would be very clever of me, and would give the Sultan a good impression of my ability, if I could discover for certain what the man's nationality was; and, with the clumsy cunning of the inexperienced, I set a trap for him.

Meeting him coming from the direction of the Sultan's marquee, I said suddenly in French, with an air of great naturalness,

"Is the Sultan in his tent?"

Ben Abu by no means fell into my trap, but, on the other hand, he evaded it somewhat obviously.

Watching his face with the utmost care, I was perfectly certain that he understood what I said. It was not a case of a sudden look of understanding being quickly suppressed, so much as of a look of stupidity and incomprehension being suddenly assumed.

Having cultivated his acquaintance, and endeavoured to make a friend of him, I told him how greatly I had been interested in Abu bin Zaka's account of his life, from the time he sailed from Sicily as a child.

"What, isn't he an Arab then?" enquired Ben Abu. "Well, well! Let us praise Allah for the diversity of his creatures!"

On another occasion I remarked upon the strangeness of Haroun bin Arrach's career. Ben Abu was amazed at the German's adventures.

In the hope of reciprocal confidence I told him my own story which seemed to amaze him more than the others.

"And so there are a Sicilian, a German, and an Englishman, in high places under our Lord the Sultan," he mused, and, just as I had given up hope, told me his own amazing story.

When next the Sultan was chatting with me about his hopes and fears, his objects and intentions, his difficulties and dangers, he suddenly said as though à *propos* of the last,

"And what do you make of Ben Abu?"

I told him that I believed the man understood French; that he was amazed and interested to know who I, Haroun bin Arrach and Abu bin Zaka, really were; and that he had told me his own story. This I repeated in brief.

When I had finished, not a little pleased on the score of my success with Ben Abu, the Sultan smiled, and for a while remained silent.

"Yes," he said, "he is an amazing chap, a very cunning dog. I should like to know something about him."

I stared in some surprise.

"My son," smiled the Sultan, "Ben Abu certainly knows French as you suspect. And Spanish. And English. And German. He knows a damn sight more about Haroun bin Arrach and Abu bin Zaka than you do; and the interesting story of his life that he unfolded to you differs absolutely, in every separate detail, from the one that he told Hussein the Brave; from another that he told Abd el Hamid; a third that he told Kassim bin Ibrahim—and incidentally, the one that he told me. All five quite different."

"You don't trust him then?"

"Oh, as much and as little as I trust anybody else," replied the Sultan rather sadly and a little bitterly. "Anyhow he's absolutely honest where finance is concerned, for I have laid traps for him a dozen times. Absolutely accurate and incorruptible . . . so far as money goes. Clever, too, with a real head for figures. Ought to have been a chartered accountant or an actuary . . . in Europe. Invaluable chap, really. I shouldn't be surprised if he is a Jew. He has played Joseph to my Pharaoh more than once."

CHAPTER XVII

The mission and convoy from the Sultan of Morocco having arrived, been entertained, and departed, the time had come for breaking camp and continuing the tax-gathering, dispute-settling, justice-administering tour, which would end with the return to our permanent home and head-quarters, the desert city of Bab-el-Djebel.

The procedure of striking this tremendous camp interested me.

Before dawn its inhabitants were awakened, earlier than usual, by a long roll of drums and fanfare of trumpets. Before this call had finished, the still and silent place became a noisy hive of industry, as men hastened, with the shouts and noise inseparable from oriental activity, about the loading of camels, pack-horses and mules, and the stowing of every kind of camp equipage and impedimenta in great nets of palm-fibre rope, or in huge baskets made from plaited palmetto leaves.

Guided and guarded by an out-flung fringe of cavalry scouts, the camel-drivers and muleteers led their beasts from the camp.

Following them, came a compact body of horsemen surrounding specially chosen mules carrying the Treasury, the Sultan's personal treasure, and the reserve ammunition.

According to custom and due and proper ceremonial, the Sultan remained with his chief marabouts—*mullahs, moulvies, darweisches,* priests—until all tents but his were struck. He being notified of this by Kassim bin Ibrahim, his camp provost-marshal, he came forth and seated himself on an improvised throne, *gadl,* or judgment-seat, about which grouped themselves his chief officials, civil, military, and ecclesiastical.

Summary justice having been executed in such cases as were brought before him for decision, a squadron of the mounted body-guard, picked horsemen, rode up and paraded in line upon his right, their commander, Hussein the Brave, two horses' length in front of them; while, to the left of the throne, the stalwart, and indeed, gigantic negroes of the infantry body-guard, fifty in number (of whom twenty-five were always on duty about his tent) stood to attention like ebon statues. In their bearing, carriage, and drill, was evident the hand of Haroun bin Arrach, once Sergeant-Major of Prussian Foot-guards.

The business of the court concluded, the officials of the *entourage* and the ubiquitous marabouts, receiving the Sultan's permission to depart, mounted their horses and, like the soldiers of the body-guard, awaited in silence the arrival of a messenger who should notify that all baggage had left the site of the camp, and that nothing and no-one remained, save only the troops, awaiting the order to march.

This information having been received, a groom brought the Sultan's truly magnificent Arab horse, followed by his body-servant carrying the royal foot-stool, without which it would be undignified for the Sultan to climb on to his horse.

The moment he was in the saddle, another roll of drums and fanfare of trumpets gave the signal for the departure of the army. Why the baggage should have taken precedence I did not know, but concluded it was either the sacred and unchangeable custom, or that there was some good reason I did not understand.

At the head of the military column rode the band, or, at any rate, the company of musicians. One may presumably call them that, as they made noises with what were admittedly musical instruments.

Behind them marched, on foot, four fours of picked men, any one of whom would have done credit to a Guards Regiment as Drum-major, such was their stature and physique. Each of these bore a remarkably long rifle enclosed in a green cover. This was supposed to be the private and special armoury of the Sultan himself, but I never saw one uncovered and imagine that nothing on earth would have induced him to fire one. Doubtless they were to him what the Sword of State is to the Lord Mayor of London or the Chief Justice.

Behind these bearers of the State Armoury, rode four horsemen, grim warriors each riding a pale horse, who, not unnaturally, reminded me of the Four Horsemen of the Apocalypse. These were the Standard-bearers appointed for proven valour, skill at arms, and loyalty. The first carried the Sultan's own banner, the second the flag of the Cavalry, the third that of the Infantry, and the fourth that of the tribe of which the Sultan was Kaid.

Behind the Standard-bearers, drawn by long teams of mules, came the Sultan's guns, weapons of which the moral significance and effect was great, the actual performance small, if real.

Next followed the infantry column, its march-discipline really surprising, and a great credit to Haroun bin Arrach, Aga of

Infantry and *Chef de Bataillon* of the First Regiment.

The cavalry brought up the rear, their order and discipline as loose and bad as that of the infantry was good. Truly irregular cavalry, these, with all the virtues and vices of such troops.

On the march, they thought nothing at all of straggling, spreading, and breaking such loose formation as they had. Not one of them had the slightest hesitation about leaving the line altogether, if he caught sight of a fruit-tree, a patch of green cultivation, nomad encampment, or other attraction—and saw fit to visit it. I conceived the hope and intention of doing for this slack-disciplined mob what Grünther had done for the infantry.

By the grace of God, my Life Guards training, and the backing of Chandos, I'd make a crack cavalry unit of that magnificent material. Guerilla troopers and Irregular Horse are—all very well; trained disciplined cavalry are all—very much better.

The whole column having passed, the Sultan, followed by his *entourage*, and a picked troop of the Body-guard, galloped along the line and rode at its head between the far-flung cavalry-screen and the front of the baggage column.

I, in my capacity of Sultan's friend, confidential secretary, extra aide-de-camp, general personal factotum and 'Minister without Portfolio' rode at the Sultan's right hand, mounted on a beautiful Arab stallion whose only fault was that he was scarcely up to my weight; arrayed like the lilies of the field in superior *haik*, *kaffieh*, *burnous* and cloak; and wearing the four-fold silk-and-camel-hair cords of rank, about my headdress.

In circumstances how different from those in which I entered it, was I leaving the camp of el Sidna el Sultan Mahommed el Kebir! The wretched slave was now embryo chief of the Sultan's Secret Service, head of his Intelligence Department, prospective Colonel of his Life Guards and Aga of Cavalry, confidant, friend and possible Grand Vizier! And it seemed but the other day that I was a miserable half-starved first voyager Apprentice, starting a three-year voyage on the wind-jammer *Valkyrie*, and almost dying of sea-sickness. . . .

That day was uneventful, but the method and ceremony of pitching camp in the evening interested me, as did that of striking camp in the morning.

First of all, an hour or two before sunset, the Sultan sent an orderly to notify Kassim bin Ibrahim that camp should be pitched at the most suitable spot in the neighbourhood. Thereupon, at a signal from the band, drums and trumpets, the whole column halted and stood easy, and the Sultan and *entourage* rode to its head.

Then followed a detail of the ceremony that I found most alarming and disturbing. Indeed, a feature to which I never grew reconciled. Kassim bin Ibrahim, accompanied by the Sultan's standard-bearer, having settled the question of the site, and notified the fact by the planting of the Standard, the Body-guard wheeled out, rode to the flag, saluted it, turned about and charged the Sultan at full gallop, levelling their rifles straight at him as they did so.

At a couple of hundred yards' range, and a signal from their leader, they fired a ragged volley over the Sultan's head, continued the charge, suddenly halted, wrenched their horses back upon their haunches, wheeled about, and galloped off to take up position by the banner planted to mark the site of his tent.

When these wonderful horsemen and indifferent marksmen opened fire, I thought our last moment had come and that I was about to witness the assassination of the Sultan and meet my own end. I was too terrified to move.

As they wheeled about, and I realized that the whole thing was merely a salute, I breathed more freely. Later, I asked the Sultan whether this powder-play was not a somewhat dangerous business—for him.

"It would be a jolly sight more dangerous for me to stop it," he replied. "They'd think I'm afraid . . . and they'd be absolutely right."

"I got the fright of my life," I said.

"Well, I've been getting the fright of my life every day of my life ever since I was acclaimed Sultan by the tribes, and shall go on getting one daily until the end."

"It's such an appalling temptation—gives such a magnificent chance—to an assassin," I said. "Suppose there were a plot and the conspirators got hold of one of the Body-guard and bribed him to . . ."

"Oh, I'm not afraid of that," said the Sultan.

"I mean that the danger is negligible," he continued. "What I am afraid of is a genuine accident. That's the only real danger."

"Why is there no fear of assassination?" I asked.

"It simply isn't done," was the reply. "It never has been done, and never will be. Point of honour and professional etiquette. Bad form. If a ruler's Body-guard decided to kill him—they'd get him all-right. But not in that way. He'd be knifed in his tent; poisoned; or, possibly, shot in the back from behind a bush."

"But supposing a man's horse stumbled just as he was in the act of firing," I argued.

"Oh, well, accidents will happen in the best regulated body-guards, but I've never heard of such a thing; and the whole lot would feel that their faces were blackened for ever, if they were such clumsy mugs and rotten shots as to pot the man whom they were saluting. . . . Rather like peppering your host at a shoot, or his favourite gun-dog. Or the footman dropping the tea-tray in the middle of the drawing-room. No, we shan't meet our fates that way, my son."

Nevertheless, I can't honestly say that I ever really enjoyed or approved the custom.

The body-guard having lined up before the Sultan's banner, his marquee was pitched close to it, and, this being done, the other tents were swiftly erected, all openings facing to the East—in theory so that the first rays of the rising sun might enter and awaken the occupants.

Meanwhile the Sultan inspected the column. At another roll of the drums and blast of the trumpets, the troops came to attention, turned left into line, and the Sultan rode from end to end of it. He then rode to his tent, the curtains of which were opened as he arrived, that, still mounted, he might ride right into it and on to the carpet spread before his divan throne, built up of treasure-boxes, mattresses and cushions.

Kassim, standing at his near stirrup, salaamed low and offered his shoulder to assist the Sultan in dismounting, and then led the horse to the tent entrance where its groom awaited it. Then, and not only then, the drums again beat, the trumpets blew a fanfare, the band broke into discordant music, and at the word "Dismiss" the ranks broke and camel-men, muleteers, infantry and cavalry, hurried to their respective lines and tents to picket camels, mules and horses, stack baggage, light fires, pile arms, divest themselves of accoutrements, and set about the business of cleaning and feeding themselves and their beasts.

Before dispersing to their tents, all chiefs, important officials, and marabouts assembled in the Sultan's tent for prayers, orders, and dismissal about their duties.

In this camp I witnessed, and carefully noted for future guidance, the Sultan's method of dealing with rulers of neigh-bouring tribes who came to pay their respects—and their taxes. Throughout the day they arrived, arrayed in their best, and accompanied by retinues varying in size and equipment with their importance.

Following the retinue or body-guard in each case, came a caravan, large or small, bringing gifts—and supplies when near a big oasis and cultivation. These consignments consisted of fresh melons, peaches, figs and grapes; live sheep and goats; as well as whole sheep spitted and roasted ready for consumption; large pots of honey, baskets of eggs and raisins; trays of cooked fowls and joints of kid, venison and mutton; as well as of contributions to the commissariat of the troops.

Being admitted to the Sultan's tent, the Chiefs prostrated themselves before their Lord who, seated imperturbable upon his divan, extended his hand for them to kiss. This they did, many of them kissing also the hem of his garment, the skirts of his burnous.

With each the Sultan exchanged long-winded compliments and blessings. Occasionally a flowery compliment, a warm and gracious blessing, was followed by a sharp rebuke, an angry accusation, and a hearty all-round cursing by reason of the fact that the recipient had brought less than the due amount of tax, an unworthy gift, or no load of *cous-coussu* or any food for the troops.

Day after day, without variation, these ceremonies of camp-breaking and camp-pitching were repeated, the latter almost invariably followed by visits from chiefs of neighbouring tribes.

On one occasion I was interested and amused to see the Sultan's method of dealing with a recalcitrant *ksar*. This was a place of some small importance, the village of a ruler who evidently considered himself sufficiently powerful to disobey and defy the Sultan, or, at least, sufficiently so to give an exhibition of reluctance. Not his the motto *Bis dat qui cito dat*.

"If you want it, come and get it," seemed to be his attitude. Definitely the Sultan did want it, and he went and got it.

Sending for Hussein the Brave and the Aga of Infantry, he gave his orders; and the inhabitants of the *ksar* awoke next morning to find the place surrounded, and the Sultan's horsemen parading the village streets.

In surprise, alarm, and the greatest haste, the Kaid of the place came forth to pay his respects and his tax, to the Sultan's representative. Having collected this, counted it and found it satisfactory, Haroun bin Arrach delivered judgment or rather, the Sultan's message of judgment. Every single carpet in the place, whether the property of the Kaid or anybody else, was to be brought forth, and all were to be placed in a pile beneath a group of palms that grew outside the village.

This valuable collection was put under guard, and news was sent to neighbouring chiefs, more loyal and more wise, that, in recognition of the promptitude and correctness with which their taxes had been paid, the Sultan had a gift for them of—rugs and carpets. And at the hour of sunset, the presents were freely distributed, and gratefully accepted.

One imagines that the Kaid, the city fathers, and the other men of the place, heard a great deal from their women-folk that night.

And in time, this majestic progress throughout the wide domain definitely admitting allegiance to the Sultan, came to an end and reached the place whence it had set forth, the headquarters, citadel and capital of the country that dwelt in the shadow of his protection and the blessing of his rule, the desert city of Bab-el-Djebel.

This great town—of which most Europeans have scarcely heard the name—both by reason of the vast wall which completely surrounded it and its position upon a ravine-surrounded plateau, struck me as impregnable and not to be reduced save by a force possessing adequate modern artillery.

The ravine which surrounded it almost completely, was deep and wide, with steep sides; and the ridge of land that crossed this was not much wider than sufficient to carry a road. Had the valley been filled with water, the town would have been an island, save for the long and narrow isthmus of rock that joined it to the mainland and made it a peninsula.

On first catching sight of this city set on a hill, I was reminded of descriptions that I had read, and pictures that I had seen, of Richard Cœur de Lion's *Chateau Gaillard*. Whoever chose the site and built the town and citadel was a military engineer of no mean order.

And here again I entered upon a strange new life as different from those of the camp and the march as they had been from my previous experience.

CHAPTER XVIII

What an amazingly adaptable animal is man.

Shall I be believed when I declare that it was not very long before life in the desert city of Bab-el-Djebel seemed as normal, natural and ordinary as had life at home in Wellingbury, or at sea on the *Valkyrie*?

Quickly I grew familiar with the routine of the Sultan's great—though stone-and-mud-built—palace; with my own daily routine of work as drill sergeant-instructor; in the care and keeping of the Sultan's horses; as Inspector-General of Cavalry; teacher and trainer of cavalry officers; and as Chief of Police, head of the Secret Service and of the Intelligence Department; Confidential Secretary and adviser to the Sultan; keeper of the King's conscience and privy purse; and general, civil and military factotum and trusted friend!

At first, life was incredibly interesting, amazingly thrilling. I lived in the atmosphere of the Arabian Nights, in a town and palace that might have been that of Haroun al Raschid himself; and, from a state of bewildered wonderment, grew gradually *blasé*, not to say bored.

My chief work and chief difficulty lay with the Sultan's cavalry, and my endeavour to turn them from a horde of magnificent Irregulars into a regiment of disciplined troops.

The Arab hates discipline as he hates the Infidel. He is a natural and magnificent guerilla warrior, and it seemed almost a pity to turn the natural article into the artificial product; but as the Sultan pointed out—when I regretted the necessity for the heavy and frequent punishment inseparable from my work—he could get all the Irregulars he wanted. What he needed was a drilled and disciplined army, foot, horse and artillery, which must inevitably defeat Irregulars; and could, if necessary, meet a disciplined army of equal strength on equal terms.

Why did a small French desert column almost invariably beat a larger force of Arabs? Simply a matter of discipline and the proper tactical use of the three branches of an army and of their weapons. Give him infantry that understood and excercised fire-control, that could drill and manœuvre, stand fast or charge; give him cavalry that could use its weight correctly in shock tactics, as well as in tip-and-run attack, and that could reconnoitre and scout; give him a battery of decent artillery and some trained gunners—and he'd make himself invincible, his sphere of influence invulnerable, his head-quarters, his capital city, impregnable. And should he wish to do so, as at present he did not, he could extend that sphere of influence as widely as he saw fit.

With ordinary Arab methods and equipment—and good luck— he could fight Arabs. With European methods and equipment, he could conquer Arabs and successfully defend himself and his people against Arab, Moorish or European encroachment.

So it was my object to do for the Sultan's horsemen what ex-Sergeant-Major Grünther had done for his infantry. Like him, I had magnificent material with which to work; and, like him, I was up against the Arabs' pronounced individualism, love of untrammelled freedom to do whatsoever seemed to him right, his lack of dogged purpose, his ineradicable objection to coercion and discipline, and to his principle of never doing to-day what can be put off till to-morrow.

In one respect my difficulties were greater than those of the Aga of Infantry, inasmuch as the Arab is, as I have said, in spite of romantic legend, a thoroughly bad, callous, and ignorant horsemaster.

I found the Arab's fond love for his horse to be a myth, founded and fostered in Europe by sentimental poems of *The Arab's farewell to his Steed* type, and by tales of the mutual love of man and horse, passing the love of woman.

In actual practice, I found, when I began my work, that almost every horse in any troop had a galled back; that no Arab loved his steed sufficiently to take the trouble to prevent saddle-sores; that horses were pushed unmercifully and unnecessarily; that, when dripping with sweat after such gallops, they were left to stand shivering in the night-wind, without thought of blanket or shelter; that horses' mouths were hardened and spoilt by the violent use of cruel bits; that the legs of every horse were ruined by the idiotic practice of bringing him from racing speed to a sudden dead stand-still, wrenching him up on his haunches, and nearly breaking his jaw and his neck, with all the rider's strength and weight.

It was up-hill work; but, steadily, with the help of Hussein the Brave and a small picked body of intelligent and experienced officers, I climbed up-hill.

These men, whom the Sultan and Hussein the Brave selected for their courage, skill, loyalty and forceful personality, I, first of all, drilled as a small troop, drilled them as a squad of recruits is drilled in the Life Guards, except that there was, of course, no riding-school.

When, in course of time, I had them drill-perfect and had taught them all I could of the care and management of the horse, I set them each to drill a troop of his own. After six months of this work, I took over each troop in turn, and put a final polish upon it. The discipline that these officers inflicted on the troopers was undeniably strict, indeed harsh, if not cruel; and, hardening my heart I endeavoured to make my own discipline even more so, but aimed at certainty of punishment rather than extreme severity.

On the occasion of Id Kebir or some other holy day, the Sultan held a grand review of all his troops, and I was rewarded when, clapping me on the shoulder and shaking me warmly by the hand, he gave me his congratulations and praise.

"My son," said he, "you are a soldier, and a maker of soldiers."

Thereafter it was his humour to allude to me as Sinbad el Askar[22], Sinbad the Soldier, and officially to confer upon me the honorific title of *el Askar*.

Freely I confess that, having trained and organized a regiment of cavalry equal, I believe, in drill and smartness, to any in the world, and far superior to most in horsemanship, horsemastership, scouting and all light cavalry work, I longed to see them in action, to see exactly what difference drill, discipline, and training made between them and an equal or greater force of the ordinary irregular horsemen of the desert.

At the same time, I can honestly say that I would have done nothing whatsoever to provoke fighting, and would have used every endeavour to prevent it.

In this again, the Sultan and I were at one. The last thing he wanted was war, and it was his firm belief that the stronger he made himself, the riper for war he kept his army, the less likely it was that war would be forced upon him. He had no intention of attacking anybody. And he wished to render it unlikely that anyone should cherish the intention of attacking him.

It is not into the house of the strong man armed, that the thief desires to break.

The Sultan's freely-expressed approval of my success and his ever-increasing friendship for me, did nothing to lessen the

---

[22] *Asker, askar, askari = soldier.*

jealousy with which I was regarded by those officers, civil and military, who had served him long and well, before I came upon the scene. That I might expect such an attitude on the part of the Arabs, if only by reason of my being an Infidel, the Sultan had warned me; but in point of fact, it was the Europeans in his service who showed me the greatest enmity, and who were the most jealous of my success.

With several of the Arab officers, such as Hussein the Brave, I got on excellently. They were fine soldiers and fine men, who freely recognized and accepted me as their superior in the art of war—which, of course I was not. I was merely a superior drill-sergeant. But with such men as the German, Haroun bin Arrach and the Sicilian, Abu bin Zaka, I always felt an undercurrent of jealousy and hostility.

I was not surprised when, later, the Sultan told me that, of all the people who had tried to turn him against me, the great majority were my fellow-Europeans in his service, of whom, in the city of Bab-el-Djebel, there were several.

I could write volumes concerning my adventures and experiences during this period of my life; of the amazing plots and counter-plots, intrigues and schemes that came to light but not to fruition; of the fascinating diplomacy, or rather policies and politics of the Sultan Mahommed el Kebir; the diplomacy by which he maintained his peace, position and importance, mainly through his wise and clever dealings with the Sultan of Morocco, the great and powerful Sheik el Senussi, the Turks of Tripoli, and the Secret Service agents (who were really the ambassadors) of certain European Powers; France and Germany, Spain and Italy among them.

I believe I was completely in the Sultan's confidence; that he hid nothing from me, and misled me not at all. Although undoubtedly far cleverer than I, and of course, immeasurably more experienced and better informed, he took no step of importance without consulting me—by which I don't mean to suggest that he always took my advice. I think that, having heard all that his Arab advisers and counsellors had to say, he liked to set the matter forth before me, that he himself might get the better view of it, as well as see how the suggested course presented itself to another European mind.

§2

And one day, as we walked apart in the Sultan's private

garden, a poor dry and dusty affair to European eyes, with its mud-built runnels of precious water—but to the Arab, a foretaste of Paradise in that barren land—Chandos, pacing beside me, placed his hand upon my shoulder, as though to lean upon my strength.

"Sinbad el Askar," he said, "I'm tired; weary to death of it all. I want a change, and I'm going to have one. Do you know what I'm going to do?"

"Not go to war?" I hoped aloud.

"No; go to Mecca. I've been going for years—and I'm going now. The time is good, and I'm going to take advantage of it. I'm going to Mecca—and you are coming with me."

I was conscious of a joyous thrill.

Mecca! . . . Why—not a dozen white men had ever set foot in the place, and come out of it alive. . . . Go with him! Would I not?

"But what about things here?" I asked.

"Oh, I'll leave everything in train, and they'll go along all right."

"Can you trust the . . . ?"

"No, I can't," interrupted Chandos. "Can't trust anybody— unless it's you, my son. I really think I'm beginning to trust you. No, I don't trust any of them out of my sight; for intrigue and plotting come as natural to the Arab as eating and drinking. Deceiving and lying come as natural to him as walking and riding. They are splendid people and have many admirable virtues; but no-one who really knows them would be so silly as to trust them. . . . One here and there, perhaps, but those are just freaks and oddities. . . . Oh, no—'there's no trusting in the game'."

"Then you aren't afraid that . . ."

"No. You see they don't trust each other; any more than I trust them. Moreover, it is shocking bad form to plot evil against a man who is doing the Hadj, making the Pilgrimage. I shall leave a sort of Council of Regency in charge, and they'll watch each other. We'll go by sea from Tangier, and I shall call on the Sultan of Morocco, at Fez, on the way. . . . Incidentally, they all know that I'd deal very faithfully with anybody who fancied himself as Lord of Bab-el-Djebel."

"What would you do, supposing—for the sake of argument— you did return to find that Haroun bin Arrach or Abu bin Zaka had won over the army, seized the capital, and made himself Lord of the Western Sahara?"

"Kick him out," replied the Sultan. "Teach him a lesson that not only he, but all the People of the Desert would long remember. It would be great fun, returning with a handful of the Faithful and finding a job like that. The tribes would rally round my banner pretty quickly; and, if they didn't, we'd go to the Sultan of Morocco. And if he were too busy to kick the interloping usurper out, which he wouldn't be, I'd either take service under him, or go into business on my own account again, somewhere else. Great fun.

"Anyhow, we are going to risk it. And, incidentally, I'm taking Abu bin Zaka with me. Safer for me—and for him. He's too clever to leave behind—and Haroun bin Arrach is not too clever to be left behind. Moreover, Abu bin Zaka is a genuine Mussulman, whereas Haroun bin Arrach is not—and could never pass as one among the Muslimin of Mecca.

"Yes—we're going to risk it. Dangerous, of course. More especially so, for you. But anything's better than sitting here and yawning. . . . I'm tired. . . . Life's dull now. . . . You've made my army too good; and no-one is going to attack me any more, till the French come—and that won't be yet awhile. Yes, we'll go to Mecca. It's high time I did my pious duty and earned the Green Turban."

The Sultan's voice changed as he added in a very sinister tone of voice,

"And I've a pious deed to do there—the payment of an account that is long overdue."

And he fondled the handle of the dagger, the hilt of which stood upright in the middle of his sash.

PART III

CHAPTER XIX

Of our fascinatingly interesting journey from the sand-buried desert city of Bab-el-Djebel to Tangier, by way of Tafilelt and thence to Marrakesh, Meknes and Fez, I have no space to tell—though, here again, I could write a whole book about my adventures and experiences in these cities, in the intriguing capital of Morocco, and at the Court of the Sultan.

There, it was evident to me that the Sultan Mahommed el Kebir of Bab-el-Djebel was not only *persona grata*, but a person of very considerable importance.

Our party, beside the Sultan and myself, consisted of Hussein the Brave; Abu bin Zaka the Sicilian; Kassim bin Ibrahim, now holding the rank and office of Commissary General and Chief-Courier; Hassan bin Yacoub, known as *el Khātil*, the Slayer, a noted swordsman; a clever subtle scribe, Abd el Hamid whom the Sultan trusted more than any other Arab save Hussein the Brave; and a retinue of a score or so of fighting men of good birth or army rank, chosen for courage, ability, personality, fidelity, and character; men who would not faint by the wayside, grumble at hardship, act rashly, recklessly or foolishly; men who would be unlikely to betray me and incidentally their master, whether intentionally or by idle tongue-wagging.

For the Sultan had made no secret of the fact that, not only was the undertaking one of considerable risk for me, but that, should I be discovered as a European and an Infidel, the whole party would probably share my fate, as a punishment. For, those who had any hand in introducing a *mleccha*, an infidel dog, a living Defilement into the Holy City, would be as bad as the Pollution himself; a deceiver worse than the thief—of virtue; and would be equally deserving of death.

Ready and willing as I was for the adventure, nay, keenly and genuinely desirous of it, I nevertheless expostulated with the Sultan on the folly of taking me and incurring the risk that my presence involved—the danger of death not only to himself but to the whole party. However, upon that subject, as upon all others, the Sultan not only knew his own mind, but was inflexibly determined to have his own way. He wanted me with him, and that was the end of the matter.

Exactly why he wanted me, to the extent of taking such a risk,

I was not sure, but believed him to have some other reason than the desire for the company of a compatriot, a congenial spirit, and a person in whom he had implicit faith and perfect trust.

As he said, he believed he could trust the Arabs whom he had chosen to share the adventure; but he knew that he could trust me—and someone whom he knew he could trust, he must have.

This was an absolute obsession with the Sultan Mahommed el Kebir. I suppose it was natural in one who had lived so long and so dangerously, entirely surrounded by people of an alien race, a foreign language, different code of honour, and different standards of honesty.

Each member of our little company had not only sworn, on a peculiarly sacred copy of the *Koran*, a most solemn oath that he would regard my life and safety as a sacred charge and duty, but had left hostages, in the person of his eldest son and the boy's mother, in charge of the Council of Regency to carry on in Bab-el-Djebel until the Sultan's return.

In choosing these men, our companions and body-guard, the Sultan had eliminated, from those whom he would have wished to take, such as were so fanatically religious that they would be likely to view my presence in the Holy City with resentment—a resentment which, inflamed by their burning zeal, might get the better of their loyalty, honour, and discretion.

All the selected men knew that I was a Christian, but also knew that I treated their religion with respect; and they regarded me as a good soldier, an honest and upright official, and a trust-worthy friend. Whether the Sultan had hinted, or stated, that one of the objects of the journey was to convert me to Mahom-medanism and to make a good Mussulman of me, I did not know; but I had my suspicions.

Anyway, every man of the party, overjoyed beyond measure at the chance of making the Pilgrimage, becoming a *hadji* and earning the right to wear the green turban of a blameless life, had leapt at the opportunity offered by the Sultan; and, whether regarding my presence as gnat or camel, had swallowed me whole and with professed gusto.

§2

Arrived at Tangier, Kassim bin Ibrahim chartered a small fleet of *feluccas* or fishing-boats, or more probably smugglers' or gun-runners' boats, in which we made our way down the coast to

Ceuta. These feluccas were big, wide, low-lying boats, carrying a disproportionately huge main-sail.

In one of these went the Sultan and I, together with Hussein the Brave; Abu bin Zaka, the Sicilian; Kassim bin Ibrahim, the Courier; Hassan bin Yacoub, the Slayer; and Abd el Hamid, the Scribe. In a couple of others were the picked fighting-men; and in the fourth, the irreducible minimum of negro servants of the cook, groom, camel-man, *farash* type, again carefully selected, some because they were deaf and dumb, others because, outside their particular duties, they were stupider than animals, or spoke no language known in Mecca—or anywhere else, save among their own tribe.

At Ceuta we boarded a dirty old tramp bound for Alexandria, Port Said and Suez, whence a regular pilgrim-ship would carry us down the Red Sea to Jidda.

It was on our last night at sea that the Sultan took me a step further into his confidence, told me his story, and gave me the real reason for his making the Pilgrimage.

Being within the prescribed distance of Mecca, we were, by the way, arrayed in the *Irham*, the white two-piece garment, as all approaching Mecca must be when within a certain distance of the Holy City. And the garb must be retained until the pilgrim has made the circuit of the *Ka'ba* and kissed the Holy Stone.

It must again be donned and worn during the days of the actual Pilgrimage itself—the three-day part of the ceremony of performing the *Hadj*, as I will describe in due course.

Women wear a *bourkah*, a kind of linen sack completely covering them from the crown of the head to the soles of the feet, with eye-holes through which to peer.

Before one puts on the *Irham*, one should shave the head, but not, of course, the beard so respected of all Mussulmans. A man thus shaven and dressed in the *Irham* is then in the state known as *Muhrim*—and in that state there are all sorts of things that he must not do, though habitual to him at other times. A kind of strict and exacting Lent.

The symbolism is that of putting off earthly things and mundane cares, assuming instead the white robe of a new virtue, humility and purity. The dress consists of nothing whatsoever but two adequate pieces of white material, one fastening about the waist and covering the legs, the other draped over the shoulders and covering the upper part of the body. Absolutely nothing else should be worn—though a good many people hide a belt and weapons beneath the upper garment. Not even the head or feet are covered, and pious pilgrims scorn to use an umbrella, even at the hottest part of the hottest day. In a climate like that of Mecca, hot and stuffy even for Arabs, the wearing of the *Irham* is something of a penance and a hardship, especially to pilgrims unaccustomed to exposing themselves to such a burning sun. It is an interesting fact that no pilgrim dies of sun-stroke even though he exposes not only a bare, but a shaven, head at mid-day to the sun in one of the hottest parts of the world. Not unnaturally, they believe that Allah tempers the effects of the sun's rays to the pious, and I should think it is quite likely that the firm belief that one cannot get sun-stroke goes far to save one from it.

Thus arrayed, and seated side by side on a carpet in the space aft, reserved for him, the Sultan talked almost throughout the languorous Red Sea night. . . .

I make a story of his story:

Mahommed Ghulamali Salehudin Yussafali Jalpur, Nawab of Aundhara, one of the wealthiest Zemindars of the United Provinces, though a very great man, proprietor and ruler of some ten thousand square miles of well-wooded country—famous for its magnificent mango-groves and vast expanses of intensive and prosperous tillage—was a bitter, unrelenting enemy of the British.

This ruling passion had been instilled by his mother, the redoubtable Zahara Nurmahal, the Begum whose admired husband, the Nawab Mahommed Salehudin Yussafali, the British had deposed and exiled to Calcutta.

But, had the young Nawab's hatred not been inherited, it would have been acquired; for, both by nature and by nurture, he brooked interference but ill.

And what else had the British done but interfere with him, from the day he ascended the *gadi*—interfere arrogantly, monstrously and treacherously?

For did not they pretend to complete religious tolerance, and profess to respect the customs and tenets of Mahommedans, Hindus and all men alike? They did. And yet, what had been his experience? The grossest, most unwarrantable interference. When some of his rascally Hindu subjects had played their beastly music, or paraded their foul idols, before Mussulman mosques, and he had treated the swinish sons of noseless mothers as they deserved, had not the British interfered and told him he couldn't do such things?

Couldn't he! . . .

And what was their prohibition of the killing off of worthless female babies but wanton interference with an excellent and salutary custom?

And granted that all his Hindu subjects, tenants, and feudal land-owners, *were* idolatrous pigs, that didn't give the British the right to interfere with their religious customs, however objectionable they might be to a good Mussulman.

Sati, for example. Why, any decent widow wished to be burnt alive on her husband's funeral pyre, didn't she? And what is more sacred than custom, save only Allah the Compassionate?

Always interfering with somebody or something; always annoying and humiliating the Maharajahs and Nawabs of Ind. . . .

What business was it of theirs how he collected and spent his revenue? What right had they to say that the bands of *thugs* and dacoits, that ravaged the United Provinces, gave him a percentage of their earnings in return for protection?

The British! . . .

Allah smite their souls to Hell and keep them burning in lowest Eblis for all Eternity, where from his throne in Paradise he could watch them writhing. Had he the power, he'd bury them alive in one great pit with ten thousand swine. Yea, with ten thousand other swine—the hypocritical defilers of religion and breakers of caste.

Caste breakers! . . . Allah knew he had no use for Hindus and their caste, but what right had the British to break their caste, utterly defile the high-caste *kshattryas*, nay, the very Brahmins themselves? For was it not common knowledge that they used the fat of the sacred cow, the Holy Mother of the Hindus, for greasing their cartridges; and, even worse, that they ground the bones of the sacred cow and mixed the bone-dust with the meal of which they made the Sipahis' chupatties.

Yes, defilers of the Faith. For was it not common knowledge that deliberately they greased the Mussulman Sipahis' cartridges with the fat of pigs; the cartridges, of which the brave fellows who were foolish enough to fight and to die for them, must bite off the ends? And, in putting the cartridges between their lips and teeth, did they not put the accursed and forbidden pork into their mouths, and did not this defile them, here and hereafter?

And then the British officers and officials would come to him for tiger and panther hunting, for deer and buffalo, for pig-sticking, and the shooting of his *jheels* when thick with duck.

And how willingly they accepted his invitations to *tamashas* at his palace by Zeerut; and how they'd shout and laugh and drink their accursed brandy-*pani*, and smoke their foul cheroots, in his banqueting-hall. Some day he'd poison the whole crowd of them. Yea, including their shameless bare-faced women-folk whom they brought to his garden-parties; unveiled hussies who shook hands with him and smiled into his face unblushingly. Yea, and for all their dislike and contempt for a "black" man, felt neither dislike nor contempt for a diamond brooch.

The British! Allah hasten the day when the swords of the Faithful should cut their throats, the torches of the Faithful burn their houses, the hands of the Faithful seize their women-folk, bear them shrieking away. . .

Allah smite their accursed souls to lowest Hell.

And when the day came—and Allah be praised, all the signs and tokens pointed to its coming—the first throat that he would cut, if he had his way, would be that of the arrogant over-bearing insolent Colonel Chandos, the man who found a Nawab's game good enough to shoot, his horses good enough to ride, his banquets good enough to attend, his young men good enough to enlist—but found him himself, the Nawab of Aundhara, not good enough to be his friend, companion, equal. Not good enough to join the Club of which he was President, and that any white Nobody could join.

By the Beard of the Prophet, the fellow thought he did the Nawab of Aundhara an honour when he shook hands with him! Yea, when the day of reckoning came, he'd bid them bring Colonel Chandos alive to him, that he himself might cut his throat with his own hand.

Yea, and he'd bid them bring, alive and unhurt, that lovely white *houri*, his wife, that pearl beyond price. What an ornament for the *harim* of Mahommed Ghulamali Salehudin Yussafali Jalpur, Nawab of Aundhara!

Stranger things than that had happened, and the Day was drawing nigh.

Allah! Colonel Chandos's throat for the knife and Janet Chandos's throat—for kisses.

Colonel Chandos, the overbearing *feringhee*. . . .

In point of fact, Colonel Walter Manny Fitzroy Chandos commanding the 7th Bombay Fusiliers, a good soldier, a martinet, and a disciplinarian, was indeed a man of somewhat overbearing manner.

Not without reason, he considered his Battalion of Sepoy Infantry to be one of the finest in the Army of East India. With much less reason, he believed it to be faithful to its salt, loyal to its service in general and to himself in particular. To himself who loved—and certainly chastened—them. Speaking of his men as constantly he did, he was wont frequently to imply that, provided they were justly punished, they positively enjoyed punishment.

Undoubtedly it was the opinion of the Second-in-Command and of the Adjutant, that Colonel Chandos enjoyed punishing the men. And these two officers, loyal as they were to the Colonel and tireless in their efforts to assist and support him in every possible way, were nevertheless agreed that—amazing paradox—no-one knew less about the 7th Bombay Fusiliers than did their Commanding Officer.

Incredible though it may seem, this distinguished Indian soldier, veteran of several wars and many battles, knew but a few words of Hindustani; knew practically nothing of India, save what he had seen with his own eyes; knew nothing of his Battalion, save its history and its chronic and present state of high military efficiency.

Of the 7th Bombay Fusiliers, on the march, and in battle, Colonel Chandos was intensely proud. As a regiment, he loved it, and would have been astounded to learn that it did not love him; that, indeed it regarded him with bitter hatred. In actual fact, Colonel Chandos would have learned no such thing. He would have refused to believe it, had an angel from Heaven come specially to inform him of the fact. He learned it eventually of devils from Hell, in the shape of his own admired Sepoys.

In his private life, his domestic relations, the charming and peaceful atmosphere of his happy bungalow, this severe ruthless soldier, apparently at once cold and violent, was a different man. To the girl, almost child, whom recently he had married on his first and last leave to England, he seemed the personification of gentleness, kindness and consideration; a tower of strength and protection; truly her lover, her adored and adoring husband, her king who could do no wrong. . . .

The heat of that month of May, 1857, was—especially to the girl fresh from Scotland—appalling, a heat such as she had not imagined; a heat that made her feel as though trapped between a burning brazen earth and a molten copper sky, a heat that frightened her.

However, the rains would come, and everyone said that it would be delightful then. Or at any rate, vastly better, if not exactly delightful: and, meanwhile, she could bear it, by dint of closing all the doors and most of the windows of the bungalow from sunrise till sunset, and seeing that the *kuskus* tatties—the fragrant-scented fibre mats—that blocked the others, were kept wet, so changing the hot dry blast into a cool and pleasant draught.

Sitting, lightly clad, beneath the moving punkah, she could read, write her letters home, sleep, and—sew tiny garments. And, at first, at any rate, dining on the wide flat carpeted roof beneath another punkah, sleeping with only the mosquito-net between herself and the diamond-studded sky, breakfasting beneath the punkah before sunrise, was fun.

The hot weather wasn't really as bad as people made out. Certainly it was not bad enough to make her entertain, for one moment, the idea of going to the Hills, as so many officers' wives did.

Leave Walter! Leave him to the mercy of *khitmutgar* and cook: to such travesty of comfort as he could find in Mess and at the Club? Nothing on earth would induce her to do so. Not even Walter himself, though he had done his best.

No. The man who ruled a regiment with a rod of iron, at whose nod men ran in haste, at whose frown they trembled, entirely failed, both by pleading and by insisting, by kindness or a false assumption of the imperious sternness for which he was famous, to move the slip of a girl, who, laughingly, sweetly and firmly, exhibited, on this one point, a determination as strong as his own.

There was a clash of wills, a loving conflict—and Janet Chandos won.

Poor Janet. . . .

"I shall be back from Orderly Room by nine, my child," said Colonel Chandos, as he kissed her before leaving the bungalow on the morning after their latest lovers'-quarrel on the subject of her going to the Hills for the worst of the hot weather, "and I shall return with a Corporal's Guard and have you deported from Zeerut Cantonments. You will have three hours in which to pack."

"I shall pack nothing, and you won't pack me—off to Simla or anywhere else," replied Janet Chandos, returning her husband's kiss.

"Well, you've had fair warning. I shall be back at nine with the men."

But Colonel Chandos did not come back with, or without, the men.

And his wife never set eyes on him again.

Nor did she ever receive any message concerning him, save the sound of musket-shots, fired at him by his beloved Sepoys as he rode on to the parade-ground. She never knew whether he was killed at once; whether he lay in agony, as he bled to death in the dust of the parade-ground; whether he were hacked to pieces as he lay.

In point of fact, Colonel Chandos rode within a few yards of the paraded Battalion, bringing his horse to an abrupt halt as his admired Subedar Major suddenly strode toward him with raised sword and a shouted order. This officer, a man of good family, a cousin of the Nawab of Aundhara in fact, a be-medalled stalwart veteran like himself of several wars and many battles, whom he had seen rise from recruit to the highest rank open to a native of India, a man in whom he had taken a personal interest, whom he had befriended and promoted and in whom he had implicit faith, was his especial favourite.

What the Devil! Had the fellow gone mad?

For his cry was,

"*Din! Din!* . . . *Maro! Maro!* . . . The Faith! . . . Kill, brothers, kill."

And instantly the loaded rifles of the men on the left of the line were flung forward, and Colonel Chandos received a volley of musket-balls in his broad chest. At the same moment, other sections shot their officers in the back, the majority falling dead; one or two, badly wounded, wheeling about and putting up a desperate fight with the drawn swords already in their hands. Probably, Colonel Chandos was dead ere the bayonets were driven into his body, and saw not the gleaming steel nor the infuriated savage faces of his murderers, the men whom so long he had justly ruled, strictly disciplined, led to victory, and in whom he had so much pride and trust.

No, of the details of his end, his wife knew nothing. . . .

After the noise of the musket-shots from the not-distant parade ground, she noticed no unusual sounds until, suddenly, she heard shouts and cries, the sound of running men and horses, mob noises, as brutally the brief peace of the early morning was shattered utterly. As the compound of her quiet bungalow, an island in an ocean of uproar, was invaded, the house surrounded by a yelling surging crowd, she could hear in spite of closed doors and windows, individual cries above the din.

"*Maro! Maro!* . . . Kill! Kill! . . . *Din! Din!* The Faith! The Faith!"

What was this?

Suddenly the door of her room was flung open, and her ayah, so quiet and dignified, so secretive and imperturbable, dashed into her presence, distraught, dishevelled, bare-headed, and flung herself at her feet.

"Memsahib! Memsahib! The *budmashes* are . . ."

As Janet Chandos rose to her feet, the portly *khitmutgar* ran into the room, his face almost pale, his starting eyes seeming to consist almost entirely of white.

"Memsahib! Memsahib! Come quickly. . . . The Sipahis have . . ."

A terrific crash, as doors and windows were burst in.

A rush of feet, and, in the doorway, thrust backward but fighting desperately with an old sword, the *durwan*, an aged Sipahi of her husband's regiment, strove to stem a rush of men . . . a deafening explosion as a musket was fired in the very room . . . thuds, shouts, a groan, as the old man fell almost at her feet . . . a surging rush of men—soldiers, street roughs, butchers, blood-bespattered fiends. . . .

Thuds . . . Blows . . . Hideous sounds . . . Fearful sights . . .

The *khitmutgar*, almost headless . . . the ayah slashed, hacked, screaming, spurting blood . . .

"*Walter! Walter!*" cried Janet Chandos.

Oh, God! . . .

Would they tear her in pieces? They would . . .

Hands at her throat, her dress . . . tearing . . . tearing.

Scream . . . Scream . . . Scream . . .

Hand over her mouth . . .

A blow . . .

Fainting . . . She must not faint . . .

Thrown down . . .

Another rush from the door . . .

The press, the crush, she was being crushed to death . . .

They were . . . they dare not . . . they *could* not . . .

A great bull voice . . . Roaring . . .

"*O-o-o-o-h! Aré, brothers! . . . Make way . . . Hands off the woman! . . .*"

Saved! . . . Saved!

"*Hands off, I say. . . . She's for the Nawab Saheb.*"

A roar of laughter. Shouts. Fumbling hands. Her necklet of pearls, her husband's wedding gift. Her watch-brooch. Her locket with his miniature. Her engagement ring. Her wedding ring. The filthy thieves. . . . The bestial brute beasts. . . . She must not faint.

"*Stand back, I say, or I'll split your skull. Give her to me! . . .*"

A heavy blow. Blood. Blood. The man had fallen upon her.

Another.

She must not faint.

"Drag the bodies of those swine off her and . . ."
Oh, relief . . . The blessed relief . . .
"Up with her . . ."
Saved! . . . Saved! . . .

And Janet Chandos was saved—for the Nawab of Aundhara.

Nor, for days, was she sufficiently conscious to realize that she was the Nawab's prisoner, his property. . . . The Nawab's—woman! She, Colonel Chandos's widow.

The shock had been too great, her injuries ere her "rescue" by Subedar-Major Yar Mahommed Ali Khan, too severe.

Slowly she returned to consciousness and realization; to knowledge and understanding that she was—what she was.

What would become of her and her unborn child?

An unusual woman, this Scottish girl of eighteen, a girl of character, strong, resolute, enduring; endowed with nerves of steel, a dauntless soul, and an unshakeable faith in the God of her fathers.

The Nawab Mahommed Ghulamali Salehudin Yussufali Jalpur found that though he had captured, he could not tame, this exotic bird. Here was no bulbul for a Nawab's delight. Rather, a hawk. But the Nawab Mahommed Ghulamali Salehudin Yussufali Jalpur had tamed many and many a falcon, wild, fierce and intractable as this. Oh, many a one.

He and his falconers had never been defeated yet, though some of the birds had died. Starvation did wonders. Opium and certain other drugs worked greater wonders still. He'd tame the pretty creature yet; turn the proud wild hawk into a cooing dove. Yes, his own milk-white cooing dove.

And if the lovely bird would not sing in a gilded cage, let it moan in a dark dungeon for awhile.

Spice to a jaded palate, this. Something really new; something different from the cloying, fawning, flattering creatures who would have crawled across glowing charcoal to his embrace; walked to his *harim* upon knives.

Untamable? Allah, that were something new! Something new indeed; if a woman, white or brown, could not be broken and trained, in the palace of a Nawab of Aundhara.

Huh! There were men there who had a way with high-spirited creatures, be they horses, hunting-dogs, hawks, cheetahs—or women.

And if he failed, what of his lady mother, the Dowager Begum?

The Nawab smiled as he thought of his mother, the Dowager Begum, Zahara Nurmahal, and how she'd handle the delicate creature; deal with a recalcitrant *harim* woman who, incidentally, was an Englishwoman!

Allah! By the time the Begum had done with her daughter-in-law, she'd be her daughter-in-*law* indeed. In the home of the Begum's law, the girl's one idea would be to obey that law, and the law of her husband's lightest wish.

Oh, between them they'd tame her. They'd teach her to be a proud and haughty, superior, self-righteous, high-and-mighty, twice-born, sneering, contemptuous Englishwoman.

Yea, something new if the Begum Saheba of Aundhara failed with a daughter-in-law!

For he was going to marry her. Marry her properly, completely, and legally. Marry her by Mohammedan law and ceremony, and by English law and ceremony too.

Yes, his wife, his property—and who could then take her from him? Not that she'd want to be taken from him, by the time she'd been in his *harim*, and the Lady Begum's care, for a while.

And what a man his son would be, with all the strength and cleverness and fighting-power of the English combined with the virtues and attributes of the Nawabs of Aundhara—a line of warriors that traced its descent far back beyond the ancestor who came to India in the train of Nadirshah the Conqueror, who defeated the Moguls, captured Delhi, and took away the Peacock Throne itself.

Yea, and now that India was about to throw off the yoke of the *feringhees*, there would be another Mussulman Emperor of India—and who was to say who he should be?

The old Mogul pantaloon, sitting there in his "capital" at Delhi writing Persian poetry all day in the Dewan-i-am of the palace, was but a puppet, a contemptible marionette dancing at the end of English strings.

He'd follow the *feringhees*—into the grave.

And who would take his place as King of Delhi and Emperor of Ind?

Brave days were coming, days when a strong arm and a sharp sword might carve out a kingdom. He might yet live to see his son seated on a throne. . . .

But this was looking ahead indeed. First beget your son and then find your throne.

However, the best-laid schemes of mice and fiends gang oft agley, alas, and, to the immeasurable chagrin of the Nawab

Mahommed Ghulamali Salehudin Yussufali Jalpur, the accursed defilers of Faith, the breakers of caste, the hell-doomed Christian dogs, shamefully, disgracefully and dishonestly refused to ac- knowledge that they were beaten. In all sorts of holes and corners, in little houses, little Residences, in two-anna forts, they kept their foul flag flying, and fought on, refusing to accept their obvious defeat.

Nevertheless, there had been great deeds and glorious doings, slaughter at Delhi, massacre at Cawnpore, murders, slaying of their officers by nearly all Sepoy regiments.

And he himself had had a heavy hand in the doings at Cawnpore; had egged on his own men as they flung the *feringhee* women and children into the well. . . .

What was the use of the British pretending that they had a chance; a hope? Look at Lucknow.

But, on the other hand, look at Delhi, contained and besieged by a wretched little army—that should surely melt as ice beneath the mid-day sun.

What if Jan Nikal Sein were there? What could he do?

But what John Nicholson did do, was to capture Delhi with his wretched little army, though he died in the hour of victory.

And then, these other hare-brained insolents, Jan Lawrence, Outram, Havelock. . . . They were making head-way, winning battles; and certain accursed unspeakable sons of dogs, and enemies of Allah, from the North-west were helping them, Pathans and Sikhs and other fools and swine that remained *nimuk hallal*, true to their salt.

And actually they relieved Lucknow, defeated the Nana Saheb, scattered the mutineers like chaff, hunted them down like rats.

Inscrutable indeed are the ways of Allah; for the tide was turning, ebbing; the chance was going . . . gone.

No longer could he ride abroad at the head of the Aundhara State Lancers, foraying, robbing, pillaging, burning, slaughtering rich Hindus, hunting out stray fugitive Europeans and Eurasians.

A new spirit was abroad, or rather, the old spirit was returning.

And bad went to worse. The *feringhees* were winning, were again sweeping across the country like a storm. Captured mutineers, and men who had raised hand against the English, were being hanged in batches; being blown from guns.

That was a wicked thing, for no Mussulman blown from a gun

could go to Paradise. The devils were inflicting a punishment that lasted to endless Eternity.

And his turn would come, for his hands were gory, his *sowars'* lance-points had been reddened, their *tulwars* had dripped with blood. In his palace by Zeerut was loot untold, rupees uncounted —and a white woman.

Yea, in his *harim*, in a thick-walled, almost unlighted room, was a bemused, drugged, half-insane Englishwoman, wife of Colonel Chandos, slain on his own parade-ground by his own men.

And how many hunted yelping dogs were there, to lift up their voices to curry favour with the British, and to avenge themselves upon the Nawab; all ready, willing and able, to prove that he had incited the mutiny of the 7th Bombay Fusiliers, by the voice of his cousin Subedar-Major Yar Mahommed Ali Khan; to prove that it was straight to his palace by Zeerut that the woman had been brought, bruised and bleeding, dishevelled and distraught, her clothes in shreds; and that he had rewarded her abductors; forcibly taken her into his harim and kept her there a prisoner?

For these things alone, they would blow him from a gun, apart from the fact that the Aundhara Lancers had made themselves a scourge and a terror, looting and torturing every *sowcar* and *bunnia*, every fat Hindu money-lender within a hundred miles of Zeerut town.

Definitely the Great Killing was over; the Great Indian Mutiny had failed; was suppressed; and all that was left was reward for those who had remained true to their salt, had helped the Sahibs in their hour of trial—and bitter punishment for all who had turned against them; punishment very bitter for those who had slain white women; yea, bitterest of all for those who had slain or abducted white women.

No man had a blacker record than the Nawab Mahommed Ghulamali Salehudin Yussufali Jalpur; and in his harim was still the captive white woman, sick of mind and body. . . .

"My son," quoth the Lady Zahara Nurmahal, Begum of Aundhara, "light of my eyes and joy of my days—heavy as the words are in my mouth and terrible to utter . . . you must go. You must flee. It is sentence of death to me to say this, but it is sentence of death for you to remain."

It had come!

His mother had put into words the dreadful thought that had haunted his mind for weeks, refusing to be cast out.

Yes, it was flight or death. Flight or death.

But whither could he flee? What spot in all Ind was safe for the Nawab of Aundhara, whose hands were red, whose face was blackened, whose *harim* contained a tortured white woman?

For that is what they would call his—and the Lady Begum's—methods of training, coercion and punishment . . . torture.

"Easy to talk, my mother," he growled. "Easy to say 'escape'. But how shall I escape? Whither shall I go? Is there one place in Hindustan . . . ?"

"No, my son," replied the Begum. "There is no place in all this land. Their arm is long; the passes are closed; the roads are theirs; and all men their friends—now that they have won. The poor Nana Saheb himself and the good Tantia Topi are hunted fugitives; chased like mad dogs across the country, living in the jungles, shelterless and empty-bellied; lying on the bare earth like the wild beasts. Great kings and princes are as dust before the wind of the *feringhees*' wrath, and there is no hiding-place in Hindustan."

"And must I, the Nawab of Aundhara, be hanged upon a tree before my palace gates; or be blown from a gun upon the terrace there below? Must I go to . . . ?"

"My son, you must go to Mecca. There, in the Holy City, will you be safe, though all the world desire your blood. There you can live in peace and piety, returning here when this is forgotten and it is safe to do so."

"*When!*" sneered the Nawab.

"And which is better, life In the Holy City, or death here in Aundhara? Yes, perhaps on a gallows in Zeerut gaol, with common malefactors of the bazaar," replied his mother.

"*This* will be forgotten? They will *never* forget nor forgive," growled the Nawab.

"They will. It is their way. There will be an amnesty, a Proclamation, that all who make peace and swear allegiance shall be reinstated; given back their lands; be taken again into favour."

"Never," growled the Nawab. "Not while there is a Well at Cawnpore. . . . Not for those who slew their women. Still less for those who kept them alive."

"Then it is flight. . . . Choose between shame and dreadful death, here in Ind—or life, honour, peace and prosperity, there in Mecca. And I will accompany you, my son. Whither thou goest, I will go.

"Aye," and the Begum chuckled evilly. "Aye . . . and the woman goes with us. *Then* with whom is the laugh? *Then* who shall gnash their teeth? . . . Jewels, money, great wealth in small compass, shall go with us, and your Diwan Facing-both-Ways, the good cunning dog, shall send us revenues also."

"*Exile!*" groaned the Nawab.

"*Safety,*" whispered the Begum. "Think you I wish to leave Aundhara, the home that has been mine so long? Better exile than death for you and worse than death for me—deprivation and captivity."

"And how should we get out of the country?" sneered the Nawab, "especially if we tried to take the Chandos Saheba. . . . Ask the Governor-General to order us a ship?"

"No, my son, we will not trouble the *Sirkar*, and we will not take the road to Calcutta with an escort, flags flying, and drums beating. We will be respectable pilgrims, neither rich nor poor. You will be making the Pilgrimage, taking *purdah* women, your chief wife and your mother. Also your aged father; that the good and pious old man may lay his bones to rest in the Holy City."

"Father?"

"Yea. Old Sirdar Iqbal Ghulam Hyder, your great-uncle, will go with us. He will be your 'father'. He will rejoice to play a part and cheat the English—and he would give his beard to become a *hadji.*"

"And the white woman? Will she not . . . ?"

"Leave her to me, my son," interrupted the Begum. "Leave her to me. You will find her very docile—and very silent. For most of the journey she will sleep, yea, as one who hath the sleeping-sickness."

"And it will not injure the unborn child?"

"Trust me, my son. I know that which I know. Your son shall be born on the sacred soil of the Holy City."

CHAPTER XX

And so the son of the widow of Colonel Walter Manny Fitzroy Chandos, the child who grew up a Mussulman and came to be el Sidna el Sultan Mahommed el Kebir, told me the story that, for simplicity, I have thus set forth.

When he had finished, a long silence fell between us, for there was nothing I could say.

"So I was born in Mecca," said Chandos, "born of Janet Chandos, the wife of Colonel Chandos, my father. *Of course*, he was my father. . . . Do I look as though I have Indian blood? Do I? Look at the whites of my eyes, the demi-lunes of my finger-nails. Look at the colour of my eyes and hair, the shape of my nose, my lips. Is there any trace whatever of native blood?"

"None," I said. "The moment I set eyes on you, when Ali bin Ahmed brought me into your tent, I knew you were a European. All the time that I was wondering what was going to happen to me, I knew that it would not be anything very dreadful, as I was absolutely certain that you were a European."

"You didn't even think I was a fair Berber? Lots of them have blue or green eyes and quite fair hair and beards, you know."

"No, I didn't."

"No! Of course I'm not the Nawab's son. I never saw my father, nor any portrait of him; but my mother used to tell me I was the very image of him. She had a miniature of him in a locket, but those devils took it away from her. And I'm perfectly certain that my mother spoke the truth. She'd do that in any case, of course. What I meant was that she'd know exactly what she was saying. It was not a case of the wish being father to the thought."

"No. And, naturally, she'd *know*, of course," I mused.

"Of course she would, but that she-devil, the Nawab's mother, bribed the *hakims* and midwives and people, to swear that I was a seven months' child. In which case the Nawab would be my father. . . . Lies, of course. Damnable hellish lies. It was only after I grew up that I realized what my poor mother must have suffered. Not only violent physical suffering, in India, I mean—and in Mecca, too, for the matter of that—but through me. I can have been nothing but a curse to her."

"Not you," I ventured to contradict. "You must have been the one thing that made life worth living and kept her from going mad. You must have been the joy of her life."

"But, don't you see—I was the *curse* of her life; for they brought me up a Mussulman, taught me to be everything she would not want me to be. Joy of her life? What, seeing me brought up to be anti-Christian; brought up to be another Nawab of Aundhara; brought up to be his son; proclaimed and acknowledged as his son; being taught that some day I should go back to India to reign in his stead—back to the palace by Zeerut where she had gone down into Hell?

"Why, it wasn't until *I* came that they could really torture her.

"God! how did she live and why did she live?

"What it must have meant to her, that I grew up among the elect of the Muslimin; to hear me praying to Allah; to see me spit each time I mentioned the word 'Christian'. Man, I can see her face now, as I stood before her, a cocky boy, and, at my father's request, displayed my new accomplishment—recited without error the words of the *Fatiha*, the opening chapter of the Koran. It is one of the shortest, you know, and used a good deal in prayer . . . I don't think I was a bigger little swine than most boys, and of course I didn't know what I was doing to her . . . but I can see her face still."

"She didn't try to make you a Christian, then?" I asked.

"Of course she did. But how much time do you suppose she was allowed to spend alone with me; and what chance had she against environment and daily teaching? When you were ten years of age, saying your prayers night and morning, taken to church twice on Sundays, filled from babyhood with tales from the Old and New Testament and the certain knowledge that God was your Father, and Christ your Saviour—could anyone who, on most days saw you only for an hour or two, have turned you into a Buddhist, Shintoist, Confucian, or even a Roman Catholic? . . . Especially if you only saw that person in the presence of the Vicar and the Curate who was your tutor.

"She tried; of course she tried; whenever we were alone together; but Christianity did not appeal to me, nor was I brought up to suppose that women were the right and proper persons to hold views on religion—much less to express them.

"Oh, yes! I must have been the 'joy of her life'! Can't you see I was the last and worst and ultimate *curse* and cruelty of her life?"

"Yes," I said. "I can."

I decided to ask a question, though this was contrary to my

custom where Chandos was concerned.

"How did you come to leave her—and go to Sandhurst?" I asked.

"Sandhurst!" he laughed shortly. "Man, I have only been to England once in my life."

"*What?*" I cried in surprise. "I imagined you'd grown up there. And on our first or second interview, you asked me when I was at Sandhurst—and remarked that I must have been there before your time."

"Well, if you had been to Sandhurst you'd certainly have been there before my time—as I was never there at all. . . . I tell you I've only been to England once."

"Well, no-one would think it," I said truthfully.

"No. They let my mother teach me English. Doubtless the Nawab thought that it would be useful to me when I went to Aundhara to claim my 'rights' as his son, the missing heir, thus enabling him to slip quietly back in my retinue, and to become the real Nawab, though nominally deposed. He got me English books, too. Sent to Cairo for them, and also for English papers and magazines. I read with the utmost avidity every English book on which I could lay hands.

"Although growing up among fierce and fanatical Muslimin, and brought up on the Koran, and rejecting Christianity as I say—I had a positive yearning to be English. It was an obsession. The blood, I suppose—for of course I am English.

"And everything that my mother told me about Britain and the British appealed to me absolutely. The Jesuits say that if you give them a child for its first seven years, they've no fear for its future. I suppose it was the same with me and Moham-medanism. And it was for more than twice that time that the *imams*, *marabouts*, *mullahs* and *moulvies* had me—for the forming and moulding of my impressionable mind, so far as religion was concerned.

"No, I did not grow up in England, nor even in Europe.

"You are wondering how I came to leave Mecca and my mother. I was kidnapped.

"No, that's hardly the truth.

"Say I was very willingly kidnapped, decoyed away without any difficulty whatever. I had got to that age and state when Mecca, and life in Mecca, weren't enough. The English blood again, I suppose. Roving spirit of the British, the *wanderlust*, the exploring urge that has coloured the map of the world red.

"And for some reason that I can't explain, I hated the Nawab.

Not that he was ever really cruel, or actively unkind, to me. And, even more, I loathed and detested my "grand-mother", the Begum Zahara Nurmahal. Somehow I knew that they ill-treated my mother. I don't mean active physical cruelty at that time, so much as mental torture. I knew that my mother suffered at their hands; suffered perpetually; and though I'm afraid I didn't love her as I should have done—partly because I saw so little of her— she had all my sympathy.

"I would have done anything for her, suffered for her, stuck up for her, and taken her part.

"Of course, a boy bred and brought up as I was, must, I imagine, be infinitely more precocious than an English boy brought up under normal conditions in ordinary circumstances. And I must have grasped the situation pretty well.

"Anyhow, I hated my alleged father and grandmother; hated life in his house and in the streets of Mecca; and was only too delighted to run away from them. No, I didn't need much decoying. . . . My one regret then, and my bitter regret ever since, was leaving my mother. It wasn't till I grew up that I realized something of what she must have suffered when I disappeared and she never knew what became of me.

"Allah! What that poor soul went through, all those years— and to think that I should add to her sufferings!"

The Sultan fell silent.

"Is she still alive?" I asked.

"I don't know. That's what I'm going to find out. I suppose I am over-ready to make excuses for myself, but this really is my first opportunity of going back. Possibly I could have gone any-when in the last year or two, but I didn't feel the time was ripe to leave my kingdom before my position was really consolidated. But for you, I shouldn't be here now. You've been a godsend, Sinbad. I almost trust the Household troops and the Cavalry now, thanks to you. And even if Haroun bin Arrach turned traitor, as he's quite capable of doing, I doubt whether he'd win over and debauch all the infantry-officers and men. And I don't believe he could win over the Cavalry you've trained, though if this is so, their loyalty—officers and men—is really loyalty to you rather than to me."

And Chandos put his hand on my shoulder—a great reward.

"Yes, it was my predecessor, Sheik Abdul Wahid Abd-ur-Rahman, Sultan of Bab-el-Djebel, who kidnapped me. He saw me two or three times in the *Haram* at Mecca and literally fell in love with me—my fair skin, blue eyes, light hair and so on. . . . Quite decently, I mean. And he attracted me enormously, a magnificent figure of a man, beautifully dressed, with lovely weapons, the *beau idéal* of a fierce desert fighting-man. He appealed to me tremendously. I made myself a sort of unofficial guide to him in Mecca—better than any *mutowif*.

"When he questioned me about my home and family, I, naturally (being Meccan born and bred), told him a pack of lies; and when he had done the Pilgrimage and was about to depart, he offered to take me with him—to adopt me in fact. I jumped at it. Here was a chance to see the world, and get away from Mecca, that stagnant hole of a place with which I was so bored.

"I went to his lodging next day, gleefully listened to his instructions, and allowed him and his servants to disguise me.

"Next day I travelled down to Jidda in his retinue, as a donkey-boy.

"We embarked in *dhows* and sailed up the Red Sea to Suez, went by camel to Cairo and, after a wonderful time there, to Alexandria, and took ship thence to Sallee, whence we travelled by caravan to Bab-el-Djebel.

"There he tried to put over some wonderful yarn about my having been miraculously revealed to him by the Prophet, in a vision at Mecca, as being his son by a woman whom he had taken to wife at Medina on his first Pilgrimage to el Hedjaz, some fourteen years before!

"He was amazingly kind to me and loved me like a father, for he had no sons of his own.

"Well, I played up to him, learned the ropes and the tricks of the trade, and did my part sufficiently well to succeed him without any great trouble or bloodshed, when he died.

"So now you know, my son—and you may imagine what it meant to me when you blew in."

"Why did you use me so badly, or rather pretend to do so, at first?" I asked. "Why did you treat me as though you thought I was a spy?"

"Because I thought you were one."

"But, as Ali bin Ahmed told you, he bought me in a slave-market."

"Yes, Ali bin Ahmed told me so all-right; and, being the truth, it sounded so much more like fiction that I didn't believe a word he said—particularly as Ali is a spy himself by profession—a spy of mine."

"A spy of yours!" I exclaimed.

"Yes, and I believe he's trustworthy, but you never know; and his story was altogether too good to be true. It struck me as much more likely that he'd been got at, and that you were a Secret Service agent."

"But you didn't doubt that I was an Englishman, surely?"

"Oh, my good ass, don't you suppose there are Englishmen in the Secret Service of every European Power? If the French were going to send a spy to Bab-el-Djebel, you don't suppose they'd send a Frenchman, do you? . . . No, you might very well have been a Secret Agent from France, Spain, Germany, Italy or Turkey."

"And if you'd decided that I had been?" I asked.

"I should have hanged you, out of hand. I fairly prayed to Allah that you might be what you pretended to be; and I thanked Allah with my forehead on the sand when I found you were genuine. . . . Allah the Merciful, the Compassionate indeed—to send me an Englishman there in the heart of the Western Sahara."

"Should I pass for an Englishman in England?" he asked.

"Absolutely," I answered. "Nobody would ever dream you were anything but a sun-burnt Englishman. You talk such extraordinarily good colloquial idiomatic English."

"Thanks to the first years of my life with my mother; to my visit to England; and to my constant study of English books, magazines and papers, ever since," said Chandos.

"I say," he added, "we'll make another Pilgrimage some day, if we get back to Bab-el-Djebel and all goes well—a pilgrimage to England. And we'll take my mother—if she's alive. Rescue her. Take her back to her home in Scotland."

I pondered this. Would the poor woman wish to go—after forty years?

"I wonder if she'll know me," continued Chandos. "I wonder if she'll believe that it really hasn't been possible for me to return to Mecca, until now.

"It is queer. I can't honestly say I really love her, you know—she's very vague and shadowy, although I remember her quite well—but somehow, I do love the idea of her. And I pity her from the bottom of my soul. . . . I do hope she's alive.

"And, by Allah, I hope my father—as he calls himself—is alive," he added, grimly.

And again his right hand went to the handle of the great dagger stuck in the front of his sash.

PART IV

CHAPTER XXI

Next morning we anchored off the alleged 'port' of Jidda, to within less than a mile or so of which, no ship can approach. Thus it is that, here, upon the waters of the Red Sea, begins the cruel swindling of pilgrims by the rapacious sharks that batten upon their piety—inasmuch as the only way of getting ashore is to charter one of the innumerable boats collected for the purpose, and to pay something approaching the iniquitous charge made by their proprietors.

Kassim bin Ibrahim, with much shouting, cursing, gesticulating and appeals to Allah, chartered a small fleet of these bunder-boats, into which we transferred ourselves and our not inconsiderable baggage.

On reaching the shore, we all had to file before the insolent Turkish jack-in-office who enquired whether we were Turks or merely Arabs. At night all cats are grey—and in the *ishram* all men are more or less alike—except they be negroes, of course.

Having passed the landing-officer, we were confronted by a mob of *mutowifs*, the next breed of pilgrim-robbing thieves. These are a combination of tout, guide and food-and-transport-contractor—the lowest form of Tourist Agency known to man. Among them are Turkish Government spies and Secret Service agents on the look-out for political undesirables who may endeavour to make their way into the country, as well as for infidel European gate-crashers of religion, who might be mad enough to attempt to make their way into the Holy City.

With these people Kassim bin Ibrahim dealt in short order, bawling that not only were we Arabs, but knew the ropes, had been there before, and that when we wanted a *mutowif* we would choose one ourselves.

I should here mention that el Sidna el Sultan Mahommed el Kebir was travelling strictly incognito. For more than one reason he most particularly desired the strictest secrecy to be observed as to whence he came, his rank, wealth, and power, and his identity. Any member of his *entourage* who let it be known that his master was a desert Sultan whose suzerain was the Sultan of Morocco would incur something more than his extreme displeasure. We were to be just a band of ordinary Arab pilgrims from Northern Africa, well-off, well-armed, self-sufficient and somewhat truculent; and he was not to be distinguished as our leader.

Later, I discovered that his reasons were partly political, partly private and personal. He desired that the Turkish Governor, the Shereef of Mecca and, particularly, his step-father the Nawab of Aundhara, should be unaware of his arrival.

As it was to be a case of "luggage in advance", and the excellent Kassim bin Ibrahim was to be the advance-agent of the party, finding accommodation for us in Mecca and bestowing our baggage therein before we arrived, we spent some three or four days in Jidda, a place of sojourn not to be recommended.

For it is the home of smells, the abode of the basest insects, the scene of the activities of the greediest swindlers on earth; and generally as comfortless as are most termini and railway junctions.

Not that there is any railway at Jidda, but it is the junction of the sea and land routes from the Red Sea and from the railway terminus of the Aleppo-Damascus railway at Medina (whence runs the Pilgrim Road to the port of Yenbo-el-Bahr) as well as the terminus of the road for pilgrims returning from Mecca to the coast.

It is a dirty dilapidated hole of a place, albeit picturesque, and one of the very oldest cities in the world. The streets, narrow, foul and filthy, run between lofty houses which, like the mosques, emulate and probably beat, the Leaning Tower of Pisa in deviation from the perpendicular.

Nevertheless, there are some quite good shops, a considerable *sûk*, and some decent restaurants. It is a town of lodging-houses, with a population of lodging-house keepers, souvenir-vendors, universal providers, stall-keeping and shop-keeping thieves, touts, guides, donkey-boys, camel-men, transport contractors, and rascals of every description, all preying on the depolarized and bewildered pilgrim. Fortunately there is always a sea-breeze, otherwise even the inhabitants would die of the stink and stench of the place—wherein sanitation is unknown. Like the poor and the pilgrim, epidemic disease is always with them, ranging from cholera and plague to opthalmia and the itch.

While Kassim bin Ibrahim, courier and O.C. transport, was arranging for baggage-camels to take him, the luggage, and the servants, to Mecca—some fifty miles distant—the rest of us sought food and lodging.

The best 'hotel' reminded me of those European resorts

wherein one can select one's own fish in a glass tank—see it caught in a net, and watch it borne off to be cooked—inasmuch as the *plat du jour*, in the shape of a whole sheep, was cooking before a brazier outside the front door. From this, great hunks of meat were detached, skewered and displayed, that the patron might take his choice.

The proprietor brandished a specially succulent portion, impaled upon a kind of toasting-fork, thrusting it beneath the nose of each passer-by, for the delight of his eye and the temptation of his stomach.

On a chunk of this excellent roast mutton and a disc of bread, we each fed full, if not daintily, thereafter scattering in search of lodgings. By order of the Sultan, his followers were to select rooms, neither rich nor poor, to dwell in them in twos and threes, and to accommodate themselves as far as possible in his immediate neighbourhood. He and I were always to dwell together and without other company, though Hussein the Brave and, Abd el Hamid the Scribe were, when possible, to be in the same house— "brains and brawn both handy", as Chandos said.

After dinner, Chandos and I sought the lodging that Kassim bin Ibrahim had selected as suitable. This consisted of two fairly large rooms, not unreasonably dirty—of which the balconies looked into the street—and in these we camped, with our bedding and personal baggage. On the floor below us, in smaller rooms, Hussein the Brave and Abd el Hamid the Scribe established themselves, and with them the Sultan quickly arranged a system of signals by means of knocks upon the floor. These, according to their number, called up either the scribe or the warrior; or directed them to gather the whole of our party with the utmost speed, and bring it to the house.

The Sultan gave special instructions to these two that any one of his followers who came to the house with news that there was a rumour abroad that an *Effrengi*—an infidel foreigner—had made his way, disguised in the Ishram dress, within the proscribed radius of the Sacred City and that the mob was hunting for him, should be instantly brought into his presence.

Our first pious duty, though not by any means essential or even very important, was to visit the tomb of Eve who is (doubtless) buried outside the walls of Jidda.

In the cool of the evening, we walked to the sacred spot, and I was amazed to discover that the Mother of Us All must have been a gigantic person, inasmuch as a domed tomb covers the resting place of her head and another that of her feet.

Having circumambulated the holy spot and said a *Fatiha* at each of the shrines, we made a small offering to the female guardians of the tomb and departed, having acquired merit.

Next day, the Sultan sent Abd el Hamid to gather the band, and we all went to mid-day prayer in the chief mosque, special orders being given that, so far as possible, he and I were always to be kept in the centre of the party, and that there was always to be someone between me and the public. Should I then make any mistake, in spite of my careful training in the drill, in the matter of rising, kneeling, prostration and so forth, it would be less likely to be noticed. And if, by any mischance, a stranger spoke to me in the mosque and I did not know the correct answer to the salutation, it must be immediately explained that I was dumb; and, while some of the party hustled me off, others soothed, obstructed, jostled or threatened the inquisitive entertainer of unworthy suspicions.

There always would be a danger of something of the sort occurring, so long as I was on sacred soil, for, to certain salutations there are, and only can be, certain answers; and the person who did not know them would stand revealed an intruder, a swindler, an infidel and a fraud—and his end would be prompt and painful.

I ran no risk whatever on the score of fair skin or western dialect of Arabic, inasmuch as quite half the pilgrims who go to Mecca are fair; very many Syrians, Russian and Siberian Mussulmans, Egyptians, Tartars, Turkomans, Indians and Afghans, being as fair as southern Europeans; while of Arabic there are scores of varieties and dialects, some of which differ so widely as to be almost unintelligible to Arabs who do not speak them.

On the next day, Kassim bin Ibrahim returned, reported himself to the Sultan, and assured him that all arrangements had been satisfactorily made for the journey to Mecca, and for the accommodation of the party there.

The question of transport had not been an easy one, and he had had to pay what seemed to him a shocking price for the hire of good camels, and then, as he explained, they weren't good—it being the local custom to keep them perpetually travelling to and fro almost without a rest, making hay while the stars as well as the sun shone, though the camels got none of it. The consequence was that the best of these hacks were weary, emaciated, and almost worn out. Apparently, it paid better to keep the camels going till they died, than to lose a minute's hire and custom by giving the poor beasts a little rest.

CHAPTER XXII

The Golden Road to Mecca from its port, Jidda, is some forty-five miles in length and is guarded throughout the whole distance by Turkish[23] posts, which are about a mile apart. Until these places were built and garrisoned by Turkish soldiers, the pilgrims were completely at the mercy of the Bedoui, and must travel in strong caravans for mutual protection, pay heavy blackmail, or be unmercifully robbed, looted, and maltreated. Until the building of the Hedaz railway, the same thing happened to the overland pilgrims who came from the port of Beyrout by way of Damascus down through Syria and Palestine into Arabia.

Prior to the officially authorized days of the actual "Pilgrimage", the traffic from Jidda to Mecca is continous, a solid and unbroken line of camels and donkeys, and the pace is that of the baggage camels—on an average, two miles an hour. To people accustomed to Saharan travel and to pacing camels, this is most trying, as one could go twice as quickly on foot.

That being out of the question, nothing can be done about it, because, as soon as the 'road' reaches the hills, some seven miles from Jidda, the traffic is compelled to proceed in single file. Thus, although we started at sunrise, it was evening by the time we reached Bahreia, the half-way house to Mecca.

This place consists of a considerable fort, restaurants, large enclosures for sacrificial sheep and goats, and shops where food and fodder may be obtained for men and beasts. And, what is more important, there is a plentiful supply of excellent water.

The admirable Kassim bin Ibrahim, having already selected a clean site, well outside the village, tents were pitched by our servants, and camp was quickly made. In spite of the fact that my back and shoulders were roasted sore, and my shaven head positively blistered, and also in spite of my excitement and thrills of half-pleasurable apprehension, I fell asleep almost immediately after dinner, and slept soundly till sunrise.

Soon after dawn, we broke camp, and again our party took its place in the river of men and animals that flowed unceasing and unending on the Holy Road to Mecca. Some idea of what that river is like, may be gained by contemplating the fact that about

---

[23] *Before the Great War.*

five hundred thousand pilgrims, and perhaps twice that number of beasts, go to compose it.

The world has seen nothing else like it. What a subject for an Arab Chaucer—*Mecca Tales*—told by typical pilgrims representing almost every social class and the people of at least three Continents; princes, warriors, merchants, priests, scribes; butcher, baker, candlestickmaker; tinker, tailor, soldier, sailor, rich man, poor man, beggar-man, thief. Thief undoubtedly, even though pilgrim about the pious business of the saving of his soul and the acquisition of merit.

In fact, one of the weak points of Mahommedanism seems to me to be the lack of connection, logical sequence, and natural relationship, between Faith and Works. So long as his faith is sound and strong and acceptable to Allah, his "works" are unimportant, a matter between himself and his own conscience; or, more exactly, perhaps, between himself and the police. But one has found a state of affairs somewhat similar, if not so glaring, in other religions.

To me, personally, it seems that a Faith that does not control and determine Works is worthless, and that the man devoid of Faith but of unimpeachable Works is surely preferable, in the eyes of the Deity, to the man of perfect Faith and evil Works. . . .

As the river of humanity flowed nearer and nearer to its bourne, it flowed ever more silently. In the early hours of the journey, while Jidda was yet close behind us, there was a certain air of holiday gaiety, a good deal of noisy shouting, a fair amount of joyous singing of unsanctified songs, and of ebullient spirits finding healthy expression in the firing off of guns.

But as we drew near to Mecca, an almost palpable atmosphere of reverence and fear compassed us about; and all men gradually grew dumb, awe-stricken by the stupendous thought that they were almost within sight of the most sacred spot in all their world, their feet about to tread soil only less sacred than that of Paradise itself.

I don't think that a non-Mussulman can really measure the depth of feeling of the pilgrim approaching Mecca. That of the Canterbury Pilgrims riding down the hill into Canterbury, of the medieval pilgrims approaching Rome, of the army of the Crusaders sighting Jerusalem, is perhaps the nearest to it. But one thinks of all these people as being lighter hearted, gayer, more materialistic; and never did they approach those Shrines in absolutely silent masses, hundreds of thousands strong.

With them, but not of them, I could not help being deeply

impressed, almost awed. Although in the brilliant sunshine, I seemed to move in a dream, so uncanny was the ghostly silence of this tremendous crowd. Not even the feet of the camels were audible upon the soft sand.

Suddenly I found that we were passing between the two white pillars of stone which mark the point at which the pilgrim first treads the actual Meccan soil—upon which no life may be taken, save under the compulsion of necessity—such as for food —and not even that while the pilgrim is wearing the *Irham* dress. Only the serpent and the scorpion may be slain, and only when this is unavoidable. No violent deed of any sort may be committed. No violent words may be used; there must be no wrangling, no acrimonious bickering; indeed, the voice must not be raised loudly in anything but praise.

And here the silence was broken—broken by a low wailing chant. At brief intervals there arose the chorus,

"*Lebeka, lebeka, Allahuma lebeka* . . . I am here, I am here, oh Allah, I am here."

Playing my part as a Mussulman, yet at the same time feeling that there is indeed no God but God, and that Allah is God and God is Allah, I too recited aloud without offence to my conscience, the oft-repeated prayer of praise and salutation,

"*Oh God, I am here! Oh God, I am come before Thee! Oh God, there is no God but Thee. For thine is the Kingdom, the Power and the Glory, for ever and ever. And Mercy is thy name and attribute,*"

Again complete silence fell, as the eyes of the Pilgrims found that which they sought, the mountain of light, *Djebel-en-Nur*, a conical hill crowned by a tomb which overlooks Mecca itself.

Soon after, we caught sight of the first houses on the Meccan road, and immediately uttered the prayer prescribed for the occasion of getting the first glimpse of any part of the city itself.

"*Oh Allah, who hast brought me here in safety, bring me in safety out again.*"

This struck me, personally, as a sound and appropriate, if somewhat sinister, prayer; and I uttered it with a fervour that was quite genuine.

Still Mecca itself was hidden from us, and again a silence an almost painful eagerness, tense and suppressed, pervaded the pious company . . .

And suddenly rounding a hill, we beheld the Holy City before and below us, in a great natural basin of stone, surrounded by high and rocky mosque-crowned hills, upon one of which was a strong, ugly, modern fort.

The effect upon the multitude, of this first glimpse of Mecca, was amazing; and if I were uneasy, uncomfortable, frightened perhaps, for my personal safety in its midst, it was quite obvious that this feeling was common to the vast majority of the pilgrims. They too were awed, frightened—some of them terrified—many flinging themselves down upon their faces, prostrating themselves with their foreheads upon the earth; others seeming literally to collapse and lie unconscious.

I can understand it. Although the sight of Mecca meant nothing to me personally, from the religious point of view, I had a sensation distantly approximating to that of the pious Mussulmans around me, as I sat upon my tall camel, gazed upon the scene, and realized that at that time probably only two other Englishmen had ever seen it—the great Sir Richard Burton and the little-known traveller Keane.

In the twelve hundred years that had elapsed since the days of the Prophet I was the third Englishman to enter Mecca and live to tell the tale.

Well—I hadn't told it yet . . .

I glanced at Chandos, to see whether his impassive unrevealing face showed signs of emotion, elation, and reverence, the look of awe that was stamped upon the faces of the other pilgrims.

No, he was only sad. His expression was definitely one of sadness . . . sorrow . . . regret . . .

And, as I watched, his mouth compressed and hardened, a look of anger crossed his face, and I guessed that he was thinking of his mother—and of his step-father.

§2

Riding on and through the gate, we passed huge barracks, capable of housing a Brigade, and on, down a long wide street to the big open square that forms the centre of the town. Here we again encountered those useful public-nuisances, the *mutowifs*.

These people are a close corporation having officially-recognized vested interests in the exploitation of the pilgrims, as guides, *cicerones*, organizers and leaders of personally-conducted tours and as general agents and contractors.

One would not have objected so much to their inevitability, their position and power, from which there is no escape, had they been priests, *mullahs*, *moulvies*, *marabouts*, *imams*, *aalimin*, learned doctors of religion—*genii loci* who had a natural prescriptive right to take over the pilgrim on his arrival, tell him what to do and how to do it, and receive an agreed fee or contribution for such service.

But, inasmuch as these *mutowifs* are really nothing but touts who know the ropes, their tyranny is irksome; and, however useful they may be, the pilgrim should surely be free to reject their services should he desire to do so. It is one thing to hire a guide because you want him and can afford him. It is quite another thing to be compelled to put yourself in the hands of a guide, whether you want him, and can afford him, or not.

But, except for its not being voluntary and free from a certain tyranny and imposition, the system is a valuable one, inasmuch as there are *mutowifs* for pilgrims of every nationality, speaking the required language and understanding the ways and needs of the pilgrim, whether he come from the Sudan or Turkestan, from China or Siberia, from Malaya or Ceylon, from Afghanistan or Morocco.

Definitely we did not need a *mutowif*, as the Sultan himself knew as much about Mecca and the performance of the ceremonies of the *Hadj* as any of them, and the attachment of one to our party would have been the source of the very gravest danger to us all in general, and to myself in particular. Were I discovered for what I was, I should be torn in pieces, and the whole party cast into gaol for trial on a charge of sacrilege, if not immediately stoned to death by the infuriated mob.

Whether the invaluable Kassim bin Ibrahim had paid a kind of blackmail to the chief of the *mutowifs* for West African pilgrims, or used his undeniable talent as a liar, when arranging our accommodation, I was not certain. Anyhow, when the band of *mutowifs* bore down upon us like a crowd of hotel touts on passengers arriving at the railway station of a holiday resort, Kassim bin Ibrahim loudly shouted that our arrangements were already made, and we were allowed to pass without further importunity.

Riding on, through wide and rather fine bazaars and arcades, which were none too wide for the vast throng that crowded them, we turned into another long road, broad and straight, until we came to a superior quarter of "desirable town residences", a district of good garden-surrounded houses, private and quiet.

This, the Sultan informed me, was the neighbourhood devoted to the accommodation of the wealthier pilgrims, usually Persians from the cities and Arabs from Baghdad. Here we should get the best accommodation, the greatest privacy, and the least likelihood of encountering pilgrims from Morocco, among whom might be some who would recognize him, having seen him in Fez.

Again he and I would live together, sharing a suite below which were rooms to be occupied by Hussein the Brave; Abd el Hamid the Scribe; Kassim bin Ibrahim the Courier; and Hassan bin Yacoub the Swordsman—a fierce courageous fighting-man, devoted to his master, and known as *el Khātil*, the Slayer. The rest of the *entourage* were accommodated in neighbouring houses.

Our own suite of rooms was really very decent; clean, comfortable, light and airy; and with the added amenity of access to a large flat roof of which we had the exclusive use.

I learned that the rent paid for this suite of four rooms, a kitchen, and roof garden, was the equivalent of thirty pounds a month.

The landlord of the house was a book-seller, as well as pilgrims' boarding-house keeper, and a man of ideas, who did things in style. We had European tables and chairs, as well as Arab divans, mattresses and cushions; and a fairly adequate collection of glass, china, and cutlery.

I took a liking to the old gentleman, he having the rare quality of simplicity, and indeed, within certain reasonably defined limits, honesty; a kindly agreeable gentle soul, very obliging, and with a pleasing gift of naively genuine flattery. He insisted on serving lunch to us, and would not hear of our waiting till our cook and servants had been to market, had procured the wherewithal, and cooked dinner for us.

To me he confided that he was so glad we were nice Arabs of the Desert—so much more desirable tenants, for a landlord who was rather particular and exclusive, than some of those horrid town people from places like certain parts of India, Sumatra, Turkey, Java, China and other places, whence often came people who had the money to pay for rooms like his, but not the manners, customs and habits to deserve them. Nasty dirty people, some of those. . . . They'd light fires and cook food in the corner of the bedroom, and show themselves ignorant of the first principles of sanitation. . . .

"Now, my son," said Chandos, as, having thoroughly enjoyed a remarkably good dinner of mutton, *cous-coussu*, cakes and fruit, we relaxed upon our divans.

"The first thing is to do our *towaf* and get out of this *Irham* kit. I don't mind how soon we get back into our proper clothes again. We'll go along to the *Haram* quite early in the morning, and get as much of the *towaf* ceremonial over, as we can, before the sun gets too hot. It's rather a trying business, as one has to run round and round the *Ka'ba*, and then to and fro between *Marawa* and *Safa*, praying as one runs. . . . When we've done the *towaf* we'll take it easy until the actual Pilgrimage, when we shall have to assume the *Irham* kit again, until it is completed. When that is over, and we are again clothed and in our right mind, we'll set about the second business that has brought me—and you—to Mecca . . ."

And the steely note, that I had come to know very well, crept into his voice.

This boded trouble for somebody—and I could guess for whom.

CHAPTER XXIII

Next morning, bright and early, we started forth for the *Haram*. The Sultan having signalled to the men below, that the party was to assemble, we were joined by the others in twos and threes as we walked through our northern quarter of the town, on our way to the *Haram*, some twenty minutes' journey. Inasmuch as we, in our *Irham* dress, were bare-footed, I found this to be twenty minutes too long.

The *Haram* of Mecca, known to Moslems the world over as *El Musjid el Haram* or *Beit Ullahi el Haram*, the Holy House of God, stands in a colossal court-yard which must be about one hundred thousand square yards in area, its four sides consisting of enormously long cloisters some sixty or seventy feet wide.

Entering through one of the twenty gates, we saw before us what is, to the Mohammedan, the very holiest thing in all the world—the *Ka'ba*.

Whether for calculated effect or not, the great stone—a cube, of which the sides are some forty feet square—is covered in black, this giving it, in contrast with the white surrounding marble of the shallow oval basin in which it stands—and which is about a hundred and fifty, by one hundred, feet in area—a strangely impressive appearance. The more the surrounding marble glitters and shines with dazzling whiteness in the bright sunlight, the blacker, more imposing, more majestic and impressive becomes the huge black stone.

This, to the pious Moslem is literally *Beit Ullahi*, the House of God, and comparable in ineffable holiness only to the Ark of the Israelites. To the majority of the pilgrims it is too holy to be looked upon—most particularly when the black covering moves. Such motion is not, of course, caused by the breeze, but by the fluttering of the wings of angels, invisible but attendant. Many pilgrims, after unbelievable hardships and unbearable burdens of expense and suffering, enter and leave the *Haram* without daring more than the swiftest glance at the *Ka'ba*, a glance of deprecation, supplication and uttermost humility.

If a profound sense of immeasurable reverence and awe settles upon the pilgrim band as it sights Mecca, who shall describe the feelings with which those pilgrims look upon the House of God itself, the House actually tenanted by Allah?

I myself, an Infidel, experienced the same kind of sensation that I experienced when first taken, as a child, to Westminster Abbey to gaze upon the tombs of the Kings and Queens of England, and saw before me the actual last resting-places of my admired heroes and heroines—a feeling of wonderment bordering upon incredulity, a thrill of absorbing interest, satisfaction and joy, deeply tinged with reverential awe. Only with this poor measure could I plumb the depths of the feelings of the breathlessly silent worshippers around me.

In addition to the Holy *Ka'ba*, the vast court-yard contains the Holy Well of Zemmen, the Arch of Abraham, and the Wall of Ishmael—the father of all Arabs—which joins the *Ka'ba*.

I learned later from the Sultan, that the *Ka'ba* is not, as I had imagined, a monolith, but a building of huge granite blocks; that it is hollow; and that access can be gained to it by way of an iron door some eight feet above the ground.

With the Sultan holding my right hand and Hussein the Brave my left, and the remainder of our party forming a chain, together with hundreds of other pilgrims, we proceeded with our performance of the *towaf* ceremonial.

At a swift walk which sometimes broke into a run, repeating, as we hurried along, the prayer shouted by a guide, we circumambulated the *Ka'ba* seven times. This done, each of us in turn kissed the wall of the *Ka'ba* at the appointed place, a stone let into the wall at one corner. This stone, the *Hagar-el-aswad*, which is some four feet above the ground, is exposed by means of a hole in the black curtain that drapes the *Ka'ba*. The stone has a thick covering of solid silver which is clearly and visibly worn away by the lips of the Faithful. What makes this particular stone of the *Ka'ba* especially sacred is the fact that it fell direct from Heaven. I have no doubt that it did—in the form of a meteor.

Next followed prescribed prayers and the second part of the *towaf* ceremony. This consists in running fast and praying hard, between *Marawa* and *Safa*, two mounds outside the *Haram*, about a quarter of a mile apart. A portion of the track between them is through the street that lies outside one of the walls of the *Haram*. Since the street was, even at that early hour of the day, pretty crowded, it was no mean undertaking to proceed at considerable pace and pray aloud at an even greater one, while threading a way through the jostling throng.

Inasmuch as we were each provided with a booklet containing the appropriate prayers, I wondered whether this performance gave rise to the expression "that he who runs may read." Probably not. In fact, vague memories of the classics and of big writing carved on a wall, crossed my mind, in contradiction of the idea.

By this time the heat of the sun was great—for Mecca is one of the hottest places in the world—and I was again miserably aware of my not only bare, but recently shaven, head; and of my unshaven, but painfully bare, feet.

Our running and praying being finished, we returned to the *Haram*, put up a concluding prayer that any omissions might be condoned, that our efforts might be found acceptable in the sight of Allah, and that all our past, if not future, sins, might be forgiven.

In conclusion, a circular patch was shaved in the stubble of each pilgrim's head; and the *towaf* ceremony was done.

We were now free to resume our ordinary clothes, and become plain and private visitors to Mecca until the time of the actual Pilgrimage. Personally, I was thankful to get back to our quarters, for I was thoroughly weary, hot and dirty; and my bare feet were in bad case, for in Mecca a road is only a road in that it leads somewhere.

§2

It was a pleasure to get back into the ordinary Arab clothing. To this I had now become thoroughly accustomed, and in point of fact, greatly preferred it to European dress—at least for wear in a hot country. A people evolves its dress in accordance with its environment and climate, and the dress so evolved is therefore, naturally, the most suitable one for those conditions.

We had now several days at our disposal, with nothing to do but see Mecca—and life—before the prescribed time for the performance of the Pilgrimage.

It is not to be supposed that the *Hadj*, the Pilgrimage, is the journey that a pilgrim makes from his home to Mecca and back—however long that journey may be. A Moslem goes to Mecca that he may make the Pilgrimage when he gets there. He might go to Mecca—as a good many do, traders who live on the pilgrims, booth-keepers, sellers of souvenirs and such—without making the Pilgrimage at all, and without becoming a *hadji*.

The actual Pilgrimage consists in proceeding from Mecca to Mount Arafat and Mina, when the new moon falls on the ninth day of the month; offering up the prescribed prayers; and performing certain ceremonies, such as "stoning the devils". The making of this Pilgrimage once in his life, is obligatory upon every true Mussulman for whom it is possible. Of course, to a vast majority, it is utterly impossible on grounds of distance and expense; though not a few make their way from their far-off homes to Mecca, begging and earning as they go, and, perforce, taking years over the journey.

During the days that elapsed between the necessary *towaf* ceremony and the making of the Pilgrimage, I had time to observe Mecca, and also the state of mind of my friend, benefactor and master, the Sultan.

I believe that nowadays every Jack is as good as his master with the numerous exceptions of those who are a great deal better; and that, indeed, but few men are so poor-spirited as to acknowledge masters. Those who have mistresses are more numerous.

Personally, I was not merely willing, but proud, to call the Sultan my master, and to admit that I was dependant upon him for all that I had, from food to friendship. In addition, I realized that he was my master in power, might, ability, forcefulness, personality, worldly wisdom and knowledge . . . a great man, a brave man, a fine man, and, considering his upbringing and antecedents, according to his lights, a good man. He has to be judged by the standards of Arabia and Africa, the desert, and the Mahommedan code of ethics.

I had been so thrilled and enthralled by the fact of being a non-Mussulman intruder in Mecca, and by the sights of this amazing Secret and Sacred City, that I had paid much more attention to objective phenomena than to subjective consideration.

Being now quite alone with him, for the greater part of the day, and having more time and opportunity to think, I thought a good deal about him. From the day I had first confronted him, until now, I had seemed to live at high pressure. More than sufficient unto the day was the work—the seeing, the hearing, and the doing. Never was the day sufficient unto the work thereof.

Now I seemed to be in a quiet oasis of time, with opportunity to look back, to look forward, to reflect, and hold a mental stock-taking.

Chandos was obviously troubled in spirit. He brooded, and, rare phenomenon in his case, was undecided. He had acquired the controlled immobility, the reflective self-withdrawal of the desert Arab; the power to sit wrapped in thought, a power and gift much more rare than is supposed. How many Europeans can sit and really think, for many consecutive minutes—and, by thought, I don't mean the vacuous state that is the opposite of thought—mere idle empty-mindedness.

Seated cross-legged on his divan, his chin in his hand, the Sultan would sit for long periods, a frown of concentration on his brow; and deeply ponder some course of action. And at times he would—not wake from a reverie, not come out of a brown study—but deliberately shelve the problem and postpone further consideration of it.

"I don't know," he would say, eyeing me. "I don't know, I'm sure. And there is nothing I hate more, my son . . ."

"More than what?" I asked, on one occasion.

"Deciding that I can't decide," he replied. "Knowing that I don't know."

I refrained from asking questions, a habit of mine that the Sultan undoubtedly approved.

"You are all against punishment by killing, I imagine," he said, after another brooding silence.

"On principle, yes," I replied. " '*Thou shalt not kill*' is not the first law I'd take out of the Decalogue."

"And yet it is your good Christian custom to hang people, isn't it? You reject the Mosaic law of your own Old Testament, '*an eye for an eye and a tooth for a tooth*', but if I broke your neck, your New Testament-professing law would break mine, eh?"

I was never to be betrayed into religious argument with Chandos, and merely agreed that in Christian countries, killing is punishable by killing.

"And you agree," continued Chandos, "that the law should punish the killer—with death?"

"Yes."

"Good. Now then—what constitutes the Law? Who makes it, and sees that it is enforced, its decrees carried into effect?"

"Well, the Government of the country . . ."

"Yes. Whether that take the shape of a Dictator, a limited Monarchy, or a Democracy?"

"Yes."

"So a Dictator has power of life and death. . . . Very well. I am a Dictator in my country. I have the power of life and death; and I use it. Do I leave that law and power behind me when I leave my country and go into another?"

"Well, you have to do so."

"So it is only a case of *force majeure*, then?" asked Chandos. "If I had the power to carry my law with me, I should have the right to do so—and to enforce it."

"I know very little about Law," I replied. "And nothing at all about International Law."

"Perhaps not—but you have glimmerings of common sense. Look here. You agree that a murderer should be punished with death. You agree that I—being, according to the preferred popular constitutional custom of my country, Dictator, with the powers of life and death—have the legal right to impose the death sentence on a murderer and see that it is carried out. . . . But not being an international lawyer of repute, you don't know whether that power travels with me outside the borders of my country. On the whole you feel pretty sure it doesn't, if only because the greater power over-rides it—the power of the law and government of the country to which I go. . . . Very well, suppose there is a murderer who has deserved sentence of death a dozen times, and whom I would most certainly execute if he were in my own country."

"Yes?"

"Suppose he is not living in my country, but comes into it, have I the right to try him and execute him?"

"Only if he commits a murder in your country, I imagine," I replied.

"Oh? Oh, indeed! That's interesting. Murder a question of latitude and longitude, eh? Killing no murder on one side of the border, and horrible crime on the other. That's casuistry, if you like."

"No. I don't make myself clear. It's not a question of which side of a border a crime is committed. It is a question of which side of the border the trial is held and the punishment inflicted. I take it that a man ought to be tried in the country in which he commits the murder, and punished according to the law of the country."

"So that if it is a country that condones murder, or doesn't take a very serious view of it, he gets a different punishment from what he would elsewhere."

"Yes, I suppose so. . . . That's just his luck."

"Well, there shouldn't be any 'luck' in the matter of a punishment for murder."

"No, I suppose not—but there it is. And, anyway, what is a crime in some countries, is a virtue in others. I don't want to be personal, Chandos, but I should serve a very heavy sentence if I married four wives in England, though I believe that if I did so in the city of Bab-el-Djebel or any other Mussulman country, I should be merely establishing myself as a gentleman of means, taste, and expansiveness."

Chandos smiled.

"Expensiveness, you mean . . . But look here, what a wriggler you are! Murder is murder, and the penalty is death in any decent country—or indecent either."

"I haven't disputed it," I said. "I was merely talking about your right to punish the subject of another Power for a murder he had committed outside your country. . . . Look here—take a concrete example. If a Frenchman committed a murder in France and came to England, the English law wouldn't hang him for it. The utmost it would do would be to facilitate his extradition."

"And suppose the French didn't bother about him?" asked Chandos.

"Well, in that case the English wouldn't bother about him either. They couldn't touch him in England for what he'd done to a Frenchman in France."

"Well, it's all wrong," growled Chandos.

"I'm not responsible," I assured him.

The Sultan waved my levity aside, and regarded me with a cold stare.

"Now then—brass tacks," said he. "There's a man in this Holy City of Mecca who murdered my father."

"But it was his Sepoys who . . ."

"I tell you he murdered my father," interrupted Chandos "by inciting his cousin, Subedar Major Yar Mahommed Ali Khan, to do it. It was he who gave the order to the Sepoys to shoot, and it was this man, my step-father, who gave orders to Subedar Major Yar Mahommed Ali Khan to have him shot. I'm perfectly certain that, left to themselves, the Sepoys would never have done it. . . .

"Very well," he went on. "This man, Mahommed Ghulamali Salehudin Yussufali Jalpur, Nawab of Aundhara, murdered my father. Secondly he abducted, kidnapped, imprisoned, and brutally treated my mother, a girl of eighteen. She has been his prisoner, from the day my father was murdered, until now.

"Thirdly, he was the instrument and means of killing unnumbered Europeans, men, women, and children, as well as Eurasians, not to mention harmless Hindus, all throughout the Mutiny days.

"Fourthly, he had me brought up, here in Mecca, as his *son*, damn him; as a Mussulman and a 'native', an Oriental, knowing me to be a pure-bred English child, the son of Colonel Chandos and of Janet his wife.

"Now then, that man's a murderer. If he were in my country, I'd hang him, five minutes after I set eyes on him. . . . Why, because he's skulking here in Mecca, should he remain unpunished?"

"Because he *is* here in Mecca," I replied. "A subject of the Shereef of Mecca; or, if he's not that, an Indian subject of Queen Victoria. Granted that you have legal jurisdiction and powers of life and death in Bab-el-Djebel, you've none here."

"And suppose he came to Bab-el-Djebel?"

"Still no jurisdiction."

"Oh, indeed? I could do nothing then."

"No. Nothing—legal. Unless his Government notified you that he was in your country, and would be much obliged if you'd kindly arrest him. But they could do that here."

Chandos stared at me thoughtfully, appraisingly, the long considering stare to which I was well-accustomed, but which still made me uncomfortable.

"I imagine you could bring an action against him here. Accuse him of murder. If you could get witnesses."

"But don't you see he's no more a subject of the Sultan of Turkey or the Shereef of Mecca than he is a subject of the Sultan Mahommed el Kebir of Bab-el-Djebel?"

"Well, you could notify the Government of India that you knew him to be hiding here in Mecca; and move them to demand his extradition, for trial in the High Court of Calcutta."

Chandos laughed.

"Extradition, my good ass! From Arabia? From Mecca?"

"Seems to be an *impasse*," I said. "Looks as though he is perfectly safe as long as he stays in Mecca."

"Well, that's just what he's not," replied Chandos grimly. "Did he but know it, he's very far from safe."

A long silence.

"You wouldn't come down to his level?" I said. "Assassination . . ."

"Assassination!" growled Chandos. "Do *you* call it assassination when your Government hangs a Charles Peace or any other murderous felon?"

"No," I said. "I don't, but . . ."

"Oh, damn your 'buts', Dysart. Look here. You were brought up with an attitude to the Law very different from mine. Although you don't know it, you put the Law before Justice. A long way before, too, sometimes. Well, I grew up here in Mecca in the belief that Justice comes before Law."

I refrained from smiling at this, for I'd seen and heard something of Oriental "justice".

"My idea of Law-and-Justice is the catching and punishing of criminals," he went on. "Deterrent punishment. Protection of society. And the spirit of the Law should over-ride the letter. Putting it otherwise, Justice should over-ride Law. . . .

"Well, enough palaver," he continued. "The thing is this. In my own benighted, dark, and dreadful way—unilluminated by the light of your countenance; and with, or without, your valuable approval—I am going to execute justice upon a murderer; a torturer; a treacherous, villainous brute. . . . Understand? . . . I'm going to punish him, after all these years. His sin has found him out; the day of retribution has dawned at last, after these decades of smug and fat and comfortable safety. . . . Now then, are you going to help me?"

"To assassinate your step-father?" I asked. "To commit a murder? . . . No."

"Thank you. I might have known that, like everybody else, you'd fail me sooner or later."

"I'm not failing you, Chandos," I said. "You know perfectly well that if you kill this man here in Mecca, you are committing a murder."

"Did you ever hear of justifiable homicide?" he asked.

"Oh, yes. But a plain premeditated murder doesn't come into that category—and you know it."

"Would you let him go unpunished?"

"Not if I could get him punished by law."

"And suppose you couldn't? You'd let him go scot-free?"

"Chandos, I don't know what I should do. But I do know I wouldn't commit a murder. I would neither kill him myself nor have him killed."

"Ah! . . . A well-brought-up young man," sneered Chandos.

"An English-brought-up young man," I replied.

"Well, I was a Mecca-brought-up young man," said Chandos.

"Quite so. And you have your own ideas and views and standards. You ask me for mine—and I've told you."

Chandos's rare charming smile illuminated his face.

"Good lad, Sinbad," he said. "I knew you'd take that line, and I'm glad you did.

"I *am* going to kill him, though," he continued. "I'm going to try him and execute him according to law—my law—as the Sultan Mahommed el Kebir of Bab-el-Djebel. And I don't care a damn whether he's in the Western Sahara or in South East Arabia; whether he's in his palace of Aundhara by Zeerut, or sitting on top of the North Pole. . . . And you are not going to help me, eh?"

"No."

"Another question. I am going to rescue my mother. I am going to take her back with me to Bab-el-Djebel and try to make the rest of her life happy. If she wants to go home, I want you to take her to Scotland. Will you help me?"

"Of course I will," I said.

"Oh . . . You'd condone the kidnapping of a man's wife, would you? You'd actually lend a hand to the wicked deed of violating the sanctity of a Mussulman's *harim*—of stealing away his wife?"

Again Chandos's sneer was bitter.

"Yes," I said. "In these circumstances. You know perfectly well it would not be a case of kidnapping, stealing, or decoying. It would be a rescue. . . . Besides, from what you've told me, she is not his wife at all, whatever ceremony may have been enforced upon her."

Again the appraising considering stare.

"You puzzle me, Sinbad. I'm glad I haven't got a conscience like yours. You'd break into a *harim* and take away a man's wife, but you wouldn't kill him, even though he'd murdered your father. . . . Queer thing, conscience. . . . Find yours gives you much trouble? Find it difficult to follow all its twistings and turnings?"

"No trouble at all, thanks," I replied. "No difficulty. All a matter of taste—and upbringing. The *harim* means nothing to me—in the way of sanctity. The forced marriage between a man and his helpless prisoner means nothing to me—in the way of sanctity. Murder does. It's a question of upbringing . . . outlook . . . different countries, different standards. Different ships, different long splices."

"So your dainty conscience won't object to helping me to get my mother out of Mecca?"

"No," I replied. "I'll do anything I can to help you."

"Thank you, Sinbad. I am grateful. I mean it. . . . And I felt sure you'd help me; and that is mainly why I brought you. You see, you are British—and my mother will understand you.

"Better than she will her own son," he added sadly. "You'll be a reassurance and a comfort to her among—savages, Arabs, Mussulmans like us. She'll feel that, in going to Bab-el-Djebel she's not going to another Mecca. And you'll know how to take her to England; how to make her comfortable; how to look after her there. . . . *Kismet!* Allah guided you; on that gun-running venture; into the hands of Ali bin Ahmed; to my camp; and here . . . A Christian and an Englishman—to take my mother home to England."

"Or a Scot—to take her back to Scotland." I smiled.

And I wondered again. Would a woman who'd lived for half a life-time in the same house, in Mecca, have any wish to leave it; to travel to the other side of Africa; to another Mussulman city; to go back to the Scotland that she had left as a happy girl? Would she know her son again? . . . Love him? . . . And, if so, having found him again, would she leave him in Bab-el-Djebel, and go to Scotland? Had a day passed on which she had not thought of her son; had not thought of Scotland?

What would she be like, not having heard or spoken the English language for a generation? Was Chandos picturing her as he had last seen her, when he was a boy of fourteen? Did she still picture him as a child?

It would be inexpressibly painful.

Yes, most certainly I would do anything in my power to help her and him. But I would have no hand in the killing of the Nawab of Aundhara.

The Sultan's voice—again cold, unemotional, sardonic—roused me from my reverie.

"Touching that tender conscience of yours," he said. "Will you find it necessary to interfere in any way with the . . . ah . . . course of justice? To convey a mysterious warning to the Nawab of Aundhara—if you can? Or to notify the Shereefian authorities that you have occasion to entertain the gravest fears that a crime is going to be committed in the Sacred City?"

"Don't worry about my conscience, Chandos" I replied. "I'll look after that. What you do, is your own business. If your conscience tells you it is your duty to—er—execute this man, it's no business of mine."

"Do you mean to say you don't feel you ought to warn him, if you could?" exclaimed Chandos in mock surprise.

"I do not feel that I ought to warn him—if I could," I replied.

"Queer thing, conscience," replied Chandos with a slight sneer. "Is yours of a special Scottish variety?"

My reply was monosyllabic, caustic, septic, and Arabic. It need not be translated.

§3

Later that day I had an idea.

"Chandos," said I as we awoke from *siesta*, for the consideration of mint-tea and Turkish cigarettes, "While we are in Mecca, and particularly while we are *Muhrim*, wearers of the *Irham*, isn't every kind of destruction absolutely prohibited? Aren't we forbidden to kill even so much as a bed-bug?"

"Absolutely, my son," was the reply. "Why? Have you caught one?"

"No, I haven't. I was thinking of the Nawab of Aundhara."

"Another bed-bug. . . . You think that while we are *Muhrim*, while we are on the Sacred Soil, while we are about our Pilgrimage, we mustn't think of taking his life, eh?"

"Yes."

"Well, don't think of it, then."

So that was that.

"Since you've raised the question," continued Chandos, "would you like to withdraw while I discuss the subject with Hussein the Brave, Abd el Hamid, Hassan bin Yacoub, and Kassim bin Ibrahim? Those wicked men, not being blessed with Scottish consciences, or with a preference for Law instead of Justice, are regrettably willing to help me to do—what I really came to do. . . . Would you rather go for a walk?"

"Of course I'll clear out, if you want me to," I replied.

"Please yourself about that. Won't you feel involved, contaminated, accessory before the fact?"

"No," I replied.

"I am disappointed in you! . . . Well, that being so, it will be quite a good idea for you to hear everything; and to know exactly what's doing. If you won't bear a hand in the—er—arrest, trial, and execution (and there's no reason why you should) it doesn't matter in the least. . . . But I daresay you won't be above helping us to escape, if it comes to that? We may have to leave Mecca in a hurry; and you might be very useful there. That all right?"

"Of course it is," I replied. "You know perfectly well I'll do anything on earth to help you, except what I consider criminal."

"Good. I don't fancy it will be necessary; but, if it is, you and half our men will have to be ready at a certain place, with fast camels. . . . I'm going to buy some prize specimens, anyway—pedigree known for a thousand years. Finest camels in the world, such as the Shereef's body-guard ride. . . . If the worst comes to the worst, you can fight a delaying action, then bolt when we've passed you. And we could do alternate rear-guard for each other, while Abd el Hamid rode straight down to Jidda with my mother. But it won't come to that, if the affair isn't bungled. . . . Yes, the more you know about what is going on, the better. So keep your ears open. . . ."

In answer to the Sultan's signal knocks upon the floor, the four men housed below came up to our apartment. Hussein the Brave; Hassan bin Yacoub, the Swordsman; Abd el Hamid the Scribe; Kassim bin Ibrahim the Courier; and Abu bin Zaka the Sicilian.

When these men had been given permission to seat themselves, and regaled with refreshment, pleasant afternoon-tea topics of conversation were politely discussed. Nothing less like a gang of conspirators, met to arrange a murder, can be conceived.

"By the way," observed the Sultan, after a silence and a long yawn, "which of you is a good actor? Able to play the part, let's say, of assistant to an itinerant Indian vendor of—trash. . . . Benares brass, made in Birmingham in Inglistan; Sind embroidery-work, made in Bombay; ebony elephants made in Ceylon; cotton Mericani stuff; silk, silver, and such . . ."

Hands stroked beards which doubtless hid smiling lips.

"A pedlar's porter . . ." gravely mused Hussein the Brave. "And who would be the pedlar, Sidi?"

"I should," replied the Sultan. "In that guise I am going to enter a house . . . if I can . . . spread my wares at the entrance to the *harim*, and speak with Those Behind the Curtain."

The Sultan's hearers looked as astonished as well-bred Arabs may. . . . What was this? Was the Sultan talking of carrying off a *purdah* woman? That would be something new in their experience of their master.

"None of you, eh?" he jeered. "Not a man in my following with enough ability to run an Indian *borah's* business . . . Now listen to me. I am going to a certain house in the guise of a merchant, a seller of goods for the *harim* women. You, Abd el Hamid, will come with me as my partner, apprentice, assistant, something of that sort; and you other three fools shall go as porters."

"There will be fighting, Lord?" asked Hassan bin Yacoub the Swordsman, hopefully.

"I trust not," was the reply. "I hope not. But knife and yataghan will go with us, under our dirty *djellabias*."

Hassan bin Yacoub grinned.

"No fighting, I hope," continued the Sultan. "But if there is—it is likely to be our last fight. . . . That's neither here nor there, of course—for to every man his last fight must come. But I don't want this to be mine. I go there to kill a man and save a woman, *Inshallah*."

"*Allahu akbar!*"

"*Bismillah!*"

"*Allah kerim!*"

"Finished?" continued the Sultan. "Then listen. The man whom I would kill is—the slayer of my father. The woman I would rescue is—my mother."

A silence of astonished bewilderment fell upon his hearers.

"Lord," said Hussein the Brave, at length, "the man is as dead."

"And the woman is saved," added Hassan bin Yacoub the Slayer.

"It is well," smiled the Sultan. "Now, Abd el Hamid will purchase, here and there, in the Indian bazaar, such goods as will be necessary—such things as an Indian pedlar would carry for sale. Each of you others will provide himself with clothing suitable to his part—the dirty dress of any *hamal*, *farash*, porter. . . . Before the days of the Pilgrimage, we will spy out the land; we will visit the house. During these Holy Days let me hear no word of violence. . . But when again we assume the *Irham* dress and become *Muhrim*, put all thoughts of this matter completely from your minds.

"Afterwards, when we have made the Pilgrimage, and when, sanctified and purified, we resume our dress and begin life afresh—we will talk more of the matter."

CHAPTER XXIV

While Abd el Hamid the Scribe was getting together a stock-in-trade suitable for an Indian pedlar, and clothing for the pedlar's assistant and porters, the Sultan and Hussein the Brave made cautious enquiry as to the whereabouts, the ways and habits, the comings and goings of that Indian Mussulman householder, Mahommed Ghulamali Salehudin Yussufali Jalpur, long resident in Mecca, who had once been the Nawab of Aundhara.

Concerning him, little seemed to be known, save that he was a very wealthy man, something of a mystery, of quiet and unobtrusive way of life, in good standing with His Highness the Shereef of Mecca—and his house itself something of a Mecca for a certain type of visitor from India.

Doubtless these latter were seditionists. What safer place for the hatching of plots than Mecca? What more ardent plotter and patron of plots and plotters than this renegade exile?

"I shall learn nothing of any real value or interest till I get inside the house," observed the Sultan.

"Will anyone there talk?" I asked.

"Money talks anywhere," replied the Sultan cynically. "Talks through the mouths of slack-jawed, fat-lipped knaves—as I know to my cost. . . . We'll get inside as soon as I've learned a bit more, and Abd el Hamid has got everything ready. . . . Look here, Sinbad, will you come?"

"Rather. I'd love to—provided you don't think I should be a source of danger."

"Of course you won't. And if you were, there is so much danger that a little more won't make much difference. You will just be a dirty load-carrying porter. No-one will speak to you, and if they did you've only got to grunt in guttural—and gutter—Arabic. . . . I'd like you to come, as I said before. You can't learn too much about what's going on and—you never know. You and I might be able to get into my mother's presence without the others, and I could tell her you are a Scot, like herself. Can you warble *Annie Laurie* or *Loch Lomond*?"

By his flippancy I knew that the Sultan was deeply moved and in deadly earnest.

"I can," I replied.

"My mother tried to teach me songs like those. I think *Ye Banks and Braes* was her favourite. I can hear her now:—

> "*Ye'll break my heart, ye warbling birds*
> *That wanton through the flowery thorn,*
> *Ye mind me o' departed joys,*
> *Departed never to return.*

"Break her heart! . . . She used to sing that to me, when I was a child, as though her heart *were* breaking. I can remember it still. . . . Man, it might make all the difference, if you came. It might just turn the scale, if she heard you speak, with a Scots lilt to your voice. Fancy good English, with a Highland inflection, after a life-time of Arabic and Urdu. She probably hasn't heard English since 1857, though my step-father can talk English—of a sort—when he wants to. Meanwhile, we'll reconnoitre the house from the outside—and I'll show you Mecca."

§2

I was surprised at the size of the Holy City. I should think it must have a hundred thousand inhabitants, apart from the half-million or so who flock into the town annually in the month of Dhu'lhagga.

On the whole, the town is clean; the streets broad and straight; the houses quite well-built and three or four storeys in height; the *sûks* and bazaars roofed like those of Constantinople and Damascus. The shops are numerous, good, and well-stocked. The shop-keepers, of course, save those who supply the inhabitants with the necessities of life, thrive on the pilgrim traffic, and cater almost entirely for the pilgrim.

The whole city is, from one point of view, itself a shop, a market; for it produces not one solitary thing of itself.

Thinking I would like to buy some souvenir, some memento of Mecca, I entirely failed to find anything that could be described as distinctively Meccan. I could have laden a caravan of camels with Souvenirs-of-Mecca made in Birmingham, Paris, Berlin, Damascus, Bombay, Benares, Pekin, Swatow, Fez, Malta, Cairo, and a score of other places; but, did I desire to take my family a Present-from-Mecca, it would not be from Mecca at all, but more probably from Birmingham.

And not only are the shops filled with assorted rubbish from all corners of the world, but crowds and crowds of itinerant traders, seasonal stall-holders, and wandering pedlars come from every part of the Mahommedan world with their wretched "souvenirs". That both the permanent and transient vendors are able to do a profitable business in such stuff, is due to the enormous variety of the heterogeneous pilgrim-assembly. Thus, to men from the Sudan, the rubbish of Bombay is a novelty; to the Indian pilgrim, the produce of Morocco is attractive; to the Javanese, that of Turkey is pleasing.

In addition to the quite good markets and shops, are the very decent restaurants and *cafés*. In these, which are crowded day and night, one can get very good meals of mutton, chicken, green vegetables, cakes and sweets. Owing to the climate and the cost and difficulty of transport, all kinds of fruit are rare and costly.

And, speaking of markets, I was amazed, astounded, incredulous, when I learned that there is an old-established thriving public slave-market in the Holy City. But, as Hussein the Brave observed,

"It's all-right—only women are sold there."

Nothing so grossly improper as the public sale of a man would be tolerated in this well-regulated market.

The place fascinated me and I visited it several times acting the part of a prospective purchaser. It was really more like a Stores than an ordinary market, inasmuch as each dealer had a show-room of his own.

In every show-room was a large dais or platform, running the length of the room; and, at the back of it, against the wall, were rows of benches on which the slave women sat. The prices asked for them ranged from twenty-five pounds to four times that amount.

When an intending buyer saw an article that took his fancy and seemed likely to suit him, he would point her out to the proprietor, who would then call her forth from the row, and she would be paraded for inspection.

The merchant would then wax eloquent upon the physical and mental virtues and the moral vices of the goods, swearing by Allah the Merciful, the Compassionate, and Mahommed his Prophet, that the woman was sound in wind and limb, extremely intelligent and amazingly vicious—in fact, everything that was desirable. Indeed, the biggest liar on earth could not say one word against her body and brain, or one syllable in favour of her character.

I'm afraid my rendering of the role of intending purchaser

was unconvincing, as I could never bring myself to prod a wretched girl in the ribs, poke her in the stomach, force her mouth open in order to examine her teeth, pull down her eyelids, accept the owner's warm invitation to feel her muscles and pinch her flesh to satisfy myself as to her excellent condition. The best I could do was to stand and look sceptical, bored, and unbelieving, as the worthy man expatiated on the unusual value-for-money that the woman represented, drew my attention to her points, and asked me what on earth I *did* want if I didn't want this amazing bargain at a miserable fifty pounds.

I got a fright one day when, having a prime slave girl offered to me for seventy pounds, I emitted a jeering laugh, offered twenty pounds, and was promptly told I could have her then and there, clothes and all, and a rope chucked in, for twenty one pounds. . . . In another minute she'd have been mine!

With a derisive yelp, I fled, just in time.

Doubtless it must appear as though I were callously indulging a morbid curiosity and in a cruel pastime by visiting the show-rooms of the slave-market, and having girls and women produced for my inspection.

In point of fact, this is not so—the one desire of these lasses being to find a purchaser, the one bright moment in their rather dull lives that when they are called up from the slave-bench to be inspected by a possible purchaser. To have one called out; to have her trotted up and down and put through her paces; to examine her; talk about her; haggle over her; and generally bring her into the lime-light of publicity for as long a time as one can spare and the vendor's almost inexhaustible patience lasts, is as kindly and pleasure-giving a deed as it is for one to go to an English preparatory-school and have a small relative or friend brought from the boring wearisome round of lessons and the class-room, out into the freedom of the open-air and the delights of the tuck-shop or the *matinée*.

The picture of the agonised, ashamed and shrinking captive, steeped in misery and grief, is a figment of the imagination. I found the majority of the girls delighted by my interest, moved invariably to much giggling, a little cheerful impudence, and an obvious effort to look bashful, blushful and coy. To be honest, I found quite a considerable number of them merry and bright, cheerful, and more than ready to exchange pointed persiflage and broad badinage, both with the proprietor and myself.

The slaves who made my heart ache were the aged and decrepit; those who—from lack of all pretension to beauty of face and form, and of physical health and strength to labour and to drudge—could scarcely hope to find a purchaser.

But even then they were no more piteous spectacles than their sisters who sat begging at street corners and in the market-place. To be old and ill and poor is terrible, whether to the bond or free.

Nevertheless, I admit that the gleam of hope that briefly shone upon the hopeless countenances of these weary old women, moved me to the point of practical effort on their behalf. Pity without relief is like mustard without beef; and I suggested to the Sultan that both he and I, Mussulman and Christian, could acquire merit by buying a number of these poor old souls and setting them free—as kind-hearted people sometimes do with caged wild-birds. But I found that my intended kindness would, in practice, be actual cruelty—like that of so many well-meaning but ignorant philanthropists.

"Buy them and set them free?" exclaimed the Sultan. "Free to do what? Starve? . . . You'd be looked upon as a monster of cruelty; on a par with a man who bought a dozen three-year-old-brats, took them a day's journey out into the middle of the desert and there abandoned them. The children would starve to death, and so would these poor old things. Buy a slave, by all means, if you want to, young or old; but you will have to keep her, feed her, clothe her, employ her, and take her home with you. If you buy her, you are responsible for her, exactly as you are for any other ass; or for a horse, or a camel. . . . You wouldn't go to a cattle-market, buy a beast, and then 'set it free', would you? Once you've bought it, you're responsible for its food and shelter."

"Can one do nothing at all for them then?" I asked.

"Absolutely nothing; except, as I say, buy them, keep them and be a good master to them.

"And," he added with a grin, "if you're going to do that, you'd better buy a young, fat, and pretty lass. . . . I'm ashamed of you, Sinbad. . . ."

And pursuing enquiries further, from people with a less spacious and expansive view of life than that of the Sultan, I found that it was so. No-one but a householder could buy a slave-woman—with any advantage to the slave or himself—and to buy one and give her her freedom would be merely giving her her homeless freedom to starve. The only thing she could do, and what she promptly would do, would be to return to the dealer in the hope that, the next time he sold her, it would be to a sane and conscientious purchaser who would not play such a wicked trick on her. . .

Without saying one syllable in favour of the foul, shameful, and abominable institution of slavery, it is only common honesty to state that, in those civilized countries where slavery is tolerated, the ill-treatment of slaves is rare, as rare as the ill-treatment of children in Institutions and Orphanages in Europe.

A slave is property, and is valued and treated as such. Moreover, an ill-treated slave has full right, and every oppor-tunity, to complain to the nearest Authority; and if serious ill-treatment were proven, it is more than likely that the Kadi, the Magistrate or Judge, would order the slave to be set free and the owner to be fined or otherwise punished. In every Asiatic Mussul-man town like Mecca, Medina, Damascus, Sanaa, Jidda, Yenbo, Homs, Aleppo, or any other such, it would be almost as dangerous for an owner to flog a slave as it would be for a British householder to thrash a house-maid.

On one occasion when visiting the slave market—and I here confess that I entertained the childishly idiotic hope of one day finding that slave girl who had smiled at me when I was a manacled slave myself—I observed to a slave-dealer in a big way of business,

"Yes, these are all very well, but . . ." and here I lowered my voice to a whisper, "what I really want to buy is a man or a good growing lad. What about it?"

The honest broker looked shocked.

"My dear Sir! My dear Sir! Hush, hush! . . . Not here! Not here! Come round to my house to-night and I'll see what I can do for you. I'll fix you up all-right, but you'll have to pay my price, you know. What do you want, a good domestic servant, a nice well-trained boy, or a sound experienced eunuch?"

So it could be done, apparently—under the rose.

On another occasion, wandering about the market, I bethought me of the tales one had read of marvellous Circassian and Georgian slaves. Invariably, in stories of Noble Sheiks of the Desert there was a most lovely houri in the shape of a "beautiful Circassian slave", a compendium of accomplishments, joys and virtues; beautiful alike to the eye and the ear—irresistible to all the senses, in fact.

There was none such, here.

I made enquiries.

Yes, one could be had, at a price—but on order only. For five hundred pounds I could have a lovely Circassian or Georgian slave, provided I gave references, gave the order in all good faith, and backed it by much good money—a handsome deposit, in fact.

No, they weren't stocked nowadays. Times weren't what they were—and they never had been. It didn't pay a dealer even to have one "on sale or return", as they were very perishable goods, and went off badly. Kept their bloom about as long as a bunch of grapes does.

No, I should have to order one, pay carriage in advance, leave a deposit, name a guarantee, and then take what came.

I refused such terms! . . .

The next most interesting thing to the *Haram* and the slave-market was the crowd itself.

I found it an almost inexhaustible pleasure and amusement, to sit outside a *café* and watch the throng go by; study the types; and endeavour to decide the nationality, occupation, rank and position of the people who compose that incredibly heterogeneous collection of representatives of almost every country under the sun; to distinguish and identify the Siberian, the Javanese, the Turk, the Chinese, the Tunisian, the Malay, the Zanzibari, the Bedou, the Egyptian, the Mongol, the Somali, the Afghan, the Persian, the Turcoman, the Swahili, the Punjabi, the Baluchi, and the rest. . . .

With due heed to the Sultan's warning to be extremely careful, discreet and self-effacing, I now began to wander about Mecca, alone and unaccompanied. I don't know why, but I was surprised to discover that the Holy City boasted Municipal Buildings, a Court-house and Post-and-Telegraph Offices.

At the time of my visit to Mecca, the Hedjaz was a Turkish province ruled by the Shereef of Mecca, a hereditary Governor descended from Ali (the cousin of Mahommet) and Fat'ma, his wife. The Arabs regard the Shereef of Mecca as a king, and, in point of fact, he lives in a royal palace, maintains a private army, and has absolute authority in his own dominion of the Hedjaz.

Nevertheless, the huge fort which dominates the Holy City is garrisoned by a Turkish regiment, as are the block-houses on the road from Mecca to Jidda. There was also a big Turkish garrison in Medina, and Turkish troops were stationed along the Hedjaz railway from Medina to Damascus.

Of the citizens of Mecca I did not form a high opinion. On the contrary, a very low one indeed. Their holiness seemed to me in inverse ratio to that of their city. In point of fact, I gained the impression that the main difference between the inhabitants of Mecca and those of the Cities of the Plain, was that they were luckier. . . .

My first shock of disillusionment came when, within sight of the *Haram* itself, almost within the shadow of the *Ka'ba*, I was offered picture-postcards that would have shocked a Port Said pimp.

When, wishing to compare my opinion and impression with the actual knowledge of the Sultan, I questioned him, he stated roundly that the native towns-people of Mecca—the permanent inhabitants, as distinguished from the pilgrim visitors—were, on the whole, taking them by and large, making all allowances, and viewing them dispassionately, canting hypocrites, smug scoundrels, rascally scum, and a uniquely foul nest of virtuous-seeming villains.

CHAPTER XXV

I have hitherto said but little concerning my companions, the Sultan's other followers.

Hussein the Brave was, by any standards, a splendid man, physically, mentally and morally; brave as a lion, as his name implied; loyal, simple, forthright and very competent; a fine fighting soldier, an excellent scout, guide and Intelligence officer, and an admirable policeman—the Arab at his best, calm, courteous, dignified, with a quiet sedateness that could blaze up suddenly into swiftest action.

He and I got on excellently. I liked and admired him exceedingly; and he, not being fanatically religious, seemed, in turn, to approve of me. Certainly he professed himself full of admiration for what I had been able to do with the drill and discipline of the Sultan's Cavalry and Camel-corps. He was one of the very few men whom the Sultan trusted; though even in him, he did not put unbounded faith, nor indeed in any Arab.

Abd el Hamid the Scribe was the antithesis of Hussein the Brave, his strong suit being subtlety, cleverness and crafty wisdom; definitely a man of the long robe and the pen, rather than of the sword. When talking with him, or listening to him in conversation with the Sultan, I always felt that, though probably he never said more than he meant, he always meant more than he said. He loved to speak in parables, in allusive cryptic speech; and invariably to leave one pondering his last remark. A man of learning, unusual ability, and the habit of thought, he was marked out for promotion to high office.

I formed the opinion that he was intensely ambitious, that he aspired to be the power behind the throne, or at any rate to be the confidential trusted Vizier to whom more and more of the burdens and affairs of State would be relegated.

Serving such a potentate as the average Sultan of Morocco, he might well hope to attain that kind of position; but in the service of the Sultan Mahommed el Kebir of Bab-el-Djebel, he could not hope for great personal power, whatever might be his reward in rank and position. The Sultan was a ruler who ruled; who used men and was not used by them.

Though it was impossible to have for Abd el Hamid the warm regard and admiration that I had for Hussein the Brave, I nevertheless liked him, and was inclined to trust him. The Sultan trusted him because, recognizing his ability and his ambition, he felt that circumstances guaranteed his loyalty, his success in life being dependant on the welfare of the Sultan.

With Hassan bin Yacoub the Swordsman, known as *el Khātil* the Slayer, I had less intercourse. A silent, self-centred man, somewhat narrow and fanatical, an admirable soldier, the devoted shadow of Hussein the Brave, and his invaluable lieutenant, his loyalty to the Sultan was guaranteed by his devotion to Hussein the Brave.

Of Abu bin Zaka, the Sicilian, I have given some account, but have omitted to state—having so many more interesting and important things of which to speak—that, as I rose in the Sultan's approval, favour and friendship; as my cavalry improved in discipline, drill, and tactics; as I superseded him (as well as Haroun bin Arrach the German; Hussein the Brave; Ben Abu, the Chancellor of the Exchequer, and the other civil and military officials of high rank and long service), this man had grown steadily and increasingly less friendly, more jealous and, indeed, definitely inimical.

What I liked least about his attitude was the fact that, while his actions showed enmity, he was always; particularly effusive, ingratiating and friendly, to my face. Where one or two genuine Arabs were inclined to show their jealousy by a surly, suspicious and unfriendly manner, the Sicilian was all smiles and flattery. Indeed, as my position improved, my rank increased, and promotion followed promotion until, from being drill-sergeant, instructor, colonel of a regiment, and Aga of Cavalry, I became Commander-in-Chief of the Sultan's army, so his apparent friendship changed to seeming deference and humility; and his flattery became positively fulsome and fawning. But, not fathoming the depth of the Sultan's confidence in me, nor being able to understand the nature of our friendship and the relationship existing between us, he made the fatal mistake of endeavouring to poison the Sultan's mind against me—a fact of which the latter promptly warned me.

He also made overtures to Hussein the Brave, suggesting that he should join him in compassing the overthrow of the upstart Infidel *Roumi*; and, finding Hussein unsympathetic, approached Abd el Hamid.

Hussein the Brave, out of sheer honesty and plain friendliness, informed me of the Sicilian's overtures; while Abd el Hamid (with a better understanding than the former's of my position in the Sultan's favour) also promptly informed me of my false friend's conduct and true attitude.

Secure in the Sultan's friendship, I took but little interest in the machinations of Abu bin Zaka, and remained completely indifferent, alike to his enmity and friendship, knowing that it would be exceedingly difficult for him to do me any serious injury. Particularly so, after the Sultan had informed me that—having carefully listened to the man's innuendo and suggestion, given him his profound attention, showed deep interest, and led him on until he had heard all he had to say—he had assured him that Abu bin Zaka, the Sicilian, would remain in good health as long as Sinbad el Askar, the Englishman, remained in good health; would thrive in corresponding degree, and would live as long—and no longer.

And of course the Sicilian had completely understood. He had made a bad mistake which he would be wise to retrieve; made a false step which he would do well to retrace. He had foolishly shewn his hand, and the fact that the hand held a dagger.

Thus was I safe, in the land of Bab-el-Djebel, from injury, from intrigue and assassination.

But Bab-el-Djebel is not Mecca. . . .

One afternoon, seated outside my favourite *café*, and indulging in my favourite pastime of observing the most varied and interesting crowd on earth, thanking Allah for the diversity of His creatures, and fully agreeing with Pope that the proper study of mankind is man, I suddenly became acutely aware of Abu bin Zaka, the Sicilian.

Now, I have a slight, if curious, psychic idiosyncrasy—a small gift not unknown among the people of the Scottish Highlands—a kind of second sight. On several occasions, during my wandering and somewhat adventurous life, I have had a brief distinct clear-cut day-light vision; a glimpse of some real happening, present, past or future. What I mean is that I have seen, for a few seconds, something that was then happening elsewhere; I have seen quite distinctly a glimpse of the past; I have seen, as in a crystal, something that was to happen in the future.

These phenomena have not been of frequent occurrence, and I cannot say that they have been, in themselves, of any particular interest or value. It is the fact alone that is interesting, for the phenomena themselves have frequently been trivial and unimportant.

I remember how, on joining my first ship, the *Valkyrie*, and being shown by the Second Mate the empty foul interior of the filthy half-deck, I distinctly saw, for a moment, the faces of its recent defiling occupants, a gang of criminal wharf-rats, low-type dock-side longshore loafers, who had, very improperly, been allowed to use the half-deck on the empty ship's run round from Hull to Glasgow. This glimpse, waking dream, or vision of these people was of no importance, help, or value; but the fact that I distinctly saw them was interesting.

Again, in the same ship, for the space of a couple of seconds, I saw the Captain, who was killed on the voyage, turn into a corpse and a skeleton; and I saw myself occupy the spot on which he stood. Definitely a peep into the future, though quite pointless, useless, and unhelpful.

Very occasionally, these intimations have in themselves been interesting and valuable; but these two are fair examples of my curious unwanted gift of the power to get a glimpse of the past, the future, and the elsewhere.

And now, suddenly, when no-one was farther from my thoughts than the Sicilian, Abu bin Zaka, I became acutely aware of him.

I looked round.

He was not among the customers of the café, who were a collection of Meccan idlers; Turkish and Arab officials, with a sprinkling of pilgrims.

He was not to be seen among the sauntering passers by.

Definitely he was nowhere in sight.

But he was near.

That I knew, although I couldn't see him. I knew moreover that he was wearing a white and yellow striped *silham*; about his waist a yellow sash; in one hand, an unattached sword that he was using as a walking-stick; in the other hand, his *sibhah*, the rosary consisting of ninety-nine amber beads—each representing one of the Ninety and Nine Sacred Names of God—the prayer-beads with which, here in Mecca, he made much play.

As always, when under the influence of this queer gift of mine, I was deeply interested and rather thrilled; the sensation being purely subjective and selfish, not objectively directed to the Sicilian himself, save inasmuch as he was the occasion of its manifestation.

Now, why was I "seeing" Abu bin Zaka; aware of what he was doing, when, in point of fact, he was not in sight, not present to the physical eye?

Deliberately I encouraged my sub-conscious mind to show

forth its wondrous works and perform its amusing marvels.

Yes, there he was, surrounded by a group of Arabs who were dressed in all the colours of the rainbow, and listening with interest to something that he was telling them with vigour and *empressement*.

I could see but could not hear, and had no particular desire to do so, being, as I have said, infinitely more interested in the phenomenon of "seeing" than I was in the thing seen.

The vision faded, and, dismissing it from my mind, I called for another cup of the admirable thick coffee, and again gave myself up to contemplation of my surroundings and to speculation as to the nationality, class and kind of the people around me . . .

Down the street came a party of brightly-garbed *mutowifs*—by their dress Moroccans. While they were still at some distance from my *café*, a figure detached itself from them and turned off down a side street—the figure of a man wearing a yellow-and-white striped *silham*, carrying a sheathed sword in one hand and a rosary in the other. Abu bin Zaka, the Sicilian, in fact. Of this I was certain, though I had never seen him wearing a djibba of white and yellow.

Arriving in front of my *café*, the band of mutowifs stopped, looked me over and approached. Suddenly I decided that it was time for a stroll, and, rising, I yawned, made the remark—half ejaculation, half-prayer—suitable to the occasion and turned to go.

A big *mutowif*, their leader, confronted me.

"Here, who are you?" he asked somewhat offensively.

"What the devil is that to do with you?" replied I, not with a desire to be equally offensive, but because I thought that a soft answer would neither turn away wrath nor avert suspicion. A bold front seemed to me to be indicated.

"A good deal to do with me," was the reply. "If you know anything at all, you know it is my business. Don't you know a *mutowif* when you see one? And don't you know that every genuine pilgrim has got to have a *mutowif*?"

Whether due to a guilty conscience or to a nervous apprehension, I don't know; but it seemed to me that there was a sinister accentuation of the word "genuine".

"Yes, I know a *mutowif* when I see one!" replied I, and contrived to make the remark sound critical, to say the least of it.

"And suppose a genuine pilgrim doesn't happen to want a *mutowif*?" I added.

"Well, I say he'd be a queer sort of 'genuine' pilgrim!" was the truculent reply.

"And what you say is of importance, no doubt," I sneered.

"That you will find out for yourself. Soon, too, perhaps," snarled the fellow. "Look here—where do you come from? Who are you—and why can't you behave like other pilgrims? . . . Since you know so much, you know that every Moslem country in the world has its own *mutowifs* in Mecca, and that every *mutowif* in Mecca has a recognized right to look after the pilgrims of the country he represents."

"Well then, you can look after me," I replied, turning my back upon him and, as I marched off, added, "and look as much as you like."

But I wasn't to get off as easily as that.

The gang followed me out into the street, surrounded me, and a couple of them actually seized my arms.

"You wait a minute," said the leader, thrusting his face close to mine. "We've heard something about you."

"You'll hear something more, if you are not careful," I replied. "Think you're the police? D'you think you represent the Sultan of Turkey? Or the Shereef of Mecca perhaps . . . ? Do you own the place now? . . . Since you want to know who I am, and it is so very important, I'm a *derweisch*. If you want to know where I come from, ask His Highness the Sultan of Morocco; and if you really want to offend a descendant of Muley Idris himself, a few more of you catch hold of me!"

My arms were immediately released, and the truculent tout who was their spokesman fell back, with a look somewhat akin to consternation upon his impudent face.

Striking while the iron cooled, I thrust past him and walked on, wondering whether I had better return straight to our lodging and let the Sultan deal with these people if they followed; or whether I had better lead them in the opposite direction.

If they were to raise a hue-and-cry, denounce me as an *Effrengi*, a walking pollution defiling the Holy City, I should be lucky if I died quickly by knife and sword—and the farther this happened from the Sultan's quarters the better for him and his followers. Provided, of course, that Abu bin Zaka had not intentionally betrayed the Sultan in betraying me.

But if he had done this, and I went straight to the Sultan, followed by the *mutowifs*, it was pretty certain that a golden plaster would heal their sores. Your *mutowif* is no fanatic, save in the pursuit of money; and though he'd see any unprofitable visitor torn in pieces without lifting a finger to save him, he would, in no circumstances, cause or, facilitate, the killing of the goose that could lay golden eggs.

Of course, I reflected, as soon as I could think coolly, Abu bin Zaka would not betray his own party, lest he share their fate; for once the mob, roused to frenzy by the cry of "*Effrengi! Effrengi!*", made a beginning, it would make an end—of all who had had a hand in bringing the Defilement on to sacred soil.

No, Abu bin Zaka would have described me to the *mutowifs*; would, having seen me there, have shown them the *café* outside which I was sitting; would have told them that I was a *Roumi* and an Infidel; and that, therefore, I had no *mutowif*.

Only too readily would the Moroccan *mutowifs* come searching for a pilgrim in Moroccan dress, who was suspected of being an *Effrengi* and was known to have no *mutowif*.

Having betrayed me to the *mutowifs*, he had disappeared, and would be seen by them no more. And if by chance they did see him and recognize him, he would merely be the good fellow who had, with proper public spirit, discovered and denounced an infidel dog, who was not only affronting Allah but defrauding the *mutowifs*. . . .

An excellent plan for getting me killed without any blame or suspicion attaching to the good Abu bin Zaka.

With the tail of my eye I had noticed, and been subconsciously aware of, an inquisitive gaping fellow of the baser sort who had thrust himself into the little crowd that surrounded me—a sort of donkey-man, door-keeper or porter, arrayed in dirty once-white clothing and an Indian turban.

Though far too occupied really to notice him, he had impinged sufficiently upon my consciousness for me, with a small part of my mind, to note that his face seemed, somehow, familiar. He passed me now, shuffling along with the bent shoulders of one who has spent his life in carrying heavy weights, a human beast of burden.

"Follow me, el Askar," the creature whispered as he passed—and the voice was that of Hussein the Brave.

I followed him. Not without difficulty, for, diving into the crowd where it was most dense, he made his swift elusive way like a fish through a thicket of water-reeds. Round corners, up side-streets, through dark-roofed market-places, under cloistered arcades, through a shop, behind some stalls, I followed the Indian turban, and, in time, reached the back of the house in which we lodged.

"You did well, oh, Sinbad el Askar," said Hussein the Brave, as we entered the garden of our house and halted to draw breath. "You were clever. Clever. A stroke of genius to call yourself a *derweisch*, for such have no country. Also, instead of denying that you were from Morocco to hint at the patronage of the Sultan of Morocco himself; also descent from the Great Marabout. But it would be well to hide for a while. . . . Or, perchance, our Lord el Sidna el Sultan Mahommed el Kebir may decree that the chief of the Moroccan *mutowifs* be sent for, taken into his 'confidence', and sent away with a flea in his ear and a gift in his pocket.

"Be told that I am an Infidel?" I asked in some 'surprise.

"No. Be told that 'for reasons of State' it were better that the Moroccan *mutowifs* took no further notice of you; and that he himself guaranteed you. They would be well content dumbly to behold a mystery—nicely gilded. . . . Let it be left to the wisdom of the Sultan to decide.

"And then for that dog Abu bin Zaka . . ."

And Hussein the Brave licked thin lips.

§2

On his return to the house, I gave the Sultan an exact account of what had happened, suppressing mention of my day-dream . . . vision . . . second-sight manifestation . . . concerning Abu bin Zaka. I did, however, mention that I distinctly saw a man dressed in a white and yellow *djibba* leave the band of *mutowifs*, and turn up a side street, when they were some little distance from the *café*.

When I had finished my story, the Sultan sat in silent thought.

After a while he knocked a sharp double knock on the floor with his pistol butt—and again—the signal that would call Hussein the Brave.

A minute later the door opened, and Hussein the Brave entered. He had changed from his disguise as an Indian coolie into his ordinary clothing.

"Sit," said the Sultan, indicating the rug spread before him. "Tell me of your doings of this afternoon."

"Know, oh Sultan," replied Hussein the Brave, bowing as he touched heart and head, "I was about your business, after mid-day prayer, reconnoitring the house that you showed us, and then buying, in the Indian bazaar, certain things of which you spoke, for the making up of your pedlar's pack. While practising my part, and bargaining angrily with a stall-holder for some silk, whom should I see go by, but your loyal and devoted servant Abu bin Zaka. At once I noted that he was arrayed in a *djibba* that I knew not, a noble striped garment of yellow and white. And, straightway, Allah put it into my mind to try to play a little trick upon him. On such small things do great depend.

"Picking up a little phial of Holy Water from the Haram's sacred well of Zem-zem, I flung down a few *nuhass*, and hurried after him. Walking beside him, I importuned him that he should buy the Holy Water, swearing that it was of especial potency and virtue for him who desired certain things—and there I mentioned 'certain things' well known by me to be desired of this faithful and profitable servant of your Highness. And, even then, he did not recognize me. No, Sidi, he knew not my face, my voice, nor my person; and my heart rejoiced that my disguise and acting were both so good. And almost I chuckled aloud when, taking the little bottle from my hand, the good Abu bin Zaka flung a coin at my feet—whether persuaded by my eloquence and curious knowl-edge of his desires, or whether to get rid of me, I know not; but, a moment later he turned aside and joined a party of *mutowifs* of Morocco, standing at their usual pitch.

"Whereat I opened wide my eyes and opened wide my ears. What was this? What business had Abu bin Zaka with the *muto-wifs* of Morocco whom we had been at pains to avoid, and whom Kassim bin Ibrahim, your Excellency's fore-runner here, had care-fully hoodwinked?

"Then I thanked Allah the Merciful, the Compassionate, that I had played my little trick on the good Abu bin Zaka, and that he had not penetrated my disguise. And scrabbling about in the dust in search of the coin that was in my hand, I listened.

"Hear and believe, oh Sidi! That dog, that father of mules and son of a bare-faced noseless mother, bade the *mutowifs* go quickly to the *café* of Abdul Izzet the Turk, in the Street called The Broad, and there behold an *Effrengi*, an Infidel dog, a *Roumi* disguised as an Arab of the Western Sahara. Yea, as a man of el Moghreb. Bade them ask him who he was, whence he came, and why he had no *mutowif*.

"It was in my mind to stab him to the heart and run, but the mischief was done. So, holding my peace, I followed—and I was filled with admiration at the way el Sidi Sinbad el Askar dealt with them—with wisdom and subtlety, with cleverness and courage—out-facing them boldly, bidding them have a care of how they interfered with a *derweisch* who owns to no country; interfered with a holy descendant of Muley Idris the Great Marabout; with an emissary, perchance, of His Highness the Sultan of Morocco himself!

"And while they stood, doubtful and confused, he walked off angrily; and, by tortuous ways, I led him here.

"I have spoken. It is the truth."

The Sultan stroked his beard; still in thoughtful silence. Again he knocked upon the floor, a signal that called the Scribe, Abd el Hamid, who promptly appeared.

"Has our good Abu bin Zaka yet returned?" he enquired mildly.

"But now, Your Highness," replied the Scribe.

"Give him friendly greetings, and bid him rest, refresh himself, and, after prayer and ablution, attend us here. We would discuss—er—certain things with him."

"Also," and the Sultan lowered his voice to a silky whisper, "bid Hassan bin Yacoub the Swordsman see that Abu bin Zaka leaves not this house until I have had speech with him. On his head and his life be it."

The ghost of an enigmatic smile hovered for a second about the lips of Abd el Hamid the Scribe as he bowed and withdrew.

A few minutes later, during which no word was spoken, Abu bin Zaka entered, salaamed smiling, and begged to be told wherein he could serve the Sultan. Ere the door closed, I had a glimpse of the grim face of Hassan bin Yacoub the Slayer.

As Abu bin Zaka's glance met mine, no change was visible upon his swarthy, smiling countenance.

"Be seated," said the Sultan, indicating a corner of the rug opposite to that occupied by Hussein the Brave; and, cross-legged, Abu bin Zaka seated himself, bowed his head and touched heart and forehead.

Complete silence fell upon the room, a silence during which I grew more and more uncomfortable, Hussein the Brave and the Sultan more and more sphinx-like, Abu bin Zaka more and more puzzled.

Minutes passed.

Almost I began to think them hours . . . when suddenly the Sultan spoke.

Pleasantly, conversationally, he observed to Abu bin Zaka,

"And the beautiful yellow and white *silham*? We had hoped to see it. Why this sombre one, with which we are familiar?"

Abu bin Zaka's smile faded not at all, but he swallowed hard ere he spoke.

"Yellow and white, Sidi?" he said with a beautiful air of puzzlement.

"Oh, am I mistaken?" murmured the Sultan. "Not yellow and white?"

"No, Sidi," smiled Abu bin Zaka, still puzzled, but humouring his master's whim.

"No," agreed the Sultan, "not yellow and white."

"Definitely not yellow and white," he repeated, turning to Hussein the Brave.

"But white and yellow," he added, a moment later.

And turning back to Abu bin Zaka he repeated his question.

"And the beautiful white and yellow *silham*? We had hoped to see it. Why this sombre one with which we are familiar, instead of the new white and yellow one—which is by no means yellow and white?"

"Sidi? . . ." appealed Abu bin Zaka in bewilderment.

"Nay, let it pass," continued the Sultan. . . . "But tell us, oh faithful servant and friend, what of the phial of Holy Water from the Sacred Well of Zem-zem, the Prophet's Own Well beside the *Ka'ba* in the *Haram* of Mecca? . . . Did you bring the phial safely home, that its virtue and potency may help you to the attainment of—certain desires?"

And the Sultan enumerated the desires mentioned by Hussein the Brave, and better left unmentioned here.

By now, the radiant smile had paled somewhat: a shadow of anxiety had fallen athwart the cunning face.

"Sidi?"

"And what of the *mutowifs* of Morocco, and your unburdening of your conscience? Your telling them of the Effrengi, the *mutowif*-less one, seated near-by in the *café* of Abdul Izzet, the Turk, in the Street called Broad?"

Abu bin Zaka glanced at me, at the door, at the windows, and moistened dry lips.

The Sultan spoke to him no more.

With a cutting contempt beyond description, he ignored him thenceforth, as he would have done a little noxious insect that he had crushed beneath his sandal.

To me he spoke.

"And you have wondered, oh Sinbad el Askar, that I put not overmuch faith and trust in every one of the men, my friends and servants, who have eaten of my bread and of my salt for years and years and years. Men whom I have befriended and raised up from nothing. . . . Tell me, what do *you* do to the gutter-bred pariah dog that you have taken into your tent and fed, and that bites the hand that has fed it?"

I pondered this.

"Drive it from the tent and feed it no more," I decided.

"And you, Hussein the Brave?" asked the Sultan.

"Throw it from the tent," replied Hussein the Brave instantly, "and then throw its head out after it."

The Sultan mused awhile.

"I think your plan the better," he said at length, "for dead dogs do not bite again."

From beneath his left sleeve the Sultan drew his pistol, and Abu bin Zaka with a scream of

"Mercy!" flung his arm across his face.

On the floor the Sultan knocked, giving the signal for the immediate calling together of all his followers.

Scarcely had he done so, when the door opened, and Hassan bin Yacoub the Swordsman stepped into the room, yataghan in hand; and the feet of Abd el Hamid and Kassim bin Ibrahim were heard upon the wooden stairs.

Hassan bin Yacoub the Slayer stood behind Abu bin Zaka, his sword-point suggestively near that scoundrel's neck.

"Lord," whispered the latter, "let me explain! I can . . ."

The Sultan's eyes met those of the swordsman and the sword-point touched the speaker's bare neck. . . .

Again the sounds of feet upon the stair, and, in a remarkably brief space, the Sultan's *entourage* were, in ones and twos, entering the room, salaaming as they did so, and were bidden to sit. It being the Sultan's order that his followers should walk abroad when he did, and be in their lodgings when he was, there were no absentees.

The door being closed for the last time, silence fell upon the assembly, and all eyed the Sultan expectantly.

"Speak, Hussein the Brave," said he. "Tell briefly, without exaggeration or extenuation, the tale that you have told me concerning my faithful friend and servant, Abu bin Zaka, and my faithful friend and servant, Sinbad el Askar.

And simply and briefly Hussein the Brave set forth the facts.

I watched the faces of his hearers as they listened to his speech, an oration the more powerful and telling by reason of its studied simplicity. On that of Kassim bin Ibrahim, I read genuine anger; on that of Hassan bin Yacoub the Swordsman, contempt; on that of Abd el Hamid—nothing, nothing whatever; on the faces of one or two of the others, a thoughtful wonderment as they looked from me to Abu bin Zaka; on one or two faces, stolid, almost expressionless, with down-cast eyes, something possibly akin, not to sympathy, perhaps, but to complete understanding of the Sicilian's conduct.

Hussein finished his story with the words,

"And returning instantly he changed the yellow-striped *silham* for the one that now he wears. In his scrip you will find the flask of Zem-zem water that I sold to him. And, here, behold the coin with which he paid me for it!"

And he sat down.

Again silence.

"And now," said the Sultan, "let our learned Abd el Hamid the Scribe go down into the room below, accompanied by our faithful servant and friend, Abu bin Zaka (*and* Hassan bin Yacoub the Slayer, on whose head and whose life be it that our faithful friend and servant, Abu bin Zaka, returns safely to this room thereafter) and let Abd el Hamid talk with him. Let Abu bin Zaka say all that he has to say, to Abd el Hamid; let him explain away this unfortunate misunderstanding; let him explain the curious matter of the changed *silham*; of his holding converse with the Moroccan *mutowifs* whom we have so carefully avoided, and so let him clear himself. And then, returning hither, let Abd el Hamid the Scribe make eloquent defence, reassuring us all as to the fidelity, loyalty, honesty, and faith of our brother, my trusted Colonel of Infantry, Abu bin Zaka. . . . Then shall Kassim bin Ibrahim question him and question Hussein the Brave; and then shall any man ask any question.

"And thereafter—when all is said, verdict shall be given—and, if necessary, sentence shall be pronounced.

"Arise, Abd el Hamid, and go to talk in private with Abu bin Zaka."

But the Sicilian threw himself upon the mercy of the Court—knowing that there was nothing he could say in his defence; that by luck, *kismet*, the will of Allah, and the cleverness of Hussein the Brave, he was caught, trapped beyond hope of escape.

He confessed the truth of Hussein's accusation, pleaded his religious scruples and tender conscience, and begged for forgiveness. But his attempted appeal to the religious susceptibilities of his hearers was without avail.

Of each, in turn, the Sultan asked what sentence he, if Judge, would propound; and in every case the answer was—'*Death*'.

"And what manner of death would you decree, oh, Hussein the Brave?" asked the Sultan.

"Were we in our own country of Bab-el-Djebel, oh, Sultan, my answer would be different. But, we being here in Mecca and the matter private, I would say—let me or Hassan bin Yacoub the Slayer, take a party of six, to be chosen by lot or who volunteer, and ride far out into the desert with—a dog. And let us return from that ride—without a dog. . . ."

And this seemed good to the assembly.

"We will think upon it," said the Sultan.

"Meantime, oh Hassan bin Yacoub the Swordsman, on thy life be it that he escape not," he added.

Hassan bin Yacoub, *el Khātil*, the Slayer, smiled.

I never saw Abu bin Zaka the Sicilian again.

CHAPTER XXVI

My next incarnation upon this dædal earth was that of a coolie or porter in the service of an Indian pedlar; and in that rôle I witnessed one of the most poignant scenes that I have ever beheld. . . .

Between them, Hussein the Brave and Abd el Hamid the Scribe had found out a great deal about the ways and habits, methods and customs, comings and goings, of the members of the household of the Hadji Ghulamali Salehudin Yussufali Jalpur, formerly Nawab of Aundhara.

Those two and their spies had, by clever intelligence-work and judiciously expended bakshish, learned that the Nawab himself was sojourning, during the present heat, at Medina, acquiring merit and interviewing certain travellers from England, Mussulmans who were on their way to India by the somewhat circuitous route of the Hedjaz Railway from Beyrout to Medina.

That he should go thither at this time of the year, was quite natural, as the climate of Medina is positively bracing in comparison with that of Mecca, being, by day, pleasantly warm, and, by night, two-blankets cold.

From Medina he would return for the ceremony of the *levée* of the Shereef of Mecca, which would take place on the day after the conclusion of the *Hadj*.

Concerning the Nawab's household, it had been discovered that he had a *harim* of reasonable proportions; four wives, three sons, and some odds and ends of daughters. One of the wives, an old woman, was some sort of foreigner, a Turki, Afghani, or perhaps a Persian or something. She had been in Mecca as long as the Hadji Ghulamali himself. It was said that he had brought her with him from India, in fact.

"No," according to the *major-domo*, "she was nobody—just an old hag of no importance in the *harim*. The real lady was the Sitt Zeinab."

With the Hadji Ghulamali Salehudin Yussufali Jalpur had gone his principal servants; his house in Mecca being left in charge of a fat and venal old *major-domo*, whose wagging tongue was stimulated by an itching palm. In the guise of a Sindhi *borah*'s tout, Abd el Hamid had interested the *major-domo* in the tout's employer; and had made promise of the usual—or better

649

than usual—commission on all business effected between his master and Those Behind the Curtain.

The way having been thus prepared, there was no fear that the surly answer that turneth away pedlars would be given when the Sind-work merchant arrived with his coolie-borne packs. . . .

I was a little surprised at the simple pleasure and whole-hearted joy that my companions took in this piece of play-acting. Far from considering it beneath their undeniable dignity to play the part of *hamals*, they entered into the plot with zest, the inherent guilefulness of their natures thoroughly approving this method of getting inside the house of one whom they had been told was their master's enemy.

And so, a few days after the incident of Abu bin Zaka and the *mutowifs*, I found myself following the Sultan through the readily-opened compound-gates of the Nawab's house, across a some-what barren garden, through lattice-work doors and into a verandah, wherein our packs were deposited and opened.

The goods being displayed to advantage, and everything being ready, the coolies were bidden to withdraw, and out into the compound they went, grouping themselves on and about the steps that led up from the garden to the plinth on which the house was built.

Through the lattice-work of the doors and arches of the verandah they, with careful carelessness, watched the proceedings. Hussein the Brave, crouching on the top step, prevented the door from being completely shut, and unobtrusively inserted a previously-chosen pebble into the hole in the flag-stone into which the bolt of the lattice-work door would have dropped, had the door been closed. Should things go awry, the Sultan's retreat would not be cut off.

Inside with the merchant, remained his clerk and his assistant—Abd el Hamid and myself.

Facing our display was an arched door-way across which hung a curtain. In this curtain were holes and, applied to these holes, were eyes. From time to time the curtain was drawn an inch or so aside, and a tiny hand and part of a face could be seen.

A delightful imp of a child crawled out from beneath the curtain, and stood clapping its hands and crowing with glee at the bright silks, silver and brass ware, bangles, necklaces and strings of beads.

Business soon became brisk, as from behind the curtain, imperious directions were given to the merchant, to hold up lengths of silk and muslin, pieces of silver, a mirror, an ornament, this, that and the other, and to name its price.

Before long, an onlooker would have imagined that the *major-domo* was the merchant, so eloquent were his praises of anything that caught the eye of anyone behind the curtain, so loud his wonder at the cheapness of the goods in relation to their quality. If we went empty away, it would not be his fault.

Business went well, and both the Sultan and Abd el Hamid discovered a, to me, quite unsuspected vein of skilful acting, drollery, waggishness, and amazing power of impersonation. I felt perfectly certain that no Indian borah and his assistant ever looked and behaved more like a jolly, prosperous, wily, keen and brisk Indian borah and assistant than those two did.

And when trade had begun to flag; when there was less bustle and excitement behind the curtain; and interest was obviously waning, the merchant stimulated it by providing a small entertainment.

Taking his *raita* (on which he was no mean performer) from his pack, Abd el Hamid played popular and provocative airs on that wicked instrument, "the Muezzin of Satan."

Thereafter the merchant sang a song of which I could make nothing. Later, I learned it was a famous Indian song, known as *Dilkusha*.

"Now then!" whispered he to me, as he finished, "Let's have *Ye Banks and Braes*, and put all the accent you can into it."

I did my best; and, whatever the cause, complete silence fell behind the curtain—a silence which might or might not have been complimentary.

"*Loch Lomond*," whispered the Sultan.

I had just finished the line,

"*I and my true love will never meet again*," when the curtain was thrust aside, and a woman stepped out into the verandah.

Before me stood Janet Chandos . . . born, bred and married in the Highlands of Scotland; widowed in Zeerut of India; imprisoned for life in Mecca of Arabia. . . .

In the second of silence in which she stared at the Sultan as he rose to his feet, I examined her face. It had been beautiful.

It was still Scottish . . . a face to be seen in any part of the Highlands. But it was the face of a woman of eighty, though she could not have been more than sixty. Her hair was perfectly white; her face almost as white as her hair; her lips almost as white as her face; her piercing eyes a pale brilliant blue.

In spite of what she must have suffered—in spite of forty years of such suffering—the face was still alive; still strong; its expression still sweet.

But it was terrible . . . terrible . . . Such a face as I never wish to see again.

And I think she was mad.

If so, I saw a mad person suddenly become sane.

I saw a dead face come to life.

I saw a ghost from another world become human.

"*Mother!*" said the Sultan, and took a stride toward her, his arms extended.

And then I beheld a miracle of change in the face of the woman.

"*My son! My son!*" she whispered as she stretched out her hands to him.

And from her fell the suffering, pain and agony of all those years.

The colour came back to the cheeks; a smile to the lips; vigour, youth and strength to the frail body.

The Sultan took his mother in his arms and held her to his broad chest, tenderly.

She laid her cheek against her son.

"*Mother!*" he said again, and raised her face to his.

"*Mother!*" . . .

But there was no reply.

She was dead.

CHAPTER XXVII

Although the Sultan had not professed to have loved his mother very much when he was a boy, and had not seen her since he ran away from her, at the age of fourteen or so, he was obviously affected by her death—or rather, perhaps, by the tragic circumstances of her death in his arms.

It was in vain that I endeavoured to assure him that she had died at the happiest moment she had known in all her life since the murder of her husband; that he had given her a moment of supreme joy, a joy greater than her heart, doubtless worn and strained by suffering, had been able to bear; and moreover, that her life having been what it had, her death was a happy release— literally release; and most certainly happy. . . .

Severely he blamed himself, and it was obvious that this self-blame was real and genuine.

He hated himself for the thought of what he might have been, and had not been, to his mother; what he might have done, and had not done, for her. I think the Englishman in his nature then rose above the Mussulman up-bringing and training imposed upon it. Perhaps for the first time he felt toward women as Christians do, and not as Mussulmans; and judged himself by the standards of an English son.

One re-action of this tragic death was an increased hatred of his step-father; an increased intention to avenge upon him all his mother had suffered. I think that the sight of her face—the first time that, as an understanding adult, he had set eyes upon it— really brought home to him some comprehension of what his mother had suffered at the Nawab's hands.

He ceased to speak of punishing the man who had murdered his father; who had denied him his birthright as a Briton; who had kidnapped him and made of him a Mussulman—and now spoke of punishing the man who had tortured Janet Chandos.

He would await the Nawab's return from Medina to Mecca, and then he would deal with him. Yea, if he spent the rest of his life awaiting him in Mecca, he would punish him.

Of that there was no shadow of doubt. The only point on which he was not decided, was the manner of the punishment. The one that he favoured was of the *quid pro quo* type, kidnapping the Nawab as he had kidnapped Janet Chandos;

taking him to Bab-el-Djebel as he had taken her to Mecca; and there keeping him in a cruel and humiliating slavery such as he had inflicted upon her.

At times, he would declare that this was a treatment too good for him, a punishment too light; and would swear that he would cut the man's throat with his own hand; would take him out into the desert and crucify him; would hang him at his own front door; would impale him to die slowly, with lidless eyes, staring at the sun. . . .

Meanwhile—to perform the Pilgrimage and attain the sanctity of a *hadji*, no matter with what passion burning in his breast, what thoughts of vengeance and murder seething in his brain.

§2

At some hour before the setting of the sun, on the eighth day of the month of Dhu'lhagga, all pilgrims intending to perform the ceremony of the *Hadj* have to take their departure from Mecca for Mina, a village some eight kilometres north of the Holy City. At Mina they must spend the night.

On the following morning they must proceed a further nine miles to Mount Arafat, and there they must spend the day until the setting of the sun. Thereafter, returning. they must sleep half-way between Mount Arafat and Mina, at the village of Nimrah.

On the next day they must return again to Mina before mid-day, and "stone the devils".

Having done this, they must continue the journey back to Mecca, perform the *towaf* ceremony again, and go back to Mina that night.

The next day, spent at Mina, is Festival Day.

On the day after that, the pilgrims finally return to Mecca, once again "stoning the devils" *en route*.

Throughout all this time the *Irham* dress must be worn; but directly the pilgrimage is finished—that is as soon as the *towaf* ceremony is completed at the *Haram* of Mecca—the *Irham* dress is finally discarded, and everyone must bedeck himself in clothing that is not only new, but of the brightest and best, the most expensive that his purse can buy.

This is symbolical (purely symbolical!) of the beginning of a new life, a higher and a better life; of all sin being purged; and of the pilgrim, washed whiter than snow, being now as a little child. . . .

The curious rite of "the stoning of the devils" has persisted since the days when Mahommed turned the religion of the Arabs from paganism, idolatry and devil-worship, to the religion of the One True God, the Islamic Allah.

Doubtless the "devils" which are merely stone pillars, mark the places where once stood actual idols; and it was to prove and confirm their adherence to the New Faith that the early converts insulted and derided the emblems of their old superstition, by flinging stones at them.

One is, of course, reminded of the stoning of the Prophets by the recusant Israelites—themselves Arabs by descent.

On the evening of the *Khuroog* or exodus, we once more arrayed ourselves in our two-piece garments of the *Irham*, mounted our camels, and set forth, our servants and necessary baggage—tents, food, cooking-utensils and so forth—having gone on ahead with Kassim bin Ibrahim.

Headed by a *hamelidari*—our professional guide, mentor, instructor and general shower-of-the-ropes—we were once again, as on our journey from Jidda to Mecca, part of a human river, flowing slowly along.

Outside Mina we were met by our ever-faithful and reliable Kassim bin Ibrahim and guided to our tents.

By the Sultan's advice, and indeed instructions, we went early to bed, for the next day was to be strenuous indeed.

At dawn we arose, and while we broke our fast, Kassim bin Ibrahim went on ahead with the tents and impedimenta. That we ever saw him and them again, was a tribute to his great ability at his job.

The road, to call it such, from Mina to Mount Arafat, now presented one of the most amazing spectacles in the world—unique in fact. Crowded into the short space between the two places, were quite five hundred thousand pilgrims—an incredible army, equivalent to no less than five hundred battalions each a thousand strong; or rather, what with mounts and baggage-animals, to a *thousand* regiments of cavalry or camelry, each of five hundred sabres.

The sound of the feet of this colossal moving mass of men and animals is as that of a hurricane, as that of the roar of a surging sea; and the dust raised by them as a column of cloud, hundreds of feet in height and miles in length and breadth.

And the soil of Mount Arafat was hidden from sight by the forms of the men that thronged it from foot to summit.

And now the roar of the column was dominated by that of voices, a mighty sound which grew intelligible as the "*Lebeka,*

lebeka, Allahuma lebeka!" that I had heard when the pilgrims first caught sight of the Sacred City from the Jidda road.

I have heard of earth-shaking sounds, and it did actually and in fact seem to me that the earth was shaken by this tremendous volume of noise; as though by the tremor of an earthquake.

Mount Arafat is a boulder-strewn hill, some three hundred and fifty feet in height, and shaped somewhat like the Pyramids. From beneath it flows the spring which forms the water-supply of Mecca. At the top is a platform with a stone monument.

Not only was this hill completely covered, but square miles of the surrounding plain was hidden by the tents, booths, and bivouacs of the pilgrims—one illimitable camp spreading in all directions as far as one could see. . . .

Again the eagle eye of Kassim bin Ibrahim, seated on his tall camel, distinguished us and, without delay, he led us again to our tents where, having rested, washed and eaten, we ascended the hill to offer up the two prescribed prayers, on the praying-platform at the summit.

At mid-day, the Hour of Prayer was announced by a salute of guns, three Turkish batteries having driven out from the Mecca Fort, for the purpose; each battery firing a twenty-one gun salute.

On the way back to our camp, I noticed that cleanliness accompanied godliness, inasmuch as the huge tanks—in which the water from the spring collected ere flowing into the conduit leading to Mecca—were crammed and crowded by bathing pilgrims.

And they were washing away more than their sins in the drinking-water of the Holy City.

Returning to our tents, we fed and rested, and thereafter strolled about the camp, which resembled more than anything else, a vast fair-ground. Of course, one could only see a small portion of it. Nor was it only the fact of the vast assemblage of tents, booths and bivouacs that reminded one of a fair; for there was a definite fair-ground atmosphere, and the last subject that seemed to occupy the minds of the mighty multitude was religion.

Toward evening, our tents were struck, and camels loaded in preparation for the move at sunset, the official moment being declared by the Shereef of Mecca, and signalized by a salute of guns from the battery.

As the first gun was fired, the vast throng of pilgrims set off in what was really a cross-country race, the object being to be first into the narrow defile through which the road to Mount Arafat and Nimrah passes. It is not only a case of "first come first through", but of "first come, least likely to be crushed to death".

Needless to say, Kassim bin Ibrahim was among the first through, and that when we reached the mosque at Nimrah, once again our little camp was ready.

The pilgrims continued arriving in their thousands, almost all night; and the noise of their feet, their shouting, the sounds of quarrelling and argument, the bubbling and groaning of camels, neighing of horses, and braying of asses rendered night hideous and sleepless.

It was thus no hardship to arise before the sun, and set forth for Mina, again well ahead of the horde; so that our place in this camp was also a good one—as near as possible to the Turkish Military Camp, a position of safety and comparative peace.

And safety is a consideration to the pilgrim to the Holy Places, for the robbery and murder of the pious by the less pious is too common to cause comment.

There is quite an organization of ghouls, probably local Bedoui, for the object and purpose of slitting the throats of sleeping men, and creeping away with their cash and weapons. Everyone is armed, but the weary pilgrim cannot keep awake all night, and it is then that he runs a risk of suddenly waking to find himself disembowelled or slashed across the throat. . . .

Here and now we had to "stone the devils". For this purpose, Kassim bin Ibrahim, the perfect courier, had laid in a store of desirable stones, and presented each member of our company with a bag containing sixty-three. Local stones, by the way, are by no means acceptable. To be effective, they must be brought from Nimrah.

To myself I murmured,

"A twenty-one-stone salute for each poor devil", for there are three of them.

And again (strictly to myself) I murmured,

"Father Devil, Mother Devil, and Baby Devil."

Father and Mother Devil are in Main Street. Actually in Mina High Street. Baby Devil is a bit farther down on the Mecca road.

As I have said, they are stone pillars. Each stands in a huge stone saucer. Early in the day as it was they were scarcely to be seen for the heavy rain of stones falling about them—a cloud of witnesses to the Faith, indeed.

As may be imagined, it is nearly as dangerous as being in a battle—a good deal more dangerous than being in some battles—to get within hitting distance of the devils.

Unfortunately it is not necessary for the thrower to hit the devil. All he has got to do, is to throw with might and main and the best intentions. If he do this from a hundred yards distance, he is pretty certain to hit at least one of the more conscientious throwers—one who has gone up sufficiently near to make certain of giving the devil a dunt.

Similarly, the conscientious thrower, being close to the devil and throwing with might and main, is quite sure to hit somebody in the crowd opposite to him, whenever he misses the devil.

Personally, I followed the tactics of the former thrower. Sixty three times I threw, and I have not the slightest doubt I hit somebody—man or devil—every time. I did my best, anyhow.

On the return from the ceremony, many pilgrims were bleeding from more or less serious cuts about the face and head. They did not seem to mind. Frequently the bodies of smitten pilgrims are left lying near to the devils. They seem to mind still less. . . .

Although we started early and set about the throwing ceremony with business and despatch, the throng was so great that it took us a couple of hours to throw our twenty-one stones at each of them and get back to our tents.

Next followed the, to me, very nasty business of the Sacrifice. Every man of that half-million must, this day, make a living sacrifice—almost always of a sheep or goat. Having slain your beast *ad majorem Dei gloriam* you can eat it, if you are selfish; you can give it to the poor, if you are a sportsman.

It struck me as an absolutely criminal piece of wastefulness, insanitary folly and stupid cruelty. Other people's religious rites are apt to seem so.

But—really! Half a million carcases left, for the most part entire, to rot upon the ground. This horror, and the practice by the diseased and the filthy, of bathing in Mecca's drinking-water, leads to terrible cholera-epidemics, these being rightly regarded by the Faithful as *kismet*.

It was written on their foreheads, and it had to come to pass. If the water-supply were protected and the slaughtered animals buried, or not slaughtered at all, there would be no such writing on the forehead, and the epidemics would not come to pass.

The Sultan, knowing the law permitted it, had our animals slaughtered by proxy; Kassim bin Ibrahim merely having to pay a small fee beyond the purchase-price of the beasts.

Having stoned the devils and sacrificed the sheep, we were now free to take the road for Mecca; and this we did, after mid-day prayer, food and ablution.

It was a terribly hot business. We could only go at a slow walk, owing to the denseness of the throng; and then had to await our turn in the *Haram*, to circumambulate the *Ka'ba* and kiss the black stone, in performance of the *towaf* ceremony again. What vigour I may have lost through my deficiency in piety, was, perhaps, more than supplied by what skill I had in Rugby scrum-tactics. Anyhow, I survived the almost fatally strenuous sport of getting at the black stone and kissing it, though more than one of our party had facial and other contusions to show, ere we escaped from the *Haram*. It is difficult, gently to present your face and lips to a very hard substance, when a surging crowd is buffeting, crushing, thrusting, bumping and struggling on every side of you, the aim and endeavour of every member of it being violently to remove you and to take your place. Quite a "wall-game".

However, determined properly to perform the *Hadj* even if I could not become a genuine *Hadji*, I kissed the black stone and, unlike Abd el Hamid the Scribe emerged from the frightful *mêlée* clothed in more than piety and virtue. The *Irham* garments are easily displaced—yea, removed and lost—in a desperate struggle of that kind.

And, at long last, came the final rite, the shaving of a small portion of the side of the head. This done (by an Elder Brother in Islam, whose piety was greater than his skill) I received the good *aalim*'s blessing—and I had then performed the Pilgrimage and, had I been a Mussulman, should have been a *hadji*.

Having returned to our lodgings, we bathed our sun-blistered bodies, rested, ate, and then arrayed ourselves even as Solomon in all his glory.

As usual, I copied the Sultan's style of dress, endeavouring to combine extreme correctness of cut and excellence of material with good taste, quietness, and absence of colour and ornamentation. White, black, a modestly cheerful sash and a noble dagger, was my idea of the correct thing for this great occasion.

Hussein the Brave was brave indeed, and wore not only every colour seen in the rainbow, but many that are not to be observed in that phenomenon. I should think that among his turban, sash, *kaffieh*, velvet waistcoat, *haik*, *silham*, *burnous*, slippers and velvet sword-sheath, there was no known colour, shade, or tint, that could not be seen and almost heard; nor did any other member of the Sultan's entourage fail to run him very closely in the matter of beauty and brilliance.

Duty done, the time for pleasure had arrived—pleasure, pious and chastened, of course, but joyous nevertheless—the next day being the First Day of the Festival.

So, just before sunset, we again set forth for Mina; and if the camp at Mount Arafat had seemed like a fair-ground, that at Mina now seemed that of paradisial super-fair, every man there being arrayed in the best and brightest clothes that he could possibly afford.

The great feature of the ceremonies of this first Festival Day was the holding of the *levée* of the Shereef of Mecca. His magnificent camp was pitched on a vast platform and surrounded by troops, part of whom were stationed as a living avenue to keep clear a wide road leading to His Highness's great marquee.

One by one, accompanied by their brilliant escorts, the different nobles and notabilities arrived to pay their respects and something more tangible, to the Shereef, seated in state at the back of the marquee. Nor were these merely local magnates.

There was the Turkish Ambassador, who brought a magnificent gift from Constantinople; Mahommedan princes from India; powerful Arab rulers; the Governors of Mecca and of Medina; and other people of high importance.

As I stood beside the Sultan, watching this extremely interesting sight and ceremony, he suddenly seized my left wrist with his right hand.

"There he is . . . the devil!" he whispered; and, within a few feet of us, with nothing between us and him but a line of Turkish soldiers, passed the Hadji Ghulamali Salehudin Yussufali Jalpur, late Nawab of Aundhara, a big heavy man whose grey beard and moustache failed to conceal the fact that his face was bloated, sensual and very evil. In his youth he must have been a powerful, up-standing, handsome man, who doubtless looked every inch a ruler and a prince. Now he looked a debauched *roué*.

As the Sultan's hand released my wrist, I ventured to seize his, for he was quivering with rage; and, knowing his quick temper, autocratic habit and swiftness of action, I was afraid that he might do something sudden and rash, then and there—in which case, whatever might be the fate of the Nawab, concerning ours there could be no doubt.

CHAPTER XXVIII

And now came detailed consideration of what was the real reason for the Sultan's visit to Mecca.

As usual, he took me fully into his confidence, and day after day, night after night, talked of the Nawab of Aundhara, talked of his mother, and talked of himself.

I had all along been somewhat puzzled as to why he should have let so many years elapse, and then taken this sudden determination to come to Mecca, rescue his mother, and take vengeance upon a scoundrel who had wronged her so unspeakably, caused the murder of her husband, usurped his place, and kept her literally a prisoner for life.

As he talked, it became quite comprehensible to me, however. It was not until he had arrived at years of discretion and seen something of life and the great world, that he had come anywhere near to realization of the unthinkable wrong that had been done to his mother. It was not for some time after this, again, that it occurred to him that he had a filial duty to perform, that he should go to Mecca and do what lay in his power to ameliorate her lot, make some reparation for what she had suffered; also to punish the man who had murdered her husband and turned the happy little heaven of her life to a dark deep hell of misery unplumbable.

Nor, having realized this and made his resolution, was it for many long years that he had the opportunity to make an attempt to carry it out with any reasonable chance of success.

He might, of course, have abandoned his position and pro-spects as an adopted son of the Sultan of Bab-el-Djebel, and made his slow and painful way across Africa and the Red Sea to Mecca; but, having succeeded in getting there, what could he do—friendless and penniless, without power, influence, or any hope of making successful assault upon the house of the powerful and wealthy Nawab of Aundhara, friend of the Shereef of Mecca, of the Turkish Ambassador, and of the notables of the Holy Cities of Mecca and Medina?

Nor, when he succeeded to the *gadi*, and himself became Sultan of Bab-el-Djebel, had he opportunity, now that he had the means and power. Throughout the years that followed his succession, he had cherished the ambition, hope, and intention of going to Mecca when he could safely leave his kingdom. But never until now had the time seemed ripe, the opportunity good, the undertaking a reasonably safe one. He had no desire to drop substance for shadow, to lose his desert throne for the pleasure of following the will-o'-the-wisp of belated vengeance across a continent—and finding himself in Mecca, a potentate deposed, a ruler of nothing but a tiny caravan, leader of a handful of followers that would soon slip from his grasp.

He was under no illusion as to the tremendous danger of taking such a step as the one he had so long contemplated; and in spite of what he had said to me about the improbability of treachery, rebellion, revolution and usurpation, the risk was both real and great.

And, in addition to the domestic aspect of the situation, he had to consider the attitude, and probable and possible action, of his nominal suzerain, the Sultan of Morocco, as well as of those European powers by whom he was subsidized—in the hope that, at the right time and place, the weight of his sharp sword might be thrust into the scales that they might hold.

Curiously enough, it was my arrival upon the scene, and my successful passing of the numerous tests with which he tried me, that led him to decide to go to Mecca when he did.

For some reason that I did not pretend to fathom, he regarded my coming as an omen auspicious to the taking of this risk—because I was, like himself, British; like his mother, a Scot.

And this was apart from the fact that my work in Bab-el-Djebel had given him greater confidence in the loyalty, as well as the efficiency, of his army; and that my advice had resulted in his doing a good deal of weeding-out of disloyal and untrustworthy subordinates, and the promotion of the more dependable men.

It has to be remembered, moreover, that the normal relations of British mother and son had not been allowed to exist between him and the unhappy Janet Chandos; that the events of his boyhood, far away and long ago, were a much obliterated memory; and that, increasingly, as the years went by, the world was too much with him.

Anyhow, I personally came to understand how it was that the action he now proposed to take against the Nawab of Aundhara had been so long postponed.

Whether he would have been as bitter, as determined, and as deadly dangerous, had his mother not died in the moment of his arrival and in his very arms, I do not know. But, be that as it may, it was now his unshakeable determination not to leave Mecca while the Nawab of Aundhara lived. Punish him he would, before he gave a thought to his own departure; and the punishment should be death—a punishment that he swore to be far too good for the dog.

Death, he growled, ought not to be his punishment at all. It should merely be the (unfortunately inevitable) termination of the cur's punishment, a termination to be postponed as long as possible.

When I observed that, of course, the question of torturing the man did not seriously arise, the Sultan demurred.

"Oh? Doesn't it?" said he. "No torture? And for how long did he torture my mother? . . . How could I, try as I might, inflict a worse torture on him than he inflicted upon a girl of eighteen—by murdering her husband and taking her into his *harim* and *forcing* her to be his 'wife' *on that very day*? . . . Try to think what she suffered. . . . Why should I not torture him?"

"Because you are not the Nawab of Aundhara," I replied. "You don't want to come down to his level."

"Perhaps you'd have me let him off altogether . . . ? Leave him to the punishment of the conscience—that he hasn't got . . ." sneered the Sultan. "You've seen his face. Do you think that that sensual devil of a debauchee has ever, for one moment, regretted the cruelty, the torture, the agony, he inflicted on my mother? . . . I can do nothing by process of Meccan law. I cannot take him to India and hand him over to the Government there. Is he to go scot-free?"

I thought of the Well of Cawnpore, of the atrocities committed by such men as Tantia Topi, Nana Sahib and Bahadur Shah in the Mutiny; of that room in Cawnpore, from under the door of which ran a river of blood—the blood of women and children, hacked to death with swords and knives—of the room that was splashed with blood from floor to ceiling, and on the walls of which were the gory imprints of tiny hands. I thought of Janet Chandos—outraged ere her husband's body was cold, ere it was buried. . . .

"No," I said, "I'd hate the idea of his going scot-free. But, of course, I grew up with the Briton's exaggerated reverence for the forms of Law as well as the spirit of Justice. To me, a slain man who is not killed by process of law, is murdered."

"Well, we won't go into all that again," replied the Sultan. "I'm going to hold a Court as I did in the matter of our late friend Abu bin Zaka . . . I don't care whether I am in Bab-el-Djebel or in

Mecca. I've got the power—the personal power, I mean—to hold a Court to try this man for the murder of my father, and the virtual murder of my mother, and I'm going to do it. I admit I have not the slightest doubt as to the findings of the Court; and I'm going to see that those findings are carried out . . . Would you care to have a seat on the Bench, or in the jury-box?"

"No," I replied. "I feel half ashamed to say it, but I wish you'd leave me out of it."

"Once again, will you feel it incumbent upon you to do anything to facilitate the escape of the prisoner or to avert the carrying out of the sentence of the Court?"

"No," I said—and gave a promise that I broke.

"Well, would you care to defend the prisoner, say anything that could possibly be said in his favour?"

"No, most certainly not," I replied.

"Right. Then you will remain entirely neutral, neither helping nor hindering me in the matter."

"Look here, Chandos," I said. "I'll do anything to help you, as I said when we spoke of this before, but I don't want to take any part in this 'trial'—and I will take no part in the execution. . . . Except for that, I will help you in any way you like."

"Good. For it's going to be difficult and dangerous; and I shall want all the help I can get—of the sort you are willing to give—before we see the last of Mecca.

"You know you can count on me absolutely," I said.

"I do . . . Good lad . . ."

"And I ask a favour, Chandos."

"Yes?"

"You're English. Your father was an English officer, your mother a Scots gentlewoman. . . . No torture."

"Suppose you leave that to me. . . . It wasn't your father and mother he murdered."

"Would your father and mother wish you to torture him?"

"Since you are keeping out of this, suppose you—keep out of it."

"No torture, Chandos . . ." I begged.

"Mind your own business."

"What you do *is* my business, Chandos."

"It will be in a minute! . . . Painful business—for you."

I made up my mind that the Nawab should not be handed over to Hassan bin Yacoub the Slayer and his men, to be put horribly to a slow and dreadful death. Not that I cared what Chandos did to that fiend incarnate, but that I cared greatly what

Chandos did to himself.

"My last word on the subject, Chandos . . ." I began.

"I shall be glad to hear your *last* word on the subject," he interrupted.

"If you do anything more than execute this man—I shall leave you," I concluded.

"You'll try to, you mean—or don't mean," was the cold reply.

§2

The capturing and kidnapping of the Hadji Mohammed Ghulamali Salehudin Yussufali Jalpur, Nawab of Aundhara, was not likely to be as easy an undertaking as that of getting into his house in his absence. This had been a comparatively simple matter, but the Indian *borah* trick would not serve twice; nor, indeed would it be in the slightest degree probable that a man like the Nawab would take the faintest interest in a pedlar's goods, or bestow so much as a passing glance upon them. Unlike the women of his *harim*—whom, Indian fashion, he kept strictly *purdah*—the Nawab could visit the shops, should he wish to make any personal purchases.

A wholly different technique would have to be adopted; different strategy and tactics followed.

Nor was the Sultan disposed to consider Hussein the Brave's suggestion that the whole party make a swift and sudden midnight raid upon the house—of which he had made a careful study—break in, stab the Nawab to death, and vanish as quickly and silently as they had come.

That, to the Sultan, smacked of vulgar assassination; plain murder; putting us on the level of a gang of Bedoui thieves. Although intending to put the man to death—in fact, to torture him to death—he shrank from the idea of what he termed 'vulgar dacoity'. What he wanted, was to try the man; punish him; execute him—not murder him in his bed. He had been too long an arbitrary judge, invested with power to put any man to death according to the forms of law—if it were only his own law—not to feel it beneath his dignity to do as Hussein the Brave suggested.

Curiously enough, had the Nawab been dwelling in tents out in the desert, I don't think that the Sultan would have hesitated for a moment about heading a *razzia*, a sudden swift descent upon the encampment, a *ghazu*, and seeing that his enemy died in the course of the raid. This would be in accordance with the custom of desert warriors, but the other would be in accordance

665

with the custom of town criminals.

Moreover, the Nawab would probably be in an extremely suspicious state of mind. The death of his aged *feringhee* wife would not trouble him in the very slightest degree—save in that she was now beyond the reach of his cruelty—but we had no means of knowing precisely what he had been told regarding her death. The *major-domo*, in great fear and trepidation, might say that she had died of extreme excitement when haggling with an Indian *borah* over some silk—which might sound plausible enough.

On the other hand, another wife, or some woman of the *harim*, might have told the Nawab that the alleged *borah* had spoken to the old lady in a foreign tongue, had embraced her, and that she had died in his arms. Whether there had been any actual witnesses of the tragedy, we did not know, nor whether someone had informed him that the alleged *borah*'s bogus assistant had sung a song in the dead woman's own tongue.

As to all that, we were quite in the dark, but the possibility, nay, probability, was that the Nawab would be puzzled, suspicious, and very much on the look-out; and that watch and ward would be most strictly kept.

The suggestion of Hassan bin Yacoub, the Slayer, that he should sit at the Nawab's gate, disguised as a blind beggar, track him when he left the house, leap upon him, and, with the help of three or four others of the party who would be watching and waiting, kidnap him and carry him off by main force, was considered by the Sultan.

It was finally turned down, however, as being excellent if it succeeded, but apt to be extremely deplorable if it did not. Should the plot fail, the Sultan would be deprived of the services of three or four valued friends and followers. That sort of thing would be extremely difficult to do in Mecca, especially at this time. Too many Turkish police and soldiers about; too many people altogether; and it was hardly likely that a man of the wealth and consequence of the Nawab of Aundhara would go out quite unattended.

No, some better plan must be devised.

It was the Sultan himself who evolved it, and I was very interested to note its reception by his hearers when he propounded it.

We were all seated about him—none being absent, as the matter not only concerned the safety of us all, but was one requiring the help of all, in our various capacities.

"No, Hussein," he said, after a prolonged and profound silence. "We won't break into the house and kill this man as though we were a gang of cut-purse town scum.

"Nor, Hassan bin Yacoub, *el Khātil*, will we spring upon him, knock him down, bind him, put a sack over his head, throw him over a camel and ride with him out into the desert—because it couldn't be done. We should have to fight our way out of Mecca. Half of us would be killed and, quite probably, the rest captured. You could only do that sort of thing here between midnight and dawn, and he would not be abroad without escort at that time of night.

"Nor, Abd el Hamid, will I entertain the thought of suborning his cook, or his coffee-maker, or any other servant, to put poison into his food or drink. He shall die, and he shall die painfully—but we are not assassins, poisoners. He shall die and he shall die painfully, but he shall be tried according to law—my law—and executed according to my judgment. We are not the Assassins of Lebanon, followers of the Old Man of the Mountain.

"Nor do I approve, oh, Kassim bin Ibrahim, of your suggestion that you shoot him from a house-top. Doubtless you could hire an upper room in the street down which he daily goes; but that again is murder. . . . Yes, yes, I know—certainly we could try him in his absence, condemn and sentence him to be shot, and you could carry out the sentence; but there are still two objections to your plan. One is that I want him to know that he was tried and condemned. I want him to know who tried, condemned and punished him, and why. And moreover, I do not wish to lose you, excellent Kassim bin Ibrahim.

"Now let all give ear . . . I myself will go openly to his house. But not too openly; for I shall be in the guise of a plotter from India, one of the seditious, who plan the overthrow of the English Government in that country. He has not beheld my face for nearly thrice ten years, and will not know me, bearded and changed as I am. I shall tell him that I am but a humble servant of the Cause, an underling; that I am sent to bid him meet my masters on the Mecca-Medina road; and that they beg him to come out, on a given day, to see them. . . . And I can tell him certain things, the hearing of which will lull suspicion. No-one who was not from India, and who knew not Aundhara, would be in a position to know what I shall show him that I know . . . I grew up speaking the Indian language and hearing much about the State of Aundhara, which once he ruled. I can deceive him and convince him. . . . I will go myself.

"Meantime, we will pack up for departure; pay all that we owe, and set forth in the ordinary way, as though returning to Jidda, for home. Should any question concerning us ever arise, the owners of this house and of the houses in which you lodge, will testify that we were quietly-disposed, well-behaved, pious pilgrims from el Moghreb, who performed the *Hadj*, did all that became them, and departed in peace."

This struck me as an admirable suggestion for the capture of the Nawab; but, to my surprise, my approval was not shared by the others. There was a completely spontaneous and unanimous shaking of heads, also respectful sounds of disapproval and the murmuring of negatives.

Hussein the Brave voiced the general opinion.

"Nay, nay, Lord," he objected. "We cannot see you go alone into the house of this man. How should we go back to Bab-el-Djebel saying,

" *'Behold we have returned without our master. We let him go alone into the house of his enemy, there to be slain'*. Our faces would be blackened for ever. Our very wives would spit upon us."

And while the Sultan eyed Hussein the Brave, Kassim bin Ibrahim added his voice.

"Lord, Hussein speaks well, and speaks, I am sure, for all here present. If you go into this house, we must go with you as we did before."

"And completely spoil the plan!" answered the Sultan.

"Then it is a bad plan," objected Kassim bin Ibrahim. "Suppose you go alone; suppose you are recognized; suppose that chief servant who admitted us before, now seeking to regain favour cries, *'Behold the borah!* . . . We should never look upon the face of our master again. We should never behold our homes, our sons, again. We could not return to them. It is a bad plan."

General approval was expressed.

"Then tell me a better," growled the Sultan.

"A far better," answered Abd el Hamid the Scribe. "Let His Highness write a letter to the man in the language of the Indians or of the English, since this man himself understands both, setting forth what should be said to him by word of mouth, and let me take the letter to him."

"And run the risk that I am to avoid?" answered the Sultan. "Moreover you know nothing of the tongue of Hindustan or Inglistan."

"Nay, Lord, there will be no risk. I am but a messenger. I am a Bedou employed by these people. I am a fool, ignorant, stupid, brainless. I carry a letter. Of its contents, of the sender, of the recipient, I know nothing. I know nothing whatever except that I want my promised *bakshish*."

The Sultan eyed Abd el Hamid the Scribe thoughtfully.

"It is good counsel," he said.

"Of course," he said to me, in English, "even granted that the Nawab failed to recognize me as his step-son, somebody at the house is pretty certain to recognize me as the *borah*—and the game would be up. . . . Yes, we'll write a letter . . . and see what it brings forth. If that fails, we will try something else; and keep on trying—if we have to wait till he goes to Medina again, and capture him on the way. If he went with a caravan and escort too strong for us to deal with, I could enrol any number of Bedoui— the lads who live by preying on caravans."

The Sultan gave his followers permission to retire.

"Now then, my son," said he. "We'll concoct a letter that'll send him back hot-foot to Medina, if it is a success. And if he swallows the bait, by Allah, we'll hook him and land him . . . I can work in some stuff about Aundhara that'll puzzle him mightily, if it doesn't convince him—which I rather fancy it will. Yes, I can make it perfectly obvious and certain that it comes from an Indian, and from someone who knows about him and Aundhara."

CHAPTER XXIX

As was his usual habit, custom, experience and *kismet*, the Sultan was successful; his letter and the acting of the carefully tutored Abd el Hamid, convincing.

On further thought and discussion, the Sultan had decided that Abd el Hamid might do better than be mere stupid letter-carrying coolie. He pains-takingly coached him in the part of an England-hating Pan-Islamic fanatic, experienced in plotting, sedition, and anti-British subversive work—more particularly in Egypt. He had been an emissary—to the Senussi; to the Sultan of Morocco; and to others, including prominent North African Sultans and Kaids—for Pan-Islamic plotters against the French; and was equally ready to give his assistance and earn his wages on behalf of Egyptian Nationalists, Indian seditionists, or other plotters against the English.

He did not know India or speak Hindustani, but he was at present working for, and with, Indians to whom he had been recommended in Cairo, and with whom he had gone to Beyrout, Damascus, and Medina, whence they earnestly wished to get into touch with the Nawab of Aundhara.

Abd el Hamid was in his element at this sort of game.

And having made Abd el Hamid word-perfect in his part, and done everything possible in Mecca, the Sultan gave orders for departure, all preparations to be made precisely as though we were returning to Jidda.

Once again Kassim bin Ibrahim set off in advance with the baggage, and we prepared to follow; this time mounted on our own camels instead of the worn-out hireling beasts which we had been using since landing in Arabia.

These new camels the Sultan had purchased with care and the sound advice of the experienced Hussein the Brave and Kassim bin Ibrahim—beautiful beasts of the kind ridden by the Shereef of Mecca's own camel-guard, his household camelry. These are of a very special and famous breed, renowned far and wide for beauty, speed, and spirit; and are to ordinary good camels what the finest race-horses are to London cab or omnibus hacks.

They indeed are racing, as compared with, or distinguished from, riding, camels; and are used to carry the Shereef's mail from Mecca to Jidda, a journey which they do at a pace of fifteen miles an hour.

For these beasts he paid an average price of one hundred and twenty-five pounds, actually giving one hundred and fifty pounds each for those he bought for himself and me. Their value may be adjudged from the fact that fifty pounds is a good price to pay for an absolutely first-class riding-camel, such as ridden by wealthy Arabs.

They were of course pedigree animals, absolutely thorough-bred, their descent being known by name and by fame, if not by stud-book, to all camel-dealers and owners of south-eastern Arabia.

All things being done and business concluded, such as the paying of rent and other costs incurred, the purchase of gifts for friends in Bab-el-Djebel, and of worthless souvenirs of Mecca—such as the curious black stone which is widely sold for the purpose and which is not a product of Mecca at all—we awaited the result of the plot.

The hour had come for putting Abd el Hamid's scheme to the test, and he was despatched upon his fateful journey, disguised as an Egyptian *effendi*. Anxiously we awaited his return, chiefly concerned with the problem of what we should do if he had obviously failed to convince the Nawab of the genuineness of the letter.

It seemed that the best plan would be to proceed to Medina and await his arrival there; or, rather, to leave a scout in Mecca who, riding ahead, would announce that the Nawab had left Mecca for Medina; whereupon we would go out to meet him. Or Hussein the Brave should suborn a menial in the Nawab's house to obtain information as to his intended journey, in time for us to encamp on the road to await him.

Abd el Hamid returned, the enigmatic expression of his impassive countenance almost a smile, to report that he had been completely successful; that the Nawab, having read the letter without trace of doubt or suspicion, had asked him a number of questions, and then bidden him return to us and say that he would set out for Medina one week after the day of the *Rugu*.

Some of the questions he had, thanks to the Sultan's tutoring, been able to answer most satisfactorily, and in a manner obviously convincing to the Nawab.

To others he had replied that he knew very little about the

matter. "He was not in the complete confidence of the Indian gentlemen, but of course they would be able to give the Nawab all the information he required."

He was careful to show that he personally wasn't in the slightest degree interested as to whether the Nawab went or not, "his real business being the furtherance of Egyptian Nationalism, though anything tending toward the discomfiture of the English was an agreeable and acceptable pastime".

§2

The road from Mecca to Medina is rough and bad; in parts so much so, that riding is impossible. Much of it runs through very mountainous country where it more closely resembles the boulder-strewn bed of a mountain torrent than any road intended for the feet of men or domestic animals. It is a thoroughly dangerous track, not merely by reason of the fact that it winds, crumbling, round precipices, and passes under great over-hanging unstable boulders, but on account of the large and numerous bands of Bedou robbers who prey upon solitary travellers, small bands of pilgrims, or indeed upon fair sized, if ill-armed, caravans.

Scattered along this road, very few and far between, are miserable Bedoui villages—places boasting a few mud huts, a few palm trees, a few filthy loafers and their women and children —where one can buy, should one wish to do so, stinking dried fish, dubious bread, and meat anything but dubious. Near each of these places, Zeyma, el Berke, Hada, Sufeineh, Gherabe, is a filthy insanitary camping-ground for pilgrims, with a market con-sisting of dirty dilapidated shacks where most scoundrelly evil-looking Bedoui swindle such travellers as are sufficiently poverty-stricken to be forced to deal with them.

Along the three hundred miles of this wretched path we rode, Hussein the Brave and his scouts ranging far and wide in search of a satisfactory place; a place, that is to say, suitable for an ambush; for a modest, retiring, and indeed secret, camp; and provided with a third qualification which was not mentioned in my hearing.

A few miles outside of Medina we again halted and camped for the night; and in the morning returned by the way we had come, finally pitching camp at a spot selected by Hussein the Brave, as the one fulfilling all requirements.

Within reach, and out of sight, of the road, we camped; and

set ourselves, with what patience we might, to await information from Hussein's scouts, that the Nawab had left Medina.

In a particularly wild, lonely and somewhat terrifying defile, where the very rocks themselves were calcined, split, and shattered by the terrific heat of summer; where the road was no road but a suitable course for a fiends' obstacle-race, inasmuch as it was itself one long obstacle to progress; where a party, be it two or three gathered together for the road, or a strong caravan, must proceed not only at a snail's pace with the utmost care, but in single file; where every prospect displeases and scarcely man's so vile, the Nawab was to be suddenly attacked by the famous and infamous Bedoui robbers who, since the days of Mahommet himself, have pursued the ever-thriving industry of preying upon the pilgrim and the traveller.

The Bedoui band, with shouts, howls, and firing of rifles and every demonstration of ferocity, was suddenly to materialize from behind rocks, shoot the Nawab's mount and those of his nearest attendants and followers, dispose summarily of any opposition, and carry him off alive and unhurt.

We were to be the Bedoui.

But little opposition, and no difficulty, was to be apprehended. The place was too well chosen; the cruel ferocity of the Bedoui too well known, and the details of the scheme too well arranged.

Another excellent feature of this method of seizing the Nawab, was the fact that his followers, fleeing for their; lives and returning to Mecca, would merely announce that one more traveller had fallen a victim to the Bedoui robbers of the mountains—as normal a fate on the Mecca-Medina Road as for a man to fall a victim to influenza in England.

The Bedoui would be blamed and would suffer nothing more than blame. Nor could one's conscience prick with any severity on their account, inasmuch as, if the Bedoui were not to blame for the death of the Nawab, they were to blame for that of thousands of other travellers. Literally thousands; for never a day passes during the time of year when men go down from Medina to Mecca, without pilgrims and travellers being robbed and killed by these professional thieves and murderers.

Worse than the raiders themselves are the foul ruffians who, in league with them, pose as camel-jobbers and drivers, and who deliberately straggle behind the armed caravans with whom they are supposed to be, and place their unfortunate patrons at the mercy of their Bedoui partners in robbery and murder.

§3

All went well. Well, that is to say, from the point of view of the Sultan and his followers.

With the utmost ease, and without the effusion of blood, the Hadji Mahommed Ghulamali Salehudin Yussufali Jalpur, ex-Nawab of Aundhara, was ambushed and captured by "Bedoui" in a lonely defile on the Mecca-Medina road; his servants, escaping with their lives and little else, returning to tell the tale of one more outrage, and to cause one more protesting grumble on the part of the citizens of Mecca against the supine indifference of their Turkish protectors.

I hope that I—when prisoner and captive in the hands of the nomadic Bedoui; in those of the villagers to whom they sold me; in those of the slave-owner who exposed me for sale in the market-place; and of Ali bin Ahmed—made a better showing than did the Nawab as our prisoner and captive.

He went all to pieces, wept, whined, implored, promised, and grovelled.

Doubtless in the year of disgrace 1857, when, as a young man he rode at the head of the Lancers of Aundhara, he was some sort of a man. Probably he was quite a fine figure of a man, endowed with hardihood, dash, and courage to match his villainy. Now he was no sort of a man at all. A poor thing—but our own.

One has to admit that the Court before which he appeared, after what must have been a terribly anxious and uncomfortable night, was grim—a sinister tribunal in a most sinister setting.

What he could have made of it, I have no idea; but doubtless he imagined that he had fallen into the clutches of some amazing branch of the wonderful British Secret Service, inasmuch as he was volubly anxious to declare and to swear that he hadn't done it—whatever it might be.

It was the Sultan's humour to conduct the trial with all ceremony, formality, and correctness; modelling it, of course, on the tribal methods of the desert Arabs, as though he were in his own province of Bab-el-Djebel, and as though his followers there present were Kaids of the fighting-tribes assembled to administer patriarchal desert justice, as from time immemorial.

Seated on his own *lahaf* as Chief Judge, the Sultan opened the trial after the *fedjr* prayer:—

"*In the name of Allah the Merciful, the Compassionate, the*

Great Lord of the Judgment Day, I declare this Court to be in session. Let each of you, called here to sit in judgment, give that judgment which—as you live and your souls live—you believe to be just and good and true."

And all the judges—or perhaps jury—murmured,

"*Inshallah.*"

"Myself, I make the charge against the prisoner; I myself, knowing all the facts of this case," continued the Sultan.

"I accuse this man of murder . . . of the murder of my father. I accuse him of the wicked and wrongful seizing of my father's wife, of carrying her off and thrusting her into his *harim*, on the very day in which he encompassed the murder of her husband. . . .

"Yea, my brothers, by Allah the Merciful, the Compassionate, I swear that this man is guilty of murder and of rape; the murder of my father, the rape of my mother; and of the slaying, the torturing and outraging of innocent men, women and children of my Tribe; not in battle; not in raid; but in cold blood. . . . He is a murderer, a thief, a liar, and a treacherous dog.

"And that is why he, a man of Hindustan, hides there in Mecca, making the Holy City as a den of thieves, a resort and refuge for hunted criminals, outlaws escaping the arm of the outraged justice and law of their own country."

Here the Nawab, grey-faced and trembling—realizing suddenly that the past—the long long ago, the almost forgotten past—was rising up to confront him, whimpered aloud and burst into impassioned speech.

"Silence," hissed Hassan bin Yacoub the Slayer, who stood beside him. "Silence, thou braying father of mules."

And in silence the Nawab listened to the Sultan's revelation of his crimes; listened to the terrible tale that the Sultan had heard from Janet Chandos.

"Hear, oh my brothers," continued the cold hard voice of the Judge, who was also Public Prosecutor in this court of desert justice, "There was a certain well . . . !

"*Bismillah!* There was a well—at a city of that country, a city called Cawnpore; and certain brave warriors, admired friends and comrades—in honourable war—of this brave warrior, filled it with the bodies of the dead and the dying; bodies not of their enemies, but bodies of wounded, dying and dead *women*; bodies of unwounded, wounded, dying, and dead *children*. By Allah! Of little *children* . . ."

There was a murmur from the members of the Court, seated

in a circle facing the Chief Judge.

"Yea, and in that foul deed, that will not be forgotten while men have tongues to speak and ears to hear, this diseased dog had a hand. Eye-witnesses testify to it. The evidence of captured prisoners confirms it. Letters that fell into the hands of the British proved it . . . And the presence of this hyena, here in this lost unknown spot, this nameless crater of rocks, many miles from the Mecca-Medina road, proves the truth of what I say. Or why is he here? Why was he on that road? Why was he in Mecca? Why is he—the hereditary ruler of a great State—in Arabia at all? Why is he not in his own country; in his own capital; in his own palace; sitting on his own *gadi*?

"Let him answer me in the hearing of his judges. For *I* . . ."

And here the Sultan rose to his feet and continued,

". . . I—am the son of the man, Colonel Chandos, whom he murdered; the son of the woman, Janet Chandos, whom he, that same day, seized, kidnapped, outraged and made his prisoner—and kept a prisoner for the whole of the remainder of her long life. Yea, I—I, the Sultan of Bab-el-Djebel, am the man whom this grave-defiling jackal declared to be his son . . . His son! . . .

"Now let him speak . . . Let him address the Court."

But that, the Hadji Mahommed Ghulamali Salehudin Yussufali Jalpur could not do.

The only words that he could find were prayers for mercy.

Prostrating himself before the Sultan, he babbled, slavered, offered fabulous sums, cried aloud, and collapsed, moaning, in a sort of coma.

The Sultan eyed him with the look I knew so well.

"He has nothing to say in his defence," he observed at length. "Nothing *can* be said in his defence. For he knows, and he cannot deny, that he murdered my father and tortured my mother.

"What is the sentence of the Court?"

Naturally it was a unanimous sentence of death; and, in fairness, I had to admit that the sentence would have been the same had the accuser not been the Sultan, and had the court been an ordinary desert court of justice in Bab-el-Djebel.

"And the method of death?"

"Impalement," said Hussein the Brave. "After torture . . ."

"Crucify him, after torture," said another.

"Hang him by the wayside, after torture, as a warning to other murderers," suggested a third.

"After torture, bind him hand and foot, and let me drag him

behind my camel till he dies," suggested Kassim bin Ibrahim.

"Lord, after torture, let me smite off his hands and his feet, and then bind up the stumps," requested Hassan bin Yacoub the Swordsman. "Let him then find his way back to his fine house in Mecca—on his knees and his elbows."

"And you, Sinbad el Askar, what death would you say was fitting for this murderer, tried and condemned by this Court of Justice?"

"Shoot him here and now—if you are going to execute him," I said.

"After torture, of course," smiled the Sultan crookedly.

"Here and *now*, I said," I replied.

"Lord, may I offer a suggestion?" asked the quiet voice of Abd el Hamid the Scribe. "There was talk of a well; of a famous well at a place in Hindustan called, I think, Karn-Por. . . . Into this well, the accused threw women and children, some dead, some grievously wounded, some alive. . . . It would appear that he favours wells as places of punishment. Near here, also, there is a well—a dry well. Disdaining to follow the cruelty with which the accused has stained his name and blackened his face for ever, let us put him into this well, gently, carefully, lowering him down with a rope so that, arriving safely at the bottom, he is uninjured, unhurt.

"It is said, as His Highness knoweth," continued Abd el Hamid the Scribe, looking round at the members of the court, "that Truth dwelleth at the bottom of a well. Let this man, for the first time in his life, imitate the Truth. . . . Let him also—dwell at the bottom of a well."

"For how long?" enquired Hassan bin Yacoub, *el Khātil*; Hassan the Slayer.

"For how long? Oh, for as long as he likes. For as long as he can. He will have plenty of food and water. For just as long as he can keep himself alive he will dwell there. . . . For—out of that well he will never come."

And with an eye on me, the Sultan approved and applauded this suggestion.

"It is wisely and justly spoken, oh Abd el Hamid," he said. "As we are strong, we will be merciful. What becometh a judge like Mercy? What is nobler than Forgiveness? We will not kill this man. We will not torture him. We will not lift up our hands against him to do him any hurt.

"Ye stand rebuked, oh ye Cruel Ones who spoke of torture, impalement, crucifixion, the lopping of hands and feet. Shame be upon ye! Ye stand rebuked. . . . We will lower him with all care and gentleness into the dry well—that he may reflect upon his sins and upon our mercy."

Smiles wreathed the faces of the rebuked Cruel Ones.

Hussein the Brave chuckled.

Kassim bin Ibrahim grinned broadly. Even Hassan bin Yacoub, the Slayer, smiled, albeit grimly.

"Let punishment, mild though it be, follow promptly upon sentence," continued the Sultan. "Let there be no law's delays. Yea, let Mercy follow swiftly upon Justice."

It having been ascertained that he had no weapon—no means of committing suicide—the prisoner, partly led, partly carried, was taken to the mouth of the long-disused, long-forgotten, long-dried-up well, lowered into it slowly and carefully by means of Kassim bin Ibrahim's spare camel-and-baggage cords knotted together, until he gently touched the bottom.

It being obvious that he had reached his destination, the light and agile Hassan the Slayer slid down the rope, the end of which was held by a dozen pairs of willing hands.

Having untied the other end from about the wretched prisoner and re-tied it about himself, he was speedily hauled to the surface again.

"And now we will pray, returning thanks to Allah," said the Sultan, "and thereafter we will rest, feast and rejoice. . . ."

CHAPTER XXX

That night I came as near to quarrelling with the Sultan as he would permit. For a while he argued with me, but, before long, was listening in silence to my appeal to his better nature, to his mercifulness, and to the teaching of his religion—for I knew that one *sura* of the Koran enjoins mercy, and praises forbearance, gentleness, and kindness of heart.

"Anything more?" enquired the Sultan when I had made the most urgent and eloquent appeal of which I was capable, in favour of prompt and decent execution of the prisoner.

"He has had a most ghastly experience, a terrible fright, and has spent the day down in that well—believing himself to be abandoned there. That's punishment and torture enough, surely —for an old man."

"Anything more?" asked the Sultan again.

"Yes. Look here, Chandos. You're an Englishman, and proud of it. Your chief bitterness against him is on account of his having tried to prove that you were his son. That was his great offence— really much worse in your eyes, than the murder of the father whom you never saw, and the torture of the mother from whom you ran away."

"Don't presume too much on my kindness to you," suggested the Sultan softly.

"If you will be honest with yourself and look into your real motives and feelings, you'll know that I am speaking the truth. You hate this man for saying that he is your father. Well then, why behave exactly as though you were his son—his worthy son, a cruel devil like himself? If you do this, you are doing far more than ever he did, to prove that you are his son—and a half-caste."

"Go on," said the Sultan, "go on . . . Don't overdo it, though."

And his right hand strayed to his dagger—quite subconsciously, I am sure. With him it was merely a sign, an infallible sign, that he was almost uncontrollably angry.

"I know that Colonel Chandos was your father. Everyone must have known it, when you were born . . . Absolutely white . . . Well, *be* absolutely white. Be the son of Colonel Chandos. Do you suppose he'd have tortured a man to death—any man, for any reason?"

"How do I know—and how do you know—what Colonel Chandos would have done to a man who had tortured his mother, a man who had murdered his father?"

"You know, and I know, perfectly well, that even if he had killed the man in cold blood—which he wouldn't have done—he'd never have tortured him. And I tell you again, you are deceiving yourself if you think that you are doing this on your father's account or your mother's . . . You yourself have told me you weren't very much good to her as a son."

The Sultan's eyes blazed and his lips became a thin straight line.

"You are doing a low beastly unworthy thing," I pursued, "bringing yourself down to the level of the man of whom you cannot speak badly enough; behaving like the savage cannibal king of a nigger tribe . . . You will be wanting human sacrifices and a cairn of skulls outside your tent, next."

"Anything else?"

"No . . . I've said all there is to say, and a great deal more than it ought to be necessary to say to any decent person. Nothing more—except that I am bitterly disappointed that . . ."

"*Don't* say that I have forfeited your esteem," he sneered. "That *would* be a blow! . . . Why, your good opinion is my most cherished possession, Sinbad el Askar."

"Oh, look here, Chandos, I thought you . . ."

"What, another appeal to my higher nature? Haven't got one. It's all one level. Just the level required for my position. This isn't England, you know, and I am not Victoria the Good. How long do you think she and her methods would keep the Western Sahara quiet? . . . What about the Mosaic law in your own Bible—an eye for an eye and a tooth for a tooth, eh? A killing for a killing, torture for torture—a well for a well. Isn't that good Old Testament Law?"

"Your mother taught you New Testament as well as Old Testament history, didn't she? We've got beyond the code of the Old Testament."

"In Europe, perhaps," replied the Sultan. "But this isn't Europe. This is Arabia . . . And it isn't the nineteenth century here, either. It's the tenth century."

"No, I know it isn't England," I agreed, "but you are English, aren't you? Well, behave like an Englishman, then. You took your adopted father's name, but your real name is Chandos, isn't it? Behave like a Chandos, behave as your father's son should, then . . ."

And again and again I went over it all until, as I have said, the Sultan ceased to argue, ceased to answer, ceased even to be angry; and began to yawn.

At length, ironically,

"You have my permission to depart, Sinbad el Askar," he said, concluding a mighty feat of stretching and yawning, "for I think I have now heard it all, if I haven't learned it by heart . . . Touching the prisoner Mahommed Ghulamali Salehudin Yussu-fali Jalpur, late Nawab of Aundhara, he will not only remain at the bottom of that well until he dies, but I shall keep him alive there as long as I possibly can. Night and morning, I will have food and water lowered down to him, and we will camp here until he dies."

"But he might live for weeks," I expostulated.

"Months, probably," agreed the Sultan, "and he will—unless he has the strength to refuse food and water. And do you think that is likely? Of course not. Not he."

"And you'd camp here for months?"

"No, I spoke in my haste, rashly. Not for months. I came to Mecca to punish this man and to kill him, and I'm going to do it—and to enjoy doing it. I am in no great hurry, but I shan't stay for months. I will have a chat with him night and morning for a few days. Probably I will allow his prayers for mercy to soften my hard heart. I will forgive him; tell him I never really meant to kill him, of course—not such a fine fellow as the Nawab of Aundhara. Then I'll send the rope down again and pull him up to the surface; let him take a good look round; and then—lower him down again . . . And when I get tired of it, when I have really had enough, I will send him down all the food and water we have got—and leave him to it . . . Or, I may let Hassan the Slayer stay behind and keep him alive as long as he can . . . Possibly delegate the job to a Bedoui tribe—extra payment for every day he lives and a handsome bonus if he is alive a year hence."

"Chandos," I began again.

"Good-night, Sinbad."

"Look here, Chandos . . ."

"Good-*night*, I said."

§2

Nor, after that, would the Sultan listen to a single word that I had to say on the subject of the fate of the Nawab. Several times I tried, but failed completely. It was quite hopeless. Nor did I try again after he had said,

"Look here, Sinbad, I'm very fond of you, and I've every reason to be grateful to you. I admit it. But if you attempt to interfere once again, I do most solemnly swear that I will put you to the humiliation, disgrace, and discomfort of being gagged, with your hands tied behind you . . . I tell you I have had enough of it . . . If you'd been an Arab, something unpleasant would have happened to you before this. Now, don't presume any further. You are my employee—you have said your say . . . now be quiet."

I spent a miserable time, though I did not despair of the Sultan. I hoped (and tried to persuade myself) that he did not really intend to abandon the man to this terrible fate.

One night, quite unexpectedly, the Sultan gave orders for the breaking of camp on the morrow. We were to start at dawn for Jidda, leaving all spare food and water for the prisoner at the bottom of the well.

For, I was told, the wretched man was still alive, and, as the Sultan informed me, consumed regularly the food and water lowered down to him. It was obvious that he did this, if the water-skin and food-bag were hauled up empty, and according to Chandos, his voice was still as strong as when he was captured.

That last night I dined as usual with the Sultan, and we talked of Bab-el-Djebel, speculating on whether all had gone well there in his absence, and how far Haroun bin Arrach had remained loyal and faithful; on what might have been happening in Morocco; on what was the latest move on the part of France. For all sorts of interesting rumours had come to Mecca with the *cortèges* of the Egyptian and Syrian *mahmals*.

And when I rose to go to my *tente d'abri* I said,

"I'm not going to make another appeal to you to spare or to execute the Nawab, but I would like to ask a question, Chandos."

"Well?"

"Are you really going to leave him alive, and with enough food and water to keep him alive for a long time?"

"I am."

"Really and truly? You are not going to relent at the last minute?"

"I am not. I shall leave him behind at the bottom of that well, with all the food and water I can give him. And I have made arrangements for a constant further supply—to be given daily, as long as he lives."

"Thank you for informing me."

Going to my tent I lay down until absolute silence reigned. I had come to a decision, thought out a scheme, and made a plan. I fell asleep . . .

When I awoke not a sound was to be heard.

I arose, put on my black *djellabia* and slowly, silently, with extreme caution, made my way toward the well.

If I could elude the vigilance of the camp sentry; if the well were not guarded; and if the cord were lying by the well-mouth, or anywhere where I could find it, I would do my best to pull the wretched prisoner up out of the well.

This might sound somewhat ambitious from the point of view of physical strength, but I was peculiarly fitted for the task by reason of my three years apprenticeship on a wind-jammer, my unusual height and weight, and a strength possibly more than proportionate. Anyhow, I could try. Incidentally it is a tribute to the honesty and loyalty of the Sultan's present followers, that it never entered my head to attempt to bribe one of them to assist me.

I could get him up somehow, and if I could get him a camel, I would—and set him on it; set him free.

It was scarcely likely that I should be able to get him a camel. The Sultan was too well served, his followers too well-trained, for me to have very much hope of such complete success as that.

Anyhow, I could lead him to the road and turn his face toward Mecca. It would then be a matter of kismet whether the first people he met were pilgrims, travellers—or Bedoui robbers. In the former event he would be safe; in the latter he would at least have a chance of persuading them that he was more valuable alive than dead; a person who could and would pay a big ransom. Quite possibly they would send a man in to Mecca to find out. . . .

The first thing was to elude the camp sentry.

As luck would have it, it was a moonless night, but the stars seemed bigger and more brilliant than ever I had seen them before.

That was all to the good, for, without light of some sort, I should have been obliged to take a lantern, unless I wished to run the risk of falling down the well, assuming that I was able to find it at all—and by taking a lantern I should, of course, defeat my own object.

Clear of the circle of *tentes d'abri*, I lay on the ground and endeavoured to catch sight of the sentry silhouetted against the star-lit sky.

Yes, there he was, standing, leaning on his rifle, near the Sultan's tent. I must move as silently as a shadow, get behind the nearest big boulder, and keep that boulder between me and the sentry in the line of my retreat from the camp.

Inch by inch, I crept on hands and knees; and, though sand is a good surface over which to crawl, I do not recommend Arab dress for the pastime.

As soon as I felt that I was beyond sight and hearing of the camp sentry, I rose to my feet and crept, crouching, on a curving course that would bring me to the other side of the well.

This spot, with which I was familiar, I reconnoitred from a short distance, unchallenged.

The well was unguarded.

At this I was not surprised, as it was utterly impossible for the strongest athlete to climb up the hundred feet, and more, of its inward-sloping sides, the well itself being somewhat bottle-shaped. Nor would it ever enter the Sultan's head, for one moment, that any of his followers would dream of interfering with the course of "justice", once sentence had been pronounced, or of disobeying his orders as to the treatment of the prisoner.

And here, curiously enough, my conscience smote me, and I found myself on the horns of a dilemma.

The Sultan trusted me—trusted me absolutely.

As he had promised, when he took me into his service, whatever happened, whatever tale was told against me, nothing but my own confession and the evidence of his own eyes and ears, would induce him to doubt me.

And here was I, not only disobeying, but deceiving him; for it was my present hope and intention to rescue his prisoner, set him free, and leave the Sultan under the impression that the wretched creature was still at the bottom of the well.

Nevertheless, I felt that this was the lesser of two evils. The man had not had a proper trial according to my ideas of law and justice; and, admitting that he was a monster, a murderer, a sub-human devil, a fiend in human form who deserved death, there is no such thing as intentional physical torture in any decent scheme of punishment.

It might be beastly of me to deceive my friend and benefactor who trusted me absolutely; but it was even more beastly to leave this old man to the unthinkable fate to which the Sultan had condemned him.

I crawled nearer and nearer to the well. Lying prone, I gazed round in all directions.

No, there was no sentry over the well. Of that I felt pretty sure. However, I had learned something of scouting, from Hussein the Brave, and decided to make perfectly sure. It was just possible that a man had been posted here and was lying down asleep—or more probably sitting in the shadow of a boulder, watching me and wondering what on earth I was doing. In either case it would do no harm if I quietly circumambulated the well-head. If there was a sleeping sentry I shouldn't wake him; and if he were awake and watchful, I should soon discover the fact.

Gliding from boulder to boulder, I made my way round, in a circle, to the spot from which I had started. Yes. The well was unguarded.

Was the rope lying beside it? Quite probably; for one of the last of Kassim bin Ibrahim's duties would be to lower our spare stock of water, bread, barley-meal, cooked meat, dried fish, olives, raisins, dried figs and so forth, down the well. Almost certainly the rope would be there. Kassim would use it, pull it up again for the last time, and then, having unknotted it, apply it to its legitimate uses.

What would he do, I wondered, if the prisoner, for some reason, failed to empty the bags that were sent down to him? Simply pull them up again and fling their contents down the well? How would the wretched man store the precious water that was lowered down to him? Of course, the bottom of the well would be of stone. It would contain natural basins. In any case he would detach the water-skins from the rope and keep them there.

Boldly but silently, I walked to the well-head.

Yes, there was the rope, coiled down ready for use.

Now then. Would the man have the sense and ability to knot the rope firmly about him, beneath his arms? I could tell him to do so; also to clutch it strongly with his hands, and to use his feet to "walk" up the side of the well as I hauled.

Lying down, with my head extended over the edge, I called, and, strangely enough, called in English.

"*Below there!*" exactly as though I was calling down from yard-arm to deck.

The sound of my voice went booming down into the depths . . . and a heavy hand fell upon my shoulder.

Literally I jumped; and it was well for me that I was lying down, and not kneeling at the edge of the well, or probably I should have fallen in.

"Giving the *shaitan* something to think about?" chuckled Kassim bin Ibrahim, and guffawed aloud. "Well, they are the last words he'll ever hear."

"Come along now," he shouted back into the darkness, "Smell your way, if you can't see it. We've got to be ready to strike camp at false-dawn."

I rose to my feet before the servants could see me.

"Yes, I've said good-bye to him," I answered Kassim, as he turned again to me.

I was defeated. Only partly though.

Secretly I took my sheathed dagger from my belt—and threw it into the well.

Mohammed Ghulamali Salehudin Yussufali Jalpur, Nawab of Aundhara, could now end his suffering himself—just as soon as he wished.

"What's that?" asked Kassim sharply. "What are you doing?"

"Er—'stoning the devil'," I replied.

And again Kassim bin Ibrahim roared with laughter.

CHAPTER XXXI

Striking the Jidda road to the west of Mecca, we retraced our steps along that most famous highway and, thanks to our long sojourn on the Mecca-Medina road, escaped most of the pilgrim return-traffic.

At Jidda we went to the same lodgings that we had occupied on our arrival at that horrible port, and there received the calamitous news that was awaiting us.

Describing himself merely as the Kaid Mahommed el Kebir of Bab-el-Djebel on the borders of el Moghreb, the Sultan had left his Jidda address at the Post Office, and directions with the owner of the house in which we had lived, for the reception and forwarding of letters and messengers.

From our lodging in Mecca he had then sent that address down to Jidda. . . .

We now learned that a messenger had arrived from Bab-el-Djebel, had been sent to the Jidda lodging and thence despatched to Mecca. Obviously he had reached our Mecca address after we had left it for Medina; and there was nothing to be done save await his return to Jidda—a thing he was certain to do when he failed to find the Sultan in Mecca. In the hope of expediting matters, the Sultan sent Kassim bin Ibrahim off on his swiftest camel, in search of him. He did this because he gathered from our landlord that the messenger was the bearer of bad news. What this was, the messenger had not divulged. Nor had he so much as hinted at it, but, from the man's anxiety and haste, and from his general demeanour, it was apparent that his task was not to his liking.

As he had only left Jidda for Mecca two days previously, he might be expected to return at any minute; inasmuch as there would be no-one in Mecca who could tell him that his master had taken the Medina road instead of returning to Jidda.

That evening, this messenger, one Mahuddin ibn Daud, who in Bab-el-Djebel was Kassim bin Ibrahim's right-hand man and understudy, returned with the latter, who had met him on the road.

Throwing himself at the Sultan's feet, he went through the motions of casting dust upon his head, and did actually rend his garments.

687

"Woe! Woe!" he groaned, "Forgive me, oh Lord! Forgive me that I am the bearer of evil tidings. The fault is not mine. Would that my tongue might wither ere it speaks the words I have to say. . . . Woe! Woe!"

And here methought the Sultan showed real greatness—that greatness in little matters, which is so indicative and so important.

"Go! Rest, bathe and eat; and be of good cheer. We will hear the tale later, oh Mahuddin ibn Daud," he said.

The man rose on one knee.

"But Lord, it is . . ."

"Peace! Go," replied the Sultan; and, as the messenger and Kassim bin Ibrahim departed, he turned to me.

"My son," he smiled, "I think you'd better get a boat for Port Said, and then the first P. & O. for England, Home and Beauty."

"What's happened, do you suppose?" I asked.

"I should think Haroun bin Arrach's 'happened'," replied the Sultan, "or . . . happened to think he'd got a chance to seize the *gadi*—and found he was right. That man Mahuddin ibn Daud is Kassim bin Ibrahim's brother-in-law; and his instructions were to come here, sparing no expense, if anything really serious happened. It is either a *coup d'état* and revolution, or else invasion and defeat."

"Suppose it's internal trouble, rebellion, and usurpation by Haroun bin Arrach or somebody else?" I asked.

"Oh, I shall go back and reconnoitre."

"Presumably he's got the army, or the greater part of it, behind him. Wouldn't he seize you and put you to death at once?" I asked.

"Of course he would, if I rode straight up—asking for it. I should go in to the City in disguise, and see what he's doing; find out who is really solid for him, who's sitting on the fence, and who's been coerced. Then make plans accordingly."

"Can you rely on the men here with you?" I asked.

"I don't know. Nothing succeeds like success. I should think Hussein the Brave and Kassim bin Ibrahim are all-right. With the others it would depend, to some extent, on how far they believed in my star, my *kismet*—and on how firmly the usurper seems to be seated."

"And suppose it is—invasion?" I asked.

"Well, depends on what's happened. If there has been a battle and we are defeated and the Citadel captured—that's that, I'm afraid. If it's France, peacefully penetrating, there is no more to be said—a case for them of *j'y suis, j'y reste*. . . . I'll go to the Sultan of Morocco and take service under him, but I don't fancy even he will be an independent monarch very much longer."

Although he must have been suffering an agony of suspense, it was not for another three hours, not until after the *asha* prayer and a meal, that the Sultan sent for the messenger and bade him tell his tale.

It was a thrilling story, dramatically told; and of absorbing though painful interest.

As I have said, the Sultan, on hearing of the messenger's arrival, had anticipated one of two calamities—revolution or invasion.

In point of fact, both had happened and his kingdom was lost, gone, irrevocably as water poured forth upon the desert sand.

And the villain of the piece?

None other than the quiet self-effacing Clerk of the Treasury, Ben Abu, Keeper of the Privy Purse, Chancellor of the Exchequer.

I had been right. The man was a Frenchman. Or if he were not, he had at any rate, been bred and born among the French, imbued with French views, aspirations, ambitions and sympathies; was a servant of France; and to all intents and purposes a Frenchman.

Whether he were pure French, pure Arab, or a man of mixed French-Arab birth, he was exceedingly clever; possessed of a long untiring patience; of great gifts and high courage; an invaluable member of the French Secret Service. . . .

Very soon after the departure of the Sultan, dissension had arisen among the members of the Council of Regency of which Ben Abu was, of course, one.

The Commander-in-Chief, Haroun bin Arrach, *alias* Sergeant-Major Grünther of the Potsdam Foot-guards, had become overbearingly truculent in his demeanour; and, before long, had flatly refused to accept any sort of direction from the Council.

As Aga of Infantry and acting Commander-in-Chief, he had at his absolute disposal a highly-disciplined magnificently-drilled and extremely well-equipped fighting force; and, provided he could win over the cavalry, he would have matters entirely in his own hands. That he now set about doing this, was immediately known to our present informant, Mahuddin ibn Daud, as his cousin was a cavalry officer and had no secrets from him.

As Mahuddin ibn Daud's tale unfolded, I got further and

further glimpses of the Sultan's methods of domestic espionage, contra-espionage, and the checking-up of the work of one officer or official against that of another.

And, there, it seemed that the Prussian methods of Haroun bin Arrach had proved, in one particular at least, inferior to the British methods of Sinbad el Askar. The German had established a name for overbearing harshness and violent ruthlessness toward the men; of unapproachability, curt unfriendliness and contemptuous superiority toward the officers.

I, it appeared, had been successful in establishing a name for fairness and justice—if without much mercy—and of severe discipline without chance of evasion, among the men; of friend-liness, camaraderie and cheerfulness among the officers.

The difference of method now bore fruit—the cavalry preferred me to Grünther.

Thus it came about that the Aga of Infantry made slow progress in winning over the cavalry, when he definitely showed his hand. One gathered that the worthy Grünther was a poor diplomatist, a man whose methods were as rough, stiff and heavy as his speech, personality and figure.

According to Mahuddin ibn Daud's relative, Grünther had, as acting Commander-in-Chief, convened a meeting of the cavalry officers, and without beating about the bush, had informed them that he had no intention of allowing the Civil authority to interfere with the Military; that he'd had quite enough of their nonsense and fooling, and would have no more of it; that he had the power, and was going to use it. Obviously the highest flight of his diplo-macy was to stir up the age-old antagonism between the civil and the military power, and to pose as the guardian of the rights of the latter.

He further informed them that he intended to hold manœuvres, contrary to the wishes and orders of the Council—who had had the impudence to pretend that the Sultan had left orders that the army was not to leave the city and its environ-ments, during his absence.

He also spoke of his thwarted endeavours to have rates of cavalry-pay raised, and various uniform and horse allowances improved; and generally prepared the soil for the sowing of as fine a crop of discontent, dissatisfaction, and disturbance, as lay within his somewhat limited ability.

His next step was to approach the cavalry officers, one by one; sound them, and endeavour to make a just estimate of their respective characters, particularly with regard to their honesty and fidelity, and their loyalty to the absent Sultan.

Cleverly and accurately, or not, he made his selection of a cabal, a junto, of cavalry officers, upon whom he thought he could rely—when the time was ripe for him to bring off his *coup d'état*, to seize the reins of power, to overthrow the Council of Regency, to put an end to opposition by putting an end to all who opposed him, and to establish himself as el Sidna el Sultan Haroun bin Arrach of Bab-el-Djebel.

Grünther's next step was the administration of a purge—a sort of Pride's Purge—to the Council of Regency, leaving a minority, a Rump Parliament, of those who were, and would be, entirely subservient—the remainder promptly disappearing into the recesses of the Citadel, probably into its dungeons. To the credit of the Council of Regency be it said that quite a majority of its members preferred this fate to throwing in their lot with the Sultan self-elect.

And now, somewhat to his surprise, the acting Commander-in-Chief found that he had an ardent supporter in Ben Abu, a man with whom he had expected to have considerable difficulty; for, like every Wazir-Treasurer-Chancellor of the Exchequer, he was a man of very considerable influence.

Of course, Ben Abu had, and had always had, his own staff of spies who served him admirably. Through them he knew precisely what was going on; and, at the right moment, presented himself to Grünther as the man who could bring over the cavalry whole-heartedly to his side.

How—and why—could he influence the cavalry officers?

Because every man has his price—and Ben Abu was in a position as Chancellor of the Exchequer to pay that price.

Among those immediately corrupted by Ben Abu's gold and Grünther's promises, was Mahuddin ibn Daud's cousin—who kept Mahuddin ibn Daud fully informed of all that was going on.

Doubtless this worthy cavalry officer was neither more nor less loyal than the majority of his colleagues; and was equally willing to receive a handsome "gift" from Ben Abu and promotion from Haroun bin Arrach, on the one hand, and to play for safety on the other, by informing his cousin of what was going on—so that, in the event of the return of the Sultan and the overthrow of the acting Commander-in-Chief, he would reap his reward as a staunch but wily supporter of the legitimate ruler. He thus stood to win either way—playing the kind of game dear to the Arab heart.

When the day dawned that the acting Commander-in-Chief,

Haroun bin Arrach, put his fortune to the test and issued orders for the army to march next day at dawn, and to camp one mile from the city gates, preparatory to manœuvres of which the special details and the general idea and plan would be issued later, he was justified of his faith in his own hold upon his Infantry Brigade and in Ben Abu's management of the Cavalry.

For the army marched exactly as ordered.

To the good Grünther it must have seemed that all went well, indeed; since he who really commands the army of Bab-el-Djebel, commands Bab-el-Djebel itself—and is *de facto* Sultan.

And then there was a sound of devilry by night, and hurrying to and fro and tremblings of distress, if no cheeks all pale which but an hour before, blushed at the praise of their own loveliness.

Certainly there was mounting in hot haste; the steed, the mustering squadron, went pouring forward with imperious speed and swiftly forming in the ranks of war.

The "choking sighs which ne'er might be repeated" were postponed—until the hangman got to work.

And a most painfully delicate and difficult situation was created for the City Fathers of Bab-el-Djebel. For here was a new master, with the whole army obeying him; about to proclaim himself Sultan; and very ready, willing, and able, to deal promptly and painfully with any who showed open opposition.

On the other hand, there was that dread person, the legitimate ruler, El Sidna el Sultan Mahommed el Kebir who—unless he could be anticipated, ambushed and murdered—would return to his country and his capital, and resume the reins of government.

And what then would be the position of those who had proved false to the old *régime*?

Nor, when the loyal, but defeated and dismissed, majority of the Council of Regency met in secret, and discussed the best course for them to follow, could they obtain comfort from one who pointed out that the Sultan Mahommed el Kebir would return with but a handful of men, and would be unable to make any head-way whatsoever against the new Sultan, even if the latter did not ambush and kill him. No comfort whatever—for it was by no means certain that the Sultan Mahommed el Kebir would return with a handful. It was much more likely that he would return at the head of a numerous and well-equipped army, provided from the Sultan of Morocco's own *hamsain*.

To these men, whose loyalty to the Sultan Mahommed el Kebir was genuine, and who infinitely preferred him to the upstart Haroun bin Arrach—whose manners and customs, breeding and bearing, they despised—the position was distressing, painful and difficult indeed. They were between the devil and the deep sea; between the present danger of Haroun bin Arrach's wrath and the future danger of that of the Sultan Mahommed el Kebir. . . .

And why should the usurper have marched the army out, to camp beyond the city? Why have ordered the manœuvres?

Was it simply because the Sultan Mahommed el Kebir had given clear and definite instructions that the city was to remain completely and fully garrisoned until he returned?

Was it so that the usurper could make a clear and unmistakable separating of the sheep from the goats, discovering immediately and unmistakably those who were for him and those who were against him; those who, on his proclaiming himself Sultan would come out from the city, visit his camp and make formal obeisance—and those who would not?

Was it so that, after holding the military exercises, he could march into the city at the head of his army, in the guise, role, and manner of a conqueror? Stage a triumphal entry; a spectacular seizure of the capital; letting all men know, from the Council of Regency to the beggars at the mosque doors, that the old order had changed, that the new ruler had arrived and taken possession?

The suggestion of the Vice-President of the Council of Regency, the aged Wazir Ali, was accepted as being the most probable—that what the new Sultan intended to do, was to make a triumphal march at the head of the army throughout the whole of the country of Bab-el-Djebel, showing himself to all the towns, villages, oases, nomadic encampments and the uttermost ends of the Sultan's tribal territory, demanding acknowledgment, homage, and oath of fealty, from every subordinate feudal ruler, governor, kaid and chief.

Having done this, and given practical proof of sovereignty, he would march upon the capital, the city of Bab-el-Djebel, and enter it as a conqueror. Should the city gates be closed, and the only approach to it be manned and held, he would probably be quite pleased; would, with the utmost ease, sweep away such feeble opposition as could be offered, and then enter, a real conqueror, with every right of law and custom to hang all prominent citizens whom he disliked, or in whose professed loyalty, fidelity, and obedience, he placed no faith. . . .

As to Haroun bin Arrach's motives and reasons, Mahuddin

ibn Daud the Messenger could only speculate; but he gave sound argument for his opinions and conclusions. On matters of fact he was quite clear and coherent—what he had not seen with his own eyes being supplemented by the information provided by his cousin.

It may no doubt be safely assumed that Haroun bin Arrach's motives in leading the army out of Bab-el-Djebel were mixed, the chief among them being the testing of his position, *vis-à-vis* the army; the display throughout the country of his *de facto* power; and the making of an impressive triumphal re-entry into the capital and citadel. In the event of his being able to carry this out successfully, he might consider himself to be the accepted and established Sultan, Haroun bin Arrach of Bab-el-Djebel; might notify the fact to the Sultan of Morocco and to any other powers and potentates interested in the matter; and then set about the matter of disposing of the former Sultan, Mahommed el Kebir.

But he had reckoned without Ben Abu, concerning whose activities Mahuddin ibn Daud was kept informed by his cousin, and by his own spies.

As Haroun bin Arrach, *soi-disant* Sultan, believed, Ben Abu had indeed won over the cavalry—by the liberal and judicious distribution of gold and promises.

The only drawback was that he had won them over not to Haroun bin Arrach, but to himself.

That most astute and amazingly competent Secret Service Agent had gained complete ascendancy over the acting Commandant and Officers of the magnificently equipped, organized, disciplined and drilled Cavalry that, a thousand strong, was, for desert warfare, the most important part of the army. . . .

The troops being encamped outside the city, all arrangements having been made for manœuvres, and one day's march of the entire force having been ordered, Ben Abu called a secret meeting of all cavalry officers above the rank of troop-leader, and disclosed to them what he described as the true state of affairs.

This, according to him, was as follows.

Their master, the legitimate Sultan Mahommed el Kebir was on his way back from Mecca.

He himself, Ben Abu, had held communication with His Highness the Sultan of Morocco, directly he knew of Haroun bin Arrach's treachery and evil intentions.

The Sultan of Morocco had ordered his own Commander-in-Chief, the famous General Mahmoud bin Hafid, to assemble a powerful expeditionary force at Fez and to march it to the borders of Morocco and Bab-el-Djebel, there to encamp and await the return of the Sultan Mahommed el Kebir.

With the help of this army of Moroccan regular troops, not to mention several important and very powerful warrior tribes, the Sultan Mahommed el Kebir would re-enter his country, re-capture his capital city, re-establish his rule, and resume his government.

What a day that would be for traitors who had openly turned against him! What a day for this upstart, Haroun bin Arrach and his followers!

Also, what a day for those who had remained loyal and faithful to their lord, the Sultan Mahommed el Kebir—especially those of the Cavalry who had proved worthy of the confidence of their Sultan and of their Commander, Sinbad el Askar!

As a matter of fact, that part of Ben Abu's task was easy. As I have said, Haroun bin Arrach was by no means popular, and they had no desire to see him established as Commander-in-Chief of the Army, nor as Sultan of Bab-el-Djebel. Definitely they preferred me, Sinbad el Askar, as Commandant, and the Sultan Mahommed el Kebir as ruler. . . .

Ben Abu's proposal then, was accepted and acclaimed—his proposal that on the morrow, the cavalry, riding out in advance of the infantry, should disregard whatever instructions General Haroun bin Arrach should give; and, led by Ben Abu, should proceed to a certain oasis—an oasis where they would off-saddle at sunset, make camp, rest, and abide in peace and comfort until the coming of the Moroccan force.

With these troops they would join, and there, the whole force encamped, would await the arrival of the Sultan Mahommed el Kebir—if indeed he were not actually accompanying the Moroccan army.

This being accomplished, Ben Abu would send messengers to Haroun bin Arrach's infantry force, to inform the officers as to what had taken place, and to invite them, while there was yet time, to declare themselves loyal to their legitimate ruler.

At the same time he would send messengers to Bab-el-Djebel, to inform the members of the Council of Regency, and indeed the whole populace, concerning what had taken place.

Thus, completely deceived by Ben Abu's plausible and probable story—as well as enheartened by his fine gifts and finer promises of favour, promotion and reward—the leaders of the cavalry fell in with the whole scheme, and agreed to his proposals.

Next morning, parading and receiving the order to march, the cavalry, troop by troop, squadron by squadron, rode away, gradually increased their pace, gradually changed their direction, and simply deserted *en masse* from the army of General Haroun bin Arrach.

Night found them at an oasis some fifty miles from their last camp, and very considerably more than fifty miles from where the infantry force halted at sunset that evening.

The place to which Ben Abu had led them was indeed a desirable spot, a green oasis beside which was a large *ksar*. Here the cavalry camped, and here at dawn, a few days later, they found themselves completely surrounded by, and absolutely at the mercy of, a large French force of Spahis, Chasseurs d'Afrique, Tirailleurs and the French Foreign Legion.

Without any prompting from Ben Abu, now revealed as a French officer, it quickly became abundantly clear to the most unintelligent private soldier of the Bab-el-Djebel cavalry that, at the cannon's mouth and the rifle's muzzle, their choice lay between prompt extinction on the one hand, and acceptance of the rôle of "friendlies" and *partisans* of France on the other.

With the somewhat treacherous help of a newly-zealous and newly francophile officer of the Bab-el-Djebel cavalry, Haroun bin Arrach was, in turn, lulled into false security, was also surrounded at dawn, and similarly offered the choice between annihilation and surrender.

Haroun bin Arrach would have fought to the last man and the last drop of his blood, but his confused and bewildered officers and men would not. They declined to fight, laid down their arms, and fraternized with their beguiling comrades of the cavalry—now friends, allies, subjects and irregular troops of France.

The unfortunate acting Commander-in-Chief, the self-styled Sultan Haroun bin Arrach, formerly Sergeant-Major Grünther of the Potsdam Foot-guards, denounced by Ben Abu for what he was, a deserter from the French Foreign Legion, was tried by drum-head court-martial and promptly hanged. This Court saw to it that he did not escape them, as he had done the last one which had sentenced him to death.

The *soi-disant* Ben Abu had, of course, kept the French well informed as to the identity and doings of the Sultan's German Aga of Infantry. . . .

The capture of the city and citadel of Bab-el-Djebel offered no difficulty whatever to the Commander of the French desert column. Led by the officer, hitherto known as Ben Abu, the cavalry and infantry—that, but yesterday, had been the State Army of Bab-el-Djebel—marched through the city gates, immediately followed by the Tenth Tirailleurs and the Fourth Spahis of the French force. While the citizens, crowding the house-tops, regarded these latter—in some puzzlement as to whether they were Moroccan Regulars—the Spahis were followed by the Chasseurs d'Afrique, and they by a battalion of the French Foreign Legion, escorting a battery of field-artillery. . . .

Bab-el-Djebel was captured—and this Mahuddin ibn Daud the Messenger set forth on his swift camel for the coast, and spared neither effort nor money to reach his master at the earliest possible moment. . . .

When he had finished his story and had answered such questions as the Sultan put to him, had been thanked, praised, and rewarded, Mahuddin ibn Daud was dismissed from our presence.

§2

"So it's both, my son," said the Sultan a few minutes later. "Internal trouble and invasion. Haroun bin Arrach and his revolution I could have settled—with my thumb-nail. But with the invasion . . ." and he shrugged his shoulders.

"The French have come to stay. As I said, with them it's a case of *j'y suis j'y reste*," he continued.

A long silence.

What could I say, in the face of tragedy so sudden, so complete? What was there to say?

It was amazing, incredible; such an utter boulversement.

And yet, astounding and unbelievable as it might seem, it was an event in the true tradition of the East, especially of the Islamic, the Arabian, East. Beggar to-day—king to-morrow. A throne in the morning—a gutter in the evening. Caliph Haroun el Raschid one day—a fugitive the next. A palace at sunrise—a prison-cell by sunset. From silken robes to foulest rags between dawn and dawn. "Sultan after Sultan with his pomp abode his destin'd Hour, and went his way." This man, my friend, who had set forth from the country and the city of which he was arbitrary ruler; immensely rich; extremely powerful; firmly established; was now all but penniless, was powerless, homeless, all but friendless—"a Sultan to the Realm of Death addrest", a Sultan dethroned, deposed, who had met his destined hour and gone his way.

> *"But yesterday the word of Cæsar might*
> *Have stood against the world; now lies he there,*
> *And none so poor to do him reverence."*

Even among us, the elect, the chosen few, there was but one upon whom he could certainly rely; but two or three in whose fidelity he could put very much trust.

In me he believed fully; in Hussein the Brave, Kassim bin Ibrahim, Abd el Hamid, Hassan bin Yacoub and Mahuddin ibn Daud he, to some extent, believed.

Of me he was sure—of them he was hopeful.

And I had deceived him.

"What will you do?" I asked.

"Get back to Morocco; spy out the land; and if, as I feel sure, Bab-el-Djebel has gone for ever—I shall take service under the Sultan of Morocco. He'll give me a job and I shall start afresh. Probably Colonel in the *hamsain*, for a beginning. Might become Commander-in-Chief some day. Or perhaps he'd take me on his Staff for a time, and then give me a Governorship of a Province, later. . . . Might strike out for myself again then."

He fell silent, wrapped in thought.

"Well, well," he said suddenly, and sighed heavily.

"What are you going to do, Sinbad? Better make for Port Said as I said, and pick up a P. & O. there. Got any money? If not, I'll give you what I can spare."

"I'm coming with you," I said.

I rank loyalty—with courage, fidelity and reliability—among the great high virtues, and I could do no less. I hadn't the pluck to break away from him in the very moment of disaster. Perhaps I was swayed by the hope of finding new adventure and employment in Morocco.

> *"Choose brave employment with a naked sword*
> *Throughout the world. Fool not, for all may have.*
> *If they dare choose, a glorious life or grave."*

Perhaps I was swayed by the fear of finding myself alone, penniless and out of work.

"Don't be an ass, my dear chap. I shall never be El Sidna el Sultan Mahommed el Kebir of Bab-el-Djebel, Lion of the Desert and Lord of the Western Sahara again. And I'm going looking for a job!" expostulated the Sultan.

"So am I," I said. "With you."

What else could I say?

"But don't you realize that it is much more than likely that I shall never reach Morocco. . . . There will be a price on my head like there was on Abd-el-Kader's. I shall be to the French what Arabi Pasha, Osman Digna, Cetewayo, Theebaw and such people, are to the English—only the French have rather shorter and sharper methods. Not so fond of palaver, humbug, and kid gloves—what they call hypocrisy. . . . I shouldn't be surprised if trouble began here in Jidda on Turkish soil, via the French ambassador at Constantinople. . . . I am clearing out, at the earliest possible moment."

"And I'm coming with you," I said.

"And supposing I do get to Morocco—and the Sultan takes the view that I am not only of no further use, but am an obvious failure, a fraud, and a nuisance. Suppose he wants to propitiate the French. I shall get one of two things, a quick death or a slow one—in a dungeon. The Sultan's prison at Fez is a nasty one: even worse than the average Moroccan gaol. . . . What will you do then?"

"Come with you," I grinned.

"Won't desert me while I've got a shilling, eh?" smiled Chandos. "Well, I *knew* you were . . . solid."

Again silence.

"Sinbad, my son," he said suddenly, "you are the only man I have ever really trusted. You've done more for me than I could ever repay—and I am not going to repay you like that. You are not coming with me. . . . We'll part here. You are the only man I ever really trusted and whom I knew would never deceive me. No, not in the smallest particular, and I . . . ."

"In point of fact, I *have* deceived you," I replied, "and—we won't part here."

"Well, you might come with me as far as Port Said; though even that is risky, because whatever happens to me will probably happen to you too, if we are together. . . . And don't tell lies about having deceived me."

"I have deceived you," I repeated, "and we don't part here. You once said you'd never listen to anything against me except what I myself told you; and that you'd only believe the evidence of your own eyes and ears. . . . Well, I'll tell you about it now; and you can believe your own ears. The last night of our miserable time on the Mecca-Medina road, I deceived you. I definitely tried to set your prisoner free. . . . But for the accident of Kassim bin Ibrahim coming a few minutes too soon, I should have hauled him up out of the well, led him down to the road, and put him on the way to Mecca—and on a camel, if I could have got one. . . . Nor did I propose to confess to you what I had done. I was going to trick you as deliberately and meanly as any of your Arab employees ever did. As it was, I threw my knife down to him, so that he could stab himself if he wished to do so—and avoid a miserable lingering death of thirst and starvation after he'd finished the water and food. If he hadn't the pluck to do it, that wasn't my fault. . . . So, you see, I've deceived you; and but for the accident of Kassim bin Ibrahim's coming . . ."

"No accident, my son," smiled the Sultan. "Kassim had his orders, and you were watched night and day. I was pretty certain that you'd rescue him, and I wanted to make sure. To *mak siccar* as my mother used to say. Yes—it interested me very much—the problem of how you'd re-act to my refusal to listen to you on the subject of torturing the Nawab. I hoped you'd have the courage of your convictions—have the pluck to rescue him. And I hoped you'd tell me about it afterwards. I felt sure you would—even to telling me of the incident of the knife.

"No, there was no deception about the knife, either. Kassim knew what you threw down . . . and it was a waste of a very fine knife—one that I'd given you, too, and had hoped you'd treasure."

"I did treasure it," I said. "But . . . I don't know how to express it . . . I treasured your decency more; and I'd sooner have put the knife to that use than keep it . . . use it to end a piece of beastly cruelty that you'd regret later. I felt perfectly sure that you'd be glad, some day—when I told you."

"Oh, you would have told me in any case, later on, eh?"

"Yes, I should."

"Well, the deception wasn't so bad, then. Sort of temporary deception eh? . . . Still, it's a pity you wasted the knife," smiled the Sultan.

"You don't think he used it, then?" I asked.

"I know he didn't use it."

"How do you know that?"

"Because he was dead. He'd been dead all the time."

"Dead? How do you know?"

"Because I had him up, that first night. He was dead. He had died of fright."

Silence. . . .

"Possibly he had a conscience," mused the Sultan. "But more likely it was pure funk. I hope to God he found the bottom of that well crowded—with women and children from the Well of Cawnpore."

"Why did you fetch him up?" I asked, wondering whether the object had been torture, or whether what I had said had borne some fruit, and the Sultan had intended to let him go, after all.

"Why did I fetch him up? . . . *Ah!* . . . I wonder . . ." was the enigmatic reply.

"Anyhow, he was dead. He had met his Fate—and found Truth —at the bottom of a well. . . . He who was so fond of wells."

"So you didn't deceive me, after all, Sinbad. It was I who deceived you—as usual."

"I meant to," I replied. "I tried to."

"You are a simple soul, my son," smiled the Sultan.

"Let's get down to the Shipping Offices," he added, "and see how soon we can get away. . . . The sooner the better, by Allah! . . . I'll drop you at Port Said."

"You won't," I replied.

"No—we might pick up a ship there that would drop me at Gibraltar, and you could go on Home while I went across to Tangier to meet the Sultan. He always spends this month at his palace there."

CHAPTER XXXII

The Shipping Offices were quite unlike those to be found in Cockspur Street, London, W.I., and their methods of business in Jidda even more different from those prevailing in London.

There was a pilgrim-ship sailing north, but when it would sail depended upon the Will of Allah.

"And what would be likely to influence the Will of Allah in the matter?" we asked.

The influx of pilgrims returning from Mecca, now comparatively few and far between, and the complete filling of the ship with such as desired to go north—Egyptians, Tunisians, Algerians, Moroccans, Syrians, Turks, Tartars, Turcomans and such like.

"And what would be the price of a fare as far as Port Said?" we enquired.

Who should say? It might be little; it might be much. It was the Will of Allah.

"And what would be likely to influence the Will of Allah in this particular?" we asked.

Demand. If a big caravan arrived before the ship sailed, prices would soar, places being knocked down—and prices knocked up—to the highest bidder.

"But suppose the ship were already full when such a caravan arrived?" we enquired.

Well, that would be splendid, of course—from the point of view of the Shipping Company; as those who couldn't pay the new price couldn't go by that ship.

What, not even if they'd already bought their ticket?

Of course not. Naturally, a man with a low price-ticket would not be allowed to go on board until all those with the new high-price tickets had done so.

But suppose they'd already gone on board?

We were not to suppose anything so silly. Nobody would be allowed to go on board until an hour or so before the ship sailed.

So it was no good our buying tickets now?

Oh, yes; certainly. Buy them now, by all means. Then we should have tickets.

But suppose the price rose after we'd bought them.

Then we could pay the extra, couldn't we?

And suppose we couldn't; and suppose all the richer men

had gone on board?

Well? Surely anybody knows a ship's elastic, don't they?

But, in the name of Allah the Merciful, the Compassionate, suppose the ship were *full*!

No ship is ever full. No ship of that Company, anyhow. Not if it dripped passengers.

This was awkward.

Although, so far as we could tell from the numbering on the tickets—which we bought, then and there, at the day's price—the ship must already be crowded from stem to stern and ought to hang out a notice *Standing-room Only*, it was not going to sail until another big caravan of northward-bound pilgrims had come from Mecca!

A few travellers, of course, dribbled in daily, but the hope of the Shipping Company sharks was that a really large party would arrive.

Anyhow, they had no intention of letting their ship depart while they'd only sold accommodation for three times as many as the ship could reasonably be expected to carry.

It was one more manifestation of the shameful and shameless way in which Moslems exploit Moslem pilgrims. It would have been bad enough had the Shipping Companies consisted of Infidels, and these contemptible dogs, these "forgotten of Allah" had robbed, swindled and preyed upon the True Believer. But these were good Mussulmans battening upon the piety of their co-religionists. In point of fact, the very best thing that could possibly happen to the pilgrims would be the establishment in Jidda of a line of pilgrim-transport ships run by a British, French, Italian or other Infidel Dog Company—ships that would offer decent food and accommodation, that would run to schedule, and charge a fixed and reasonable fare . . .

Daily the Sultan sent Kassim bin Ibrahim down to the offices of the Company that owned this only northbound ship; and, daily, Kassim returned fuming, boiling with rage, at the impudence and insolence with which he'd been told,

"No. The ship won't sail to-day."

And in reply to his question,

"When will it sail?" jeers and sneers such as,

"How do we know? We are not prophets. It'll sail when we think fit—and that'll be when it's full."

On his enquiring patiently—and Kassim was not a patient man—whether we might hope to get away that week, he had been told . . .

Why, certainly! Certainly! Of course he might hope. Hope's free. They charged nothing for it. He could hope all day and all night, if he liked. Meantime, he'd better clear out, and do his hoping in the street . . .

"Let us go down and hold converse with these merry gentlemen," said the Sultan grimly; and, that morning, a large party crowded into the offices of the Syrian Syndicate, the shipping firm trading under the name of the *Jidda, Suez, Port Said, Haifa, Smyrna and Constantinople Shipping Company.*

This company appeared to consist of three fat rascals from Beyrout; oily, overbearing, insolent, swindling rogues for whom flogging would have been too good. I'd have liked to have had them in my Watch on a wind-jammer rounding the Horn.

"Hold the door," said the Sultan to Hassan bin Yacoub, the Swordsman. "Let no one in. '*By orders of the Company*', say . . . Now then—out swords and follow me."

And, passing behind a sort of counter where a supercilious clerk sat at the receipt of custom, he made for the stairs leading to the rooms above.

The clerk leapt to his feet with cries of indignation and rage. The Sultan laid his hand upon the man's face and pushed.

The push was of such vigour that it needed not the extended foot of Hussein the Brave to cause the unfortunate man to crash heavily upon his back. Nor was his fall so light and negligible that there was any occasion for Kassim bin Ibrahim, in turn, to put his foot upon the mouth of the unfortunate fellow, while an over-zealous supporter endeavoured to drive sounds from it by stepping on its owner's stomach.

I gathered the impression that Kassim bin Ibrahim had already had words with this particular clerk, and that the clerk's words had been rude.

Up the rickety wooden stairs we clattered, a score and more of scowling ferocious-looking men—in the right hand of each a gleaming sword, in his left, an ugly dagger.

I had never taken passenger-tickets before.

In the big room above, by the window, sat, cross-legged, two of the Syrian Syndicate, on the low once-white divan that ran round three sides of the room. Their mouths fell open, their eyes goggled almost from their heads, as led by the Sultan, we burst into the room.

"Who are you? What do you want? What do you want?" squealed one of them.

"Blood!" growled the Sultan. "Blood! Your blood. Lots of it."

And, striding across the room, he raised his sword above the head of the speaker; while, beside him, Hussein the Brave presented the sharp point of his weapon at the throat of the other man.

Around them crowded the score or so of clamorous desperadoes.

The threatened shipping magnates cowered, begging for mercy.

"When does the *Beyrout* sail?" asked the Sultan, bringing his sword down from the cut position to that of the thrust, and approaching it unpleasantly close to the fat bosom of his victim.

"To-day! To-day! At once! At once!" replied the man.

"It had better," was the answer. "Unless you want to sail with it, and be thrown overboard to the sharks as soon as we are tired of you. . . . Now—look! We've paid our passages, and so have hundreds and hundreds of other pious pilgrims. And they've had enough of your game. Do you hear, you bloated vultures? And they have elected us their representatives. Do you hear? And unless that ship sails to-day, we'll either hack you to pieces here in this room and throw lumps of you down to the dogs in the street, or we'll take you in sacks on board the *Beyrout* and there decide whether to push you into the furnaces or hang you at the yard-arm."

The Syrians swore by their heads, by their beards, by their lives and the lives of their eldest sons, and by the Ninety-and-Nine Most Sacred Names of Allah that the *Beyrout* should sail that day, or—allowing for unforeseen circumstances—at the very latest, on the morrow.

"Well, then," growled the Sultan, "we'll spare your lives—but look you, if there's any trickery, we will not only come here and deal with you ourselves, but we will start a riot. We'll lead the whole ship-load of pilgrims here, and burn this place down and you inside it. . . . And don't you try any games with the police, either. If anything happens to any one of us, through information laid by you, some of us may go to gaol—but *you'll* go to Hell, for we will arrange for your assassination. Now then, that ship's full—bulging. You've sold the proper number of tickets for her, twice over. You get her out of harbour quick, and get yourselves out of a mess, if you value your lives—not to mention your property."

The Syrians oozed, nay spouted, acquiescence, reassurance and promise.

The Sultan listened for a brief space.

"Very well, then. Now I'll tell you what we are going to do. We are going on board now, straight away; and we are going to send word round the town that all the other pilgrims can come on board too, and when all those who've got tickets (and don't you sell another single one, you swindling swine) are on board—up comes the anchor."

"But you can't! You can't," screamed one of the rascals, and squealed even louder as something pricked him, apparently rather severely.

"*Can't?*" ejaculated the Sultan. "*Can't?* You watch us!"

"I say, Sinbad," he said, turning to me, and speaking in English. "You've been a sailor. Could you take charge and get her out? We'll make you Captain, and we'll all do what you tell us, of course."

"No," I regretfully replied. "Might have done something if she'd been a sailing-ship—but I don't know anything about steamers. Never set foot on one. I could navigate her all right, but we should be absolutely in the hands of the engineers."

"Well, we could bribe them," objected the Sultan, forgetting that he was a Sultan no longer, and that the days of his affluence, autocracy, and high-handedness were over.

"And suppose we could? What's going to happen when we touch port? It would be gaol for the lot of us, and a very heavy sentence too, for piracy, barratry, theft, sailing without proper papers, infringement of Port Regulations—God knows what crimes." I pointed out. "I should think we are fairly well on the wrong side of the Law, with what we are doing here now, aren't we?"

"No more so than these swine are, anyhow. They'd be the last people to invoke the Law . . . Don't you think we could steal the ship—and get away with it?"

I thought of the *Valkyrie*. Was my young life to be always haunted and darkened by the crime of ship-stealing?

"No. Absolutely impossible," I assured him. "Suppose you could bribe everybody on board, and we attempted to put out to sea, we should have more than these scoundrels to deal with. It'd be out of their hands, and a matter for the Port Authority, if we tried to slip away without clearance papers. We should have a Turkish gun-boat after us in no time, if we got out at all . . . And, as I say, our first port of call would be our last—and we should spend a long time in it. In its best prison too; or its worst."

"Pity!" said the Sultan. "I should have loved to steal the ship from these thieving swine, and scuttle it when we'd done with it.

Oh, well . . ."

And he turned to the trembling Syrians again.

"Now then. Understand? We are going on board that ship *now*; and we are going to invite all the other passengers to come too. And the ship's going to sail to-day or . . . or . . . we'll know the reason why! Yes—if we have to come back here, a thousand of us, and hang you, out of your own windows."

§2

Sending Kassim bin Ibrahim and the servants back to collect our baggage, we made our way down to the water-front, chartered a bunder-boat and went out to the *Beyrout*, which lay about a mile from the shore. She was a big wooden tramp steamer that could scarcely have been as aged, decrepit and filthy as she looked:

Swarming up the accommodation ladder, we boarded the ship somewhat in the manner of pirates—so truculent was our mien, so violent our manner, so bad our manners.

Most certainly we were not expected. On the contrary, our arrival caused the utmost surprise, not to say consternation and alarm. Definitely we were not welcome.

Promptly we were informed, by the senior officer aboard, that there was neither accommodation nor food for us.

Promptly he was informed by the Sultan that there was accommodation for him in the sea, plenty of it; and food for the sharks—and for plenty of them. Nor did we care how soon he went overboard, nor how many of his crew followed him.

In short, if not pirates, we were definitely a type of pilgrim to whom the personnel of the *Beyrout* were unaccustomed.

However, had we been pirates, we could hardly be bigger pirates than the swindlers who owned the ship and the scoundrels who manned it.

Her captain and officers were Turks and Syrians; the deck-hands were Lascars, and assorted Red Sea ruffians of the type that man Arab dhows, gun-running, pearling and slaving boats; the engineers were likewise Turks; the stokers and trimmers, negroes of the sort that coal ships at Aden.

A hundred eyes must have watched our irruption into the offices of the *Jidda, Suez, Port Said, Haifa, Smyrna and Constantinople Shipping Company* and our eruption thence; a thousand must have watched our sailing out to the *Beyrout*. Word must have gone round with that speed with which rumour can travel

707

only in the East; for, even while we were abusing and threatening the officers of the ship, pilgrim-laden boats put out from the water-front.

Before long, a crowd of boats jostled one another at the bottom of the companion-ladder, and a steady stream of pilgrims poured on board.

I should think that, by evening, there were a couple of thousand of them!

Anyhow, the ship—which had been converted from tramp-work to the requirements of the pilgrim-traffic, and consisted almost entirely of cleared decks, tier above tier—was crowded to suffocation. There could have been but few proper cabins left on her—the Company's idea of accommodation being sufficient bare deck-space for a man to lie down upon—or rather, to sit down upon, with his feet tucked well under him. I never saw an enclosed area more tightly packed with human beings.

And each of these human beings had to sleep, wash, dress and undress—and, moreover, cook his food—on the few square inches of deck allowed to him in return for the exorbitant sum that he had paid for his fare.

CHAPTER XXXIII

I hate to write of what followed. . . .
After all these years, I hate even to think of it.

How or where the fire started, I do not know.

I wonder whether the ship's officers—Turks and Syrians to a man—knew when and where it started; knew when and where it was going to start?

If they did not, why were those noble souls, worthy servants of the *Jidda, Suez, Port Said, Haifa, Smyrna and Constantinople Shipping Company* the first, and the only, people to leave the burning ship?

It is an unspeakable thing to say, an unthinkable thing to think, an incredible thing to believe—but I *do* believe that this ship, packed from stem to stern with pilgrims, was heavily insured and deliberately set on fire. Otherwise, why did every officer on board—deck and engine-room—get away in the two best boats—watered and provisioned, well-prepared for a sea voyage, and adequately manned with quarter-masters and useful deck-hands?

The first thing we knew of the beginning of this terrible tragedy, was a confused uproar and the sight of two boats pulling away from the ship, boats on which there was not a single pilgrim passenger—man, woman, or child.

The next thing was a wild stampede, screams, clouds of smoke, a horrible smell of burning, flames, a rush for the remaining boats. For the boats—of which none contained oars, mast or sail, food or water; and the only one of which that ever reached the water hung perpendicular, its stern-sheets submerged. I doubt if the others could have been lowered by a crew of Able Seamen. Probably ours was the only one of which the falls had not been put out of action; and that only because we, a truculent, high-handed, and dangerous band, were encamped in and about it.

I have been told by those who should know, that a violent blow on the head which causes prolonged unconsciousness, invariably causes loss of memory also; loss of all recollection, for a period which may be long or short, of happenings immediately

709

preceding the blow.

Certainly this occurred in my case, and, moreover, I have but a confused recollection of what little I do remember.

We were seated in a circle, feet almost touching in the centre, while the Sultan was telling us what he was going to do, in the light of the information brought by Mahuddin ibn Daud; and advising us as to what would be the best thing for each of us to do in the circumstances.

I like to remember that each one of us stoutly swore—with, at any rate, every appearance of absolute sincerity—that he would follow the Sultan to the end, be it what it might; that he would in no wise make his way back to Bab-el-Djebel and take service under the French; that he would abandon everything—hearth and home, wife and child, possessions and prospects; and cast in his lot with the Sultan, live to ride at his back through the gates of Bab-el-Djebel—or die at his side.

They died at his side.

To go back . . .

I noticed that the throb of the propeller had ceased, and idly wondered whether the wretched old tub had already broken down within a hundred miles of Jidda.

There was a curious and prolonged silence.

Had not the Sultan continued talking, I should have been more interested.

After a while, I was conscious of a rising murmur of voices and then of shouts.

The murmur increased to a roar.

As the tumult arose, the Sultan stopped speaking.

As it increased, he rose to his feet.

As shouts of,

"*Fire! Fire!*" rose above the babel of voices, the screams of women, we gathered round him.

"By Allah and by Allah!" he cried. "The ship's on fire . . . And *look* . . ."

And he pointed to where, a couple of cable-lengths away, oars were being taken in, and sails hoisted on those two boats.

The next definite and distinguishable movement in the hellish pandemonium that now arose, was a rush for the boats that remained—of course utterly inadequate in number and size, and utterly unseaworthy, even had it been possible to launch them.

I should say that, given ample time and every facility for getting away, there was not accommodation for one-tenth of the number of the people on board. What strengthened my suspicion, or rather confirmed my certainty that this was arson, that the whole thing was carefully planned, was the fact that the rush for the only useful boat, the boat by which we were standing, was made by sailors and others of the personnel of the ship.

These men knew that this was their boat, the only sea-worthy boat, the only boat that could be launched; and they made for it.

I am glad to remember—and I do most clearly remember—that it was the Sultan himself who shouted that there were women and children on board.

"Get the boat lowered, Sinbad," he cried, knowing that I was a sailor, "and we'll put the children—and women—in it."

Easier said than done—and what hope was there that, once the boat was in the water, these Lascars would wait for such things as women and children?

However, the first step was to get the boat lowered. I might then, somehow, prevent her crew from pushing off.

I remember shouting orders; fighting to prevent the sailors fighting each other, hindering each other in lowering the boat, and trying to get into it; fighting to keep my feet; to use my hands, to prevent maddened fools from knocking aside fumbling fools who struggled round the davits; being myself swept aside by sheer weight of numbers, as a rush of pilgrims followed a rush of sailors; struggling to my feet; and striking out with all my strength, to clear a space, to get them to do something; to get at the davits. . . .

I remember hearing the clash of steel and seeing the Sultan surrounded by his body-guard, fighting as though in battle.

And it was a battle.

I remember seeing him fighting to drive the mob back from the boat; swords rising and falling like flails; men falling at every blow; the decks slippery with blood; a semi-circle of his body-guard forming about the boat, facing outward, hacking and hewing; the Sultan, backed by his men, giving his life for others; shouting aloud above the tumult,

"Bring your wives, you dogs; your children, you hell-damned bastards . . . your . . . mothers . . ."

A sudden swish of rope through sheaves; the boat falling, stern first and hanging perpendicular; blood-curdling, heart-rending screams from every part of the ship; dense swirling

clouds of heavy smoke; a hissing as of ten thousand serpents; swirling blinding steam; a terrific explosion; a sheet of flame; an irresistible wild rush that bore the half-circle of swordsmen back, back; men leaping overboard . . .

Steam: smoke: fire: shrieks: pandemonium: hell upon the waters . . .

The boat was useless. I hacked at the jammed rope that kept it dangling perpendicular . . . It fell, stern first—filled, and sank.

I remember springing to my feet and getting to the Sultan's side as a great Nubian swordsman brought his heavy cross-handled sword down upon his head; smashing my fist into the mad black face; falling across the Sultan as a sword struck the side of my head; his face close to mine; seeing the blood that streamed down my face mingle with his, and saying to myself,

"He's dead! . . . He's dead! . . . His blood and mine . . . !": getting once more to my feet, clearing blood from my eyes.

No, I can remember no more.

I can pick out those few incidents as realities, from among a thousand dream memories . . . glimpses . . . visions.

Did I see Hassan bin Yacoub the Swordsman, the Slayer,— spinning like a dervish, bounding like a tiger, fighting like a fiend—slice a man's head clean from his shoulders with one blow? And did a fountain of blood spurt up in a column six feet high into the air, ere the body tottered and fell?

Did I slip as I struck at a man, and fall heavily upon the hacked body of Hussein the Brave, driving the air from his lungs in a great gasp, as though I'd hurt the dead?

Did I, catching up a sword and lunging with all my strength, drive the point straight in a gaping mouth—and through—so that the hilt clashed on teeth?

Did I see a man pull himself up, clutching the leg of Kassim bin Ibrahim—pull himself up from the deck, bite, and hang on like a bull-dog as Kassim bin Ibrahim, looking down, stabbed him, just as a yataghan split his own skull?

Did I see Abd el Hamid, his clothes on fire, leap shrieking into the sea?

Did I, that time I fell upon the Sultan's body, press gory lips to his brow ere I rose for the last time?

I don't know . . . I cannot remember . . .

§2

I recovered consciousness in an Arab *dhow*, a swift and sinister boat manned by a crew of evil scoundrels—slavers, pearl-poachers, gun-runners, hashish-smugglers.

They had pulled me out of the water and were in two minds as to whether to throw me back again, or whether to keep me for reward, ransom, or indeed, simply for sale.

Luckily I was mad, incoherent, delirious—and no Arab ever injures the mad, the Afflicted of Allah.

Anyhow, keep me they did.

And, how long after I cannot say, the *dhow* crept ghost-like, one night, to anchor off the port of Djibouti in French Somaliland, promptly to be seized by a Revenue cutter or some such official craft.

On the beach we were flung down, bound hand and foot.

And I was back where I had been—a captive on the shores of Africa. On the opposite shore this time—and in the hands, less cruel or more cruel, of civilized captors.

Apparently the Captain of the *dhow* was expected, welcomed with open arms; and joyfully seized. He, his crew, and I, were cast forthwith into gaol to await sentence—if not trial—for every crime known to the French Maritime Penal Code.

Personally, I didn't care.

At the time, it would have been all one to me whether I was sentenced to death, to imprisonment for life, to the chain-gang that scavenged the streets of Djibouti—or to the Governorship of French Somaliland.

However, I did take the trouble wearily to tell the truth and to state the simple facts of the case—that I was an Englishman, recently in the employ of the Sultan of Bab-el-Djebel, and probably the sole survivor of the pilgrim ship *Beyrout*, burnt and, as the crew of the *dhow* stated, sunk without other survivors, a day's sail from Jidda.

My story deeply interested the Court. Moreover, it amused it. Relations between England and France were somewhat strained, just then.

"*An Englishman*, was I . . . ? On a pilgrim ship leaving Jidda . . . ? In the employ of the Sultan of Bab-el-Djebel . . . ?

"Ha! Ha! . . . Ha! Ha! Ha! . . .

"*Espion!* A spy! A spy!

"*Perfide Albion!*

"Aha!"

In the end I was given the choice of enlisting in the French Foreign Legion or of suffering—that which I should be condemned to suffer.

It was all one to me.

"*Monsieur le Juge*," said I, "or *Monsieur l'Administrateur* or whatever you are—I really do not care. I really am not interested."

"Well! Your fellow pirates have been shot, Mr. Arabic-speaking Englishman or Mr. English-speaking Arab," was the reply.

"Then their troubles are over," said I.

"Yes. But yours, I think, are just beginning," smiled the Judge.

. . .

Available P. C. Wren Titles
from
Riner Publishing Company

The Collected Short Stories

Volume One: ISBN 9780985032609
Volume Two: ISBN 9780985032616
Volume Three: ISBN 9780985032623
Volume Four: ISBN 9780985032630
Volume Five: ISBN 9780985032647

The Collected Novels

Volume One: *The Geste Novels*
   Part A: ISBN 9780985032678
   Part B: ISBN 9780985032685
Volume Two: *The Sinbad Novels*
   Part A: ISBN 9780692639382
   Part B: ISBN 9780692639429
Volume Three: *The Foreign Legion Novels*
   Part A: ISBN 9780999074909
   Part B: ISBN 9780999074916
Volume Four: *The Earlier India Novels*
   Part A: ISBN 9780999074923
   Part B: ISBN 9780999074930
Volume Five: *The Later India Novels*
   Part A: ISBN 9780999074947
   Part B: ISBN 9780999074954
Volume Six: *The English Novels*
   Part A: ISBN 9780999074961
   Part B: ISBN 9780999074978
Volume Seven: *A Mixed Bag of Novels*
   Part A: ISBN 9780999074985
   Part B: ISBN 9780999074992

Further information can be found at
rinerpublishing.wordpress.com

www.ingramcontent.com/pod-product-compliance
Lightning Source LLC
Chambersburg PA
CBHW032248020726
47495CB00001B/11